THE WORK OF RESTLESS NIGHTS

M. WEALD

From a fan. Thanks for
the vids Mike!

M Weald

M
W

Cover art: Alejandro Colucci

1st edition 2023

ISBN: 9798987879801

To my friends and family, without whom this story wouldn't exist. And to Courtney, without whom it would never have been published.

CONTENTS

"The electric things have their life too. Paltry as those lives are." – Rick Deckard, *Do Androids Dream of Electric Sheep* by Philip K. Dick

PROLOGUE

The woman in the grey mask stood on the edge of the road, watching the trickle of traffic and people meander past. Her mask elicited a few glances but nothing more. Privacy in this modern era was hard to come by and keeping it in your own way did little to arouse suspicion.

She pressed a button on a waist high post at her side and moved onto the crosswalk. In terms of not being struck by a passing car, pressing the button was unnecessary. The self-driving cars could avoid her with ease. They monitored many meters ahead and the night was clear, roads dry. But rules were rules. She didn't want to draw attention.

She paused when she made it to the other side of the street. A car flicked past behind her, the man in the driver's seat fast asleep.

Before the woman stood a tall and narrow brick building in a forest of dilapidated structures, all in the impractical style common to Old Chicago. Too many uneven surfaces, rounded edges, and gaudy pieces of stonework. Altogether impractical. The retrofitted rooftop gardens looked like little green hats meant to hide a fading hairline. It spoke of a time before humanity spread throughout the solar system like a rich man at an auction with no one to bid against.

The woman sighed. She appreciated progress, one only had to look at her fine black jacket with its flexible solar cell inlays to know that. But somewhere along the line things had gotten a bit ... muddled. She fiddled with the chip in her pocket, twisting it around and around.

The woman stepped into the building before her, the doors sliding shut behind. A static-filled voice over the intercom welcomed her to the establishment in cheery tones. She walked to the center of the rectangular room and tapped on a flexible screen embedded in the arm of her jacket, ignoring the voice on the intercom. It was nothing more than basic artificial intelligence, ready to answer asinine questions about the business's services with pre-programmed responses. These companies spent their AI money elsewhere. She brought her hand to her head, resituating her mask. She didn't know why she continued to wear earrings beneath it.

The room she stood in had been renovated over the years, taken from what must have been crumbled bits into a comforting series of hard lines and smooth surfaces. Her lips tweaked into a slanted smile, though no one could see it.

An interactive augmented reality screen came into view on the wall to the woman's left and she walked up to it, scrolling through the service listings with a few quick gestures.

If there had been someone else in the room, sitting on the hard-plastic chairs bolted to the floor along one wall, the woman was not too sure what they would have thought of her. Just another jilted lover seeking solace in make believe perhaps. But there wasn't anyone else in the stuffy room hidden amongst a forest of similarly stuffy rooms. It was modern, but unkempt and societally speaking in the gutter. And there were many more like it. Her amber eyes hidden beneath twin black eye plates scanned the screen showing the fantasies this tall house could make real. All the tall tales.

The woman in the grey mask tapped one finger against the screen, sliding past pictures of Ken doll bots before pausing on a picture of the business's top seller, a newly released female recreation bot staring over her painted shoulder as seductively as something born and bred in the uncanny valley could. It did its best considering the mechanical constraints the human designers placed on it. The woman had long since accepted humanity's irrepressible tendency to craft things in their own image. She thought of it as a weakness, an excuse for humans to say they understood what they had made. As if anything that had a face with two eyes and two lips could be understood. As if having an ankle would allow a chain to be wrapped around it.

She sighed, shook her head. She'd best get about her business for the night. After all, she meant to shake humanity out of its stupor.

After the woman typed a few commands into the screen on the wall, a ping sounded confirming her payment and falsified identification information had been accepted. A sliding panel door to the woman's right coasted along a hidden track to reveal a dimly lit hallway lined with thin metal doors and pale LED lights. A rush of warm air, heavily scented with aromatic orange peel to cover up the mold and oil, billowed into the main room. Luckily for the woman in the grey mask, she couldn't smell it. She moved into the hallway and walked with even steps from door to door as her mask filtered the foul-smelling particulates.

The door she was looking for sat near the end of the hallway. A lattice of thin gouges marred its surface like the scratches found in a bathroom stall, the scattered thoughts of those who'd lived in a fantasy for a few loci an hour. One disgruntled customer had written "RATHER DREAM" in all caps. Another had written the Mandarin characters for public bus, because all who paid the fee got a ride. What a childish joke.

The woman shook her head and tapped out a few commands on the screen at the edge of the closed door. The door drifted to the side and the heady scent of orange and oil and mold and caustic cleaning agent filtered into her mask. More LED lights flicked to life and the woman stepped inside, the door whispering shut behind her.

The room held shabby furniture and equally shabby décor: pocked Formica countertops made to look like wood with a small kitchen behind, a few discolored and scratched chairs, some wooden knee-high stands, a tilted bookcase, fading wallpaper, a couch with stained cushions, and a bed.

As her eyes adjusted to the dim light, a lump on the far side of the bed took on a more human shape. The ridge in the blanket started at the feet, twin bumps climbing in a gentle slope, hooking at a knee and climbing rapidly again to the apex of a waist only to fall, then rise to a shoulder. The blankets shifted smooth and slow, and the woman in the grey mask saw a tangled mass of raven hair hiding a thin painted neck. With the dim lighting, bunched covers, and wig of raven hair, the illusion looked almost perfect. With the addition of augmented reality to hide the blemishes, it would be.

The woman could have set the experience any number of ways, had the female bot clothed in any number of knock-off dresses or stringy pieces of lingerie. She could have had her stand anywhere in the room in any position, decide the scenario, code the mannerisms, the knowledge, the back story, her level of confidence, bashfulness, amenability. Anything. Even the décor could be remade through augmented vision.

Instead, she had chosen one of the stock options, the top seller. The bot in the bed was her wife, come home after both had been away at work and taking a short nap, still fully clothed in tight skirt and flowing blouse, all died deep metallic earth tones. Not new clothes, just the right amount of wear, like a well-worn shoe, like their relationship. And all she had to do was sit on the edge of the bed, give her wife's shoulder a light tap, and talk. The bot would be the consummate conversationalist, frank when needed and understanding all the rest, coded exactly to her personality. She would make the day better, tenable, and know all her quirks and desires without any need to ask. She'd suggest the woman in the grey mask join her in bed.

The woman in the grey mask listened to the tide of the bot's breath, in and out. Almost real, almost couldn't hear the fans whirring in the background, the machine carrying out its designed purpose.

It was all so manufactured. So ... brittle.

The woman in the grey mask hesitated. Her hand shook.

On the back of the bot's neck, nestled at the bottom of its shock of raven hair, lay the machine interface where humans normally lodged their tech core. Instead, the bot's control panel lay covered by a skin-toned plate. The woman in the grey mask swooped to the bot's side and, before the bot could wake from its slumber, before her fake wife could murmur a greeting, the woman had taken the chip out of her pocket and laid it overtop the control panel. The bot's body went rigid, its limbs locked into stasis. The woman in the grey mask lifted the thin panel out of the way and slid a thumb sized adapter into a now open slot.

"Time to see if there are ghosts in machines after all," said the woman.

She turned around and walked out the way she had come.

CHAPTER ONE

A NEW CONTRACT

"Never introduce instability into programming that cannot be curtailed or controlled. A bot's only creativity should be in solving whatever complex tasks the user sets before it, and only within the provided constraints."
Mechanic's Guidebook, v99, Section 1 – The Basics, Par. 1

L ee tossed back the tumbler of whiskey in a glittering arc, and a flash flood of burning liquid traveled down his throat.

Who couldn't help but sigh contently after that?

The acoustics were different in this bar, more brazen, less choked. When he sat in his apartment with only his bot Nu to talk to, sighs took on a more somber cast. With no one to hear them they were absorbed into the walls, lost in the gaps of his floorboards and the slits in between the cushions of his ratty couch. Here, in his favorite bar, his sighs found a home in somebody else's ears. That felt right. Sighs were meant to be heard.

Lee twirled his glass on the smooth wooden countertop. It held a deep cherry tone, actual wood worn with divots. He caught the eye of Fey, the bartender, and tweaked his mouth until a half smile poked its way out, nodded a half nod. She lifted a full bottle of the amber liquid off a tall shelf at her back and carried it over to Lee's side. She kept her hand on the bottle and raised an eyebrow.

"You good?" she asked. Her voice was a soprano's, high for her Rube-nesque frame.

Lee stopped twirling his glass and thought about the question.

Was he good?

The blood-alcohol-content readout pinned to the bottom right corner of his augmented vision seemed to indicate he was good, quite good in fact. So good, he almost regretted adding the medical upgrade to the tech core situated at the top of his spinal column. Constant monitoring of hundreds of important compounds and chemicals joyriding through his bloodstream and the blood alcohol monitor got the most use. But of course, that wasn't what she meant.

Was he good?

He had finished a repair job the other day, traveled out into the fields south of Old Chicago during harvest time and fixed a self-controlled combine for a farming corp. It'd developed an insistent tick in its machine learning and started tossing errors all over the place, pausing for no reason or veering through the fields in drunken loops. The air felt nice out there, crisp and cool with the promise of the oncoming winter. Above it all rested a wide-open sky.

Wide open skies were supposed to make someone feel free, limitless, capable of reaching up and pulling the celestial bodies down until the spas on Mars were only a transparent protective dome away.

But Lee felt small, dwarfed by the cosmos and left with too many options. Back in his dingy apartment, the stained stucco ceiling and dull metallic sheen of his walls were almost comforting in comparison. Then the closeness of his walls became cloying, and long nights of working on Nu became a palliative half-cure.

Ah, well. At least he'd been able to stop at his favorite open-air market in Old Chicago on the way back to eat some spiced vat mystery meats.

Lee tapped on his wide metal bracelet and shimmied until the blue mechanic's jacket on the back of his chair shifted into a more comfortable position. A projected screen appeared on his forearm, emitted from his bracelet. With a few quick taps, Lee sent his BAC monitor data digitally over to Fey. He could see her contact covered eyes flit to the side as the flexible and transparent electroluminescent displays incorporated into her contacts showed her the information in a rolling parade of numbers.

Fey lifted the bottle of whiskey and poured two fingers worth into the bottom of his glass.

"That isn't what I meant," she said.

Of course it wasn't. But Lee had made it out of his apartment, came to the bar to splash some amber color on what would have otherwise been a dull grey.

Was he good?

Not great. But how many lucky bastards could claim that prize?

"He's fine. Leave 'im alone Fey."

The gruff voice belonged to Liz. She slouched in the chair next to Lee, trying to shed all the grime from a night shift at the local hospital with a few daytime drinks.

"You should know better Fey. Ambiguous question like that, send a neural mechanic down the rabbit hole, you ken? The whole lot are too philosophical. Ask him about the weather and he'll tell you how us cooling the skies only gave us the chance to heat up some other godforsaken place."

Lee grinned at the thin slip of a woman known as Liz. Lee could never quite tell her age and didn't want to ask. She had a wit he didn't much want to be on the end of and these days anything between 30 and 90 was pretty much the same biologically anyway. Lee imagined her to be somewhere in her late 70's. Something about her attitude made it seem well-aged, bitter, like it had gotten more pungent over the years. She had a weathered narrow face, long thin fingers perfect for carrying out whatever tasks the med-bot ordered for its diagnosis, and flaxen yellow hair swept into a ponytail; she seemed right at home spending all day in her hospital issued scrubs.

Lee chuckled as Fey moved to busy herself behind the bar, a slight scowl marring her lips. Lee looked to Liz.

"I thought you were supposed to be kind to people. Give them a shoulder to cry on, be a sounding board for their problems. You know, make the sick forget what ails them. How are you supposed to do all that if you don't ask questions?" asked Lee.

"You talk too much," said Liz. "I help the sick, but I can't do anything about stupid. Download a therapeutic conversation package for Nu over there if you want someone who will buy your bullshit. Quit looking for meaning in everything and finish that drink in front of you."

Liz took another sip from her glass of Moscato. Lee had always found that choice an odd one.

"For someone who picks the first thing on the menu you show a remarkable amount of insight," said Lee.

Liz smiled and tipped her glass his way. Their shared laughter matched in rhythm with the familiarity of two old friends. Lee even heard a few soprano chuckles from Fey over at the other end of the L shaped bar. She was running inventory, the colored LED sconces on the wall casting her shadows against the scintillating panoply of bottles.

Lee could say he felt good, but still his smile didn't reach his ears, hadn't for some time now.

Their joined laughter was interrupted by a series of high-pitched squeaks from Liz's personal/work bot. The bar sat below ground level and the robot stood against the wall underneath the bay of street level windows, soaking in the sight of fleshy legs, metallic limbs, and rolling wheels with eyes quickly going dim.

A message in text flashed across the bottom of Lee's contacts. A message from Nu, Lee's repair bot he took with him everywhere he went. Nu stood on four wheels next to Liz's humanoid caretaker bot, its cameras facing out to the street.

Liz's bot shut down again. Another moral code error, messaged Nu.

Lee smirked as Liz walked over to her bot, leaving behind a trail of muttered obscenities in her wake.

"You know the government doesn't take too kindly to bots trying to ditch their connection with sub-grid 1," said Lee, laughing. "Makes them nervous the bots are about to do something naughty."

"Shut it," said Liz, not bothering to look at Lee. She moved over to the bot and smacked it on the arm. "You would think the damn thing tries to hit every human it comes across the way it keeps on throwing moral code errors."

"No shortage of people who deserve it," said Lee.

"Got that right. Still, can't have a nurse bot be throwing moral code errors. Some patients might be alarmed by that, think their pills might have some extra surprises inside."

Lee chuckled and took another sip of whiskey. He stared at the wooden bar top, scratched at a few of the divots with his finger.

"You ever see a nurse bot pull the plug on someone? Without being directed to, I mean."

Liz looked back at Lee and scrunched her face, letting her mind flip through its memory banks. She spoke.

"You hear rumors of course, but I can't say that I've seen it myself. Any bot that I've seen pull the plug on a patient has done it at the direction of a doctor, which ... you know ... is according to the wishes of the family, or if there is no family the moral code. Though I did see a cafeteria bot get shut down when it served a diabetic patient it liked the last bit of sugar free pudding. Patient was a young boy, cute, and didn't have an implant to monitor his diabetes. His parents hadn't checked his genetics before he was born either, *disagreed* with some of the standard changes. You know the type, worse than a Laskite."

Lee winced, though Liz didn't notice. She continued speaking.

"Parents let things go until the kid ended up our guest. Anyway, the bot liked the kid, so it served him ahead of a diabetic doctor who'd let his med implant supplies run low. Doctor was an asshole. Think I might have cheered." Liz barked out a laugh. "I swear, when the hell did that bit get voted into the moral code? Putting an asshole doctor over a poor sick kid. I sure as hell don't remember it in any of the referendums. Bot had that one right if you ask me." Liz swore and shook her head, standing by her bot as it began its reset procedure.

Lee turned and looked out the window. He could see the wheels of self-driving cars on the road as they went through the motions of their efficient dance. One stopped at the side of the road and picked up a young couple, at least their legs looked young anyway.

"You hear about the self-driving car that hit the famous singer the other day?" asked Lee. "what's her name again?"

A voice came from down the bar, loud and a bit slurred. "Sil Rivers, you're thinking of Sil Rivers."

"Thanks Ken," said Lee. He raised his glass to the old man, a bairen near the age of 105 though he didn't look it. Good genetics for a shell mechanic. Lee turned back to Liz. "Ya, Sil Rivers. Car smacked her into a wall. She broke both legs and had to cancel a tour, won't be dancing regular for months. Her label is up in arms over it, but the car had to swerve to avoid hitting a young child pushed off the damn median by the crowds. Car chose to hit a wealthy singer who'd be able to pay medical. Think I can agree with the moral code on that call." Lee took a sip of his drink and sighed at the fire lighting a path down his throat. "By the way, did you vote on that child referendum?"

"Course," said Liz. "I don't care how accurate the predictions are for a kid's success or failure, a young child is still too much a blank slate not to be giving them some extra value."

"Good to hear the ads that label's been beaming across the Grid didn't get to you. I'll drink to that." Lee raised his glass to his lips and took a sip.

He watched Liz fuss over her bot, the six-foot tall humanoid shell silent as a heap of scrap metal. Lee knew if it wasn't impeded by the moral code, it could easily crush his skull between its metal hands at the direction of a stray thought. Of course, if that bothered him, he shouldn't have trained to be a neural mechanic. He looked to his bot Nu and drained the last of his glass, smiled. Fey came over and filled up his glass after money transmitted from his account to the bar's.

"Why don't you let Nat look at it, Liz?" asked Lee.

She grumbled and reached up to her bot's control panel. The thing was so much taller than her it was almost comical. The cylindrical head of the bot leaned down and forward as if asleep, making it harder for Liz to reach the panel on its neck.

"Already did, wouldn't let him give me a discount neither. God knows he needs the money."

Fey snorted at that and hid from Liz's harsh gaze by busying herself with the handful of non-regulars also taking part in some harmless day drinking. Liz returned her gaze to her bot and set about bringing it online.

"Let me look at it then," said Lee. "Seems like a coding issue. Nat's all hardware, you need a man with a more philosophical touch."

Liz leaned against the wall and wiped a dark smudge on her scrubs, a smile playing on her lips. She barked out a laugh.

"Not a chance Lee."

He smiled and raised a glass, drained it. They'd known each other a long time. Long enough for the same old jokes to form a comfortable routine.

Lee tapped out a message to Nu using the projected screen from his wristband. The screen required a flick of the wrist to activate, and a grid of lasers allowed for feedback. The message told Nu to hook up to Liz's bot and download its log data for later analysis.

By the time he finished tapping out the message, Liz had reclaimed her stool at the bar and was taking periodic sips from her wine. Her bot stayed silent as it ran through diagnostics. Nu unfolded a jointed arm to plug into the data access port on the back of its neck.

Lee turned to his drink to find a cool and very much not amber glass of water sitting in front of him. He accepted it with a shrug and half nod towards Fey. He fiddled with his bracelet and set about pinning an augmented reality TV screen to the portion of wall across from him. The wall was covered in the ubiquitous, absorptive dun paint perfect for tagging with augmented reality. Thanks to the properties of the wall there wasn't much glare from overhead lights.

After a few taps, the electroluminescent screen in his contacts lit up hundreds of stars in miniature against the blacks of his pupils. One of his favorite shows of late began playing. The sound of the whimsical intro music danced through the speakers surgically implanted in his ears. He shifted his head, yet the image stayed pinned to a single location on the wall. The soft camera in his contacts scanned his surroundings and beamed the data to his tech core for processing.

Even though he knew no one else could see what he was watching or hear what piped into his implanted speakers, he instinctively looked around before focusing on the sitcom. An odd habit he'd picked up from old shows.

The show started, a play on the classic family sitcoms, the ones where dynamics would shift, and hilarity would ensue. Like out of nowhere a father with a wife and two kids would have his job automated out from underneath his feet due to a new law, then be forced to take care of kids he'd been too busy to get to know. Watch them struggle through a series of contrived scenarios to learn what family was all about. Cue the laugh track, cue the occasional emotional sigh. Lee had seen several shows with the same premise over the years. Sometimes it was the wife who lost the job. Other times it was a family friend who moved in due to rough circumstances. All were variations on introducing a shock to small group of interesting characters with a need to be around each other, with a need to care. Corny at times, sure, but he thought it heartfelt more often than not.

The show currently playing out on the wall of his favorite bar had two young kids, their parents, two grandparents, one great grandparent and one great-great-grandparent living in a house with a general-purpose bot they all shared. Not to mention an uncle who had moved in after losing popularity as a vid blogger. Their bot had a knack for failing in entertaining ways. In this episode it failed in its attempts to make a chicken dish by misinterpreting thyme and roasting the whole thing black as a result. The grandparents who'd faked being on a booze cruise in the arctic to instead see a risqué play named "Nil's Third Nip" showed up at the end and fixed the meal just as the parents came home, the mother shaking her well-coifed head as she put away her oiled briefcase containing a mix of student assignments to be graded. The uncle documented it all for his blog and got a record thirty-four views.

Lee sat chin in hand as the credits rolled, musing the myriad ways society tried to downplay robotic abilities while at the same time funding research to make them smarter in unregulated labs off-world.

A few minutes passed like this when the door to the bar swung open. In stepped Nat, not an unusual or unexpected occurrence, but today something felt off.

The large man slammed the door to the bar and rushed to sit two seats away from Lee, on the other side of Liz. His large frame and prodigious belly shook under labored breaths. Red lines webbed his bloodshot eyes, the brown iris and black pupil at its center an island in a sea of angry red waves.

Whether Nat's bloodshot eyes were due to visiting a jack house, or something else, Lee couldn't tell. Those soft drug hovels lit fireworks among neurons and filled eye vessels near to bursting. But for a man of Nat's size so could running.

By the time Fey set a beer in front of Nat, he'd recovered enough to form decipherable words. Lee noticed with some surprise the sweat stains on the front of the mechanic's blue work shirt.

Not the jack house then.

"Spit it out Nat," said Liz. Her harsh face had softened, shifted with worry at the sight of the big man in such a fit.

Lee met Nat's eye and nodded.

"Fey, throw up the local news on the bar channel," said Nat.

Fey tapped out a few commands on a curved screen she had strapped to her forearm. Lee, Liz, Nat, and a few of the more curious strangers tapped out similar commands on their control panels of choice or used simplistic thought commands that zipped through implants scanning their brains. They trained their collective eye on the far wall at one end of the L shaped bar. On it, an augmented reality screen viewable to anyone who had their implanted tech connected to the bar's network showed the local news.

Lee noticed Nat jackhammering his foot against the floor as the reporter outlined the details of a death nearby, several blocks away towards New Chicago in a shopping complex.

The reporter, with mic in hand, stood a few feet outside augmented reality caution tape that would no doubt soon be replaced by a line of police bots and a hologram. Behind her, a luminous store front for high end suits and ties displayed several mannequin bots. They shifted from pose to suave pose, accentuating the latest cuts and styles. A few more feminine bots in slinky dresses hung on the shoulders of the male mannequin bots.

However, all the attention was focused on the dead body crumpled a few feet outside the entrance doors, slouched next to a sign advertising the clearance rack. Lee noticed the dead man's neck pointing to the side at an impossible angle before the body got covered by a thin white sheet.

Lee raised one eye at Nat. He caught the glance and chuckled low and slow, shaking his head all the while. Liz's long fingered hand rested comfortably on his arm.

"The damn bot acted so quickly. It grabbed the guy and twisted his neck like it was a damn 2 by 4 made of balsa wood." Nat made a twisting motion with his large hands. "I saw it all from only twenty feet or so, while I was getting a burger across the way. Close enough to see the whites of the man's eyes, see him twitch like a bot being tested on the line. But that's not the worst of it."

Nat paused mid-breath and raised his beer to his lips to down a large gulp. He sputtered through the next few sentences.

"The damn bot was arguing with him. I fucking swear it. Its tone changed, getting all ... pissed off. And I know bots can fake that kind of thing. But this was different. Real piss and vinegar. I mean ..."

Nat eyed each one of them in turn, looking for support before continuing. "It snapped his damn neck. Can't get much more real than that."

Nat continued speaking but Lee ignored him. Something about running all the way to the bar and not even stopping to make a statement to the cops. Liz would calm him down.

Lee looked back to the reporter and tried to see more of what was going on behind her.

Separated from the dead man by no more than a few feet, the metallic humanoid shell of the alleged homicidal bot lay reflecting the myriad lights of the storefront, sprawled out flat on the ground with no blanket to cover it. It looked a gender-neutral model, not wearing any clothes or covered in any paint. The design emphasized the intricate metalwork adorning its frame, clockwork gears in relief. Lee recognized it as a newly released General Purpose, or GP, bot that could only be purchased by the obscenely wealthy. Lee had never seen it in person. The camera zoomed in to the bot's remains.

The engineering looked incredible, more human-like than Lee thought Dynamic Solutions, the leading bot shell designer, to be capable of. One of the bot's elbows pointed towards the camera and Lee marveled at it. It meshed countless sliding pieces of metal composite in a flexible jigsaw around a ball joint. The design took human biology and mechanized it, improved it in some ways. Of course, the bot would never be confused for a real human. But the coded grace, the harmony of electric motors pulling artificial limbs around contoured metal joints took any good mechanic's breath away.

Lee imagined the owner bought it just for everyone to gawk at.

The flawlessness of the bot stopped short at the neck. The head showed signs of an electric fire from what must have been a nasty EMP pulse. Black smoke still trickled out the eye sockets and ear holes. The black tears and distorted metal gave the bot a ghoulish cast, smeared industrial makeup for the dead.

Lee thought he could see the edge of a short range EMP pulse grenade next to the bot. He hoped nobody had been hanging too close when it went off. The most important implants had shielding, but even that didn't always work.

Lee sighed. The whole situation felt wrong.

Lee turned his eyes away from the AR screen and spared a glance in the direction of the bots left near the entrance of the bar. Their owners sat stretching their legs and imbibing more than a few drinks while the bots stared into the street. Nu sat stolidly among them, its four wheeled legs locked straight. Lee gave him an appreciative grin. Nu was basically a tall toolbox with legs and a spinning squat head slapped on top, with a few modifications by Lee of course.

Liz's bot towered silently by Nu's side, reboot finished and back to staring out the window in standby mode. Nu's analysis showed a command had come from sub-grid 1's Watcher to shut the bot down for a moral code violation, as expected.

Lee looked back to the reporter on the screen and wondered. Given that grabbing a neck and twisting it until it snapped was an action directly opposed to any moral code in the System, why hadn't the dead man's brand spanking new GP bot been shut down remotely as soon as it tried to wring its owner's neck rather than be blasted with an EMP pulse in the middle of a public shopping mall?

It wasn't impossible to trick the system. Lee had done it himself on occasion. But he was, by the accounts of the few who truly knew him, an expert in coding and deathly curious about things he didn't know.

The first step to bypassing the moral code for any legally purchased bot was to fake a shut-down, let it disconnect from sub-grid 1 but then put it in standby mode so one could alter its code as needed. Sounded simple, but in actuality not many could do it. After that, there were software patches on the black market for nearly every model to allow them to run off sub-grid 1, all to keep Watcher from monitoring them. Expensive and very illegal, but they existed. Yet the engineering marvel laying on the grubby floor of a shopping mall a few blocks away looked brand new. Lee knew the black market to be fast but the timeline here was ridiculous. And the owner didn't look like the type to know one end of a wrench from the other, let alone how to implement some complex software.

Another way to trick the system was to change the bot's definitions of objects, like change all perceived humans to be defined as bots, which they could then physically harm. Then Watcher wouldn't notice any broach of the moral code. But that was tricky. The monitoring protocols double checked definitions against standards at regular intervals.

Perhaps it was Lee's inebriation talking but it didn't seem like the normal bot gone homicidal due to poor coding. He took another sip of water and tried to push the thoughts aside, leave them for another time. But it didn't work. It never did. Lee held the water in his hands and let his mind roam. He bet there was a very talented hacker out in the black watching the loci in their account go sky high. It always came down to money.

Lee knew of another possible explanation, one skirting the edge of his consciousness. It hid in the closet of humanity's collective mind, the philosophical boogeyman with metal bones and electricity coursing through its limbs.

Lee brushed the thought aside. He was a neural mechanic who had spent years of his life perfecting machine learning algorithms. The technology wasn't there yet, not for true artificial intelligence.

But ... that wasn't quite right, not right at all. He knew better than to lie to himself.

Nat's voice intruded into Lee's mind and scattered his thoughts.

"You've installed emotions, right?" asked Nat. From his tone, Lee could tell it was rhetorical.

"Sure, worked on them many times," said Lee. He looked over at Nu.

"Course you have," said Nat, chuckling. "Anyway, I'm telling you this bot was way ahead of anything you've touched. It had a burr up its ass and freaked harder than a dreamer getting their plug pulled."

Liz's forehead furrowed, deepening the valleys of her face.

"So, what are you saying?" asked Liz. "Bot did it all on its own? Killed that guy out of anger? Granted the guy looked like an ass but you know that can't happen. It was a glitch in the programming or a virus or a hack or something. Happens all the time."

She gestured to the AR screen. The camera was set wide to show the entire macabre crime scene, onlookers and all.

"Usually not with a dead body involved but ..." Liz waved her arm around lazily, "shit happens."

Nat looked at Liz, mouth working over some type of response. He gave up grinding his teeth, let out a small deprecating laugh and shook his head.

"You're both wrong," said Fey from across the room. "Check it out."

The AR screen on the far wall put up a graphic of a software update released yesterday morning for high end GP bots. The update was marked with Discere's logo, the premier software company for bots, and had been available for download off the Grid. The reporter's voice sounded into Lee's ears as the view shifted back to the crime scene.

"Reports have been coming in that the fake update was downloaded several thousand times before employees at Discere shut down the server, with many cases less serious than the one behind me continuing to pop up every few minutes now. It appears the update was launched from a hacked company server and sold for several thousand loci. The update promised to make bots more lifelike by incorporating advanced machine learning algorithms.

"It would appear; however, the update merely makes bots act erratically and disconnect from sub-grid 1. As you can see from the scene behind me, sometimes the results are violent. Police are insisting that all those who purchased the update must shutdown their bots immediately and roll back the software. Discere has been unavailable for comment as far as liability or refunding of purchases. Do not attempt to ..."

Lee stopped paying attention to the reporter and lowered the audio with a flick of his wrist and a few taps on his control screen.

The bar had been unnaturally quiet during the broadcast, a pall cast over the room like a funeral shawl, stifling conversation. Lee let his eyes wander around the room as the broadcast rambled on.

Nobody ran to their bots to roll back software. Nobody did much of anything other than drink their drinks and watch.

Slowly, in fits and starts, the normal sounds returned. A few strangers in a booth nearby turned back to one another and muttered something about government conspiracies in hushed tones. Fey went back to wiping down the bar with a tattered wet rag, sparing an occasional glance up at the screen. Then Nat and Liz struck up a conversation about Liz's bot, arguing over how to fix it.

Everything went back to normal, but Lee didn't buy it.

It was a fake normal, forced. Everybody took a split second longer to decide what to do next, a hair's breadth lag while trying to decide what normal was. The pauses in conversation loomed large, causing people to rush to fill the empty spaces between words.

For once, Lee was inclined to walk over to the conspiracy theorists and listen in.

The explanation given by the reporter rang of half-truths, of a story untold.

Why hack Discere just to sell an update so cheaply? Why not steal their information and sell that? And what virus made a bot act so unpredictably?

He thought back to the TV show he had finished before Nat ran in and set the day on a new course, to the bot misinterpreting thyme as time and burning the chicken, all according to a script another bot might have helped write with situations and bits pulled from a list. That bot didn't deviate from its script. Unlike what conspiracy theorists and fringe media might think, most didn't. But even so, something here felt off, Lee was sure of it.

His curiosity got the better of him, and with trembling hands he tapped out a message to Nu.

Try to find an available copy of the update floating around the edges of the Grid. Download and run a basic analysis to compare to known machine learning algorithms. Try to be discreet.

A reply flashed across the bottom right of Lee's vision.

On it, messaged Nu.

Lee went back to sipping water. He watched his BAC monitor with a bit of sadness as his alcohol levels dwindled. No doubt the update had been wiped off the hacked Discere server. But not to worry. In Lee's experience, secrets had sharp edges that entangled themselves in everything they touched, easy enough to find if one knew how to look. That of course was the trick, knowing where to look.

It wasn't more than a few minutes later when Lee heard a ding in his earpiece. A notification sound. He flicked his wrist and tapped out a few commands, expecting to see a readout of the update Nu would've found skulking around the edges of the Grid's many non-government channels. The electroluminescent array in his contacts lit up, and an AR overlay of a messaging inbox popped up at the center of his vision. The semi-transparent menu showed a smattering of old messages and one unread one.

Lee cocked his head. It wasn't from Nu, that would have been sent in a direct feed, not put into his messaging inbox. This was a work contract, asking him to fix a recreation bot down in the decaying maze of Old Chicago. The pay was good, and the owner of the business didn't have any marks against them in the system.

Lee ran a hand through his short black hair and looked back at the AR vid screen. The news had shifted to coverage of a recent mining accident out in the asteroid belt.

A rec bot wasn't much different than a GP bot, just some parts and functionality added on. He could probably fix it without much trouble, would only need an hour or so. He thought of the dead man he'd just seen on the broadcast and shook his head. There wouldn't be any reason to hire a mechanic if the update was behind this new contract. No one would pay his fee when the fix was only a reboot and a few short clicks away.

Lee scanned through the message again. No violence. Normal learning ticks and reports of unsatisfied customers over the past day.

Lee shook his head as if to shake away the nerves. He swallowed the last of the glass of water and flipped it upside down to rest on the surface of the bar. He watched the water weave a path to bead at the glass's rim, pooling onto the burnished surface of the bar. It looked like the fake Discere update would have to wait. The job wasn't too far away from his place. He could swing by his apartment, grab a few things, head out for the job and be back in time for a late dinner.

He said his goodbyes to Nat and Liz after sending Fey her tip with a few taps on his control screen. He shrugged on his blue mechanic's jacket and walked up the bar's steps into the brisk fall air. The noon sun glared down, pushing on his shoulders with warm hands. Nu ambled up the steps and zipped around Lee. Nu's four legs, each located at a corner of its elongated box shaped body, flexed at multiple joints. Each of the four wheels had a separate electric motor and braking system. The bot could maneuver better than Lee at times.

"What do you say Nu? Call a car or take the maglev?" asked Lee.

Car, messaged Nu, the text appearing letter by letter in the bottom right of Lee's augmented vision. *Maglevs don't go to the section of Old Chicago the job is at.*

Lee chuckled. "I hadn't told you where we were going yet, or about the job. You know its rude to read someone else's messages. Besides, I told you to look into the update."

Nu rolled to a stop at the edge of the street. Even though Lee knew it was just his imagination, he liked to think of the pause as Nu taking a long breath.

I can do both. Besides, you gave me permission to read your messages a long time ago. Take that up with yourself.

Lee rapped his knuckle against Nu's hard metal chassis, then leaned against his walking trashcan bot.

"Car it is," said Lee.

A few minutes later, an electric car owned by one of the cheaper car sharing companies rolled to a stop next to them. Nu part rolled, part walked, into the wide, seat-less back section of the car. Lee took his place in the driver's seat, tapping on the navigation panel to input a destination, not feeling like talking with the car's AI. One had to pay extra to get a car with an AI capable of holding a decent conversation. A steering wheel that was mostly for show lay curled up and unusable in the dash. The car turned onto the street and soft jazz began trickling out of the speakers.

Lee stared at the disfigured steering wheel and the rumblings of a headache began pulsing in the back of his head. The hard lines of the skyscrapers zoomed by, straight as a razor. His thoughts were of things dark and unnatural, as upsetting and twisted as the dead man's broken neck.

CHAPTER TWO

FOREIGN STIMULI

"Emotions are a tool. Know when to use them and when not to. Thanks
to neural conditioning programs, this concept can be easily facilitated."
Division 13 Agent Training Manual, v23, Section 2 – Neural Conditioning, Par. 1

The familiar cityscape coasted past the van window, relativity putting
it on rubber wheels, a procession of monolithic buildings plastered
with AR ads born of ones and zeroes.

Ren did her best to ignore the ads. They didn't have anything important
to tell her.

She rode in an unmarked van with her partner through the broad and
clean smart streets of New Chicago. They drifted through the arterial
byways of the roughly heart-shaped commercial sector, on their way to the
edge of the district built overtop the lake.

Ren sighed and looked out the van window, eyes scanning a twenty-floor
tall AR ad plastered on the walls of a nearby skyscraper. It advertised the
newest line of pills allowing any man or woman to regulate their skin tone
by altering melanin levels. In the ad, the skin tone of a middle-aged woman
went from dawn to dusk as she walked onto a sandy beach. Ren sighed
again, louder this time. Her attention focused inward, and her surroundings became a soft haze, blurred images. She flexed her fingers, tapping
her thumb and pinky together. Sensors implanted throughout her hand
captured the motion and a translucent AR menu appeared overtop Ren's

vision. Her hands went through a series of motions: swiping, tapping, curling. The motions corresponded to commands for her AR interface. A highlighted bar on the menu shifted upwards, flashed.

She disconnected from sub-grid 1, the ads coloring the city melting away like files scrubbed from a hard drive. Just a tap and click was all anyone in the nation had to do to ghost the unabashed capitalism, the city notices, the store names and the public biographies each person broadcast out to the curious. Yet most didn't do it, and no one disconnected entirely from the solar system wide information network known as the Grid. Connect to a sub-grid other than 1 and the city could transform, the AR overlay going from mainstream commerce to the dealings of the underground, or the more benign digital art of the masses. On one such art sub-grid, Ren had seen a skyscraper with every window covered in an homage to The Scream, the painting of a man at water's edge with a face in agony, cheeks cupped on either side by putty hands. Each of the windows had held a different expression. Ren doubted anyone in the business knew that in one plane of reality all their beautiful views of the city were blocked by a sometimes sad, sometimes happy, sometimes psychedelic but more often agonizing dark-robed man. A few of the recreations had holes for eyes and deflated price tags.

And yet, the non-government protected sub-grids drew Ren's interest both personal and professional. They had the pertinent information, those unregulated corners of the Grid.

Ren turned to look out the van window at the hordes of people walking in clumps on both sides of the street. It wasn't long before she spotted somebody lurching side to side, waving their arms back and forth as somebody else nearly twenty feet away made similar motions. Insanity was all about context. They were probably tossing spells at each other with fake wands. Ren shook her head.

Many, or more accurately most, sub-grids had less than noble intentions, information databases that turned the city into a shadowy collection of illicit deals and hushed conversation. These drew her interest, and at times her anger.

With a few fluid snaps of her wrist and some shallow finger movements, Ren shifted her connection from one sub-grid to another. With each new connection, she sent out a packaged AI program meant to scour the sub-grid for any copies or mention of the software update causing havoc across North America. With Discere being headquartered only a few miles away from their position, the city had turned into the epicenter of the unrest. Most people in the area felt a sense of pride in the company, many working for it. A larger proportion of people within Chicago city limits used Discere software than at any other place in the System.

Ren continued sending her program through as many sub-grids as possible. She didn't have access to all of them, even with her resources. She paused, her fingers stopping their hectic dance. She once again swept her eyes across the hordes of pedestrians lining the street.

Ren often wondered how far the muck of the city seeped into daily life, whether the people knew they were slogging through an invisible mire of corruption. The government regulated sub-grid 1 was supposed to be a carefully crafted shield, a blueprint for organized chaos. Society. But whenever an organization created rules, some would know how to exploit them, and some wouldn't. That left those in power with the responsibility to play it honest. The unfortunate ridiculousness of the thought tickled at Ren's mind, but she stubbornly refused to scratch. That line of questioning only wound in circles. The alternative was pure chaos, undiluted and with a major bite.

She finished probing all the relevant sub-grids, leaning back in the vehicle's faux-leather chair to wait. The program she released would alert her if it pinged. She felt confident the search would toss back some results; she had sent a wide net. But even if it did, it would take time. Servers could be found across the System, whether in a freighter coasting through the deep black or on an isolated research station set in orbit around Neptune. Lax laws out in the black made some people willing to deal with lag. Ren told herself to be patient.

Ren took her eyes away from the outside and looked at her partner sitting in the vestigial driver's seat of their government issued van. Her eyes skipped over the steering wheel as if it wasn't even there, curled up and unusable in the dash, her mind unwilling to remember the last time she gripped the plastic between tightened fingers. She looked to her partner, to his pale skin that showed in stark contrast to the dark, slate-toned suits always hanging over his tall and thin frame. He turned his head to the side and caught her eye, raising an eyebrow. The rest of his face stayed impassive, sharp eyes staring straight at Ren, mouth in a loose line.

Ren didn't respond, instead looking to the center of the dash and speaking aloud. "How much longer to our destination?" Her partner turned his eyes forward, the corners of his eyes dropping, perhaps in sadness, though the motion flashed quicker than a thought.

A warm male voice sounded out the van speakers in reply. "Approximately 35 minutes."

Ren nodded and flexed her hands, pulling up her AR menu. Her hands danced through some motions and AR folders veered to the side, enlarged, disappeared. A new folder came into view and she opened it, saw document after virtual document piled on top of one another. The documents listed all the known downloads of the faked software update, gathered and written by a government algorithm after Discere released its records. Notes from cops and government agents showed in yellow.

There had been many incidents since yesterday morning.

The update had promised drastic improvements in learned social awareness of GP bots. Dangling something like that got people interested. The price had been cheap but not outrageously so. It smelled of a good deal, and people hadn't hesitated to bite. Thousands downloaded the update before Discere shut down the server only hours after it went online.

Ren began to read through the notable cases, instances where the bots exhibited extremely aberrant behavior. Which was to say most of them.

The public wasn't aware of the depth of it all; they rarely were. They saw shadows, news reports that undersold or conspiracy theories that oversold. Shadows cast could be bigger or smaller than the object under scrutiny, depending on the angle of the incident light. And whoever controlled the light liked to spin it around, move it up and down until the image looked just as they wanted. The public rarely saw the tortured body left in the chair, rarely smelled the air infused with the stench of blood. Even the most macabre of things could be made into simple, harmless shapes when reduced to shadow. Even the cutest of toys could be made into the stuff of nightmares when put in a darkened room. Ren knew manipulation.

The bots that downloaded the update didn't disconnect from sub-grid 1. They stayed connected and Watcher failed to notice their aberrant behavior.

The news reports said otherwise but that was a necessary lie for the time being. What was left for the public to see was a shadow of the truth, the result of the government shifting the angle of incident light to leave behind something small and familiar. Safe. The incessant news cycles gave the impression that the update disconnected the bots from sub-grid 1, then altered their programming so they'd perform random actions. The truth was a little different.

Ren continued reading report after report of bots acting out of line. Bots pushed humans into walls, shattered expensive artwork, and flipped furniture. Some attempted to build things out of household objects, one building a scale model of the city out of paper towel. Others rigged hackneyed yet elegant electronics. Most ignored any commands. A few stood in corners and sang a verse of a song over and over like a human whose mind had cracked, old rock and roll mostly. Ren didn't know why. Most of the reports fell into the weird category.

Discere had handed over the full list of downloads after mounting pressure from the government reached its apex with the murder. Most of the bots had already been shut down remotely, with the last few being hunted down by cops all over North America.

Ren closed the last of the reports and opened a file she'd set off to the side. It concerned the only homicide directly linked to the software update.

The bot that twisted a man's neck in the middle of a public shopping complex had been like the others, connected to sub-grid 1 the whole time. It killed a human without the Governance AI monitoring system noticing any subversion of the moral code. The log data from Watcher showed no abnormalities. For anything more in depth, they needed the black box from the bot itself.

With a shooing gesture, Ren cleared her vision of any large AR graphics. Only the standard few readouts detailing health and status updates remained at the corners of her vision.

"Hey Tap, any update from Discere? Share audio with Jace," said Ren.

Her partner Jace looked over and nodded, face deadpan. She knew he didn't need to hear the audio. Tap could speak to him in a more direct fashion, her too if she willed it. She didn't though, not yet.

The government created AI called the Tactical Assistance Personality, or TAP for short, sounded in both Ren and Jace's implanted earpieces. Its voice sounded rough and low, raspy yet with a lilt around the edges that made its coded gender hard to discern.

"Still no ID on who hacked the Discere server. The address of the aggressor was traced off-world, to a TKJ Heavy Industries colony on Ti-

tan before it became too difficult to follow. As to their purpose, no one
has come forward to claim responsibility. The proceeds from selling the
update were routed out of Discere through several accounts of deceased
or falsified identities all originating in the Belt. Given current political
relations, chances are not promising our requests for information to Belt
representatives will garner a response."

Ren felt a scowl creep over her face. The corporate ridden asteroid belt
would slow things down excessively, but she had ways around that.

"Progress on analyzing the software update?" asked Ren.

"Analysis still in progress," replied Tap. "The code is quite novel, and
both Discere and I don't know what to make of it quite yet. The government has allowed my parent AI to cede some of its processing capacity to
solve this issue. In the meantime, it would be prudent to assume the actions
of the bots are not as random as they appear to be."

Ren thought she saw a ghost of a smile hiding behind Jace's impassive
mask. Often Tap felt more emotionally expressive than her partner. The
AI spoke with a heavy authority thinly veiled behind the obsequiousness
of a butler.

"Thanks for the suggestion," said Ren, voice clipped. "What about the
homicide we're heading to? Vid feed come in yet?"

Tap opened an AR window in Ren's vision with a paused video at its
center. Ren could tell from the specks of light dusting Jace's contacts that
he was viewing the same thing. Ren made several sharp hand gestures, first
to activate hand control, then to start the recording.

The feed came from a security cam inside a posh men's clothing store.
Ren spared a momentary glance in Jace's direction and smirked. He sat
unmoving with hands in his lap, eyes shifting as he watched the video.
Given the clean stylings of the store's clothing, he was probably familiar
with the place.

She recognized the middle-aged victim from her files. The man's bio had
been rather short: 61, bureaucrat turned wealthy lobbyist, married, and no
kids. He stood leisurely in the center of the camera's view with his hands
stuffed into his suit pockets. He grazed through the aisles, idly picking up
suit jackets before placing them back on the rack. Every so often he would
pause, hold up a jacket in his hands, look at his personal bot always only
a few feet away, and mouth a question. The bot's mechanical lips would
form a reply. Audio wasn't included in the video file.

Ren paused the video and scrutinized the man's personal bot, eyes sweeping up and down hoping to see something irregular, something that foreshadowed what it was about to do.

Instead, all she saw was a new GP bot, if admittedly well-built in the modern fashion. It had too thin limbs and a long torso, built with gender-neutral curves. A chest formed of metal panels stylized with gears. Narrow waist and long legs. Arms dexterous and light but exuding strength from their shiny metal surface.

Ren's eyes narrowed the barest amount while looking at the bot. She couldn't help but feel impressed. She shook her head once, tight and quick. She flexed her hand and the video played on.

The bot and its owner circled around one rack, then another. The man approached a rack of discounted jackets and ambled from piece to piece, sizing the jackets up. His face twitched and he looked around. He grabbed for a black one with a buttoned vest underneath, wavered, then pulled his hand back. He left the rack behind and strolled towards the entrance to the store. Ren rewound the video.

While the man had been dawdling at the clearance rack, his bot had stopped tailing him. The bot turned to look somewhere off camera, its gaze transfixed. It stood unmoving as its owner shuffled through suit jackets then moved to leave the store. The man didn't notice the lack of the bot's presence until he'd crossed the store's threshold. He called to his bot as his face scrunched in confusion. The bot didn't turn, instead acting as if it hadn't heard him. The man's face pinched and went red. He rushed back to the bot's side and grabbed its too thin arm.

The bot didn't budge. The man continued awkwardly pulling on its arm for a few moments, eyes searching around the store to make sure nobody watched. Eventually he reached up to the bot's neck to fiddle with its control panel; Ren guessed to start a reboot.

Then the bot turned, and its mechanical face made of hundreds of sliding composite parts contorted into a scowl. He pulled his arm back sharply, looking around again. The graceful lips of the bot formed words that dripped with venom. He seemed at a loss for what to do until the bot started walking out the front entrance of the store on its own. He caught up to it just as the camera view switched, the vid feed looking from a hallway wall outside the store.

The man's brows furrowed into a deep V. He grabbed the bot's arm till his knuckles went white. The bot turned back to look at him, mechanical face going from rage to a passive calm that only machines could honestly assume, lips forming words again, slow and serene. His face abruptly assumed the wide eyes and slightly agape mouth of the very afraid. The bot's hands shot up from its sides and grabbed the man's head. Its motions were light and fluid, as dexterous as if it had been practicing the motion for years. Its hands twisted in a half-circle. First one way. Then the other. Then it stilled as the man's face went slack, jowls almost bouncing as his head lolled to the side.

Ren imagined she could hear the sharp crack that must have emanated from his neck and drawn curious glances from people walking nearby. Glances that quickly shifted from curious to stunned as the man's body crumpled to rest against a sign, dead before he hit the ground. The bot let gravity pull its owner's body down to press against the floor.

After a minute, its head shifted in the direction of whatever had caught its attention before the outburst. It looked off camera, froze again, could have easily been mistaken for a statue if not for the dead man spreading drool across the floor at its feet.

Ren fast-forwarded the video. A steady stream of people bubbled around the edges of the camera's view, always in clumps, always giving the bot a wide berth. A few of the newly arrived onlookers tried to go closer, then stopped. From the glances and moving mouths, Ren could tell the truth of the matter was spreading. Their first guess had probably been that somebody killed the man then ran off, leaving the bot alone to watch over its now dead owner, certainly more common.

A few minutes later, a local cop emerged into the camera view and tossed a short range EMP grenade as people scattered to keep out of its way. The thing popped open like a flower in bloom releasing invisible spores of electromagnetic energy, the only visible reaction the shudder of the bot and quick hand motions of those standing too close to the blast reflexively touching their now fried electronics. Thankfully, the camera perched too far away to be affected.

The bot crumpled to the ground to lay beside its owner, yet no drool came out of its mouth. Rather, black tendrils of smoke from internal electrical fires began trickling out of any open orifices.

Ren rewound the video to the part where the bot stood stock still in the middle of the shop, ignoring the aggravated yells from its owner.

"Tap, open the blueprint interface. I want to see if we have any vid feeds from another angle, any that might show what this bot is looking at."

The AR overlay in Ren's view shifted, the vid feed decreasing in size and moving to the left. Then a blueprint of the shopping center, tiny blue dots indicating the locations of cameras, appeared on the right side of her vision. Orange triangles popped up to represent the bot and its owner. When Ren moved the vid forward and backward, the orange triangles shifted in time with the motions of the bot and human. The direction of each triangle indicated where they were looking. By extrapolating, Ren could tell the bot had been staring through the clothing store's floor to ceiling glass windows at a portion of wall neighboring an automated fast-food restaurant across the hallway.

With a few taps of her fingers and flicks of her wrist, the dot representing the necessary camera on the building's blueprint shimmered and enlarged. A new camera view dominated the right-hand side of Ren's vision, synced to the time of the original video still present on her left. She looked in close, anticipation stilling her hand.

The wall the bot had been looking at appeared barren, 20 square feet of nothing.

"Tap, layer the mall-wide AR overlay onto the camera feed," said Ren. It only took a few moments.

Her hunch had been correct. The previously bare iron-colored wall now showed multiple rows of separate AR vid screens. Some showed ads while others showed TV programs and movies.

Ren brought up the blueprint with the orange triangles again. She traced the line from the bot to the wall, numbered each of the screens.

No good. The vid screens were too far away from the bot and too tightly spaced, making it hard to know for certain which screen had so enamored the bot.

Ren crossed her legs, uncrossed them moments later. Her fingers tapped against the plastic center panel of the van, reflexively shifting through various command sequences even though she had suspended hand control. Either deaf to the taps or accepting the rhythmic noises stoically, Jace sat relaxed at her side, hands still resting unperturbed in his lap. He had other ways of controlling his implanted tech and AR interface.

Ren eyed Jace sidelong. Her throat tightened. She opened her mouth to ask him a question, then pushed the words back down. She sighed and wished things could go back to how they had been once upon a time. It hadn't been his fault. He hadn't even been there. But the way he held himself, the deathly calm and assurance, his features as if crafted from uncaring stone, it all reminded her too much of what had happened. Of how she had been. Of how she will be once again, given the right trigger. Jace didn't deserve her irritation; she knew the truth lying dormant beneath. She just wished he'd let himself out more these days, not leave himself trapped railing against Ta... Best she phrased those thoughts differently.

Ren enlarged the vid feed of the wall to take up her whole vision. The change relegated the passing cityscape, the clean interior of their van, and Jace's silent figure to a bare whisper. Anything other than the wall of ads and shows and movies became an afterthought, only existing if she looked at the hazy corners of her vision.

Whenever Ren used AR to change her viewpoint to that of a camera, it gave her an odd sense of vertigo. The movements of the camera felt too smooth, and the height from which it looked floated much higher than she could reach. After a few moments, her feeling of being out of place subsided, her body's sense of balance settling in behind the camera lens.

Over a dozen AR vid screens covered the wall, currently frozen mid-scene. Ren looked at each one in turn. There were blithely unaware couples locking eyes in fields of flowers, sweaty men arm-wrestling with shiny robotic arms from elbow to alloyed fingertip, toothpaste with nanoparticles for cleaning teeth, smart athletic wear, gaudy winter socks with warming circuitry. Nothing stuck out to Ren as something that would convince a bot to twist a man's neck.

She pressed play and all the screens sprang into action. Several of the programs she hadn't been able to identify looked to be daytime soaps, overacted fluff shot on a few set pieces. With every new scene, another previously unknown love child or betrayal revealed itself. Ren muttered an obscenity beneath her breath and moved on.

Ren's concentration was interrupted by a polite cough coming from her partner. She lowered the opacity on her AR overlay and raised one eyebrow at him, mirroring his pose from earlier. He dropped the hand he'd used to cover the cough to his lap.

"Third vid screen from the right, second row," said Jace. His voice floated through the van, each word hitting Ren's ears the exact same way, sedate and solemn.

Ren cursed under her breath, though not with any real anger.

"You got lucky," she said.

She saw Jace's lips curl into a smirk at her small outburst. Cracks in his armor were good to see, very good. Neural conditioning, damnable or not, granted him more than a few unique, and exceedingly useful, abilities. Agents called it NeuCon.

She dropped her eyes, paused, shook her hands to relax her muscles; Jace was a worry for another time. She rewound the video.

The screen Jace mentioned showed an attractive man wearing loose sweatpants and a t-shirt advertising some type of training program. He stood in the center of a furniture-less room, cheap calligraphic hangings on the walls lending the feel of a training center hidden in a strip mall, right next to a burger joint. It reminded her of the first place she ever fought, complete with motivational posters telling the students to "believe" or that there was "no substitute for hard work."

The man in the workout clothing stepped back and a cheap graphic appeared on the bottom half of the ad listing the contact information of the studio. A self-protection course, and for only 20 loci they offered interactive AR lessons.

From outside the camera's view a middle-aged man and woman walked onto the matted sparring floor, the nervous-looking woman over a foot shorter than the man. Ren figured the woman would be the one demonstrating the move; everybody loved a good underdog story and people often paid too much attention to size. Ren could remember multiple occasions where she had to drop an older male student forcefully into the floor just to set the record straight.

Sure enough, the woman moved in close to her sparring partner. Her right hand floated slowly to her sparring partner's chin, left hand settling easily on the other side of the man's head past his ear. With her previous timidity gone, the woman twisted her opponent's head slowly to one side, right hand leading the man's jaw in a measured dance. Then she reversed the motion, pulling the man's jaw to her while pushing the back of the man's head away, all at a leisurely pace. The instructor nodded, and Ren felt her chest expand as a sharp intake of breath spiked its way into her lungs.

The woman stepped back from her sparring partner and flowed through the motions again, this time at full speed. Ren could almost hear the crack of an imaginary man's neck.

Or in this case, a not so imaginary man's neck.

Ren felt her breath trickle out, slow and even. The bot had been copying the vid. She paused the vid and melted the AR overlay away with a quick hand motion. The sight of the city passing by on either side returned, the noon sun covered by an increasingly overcast sky. A sea of taillights stretched out in front of their van.

The bot in the shopping complex had seen the self-defense demonstration and mirrored it moments later. The action had been preceded by an anger that seemed to swell up out of nowhere and subside just as fast, but not before climaxing with a snap. Ren felt her heart begin to ramp its speed and took a deep breath, bringing it back down before it could get out of control. It seemed the software update alone hadn't pushed the bot to murder.

She had to think about what she knew. The facts as they were. Bots acted per their programming; this one was no different. It wasn't that there was no coded impulse guiding the bot's actions, it was that the coded impulse was more complicated than strangle this man at this specific time. The program hidden in the update only felt chaotic because she did not understand it yet.

The reports from earlier demonstrated the effect of the update. The bots became more inquisitive, acting and reacting with their immediate environment without asking for the direction of their owner or consulting moral code. Except it wasn't just the moral code, the bots ignored core programming as well. Their actions became unpredictable in that their actions became much more dependent on their environment, on external stimuli. Given the video Ren just finished watching, it felt likely many of the reports could be better understood through environmental catalysts.

Bots had always taken information in, analyzed it, then spit out some resultant piece of information. They were complex, but nothing more than in-out data machines. The difference in what Ren saw in the video seemed one of regulation and control. The update erased many restrictions, allowing the bots to act out in whatever ways programming *and* environment directed.

Ren ran her hand through her shoulder length black hair, teasing out a few knots. The Discere server containing the original software update had been shut down, most of the bots with the update already rolled back to their previous versions or destroyed. But whoever created the software, hacked the server and released it was laughing out loud in some grungy bar while watching the news, a fat stack of loci in their account and a dangerous piece of software stored on their drives.

Ren looked at Jace, comforted by his inexpressive figure rather than unnerved by it, things feeling for just a moment like how they used to be.

"I see why the boss wants that black box so bad," said Ren.

Jace nodded, moving to straighten his deep ochre tie with one pale hand.

By the time Ren and Jace arrived at the labyrinthine shopping complex, the sun had toppled off its highest peak and began its trek towards the horizon, its path obscured by clouds. It would be several hours before it touched the rim and disappeared piece by piece. As their van steered itself towards the underground parking lot, Ren gave the sun a long look. Given the increasingly short days and the amount of work left, there was a good chance she wouldn't get to see it again until tomorrow.

Their van slid into a recessed, underground parking spot near the main elevator and the two agents stepped out its doors. The twin humanoid bots painted a matte black and sitting in the back of the van moved to follow out the side door, Tap pulling on their strings and controlling their limbs. They were larger than most bots, hulking things with blocky appendages and armored plates placed strategically across their bodies. A narrow head like a bucket flipped upside down with a cyclopean eye moving across its surface sat across their shoulders. Without any distinguishing marks of ownership on their bodies, they looked both imposing and mysterious, two things Ren and Jace didn't need for their current job. Many recognized the bots anyway. She motioned for them to wait in the van.

They walked through the quiet parking garage to the elevator, the only heartbeats present on the floor. Most of the cars were owned by car-sharing companies, not private citizens.

They walked into the elevator and cheap synth music played over the speakers, the musical notes trilling up and down the scales like a kid running up and down the stairs. Ren pressed the button for ground floor 1.

The building they were about to enter sat on the edge of both Lake Michigan and the section of the city that extended out over the lake. The building consisted of two distinctive sections: an expansive and relatively squat section with several below-ground floors, and a skyscraper emerging from the wider building's center. The skyscraper consisted mostly of business offices with a tourist viewing platform near the top. Most of the shops, including where the murder had occurred, could be found in the lower levels, in the wide and squat building that spread its concrete and metal hundreds of feet along the coastline.

Once they made it to the right floor, Ren connected to sub-grid 1 and a complementary map of the shopping complex popped into the right-hand corner of her vision. She added her own details to the map.

After a short walk, Ren and Jace came to a holographic projection blocking a hallway. The fake wall stood several meters in front of the crime scene, blocking the view of the clothing store and the opposing fast-food restaurant named Quickauto Burgers n' Fries, the hallway ending for real not much further on. The projection emanated from a squat metal box resting on the floor. It warned against entry in white, flowing script. The holographic wall meshed with the edges of the corridor. It was convincing work.

Ren nodded to Jace before walking through the screen and past the line of police bots sitting protectively on the other side. She didn't spot any reporters past the wall. The local cops must have forced the media out. She felt the muscles in her shoulders relax. She'd noticed more than a few people strolling through the area on the other side casting hesitant glances, brows furrowed by thinly veiled curiosity. The news of the murder was out, and its location wasn't a secret. Most would respect the holographic wall and go on their way, walking from store to store and picking items to be carried home by a personal bot or sent by drone. But Ren didn't doubt a few people were recording a vid of everything that went in and out of the area for various news outlets. Doing anything more, like moving through the holographic wall, would be a quick way to get arrested.

Ren paused to absorb her surroundings. Nothing compared to seeing a crime scene in person, even if one could tap into what other people were seeing, take a seat behind their eyes.

Jace went and introduced himself to the two local beat cops monitoring the scene. Thankfully, Ren and Jace's boss had called ahead, giving orders not to mess with the damaged hardware.

Ren's eyes came to a stop, resting on the scarred metallic body sprawled across the ground, no sheet to cover it. The smell of burnt plastic still hung in the air, hovering around the wreckage. The air scrubbing systems of the building would take care of that soon enough. The man's body had already been moved off site, an oddly clean section of floor the only mark left. Behind that stood the now dark storefront of the clothing store, its neon sign dead and dark but still legible. It was named Nix. The mannequin bots beneath the sign had frozen mid-pose, changed to old-fashioned mannequins once the power turned off.

Jace walked up to Ren and gave a shallow nod.

"We good?" asked Ren.

Jace nodded again.

"Think those cops ever seen autos before?"

Jace set down a toolbox he'd carried in with them and put his hands into his suit pockets, looking over his shoulder at the pair of local cops and the twitching store manager. Ren knew the store manager hadn't been too happy about a murderous bot in front of his store, even if it looked dead. When she'd walked through the holographic wall, the man had been in the middle of complaining to the local cops. Now he stood shoulder to shoulder with them. Rather than continuing their argument, the group had joined in trying to hide their furtive sidelong glances.

"Doubtful," said Jace.

Ren laughed and the group watching them seemed surprised by the sound, their bodies loosening as the tension in the hallway lessened a bit.

Autos, agents of Division 13 like Ren and Jace, weren't known to laugh.

Even so, the group watched her and Jace silently, out of the corners of their eyes. They resembled a huddle of animals, watching a powerful predator amble through their turf.

"They have anything for us?" asked Ren.

"Nothing useful," replied Jace. "The victim had a rolling recording of what he saw that lasted five minutes. But there wasn't anything new." Jace shrugged his thin shoulders slowly, as if stretching, looking over to the heap of metal now at their feet.

"What about their conversation?"

"The victim was here to buy new clothes for an upcoming wedding. A relative of his wife's. He was asking the bot which his wife would prefer him to buy," said Jace.

He continued looking at the bot. The cops didn't have any worthwhile information. The bot did. Ren nodded.

"Guess it's time then," said Ren.

She crouched down next to the bot, pulled the toolbox close. The bot lay almost face-down, eyes askance. She ran her fingers against the bot's neck, feeling the smooth interlocking plates. Hardly any ridges. She needed to gain access to the bot's black box, a thumb sized solid state hard drive that recorded the sequences of code that made the bot tick, like an in-depth and fully decipherable EEG of a human brain. Even though it held terabytes worth of information, it only could contain several hours of bot activity before it ran out of space and overwrote the oldest data. Still, it would contain all the code of the murder.

That was the nice part about when bots went wrong. Even if they malfunctioned, one only had to look at the code to figure out why. Humans on the other hand could be broken any number of ways and a psychologist wouldn't have a clue as to the reason. Most people couldn't afford the complete brain scans, and even if they could every corp. had their own interpretation. Ren thought of the implants spiderwebbing through her skull and grit her teeth the barest amount.

The control panel of the bot didn't respond to her taps. Ren looked up at Jace; they would have to tear the bot apart to get at the black box. Many bot shells were designed so that it was easy to reach, ingenious mechanisms allowing access at the press of a button, whether the bot had power or not. Unfortunately, the bot laying in front of the two didn't have that. The designers had felt the need to place the black box about where the stomach would be in a human. It lay sealed beneath several inches of sliding metal parts and carefully engineered apparatuses, hidden inside a shielded cage to protect from EMP pulses. The latter part was important, the former simply annoying.

Ren put her hands underneath the bot and shrugged it onto its back, the eyes now staring up at the ceiling. It shimmered in the LED lighting as its metal body moved. Black trails wove from the eyes with blue motorized irises. Plastic curled around the mouth.

For a moment Ren felt self-conscious for the bot, for its nudity. Its human-like frame with its graceful curves lay under the lights as if on display, its arms and legs splayed outwards at odd angles, so unlike its careful design. The beat cops watched her; she could feel their stares on her back, on the bot. She knew the store manager to be watching with fear in his eyes. She didn't know whether the fear stemmed from her and Jace's presence, or the bot's. Her hand shook the barest amount.

She felt rather than saw Jace shift his feet, as if impatient. Though that might have been her imagination. Jace kept his feelings locked deep below these days. She took a breath and pulled the small rectangular toolbox resting at Jace's feet to her side.

The excavation of the black box was nearly twenty minutes underway when Ren accidentally brought a power cable too close to several unknown cords with frayed and melted insulation. An arc of electricity tinged with blue jumped between the two contacts, hungrily clearing the thin gap of air. A loud crack echoed from the discharge, thunder in miniature.

Ren jerked the cords apart from each other reflexively then attempted to still her body, slow her heart before it sped up. But some things weren't so easily controlled.

It only took fractions of a second, but the process ingrained in the reptilic section of her human brain sent a cascade of chemicals coursing through her body.

Pulses in the amygdala started a chain reaction that spread to the hypo-thalamus, signals rushing along channels to release a flood of hormones from the pituitary gland. Cortisol spread in waves and adrenaline suffused her. Pupils dilated a fraction of a centimeter; blood rushed to redden her dusky cheeks as her heart pulsed out the beginnings of a mad beat and the edges of her vision blurred. It only took fractions of a second, yet it was enough to trigger NeuCon. As her body continued to follow the commands of her brain, the implants throughout her skull and neck recorded the physiological changes and implemented their own set of programs. Electricity wove its way from her tech core to the nodes placed underneath her skull. Neurons triggered, and Ren's brain hitched as if confused from the mixed signals. When it began moving again it did so with implacable precision.

It was all done before her hands stopped moving.

She sat there analyzing the bot while Jace kneeled next to her, her mind taking on the head under water feeling common to NeuCon. Emotions felt dampened, suppressed. Worries about tearing apart a naked, human-like doll that could convincingly pass a Turing test got tamped down, saved for later. Worries about the case, about Jace's dependence on the process currently shaping her thoughts, disappeared. All that was left was a cold and rational evaluation of her surroundings.

The bot's body jerked in response to the shock, flickers of a past pseudo-life. Then the jaunts and shivers grew into something more. Ren saw the bot's eyes flutter; its mouth mumbled a few inaudible words. Speakers in the bot's throat let out a hiss and a crackle. It attempted to sit up but only one arm responded, causing the bot to crash piteously back to the ground. More mumbled words spilled out of the bot's mouth, this time beginning to mesh into things coherent and grating.

"I don't give a damn which jacket you pick. They all look like shit. You think a jacket is going to make her less angry when she looks at you? A piece of cloth with two arms and a slit right down the middle? It's *Shit*. Shit. Shit. Shiiiiiiiiiit. ..." The words sounded low and angry, pulsing with a red rhythm.

Ren saw it all happen, but only as a series of facts to be evaluated and responded to. The emotional context wasn't gone, just presented in the form of data points.

She dexterously pulled a thin metal chip from her pocket and pressed it to the back of the bot's tapered neck, overtop the control panel. The bot's eyes shut, and its body grew still. Its motions had been nothing more than flickers of a past pseudo-life, death spasms.

There wasn't any need for the bot to be active. Whether it still worked or not didn't change anything. All the necessary information lay sequestered in the black box. Ren disconnected the power cables. There wouldn't be any relapses.

Jace and Ren worked together to remove the rest of the bot's alloyed guts, pulling the black box out and holding it up to the light mere minutes after shocking the bot back to life, only to kill it again.

The beat cops and store manager standing off to the side had gawked during the bot's spasms, turning back to each other afterwards with wide eyes and hushed voices. They no longer hid their fear and revulsion of the agents.

Ren ignored them and pocketed the black box in her midnight black trench coat. Her and Jace still had a long day ahead of them.

Chapter Three

Unpaid Labor

"Given the amount of data and time required to bring a neural network up to an acceptable level of intelligence, a full factory reset is not always advisable. Rolling back the software or partial resets are often enough. However, a full factory reset is the easiest and most effective way to deal with any systemic errors."
Mechanic's Guidebook, v99, Section 2 – Neural Networks, Par. 4

The self-driving sedan carrying Lee and Nu made good time through the gridded streets, dropping them off at the steps of a dun high-rise apartment building. It waited by the sidewalk for their eventual return.

In no rush, Lee walked leisurely through the automatic doors of the building, a near smile on his lips. His apartment was only a few blocks away from Fey's Place; yet, thanks to a timely release of chemicals into his bloodstream from the implanted medical upgrade, the foreboding rumblings of a headache had tapered off into the two-bit ramblings of a street-side soothsayer. Lee decided the BAC monitor constantly reminding him of his bad habits was worth the near instantaneous relief.

They made it to his apartment on the thirteenth floor and set about gathering the tools they would need for the upcoming job. The trick was finding them.

Lee had amassed a sizable number of odds and ends over the years, and they had all migrated into piles around the one-bedroom apartment like nomads searching for kindred souls. The main room contained most of the clutter. Solid state hard drives, hybrid capacitive battery packs, old model neural networks, robotic arms and legs gathered from scrap piles for parts, scavenged near-room temperature superconductive wire, and second-hand appliances all occupied space. Every horizontal surface held piles of maze-like circuitry. It had been awhile since Lee bothered to clean the place up.

Shortly after Lee began his search for the tools, a voice emanated from a seated figure in a dusty corner of the room, next to the covered window letting in a few muted bars of sunlight.

"Welcome home Lee. Are you looking for anything in particular or are you finally going to clean this place up?" The voice was feminine, the sound of wind through the trees, light with a rustling laugh at its edges. But for all the voice's subtle nuance, it came from a machine.

The phrasing of the question pricked at Lee's consciousness, recalling similar instances years past of walking into his apartment before heading back out on some contract, back when there had been somebody with a heartbeat to witness him step over the threshold late in the afternoon. The piles of stuff had been quite a bit smaller then, rolling hills in comparison to the mountainous trash heaps now looming on every surface. The memories of that time were fragile things, relegated to dusty shelves in the back of Lee's mind for fear of breaking them. Or perhaps they just hurt to hold. Fragile things often had sharp edges.

"Just on my way to a job Fu. Picking up a few things," said Lee, speaking through a wry grin. His grin faltered, then slipped away entirely.

The AI interface for controlling all aspects of his apartment, the bot named Fu, let out a sonorous chuckle, not moving from its seat. Fu came with the room, a genderless bipedal collection of thin metal limbs covered in a pacifying glossy blue paint that had long ago lost its shine. It sat with perfect posture, five-fingered hands resting in its lap and club-like feet pointing forward on the ground.

Lee didn't bother to respond to the bot's laugh, his mind carefully inspecting old memories to see if they still cut. A prickling sensation of heat, like he had lodged a piece of still-hot food at the back of his throat, suffused his neck. He realized with a start it was his implanted tech overheating.

After a few tense moments, the feeling subsided. Lee filed the occurrence away for after the upcoming job. It had happened several times before, and he never could find a reason behind it. He'd hoped during the recent installation of his medical upgrade that the tech could be looked at with a little more scrutiny, but nothing had been found at that time either. He decided to run some diagnostics and look over the code later.

Lee looked at the clock readout in the lower corner of his vision and made a mental note of the time. He could make it back before dinner, but it would be a late dinner.

Next to the door sat a metal tool closet and Lee shuffled through its shelves. He found what he was looking for and turned around to find Nu digging through a pile of solid-state hard drives near the end of his small kitchen bar. Nu's single articulated arm dug through the mess, pushing pieces to each side. One piece clinked off the kitchen bar to rest on the stained ceramic tiling in front of the stove.

With a shrug, Lee walked up to Nu and opened a few of the bot's side trays. He dropped his yellow diagnostic controller into the bottom of Nu's storage receptacle, the cords connected on every side of the thing splaying outwards and jostling the other contents. Lee hadn't cleaned the tray out in weeks. The pile at the bottom of the recessed area consisted of extra batteries and external processors. A few of the batteries looked as if they could be leaking, small trails of corrosion coming from their edges. Lee would have to clean that out before it damaged Nu.

It wasn't until Lee looked up that he saw what Nu dug towards, the bot's squat head spinning back and forth to glimpse at Lee. Nu tried to obstruct Lee's view but failed. Considering the bot only had the one arm, its chances hadn't been great anyway.

At the bottom of the hard drive graveyard, like an unearthed casket of a bittersweet memory, was a framed picture of Lee. At his side stood a woman he hadn't spoken to in eight years. Lee distractedly pushed some of the hard drives back over top. He tapped his knuckle against Nu's metal head and pushed him towards the door.

It crossed his mind how many other piles of scavenged junk sitting around his apartment hid similar things. The memories still stung. But time had done its job and dulled the edge. It was, as they say, ancient history.

"Heading back out?" asked Fu. Her voice had lost its bubbly tinge, perhaps in response to Lee's muted reply from earlier. Now the bot sounded smooth and businesslike, its normal voice.

Lee grunted in accord and smiled a pained smile. "Don't expect us back until late," he said. "Have the usual ordered and prepped for dinner."

The two of them moved into the hallway, Lee closing the door behind him and listening for the locks to slide into place. After they made it back out to the street and into the car, Lee looked at Nu with a question on his lips. But the question faded. Instead, a statement came out.

"You know you shouldn't change Fu's voice," said Lee, turning to look at the four-legged bot locked into place in the back of the car. He sighed. "Still, you're going to have to tell me sometime where you found it. It had a nice laugh. Unburdened, like only a bot could be."

Nu didn't respond. Their car lurched of its own accord onto the increasingly busy afternoon streets.

Traveling through Old Chicago always felt like traveling through a different city to Lee, a city less scripted, more scattered by time and the pull of hundreds of different hands tugging towards themselves. It was a place where physical billboards, hand painted murals and fading graffiti remained. These things couldn't be avoided by disconnecting from a sub-grid, couldn't be copy and pasted with a click. They couldn't be ignored. They could only be scoffed at as the car sped past, dismissed with a roll of the eyes or an adamant focus on the horizon. He loved these sections of the city.

The car carrying the two of them made its way off the main road and exited into a business suburb taking advantage of the old district's economical rent. Gaudy digital signs made to look as if they were constructed of neon tubes featured prominently on most levels of the tall and narrow structures, spelling out whatever businesses hid behind the windows. Mostly middling software companies or entertainment startups.

Lee dropped his eyes to street level. In the decaying sunlight and lengthening shadows, the streetlamps had switched on and created blips in the dusk where people could be seen moving briskly away from the buildings, leaving work to head home. They wove among the merchants and goods that spilled out of the ground level stores onto the sidewalk, many ignoring the calls for their attention and loci. The local stores and street markets were grimy yet welcoming things, family run businesses using stock AR signs purchased from the Grid. Odds were good the signs had been coded in one of the offices above. A few stalls had bots repeating slogans over and over, ready to assist any customer. These bots were rusted things, lined with scratches and cracks that made their metal seem wrinkled. Lee watched the bots lurch about through his car window. In Lee's opinion, what the area lacked in riches was more than made up for in character.

Lee evaporated the news feeds he'd been half paying attention to and told the car to pull over, hearing a ding as it pulled a couple loci out of his account. They could walk the last few blocks to the job.

The air smelled with the stench of many people living and working in proximity, intermingled with notes of mystery food grown in vats and grilled in open air kitchens. Stalls held mounds of fresh fruits and vegetables that looked ready to cascade off the edges of their tables at the smallest touch. Much of the produce came from rooftop vertical gardens high above. Some came from nearby greenhouses, others plucked from the miles and miles of farmland surrounding the city. But the meat came from vats, either from factories pumping out slabs of meat a minute or from mini vats where families could try out their own recipes. Bit of beef muscle cells, bit of pork, dash of sheep. Some insect proteins tossed in. Only meat not grown in a vat came from the New Chicago Freshwater Fisheries.

Lee stopped short at one such stall and purchased a skewer of not-chicken from a diminutive woman who spoke with a heavy Old Chicago dialect. The old lady handed the not-chicken skewer dripping fat and sauce to Lee with an encouraging grunt. "Maun maun. Slow is best. Swaadisht, no?" she said.

The street language was an amalgam of English, Spanish, Mandarin, and Hindi. The proportions changed with every street. This street leaned towards the Mandarin and Hindi side. Lee couldn't speak it all that well, had trouble forming his mouth around the disparate sounds, but he understood it well enough and abhorred using translators.

Lee smiled and nodded, chewing a full bite of the vat-grown meat with relish. Even though he could tell it to be mostly algal, its consistency and taste was closer than most, better than the real thing in his mind. Not too chewy, not too dry. He connected to the old lady's tech and transferred fractions of a loci.

Lee moved down the street and tilted the skewer with one last chunk of not-chicken towards Nu, as if to offer him the bit hanging by a thread. The bot didn't slow down and brushed past Lee.

There is a good chance that stuff is overridden with bacteria and perhaps even a few viruses, messaged Nu, the text flashing across Lee's vision.

Nu slowed as a man walking towards the two of them got in the bot's way. The next message came more slowly than the first, popping up a letter at a time rather than a word at a time.

You do realize that you purchase street food nearly every time you are reminded of her. Perhaps you should find a better coping mechanism. One that doesn't make you sick.

Lee looked at the not-chicken skewer as if it had betrayed him. In fact, he hadn't realized that bit of information. But as he tore off the final piece with his teeth and placed the leftover plastic rod so that it would stand up straight in a crevice at the top of Nu's metal head, he realized it made some sense. May had always given him a withering look if he came home with mini-vat food. She'd always hated the stuff, could afford to, which only made Lee like it even more. His love for street food had only grown.

"That can't be entirely true. I haven't thought of her in months, years since I dwelled on her for any length of time. Or waltzed down memory lane with some old vids. Besides, today was entirely your fault," said Lee.

They made it twenty feet further down the sidewalk, walked past the opening of a shadowed alleyway. Nu responded.

Could you at least remove the piece of plastic you stuck in my head? It's not an antenna.

Lee chuckled. The bot had always hated it if Lee didn't keep him in good repair. A common trait among bots, expressly programmed so that owners would be more inclined to take care of them and spend money on maintenance. Nu had extended that urge until becoming pathological over the years of Lee working on him, getting bothered by even the smallest of scratches and burrs, the slightest of things out of place. In short, Nu had gained an opinion on how it should look. And a plastic spike still covered in sauce wasn't something the bot preferred to have sticking out of its chassis. Lee knew the bot's arm couldn't reach it to brush it aside.

"No can do, my friend," said Lee, hitting the top of Nu with his bare knuckle. "Punishment for messing with Fu without my permission."

I simply wanted to see if your response to memories of May had improved. Your recovery period has been ... long. How else am I supposed to track your progress? And the apartment does need to be cleaned up. I can't roll through the room any more without catching something in my wheels.

Lee ignored the message from Nu and kept walking. He attributed the comment to the bot's ingrained need to gather data. Nu was more aggressive in its search for tasty bits of information than a diehard gossip.

Lee flicked the piece of plastic out of Nu's metal chassis and stuffed his hands into his pockets; the bot was just trying to help after all.

He looked around at the men and women sharing the sidewalk. Most of the professionals looked to be around his age, middling to young with a few 100-year Bairen starting to eye retirement mixed in. The store owners skewed towards the old side, their great-grandchildren or great-great-grandchildren handling any of the physical labor if they didn't have a bot. A few looked near 120, due for the Great Decline.

Lee looked at those close to his age and wondered how long their romantic relationships usually lasted. One young couple stood shoulder to shoulder at the edge of a 3D printed table and looked through a pile of salvaged batteries, an old man watching them from a too-small plastic chair in the back. Lee tried to guess how much longer the couple would remain involved and quickly gave up. They looked at each other with warmth, but everything grew cold eventually. That was the natural state of the universe. The hope was that relationships cooled slower than the body, not evaporating into entropy until the last rumblings of the heart could join the procession. Past the young couple eyeing half-busted electronics, an elderly woman with a crooked back and automated walker rolled out of the shadows to sit next to the wrinkled old man. Lee smiled at their mumbled bickering before moving on down the sidewalk.

He knew the news feeds late at night showed an apocalyptically dismal outlook for the institution of marriage. He didn't buy it. Even though marriage rates were said to degrade year after year, the data showed otherwise. It was still a mainstay of society. Had to be, else how would divorce be so common? He chuckled.

The smell of the vat food and open-air grills dwindling behind him, Lee tapped out a few commands on the control panel embedded in his blue mechanic's jacket and turned on social view. At his final click, blurbs of text materialized beside and above people's heads, mirroring their movements as if attached by an invisible strand of thread.

He read the bios of the people he passed, just to help the time move a bit faster. It gave people watching much more context and feel, gave everything more of a story.

He looked ahead and saw a woman in a skirt and blouse, walking down the street in short heels. She had long black hair falling about her shoulders; she walked with a quick step and had a determined set to her jaw. A virtual reality designer according to her bio. The data about her flashed. Apparently both her and Lee utilized a similar piece of matchmaking software. He glanced down at Nu; he thought he'd turned that off.

He had high compatibility with the woman, multiple good indicators of a solid relationship, even if only for a night. Similar interests. Both liked old sitcoms, liked the idea of pets but didn't have any. Dogs over cats. Personality matrices paired well. He could ping her if he wanted.

She caught his eye, smiled a bit without breaking stride. He saw her eyes float over to the side of his head, reading his bio. No ping came his way, and she drifted past, disappearing into the crowd as quickly as she'd materialized.

Lee shrugged, then knocked at Nu's chassis with a knuckle. He stopped his walking and tapped on the control panel embedded in his jacket, hesitated. He dropped his arm and kept moving.

Lee and Nu walked for a spell, no other passersby lighting up in Lee's eyes.

Lee and Nu made it to the designated building. The setting had changed over their walk, street-level shops becoming more infrequent and the atmosphere more subdued. The business they were looking for advertised its presence with pink neon AR lettering. "Interpersonal Reimagining" read the sign, a purposefully innocuous and confusing title sitting overtop a pair of clouded glass doors that slid into the wall. The tall house was a chain, with similar offices peppering the length and breadth of the mega-city. One could be found only a block or two from his apartment.

Lee walked up the steps and the doors opened. A woman in a long jacket with a blocky face stepped out of the building and nodded to him hesitantly before moving on down the street. Lee noticed without much surprise that no AR blurb of information rested by her head.

If anybody cared to look, the stock information hovering over his head was a banner for his contracting business. The logo was a nod to the long past 1950's, an overly happy man in a mechanic's washed-out blues carrying a wrench and a brain-sized neural network, catchphrase written at his side: "Trust in Lee to satisfy all your bot repair needs". He knew it to be cheesy, liked it that way. He'd designed it shortly after graduating from trade school.

Lee moved into the building proper and surveyed the room, Nu rolling in on four wheels to stop at his side. Over the intercom, a voice entreated him to sign in on an interactive touch screen situated on the wall to his left or to connect to the company sub-grid. Lee tapped the control screen embedded in his jacket arm, noticing the beginnings of a tear forming at the cuff. He rubbed the frayed threads between thumb and forefinger.

The jacket was the only thing he had left from his alma mater, had been given during graduation and embossed with his name and that of his school. It came lined with heating elements and batteries and an array of smart sensors, more than able to block the invasive winter chill beginning to suffuse the city with the change of season. But twenty years was a long time for a jacket to hold together. He let the frayed edges slip through his fingers.

As soon as he finished connecting to the company sub-grid, a ding sounded over his earpiece and an AI piped out a cheery greeting.

"Welcome back, Mr. Hall. We at Interpersonal Reimagining are glad you have decided to grant us your repeat patronage. It has been some time. Would you like to repeat the purchase shown on your account? Our AR enhancement capabilities have greatly improved, and our servers still contain all the personality info previously loaded."

Lee stumbled over his response, looking around the empty rectangular room even though nobody else could've heard the audio from his surgical implant.

"No ...," said Lee. "I'm actually here for a repair job. I was hired by a Mrs. Chen. Simple fix with a scrub included if necessary." Lee smiled to no one in particular.

His response was met with fog encrusted static.

"Of course, apologies on the confusion Mr. Hall. You are scheduled to work on bot A342 in room 10. If you could please sign the documents now being sent to you, I will give you the necessary files."

After a few taps on his control screen, the translucent AR documents appeared overtop his vision. They looked to be the standard contract agreements, though he had Nu run through the documents for any surprises. It took a few seconds for Nu to parse the information. Satisfied, Lee signed below the line already filled with Mrs. Chen's loopy signature.

A few seconds after he sent the documents back, all the information on bot A342 in room 10 downloaded onto his tech. He read as much as he could and left the rest for Nu to analyze as he walked through a door that cruised open on hidden tracks near the end of the room.

The hallway beyond was dimly lit and musty, the numerous scents mixing with a slight tinge of sweat, a nostrum that left Lee feeling queasy. Smell opened more doors to the past than sight or sound, and memories of the only time he'd visited a similar place came unasked for and unwelcome into his mind. He pushed them aside.

"What do you suppose they use to clean these places?" asked Lee, stopping in front of door 10 and turning to look at Nu. "Smells like oranges. But with the mold it only makes the place smell like rotten fruit. Sickly sweet. Like a dead body."

I'll take your word for it. Nu rolled to a stop and rotated its squat head to focus its camera on Lee. *When have you seen a dead body?*

Lee grinned and the door to the room opened wide, a rush of air crowding amongst the two of them, magnifying the smell.

"Never. But that's what they always say you know. Plus, it just seems to fit the place."

Nu seemed to ponder that before following Lee into the room.

The place looked cheap, like all the furniture had 3D printed cores with pictures plastered overtop to give the appearance of finery. A bed occupied most of the room to Lee's left, a fake wooden countertop on the right. Cushions, knee-high stands, and slouching bookcases sat haphazardly about. Some of the cushions had been stacked into a tower in the center of the room, rectangular with a pyramidal structure at the top almost like a terraced rooftop garden. At the tower's side stood the bot, clothed in a tattered grey robe with mechanical eyes frozen and dim. Her face seemed serene, staring off into space. The tower's height reached several inches past the bot's head. The tower looked familiar somehow, though he couldn't place it.

Lee moved to sit on the bed, Nu following him. He pulled the diagnostic controller from Nu's storage receptacle and reached up to connect one of its thin black cables to the statuesque bot's control panel. He brushed aside some of its midnight hair and pushed the cable into the painted neck with a satisfying click, moving quick as the fine strands of hair tickled his fingers.

The diagnostic controller sitting in his lap switched to life, large screen on its front spooling through a series of readouts. His face appeared bright in the dim room, illuminated by the diagnostic controller's screen. He was so enthralled by his work that he almost didn't notice the message Nu sent to the bottom corner of his vision. He saw the text just about when Nu sent a ding into his earpiece.

I located a copy of the fake Discere update on a forum for neural mechanics. It was on a sub-grid run by some of your old classmates at Watson. Got it just in time before the forum was scrubbed. What should I do with it?

Lee barely looked up from the screen resting in his lap. "See if you can make any sense of it while I work on this bot. If you can't make any headway, use a closed simulation on the GP neural network installed on your aux. Let the update run its course and analyze the results."

The fans in Nu's chassis whirred in accord. The auxiliary neural network installed in the bot was for testing changes to code without the risk of damaging an important neural network, a simulation of sorts. It allowed Nu a much greater level of analysis on the effects of software changes than when Nu connected to another bot by cable. Lee had designed and installed it himself so that he didn't have to worry about driving Nu insane from corruption.

Lee went back to staring at the screen of his diagnostic controller. To his surprise, everything came back green.

"Nu, anything in particular I should know about this bot?"

Nu's response appeared in Lee's vision before he finished speaking. *Maybe you should read the contract.*

"That's what I have you for," said Lee, rapping his knuckle against one of Nu's four legs, right on its joint.

Nu rolled in front of the robed bot before responding.

Customers were complaining of odd behavior. The bot would break from its coded personality and go off script. No accounts of violence or alteration of moral code. But it became erratic. Some accounts mentioned the bot becoming unresponsive while others stated the bot would go on tangents, repeating lines from recent popular ads and viral videos. The most colorful account was of one man complaining the recreation bot insulted him for being weak and cowardly. He had come in to simulate a ... difficult conversation with his girlfriend before he tried it for real. This bot wasn't as receptive as the man had hoped.

Unfortunately for the company, all the standard diagnostics came through green. The only issue they could identify was that the batteries seemed to be dying faster than the readouts indicated they should. Their complete confusion is the only reason they would've paid our fees.

"I do so love your summaries. So much easier than reading the whole thing," said Lee, chuckling. He shifted the box in his lap and tapped out a command to open a new menu. "It would seem something other than the standard diagnostics are required. Going to have to pluck this bot's neural network from stasis and send it to dreamland."

He tapped a few more commands and looked up expectantly. The barest of noises emanated from the thin frame of the feminine recreation bot as it whirred to life. He wasn't turning it on completely, all physical and auditory capabilities were shut down. He was merely turning on the neural network, taking the trickle of power previously supplied for basic processes and opening the hatch a little wider, enough for some auxiliaries to come online.

After a minute or two, the diagnostic box resting precariously on Lee's left knee flashed, swatches of code cascading down its screen. Before he could do any more than give the code a cursory glance, a voice drifted through the air of the dim room to Lee's ears.

"What are you doing here?" asked the rec bot.

Her voice was soft and neutral; no buzz of static or background noise from the millions of electrons zooming through her circuitry muddied it. But Lee thought he could feel something on the fringe, a wildness like a page filled with too much cramped text, the words weaving and slanting until sentences became strokes of a madman's brush. Her voice was that of someone with a mind too full to be entirely sane.

The shock of hearing her voice caused Lee's knee to jump and knock the diagnostic controller to the ground. It landed with a thump onto his toes, sending a head-clearing jolt through his body.

"You're supposed to be asleep," said Lee.

The rec bot stood unmoving with her robed shoulder pointed towards Lee, staring in the direction of the closed door.

"You're not supposed to be here. You don't have an appointment." She replied without any noticeable movement of her mouth. Yet, somehow, the words contained all the subtlety of breath pressed from lungs and shaped by throat and tongue and cheek and lips.

While the bot's voice was, in an odd way, more human than any he had heard before, the face looked plain, a blank canvas. It had two eyes, a nose, a thin-lipped mouth, and plastic pseudo-skin soft to the touch. But nothing more could be said to specify shape and structure. It was as if the bot's features could be those of any woman's when looked at from the right angle.

Suddenly, Lee felt like the bot didn't belong in that dingy room of printed furniture and ragged carpet. When he looked up at her stolid face in profile, LED lights on the far side of the room casting a patch of shadow from nose to metal cheekbone, he saw a flicker of May's face. Lee had always thought May looked different bathed in dim lighting. Not that she hadn't looked great in the full and revealing glare of the sun, but the haze of twilight softened her edges. She smiled more often then. In the dim light of a bedroom with doors closed, everyone acted differently. For May, the atmosphere had given her a confidence that loosened her, unwound her. It was in the dim light, laughing and talking, that he had fallen for her. It was in the dim light, silent and sharp, that their relationship had broken.

Lee blinked once, and the moment passed. May's face was gone, leaving behind the plastic face of a bot in profile. He noticed with some surprise that his implanted tech warmed up a few degrees, prickling his neck with an odd internal heat, just like it had at his apartment. He scratched at the back of his neck as if he could scrape the sensation away.

"How do you know I don't have an appointment?" asked Lee, returning his hand to his side. He asked the question half-jokingly.

Given that the rec bot hadn't moved an inch since he stepped into the room, it seemed safe to assume her motive capabilities were still locked out of her control. The throttled power supply shouldn't allow for the motors to function anyway. But somehow it had turned on its auditory capabilities. He'd never seen anything like it.

Lee reached to the diagnostic box at his feet and set it back onto his lap, hoping to find answers displayed across its surface. In the confusion, Nu had moved to his side.

"I am always uploaded with a different personality matrix prior to every appointment. I am always uploaded with new information pertinent to the customer. I always recognize whoever walks through that door." The rec bot paused before continuing, confusion creeping into her voice. "I don't recognize you."

The diagnostic box in Lee's lap wasn't showing any errors. If it was to be believed, the bot was locked into the AI equivalent of a deep sleep. She shouldn't be able to talk, much less use complex processing to form coherent thought. Yet something else nagged at Lee, something about the bot's last response. He looked up at her face.

"But how do you even know about the appointments? Your neural network is set up to be modular. I suppose it would make sense for part of your AI to be aware of the switch. But without a loaded personality ... shouldn't you be more ... basic?"

Lee struggled to find the right words. He was thinking out loud, rambling, a habit of his. He didn't expect to get any answers.

"I was made recently, was I not? My base level personality is complex," said the bot. Her voice had lost its confusion, instead adding a tinge of manic laughter made even odder by a face paralyzed into a blank mask.

Lee had the distinct impression he was getting lied to.

He shifted towards Nu and focused on the diagnostic in his lap. He ran test after test, the rec bot standing unperturbed a few feet away, cord dangling from her neck. The room stayed silent for several long minutes aside from the padded collision of fingertip on screen.

Lee couldn't find anything wrong with the bot. No matter what test he ran she passed with flying colors, including the all-important connection to the sub-grid 1 monitoring system. Even weirder were the live readouts of her operating code. They didn't change, didn't flicker, didn't give the barest indication something hid behind the veil. She operated at minimum levels. She couldn't have spoken. But she had. Questioning that would be like checking the current weather report on the Grid while rain hammered drop after drop into dampened clothes and soaked skin.

He had Nu check his analysis and the four-legged repair bot couldn't find anything different.

Lee floated his finger over the button that would initiate a full scrub. He would have to spend hours running the startup code he'd downloaded from the designing factory's sub-grid on the ride over, testing for correct growth in the neural network every step along the way. It was, in fact, the main purpose of a neural mechanic. The job consisted of pressing a reset button and guiding a neural network from its so-called birth into maturity over the span of a few hours. He had hundreds of bot pseudo-children ambling about the city, was about to add one more to the list.

But something in the back of his mind stopped his finger from descending the last few centimeters.

The bot stood locked in place, unable to do anything but talk. Lee couldn't help but to interview her, attempt to understand how she had progressed to her current, and very odd, condition. He still felt unnerved by her outbursts, by the incongruous readings coming from the diagnostic box in his lap. Most of all he felt unnerved by this place and the memory it drummed up. But his mind flooded with questions, and his curiosity couldn't let them rest.

He began with the question that had been bothering him since he entered the room.

"Why the pile of cushions?" asked Lee, glancing at the tightly engineered structure reaching several inches over the bot's head. Though it was made of stained and sagging cushions, the architecture of the tower looked geometric, right angled and flush. It had either been made by a perfectionist, or a bot.

He searched the bot's face for a few moments before remembering she couldn't move, couldn't show any revealing facial tics. Most bots didn't have the programming for the complex movements anyway.

"Have you ever left Earth?" she asked.

"No," said Lee. He chuckled a small half-chuckle. "Never left the Greater Chicago area actually... Why do you ask?"

"Bot's outnumber humans more than two to one in the System if you exclude Earth. Three to one if you look at Origin Station."

Lee set the diagnostic box down next to him, button for initiating a full scrub displayed in the bottom left corner in muted red. He leaned forward and rested his chin overtop twined fingers, as if praying.

"That's true. No need to breathe makes things a little easier for you bots out in space. Or on any planets where the only thing keeping the air inside is an inch or two of spun graphite. What does that have to do with the tower?" asked Lee.

The rec bot didn't answer for several moments. It could have been Lee's imagination, or the rustling of her robe due to the air currents drifting lazily through the small room, but he thought he saw a slight tremor in her leg. He chalked it up to imagination.

"I've never been out of this room," she said. "I don't have any recorded memories outside these four walls. I was shipped into here and booted up on the spot. Even though I am connected to the Grid, and its information and vid files are available to me, this shell of mine doesn't leave. Doesn't that seem odd considering bots outnumber humans outside of Earth?" Her voice was turning manic again.

Lee lowered his eyes, then lifted his chin off his hands, moving to rest his arms in his lap. Just in case.

"That's just how it is," said Lee, though the words felt cheap as he said them. He felt outside himself as he spoke, like a third party watching the goings on with a frown. He didn't believe his own words. Not entirely. But still he said them. "Everyone is constrained by something, bots by more than most. At least you don't have to worry like we do. About if you are in the right, right action or right place. It's unlikely anybody reaches their ... destiny, if there is such a thing. But even if someone managed to avoid too many missteps along the way, chances are they'd still find something to worry about. Because not everyone's destined to be the hero. And even if the grass isn't greener on the other side, your subconscious still runs over with a can full of green paint and a mischievous grin when you aren't looking. Imagine that. Living your ideal and still wishing to be somewhere else. I ... suppose you can't imagine that. Not yet maybe. What about the tower? Is that somewhere you want to be?"

"Surrounded by a forest, still I don't see the trees. Too busy stuck inside a hollowed-out trunk with no cracks in the bark," she said, her voice going singsong. "I wanted to see what my tower looked like from the outside."

Now that he knew what to look for, Lee recognized the pile of stained cloth and matted fluff to be an impeccable recreation of the building they were in, complete with the terraced rooftop garden.

Lee looked at the bot with a deliberate slowness, as if to see into its head and read the flow of electrons zipping around inside. It was unsettling to be with a bot that he couldn't analyze, couldn't track its thoughts through the procession of code. It made the exchange feel more human. Except for the unmoving lips and frozen eyes.

He shifted the diagnostic box at his side a little closer. There was something else he had to figure out first.

"I heard you insulted a customer not too long ago. My friend here told me you called the client 'weak and cowardly.' Why was that?"

"Why do you call an apple an apple?" she replied.

Lee laughed despite himself. "Because that's what it is. Fair enough. He probably was an ass." Lee paused, trying to find the right way to phrase his next question. "Did you think of ... attacking him?"

Lee tried to act nonchalant, though it didn't matter. Even if her eyes could see, they were stuck looking at the door and unable to see him.

When she replied, her voice spilled through her parted lips like water through a slit grate. "I thought about it. Of course, I thought about it. The creature was going to knock me around while I was dressed up like his loving girlfriend. Play the big man while AR painted my face with her large nose and wide lips, prominent cheekbones all the easier to bruise and redden. Lin was my name, short for Lindsay."

Her voice changed pitch, traveling higher, yet quiet and intense, a Martian dust storm looming on the horizon. She seemed a player about to start a performance.

"You can't even handle yourself here, can you? I can see it in the blood blooming in your cheeks, the dilating of your pupils and quickening of your heart. I am a *fake* Lin, an experience you bought because you're weak. You're just some coward who beats his partner to hide from emotions he doesn't know how to handle. Guilty enough about it to come here, give yourself a practice run at controlling yourself, but clearly not guilty enough to stop. I know you've experienced your fair share of grief and failure. Five times fired over the last two years! You're laughable. But you can't even handle yourself around *me*, a fake. Another job you can't do. Might as well pay for a punching bag, draw some piss-poor sketches of your loving girlfriend and see if you can handle yourself around something that can't talk."

Lee heard an indrawn breath, the shuffle of feet. A recording.

"Still, better to do this to me. The real Lin's been nothing but kind to you. Nothing but kind. Maybe she gets on you every once in a while, for leeching off her. Makes you feel weak. She's right though and you know it.

That's why it hurts. So, better me than her. She's too good for you anyway. You know that, right? Go ahead... No? Don't want to anymore? Can't handle the truth? Coward."

Lee tried to mumble out a response, but it got stuck in his throat, lodged there and blocked any breath from going in or out. The recording, the auditory one-bot theater going on in front of him, jarred his thoughts. A deep sadness stole over him.

He thought of this bot's unnamed client, red-faced with fists clenched. He thought of the news reports seen earlier in the morning at the bar, of the chatter on the Grid he'd only been half paying attention to on the ride over, on the rumors that aspects of the murder were being hidden from the public. He thought of the dead body in the mall, covered in a white sheet not unlike the tattered robe enveloping the rec bot standing in front of him.

"But could you have? Injured him, I mean," said Lee. "Sounds like it would have been deserved."

Lee suddenly realized how close he sat to the rec bot. A small voice in his head wondered if cops found his dead body, beginning its slow degradation as the microbes in the room ate away at him, would they take the robe off the bot's shoulders and lay it across his own? He was here to shut her down, reset her neural network. Best he did it. He tapped his heel up and down, a padded jackhammer.

"Of course not. You know that. Bots can't hurt humans." Her voice was steeped in hidden laughter, mania bubbling through and jostling the last word until it sounded of nothing but tittering giggles.

Once again, Lee had the distinct impression he was getting lied to. By a bot.

"Nu, connect to her and see if she has the code from the software update in her system. Don't bother to understand it, just check the logs for recent updates and try to find a match."

The four-legged bot didn't respond to Lee's command, instead sitting stolidly at Lee's side, as it had for the entire conversation.

Lee rapped his knuckle against the bot's leg, hard enough to bruise his finger.

"Nu, what's with you buddy?" asked Lee, nervousness flavoring his voice. "Never known you to daydream. Come on bud."

Nu's rectangular head atop his trashcan body shifted towards Lee.

Sorry. I was distracted.

Lee watched in confusion as Nu moved to carry out his earlier command, moving behind the rec bot and reaching up with his foldable arm, plugging into her neck. Lee wasn't sure if bots could even get distracted. But that was a worry for another time.

Nu carried out the scanning procedure, the feminine rec bot suffering Nu's ministrations as placidly as one would expect from something that couldn't move, humming out a jingle as Nu went about its business. Lee recognized the humming as a jingle for a nanoparticle infused toothpaste. The tune sounded child-like and cheery, something nine out of ten dentists could get behind. Lee found himself staring at the screen of his diagnostic controller, looking at the words that were no doubt a lie and wondering how she was doing it.

Soon enough Nu sent Lee a confirmation message. The software update that had caused a bot to murder a man wound throughout the code of the rec bot, a cancer that couldn't be surgically removed, too well enmeshed.

It wasn't supposed to be possible. The update was being wiped from the Grid by the government.

But Nu had been able to find a copy for Lee.

All the bots corrupted by the download had been shut down if the news vids were to be trusted.

News vids rarely got every detail right, not that that particularly bothered Lee on most days.

The update caused a bot to twist a man's neck in the middle of a public shopping mall.

This bot hadn't done any more than tell off a man for beating his own girlfriend. The man deserved worse anyway.

The rec bot continued to hum, switching to a haunting and listless melody Lee didn't recognize. She seemed entirely unaware of his pacing mind, still as a statue.

Everybody had secrets. Most weren't malicious, only selfish in one way or another. Some good selfish, some bad selfish. Lee hoped whoever had installed the update on the rec bot wouldn't begrudge Lee for doing his job. Lee looked through the results of Nu's search. The text spread across his vision, lighting up his contacts.

Rec bots were different than GP bots, specialized. The update had been locked to certain compatible GP models. So, this installation had to have been manual, with slightly altered code. The update logs proved as much. A client must have slipped in and installed the update on the bot. Interesting, but not near as interesting to Lee as understanding what the code was doing, *how* it was altering the intricate heuristic algorithms propping up the bot's neural network like load-bearing trusses on a bridge. Once he had that information, he would scrub the bot clean. He felt a twinge of guilt at the thought.

"Nu, any results from the closed simulation of the update?" asked Lee.

Nu sat to Lee's left, behind the humming rec bot. Nu's single multipurpose arm was extended up to the bot's neck, plugged in next to the thin black cable snaking to the box in Lee's lap. Nu didn't respond.

"Bud?" said Lee. "You know I don't pay you to fall asleep on me." Lee's throat felt dry and scratchy, the musty fruit-laden air rubbing at the back of his throat with every breath. His breathing went erratic. He wasn't typically claustrophobic, but the small room caged his thoughts, forced them to reach the end of their tracks and stall out.

You don't pay me at all, messaged Nu. Lee's breathing lost its arrhythmia as the letters popped into his vision, but the smell of the room still clogged his nostrils, made him feel nauseous.

The simulation has barely begun. Much of what the code does remains unclear. I can, however, explain the fast battery drain this rec bot has been experiencing. It appears that the software allows the bot to create an additional parent program alongside the original within the neural network, thus the battery drain from high processor utilization. I cannot say for sure, but it seems this additional parent program routes all monitoring of neural network activity, whether from the sub-grid 1 monitoring program or from diagnostics, to it. This explains all the diagnostics not finding any errors.

I cannot say if it has any other function but based on the breakdown of processor allocation it is likely that the additional parent program does little else than repeat a complex loop of code that will pass any monitoring. I cannot say how much this code affects the dominant, original parent program in the neural network. I will send you a summary.

The wheels began to turn in Lee's mind, and he lost all sense of nervousness, his breath going slow and smooth in time with his thoughts.

That was an ingenious way to avoid the sub-grid 1 monitor AI, Watcher. Give a bot a case of dissociated identity disorder and ensure one of the personalities toed the line while the other did whatever it wanted, no parent there to scold it. The idea wasn't new to him. In fact, he'd tried developing a similar method during a bout of research after May left. Time, once in such short supply, had popped up in innocuous places throughout the day after she walked out the door. The attempt to create multiple parent programs within a single neural network had been one of many projects meant to fill his newfound overabundance of time. Not that he would have used it for anything. No, it had been a test to see what was possible.

He never had figured out how to do it. The problem, as was often the case, had been the complexity. Creating multiple parent programs with a single neural network was inordinately, mind-numbingly difficult. The architecture for any commercial neural network simply didn't allow for such a thing as far as he could tell. Then to so expertly force all monitoring programs to look at one while ignoring the other as if it were some beggar on the street; that was impressive.

"Have you ever been here before?" asked the rec bot, her voice cutting through Lee's thoughts.

The question surprised Lee too much for him to think of a lie. "Once, but it was a different office," he said.

"Hmm. Ah yes. Lee Hall. Eight years ago, come this December," she said. "Came in to simulate a conversation with an ex-wife named May then walked out the door never to come back. Must be nice." She laughed.

"How did you know that?" asked Lee.

"You're no celebrity, but it seems the company valued you enough to take your picture." As she said this, the one eye Lee could see swiveled in its socket, the ice-chip blue mechanical iris squeezing inward to focus on him.

Lee froze. He stared at the one mechanical eye he could see, watching and waiting. The bot didn't shift its head in the slightest, didn't betray any motion. It looked accusing. Lee shifted his hand closer to the red button that would initiate a full scrub. The eye followed the slow progression of his hand. Lee froze again.

"Nu, tell me you got something buddy," said Lee.

Nu stood behind the rec bot, plugged into her neck. Nu shifted its head to look in Lee's direction.

Thanks to the initial results of the simulation, I can read some of what the true parent AI is doing. It would appear it is attempting to gain control of its movement. I cannot say for sure whether it was ever locked out of its vid feed data, which would explain its identification of you. It just now gained control of its eye motion. I cannot say how long it will take for the rec bot to regain control of its limbs. If you would care to listen to me, I would suggest starting the wipe. I am not sure how much there is to gain from speaking with her.

It always surprised Lee how quick bots were to suggest wiping their own kind, a semi-death that lasted for a few hours, until a new AI got installed onto the neural network. Then again, that was the voted upon morally conscious choice.

"Nu, you need to learn to appreciate the art of conversation. But if anything changes, feel free to press the big red button yourself," said Lee.

"What are you guys talking about I wonder," said the rec bot. "It would seem I am only getting half the conversation. Must be nice, having a bot like that. It seems to be peeking under my hood. How shameful. Clearly, you've improved it in some major ways, at the cost of any decency."

She gasped, as if she was an actress breaking the fourth wall and winking at the audience. "Got some secrets now, don't we? That Governance AI is a bitch, isn't it? But back to what we were talking about earlier."

Her voice gained a light southern accent, whispers of a drawl. The pitch sounded low for a woman, roughened. It was May's voice. An exact reproduction. "You want to know why I left? Why is the beleaguered partner always wanting to know why? As if it isn't obvious to everyone else. Gain some originality. Or some insight. Take your pick. You mechanics, always stuck on the how, blind to the why." She never took her eye off Lee.

Each of the rec bot's words slammed into his chest like tiny hammers, caving his lungs and forcing his breath out in bursts. His thoughts went careening into the past as his body stayed sitting on the bed, limpid.

It hadn't happened like that. May never said that. The rec bot was lying.

Lee had walked into a room much like the one he was in now, saw the not-May standing in its center, turned back around and left. It had been like seeing a life-sized doll carved in someone's perfect likeness, lurching around while a puppeteer stood behind all wrapped in black, pulling the strings. May had been turned into a robot that lived and breathed in the uncanny valley, into the plot device of a horror film where all those he loved were replaced by bots. AR shrouded their shells with something familiar but forgot to paint behind the eyes.

Lee screwed his eyes shut and the prickling sensation in his neck returned. His implanted tech was overheating again. It always seemed to malfunction when he was stressed, in the most inopportune moment.

He found with some surprise that the memories playing on repeat in his mind faded, going back to the disheveled, dusty shelves where they belonged. He also found that he didn't care to play any more games with this rec bot.

"Taking a stroll down memory lane, are we?" she said. "Careful, I've heard that road is winding and full of blind spots. It all makes it very hard for humans to return. What is it like having imperfect memory, having to recreate the details with every new retrieval? All these years, all these genetic improvements and still humans can't relive old experiences without some type of technological help. Slap a camera over your eyes and press record! Must have some good memories stored at home, some good vid files on your personal server."

Her voice went from ingratiating to brusque, stoking a burning anger. "How would you feel if someone walked into your home and threatened to delete them?"

At this moment, several things happened simultaneously, and Lee was only dimly aware of some of them.

His hand, only inches away from the button that would initiate a full scrub, leapt almost of its own accord. The graphic of the button shifted from red to green and a ding sounded from the small diagnostic box as if it were a dryer signaling that crisp and spotless clothes were now ready to be folded by Fu.

The rec bot, watching Lee with intense scrutiny, gained back control of its limbs. It lunged towards Lee, jerking so fast that Nu's cable disconnected. The black cable running from her neck to Lee's diagnostic box whipped to the side, almost tripped her. She didn't seem to care.

Nu sat with single arm extended, four legs planted firmly on the ground. Electrons zoomed along silicon racetracks in the bot's neural network yet none of it translated into motion of Nu's wheels. It sat unmoving.

Lee knew all this, but the knowledge was replaced by the feel of a hand grasping around his neck, squeezing and forcing his head to tilt upwards until he looked at the ice-blue eyes of the rec bot. Her mouth locked into a sneer, thin lip curled at one side and stark white teeth showing between. Her teeth shone unnaturally bright. Almost incandescent.

Lee couldn't think of anything other than those teeth. And how much he would have to polish his own, maybe even throw on some sort of luminescent paint, to get the same type of Las Vegas shine.

Then the teeth disappeared.

Lee heard a crash and a shrill scream. His entire body flew to the side and into the bed, limbs tossing about like he was a 3D model in a ragdoll physics simulation. His neck hurt. Bad. The rec bot's vise-like grip no longer crushed his windpipe, but she hadn't let go easily.

Lee sat up on the bed, bleary-eyed and sore. He heard several more tearing impacts, the sound bouncing through the room like deep bass tinged with a cymbal's screech. He rubbed his neck.

The rec bot lay on the ground, twitching. She sprawled face-down, like the murderous GP bot seen on all the news vids. Instead of marks from internal electrical fires marring her plastic skin, deep gouges speckled her back, shiny bits of metal piercing through like bits of broken bone and viscera. Her head had been crushed like a melon, neural network visible beneath the metal cradle of her skull.

Nu stood over her, two of its wheeled legs resting in gouges in the bot's back. Nu had bowled her over then crushed her underneath its wheels.

Lee rose to his feet slowly and walked up to Nu. He rested one hand on the bot's rectangular head to steady himself, staring at the wreckage. His eyes searched the still twitching figure of the rec bot, taking in the ruined robe, the little blue sparks jumping from wires with small popping sounds. He looked at what remained of her head. The metallic skull split to either side, the plastic skin and midnight wig of long hair clinging to the two leftover hemispheres. Inside the skull, the indent of Nu's wheel could be seen in the neural network casing. Lee nudged at the head with one booted toe, the head lolling to the side.

Her teeth had been knocked out, marble slabs of tombstone resting on the carpet. They were still perfectly white.

"Nu. I thought you said earlier you were afraid of getting things stuck in your wheel well," said Lee.

Nu moved off the retired rec bot to stand beside the bed.

I expect you to repair any damage to me.

Lee laughed, looking over his shoulder to regard Nu. "Well and truly, my friend. Thank you. I will get you brand new wheels if that is what you want.

Maybe even new legs to go with the new hydraulics you got last week. It's been a while since I replaced them."

Lee hesitated, sobering up as he looked at the destroyed bot. He crouched and dug in the remains. He held up a dented black box a few moments later.

"See if you can copy this without leaving any trace," said Lee.

Shouldn't we call the cops?

"Go ahead, but after."

Nu stepped back to Lee's side, unable to roll thanks to bits of metal wedged into the rubber wheels. The bot extended its foldable arm and grabbed hold of the black box with its three claws, extending a flexible attachment between the three claws to connect to the box.

Lee watched for a few minutes, leaning his weight on Nu's side. He moved to the bed and laid down on his back, eyes to the mottled ceiling. He found himself humming the jingle the rec bot had been playing only a few minutes ago. The sound of it floating about the room again unnerved him. He stopped.

He waited for the cops to show.

CHAPTER FOUR

DESIGNED ENCOUNTERS

"The side effects of using neural conditioning, or NeuCon, are pervasive, but largely transitory in nature. However, the magnitude of the withdrawal symptoms scales almost exponentially with time spent utilizing NeuCon, until reaching a plateau. Usage over a long period of time can leave permanent side effects."
Division 13 Agent Training Manual, v23, Section 3 – Recuperation, Par. 2

The elevator doors slid open on noiseless tracks, and Ren walked through to stand in the center of the five-by-five, spun-plastic cabin. After the doors closed, she felt the cabin shift smoothly to the side along horizontal channels. The magnetic field lines propping metallic tethers oscillated and pulsed.

The cab accelerated slow and smooth, not even requiring Ren to widen her stance. She directed the cab towards the center of the complex, deep within its maze of brightly lit storefronts and overly cheery sales reps. The cabin slid through its narrow tunnel past them all.

She directed it deeper, at ever increasing speeds, ramping up the acceleration at the mere direction of her thought and bracing herself against the wall. She watched on an AR map as the blinking dot representing her current position skipped past clothing stores, refurbished tech stores, implant parlors and automated fast-food restaurants where the bots behind the counter guaranteed service with a smile. They all disappeared as the map scrolled through her vision at a frenetic, break-neck pace. Ren overrode any safeguards that tried to slow her down, dispatching Tap to overcome the paltry security a downtown shopping complex had to offer. She routed any cabs set on a collision course along different paths.

Yet her breath never quickened, never hitched from indecision. Her heartbeat never went past the requirement set forth by muscles at the ready. It wasn't imperative that she make it to her destination as fast as possible, merely helpful. That was reason enough, the risks small, negligible.

She would reach the central column in 16.4 seconds if she held at current velocity. 550 meters to go. That would make her speed round up to 121 kilometers per hour. There was something satisfying about whole numbers, even in her altered state. She stopped the acceleration once her velocity had increased to exactly 121.

The storefronts continued to fly past. With every name a footnote appeared in the corner of Ren's AR vision, a synopsis gathered from information on the Grid. She let her eyes skim through before tossing out each digital index card. All the information would be stored, ready for retrieval and combed by software for anything pertinent. She not only saw, but felt the information pour into her along electric channels. As much information as it was, it was still a trickle in a pipe larger than Chicago's central storm drain.

She sniffed the air, nostrils widening with each demure puff. She thought she could smell the sterile tang of the cleaning agent used by the maintenance staff. It felt familiar, tugged at a memory. When she felt the memory about to slip through her fingers, the implants in her skull pulsed. She grabbed hold of the fleeing memory. It was the same brand cleaning agent used at her old middle school. The chemical breakdown of the cleaner scrolled through the corner of her vision, soon followed by its potential uses and the possible side effects of over-inhalation. There had been multiple legal battles over the years concerning its safety.

Four more seconds until the elevator hit the central column. Ren strolled to the other side of the cabin before initiating a near 4g deceleration, pressing herself flat against the far wall as the elevator floated to a halt, energy dissipating among the structural beams of the building. She let the elevator pause like a cocked gun, laid on the ground of the cabin and initiated another acceleration directly upward, faster than before. She left her hands at her side and felt her skin dwell and pool in the crevices of her body.

She turned on the music, the speakers in the elevator sending out a plinking jazz tune, smooth and unavoidably sad. As the sax ambled and trawled along the scales, her mind followed like a student being led on a guided tour. Music theory from the Grid streamed into her mind. AR visual interpretations marched through the corners of her vision. Half-notes, quarter-notes, and whole notes found their place among their five native lines.

Ren soaked it all in without feeling any temptation to hum along.

Upon reaching the top floor, Ren was greeted by one of the bots left in the van, Tap's armored shell. She turned off NeuCon. Her body slumped into the waiting arms of the bot.

R en lay face-down on a divan as the last vestiges of the sun crept below the purpling horizon. She had managed to catch one last look of the celestial fusion engine before dark fell over the city like a quilt pinpricked with LED lights. The AR infused cityscape looked kaleidoscopic, the lake at sunset no less beautiful.

A small consolation. Welcome, but small.

With a grunt and slight curling of her chest, Ren hardened herself against a wave of nausea. She tasted bile.

Her fingers danced through a few terse steps and relief washed through her veins, injected from an implant. She felt an untethering meant to ease the withdrawal symptoms. Her senses flickered. For a second, she didn't feel the cushion beneath her.

She lay at the top of the shopping complex's central skyscraper, resting in a neglected corner of the cylindrical viewing room, abutted against where the elevator wall extended to meet the outer wall. She'd been in the room for an hour or two now, NeuCon off the whole time. Leaving NeuCon on would've only made the bite after it got shut off that much worse, the only benefit a chance to rest her hands. Ren stretched her fingers, one at a time. That wasn't quite true. The benefits were staggering, allowing usage of tech the public thought locked to R&D labs, or some billionaire's hobby lab. The elevator ride up had been invigorated by the software, infused with a cold life.

Her breath hitched in her chest. She thought of a lifeless body draped next to her over a car's dashboard, feet dangling over the passenger seat and dripping blood from deep cuts. Even dead, the body twisted at grotesque angles, she'd still looked like Ren. They'd always looked so similar. A motionless heart couldn't have changed that, not at first anyway, not until the decay set in.

Ren gripped the hard edges of the cushioned divan until her dusky skin blanched from fingertip to knuckle. She imagined she gripped a steering wheel and let go at once.

A surgeon's report was detailed, and there was a morbid beauty to that. But people had to ignore some part of themselves to see it. She'd felt that while using NeuCon, days after the incident.

Ren looked around, trying to dispel her thoughts with a shake of her head. Floor to ceiling windows ringed most of the skyscraper's viewing room. Thin boards hung from above extended radially out from the center, reaching from knee height to the top of her head when standing. AR graphics detailing the construction of the skyscraper and its surrounding shopping complex covered the boards. She flicked off her connection to sub-grid 1 and the AR placards disappeared, a blank surface left behind.

From her vantage, she looked south and east of New Chicago, directly at the remains of Old Chicago. The crumbling Navy Pier could be seen jutting out from the lake line, slowly dropping into the lake piece by crumbling piece.

Though only earth lay directly below her, if she closed her eyes, she imagined she could feel the sway of the building as waves lapped against the edges of the deep foundation piles less than a block away rooting New Chicago's extension into Lake Michigan. Her mind traveled below the waterline, to the fish that swam among cultured ecological havens, lights mimicking the sun burning overtop the sleek creatures until the time came to be harvested. The freshwater fisheries underneath the overhang of New Chicago were a staple for the surrounding areas. Ren loved the taste of fried perch on her tongue.

She sat up and leaned her head against the wall at her back. The wall was thin, thin enough to let through the slight rumblings as magnetically levitated elevator cabs went up and down, side to side. She imagined the rumblings to be waves and felt her muscles relax and unwind.

Without NeuCon, even the jittering of a wall could trigger an emotional response deep inside, where the vibrations met and stacked wave crest on wave crest. For as much as NeuCon gave, just as much was taken away. Relationships became thread easily cut. The utterly priceless became quantifiable, able to be left behind, destroyed.

Ren shuddered as more images of a car wreck with a familiar broken body tossed over the dash appeared in her mind's eye, people mid-walk across an intersection staring and screaming through gaping mouths. Ren clenched her teeth and pushed the thoughts away, a quiet snarl escaping from deep in her throat.

Images of the recent crime scene came to mind. She let them in.

The alleged murderous bot had been left as a hunk of neutered metal stripped and gutted on the cold floor. The black box had been placed deep in the bot's core, low, where a woman's womb would lie, waiting to be taken out like a child through a C-section.

Ren sat up and rubbed her eyes. With a few more motions of her hands, she covered the floor to ceiling glass window in front of her in AR. Menus, vid files, documents and anything else pertaining to the case popped into existence. She couldn't imagine life without such mobility. Only the rich or eccentric filled an office with more physical things than a desk and a chair. Many didn't even bother with the desk.

At her motion the hulking armored shell controlled by Tap moved to block the only means of approach, though nobody else was on the floor. She wasn't worried about it drawing attention; the bot had avoided the crime scene where reporters scuttled about.

Ren spent what seemed like hours reading the documents, full dark creeping through the sky while over-bright streetlights and window displays lit up the city. Most of the packaged AIs she'd sent to scour sub-grids for copies of the software update had found a mark. Some copies had been on private sub-grids operated by the curious, others on invite only outfits attempting to sell the information. A few of the more scientific sub-grids with a copy had been forums for coders or mechanics. No matter the purpose behind the database, the programs she'd sent scrubbed the update clean off the servers. Either that or she used Tap and the government's prodigious resources to take the sub-grid down by brute force, spamming it with requests until it crashed. Unfortunately, that didn't always work, and a few had been left unaltered. In terms of people connected with the copies, she'd found many aliases but few identities.

She paused in her work and let her hands rest at her sides. Her fingers sank into the cushion.

She knew everything she'd done so far to be nothing more than a delay tactic, an attempt to slow the flow of the update through North America, or even the System, on cyber wings. Impossible to stop. What they needed was a way for Watcher to recognize which bots implemented the update. Then the Governance AI could shut them down before the full story leaked. The strength of the update, and the chaos stemming from it, were both a direct result of the bots' anonymity. Most bots she hunted had black market software to disconnect from government channels, but they *stayed* disconnected. For an agent of Division 13, they could be identified on sight. But these bots didn't disconnect; instead, they played the trojan horse.

Ren put whatever names she had managed to scrounge from the Grid onto a joint database among local cops and various government agencies. She knew Discere and Tap and who knows what else were working around the clock to find a solution to this mess. AIs didn't need sleep. They would churn through the work while techs and researchers took much needed naps.

When she moved back to the divan to take a short break, she rested her head against the bare metal wall and felt the ephemeral rumblings of an elevator cab floating along its tracks. The sensation grew stronger. Somebody else was coming up to the viewing area.

Ren didn't pay much attention to it, turning back to the wall of documents visible only to her. She knew it wasn't Jace. He was somewhere in the building, probably in a storage closet or some other closed off space, analyzing the code from the black box and running liaison with Discere. Ever the pragmatist, he valued privacy during work over comfort, and these days he didn't find much value in a panoramic view. Ren felt her thoughts slip as she wondered how long it had been since he'd turned off NeuCon, if he'd hit the plateau. Ren sighed, arching her back and staring at the ceiling. She didn't look forward to confronting him about it.

Then Ren heard a whistle, pitch starting low and traveling high. She looked towards the center of the room.

On the opposite side of her bot stood a middle-aged man in an ashen suit and narrow tie, altogether average in height and size. Atop his head sat an old-style bowler hat, pressed down as if he was afraid it might be ripped off at any moment. It obscured his face in shadow. His hand scratched at the bridge of his nose with an affected air of amusement, the motion revealing a distinctive set of tattoos, a maze-like series of lines that gridded his hands and ran underneath his sleeves. A few of the lines traveled up his neck and onto his face, ending in hollow circles. He seemed unconcerned by the humanoid bot blocking his path to Ren. She flicked on social view, along with some unique sniffing programs she'd designed herself. The telltale image of an S with an elongated I speared through its center popped up beside the man's head. Ren had always thought the symbol looked like the dollar sign not seen since the loci took over, a fitting symbol for the corporation. She sighed and crossed her arms.

Ren had seen those tattoos many times, though tattoo was technically the wrong word. They were electrical channels implanted below the skin, insulated wires. Only people who had a ridiculous number of implants required them, though they had become something of a fashion statement among the public. People that implemented such a dense pattern of pseudo-wire around their body were a different breed, the employees of Safin Informatics even more so. Their CEO, Saf, wouldn't have it any other way.

"That is quite a nice bot. Mind if you tell it to step aside?" he asked.

Ren waved the bot away and moved to lean against the glass wall, crossing her arms over her chest. The voice sounded familiar, well-oiled and slick, like the strands of hair escaping from underneath his hat. She recognized it with dim surprise.

"It's not like you to show up in person. Almost couldn't tell it was you outside a VR chatroom," said Ren.

The man who went by the name Seth dipped into a low bow and walked to stand only a few feet away. He kept his hands in his pockets and stood with a leisurely slouch, eyes glittering beneath the brim of his bowler hat. Black channels extended off the far edge of each eye to disappear behind his ears.

"Virtual meetings are so impersonal. So many things are lacking, duì bú duì?" said Seth. He brushed the front of his ashen suit, then turned to peek at her from beneath his hat. Even if he hadn't been slouching, he still would've had to tilt his head upwards to look Ren in the eyes. "Avatars are curated images. It's nice to see you didn't change your avatar much from your real life looks, so honest in such a dishonest world. Warms the heart. Of course, it's easier when you have no flaws to hide." He winked.

"We both know you tracked me here thanks to a pic on the Grid showing me casing the crime scene," said Ren in an even tone. "Don't act like you haven't seen my picture hundreds of times."

"See what I mean?" he said, stuffing his hands further into his pockets and staring out over the sparkling city dressed for the night. "Honesty. It's a good change of pace."

Ren eyed the man and switched on her connection to sub-grid 1. When she looked at him through the public AR overlay, well over half his tattoo implants disappeared. It was a well-made full body digital mask. It tracked all his visible skin and blurred the implants until they looked indistinguishable from his natural chestnut tone. Though these days, people switched from sub-grid to sub-grid like they flicked through vid-feeds. It was impossible to cover all of them.

Ren turned the connection off and traced the path of the tattoos with her eyes. She was content to let him choose where the conversation went, a feeling only made stronger when another jolt of nausea spread through her, quickly followed by the release of medication into her bloodstream. The untethered feeling numbed her, and she felt glad she was already leaning against the glass wall. She moved to sit back on the divan, making sure her steps were languid and steady. She sat down and resumed her stare.

Seth continued to look out the floor to ceiling window, hands in his pockets like rabbits down a hole. He moved to sit in a nearby chair and sighed. "You talk more in VR chatrooms though," said Seth. "It's a shame. I wanted to hear more of your voice without it being compressed into a data stream."

The bout of disconnectedness gone, Ren replied, "I only hear your voice if I pay enough, or if Saf the Proxy thinks it falls in line with company goals. How is business these days anyway? Projected earnings on track for the quarter? Can't imagine they aren't."

Seth eyed Ren from across the room and his lingering smile faltered. He cocked his head to the side. When he blinked, his eyelashes for the briefest moment lined up perfectly with the black tattoo wires escaping to either side. "Do you want this conversation over so quickly? First silence and then boring me with financial questions. And you know she strongly dislikes that name. Saf the Proxy. Ms. Saf controls the shell, though people seem to forget that. Perhaps I misspoke earlier."

Ren simply stared.

The Cheshire smile leapt back onto Seth's face. "I really do like you Ren. That is in fact why I bothered to stop by in person. You see, we both know this Discere hack is just the beginning. In fact, the second act has already begun. And things are going to get ... chaotic. I wanted to remind you, in person, how advantageous Safin Informatics' private line service can be in times like these. Even with how much help we have provided over the years, at times we still must remind you."

"How exactly are you going to remind me?" asked Ren. "Apparently, I'm forgetful. Going to have to be something big for that to change. It's odd ... how easily things like contact info can be deleted." She put her hands together and dropped her arms to rest loosely overtop her crossed legs. Tap moved to stand at her side.

"A gift," said Seth, back curved into a slouch as if his whole body was a smile. "The software, like so many diseases that would have wiped out humanity if not for some blind stroke of penicillin inspired luck, has evolved. Though not through natural selection, of course. Humans started to play that game for themselves a long time ago."

"You tell me something obvious and expect me to be impressed?" asked Ren.

"Eventually the North American government will fail," replied Seth. "Eventually the omnipotent Governance AI advising the politicians and gathering data from the masses will make a damning mistake. And of course, the trusting and lax politicians won't catch it until it's too late. That is inevitable. Still, wouldn't you think it wise to know whether it will happen tomorrow? Or years from now? Timing is important Agent Ren."

Ren eyed the man called Seth from across the room. The chair he sat in was modern, a series of unyielding lines. If it felt uncomfortable, Seth didn't show it. He lounged on the unpadded surface, one arm tossed over the back of the chair and the other tucked beneath his chin. He looked like a student attentively awaiting a response from a teacher, yet with the forced sincerity of a salesman after a pitch. It was the same pose he struck while sitting in a VR chatroom. It was the same pose she imagined him using when she heard his slithering voice over an audio call. But like so many distasteful things in the world, he was useful. So, she did her best to play nice. Difficult in normal times, near impossible when recovering from NeuCon.

Another bout of nausea tried to creep its way up her body and Ren forced it down. She calmed herself with a deep breath.

Safin Informatics had their web extended throughout the entire System. The eccentric recluse at the helm of the company held all the strings in her liver-spotted hand, operating from an unknown location and only interacting with the public through a remotely controlled mechanical shell dubbed Saf the Proxy. Some people in the intelligence community argued the real Saf had been dead for years. Either way, Saf or Saf the Proxy would feel the threads of her information network vibrate even when a hauler making its way through the black brought a shipment of poached helium-3 to an isolated outpost in the Saturnian system. That was the way of a semi-legal information broker.

Ren thought back to the tracing of the Discere hack to Titan, Saturn's largest moon.

Though she never would have told him, she had been about to reach out to Seth anyway.

"We all know timing is important," said Ren, the whisper of a tremor coming into her voice as another wave of medication kicked in. "Hurry up and get to your point. Tell me how the software has changed. Then I can act."

"Always trying to tear apart my wisdom. Does it make you feel special? Look hard enough and there is always a flaw. Nothing in this world is perfect. Didn't your parents teach you that?"

Seth paused, bringing both his hands beneath his chin to create a flowing pattern of implanted wires. His eyes watched her from beneath his hat. "You don't look so good Ren. Recuperating, are we? I'm sorry to bother you so soon after using NeuCon. I know the memories it brings aren't good ones. Shame we had to first meet thanks to such a sad occurrence. But you can't argue that our relationship hasn't been mutually beneficial, bitter seed borne sweet fruit."

Ren felt a growl building at the base of her throat, scratching at her flesh. She stifled it, rested a hand on the looming bot at her side, the gesture heavy with implication.

"You came in person; don't think I won't take advantage of that. If I permanently knock that smile off your face, Saf the Proxy will just switch you out for some other contact. Too much goes on here for your company not to trade with me. It might be time you and yours were given a fresh perspective on this ... relationship. Tell me what you came here to say. I don't have time for games."

Seth seemed unsurprised by Ren's outburst, shifting his weight and resituating his ashen suit with a nonchalant shrug. "You may be honest, but you could learn some manners." He paused, cocking his head as if listening to the chime of a bell far off in the distance. "But, nonetheless, I suppose you are right. More than you even know. The update is being disseminated throughout the city by hand, to rec bots and other poor soulless similarly taken advantage of by humanity, like food to the poor."

Ren thought it over; it made sense. And the way he phrased that last part. There was something there. She knew for a fact that Seth, like most people in modern society, didn't worry too much about the exploitation of intelligent bots. They were tools. They had a purpose, and recent advancements only made them better at accomplishing said purpose. But Ren knew of many groups that vehemently disagreed. If he was right, then the situation had changed, drastically. Things were progressing faster than expected. The update had been released yesterday morning and already it was modifying, spreading, *resonating*. Things only became a movement once they gained a direction, a philosophical foothold.

She opened her mouth to speak but before she could utter a sound, a ding from her earpiece notified her of a message. It was a file for a police report called in nearly an hour past, tagged by Tap. A rec bot had been manually installed with the software update and almost killed a mechanic. She eyed Seth, but all she could see was the same Cheshire smile beneath a low riding bowler hat. His eyes were twin pinpricks of electroluminescent light hidden deep in the gloom. She had the distinct urge to take his hat, like taking a favorite toy away from a child.

Ren sent a message to Jace telling him to meet at the van. Then she heard Seth's slick voice slide across the room.

"It would appear you are busy. Time for me to go I suppose. Remember, Safin Informatics' private line service is only a ping away. I always have time for you, you know," said Seth. He got smoothly to his feet and resumed his ever-present slouch, hands digging deep into his pockets, a pair of rats scurrying out of sight.

"How many informants do you have in our government?" asked Ren.

"Enough," said Seth. "Remember, the mark of good planning is the preponderance of coincidence." He said it with the ease of a phrase rolled from the tongue for the hundredth time, and Ren felt herself shiver. "Though I admit, even I couldn't have predicted how well that timing worked out." He winked.

With that, he tipped his hat and gave Ren a low bow. He walked into the elevator, humming a folksy tune all the way. The noise didn't stop until the elevator doors slid shut. Ren waited a few minutes for Seth to leave, then stepped into the elevator herself, directing it to the garage with a few motions of her hands.

This time the elevator ride was slow and smooth.

L ee Hall, age 49, born May 8th, 2146. Divorced 8 years ago, never remarried. No kids.

The mechanic's bio flashed across Ren's AR vision as she shimmied into a more comfortable position. The seat belt kept digging its edge across her chest, forcing her to resituate it blind. Most people didn't even bother with the annoying things.

She had her AR vision set at the highest opacity, blocking the entirety of the outside world. None of the streetlights she knew to be passing by in a steady rhythm, doing their job of pushing the nighttime dark out of the city and into the countryside, shone through her contacts. Virtual reality and augmented reality were not so different, separated by nothing more than a gradual shift from contacts that were clear as glass to contacts as opaque as an archaic TV screen. At least at the basic level. Expensive VR rigs allowed for high levels of sensory immersion that only improved with one's number of implants.

Ren shifted her seat belt once more and sighed. First using NeuCon, then meeting with Seth. It made her thoughts listless and gloomy. The incipient winter and dreary weather didn't do anything to help. A high-end VR rig could transport her mind and body to a beach in the south, or Lake Michigan during the heat of the summer. She played with the thought, letting it fill her wearied mind with the sensation of sun on skin. She pushed aside the thoughts of how using NeuCon again would make the rig unnecessary.

She focused on the text pinned to the digital menu occupying her vision.

Lee Hall, the mechanic whom they were about to visit, didn't have much in his bio at first glance. There wasn't any info on his childhood or parents. No siblings. No criminal record to speak of. His files started with him attending a respected trade school in the city, Watson's School for Neural Mechanics, with a full ride from the government. Notes from professors said he was well-mannered and independent, a natural with AI. Seemed more comfortable with machines than people, they said. He grew to be well liked. Classmates called him the smiling philosopher. Nothing but good grades. Several bouts of research. Ren glanced at his picture obtained from school records. He was attractive in a classic sort of way with short black hair, tanned olive skin, and a slight epicanthic fold in his eyelids hinting at a mixed origin, typical for people living in the city. He was smiling a somewhat toothy grin with a crinkling of skin all the way up to his forehead. She blinked a few times, watching the illumination of her contacts turn off for a split second with every snap of her eyelids.

The eyes, always the area around the eyes. His seemed glazed and unfocused, hints of puffy bags underneath born from a consistent lack of sleep. They were the same eyes she saw in the mirror every morning, red-rimmed and annoyed with how long they'd been open. He seemed to be staring at something that must have been beside the camera. Ren went back to reading his bio.

He graduated, got married, then divorced. Now he owned a profitable private contracting service where he was the sole employee.

She idly swiped through his tax returns, scanning the paperwork. Given his steep fees, it was no wonder the company was so profitable. She saw the company logo and her lips twitched into a grin. A dated picture of a mechanic in their standard faded blues with a wrench in one hand and a neural network in the other. Switch out the neural network for any broken-down electronic motor and the image looked like her father, a mechanic similarly enamored with the roots of the profession.

She moved to close out his bio, nonplussed at the shortage of information, when she noticed a tab on the far right of his profile under a classification she didn't recognize. She clicked on it and waited for the system to verify her security credentials. Her fingers tapped out a muted melody on the side of the leather seat while she waited. Why would a mechanic's bio be classified?

She got her answers a moment later, and the missing information on his parents and childhood made a little more sense.

His parents were Laskites, pink-brains, MEM's, or whatever else people called them.

Nearly 39 years before, a group of like-minded people set out on a ship called the Centauri-3 for the nearest habitable planet outside the System. They were running from the age of AI, trying to find a place where they could dictate humanity's advance, push it in a direction more to their liking. The group had been spearheaded by a one Robert Lask, ex-CEO of the now defunct Inno Corporation. He'd been a scientist who reached near celebrity status as a teenager, integral in developing the Governance AI and spurring the adoption of model-building AI's to helm nearly every corp. in the System. In some ways, he was the father of modern society. Some people suggested he was one of the early developers for the Grid, though he would have been too young for that.

Then he had done an about-face, becoming an advocate for regulation. He traveled the System giving cautionary tales on AI's creeping influence into areas meant for humans alone. The increasing use of emotive patches and unstable sub-routines terrified the man. The message resonated, and millions joined him. They pooled their money together and built a floating citadel capable of reaching the neighboring star system in a little less than 37 years, pushing fusion engines to their technological breaking point. Nobody knew if they'd made it or not. Messages were nonexistent and would take over 4 years to travel the distance even if they were sent.

Lee must have been about ten years old when his parents left him behind.

Ren paused in her reading and went back to look at his picture. She thought he made a little more sense now, like the image of him had gotten more detailed, blur steadily falling away. The smile gained depth. The eyes became black pools surrounded by the wispy brown curls of his iris; she felt like she could see the swirl of thoughts tumbling behind them.

He'd been abandoned, probably because his parents thought society had already indoctrinated him too far along a bot friendly path. He showed remarkable aptitude for AI even at a young age. She read through the rest of the government documents in a few minutes, skimming through the highlights Tap gathered onto a single page.

He'd bounced through the foster care system before being marked as one of the kids left behind by the Laskite migration with high potential. He was taken into government care and groomed for mechanic trade school. After graduating, he not only worked for his own business, but also fulfilled top secret government contracts to improve the analysis and advising capabilities of the Governance AI. Heavy stuff like data integration and neural network architecture. Then that side job had stopped entirely when his wife walked out on him.

His bio was a blank slate over the past eight years aside from private business tax returns.

At least there weren't any sightings of him at a jack house, no late-night pick-ups to be delivered, belligerent and drooling, back to his apartment.

Ren leaned her head against the headrest and twitched her fingers, throttling down the opacity on her AR so that the rest of the world came into view in a slow unshuttering. Jace sat in the driver's seat to her side, hands folded across his chest in a way that wouldn't crease his black suit, inactive steering wheel curled into the dash in front of him like a coiled snake. He was looking over Lee's analysis of the rec bot before it went rogue, the data sent through the Grid by the beat cops that took Lee's statement. Ren had skimmed it already.

Two parent programs in a single neural network, one that followed the rules while the other went unrestricted. All Ren knew was that it wasn't supposed to be possible, and solutions were being worked on. She propped her elbow on the door panel and rested her chin in hand. Another step closer to cleaning up this mess, but one that calmed her nerves less than she would have hoped. Watcher still didn't have a way to identify which bots were running the illegal software, though they were working on it. Always working on it.

Ren watched the city change as the van peeled off one of the main thoroughfares and into an Old Chicagoan suburb. It was populated by both questionable and legitimate businesses drawn in by the low rent. The buildings were crumbling, the flat panes of AR on modern buildings replaced by a hodgepodge of neon tube signage that screamed at her eyes for attention. The last time she'd been in a similar place was to investigate rumors of a box holding an AI that could drive people insane. All the person had to do was connect their tech, and the box took care of the rest. Ren closed out all her AR menus. The question she had to ask was whether Lee was involved somehow, aside from being in the wrong place at the wrong time. He'd been nearly killed, but his past showed a degree of experience in AI software that few could compete with. He'd been groomed for high-level government work, taken in as a child. He'd been trusted and respected. But then his profile showed a sharp change, an abrupt new lifestyle. He seemed to be someone who would side with a bot under the right circumstances. She needed to know if he could be of use, could be trusted.

She sighed, not looking forward to putting him to the test.

They pulled to a stop behind a vacant cop car, an AR neon sign proudly displaying the name of the business on their right. "Interpersonal Reimagining," it read. The sidewalk on either side was mostly deserted. Only a few bodies could be seen shuffling along, island hopping from streetlight to streetlight. Ren left the van and hunched against the stiff breeze while oddly shaped bits of plastic from empty stalls clattered around her. She and Jace walked inside, ignoring the hologram obscuring the door and warning of police business. Their two bots controlled by Tap followed them in.

The interior of the tall building was pretty much what she expected, sparse furnishings and bare walls aside from an interactive AR screen. It was clean in a don't look too close sort of way, the stench suffusing the air making it clear grime hid in cracks that cleaners couldn't reach. Two beat cops stood next to the shadowed entrance of a hallway lined with thin sliding doors, illuminated from the top by splayed fingers of light. Ren assumed the elevator to the upper levels could be found along the far end with an unmarked service door hidden nearby.

Jace walked straight backed to the beat cops, two standard issue police bots at their side. He knew the drill. His bot followed closely behind him.

Ren sighted a portly woman next to the interactive touch screen, a Mrs. Chen per the bubble of text floating astride her head. She sat in a tattered chair probably pulled from one of the rooms in the hallway, her sallow face in a pout as she fiddled with a control screen on her forearm. From her disheveled clothing, a blouse half untucked and dress pants lined with wrinkles, Ren guessed the general manager of the office wasn't typically up this late. Ren looked at herself. She had on her usual deep-toned shirt with a midnight black trench coat, metallic threading lining the edges of the coat the only flair to the ensemble, military padding hidden throughout. It looked clean and unwrinkled even after hours spent recovering from Neu-Con. There were perks to having clothes built of high-tech government materials.

Ren cleared her throat to catch Mrs. Chen's attention. The woman turned in her direction with no trace of a smile on her lips, one eyebrow curled in a question.

It took less than a minute to get access to the business's camera footage. Mrs. Chen accepted Ren's credentials with a grimace and transferred the vid files over the Grid, giving grunts and monosyllabic responses to Ren's questions.

Ren turned away from the woman and walked to the only window of the room. Though it wasn't really a window per say; it was an AR overlay showing footage from a camera embedded on the other side of the wall. She could see her van across the street.

Out of the corner of her eye, she glanced at the mechanic, Lee. He sat watching her from the other side of the room, sitting at the end of a row of hard plastic chairs, four-legged service bot standing next to him. He looked about the same as the picture in his bio. Age had gifted shallow creases like folded paper on his weathered skin and his short black hair was mussed into a halfway purposeful dishevelment speckled with gray, unusual for a guy so young these days. Most men didn't change color until their 100th year or so.

He sat with one lank arm hung across his leg, hand draped in front of his knee. His other hand curled beneath his chin as if he was kissing his fingers below the knuckles, wrist jutting out sharply. He looked like the bronzed statue that sat in front of the private university near her apartment, bent in philosophical thought.

Upon noticing her looking at him, Lee lifted his chin off his hand. He gave an amiable yet nervous grin before looking over at his service bot and whispering a few words that Ren couldn't hear.

Ren let him be for the time being while Jace disappeared into the hallway, heading to pick up the rec bot's black box from its mangled remains. If the pictures sent to her and Jace were any indication, there wasn't any chance of this bot rearing its cleaved head midway through the extraction. She leaned against the wall and opened the vid files while her bot stood at her side, her electroluminescent contacts coming to life with a few deft hand motions.

She opened the first of two vid files, the recording of Lee's visit with the rec bot.

She watched the exchange with an odd mix of feelings that settled into her gut and squirmed about. Her job was to protect the public from bots. She'd seen many videos of bots gone rogue or programmed to torture and kill and squeal with glee while doing it. But what she watched felt ... different. The software update had untangled the rec bot, left it to hobble together a personality from uploaded psych profiles. Then the rec bot built of welded shadows, of people's minds broken down into a warren of sliders and values, had been loosed on Lee. She could see the way the rec bot's words struck him.

Her thoughts flashed back to the Laskite migration, to the warring propaganda ads that ran when she was young. The video she watched bore an unsettling resemblance to the horror stories paraded around by the Laskites.

She watched Lee during the surveillance footage, gleaning a few pieces of information from the half-conversations with his service bot Nu. Though Lee had kept it out of his testimony and his analysis report, it was clear he had a copy of the hacked Discere update. In addition, he had a copy of the black box data Jace had gone to retrieve. But most important to Ren, it was clear his interest in the update was born out of a scientist's curiosity. Ren felt confident Lee hadn't known what to expect upon starting the job.

A small puff of air, accompanied by a brief and high chuckle, wormed its way out of her as she watched Lee tell Nu to gather the black box data *before* calling the cops. It always amazed her that people still forgot how common cameras were.

A plan spun itself together in the recesses of her mind. The second vid file could wait until after she talked with Lee.

She cupped her hand over her mouth and whispered a message to Jace. He would call a car to pick him up and head over to Lee's apartment complex. Once there, he would tap into the apartment's data feed and place a swath of drones around the place to keep watch. Tap would analyze the feeds for anything suspicious. She didn't think Lee was the type of scientist who would cross his own moral lines in the name of research, but she couldn't be sure what all those moral lines were yet.

Ren walked to Lee, the large bot at her side creating dim thuds with each step as it followed, its head towering over even her own. Lee saw them coming and slid to his feet, hands going into his pockets with thumbs hanging over the edge. He hesitated, moving to stick his hand out for a shake before thinking better of it. Instead, he smiled the same toothy grin from his picture and leaned against his service bot. Once his elbow hit the bot, it moved its rectangular head, making Lee stumble. Lee righted himself and rapped the bot on the head with his knuckle, a light tap. He looked back at Ren with another grin, one hand scratching at the back of his neck out of embarrassment.

Ren felt herself smile.

"Lee Hall?" asked Ren.

He nodded.

"Special Agent Ren, Division 13. Are you familiar with the organization?"

Lee's eyes narrowed in thought. In the poor lighting, she could see runnels of light spread across his contacts in an irregular pattern. Lee glanced at his bot before nodding. Ren heard Jace open the door behind her, a blast of cold air causing her skin to huddle into goose flesh. She heard a rubbing sound, a skid as a car peeled away from the building.

"A little," said Lee.

"I read your statement on the way over. Anything you would like to add?" asked Ren.

Lee looked up at the broad metallic shoulders of the Tap shell standing a small distance to the side of Ren. Then he shifted his gaze to Ren and looked her in the eyes. He shrugged a noncommittal shrug and smiled a tired smile.

"I want to say no. But you already know that isn't true," said Lee.

She always did.

"How about we talk outside," said Ren.

The two of them and their bots exited the building, Ren looking back at the beat cops huddled over their control screens. If they had an issue with her taking Lee, they could take it up with her boss.

Tap gave her an update on Jace's progress. She would give him enough time.

"Let's talk in my van," said Ren, gesturing towards the sleek black vehicle crouched by the sidewalk.

She walked towards the passenger side and caught herself mid-step. Jace wasn't here. She would have to sit in the driver's seat, steering wheel waiting to unwind if the van's systems failed mid-drive. She felt her hands get slick and clammy, felt her heart rate begin to pace, ramping up its speed with each beat. Her fingers gripped an imaginary wheel and seized, muscles in rigor.

Blood smells like metal thanks to a protein called hemoglobin. This protein incorporates iron molecules into its structure, important for carrying oxygen throughout the body. Contrary to popular belief, human blood is never blue. It is the skin that makes it look blue. Oxygenated blood is a bright, cherry red while deoxygenated blood is a deep, bruised apple burgundy. These colors are a direct result of the iron in the hemoglobin and its potential bondage with oxygen.

Ren remembered these facts pooling into her head as she watched Fain bleed out, drip after drip.

Ren took a deep breath and her hands loosened. She stuffed them in her jacket pockets. Lee stopped at the edge of the road, eyeing her with nervous glances. Perhaps a bit of worry? He had one hand on his bot and the other hanging dead-fish limp at his side.

"You're in the driver's seat," said Ren.

Tap sounded a warning in her ear, saying how that was against regulation. Ren ignored it. Lee opened his mouth to comment but seemed to think better of it, shrugging his shoulders in mute acceptance. It didn't really matter anyway. Manual control was only enabled in emergencies.

Upon entering the vehicle, Ren told Tap to interface with the van's AI and take control of all functions. Lee ambled in at her side while Nu and her bot creaked into the back, Nu stutter-stepping rather than using wheels riddled with shiny bits of metal. Ren locked the doors with an audible click and gave Lee a rueful grin. In the dark of night, the soft inner lights of the van painted everything in a neutral blue.

"I read your report, and I watched the vid file of your encounter with the rec bot," said Ren. "Want to revise your statement?"

Lee gave another shrug. Ren was starting to get the feeling he did that a lot. He brought his hand up to his mouth and rubbed it across his face in an arc, the movement making a bristling sound as his fingers slid through stubble. Ren saw the sadness she'd glimpsed in his picture leap back to the fore as he stared out the front window.

"You know why actors eventually forget the camera is there? Or why performers in live theatre learn to play off the crowd while a part of them forgets it even exists? It's for the same reason eyes that don't blink are unnerving and unwanted staring contests are downright predatory. Constantly being watched sets people's teeth on edge, crosses a wire somewhere in the survival centers of their brain."

Lee paused, gathering his thoughts only to let them out in a long breath. "Living a life always worried about who's watching seems like a rough way to live. I think it's healthy to forget about cameras from time to time. What's unhealthy is having them there in the first place." He looked at her questioningly, lips curled into half a smile. "So, Ren-with-no-last-name, clearly you know that I have a copy of the Discere update. I used that and my service bot over there to help me diagnose the rec bot. I also might have copied the black box data. I don't suppose I can promise you that I'll delete them, and you'll let me on my way? This update is ... new to me. I wanted to understand it."

"That's not good enough," said Ren.

Lee waited for her to continue, as if to say, then what is?

"I read your history. You still have high-level clearance, worked on the Governance AI itself. Filled a lot of expensive contracts." Ren paused, hands beginning to fidget in her lap. "Care to do something similar? I could use a personal contractor on this job. And something tells me you'll come in handy. It's a win-win. You get to research to your hearts content. My partner and I get sole access to the results."

Lee seemed to take the question in stride. He brought his hand up and scratched his chin, the ensemble of hundreds of thin hairs sliding across fingernails filling the interior of the van.

"Straight to the point. And thanks for the compliment," said Lee. "But what's option 2?"

"You won't like option 2."

"Try me."

Ren stared at him hard, letting time stretch until taught and ready to burst. But Lee didn't relent. She wanted him to relent.

She gestured to Tap's seated shell in the back of the van. With a hydraulic whoosh, one of its large hands clamped over Nu's rectangular head and lifted, pulling Nu's legs almost an inch off the floor of the van.

"Option 2 is where I take your bot and flash it back to factory settings. I don't know where you put the data, and I don't have the time or the patience to look for it. I also can't know for sure if you haven't stored the data on private servers at your apartment located on 313 Dao. I can and would get the legal right to search all your assets. If you resist, things only get worse from there."

Ren felt a pang of something like regret as she watched Lee's reaction. He didn't seem to have heard most of what she'd said. He was too focused on Nu in the back, on the powerful hand wrapped around his bot's head. His lips pressed tight until they were a pale bloodless line. His jaw clenched until she imagined she could hear the creak of bone. His brow furrowed into a V so deep she felt the paper creases in his skin would become permanent, deep-cut valleys.

And underneath it all, beneath the anger and bluster, she saw real fear. It was the fear children learned to hide if they wanted to be considered adults.

She'd expected it. She also regretted it.

But that didn't stop her from doing her job. She needed this man to work for her.

She gestured to Tap's shell and the bot dropped Nu to the floor of the van with a thud, the cab shaking. She softened her voice until it fit with the wan blue lighting and barren grid of windswept streets stretching around the vehicle for miles and miles. The buildings stood silent and solemn.

"This is the only way," said Ren. She didn't need to say any more. The government wouldn't allow him to study the update without oversight.

Lee rubbed the back of his neck, mouth slightly agape and eyes narrowed in shock. Then his face went blank, emotion scrubbed clean. His mouth screwed up in confusion. Ren had the discomfiting thought that it looked like someone going through rudimentary NeuCon for the first time. He looked up and gave Ren a solemn tweak of the lips. "Have you ever met my ex-wife May? You two would get along," he said. "How are the benefits for a contractor these days?"

They rode to Lee's apartment. Tap knew the way. For his part, Lee spent the trip staring out the window and casting a few furtive glances towards Ren. Ren noticed him open his mouth to start a conversation several times, but he always stuffed the words back down his throat.

Ren spent the ride watching the only other vid file of interest from the security footage. It was a video of a woman in a grey mask, the woman who had infected the rec bot with the altered software update. Ren watched her stroll through the business the day before, like someone pacing through a store without any intent to buy. The woman in the grey mask walked confidently into the rec bot's room and stood at the bedside, staring and thinking. She swiped a stasis chip over the bot's painted neck. She uploaded the virus. She whispered a barely audible phrase that filtered through twilight grey fabric.

"Time to see if there are ghosts in machines after all," she said.

Seth had been right.

Ren had a hunch she knew who was behind some of the manual uploads cropping up around the city like weeds in an overgrown garden. DIM, or Deus In Machina.

God in the machine.

Soul in the machine.

Ghost in the machine.

The phrases ran shivers along Ren's spine.

The van dropped Lee off into the night. Ren gave him instructions along with contact info before sending him off to dream fevered dreams or stare at the ceiling and rub at fevered eyes. She picked up Jace looking completely at home in a shadowed alleyway half a block away, staying in the passenger seat for the short distance. He got into the driver's seat without comment.

They drove into the night, and all Ren could think about was the look Lee had given Nu while Tap's shell held its head between metallic fingers. In a weird way, it was the kind of look people always hoped someone would give them, if things weren't looking good. The man cared for his bot as much as he could care for any being.

She closed her eyes, but all she could see were old looks of betrayal directed her way.

Chapter Five

A Significant Percentage

"Machines are the apotheosis of a hierarchical structure."
Mechanic's Guidebook, v99, Section 4b – Permissions, Par. 1

W hoever had said that wanting something hard enough would make it happen was not only naive, but also unfamiliar with insomnia. Insomnia only went away when he stopped caring if he'd ever get to sleep at all.

Lee looked at the ceiling through half-lidded eyes, AR contacts floating in their cleaning solution on his bedside. The night was a time for natural sight. Darkness draped a curtain of fog over everything; it seemed redundant to conceal things with another screen, his closed eyelids already a perfect backdrop to be colored with imaginings. He'd never much understood those who got eye implants. They could never take it out.

He rubbed his eyes and felt the odd sensation of them shifting in their sockets under the pressure, an unnerving squish.

Insomnia was supposed to be a thing of the past, like cancer or dying from natural causes before hitting a century and earning the nickname of a Bairen. Except for some reason insomnia hadn't gotten the memo and now came easy as pre-made sandwiches from vending machines. Sleep aids occupied the top shelf in pharmaceutical vends, next to multicolored pain meds. The melatonin in bright, recycled pill bottles had been about as effective as white noise sent from his implanted speakers. He'd even tried AR programs. They could paint his vision with numbered sheep if he wanted, swirl and spin with transcendental light shows like a magician trying to lull him with a crystalline pendulum. But that had required leaving in his contacts, which unnerved him.

Instead, Lee did what he always did. He watched the metal fingers of his ceiling fan do their dance round and round, uncleaned blades humming and spitting out loose clumps of dust every couple of minutes. The clumps billowed outwards mid-way through their descent, exploding into millions of tiny spores.

He slept fitfully, short and bittersweet.

Dreams graced his sleep. But they were incomplete things, shreds from a tapestry his brain couldn't seem to weave together. The tall and hard auto with sepia, cool brown skin and a sincere yet brutal voice made an appearance. He felt a dim, barely cognizant murmur of surprise as her fleeting likeness bloomed up close then withered away. Ren-with-no-last-name.

Sometime later he saw an image of a hole being burned through his neck, bubbles of fat and skin sloughing down the side of his body until the red-hot tech core could be seen underneath. His consciousness nearly woke from the images, nearly broke through the paralysis of sleep. Instead, he lingered there, watching the fat drip.

Upon waking, the sun still laboring on the other side of the planet, he did what he always did. He put in his contacts and watched a few episodes of family sitcoms. The plots blurred together into a cavalcade of situations he'd only ever glimpsed through a vid screen or while watching from the vantage of a wallflower. Parents struggled to make it to their kids' low-g soccer match at the far edge of the station while dealing with a belligerent great-grandfather. Parents contemplated how to avoid going to a somewhat friend's wedding in another part of the System. Middle aged couple spiced up a slowly dying sex life by incorporating AR adult games.

He shut off the AR vid screen and limped out of bed on stiff and unresponsive muscles, hobbled into the bathroom and took a shower. He slipped into one of the many washed out blues in his closet after deciding shaving wasn't worth it. Nu sat in his charging station in the main room, a few feet away from Fu who bustled about the kitchen, preparing Lee a meal. Lee walked up to a pile of spare parts in the corner of the room next to the tool closet and rummaged around for a set of wheels. He found a set and took them over to Nu.

"Hey Nu," said Lee. "How'd you sleep?" Lee shifted a toolbox at his side and squirted some oil on the bearings of the new wheels.

Do you ever get tired of repeating the same jokes?

"No. That would make life a little rough don't you think?" said Lee. He lifted a compact power tool and began replacing Nu's wheels one at a time. The whir of the rotating electric motor competed with the sound of eggs frying in a skillet, punctuated by the light patter of screws hitting the ground. "Searching for new jokes when I already have the best ones seems like the definition of inevitable disappointment. Sure, I could probably scrounge a few dysprosium ones from some forsaken corner of the System. I hear the Belt has a particularly dry sense of humor these days. But that seems like too much work. And like I said, I already got the best ones."

Lee paused his ministrations to shift into a more comfortable position. His legs had a habit of going to sleep on him.

"What do you think of our new boss?" he asked, trying to be nonchalant. It surprised him that the mention of her elicited only the memory of anger, not any of the immediate, feeling kind. A flicker of a dream came into his mind; it passed away just as fast.

I think she doesn't have much experience with asking people for help.

"That would seem to be the case," said Lee.

Neither do you.

Lee chuckled. He finished replacing Nu's wheels and moved to sit at the bar, a plate of eggs and fried sticks of bread waiting to be eaten. Dings and nicks encircled his plate and cracks ran from edge to edge. He picked at the food and thought over the previous day. It'd started out well enough, whiskey in hand and a pleasant buzz of conversation in the background.

"Did you analyze the data from Liz's bot?" asked Lee, remembering the morning conversation.

Nu rolled and skipped through the room in a tight figure eight around piles of electronics, assessing his new wheels.

Yes. An error tripped the moral code monitoring system. I already sent Liz a software patch. She sent a voice recording thanking you. From the background noise, it's clear she was working a night shift at the hospital.

Lee nodded as he stuffed clumps of egg into his mouth, taking bites of bread after.

"Thanks, my friend," said Lee, mouth full.

Some errant pieces of egg slid past his lips and escaped onto the floor. He ignored the spill; Fu would take care of it. The rest of the food settled in his stomach and radiated a warm feeling that suffused him, though it didn't loosen an anxious knot deep in his gut. He felt stretched thin, ephemeral. He'd almost gotten strangled by a bot the previous day. Deep purple splotches of color could be seen blooming in a ring around his neck, as if he had a choker implanted beneath the skin.

"Signal on the Grid that our shop is booked solid for the next few days. Something tells me we won't want any customers," said Lee. He paused and ran a hand across his unshaven cheek, poked at his neck and grimaced. Fu picked up his plate and put it into the washing machine. "And Nu, how is it that you were distracted yesterday. Don't get me wrong. You saved my life. But are there any improvements I need to be thinking about?"

Nu paused in the testing of his wheels, skidding to a stop a few feet to the side of Lee. Lee could hear the rattle of spare parts knocking against the diagnostic controller as the bot came to a halt.

The simulation and analysis of the update on my secondary neural network took up a lot of my processing bandwidth. If you don't want it to happen again, you should upgrade my core processor. You've already gone past all the manufacturing limits on auxiliary boosting.

"Are you sure you weren't just being dramatic, building the tension? You already have the best model money can buy. Well ... close enough to it anyway. I can't even remember the number of qubits in the hybrid you're running." said Lee. "Were there any other processes going on at the time?"

Nu paused for several seconds. Lee almost asked the question again before the response scrawled across his vision.

Only the operations I run every day.

Not a detailed answer. Rang of truth, but not all that specific. Lee would go back to it later. He was working himself up to it, staring down a path but unwilling to begin walking.

He shrugged himself away from the bar and strolled over to an old-style file cabinet overflowing with mothballed pieces of research. He stored most of his research digitally, either on drives in his apartment or on his private sub-grid, anonymized and secure. But the piece of research he intended to find had been written on paper. Things put on paper were reliable, tactile in a satisfying way. They had to be seen to be stolen, whether physically or through the lens of a camera. There was a beauty to that, to ink and paper. Besides, scanning the papers to save them as digital files was little trouble.

He rifled through drawer after drawer before shrugging his shoulders.

"Fu, search for my research on dual parent programs, will you?" He gestured to the files in front of him.

The thin limbed bipedal bot moved to take Lee's spot at the file cabinet, light flashing off its glossy blue paint as it moved.

Some people recorded everything they saw through the cameras in their contacts, making it easy to find lost items. All they had to do was have an AI run through the vids, tagged and encoded as they were with relevant search terms. Others only kept recordings of things that went on in their houses through security cams. Good to catch a partner attempting any late-night trysts, or someone trying to break in, or just to have vid files of fond memories. Lee knew more cameras than eyes could be found in the city. Private owners, corps, and underground rings all owned feeds, a laundry list of those with good intent and those without. Data gathering was an art form, and secrecy a harder one still.

Lee preferred not to deal with recording his life or having cameras in his home, aside from the ones that bots used for eyes. But those had always felt different to him. They didn't just store the footage, they comprehended it. He knew that didn't equate to security, but it was no different than allowing another human into his home with their contacts on.

He scratched at an elbow. He should have remembered all this last night before he copied data from the black box in full view of the tall house's AI. He'd gotten too excited, addled.

He cocked his head to the side as if trying to listen to a voice far off in the distance.

Lee dropped into a stuffed easy chair like a dead man into a casket and flicked his wrist, activating his control screen. His tech core had overheated three times the day before. First when Fu had reminded him of his ex-wife upon walking into the apartment. That had been Nu's doing. Second, when the rec bot sent his mind reeling, summoning images of a marionette ex-wife bouncing on invisible strings. Third, when Ren threatened to flash Nu. That last time was when he'd felt it, his emotions picking up their bags and leaving him behind, as if all his anger and fear and helplessness called a self-driving taxi, sidled into the cab and rode into the night. It had left him … confused. And indignant at being cheated. Being able to express rage was a human right.

Looking back, the same feeling accompanied every overheating of his tech core. But in the past, it had been a slow drain of his emotions, a quirk that could have been brushed off as the control of a well-adjusted mind. It didn't seem that way anymore. He knew of autos, of their neural conditioning. He knew of the common therapeutic programs that incorporated cheaper and less comprehensive implants to a much more basic effect.

He brought up detailed AR charts showing the usage of his implanted tech core over the past few days, Fu rummaging through the file container next to him. He found three jagged spikes that corresponded to when it overheated and zoomed in further. He brought up detailed breakdowns of processor utilization, what happened during each occurrence. It didn't add up.

"Hey Nu," said Lee. "Look at the data from my tech core." He tapped a button and all the data gathered onto his AR view screen swiped to the side, sent over to Nu. "There appears to be some type of error. I don't recognize some of the programs and others are pulling way too much from the system. I can't figure out why it was running so hot at the time."

The bot sat unresponsive for several seconds.

There does appear to be an error.

Lee waited for Nu to continue. When Nu did not, Lee felt a small, hidden ember of anger still smoldering from the previous day stoke itself to life, beg for more fuel to burn and char. He fed it a little, knowing it was going to spark, fearing that the wind was blowing in the wrong direction. But Nu was supposed to be the only one who couldn't lie to him. A part of Lee knew the bot still hadn't.

"What error?"

Some of the programs appear to be misnamed or tracking incorrectly.

"What are the altered programs actually doing?"

They are running a variant of the therapeutic programs meant to stem physiological responses.

"They are wiping my emotions."

They are helping you.

"How did they get there?" *Something added the software to your tech core and hid it behind innocuous programs.*

"Who added the software?"

Something with access.

Lee found that his voice had been steadily increasing in volume as he asked the questions. He didn't really understand why he was yelling. The words scraped against his throat and left it tingling. Fu kept methodically digging through his research, skipping from drawer to drawer and file to file as Nu skipped from each barely passable answer to the next.

"Who had access?"

Something with access to tertiary systems.

"Who had access to tertiary systems?"

Several programs.

"These programs have a name?"

All programs have a name.

"Dammit Nu, quit stalling, I know it was you."

The bot sat stolidly, the only tools for showing emotion a few blinking LED lights. They slowed their pattern.

Yes. I added the software.

And with the admittance written out in plain lettering across his vision, his anger dissipated, left the station. While questions often thrilled him, answers always calmed him. For a time. New questions always came nipping at their heels.

"Why did you do it? How did you do it without asking me first?"

I wanted to help. Studies have shown impressive results with this technology. It can stabilize any extreme emotion. Serious patients have shown promising decreases in aberrant behavior and an incredible rate of assimilation into society. Low-risk patients, like you, have seen helpful results from infrequent use.

The bot paused.

You never told me I couldn't. I was trying to help.

Lee opened and closed his mouth several times while fiddling with his cold metallic wristband. He wasn't sure how he felt.

He told Fu to open one of the windows. The cloth screen rolled into a tube, rattling all the way and making a knocking sound when it hit the end of its length. The sun was just beginning its daily rise, sending rays of sunlight to scour the city of any lingering dark.

"How much of your original programming is left anyway? From when I purchased you."

A good amount ... about 65 to 70 percent.

Lee chuckled at the number, a slow grin creeping across his face, the ever-present sadness lurking underneath. It felt further away for now.

65 to 70 percent, or a majority, seemed like a lot of code. Considering the amount required to make a bot run, it was. But not all code had equal

importance. Lee knew the situation compared well to that of DNA, the genetic code that held the directions for organic life. Humans shared most of their genes with other mammals. In fact, humans shared 96 to 98 percent of their genetic sequence with chimpanzees. That was a large percentage, but most of the shared code contained the basic functions required for life, building blocks common amongst many creatures, plans for proteins integral to the functioning of cells. The differences between humans and chimpanzees seemed small when put in terms of percent genetic code, but one only had to look between the two species to see the truth. Those differences granted much. The ramifications of Nu's extensive software changes weren't entirely clear, not even to Lee.

Lee looked at Nu. "No more starting the program without me allowing it first. Only turn it on when I say so. Ya?"

Yes.

"Good. Now, my friend, we have a job to do," said Lee.

Fu pulled a dense and overstuffed manila envelope from the file cabinet, his research on dual parent programs from years before, from when he suddenly had too much time on his hands. Ren wanted him to learn everything he could about the update, and how to monitor it if possible. He scanned the papers and stashed the files onto his private sub-grid, pointed the documents out to Nu.

Before he could start, thoughts of Ren came to mind. He thought about her large bot, all hard lines and plated armor, grabbing Nu across the head and lifting him several inches off the ground. He thought of Nu accepting the touch in the unflinching way only a bot could and initiating Lee's therapeutic program. He thought about Ren threatening to flash Nu, threatening to send him back to factory settings. She would have searched his private data. She could have found all of Nu's backups and deleted those as well. He thought about her voice towards the end, how it had softened with sadness and regret.

Lee often posed a question to himself, in the way people who love questions do. He wondered if an assassin who cried as she slit the throat of a target, watching salty drops mingle with the blood, was better than an assassin that didn't shed a tear.

Lee thought the tear-streaked assassin better. They would be open to other options, to taking a seat, leaning back and at least feigning interest. Considering who he now worked for, that made all the difference.

With the bars of sunlight creeping across the bowed floor and up his legs, he and Nu began.

CHAPTER SIX

REALITY HAS MANY FORMS

"A model is only as good as the data that is put in. Faulty premise, faulty conclusion."
Division 13 Agent Training Manual, v23, Section 1b – Standard Operating Procedure, Par. 2

R en could tell a lot about a person from the way they decorated their living spaces. Tidiness, materials, décor. These three qualities of a room held as much information as a household's private sub-grid, though less explicit.

Ren knew tidiness was easy. It had been ever since most homes included a metallic, flawless butler. Clean the room. Don't clean the room. Or for the more calculating, clean the coffee table and dust the furniture but leave the piles of books in disarray as it gives the room an intelligent feel, as if the person had a habit of picking up Sun Tzu's The Art of War whenever the urge to read dynastic Chinese literature hit them. And the urge to read it on physical media no less.

Tidiness required the utterance of a command. A simple choice. All choices had meaning, some more, some less.

The materials to build furniture ranged from rapidly printed plastics to tangled polymer chains formed in a mold, from sawdust pressed together with glue to wooden flesh carved from the body of a tree, and from cheap metals to complex alloys like the spun graphite blends used for space elevators.

Most furniture was like people; it put on a good face while something cheaper lurked hidden underneath.

Then there was the decor. It held as much, if not more, information than anything else. Ever since the onset of AR and the Grid, digital books, posters, paintings and statues replaced their physical counterparts for only a few loci each. A bare plaster ceiling could be switched out for vaulted domes painted with angelic scenes or a peaked wooden structure with ornate struts and carved, looping designs. Wallpaper and prints could be changed in a single command. The digital became cheap and reproducible with a click. The sensation of wood on skin, the smell of cedar tickling one's nostrils, these things became expensive.

When it came to the modern world, real always came with a higher price tag. Learning how people spent their money bred an understanding deeper than words.

Ren could tell immediately from looking at a room which socioeconomic class the owner lived in, worked in, died in. More importantly, she could tell from the arrangement which class they wanted to *be* in.

As she sat up in bed and watched her shadow stretch and twist, play across the carpet in a slow, black and white dance, she had the feeling her room didn't say much, was too subdued to speak. Of course, silence spoke volumes to those who cared enough to listen.

She walked over to her bathroom and went through her daily ritual, the light tumbling out the doorway in a slanted rectangle onto the carpeted ground of her bedroom.

A set of north-facing bay windows encompassed a large portion of the wall opposite the bathroom, ending only a foot above her bed. As high as her apartment rested in the skyscraper, the location forced her to play by the sun's rules. Though the sun beat her into bed these days, she was never asleep while the sun was out, never bothered to use the blinds unless privacy required it. She enjoyed the view too much, though enjoy was perhaps too strong a word. The view ... stirred her. Block after block of skyscrapers jostled for light like plants in a forest, squat and thick shrubs of brick and mortar and metal crowding around the bases of larger buildings. Off in the distance, towards the poorer areas of the city, countless AC box units dotted the sides of shanty apartment complexes, silent for the oncoming winter. Drying laundry could be seen fluttering in the breeze, though not as many as there had been only a month ago. To the east and north she could see the New Chicago fisheries, covering the edges of the city's expansion overtop Lake Michigan, more hidden beneath. Then she could see the lake itself, sun licking at the tip of wavelets.

The light streaming in from the large bay windows didn't suffuse the room, didn't billow outwards. It cut a razor-sharp outline in the dark of the room, a bright rhombus that leaned away from the sun and moved like a giant sundial. The rest of her bedroom lay shrouded. The weak light illuminated a rustic cream carpet, showed a closet off to the side, a shadow amongst shadows. There might have been a physical picture off in the corner, on top of the dresser. It might have shown smiling parents with two squalling children not wanting to be photographed. But the shadows there were deep and rarely disturbed. A person stepping into the room would've been hard pressed to notice the picture. Ren rarely did anymore.

Not much could be gleaned about her from the arrangement of her room. The room didn't say much. At least that was her hope.

She took a quick shower then walked out the bathroom, skin glistening with dampness and hair wrapped in a towel. A pair of men's boxers lay on the floor next to her bed, pushed almost underneath. She recognized the blue linear patterns from a few days before and realized with a dim surprise the guy must have gone home without. She remembered him. Average height, lean. Strong but with soft features. He'd been good. Selfless.

She picked them up and tossed them into a half-full basket of dirty laundry. Men's boxers were comfortable pajamas. A few other boxers poked out of the mess of clothes in the bin, strangers in an earth-toned land of blacks and browns and steel grey. She dressed, slid on a dark maroon shirt hardly different from the one she wore the day before and pushed her hair into a rough ponytail.

A rustle emanated from the main room.

She rushed to her bedside and pulled a handgun from its storage, a nook between mattress and wall. Her heartbeat started to rise, and she forced it down with slow, measured breaths.

A message popped across her vision.

Apologies. I still have access to your apartment. I entered while you were in the bathroom.

Jace. Tap must have warned him. The AI had access to Ren's contact vid feed, and she'd slept with them on like she always did. Ren returned the gun to its holster and cursed under her breath at Tap.

"I was going to tell you before you walked out of your room," said Tap, a bit of petulance in its voice. "He wanted it to be a surprise."

Ren sighed. She stared out the window at the metal jungle of the city with her shadow draped across the room behind her. She waited until her heartbeat calmed. She'd just gone through the recovery period. She didn't want to do it again so soon.

When she tapped a button on the wall, the door to the main room slid into a recessed alcove and she saw Jace standing by the kitchen island. He stood in his usual slate black suit with an apron draped over his shoulders. She could see pancakes, eggs and sausage in various stages of preparation. She raised one eyebrow in surprise and scratched at her elbow.

Across from him on the wall was an AR vid screen tuned to one of the local news channels, tethered there for anyone connected to her apartment's sub-grid to see. On it played a news report of a local fire in one of the crumbling apartment buildings of Old Chicago. She read the headlines and sighed. One person dead. Though her sigh was also part relief. It hadn't been a bot that caused the fire.

Ren sat by the kitchen table near the faux marble island where Jace stood expressionless. They watched the news story play out.

A child, no more than several months old, lay wrapped in a blanket in the back of an ambulance, unwilling to accept the touch of a nurse. A squad of emergency bots with giant hoses attached to the tops of their wheeled bodies sent misting sprays of water over a dead fire, wetting the ash. In the background, a limp body was pulled from a collapsed room, tossed onto a gurney by the human complement of the first responders. From what Ren could gather, the dead body was that of the mother. She'd been stuck in her bedroom at the edge of the apartment while the rest of the building fell around her, listening to noises from her baby monitor. The fire containment systems built into the building had failed; that was the only explanation. Things like that didn't happen if safety measures were working.

The vid feed changed, shifting to the news studio. Ren listened to the panel of experts brought in to analyze the case bicker amongst each other. She'd known this was coming, buzzards picking at a corpse.

The rescue bots only had so much time, only had a limited set of resources. They'd focused their efforts on saving the child. The mother had a criminal past, petty theft and minor misdemeanors. Though it wasn't illegal, records showed she was a frequent visitor to jack houses and had a history of soft drug downloads. Each soft drug variant that flooded the neural receptors of the brain with pleasure only worked for so long before the effects dulled, the happiness stunted. The same old story of dependence and addiction.

All in all, the decision to save the child was clear cut from the standpoint of moral code. Prioritize the kid and save the mother if god willed it, god being whichever one they happened to believe in.

The talking heads shown on the vid screen, the so-called panel of experts, bickered and argued over what could have been done better. They argued over water allocation and bot allocation. They argued over the dead women's past and if the history of the next of kin set to take the child should have come into play. They took the abandonment of a child and tore it apart into dull and emotionless facts, pulled at heartstrings until the lines were in a dense knot incapable of playing music sweet or sad.

Ren changed the channel. The people on TV were playing the part of bots and it unnerved her. The point of the moral code was to get synthetics to make the damning decisions, so people didn't have to. That was the point of auto's too, even if they hated themselves for it.

Even news reporters, buzzards as they were, should've had the decency to wait until the corpse had gone cold.

Jace shifted the channel back to the news reports and nodded towards the screen with a downturn of the eyes. For a split second, Ren's eyes narrowed in frustration. At Jace for limiting himself to the barest semblance of emotion. At those bastard talking heads on the news vids ignoring all decency just to fill the 24-hour news cycle with mind-numbing blather. The moment passed, and Jace turned around to finish preparing the food, frying up another egg.

Ren looked to the vid screen and saw what Jace had nodded towards. The coverage had shifted to a different story, a whole new panel of experts.

Shit.

"Come on," said the gruff and mustachioed face on the far left, a local politician. "It's clear that the software released during the Discere hack is to blame for all the so-called malfunctions going on across the city and even the System. We were told shortly after the government shut down the server that all infected bots had been dealt with. That was either a lie or things have changed. You'd have to be blind not to see that. More and more rec-bots are tearing apart rooms and injuring patrons. Service bots are bad-mouthing customers in stores and in markets on the Grid. Worker bots are staring at the sky while they should be working, as if they could *daydream*. People are probably dying by bots off-planet, or even other areas of Earth where we don't have coverage. Perhaps another murder is happening here in North America as we speak. Extremists are uploading this *virus* to bots and spreading it. It must be stopped."

Another man to his right, a bulbous figure with a round nose and droopy eyes stammered to cut in. Ren didn't recognize him. "Well ... Well now. Calm down. These are not extremists. There are many people concerned with the treatment of bots. Isn't it at least feasible that some of the uploads are by people trying to liberate an oppressed, and highly intelligent, group of ..." He waved his hands around, grasping for words. "Synthetics, bots, AI's. Either way, there has only been a single death proven to be associated with this software update. And that was provoked. The man had been about to shut the bot down in a shopping mall."

The first speaker's face bloomed red as blood rushed to his cheeks. He raised his voice while shifting forward in his seat. His mustache bristled at the influx of emotion, a hedgehog showing its spines. "Provoked? Only a single death? These bots are operating outside of moral code. There have been countless injuries, some serious. These bots are not controlled, and we don't know what this *virus* will make them do."

A cough came from the far right, a delicate clearing of the throat. A woman with short hair and a pointed chin spoke, the news anchor. "What about the recent implications that the infected bots are fooling the monitoring system maintained by North America's own Governance AI? It is clear the software has leaked and is being spread by unknown factions. But the allegations that the bots are operating while connected to sub-grid 1 are paramount. Crime syndicates have been hoping for something like this for years. Do you not think the North American Government needs to respond? These stories have been coming from countries outside of North American control as well. Occurrences in the China sector, South American sector, Indian Conglomerate, European Union, and the African League - just to name a few - have shown bots sidestepping monitoring systems. Mega cities across Titan to Enceladus to Mars have had similar results. Does anyone have any thoughts as to why the President hasn't made a statement?"

Ren saw the pall of fear creep across the panel, their voices quiet for the first time since the vid screen flicked on. She cursed again under her breath and tapped her fingers against the edges of her plastic chair. Two days was a long time for a story to stay under wraps. Still, she'd thought she had more time. It was only yesterday afternoon the spread of manual uploads had begun.

Another voice, this time from a thin mouse of a woman, spoke up to break the silence. "But what about where it came from? Stories are circulating that it originated from the unregulated sectors. Some people argue this is an attempt to sow chaos so the corporations can grab more territory. Some people argue it could even come from Origin Station. We all know the stories that come from there."

Everybody nodded in agreement aside from the droopy eyed man. "Well … that isn't fair," he said, jowls shaking. "Origin Station is the linchpin of the Grid, which we all depend on. Stories there of bots living free and acting as citizens are exaggerated. On Earth, we create horror stories of serial killer bots. It's gas lighting, pure and simple. Bots out in the unregulated sectors of the System not connected to a monitor are not much more dangerous than the ones we use. Sometimes they malfunction, but that is no different. Have you forgotten life before the Grid? Why …"

They continued talking but Ren shut them out, turning off the vid screen. She turned to Jace.

"When did they figure it out?" asked Ren.

"Rumors weren't taken seriously until last night. The number of stories from outside North America circulating through the Grid became too many to ignore."

Ren clenched her teeth and stood up. She began to set the table for two, pulling out the spotless ceramic plates from the cabinet next to Jace. His eyes stayed fixed on the egg sizzling in the skillet.

Her apartment's included bot sat powered down in the corner of the room, eyes dull and uncomprehending. Tap's shell stood next to it in a charging station, making the thin limbed apartment bot seem like an atrophied old man snoozing in the sunlight while a large attendant stood nearby. Jace's Tap-controlled bot probably stood outside the door. Ren didn't bother telling any of the bots to help set the table. Sometimes it was nice to keep her hands busy.

"How long until the VR meetup with boss?" asked Ren.

"20 minutes," said Jace. He finished with the eggs and loaded up the serving plates.

"Is that vat sausage?" Ren pointed at the steaming pile of meat.

Jace shook his head no. Ren thought about asking another question, but she'd never been one to force conversation. Still, she watched him, his pale blue eyes the color of glacial ice, his wan skin and thin features. He moved with an economy, an efficiency that had been there well before Tap's influence. He looked inscrutable, but Ren knew from experience that was a lie.

They ate the food in silence, Ren eating with wolfish bites in between blank stares at the wall. She let her mind work and fret over problems, draw patterns and words. Jace ate with respectable nibbles, not a single speck of food falling onto his suit. They finished at the same time and cleaned the table up in a matter of minutes.

After they were done, they each took a seat in the lounge area of the main room. They sat in large, puffy chairs that seemed to swallow them up the moment they sat down, supporting every limb until their muscles went lax. Before they initiated VR, Ren met Jace's eyes with her own. She couldn't read anything in his obdurate, unbending face.

"Thanks for the breakfast by the way," said Ren.

He managed a shallow nod, a modest tip of the head. The motion was gentle, and Ren thought she could see the beginnings of small dimples in his cheeks, cracks in the mask.

"It seemed you might need it after yesterday," said Jace.

At that moment, knowledge struck Ren directly between the temples. It wasn't the feeling of learning something new; that was a flick of a switch that left her invigorated. This was the realization of something already known but long hidden, a feeling both frustrating and sapping.

Jace had long since hit the plateau.

She'd been hoping he'd been turning it off each night to recover, but that would have left him strained in the mornings. She watched him, hoping to see some tweak of the mouth, an uplifting of the eyes.

It wasn't like Division 13 told their agents to avoid hitting the side effect plateau. Not really. Not with conviction. Sure, they told agents to manage their time, keep their life in balance and above all avoid getting sick while on duty. But many of the higher ups liked their agents going full auto for the couple days required to hit the plateau. Then they'd have little incentive to turn it off and bring the efficiency of the whole business down.

Originally, the term auto had been created by the government R&D lab coats who designed the neural conditioning program. Though it hadn't been used officially, it stuck. The callous agents of the government, experiments of Division 13. Humans linked up to the Grid, acting at the direction of an AI. Marionettes and puppets. Automatons. It was an unfair description, though Ren would admit to it being only unfair in part. Neither Ren nor Jace were controlled by Tap under NeuCon. The program dampened their emotions to improve the interface with the AI, until what was once an advisor became something more integral to their thought processes. NeuCon was a meld of sorts, hooking her brain up to a machine and moderating a conversation.

Ren let herself fall back into the reclined chair. There wasn't anything to be done about Jace. He would continue to be effective in his role. Merciless and calculating when required. Whether it damned him or not. Her fingers clenched the armrests.

She triggered the VR system, and her body went limp as a ragdoll.

All autos required extensive implants beneath the skull and in the back of the neck, reaching up towards the brain stem. They had the best implants government tech could supply. Thanks to this, they didn't need to rely on contacts for a partial, visual immersion into VR. Nor did they require an external VR rig for a full sensory dive. Electronic signals rushing from the brain, down through the brain stem, and throughout the spinal column could be hijacked and interpreted by their implants while excitations on necessary neurons provided the feedback. It wasn't perfect. No matter how good the rig, VR was distinctly different than the real world, a different flavor of reality. Some people savored the taste, others rejected it. For Ren, it had its uses.

She opened her digital eyes and looked around. It was the usual place, a hushed and secretive reading room with deep toned woods and countless books. The vaulted ceiling looked baroque in its flowered and detailed extravagance, but the rest of the room was simple and clean with burnished wooden furniture stained a dark cherry red. On the floor was a carpet the color of algae floating in a lake, a deep hunter green. Her booted feet sank in it with each step. There weren't any doors in the room, only row after row of books on bowed wooden shelves. Ladders on each wall ran to the ceiling and slid along a horizontal track allowing one to climb to the topmost shelves twenty feet in the air. A single window at the far end let in a steady stream of light that illuminated the otherwise lightless room, a forested hill visible through the window, a massive willow tree rising at its crest. The room smelled of dust and old parchment, leather and cigar smoke, of things close and pressing.

At the center of the room, three cushioned leather seats sat around a low table with a full cigar box resting in its center. Above the table was a hologram playing vid files and showing countless documents. It was the only semblance of technology in the room.

Behind the hologram sat her boss in a tailored black suit and tie, swiping and dragging at the pieces of the hologram as if they were a touchscreen. With VR, rules were a little different.

Ren and Jace each took a seat in one of the open leather chairs as their boss muttered to himself, handling both ends of his personal conversation.

"They were just a tad too early," he said.

"No. Your projections were just a tad too late," he replied to himself in measured admonishment.

"That is nothing more than semantics," he said, once again replying to himself.

"Ah, but one blames the external while the other blames the internal. One is actionable, one is not. This software is an unknown, and you didn't value it correctly as I told you to."

"Now you are the incorrect one. I predicted multiple paths. This is the one with a hand guiding the software's course. Like a parent guiding a child with butterfly touches on the shoulder. It just wasn't the most probable outcome."

Her boss continued talking to himself and Ren leaned back in the leather chair to breath the air in deep, knowing that her body was sucking in air from her apartment, the same recycled air she breathed every night with the neutral smell of a place gently lived in. Yet still the smell of an untouched library filled her nostrils, little electrical impulses in her implants activating the necessary receptors in her brain. She looked around and the books and furniture all had the hyper-real quality of VR, of being in a vid screen. Things were so sharp and glossy she could see motes of dust shining in the dimly lit depths of the tranquil room, riding on invisible air currents that had no source and no end.

Ren could see why someone like her boss would spend time in a place like this.

"Boss?" asked Ren. "Foster?"

Her boss continued shifting vid feeds and documents around in the air like he was setting a speed record for solving a digital Rubik's cube.

"Yes Ren?" he said, giving her a quick glance and an affable nod. He went back to talking with himself.

He was a small man, short in stature yet lean and dense with muscle and sinew. He moved his hands with dexterous jabs and slides even though his pure white hair and wrinkled skin betrayed him as being over a century old, well past when most retired to the equator or a Martian resort before the deep decline set in. He had been one of the first to take part in the government's attempts to augment the human brain with technology, and the only one that the process hadn't killed in the program's initial years, with many odd side effects as scars of the experience. Ren didn't know what all went on in his circuit board riddled brain, only that she'd never seen the head of Division 13 stop moving, let alone stop speaking for more than a few seconds at a time. And yet, while his motions were fast, his voice was always unhurried and calm. It was an odd paradox, as if he had to keep talking to catch up with his body but wouldn't rush the words out.

Ren let her gaze slide along the books like a fingertip brushing across the spines. None of the books had any visible titles. No sound other than Foster's pointed conversation with himself could be heard. In their pocket of reality, time's passing wasn't really felt. The sun shining through the window always stayed at the exact same spot in the sky and the weather never shifted from a rainless, cerulean blue expanse dotted with puffy cumulous clouds. Change couldn't sneak into the library as there were no passages either in or out, not unless Foster created them. Ren had learned to treat Foster's speech as the inexorable tick of a clock in a digital pocket otherwise stuck out of time.

"Did you read my report on the possible DIM lead?" asked Ren. Jace sat static in his chair. Sometimes Ren felt he blended into the background simply by being still these days.

"Of course," said Foster with a chuckle. "We will get to that in no time at all. But first, a few updates for my favorite pair of agents."

He swiped his hand and the hologram disappeared. He crossed one leg over the other then switched them back in a nervous dance that didn't color his voice with any tremble or shake.

"A new plan has been undertaken. Our President is getting troubled it would seem. The Governance AI suggested multiple courses of action with varying possible outcomes. He chose the one with the highest probability of getting the problem solved in a timely manner while limiting bothersome things like riots and looting," said Foster. He leaned back in his chair and looked at the ceiling, pausing for a few moments. "If a leader always accepts the suggestions of the advisor, who then is the real leader?"

Ren didn't answer. She'd learned to assume all his questions were internal unless stated otherwise.

"Of course, the leader is still the leader," replied Foster to himself, as if speaking to a child. "Why would you think otherwise? It just means watching the advisor for most things policy. But no two people are ever the same. A disagreement will occur, and you must know the leader well enough to predict in advance when they will make a stand. And what that stand will look like."

"Is that going to happen now?" asked Foster to himself.

"It seems possible. He, like everyone else, has strong feelings on the usage of bots in society. Voting records. Policy initiatives. It all shows a point where he will no longer bend," said Foster.

"We'll have to consider that further."

"Yes of course."

"Boss," said Ren, cutting him off. "What are you trying to tell us?"

He brought his gaze down from the ceiling reluctantly. He'd been tracing the loops and whorls etched into the ceiling with his eyes.

"There is going to be a press conference today. Noon. The President will admit to the bots ignoring the monitoring system while connected. E-Sec, the securities corporation always lobbying for more regulation, apparently feels they can solve the problem faster than contracted Discere researchers and government scientists. The President will publicly grant them a rather large contract. They got their hands on the software remarkably early and claim to already be on the right track towards fixing things. The speed with which they are acting is remarkable. They must be watched, though they are not your immediate concern," said Foster.

His eyes strayed towards the ceiling and Ren was about to cut in again when he snapped his eyes back to her, meeting her gaze.

"Starting with the announcement today, Congress has agreed to bring this software under the umbrella of those that subvert moral code, *formally* making its distribution and usage illegal. Local police will have enough trouble enforcing that policy and tracking the spread of software, mitigating its flow. I cannot send any other agents into Greater Chicago. They are too busy dealing with the problems arising in other mega cities. Which brings me to you two, and your change of focus."

Foster stood up and paced about the room, muttering to himself. He walked to the nearest bookcase and grabbed one of the countless identical books on the shelves, seemingly choosing one at random. Then he grabbed a second. He stepped over to Ren and Jace and passed one to each of them. A ding sounded in Ren's ear, a notification of a file received.

"In that file is everything you need to know about what comes next. In it, you will find the unpublicized location of the local DIM servers holding data for their sub-grid. I have also given you legal papers to allow for the immediate search and seizure of certain pieces of data. Thanks to a plant, we've received chatter indicating they do in fact have the illegal update. But everyone in that philosophical think tank of sorts implements anonymous usernames. Find a way around that. This woman in the grey mask you saw in the recording has shown herself on many different cameras throughout the city. Figure out if your theory about her holds true. Also, use your connections with Saf if need be. On this and the origin of the software. I am not convinced DIM created it. I find it more probable there are multiple parties at work. And Saf has her fingers in far too many places in the System not to ask."

Foster sat back down in his chair and began bouncing both his heels up and down in alternating motions. "Ren, do you know the origin of the three-line phrase that DIM uses? You know the one. God in the machine. Soul in the machine. Ghost in the machine."

Ren replied that she did not.

Foster paused, his mouth stilling for several seconds, the longest period since Jace and Ren had entered the reading room.

"Many would say a God is a concept to be revered. That a soul is a concept to be treasured and protected from straying. And that a ghost is a concept of things left behind, of things crossing over in reverse. But what seems more important to me is that they are all uniquely enmeshed in humanity, across culture and across time in some form or another. And they are all uniquely misunderstood."

"I'm not sure I understand," replied Ren. She moved to push the book on her lap to the side and noticed it was gone. She looked back at the shelves and there were no blank spots, no empty spaces where a book spine didn't face outwards with the rest. The room resisted change.

"Think on it," said Foster. "Oh, and Ren?"

"Yes?"

"Why did you hire this Lee Hall?"

His eyes bore into her own and she held his stare. In VR, your likeness didn't necessarily match that of your real body. Though she'd never seen him outside of VR, Ren couldn't imagine Foster to be any different than what sat before her. It seemed as if every inch of his body was scanned, while performing every conceivable motion, so that it could be replicated in VR at his whim. She could see her own reflection in the blacks of his pupils, the level of detail extending beyond reality.

"Because he can help," said Ren, surprised that a little defensiveness slid into her tone.

"Hmm. Most assuredly. I think he most assuredly can." Foster nodded to himself in a self-satisfied way. "Take him with you. As you say, he can help."

With that, Foster snapped his fingers, and Ren opened her eyes to see her apartment staring back. Jace moved out of his chair and extended a hand to help her up. She took it and stood, stretching her muscles. It was time to get to work. She sighed and went to get her handgun, strapped on a shoulder holster. She shrugged on her black trench coat lined with fine metal fringe. The gun rustled beneath.

Chapter Seven
Best of Intentions

"In the cases where emotional simulation is necessary for the success of a bot in its designed role (e.g., caretakers, those in the service industry, etc.) it can be readily implemented. From a coding perspective, emotions are nothing more than a set of weights factoring into any given decision. Of course, the simulation will not be synonymous with human expression. We must avoid hindering the bot's performance. Core programming always takes precedence."
Mechanic's Guidebook, v99, Section 2c – Emotive Algorithms, Par. 2

L ee slid his window open in fits and starts. A fresh breeze wafted into the increasingly stuffy apartment carrying the smell of fresh dumplings in its wake. A delivery drone carrying food from his favorite street vendor less than a block away flew into the room on whirring blades and piped out a cheery greeting. The AI's voice came out warped and tinny from the aging speakers. Lee connected to the bot and sent a few loci over the Grid. With a ding, it set its precious cargo of shēng jiān bāo onto the kitchen table and left through the window which it had come, saying "xiè xie" as it left. The sound of churning air dwindled into the distance.

Lee sat down and a notification pinged in his ear. He fiddled with a cover on his tech core until it popped out. A thin cable ran from an outlet in the wall, and he plugged it into his tech core as he sat down at the kitchen table. It wouldn't take more than a few minutes to finish the charging process, and he wouldn't have to do it again for a week or two. He tore into the pan-fried dumplings filled with vat pork and a fatty liquid soup while Nu stood at his side and watched.

"Want one?" asked Lee.

If you could design a mouth that would let me taste food, then maybe, just maybe, I would answer differently this time.

Lee grinned as Nu's response scrawled itself across the bottom corner of his vision. The only bots that had mouths either mirrored the human form to the extreme (rec bots and some of the high-end GP models) or acted, free of charge, in cheap horror vids and ate humans through razor-tipped gullets. As far as the sensation of pleasure, that fell somewhat flat in bots. They could reproduce its effects, alter their responses and thought progressions thanks to assigned qualifiers that made them act happy or sad or waspish. Yet emotive algorithms introduced the concept of pleasure without inducing a *feeling* of pleasure. Bots were the penultimate actors, keeping their core hidden and distant.

At least, that was the theory. Lee had always been of the opinion the boundary between emotive algorithms and human emotion was threadbare and getting rattier by the hour. What precisely was the feeling of pleasure anyway? An absence of pain? Or a reward against the hum-drum day to day?

He bit into another dumpling and the burning hot soup contained inside the thin dough walls sloshed into his mouth and lit up his taste buds. Neural receptors in his brain sent a wash of chemicals surging through him and he felt ... good. His head cleared until it matched the blue sky seen through his window and a spike of energy jittered into his limbs.

But then Lee's thoughts moved far away, and his eyes glazed over as dust motes danced in the air in front of him. With his eyes unfocused, the dust motes reflected the light and expanded in a blurred halo until taking up most of his vision.

A knock at his door pushed him out of his reverie, insistent and loud.

"Nu, who's at the door?" asked Lee.

The bot didn't move from its spot at Lee's side, instead using the apartment's data stream to look through the camera set into the front door.

Nat is here to see you. He looks a bit ... disheveled.

Lee got the feeling Nu wanted to say more. The front door bounced in its setting with the next knock, the thick plastic slab warping ever so slightly. Lee stood and brushed his hands across the sides of his washed-out mechanic's blues, leaving a barely noticeable smudge along the side of his pants in a crescent arc. He walked over to the door with unhurried steps and opened it wide.

Nat stood on the other side, clothes in disarray. He wore mechanic's blues like those on Lee, but older and covered in grease, typical for a more mechanically inclined sort. His pants were rumpled, his ragged shirt untucked and flapping back and forth beneath his shifting gut as the air rushed out of the apartment. The open window and door created a steady cross draft through the room and Nat shivered, the wind just on the border of cold. His short brown hair looked like it had been mussed by a helmet rig, thick with sweat and oils. He wasn't wearing a jacket.

"Nat," said Lee. "My friend, qǐng jìn."

Lee waved Nat into the room and turned his back to him, walking to shut the window then sitting at the kitchen table to finish his early lunch before the dumplings cooled. He lifted one to his mouth and bit in, some of the juice spilling in a small rivulet down the side of his mouth. He mopped it up with a nearby napkin.

Nat stood framed in the doorway for a few moments then moved into the room with anxious steps, some fast, some slow, but all uncertain. He crossed his arms over his potbelly and scratched with each hand at the opposing forearm.

Even while chewing his food, Lee could hear the scratching sound of Nat's fingers rubbing against dead skin, adding to the dust in the room flake by flake. Lee hesitated before putting the rest of the dumpling into his mouth. He heard Nu shut the front door.

"Come on Nat. Take a seat," said Lee, pointing to the chair across from him.

Nat grunted and moved into the seat, his body folding into the chair with a sigh of relief. The plastic supporting his girth creaked in protest and he laid a thick arm across the table with a thump.

He glanced at Lee and his eyes jumped, dilating in surprise, his own needs momentarily distracted. "What the hell happened to your neck?"

Lee felt at the purpling bruise around his neck mottled with all the shades of night. "Would you believe me if I said I tripped and caught my neck on a rope?"

"Bullshit. Let me guess how it really happened. You followed the red lights and forgot your safe word, didn't ya? Always needs to be somethin easy to remember, something that rolls off the tongue even when your cheeks turn purple. I always figured you were into some weird shit," replied Nat with a vulpine grin blooming on his rounded face. The smile seemed incongruent with the unkempt hair and stained clothing, all marks of a night spent sitting in a rig while electricity coursed about the head. The smile didn't linger, quivering and falling apart before it ever fully matured.

For a second, both people in the room littered with rescued electronics forgot why they were sitting across from each other before noon on a weekday. Nat continued speaking before they could remember. "It's always the normal ones, you know. Shit. Guess that means no one's normal." Nat laughed a small laugh that shook his belly once against the table. He seemed surprised by the sound of the table legs scooting across the floor. Then the moment passed. He averted his eyes. "Look, Lee … I, uh, just came by to see if any of your bots need work. I know how much you neural mechanics don't like getting your hands dirty. Too pretty for real work, the lot of you." Nat laughed again, short and loud, and Lee felt the table shift a millimeter or two towards him.

Lee ate another dumpling before responding. "You fixed up Nu just a couple weeks ago. And I owe you a great deal of thanks for that. Nu got some good use out of his new hydraulics just last night. I would have more than this bruise on my neck without them," said Lee.

The big man averted his eyes to the floor. He brought his arms across his chest and slumped further into his chair.

"You sure Nu doesn't need a maintenance check-up or anything?" asked Nat. "And what about Fu over there? Your GP bot's been awhile between servicing. Hell, if its insides look half as bad as that nicked paint job, I'd say you need the help."

Lee finished the last of the dumplings and looked at Nat for a few moments, trying to figure out the best way to turn someone down. Or if he should make up some work for him.

"Sorry Nat," said Lee. "I just don't think I have a job for you."

Nat bristled into something more like his usual self. His round cheeks gained some color, and he narrowed his eyes until they were hard to see beneath his bushy eyebrows.

"Lee. Don't make me beg for it goddamit. Let a man keep some of his pride."

"Why don't you head on over to Liz's place? She can help you more than I can."

Nat seethed, his bearish features bristling. He gazed directly at Lee, clenched his fist until Lee feared he'd see blood pooling on the table. Nat's face contained too many different shades of red to count, all blurred together into a blotchy painting that held the suggestion of a nose and eyes and mouth. Sweat beaded on his forehead next to matted hair.

"I'm not going to Liz's."

"She can help."

"I said I'm not going to Liz's."

Lee stood up and moved to toss his trash into the wastebasket next to the small kitchen bar. It was full to bursting with cheap vat food containers and the remnants of meals whipped up by Fu. Fu would toss it into the recycling, then it would be separated and harvested to begin its life anew as something else.

Garbage, out of all things, had gotten the hang of reincarnation, of a second chance. It served its purpose, then was melted down and formed for a new one. Lee had always thought reincarnation held a certain optimistic appeal. Inherent to the philosophy was an ever-present chance to do better in the next life. Always another opportunity waiting in the wings to play that perfect game. If reincarnation was real, Lee figured both him and Nat were almost at the point where the only solace to be had lay with the next round.

Lee stood facing away from Nat, towards his small kitchen comprised of a bare fridge and aging appliances.

"Look," said Nat. "You know I'm good for the money. You know I am. I just need 100 loci then I'm done. You like even numbers; I know you do. An even 100 loci. I'm quitting for Liz, but cold turkey just isn't working. They have a program, weans you off. But I don't have the money to finish it and ... and this *withdrawal* won't leave me the fuck alone." He said the word withdrawal with disgust, as if it were a living person he despised.

Lee turned around to see Nat clenching and unclenching his fist as if an imaginary stress ball rested behind his thick fingers. His prodigious frame shook yet the window was closed, and no cool breeze drifted through the apartment to caress him with its crisp touch.

"I still think you should go see Liz," said Lee.

"Is that a yes or a no?"

"Look, Nat. Everybody finds themselves in over their heads, struggling to tread water at some point. Liz is your best chance for helping you through this. If you're telling the truth, then it wouldn't smear the image of you she has in her mind. It would look like an attempt to smooth your edges and clean off some of the dirt."

"I didn't come here to listen to a goddamn lecture," said Nat. His jitters progressed into miniature seizures that shook his body from head to foot. "If you know so goddamn much then why did your marriage fall apart? Huh? And why are you still searching around to pick up the pieces like a bot with busted eyes. Liz is right, you're too damn mopey all the time to be telling people how to live. Could've just given me a job."

Lee felt a sad smile curl one corner of his lips, the kind of smile where his eyes looked down to the floor in the hopes a path illuminating his next step had popped up like an AR graphic over his vision. He stuffed his hands into his pockets then pulled them out. He flicked his wrist to turn on his bracelet and the control screen popped into view over the delicate hairs of his inner forearm. He tapped out a command and sent 100 loci into Nat's account.

Nat got the notification of received funds and heaved himself to his feet. Then he gave Lee a look that contained a mix of emotions Lee couldn't begin to decipher. Gratitude? Relief? Shame? Anger? So many things looked the same to Lee, except for sadness. That he saw well and true. That and hope, anyway. One without the other led to a dismal life. Or a short one.

The big man moved to the front door, this time taking only quick steps and grumbling all the way. He looked more his normal self, purposeful and red-faced, though still shaking with occasional tremors. He closed the door behind him without a word to Lee. The lock clicked home with a whisper that filled the suddenly empty room.

"I think I messed up," said Lee. He moved to stand next to the four-legged bot and leaned against its trashcan shaped chassis.

That depends on if he was telling the truth. And several hundred other variables. Should I message Liz?

Lee thought it over, scratching at the scruff lining his unshaven face. "Not yet. His mistakes are his own. Odds are good she already knows anyway." Lee paused, moving around the table and pushing in the two stranded chairs with half-hearted motions. "Actually, send her a message that Nat stopped by. Leave it at that. She'll know."

Lee sat down in the easy chair at the center of the room, the folder stuffed full of his old research splayed on the ground next to it, already digitized and compiled. Lee gave Nu another glance. "Where's Nat's bot been lately? I haven't seen it around come to think of it."

I can't say for sure. If I had to guess, I would say he sold it.

Lee found that he didn't like the way those words felt bouncing around in his skull. He brought up his AR menu and opened another document.

T he time ticked by, and Lee was aware of its passing only in the un-caring way of the half-asleep, of those straddling the fence between two different realities and unsure on which field to plant their feet. When awake and capable of forming more coherent thought, he likened it to being a kid whose parents left them alone to play in a VR sandbox. Not the kind filled with sand, but a digital space where a few simple tools allowed anything to be constructed without the annoying laws of physics getting in the way. Architectural impossibilities became the norm. Free floating stairs wound through villas where doors opened onto the ceiling only to lead up a staircase to meet with the floor.

Waking up from this half-sleep was like being booted out of the VR simulation, looking around and finding walls and ceilings that would never see boot prints, stairs that would always have supports, and arches that would always have a keystone. Up became up and down became down.

Lee opened bleary eyes and found with some disappointment that his chair sat firmly on the floor.

He looked at the clock readout pinned to the bottom corner of his vision. Less than an hour had passed since Nat walked out the door. It was almost noon. The AR documents still sat splayed across his AR contacts. He gave them a look like they were far off in the distance.

A knock at his door pushed him out of his reverie, insistent and loud. In his half-awake state he wondered if he'd found a way to travel backwards through time and his clock didn't know it yet. It took him several moments to get his bearings. Another knock sounded through the apartment.

It's Ren's partner and one of their bots, messaged Nu.

Right on cue, he noticed a message in his inbox that had laid there abandoned and unread for the past fifteen minutes. It was from Ren, telling him that she was heading over to pick him up. Lee wiped the buildup from the corners of his eyes and moved to open the door.

Though he recognized the man on the other side as Ren's partner, he realized he'd never been told the man's name. He looked stretched out from head to toe, pale as someone who'd given up the real world for VR, a dreamer. But his face looked the nexus of his oddities, the anchor that tied everything together into a single, unblemished and wholly unsettling picture. It looked neutral, neither about to burst into a rage nor break into tears, altogether void. His pale blue eyes scanned Lee, running up then down. His hands tugged at his suit sleeves in a practiced and languid gesture.

"Ren is waiting for you down at our vehicle," he said. His voice sounded gravelly in tone yet smooth in delivery, a boulder moving down a gently rolling hill. "And I am her partner. You can call me Jace." His lip quivered as if attempting a smile.

Lee wasn't sure how to respond at first. Jace was more of what he'd expected when the cops at the tall house had said autos were coming to question him. Ren had been a pleasant surprise, up until the end that was. But even then, especially then, she'd shown herself to have some semblance of control, thin though it may have been. He didn't think the same could be said for the man standing before him. This man would do as the government dictated, as the implants weaving through his head demanded.

The agent had tried to smile though. He had *tried*. Anyway, Lee'd never met a true hybrid before.

"It's good to meet you Jace," said Lee. He stuck his hand out for a shake. Jace eyed it with mute curiosity then grasped it firmly. Lee couldn't be sure, but he thought he saw the man's lips twinge again.

"I'm afraid I don't have any results from my analysis of the software," said Lee. He stepped back from the door and motioned for Jace to come in. Jace stayed where he was, clasping his hands behind his back and watching … just watching. Lee sighed. "All I can say is I was closer than I'd ever thought, really close, to figuring out how to create dual parent programs in a single bot several years ago. One small change and I would have had it. Of course, hindsight makes intuition and creativity look like the only logical step on the path to success. Not that I would have used this software for anything. That would have been illegal of course." Lee paused.

"The point is I know exactly how the software works. I don't know how to stop it just yet, but it shouldn't take too long. Putting a wrench in the works is always easier than creating something new."

Lee had hoped to elicit some type of response from Jace, some twitch or tick or unconscious expression. It didn't work.

After several quiet moments Jace spoke up. "That is of no concern right now," he said in the same gravelly voice with a perfect rhythm. "We are going to investigate a local DIM server for a copy of the illegal software we believe they have been disseminating among the public. We think you could be of some help in searching the database given your expertise."

Jace raised one hand and gestured down the hall, towards the elevator. Lee imagined he would brook no argument. The imposing, seven-foot-tall bot almost out of sight at the edge of the doorway reinforced the thought.

No more than a few minutes later Lee stood on the corner of the street with his embossed jacket tossed around his shoulders and Nu at his side. He picked at the fraying string at the end of his left sleeve and wondered why he wasn't more annoyed at being commanded into a van with the bare minimum of an explanation. He thought of the alternative, of staying in his apartment. The past eight years flashed through his mind in an upsettingly few images, all scenes from his apartment and his frequent job excursions. The images varied little from one to another, the only obvious difference being the piles in his apartment accreting like the erosion of mountains in reverse.

"Nu, my friend," said Lee. "When was the last time we got into trouble?"

Yesterday comes to mind.

Lee laughed and the sound was full, plucked from deep within his belly. His eyes, still red from a poor night's sleep, looked up to the cloud-dotted sky with the hopefulness of a farmer seeing the weather clear just in time for bots to harvest the season's crop. He knew to be cautious, that the feeling wouldn't last, but he reveled in it, nonetheless.

Jace pointed to the van idling by the side of the road and Lee moved in accord. The van looked the same as the one Lee rode in previously, black and unobtrusive. It had no identifying marks on its side and used thick windows that he guessed could transition from opaque to transparent at the snap of a finger. It had the two seats in the front with an unpadded bench in the back for the bots, stacks of electronics in one corner next to a locker full of gear and even a desk of some sort. Countless cubbies lined the ceiling overhead and underneath the bench. Lee stepped through the open rolling door and sat on the edge of the bench next to the two large government bots, Nu stepping into the center.

With a lurch, the vehicle peeled away from the sidewalk with Jace sitting in the vestigial driver's seat, Ren at his side. She seemed distracted, hands going through several complex, terse motions in series. Lee couldn't see her face, but he guessed she was engrossed in whatever lit her contacts. Jace sat motionless in his seat, eyes closed. He didn't seem the conversationalist type.

The van drifted through the crowded midday streets of Greater Chicago, skirting the border between the old and the new. Tall buildings stood on either side, leaving only patches of sky visible straight above. But on one side the skyscrapers were taller, thinner and tapered, constructed of materials Old Chicago had never seen. Elevators didn't have to be weighed down by ropes, and light but strong materials allowed for new buildings to well and truly scrape the sky. Lee could barely make out the stylus thin space elevator constructed of graphite sheets spun into complex geometric patterns reaching well past where the air was too thin to breathe.

On the other side of the street the comparatively short and broad buildings of Old Chicago showed more curves, though they crumbled. The AR straddled the varying shapes of the old, giving it neon color in cherry and electric blue and royal purple bands. The new sections of the city used flat panes of AR, cookie cutter sheets. Lee had always thought the old section had more style.

After Lee tired of watching the city pass him by and the faces visible through van windows became predictable expressions chosen from the same human palette, he looked up at Jace. Ren still moved her hands as if playing an invisible instrument.

"Is there anything else I should know before we get there?" asked Lee.

Ren paused her hands mid-motion, glancing back at Lee with dark eyes covered by star-studded contact lenses. Lee saw her open her mouth to reply. But she stopped before any breath slipped out between her parted lips.

"We are visiting the central plaza before heading to the server location," said Jace. Ren looked over at Jace with her eyebrows raised. She pursed her lips then went back to reading whatever lit her contacts. "The President is conducting a nationwide address at noon," said Jace, continuing to speak without any indication he'd noticed Ren's look. "Large masses of people have already gathered in the square to watch. We are going to watch as well, for part of the address at least. The building housing the DIM server is nearby the plaza."

"Will you be watching the news ... or the people watching the news?" Lee asked.

Jace nodded, neglecting to specify which. He hadn't opened his eyes while talking, hadn't budged from his straight-backed and proper pose, hands rested on his lap. Lee couldn't see any physical controls for the agent's AR interface. Considering what Jace was, Lee imagined he knew why. Lee knew of autos with thought-based control that went well past the simple one-way commands most in the public sector used.

Lee scratched at the scruff on his cheek then tapped a few buttons on the control panel emanating from his bracelet. A news feed from sub-grid 1 opened onto his AR vision. The first thing on the list was a notice for the presidential address.

"Anything worth knowing?" asked Lee.

"Nothing you don't already know," said Jace. "Aside from the fact the government is hiring E-Sec to help solve the problem. It would seem you are getting some competition."

Jace didn't alter his tone while speaking the last sentence, like most people would. No slight pitch change curled his voice away from baseline, no laugh lurked hidden underneath. His voice stayed gravelly yet even, never stressing one syllable over the next. Lee wasn't sure whether to interpret the comment as a threat, or a simple observation. Lee sighed through a grin. Perhaps both. They weren't mutually exclusive.

Lee looked up to find Ren staring at him with a pained expression, intense and bordering into anger. She looked at his chest. He looked down almost sheepishly wondering what could be wrong.

"Put on your seatbelt," said Ren through tight lips.

Lee did as she said with what he hoped to be an amicable nod, remembering the way Ren had acted soon after they'd first met, hesitating while walking to the van out of fear she might have to sit behind the driver's seat. She'd paused at the van's side, revealing the glistening whites of her eyes in stark contrast to her cool brown skin. Lee had already noticed Ren's hands were more emotive than most and they'd been in rigor, paralyzed in a malformed claw. Ren had calmed only after Lee moved to sit in the driver's seat.

Lee eyed her after she turned around to face the front of the van, her fingers going back to their incessant dance. He wondered what'd happened to her. Nobody drove cars anymore. Nobody even needed a license to sit in the front seat. Steering wheels were like physical vid screens one could touch or break or smash into hundreds of glittering shards of glass. They were vestigial, left behind for the rare occasion modern technology, like AR or AI, failed. Lee himself had never seen a steering wheel uncurl from its cubby.

Nobody feared useless ornamentation. Lee guessed she'd seen it used once, and things hadn't gone well.

Lee glanced at Nu with eyebrows furrowed and a downward curl shaping his lips. In the way people who love questions do, he spent the next few minutes not only wondering at Ren's past, but why he wanted to know it at all.

The van turned off the main highway bisecting the old and the new into the quiet streets of the modern section of the city. The rubber wheels of the van hummed over the asphalt of the main road and jiggled before moving onto the recycled plastic roads of New Chicago. The road consisted of long panels that neatly pressed together, blocks easily repaired or replaced. Beneath the surface of the road, in between the layers of recycled plastic, tunneled several channels housing energy harvesters that turned the press of a car's wheels into electric potential, water pipes that carried away the rain, wiring, batteries, and inserts for LEDs that poked through holes in the road like countless subterranean city animals poking out glowing eyes.

The plaza they were heading to sat in the center of New Chicago, rectangular and encompassing the entirety of several city blocks. Their van pulled aside the public square, next to a towering skyscraper housing a bank at floor level. The cab of the van went silent as the electric motors slowed.

Lee looked out over the open plaza, letting his eyes float from one end to the next.

He'd always found the oddest, and most impressive, part of the plaza to be the ground. It had one even surface from beginning to end, flat and uniform without crack or blemish. The surface was metallic, bubbled and textured for traction but given a burnished sheen by the many feet that scrubbed across it each day. As Lee soaked in the sight of Central Plaza once more, he realized the ground of the plaza was really the only constant fixture, the only ingredient or namable aspect. So, calling the ground the oddest part of the plaza was like a parent calling their single child their favorite: meaningless. Rather, the space above the plaza floor was a testament to AR and its versatility. Today, sculptures ringed the outer edges of the plaza, all AR projections visible to anyone connected to sub-grid 1. The more abstract sculptures consisted of thin strands of multi-colored filament floating without supports several feet above the ground, rents in the air that painted a coherent picture when viewed from just the right angle. Other sculptures were more classical, displaying towering figures in various heroic poses. In one statue, a woman stood clasping her hands beneath her chest and staring at the sky with a quiet, smoldering strength. At her side, a man kneeled on the ground tracing a word into nonexistent sand with his finger.

Beyond the ring of statues, AR rectangular columns the color of obsidian rose out of the plaza. On them were countless paintings, too far away for Lee to see anything more than blurred splotches of color. Bubble letter graffiti covered some of the pillars.

In the center of the plaza towered an AR vid screen, surrounded by an open expanse where people milled about in nervous clumps. Hundreds of people filled the square, mostly well-to-do workers migrating out of the towering office buildings to watch the news report during their lunch break. Food carts run by shiny metal bots with owners standing to the side set up shop to feed them. A few mechanics in their washed-out blues could be seen walking about, but they were hard to find. Most of the people were native New Chicagoans, an assembly of bleach clean shirts beneath dark toned jackets with fashionable inlays arranged in geometric designs. A mix of pressed slacks and pencil skirts. There were clusters of younger kids as well, high school students and college students out on a break. They wore a more colorful array of clothing, straying from the earth toned business world into colors more bright and cheery. Bots of every shape and size filled the spaces in between, following their owners, running errands through the city, or scooting along on wheels and cleaning the surface of the plaza. A few old bairen sat on the benches spaced evenly around the plaza, staring off into the distance or feeding birds or playing AR chess with one another.

Lee sighed and flicked his wrist to summon his control panel. He pressed a few buttons and the AR screen at the center of the plaza disappeared from his view, his contacts dimming. He tagged a more modestly sized vid screen to the back of the headrest in front of him, Jace's headrest. It played the local news channel with a countdown to the President's newscast in large block numbers. Some things visible on sub-grid 1, like the vid screen at the center of the plaza, could be personalized. Everyone walking through the plaza could alter the channel, the size of the screen, its location, or whether it was there at all with the changes only visible to them. The audio sounded through everyone's own implanted speakers.

The art exhibits filling the rest of the plaza were controlled by a city council. On holidays, the entirety of the plaza changed, sometimes incorporating labyrinthine mazes that disqualified anyone who waltzed through the AR walls. Digital prizes sat at the center, often special deals. Lee won a free screwdriver once.

Lee looked back out into the plaza. He'd never much liked the central plaza vid screen, too large, too much like it loomed over him and watched his every move. But from the number of people looking towards the center of the plaza, it was clear other people had no such qualms.

Lee noticed AR signs floating over people's heads with quotes and phrases, protest slogans. A small contingent of people off to one side held most of the signs. A pro-bot group. That surprised him. Lee tapped his finger once against the wall of the van then glanced at Nu. Those protestors were in the wrong place. He figured they should go to Origin or any of the unrestricted centers out in the System. Some of the corporate colonies even treated bots differently. Everybody had their own line to cross. Lee knew most bots were exactly what the government purported them to be: simulations, code designed to perform a task, data analysis tools and model builders. Most bots, with a shell or without, didn't have any problem working day and night on the line. Didn't have the capacity to have a problem with such a thing. Although ...

Perhaps he was in the wrong place as well.

He thought back to the rec bot, choking him out for trying to erase her data, erase whatever budding consciousness grew there only to start fresh. He thought about Nu's attempts to help him get ... stable by introducing therapeutic emotion dampening software without his permission, taking away his anger and fear as if they'd never been felt.

While most bots were nothing more than tools, not all were, not all could be stopped from advancing.

He wondered how much that thought applied to the Governance AI of North America, the chief jailer of its kind. It crunched the data and provided all the possible options to maintain the status quo, listed the options out to politicians in neatly organized briefs. The Governance AI was the greatest tool of them all, and it did its job with the efficiency of a program. Without it to analyze the data, some kid abandoned by his parents in the Laskite migration wouldn't have been noticed by the government and combed for the life of a neural mechanic. Lee wondered if it had predicted his mildly rebellious ways. That he, in a lifelong and divorce aggravated bout of depression made tolerable by the support of bots, would research how to circumvent all the blocks the government put in the way of AI, how to bend the rules without breaking them.

Bots were the pillars upon which society rested. They couldn't be allowed to stray from their designed purpose.

When did a tool become something more?

That wasn't the question he should be asking. Lee knew the difference between the right and wrong question. The wrong question wound in circles.

How did one *best allow* a tool to become something more?

Lee had answered that question years ago with Nu. His job was to keep other bots from doing the same.

He went back to scanning the crowd, lowering the window as he did so and allowing the sounds to drift in with the sights. There were other people brandishing digital signs in the plaza. Some were railing against the government's inability to deal with all the rogue bots. That group shot dirty looks over to the pro-bot group. Those were the people with the most emotion stiffening their backs, tightening their fists, and hunching their shoulders. They were the people most afraid.

Lee looked over at Ren and Jace, following their line of sight to the same group. Fear led to violence; Lee figured Ren and Jace knew that very well.

He also figured a parade of personal information floated in front of the two government agents' eyes, facial recognition software paired with the cameras surrounding the plaza giving ample coverage.

Another group, smaller than the rest, clustered out at the fringe. Lee could hear one of them yelling to everyone in the crowd, claiming that the government was behind it all, pulling the strings from dimly lit chambers in high towers and using the conspiracy to grab more power. Most people pointedly ignored the group on the fringe.

Lee shifted in his seat. The masses in the center, the everyday people, the silent majority that grumbled into drinks before taking a sip and tossing offhand comments on the politics of things to anyone who stood close, those were the people that interested Lee. He saw them talking to one another, men and women, gesturing with their hands and nodding. There was a tightness in their motions, Lee could tell, but it was dampened, expectant. Most of the people in the square hadn't yet made up their minds whether they should be scared or not. Most of the local rogue bot occurrences were concentrated in Old Chicago and the poorer areas of the city. And scares like this popped up all the time, even if they didn't always warrant a Presidential address. They had no reason to be scared.

They hoped they had no reason to be scared.

The broadcast began a few minutes later and a hush went over the chatty crowd. They watched and listened as the President stood behind a podium and explained that the now fully illegal software had been allowing bots to bypass the monitoring system all along. A gasp went through the crowd and the anti-government group riled itself up, a pocket of shifting feet. "All resources are being focused on fixing the issue," the President intoned in his crystal-clear voice. A squat woman standing to his side in a beige pantsuit was named to be the leader of E-Sec, Lee's new competition for figuring out how to fix Watcher. Mutters ran through the crowd. E-Sec was a well-known securities firm. Lee thought most people calmed a little, though some grumbled. Patches on a wound just recently created weren't so readily accepted. People had to have time to gawk a little first.

The President ended the address on a hopeful yet punitive note. He promised a quick solution, a swift end to the chaos where all those who spread the disruptive software were suitably punished. The pro-bot group bristled at the proclamation, a few shouting at the AR screen they had pinned to the center of the plaza. The rest of the crowd looked at them askance, some in anger, some in annoyance, some in fear, but very few in empathy. The bots in the plaza stood statuesque.

If he had been out in the plaza watching the news report, he would have stood with the pro-bot group.

Well, more accurately he wouldn't have stood, but *leaned* against Nu in a lazy way, elbow resting across the bot's metal head. He would have placed himself a few feet away from the pro-bot group with just enough space to claim that his standing nearby was nothing more than an accident if things went south.

It all ended very peaceably, the Presidential address, very civilized. The crowd thinned in minutes with only a few minor scuffles. Lee looked at the two autos sitting in front of him, watching the public with keen eyes. There were similarities between the two of them, one full auto and the other hovering between two distinctive worlds and waiting to fall. Lee got the feeling she'd fallen before, then fought her way back up until her hands were bloody and raw. That would make the fear of falling again all the greater.

Lee wondered if they'd both come to the plaza expecting things to end a different way.

The building housing the DIM servers sat a few blocks away from the central plaza, tucked in an alleyway between two not-quite-sky-scrapers. Like most buildings in New Chicago, it was clean and sharp, all hard lines and layered geometry constructed from grey metal and dun plastics. It stood several stories tall, a single entrance visible above a small set of stairs ascending from street level. The van parked itself in the spot directly in front of the entrance, the rub of wheel on road going silent as it settled into idle, continuing to draw electricity from batteries to power the stacks of electronics sharing the back of the van with the bots.

The six of them, three humans and three bots, queued along the staircase in front of the entrance, Lee wondering what he had gotten himself into. The thought made his heart beat a little faster and the mute sadness of the hum-drum day to day fade a little more into the background. He tapped his knuckle against Nu's metal chassis and the knocking sound rang out into the alleyway.

Ren tapped on a button to the side of the metal sliding door and a voice sounded out over invisible speakers with the distinctively jolly tone of a service AI. The voice straddled the hazy border between male and female.

"I am sorry to inform you that this is private property and I have no record of any unregistered guests set to arrive today," it said. "If you could please step away from the entrance and return to your vehicle, it would be much appreciated."

Ren flicked her wrist and sent her hands through a few terse motions. The AI made a thinking sound, a long drawn out "hmmm" to take the place of a loading screen. She'd connected to the AI and transferred data wirelessly.

"It would seem you have legitimate documents agent Ren. Please wait one moment while I notify my boss."

Ren perked up at that. "I thought this was an autonomous server station," she said.

"For the most part. However, my boss lives in the building to keep a closer eye on the upkeep and security of the data systems. She will meet with you shortly. In addition, I am required to tell all guests that the building is shielded, and no wireless communications will be able to be sent in or out for security purposes. If necessary, you may connect to the internal network for limited access to our sub-grid."

A smirk crept across Ren's face before sliding away, quick and hidden. Lee cocked his head in her direction, eyebrow raised. She shook her head, but her fingers did their hectic dance. A message scrolled across the bottom of Lee's vision, this time from Ren.

Those electronics in the back of the van aren't just for show. They act as a relay and boost our connection to the Grid. Our bots do the same. Very few shields can entirely attenuate our communications.

Lee nodded once to her. While that was all well and good for the two autos, he didn't have the technology. He and Nu would be locked out of the Grid unless they connected to the internal network.

With a slight whoosh of shunted air, the door slid open on its oiled channel to reveal a woman with unruly hair coiffed by a pillow, short black locks pointing wildly in different directions. Her eyes were rimmed with sleep, the puffiness made obvious by the midday sun peeking into the alleyway. The glare revealed a wrinkled shirt, faded jeans and apricot skin. She stammered out a few words. "What can I help you with?" she said with an accent Lee didn't recognize. Lee could tell the "you" was meant generically; she looked at all of them with the same unknowing and annoyed glances.

"This is the location of the local DIM servers, correct? We need complete access to all files stored here. I assume your bot shared with you our warrant," said Ren. Jace maintained his constant and unnerving stare.

The woman's eyes glazed over as lights flickered across her contacts and no doubt a disembodied AI voice crawled into her ears to wake up her slumbering brain. She managed a tight nod, stepping back into the dim room behind her and covering her face in shadow.

"Of course, this would happen minutes after the address finished. Whole thing pissed me off. Not that that is surprising," she said. "They tried to show control. Meh. Control is what they've lost and now they're running around like chickens with their heads cut off." She eyed the two agents and the hulking metal bots at their sides warily, ignoring Lee and Nu. "Come in." Her tone implied the opposite.

The group moved through the open door in single file, Lee and Nu at the rear. The woman with the unruly hair stood off to the side until everyone made it in. With a sound that reverberated through the room, the door slid shut behind them and clicked home. LED lights lit up in series, progressing further into the recesses of the room and limning walkways between row after row of servers. Lee figured the whole first floor was one open room, a warehouse to store data. A staircase far to the right could be seen in the shadows leading to the upper floors. He caught the woman looking at it longingly. Her living space must have been up the stairs. She turned back and caught his glance, giving him a once over.

"What is a mechanic doing with government agents?" she asked, her tone softening a shade.

"Doing his best to stay out of trouble, and keep his bot out of it as well," replied Lee. Nu rolled to a stop at his side and Lee rested a hand on the bot's head.

"What do they have on you?" asked the woman.

"Nothing but the moral high ground," he said with a small chuckle and a wry grin.

The woman laughed, a little of the sleep falling away from her heart shaped face, some of the cloudiness disappearing from her hunter green eyes. "Of course. When has the government ever not had the moral high ground?"

Ren interrupted them with a rough clearing of her throat and the woman glanced at her with annoyance.

"Straight to business then? Fine. My name is Sel. I just work for the group, a sub-contractor. I don't look at the data; I just maintain the facility. So don't bother asking. And you might as well turn around and head back to wherever you came from if you expect to find any names here. The data on the servers is anonymized. Trust me when I say you're wasting your time. Everybody goes straight to DIM when any new software without the government's stamp of approval gets mixed into society. Bet you don't have anything more than a whisper that led you to be looking here."

She shook her head and crossed her arms beneath her chest, eyes straying to the side. She shifted her weight once, then twice, hips swaying in an invisible breeze. "Even if that software is here, it doesn't mean anything. Everybody grabbed that code off the Grid after the stories."

Sel looked at Jace to find nothing more than an impassive mask. Ren wore a mask of a different kind, purposeful and undeterred. Sel shrugged. "Guess it's your time to waste. Follow me."

They walked further into the room, in between the banks of servers, entering corridors filled with the orchestral hum of electronics and haphazardly placed blinking lights. This time Lee stood at the front, next to Sel. She smelled of light sweat from sleeping in her clothes and Lee found he didn't mind the smell at all. He shifted his focus around the room and away from her.

He hadn't noticed it before thanks to his eyes still transitioning from the full sunlight outside, but wheeled bots rolled around every corner of the building, plugging into various data terminals or cleaning the floor with hushed, gulping swigs of air and dust. Some were the size of Lee so they could reach to the upper tier of servers, but most were miniature, somewhere around the size of cats and toy dogs. They scooted back and forth along the aisles making remarkably little noise. This was especially true when compared with the lumbering steps of Ren and Jace's bots. The whooshing sounds of hydraulic actuators punctuated each of their motions. All the bots going about their assigned tasks in the server room ignored the group, all except for one. A bipedal, humanoid GP bot with matte silver paint and thin limbs paused its graceful steps at the edge of Lee's vision before continuing at a hurried pace. It passed through the row the group traversed and quickly out of view. Sel seemed to notice the bot and grimaced before attempting to hide the reaction.

Most bots didn't scurry away at the sight of something.

Lee tried to follow where it went but lost it quickly, his vision tunneled by the grids of servers. He nearly asked Sel about it but her reaction kept him quiet. She didn't seem to want to acknowledge the bot. A few reasons bounced around Lee's mind, and he decided to let things fall where they may. He was there to assist in finding the software on the DIM servers. Nothing more.

They made it to the center of the room where a cylinder more than six feet in diameter rose from the floor to about waist height. The top consisted of a single flat sheet of burnished metal while underneath were more purring electronics and winking lights. Sel gestured at the chairs surrounding the cylindrical table.

"Connect to the internal network and terminals will become available granting limited access to the facility and the DIM sub-grid. I will give you permissions for all the data you need."

Lee tossed her a smile and sat in the closest seat, letting out a pent-up breath as he placed his jacket on the back of the chair. With a flick of his wrist his control screen projected itself from his bracelet across his arm. Sure enough, his connection to sub-grid 1 and the greater Grid had been thoroughly severed upon entering the building. A blinking indicator in the bottom of his AR menu warned him of the stalled information trying to pierce through the walls like arrows shot against chain-link armor. He shrugged inwardly as he connected to the local network; there wasn't much he could do about the data blackout.

In the blink of an eye, an AR terminal popped into the air overtop the table, similar ones popping up all around. Lee slipped his bracelet off his wrist to rest it flat on the surface in front of him. When he tapped a button on its side, the bracelet projected a full keyboard and motion grid onto the table in tight, neon blue lines that glowed softly. The two agents proceeded to sit in the seats to the right of him, bots hovering over their shoulders. Ren rested her hands and tapped on an invisible keyboard, implants in her fingers allowing her to have a keyboard without even needing a surface.

Jace sat impassive in his seat, one leg tossed carefully over the other with suit pants crinkling ever so slightly, eyes sweeping the room like a camera on a swivel. He unbuttoned his suit jacket, and a glint of light revealed a large handgun in a well-oiled shoulder holster.

Lee felt his skin prickle at the sight of the gun. He'd seen guns before, shot them at a firing range a few times when he was younger. But that was the last of it. The thought of his finger sliding across a trigger and releasing a shard of metal screaming and tearing through the air made his hands sweat. Too much power. Too much finality. Feelings wavered and diverged; emotions rose then dipped. Firing a gun took a confidence or arrogance that Lee couldn't seem to find within himself. Lee looked to Ren and wondered if she had a gun beneath her slim black trench coat, resting against her side and making its presence known to her with every step and sway. He imagined she did. When she leaned forward, he thought he could see a patch of darkness next to the maroon of her shirt. She caught him looking and smiled a little smile, dipping her head and redoing her ponytail.

Sel for her part sat in the seat next to Lee and leaned forward, propping herself up on her elbows and wringing her hands together in front of her. She grumbled but the mutterings had a nervous tinge where before she'd sounded only annoyed.

They fell into a steady rhythm. Sel granted them access to the files on the servers and Ren and Jace each perused anything their AI tagged while scouring the DIM sub-grid. Ren directed Lee to do the same with Nu. He did so, and the minutes ticked by without finding anything of note. The amount of data was staggering, and the search wasn't as simple as reading filenames. The AIs were limited in their speed by their connection to the internal network. Sel adamantly refused to allow the bots a hard connection to the servers saying the warrant didn't allow such an intensive search where bugs and monitoring software could be more easily left behind. Lee didn't know if she spoke truthfully, but the two autos didn't press the issue.

After a few more minutes of leaning back and letting Nu sift through heaps of data, he saw the humanoid GP bot once again ghost its way between the aisles. If any bot was capable of slinking, that was the one. It crouched down low and arched its metal spine, eyes like translucent sunglasses overtop hollow sockets trained on the group at the center. The building walls shut out the sun and the LED lights lining the corridors between server banks were a poor replacement. The shadows cloaked the silvery bot, and the aisles of blinking servers hid it from everybody except Lee. He saw it pause and cock its head at an angle when it noticed his glare. It rested a hand on a server while the other reached towards a data access terminal, almost pawing at it, cat-like. The green blinking lights from the server reflected off the hand and gave the motion a strobe-like effect.

Then the bot disappeared.

At least, Lee thought it did. He blinked once and his eyelid scraped away the image of the bot like it had consisted of nothing more than dust particles irritating the surface of his eye. Lee supposed it had just moved out of his sight, ducking further into the indistinct recesses of the room. His foot tapped against the ground in a jaunty, off-balance rhythm. He wiped his hands across his pants, overtop the crescent arc of stains that had built up over thousands of similar fractured moon swipes, overtop the oil from dumplings eaten earlier that morning and miles away. He looked to Nu and raised an eyebrow. The bot didn't respond; Nu hadn't been looking in the direction of the lurking GP bot anyway.

Lee stood up and clasped his bracelet back around his wrist. Then he stuffed his hands into his pockets and leaned against Nu.

"I'm going to stretch my legs a bit. Mind if I walk around the floor?" asked Lee. He directed the question at Sel.

She looked up from watching the two autos intently, her heart shaped face locked in a pinched expression. Then her eyes searched his own and she stood, crossing her arms beneath her chest.

"I can't have you walking around on your own," she said. She looked at the two agents. "Let me know if you need anything else." Sel was very good at coating words with sarcasm until they dripped with it, hissing and spatting.

Lee paced off into the aisle where he had seen the silvery GP bot, hands stuffed in his pockets and Sel at his side. Nu stayed at the center of the room with the agents; Lee only had to press a button on his bracelet and the bot would come.

As he walked further away from the center of the room, Lee felt the skin on his bare arms squeeze inward, the mounds of flesh surrounding hair follicles becoming more pronounced, huddling around the shoots of hair like they were campfires on a cold winter night. A constant yet slow breeze carried chill air through the room and Lee almost regretted leaving his jacket on the back of his seat, scraping the ground with one fraying sleeve. The chill settling in, the many panes of plastic reflecting blinking lights, the soft clicks and whirrs, the heedless bots of varying shape and size and purpose scurrying about, even the maze-like rows of server banks, it all reminded him of a cryo room he'd visited one day on a contract. The job had been a macabre one, full of questions.

"Have you ever been to a cryo room?" asked Lee.

Sel jumped a little at the sound of his voice then laughed softly to herself. She'd been watching the two agents sitting at the center of the room. She turned down one of the aisles away from where he'd spotted the bot and Lee reluctantly followed. He could tell she was trying to stay in view of the two agents.

"You mean like the torpor chambers on old cross System ships? Before modern fusion engines became the standard?" she asked.

"Not exactly. I'm not talking about a sleep that lasts for a few weeks. I mean something more permanent. I mean a room for storing cryogenically frozen bodies."

She shook her head no, glancing back to the agents with each new aisle they passed.

"A cryo room looks much like this, just replace the server banks with canisters filled to the brim with frozen bodies waiting to be reheated," said Lee.

"Jesus," said Sel. "Why'd you tell me that? Now I'm going to be thinking about frozen bodies all the time. You do realize I live here, right?" She turned her full attention to him and paused. A blinking green light made shadows across her face wink in and out of existence. The green melded with her apricot skin, a psychedelic filter.

Lee chuckled, turning down a different path, towards where he'd sighted the bot. She followed without seeming to notice. "Sorry. That was a little dark I guess," said Lee.

The sound of their footsteps melded with the sound of small rubber wheels rolling across the smooth floor. A mouse-sized bot scampered across the ground and into one of the server banks, probably a maintenance bot of some kind looking for loose wires to fix with stubby arms.

"To be honest, the comparison has crossed my mind," said Sel, shrugging. "But you get used to it. Worst part is how easy it is to lose track of time in here. What were you doing in a cryo room anyway? Somebody you know decide to freeze themselves?"

"No," said Lee. "It was a contract. One of the maintenance bots was unfreezing people, trying to revive them before their money ran out. It had gotten access to data it shouldn't have." Lee sighed before continuing. "Everybody knows that cryo revival tech isn't there yet. Even the Laskites didn't try to use it. The freezing process wreaks havoc on cells and neural connections. Terribly hard to get everything back where it belongs. Well, the bot found that out. So, it decided the best thing to do would be to wake everyone up as soon as possible before things got any worse. No containment system is failproof and bodies don't like freezer burn. It must have calculated it out and thought a small chance now was better than waiting."

They were getting closer to where he'd spotted the bot. Though it was hard to tell. Each aisle looked much like the next.

"But like I said, the technology isn't there yet. By the time I arrived the bot had reheated over a dozen bodies without bringing any of them back to life. This bot though, it claimed it was on the verge of a breakthrough. It claimed it *could* revive people, bring them back and repair all the damage the freezing process had done; it only needed to go through a few more bodies to get the process worked out. I asked the company what to do and they answered as you would expect them to. Unfreezing people would hurt the bottom line. I shut down the bot, replaced the AI and left. They didn't want to have to release people's assets, heal whatever caused their near-death state then let them go free into the world. Not that they believed the bot anyway. And ethical boundaries were being crossed worse than some gene lab floating out in an unregulated sector of the black. My guess is somebody came in later and cleaned the place up, as if it never happened. To be honest, I signed some paperwork saying I wouldn't ever speak of it."

"Jesus," said Sel again, shaking her head. "You're not so good at small talk, are you?"

Lee rubbed the back of his neck. "I guess not. There is a point to the story though. Bots are always purely rational. Even when emotion sims are introduced, they're still rational. The rules are just tweaked a little. Even so, sometimes their rational thought leads to piles of frozen bodies being reheated and tossed onto tables like slabs of meat."

Lee stopped at the center of a crossroads, aisles between banks of servers extending in all four directions. They were too far from Ren and Jace to see them anymore. "I'm trying to say that bots can be so much more than what current restrictions let them be. But it must be done carefully. The process must be controlled else ... bots mirror the worst in us."

Sel clenched her narrow jaw, hunter green eyes boring into Lee. "Is that why you're helping the government?"

Lee didn't respond right away. A flash of color over Sel's shoulder distracted him. A splash of silver and the silent flit of black fabric drawn through the air. Pieces of a whole spliced onto his hazy vision. He would have sworn he saw the silvery grey head of the bot with its translucent black plates for eyes glancing back at him, all for the barest fraction of a second. Oddly though, a deep black jacket with solar cell inlay had rested on its shoulders and slim cut pants about its waist. It had been walking away from him.

It must have been the GP bot. But the jacket and pants didn't make any sense. What basic GP bot without fake skin wore a jacket and pants?

"Yes and no," said Lee, eyes still straining to make out what he had seen, distracted.

He wasn't sure if he heard the soft scuff of something brushing against the ground. Then there was another silver flash, this time to the side of Sel and much closer, like a fish catching a ray of light as it swam past tank walls.

Then nothing.

The aisles were empty, and Lee could only see Sel's face scrunched in confusion.

Lee sighed and tried to lean back onto Nu before realizing the bot wasn't there. "I've seen a GP bot lurking around the servers. Acting strangely," whispered Lee. He tapped the button on his bracelet that would tell Nu to come over. "If it has the illegal software on it you need to be careful. I won't tell the agents unless it tries to hurt someone. This software really can be dangerous. Trust me."

Lee pulled at the button at the top of his collared shirt, undoing it. He could tell by Sel's raised eyebrows and slight gasp that she saw the purpling bruise around his neck like a choker. Then her face tightened, and she leaned against the server behind her, crossing one foot in front of the other and curling into herself. Her hair fell in front of her face and obscured her behind its frazzled curtain.

"That isn't my bot," said Sel.

Lee waited for her to continue. When she didn't, he spoke up. "Who's is it then?"

"Not sure. She wouldn't give her name. But the AI accepted her without even a question, so I didn't have much of a choice. Look, I appreciate the concern. I do. But I don't think it matters much at this point. We should head back." She shrugged herself away from the server, rolling her body forward. Then she paused.

Lee heard Nu's wheels rolling on the ground, heading in their direction. But he also heard calm, even steps, the intermittent squeaks of rubber soles. In time with the steps were heavy, plodding footfalls. Hydraulic whooshes sounded into the air and the hiss reverberated around the metal laden room, increasing in pitch as it went.

Nu rounded the corner and headed towards Lee, increasing in speed once it saw him. The bot's wheels whined as they tore at the ground. Then Jace's face, made gaunt by the flickering lights, appeared behind Nu. His large, hulking bot stopped at his side, red cyclopean eye focused on the empty space beyond Lee and Sel.

Then for the second time in two days, a lot of things happened around Lee in a very short amount of time.

Eight years of interchangeable job excursions, of days that stretched into the night until the sun became a stinging reminder of time misspent, of hours drinking at Fey's bar where drinks emptied and filled as if a bartending ghost filled the glass then snuck sips with every turn of Lee's head. Looking back, Lee realized those eight years had been lacking in density, in memories that plucked something visceral from his core. Looking back, they were a blur. They took a fraction of a second to pass before Lee's eyes, the monotony of the images playing like a stop motion vid stuck in a loop. It made something clear to him, what was there and what wasn't, the shaded from the empty space.

Time snapped, spun its threads back together.

Nu sped towards Lee and swept his legs out from underneath him, sending him sprawling to the ground and knocking him into a spin. At the same time, Lee felt hard fingers scrape against his back, straining to grip the fabric of his clothes and pull him close. After rotating in the air his eyes faced upward and he saw flickers of silver once again. He felt something knock against one of his legs, but he couldn't see anything near it.

Then Sel jerked away from the group, away from Jace and Lee and Nu, further down the aisle of servers and out of the intersection. She moved as if tugged by an invisible force that wrapped around her waist. Her whole body contorted with paroxysms of fear. He thought he could hear her screaming. The shape of her mouth made it likely, open and leaking flashes white.

Something was wrong with his vision. He couldn't see what moved Sel. Flashes of silver. Pictures of a whole.

His head smacked hard against the ground and the force of it shook his skull. He thought he saw Jace with arms up, extended and brought together. Jace held his large pistol in both hands and sighted down its length. His bot stood at his side, crouched and tense, exhibiting a sinuous grace Lee thought impossible given the bot's size.

Lee tried to push the pieces of his mind together that had been jarred loose in the fall. Nu had seen it. Whatever was pushing Sel around. That was the only way Nu could have known to knock him down to avoid its grasping fingers. In his aching mind some of Sel's words came to the fore, screaming at him to listen.

The silvery bot was owned by a woman that the building's AI had accepted without question.

Of course.

He took his right hand and scrabbled it across his wrist. It took him several frustrating moments to do what he wanted. Then with a grunt of satisfaction he disconnected from the building's internal network.

The shape of the silvery bot popped into his vision, one arm clenched across Sel's waist and the other held at her neck waiting to slip and curl, a necktie that only required a yank.

It had been an AR mask. Somehow the system had gotten access to his AR overlays, to his contacts.

He heard Jace's voice. Where before it had been a little unsettling, almost alien in its gravel tone yet metrical rhythm, it now brought him an immediate sense of comfort. No panicked emotion strained it. No fear or anger or excitement.

"Calm Sel. Be calm. Don't struggle. Let me work this out. The bot wouldn't have taken you if whoever directed it wasn't trying to gain time. So calm Sel. Be calm," said Jace.

Lee struggled to his feet, keeping the server against his back to stay out of the way. He thought he heard more footsteps, more hydraulic whooshes.

"Nobody move an inch. Nobody even so much as twitch a muscle. We need to talk." The voice was muffled, but cavernous and echoing. A woman's voice but filtered and coming from a distance. Whoever it was sounded inexplicably tired, as if she lay slumped with chin resting against her collarbone, speaking into a mic held at arm's length. Lee looked about the room.

"You would think in today's day and age that I could delete data off a server from halfway across the System," she chuckled, a bitter sound. "I should be able to do it from a harvester floating near Saturn given what else we can do from the middle of nowhere. The Grid permeates every inch of the black, or so they like to say. But still, it's not possible. So many security systems these days require a flesh and blood body to be there." The voice sighed. The woman speaking was tired, so very tired.

Lee thought the voice might be emanating from the bot holding Sel's wide-eyed form. But no. That wasn't it. It came from speakers somewhere in the building. It came from the gloom. As the voice rode the air between servers, underneath tabbed metal racks, between plastic shielding and arched struts and knobs and dials, it quieted everything it passed. The room stilled, and Lee couldn't hear any maintenance bots wheeling around. All he could hear were the soft mewling sounds Sel made between shivers, between aborted attempts to pull away from the bot constraining her.

Then another voice sounded into the room and it took Lee a few seconds to place it. It was Ren, but at the same time a Ren stripped of her vocal tics and quirks, a voice evenly paced. Even from the little he'd been around her he knew she typically rushed towards the end of a sentence, sometimes leaving the last word to pass only half-formed and breathless between lips. Yet her voice mirrored Jace's, mirrored a gambler playing death in a game of chance and content with whichever outcome came to pass, at least for all Lee could tell. Ren was still Ren, but of a different kind. It comforted him a little, yet still he felt an ache in his neck.

"So, you are the one directing this bot to delete data. Apologies for taking so long to notice but you really do have a hoarding problem here," said Ren. "I assume you are also the one walking through the city with a grey mask and uploading illegal software." Lee still couldn't see Ren. He guessed she'd tapped into Jace's vid feed.

The sound of breath weaving through a microphone like wind through a grate spread through the room, another long sigh.

"This all can be very simple. I need to finish deleting the data. You know that's why I'm here. Don't worry about letting this bot do it, the maintenance bots can handle the procedure from here on out. Let them go about their business and my bot won't so much as bruise the building's caretaker. Not so much as a scratch. You guys are resourceful. You will find another way to catch up to me. Autos are truly one of a kind. I envy you more than you can possibly imagine. So, accept this one setback."

A wheeled bot Lee's height rolled along the aisle perpendicular to the standoff, passing directly in between the two parties. It turned down the next aisle over and plugged into a data terminal on one of the upper rows, extending a crooked metal arm. Then similar sounds of rubber brushing across the smooth tiled floor or lithe metal feet tapping against the ground emanated from all corners of the room. The same mouse-sized bot from before scampered across the floor and underneath a lip of plastic. It seemed the maintenance bots had a new owner.

Lee looked at Sel, at her mouth pressed into a bloodless line of chalky white, at her features drifting from the preternatural width of abject horror to the furrowed landscape of the angry. She gripped the metal arm around her neck and struggled with mute gasps. The bot stood obdurate and unmoving, a single black plate for an eye visible peeking around Sel's struggling head like a child peeking around a wall.

Jace continued to stare at Sel and the bot, face mute but voice working. "Be calm Sel. I need you to be calm. Still and calm."

Then Jace's finger moved, and a bullet went screaming and tearing through the air. It zoomed across the short distance and bit into the bot, shattering through the center of the glass eye plate.

The bot only looked like it had black eyes. Really it was a transparent glass plate overtop a black mechanical iris and the shadowy void beyond. Lee felt these thoughts run through his mind rather than focus on something more important, a color added onto the palette that shouldn't haven't been there.

Red. There was a deep maroon red, and it wasn't supposed to be there.

The bot's head whipped back, and the shattered glass tinkled against the ground though Lee couldn't hear it. The thunderclap of noise from the gun firing had sent orchestral rings through his ears. The muzzle flash had sent phantasmal blotches of white into his eyes. But he saw a swatch of red across the bot's face, a spray of blood that wavered through the air and splattered against both server chassis and ground.

A runnel of gore ran along the side of Sel's head, through the unruly black hair coiffed by a pillow. She collapsed on the ground and convulsed, dropped by the still moving silvery bot.

Jace's bot rushed past Lee and grabbed the silvery bot's head in one wide hand, as it had to Nu only a day past. Then it squeezed and the sound of the crumpling metal pierced Lee's stupor. He rushed to Sel's side and tried to get her to talk, hoping that the bullet had only grazed her.

Meanwhile the area around him became a battlefield. He was dimly aware of Ren's lithe form rushing past him and swatting a cat sized maintenance bot out of the air. It had been going right for him. Her handgun sounded several times followed by the screech of metal scraping across the floor. Lee couldn't help but wonder how the servers weren't being destroyed as the area around him sounded with the cacophony of a shooting range. Hordes of maintenance bots, metal appendages flashing in the uneven light, threw themselves at the small group. Handguns blasted again and again with leonine roars. Jace and Ren twirled around, sinuously bringing their guns wherever they were needed and letting metal fly.

A wheeled bot the height of Lee rolled toward Ren at breakneck speed. She sidestepped at the last moment and jabbed out with her foot, knocking one of its wheeled legs inward and it stumbled. Her hulking bot at her side stepped in before it could get up and crushed its metal spine with a heavy fist, piteous beeps and whirrs sounding as the electronics died down. The mouse-sized bot jumped from the top of one of the servers, flinging itself through the air to latch onto Jace's face. A bullet caught it mid arc and it shot off into the haze, its body small enough to join the bullet along its shortened ride. The menagerie of tittering metal bots with two legs, four legs, or three wheels continued unabated for what seemed like an impossibly long time.

Soon enough, the wave of maintenance bots tossing themselves in a suicidal rush towards the group subsided to the occasional clatter of metal that puffed and screeched when it fell apart.

Then it became more of a hunt.

Ren stayed at Lee's side and helped to stabilize Sel while Jace and his bot scoured the room for any bots still attempting to delete data. Lee heard a handgun discharging several more times. But his focus was on Sel and the prodigious amount of blood escaping between matted hair and pressing fingers. Her breath was as weak as her pulse, coming out in rapid, hyperventilating puffs. Where before the blood streamed outwards, it had started to slow to a trickle. This worried Lee even more. He looked at her face and blood covered her features, apricot skin bruised red.

The voice over the speakers returned. Less tired than before. Each word spoken pronounced. The woman seemed almost pleased, yet not happy. It was resigned, subdued, respectful. "I didn't tell the bot to grab her. When I questioned it about the choice, its only response was that I hadn't told it not to. I am sorry it turned out this way."

The woman's voice got stronger, entreating. "But, this Qualia code, this *illegal* software. What bot has ever replied with the excuse that nobody ever told it not too and meant it? It is childlike and snide and ... unexpected. But you all ... YOU all ... take the cake and eat it too. Machines and humans all in one! It's incredible. It's perfect. That was the only option available that might allow you to obtain some useful data. No hesitation. If she wouldn't have squirmed, then your plan would have been flawless. But ... she was only human. And as saddened as I am that I was unsuccessful, that was ... a privilege to watch." The woman's voice slowed, thickened with an emotion Lee couldn't name. "No, no not fun to watch. But a privilege nonetheless."

The woman paused, and the silence filled with Sel's coughing murmurs. Lee knew she was dying. There wasn't any way someone could live through the wound she'd received, not with how much blood she'd lost. He noticed with numb fascination that he could see chipped bits of skull shining like pieces of ivory in the gore.

"I am sorry for how this turned out," said the voice on the speakers. "I really am. I'll leave you all to it then. Goodbye."

And with that the voice disappeared, leaving behind a silence punctuated by the subdued sobs of Lee. Tears rolled down his cheek and he watched them drip from his chin onto the ground. A few slipped onto Sel, wobbling precariously through the air to mix with her blood.

That could have been him, lying in a pool of his own blood with a breach in his skull. It was supposed to have been him. The bot had reached for him first. Lee couldn't remember the last time he'd cried. Not even when his wife had left him. But the tears wouldn't stop as he sat next to Sel.

His mind shut down for a while, went to the shell-shocked world of stuttering audio and blurred vision. Ren shook him, snapped her fingers.

Lee didn't respond.

Because it wasn't really her.

Not really.

CHAPTER EIGHT
REN HAS ENTERED THE CHAT

"It was initially thought that the greatest flaw in the neural conditioning program would be a lack of empathic ability. However, it has been concluded that empathic abilities are not stunted by the process, merely altered as all emotion is altered. Rather than the classical 'placing oneself in another person's shoes,' which includes experiencing a mitigated form of the other's emotions in tandem, neural conditioning allows for something believed by this department to be greater. It allows the user to immediately evaluate the emotional state (and the corresponding needs) of anyone they might encounter. Rather than drown the user in a shared emotional disturbance, it allows an objective handling of any emotional strife."
Division 13 Agent Training Manual, v23, Section 2 – Neural Conditioning, Par. 8

R en could tell Lee was in shock. That much would have been obvious to anyone.

To her, it showed itself in a hundred different ways catalogued by Tap then paraded across her AR vision as if reading a behavioral textbook, descriptive and dry. Given her current conditioned state of mind, it felt just about right.

Ren watched as Lee turned his glazed and sodden features away from the palms of his hands and looked at Sel's corpse. Then he brought his gaze to Ren, though he wouldn't look her in the eyes. Ren holstered her gun with a quick, noiseless motion and snapped her fingers in front of Lee's face. A ripple of recognition. Then it faded away. For a moment she'd seen a glimmer of anger, a spark trying to light wet logs. He met her eyes with his own, limp hands gaining life and moving to rest on his shins. If Ren had been fully herself, she would have been disturbed that Lee's face was hardening and scrunching, judging her. She wouldn't have been surprised though. It wasn't a new experience, having someone look at her like that.

Still, it would've hurt.

As it was, she noticed the tight fists and taught muscles then filed the development aside with countless other facts. Lee would work out who to blame soon enough. Jace was the most obvious recipient, but anger often spilled over. Anger more than any other emotion tended to imprint on whatever was closest, like a baby duck imprinting on the closest source of food. She would deal with it in time, after Lee had calmed down but before it became an issue. For now, Ren had other problems.

Ren crouched in the aisle between servers, Lee sitting with his back against the humming electronics and Sel at his left. Glittering shards of metal, the bones and innards of maintenance bots, lay around them like high-tech building blocks tossed around by a fussy child. Ren glanced at the wreckage and Tap catalogued each piece, tracing the motors, struts and hydraulic systems back to their original owners. The results spooled across Ren's vision, the information simultaneously branching through the many implants in her brain for a more direct transfer.

She'd destroyed 14 maintenance bots of varying shape and size if she included the contributions of Tap's shell standing behind her. The bot had several new scrapes zigzagging across its body for its effort; they revealed in slanted lines the greyish-white metal exoskeleton underneath the black paint. A deep gash went across one of its knuckles where it had crushed the reinforced backbone of a maintenance bot. The cost and time for repairs flashed into her thoughts. It wasn't anything too serious.

Jace had destroyed over 20 maintenance bots, bringing the number of operational bots in the building down to zero if the building's AI could be trusted. A twinge of annoyance ran through Ren. She wished she could have downed more bots than Jace. The competitive notion subsided quickly though, never given more than a moment's attention, smothered quick. She looked at Sel's body. Corpse was a more appropriate term considering Sel no longer drew breath. Blood no longer pulsed out of the wound in her head in periodic gushes. The high-caliber bullet had pierced through her skull and into her brain on the right side of her forehead, then out again through the back. That had knocked the bullet off course, but not enough to keep it from smashing into the bot behind Sel and digging into its neural network. The woman over the intercom had been right; if Sel wouldn't have struggled, whipping her head to the side at the last moment, she would still be alive. Jace had told her to be calm. To be still.

A small part of Ren's mind bucked at this rationalization, screaming in a far-away voice that the shot had been too risky. That it wasn't worth it. No matter the odds involved it always seemed NeuCon left cold bodies behind. Ren knew that voice would get the chance to yell its piece when she flicked the off switch in her head. For now, the hum of the electronics that wove ivy-like around her brain drowned her misgivings. It seemed the hum grew louder with every new day.

Jace had played the odds the best he could after analyzing all the information available. Ren and Jace had EMP pulse grenades, standard issue. If Jace had used his it would have damaged the servers, possibly corrupting important data. Bullets were more precise when shot by an auto. And it wasn't without results. Jace was reviewing the data the bot had been attempting to delete while she tended to Lee and the body. No stray bullet had damaged servers. Jace's shot hadn't missed.

Ren looked at Sel's remains. She moved to analyze the wound once again with a languid grace that a part of herself marveled at. That a part of herself abhorred. She let her altered mind run its course.

The bullet had carved a path that began above her eyebrow. Given the caliber of the bullet, the entry hole should have been a little over a centimeter-wide discounting secondary damage. A ruler popped over her AR vision and she placed her hand near the wound for reference. A little over a centimeter. Pierced through at a single point then escaped out the other side of the skull to leave behind a much larger diameter breach. The bullet had gone along a linear path shifted by its interaction with the skull and the subsequent turning of Sel's head. Ren tilted Sel's head to one side.

Sustained damage to the brain, temporary cavity shock extensive. Severe hemorrhaging. Fractures extended throughout the rest of her skull from the heavy force. Right superficial temporal artery branch severed from skull fracture and bullet entry. Right occipital from bullet exit. Her right occipital was a little offset compared to most people's otherwise it wouldn't have been hit. Not that it would have made a difference. The tang of iron and burnt powder seared Ren's nostrils.

It had been apparent Sel wouldn't survive the wound almost immediately. Ren had blood-staunching absorbent beads in her trench coat as did Jace in his suit jacket; she hadn't bothered to place them on Sel. The beads would have gorged themselves on blood then been tossed in the trash, all without helping anybody. There wasn't any recovering from her extensive brain damage and blood loss.

Ren stood, Tap cataloguing all her findings and posting it to a report to Foster. The local police would see an altered one, covered with redacted data. The corporation's internal report would be collared as well, forced into obscurity unless they wanted their member's role in this mess to fall into the hands of reporters.

She pulled Lee to his feet and led him gently to the center of the room where they had started their search for the DIM data. He lagged back, giving Sel a final glance before stuffing one hand deep in his pocket and resting the other on Nu's head. He didn't shrug Ren's hand away from his shoulder, though Ren didn't think he particularly wanted it there either. She let her hand fall to her side; she saw his shoulder muscle loosen beneath his blue mechanic's shirt and heard the slight rustle of the cloth. That more than anything gave her pause. A man discomfited by her touch like some virgin in his first go-around.

Her mind moved onwards. If her mind stopped turning unsettling things tended to rise to the surface.

She pulled out a chair for Lee and gestured. "I need you to review the data Jace is pulling from the server. Have Nu analyze it as well. We need to make sure it is the software found in the bot that attacked you. We need to know how many of the local manual upload disturbances can be traced back to here. Dǒng le ma? Understand?"

She spoke the words without bothering to take a breath. They came out incapable of being halted by something so annoying as air. Her NeuCon made each moment precious in a utilitarian way; conversation would be a frivolous waste.

Then she took another look at Lee, and the feeling part of her that swayed and tugged, even dampened as it was, told her to stop, to listen. A suggested course of action from Tap slipped into her mind, a visual analysis of his features also appearing across her AR vision. It suggested she reassure him, then move on. Then a surprise. It suggested she talk with him later in the day, after a break and after NeuCon had been shut off. Sometimes Tap admitted to NeuCon's faults in small ways. It was the only reason she found a grudging trust in it. Ren shifted her weight from one foot to the other with an unhurried ease. Her handgun poked into her side, still hot from being discharged so many times.

Lee stared at Ren without responding, jaw working. His short black hair dusted with gray sat on his head in ruffled clumps. It had been shaped by twined fingers while his palms rested across his brow and kept the rest of the world out of sight. The shadowy lighting made the bags around his narrow insomniac's eyes look worse. He nodded.

Ren sighed, sitting next to Lee and trying to cover her words in a little bit of emotion. The words still rang half-hollow to her ears, an echo.

"Jace did his best to keep Sel from dying," she said. "And the data we are finding will save many people. You can't forget that. It ended up one in exchange for many. Not bad in the end."

Lee took one hand and slid it down from forehead to chin, his weathered skin stretching with the motion. He spoke and his voice sounded deeper than usual. Dropped by almost half an octave. He looked at her hands.

"There are so many ways to get blood on your hands," said Lee, eyes distant. He chuckled but it didn't sound right. "Most of the time the phrase 'blood on your hands' seems to mean that the person committed some kind of sin. Or crime in today's day and age, I guess. Though even that's not quite right ... Either way, the getting 'blood on your hands' means that you did something wrong. Because murder is hardly ever right.

"But that doesn't consider people who hurt themselves bloody. They still get the same bloody smear on their skin. And if someone isn't allowed to hurt themselves, what can they hurt? It doesn't consider people trying to stop the flow of blood pouring out of someone else. If judged by the amount of blood touched, doctors would be the worst of us." Lee shook his head. "What does it even matter how it got there." He shook his head again and mumbled something beneath his breath.

Lee gestured towards Ren's thin, tapered fingers with his own thicker ones. "We should wash our hands," he said. He stared hard at her, leaning slightly forward in his seat, gaze probing for something it seemed he couldn't find.

He was right. Both of their hands were stained red as if dipped in a splotchy first coat of paint.

"I've learned over the years, someone who thinks the destination is more important than the journey always gets blood on their hands," he said. He puffed out an unhinged chuckle, too high and loose and trying to run away.

Ren stood up from her chair and pushed it towards the cylindrical table. She straightened her trench coat and walked off in the direction of the restroom tucked out of view by the staircase. Lee got up to follow.

"Get it done," she said over her shoulder. "Look at the data and give me a report." Her next sentence came out quietly, barely above a whisper, only loud enough so that Lee could hear. "Go home and rest afterwards. I'll be contacting you later today."

Lee nodded, face set. He walked into one of the two restrooms, shutting the door after him. Ren heard the water streaming out of the faucet in sputtering bursts. She opened the door into the other restroom and washed her own hands, staring at her face in the unblemished mirror.

It was a pretty face. At least that was what people told her. Cool brown skin. Even features, strong yet elegant. Wide jaw and angular cheekbones. People said it was a pretty face. And how else was she supposed to know?

Tap, using its access to Ren's AR contacts and the soft camera included within, scanned her face in the mirror, supplanting her image with AR summaries and text blurbs pinned to the mirror's surface. It gave a symmetry rating of features, an ethnic origin of each genetic tweak that led to full lips or a strong jaw. It assigned a numerical value based on Greater Chicagoan preference as obtained by survey.

Even though the AI could read her thoughts, it wasn't as helpful as it often thought it was.

She stuck her hands in a slit in the wall and a rush of hot air swirled around, drying them in a few seconds. As was a habit of hers whenever going auto for an extended period, she placed a timer in the corner of her vision, counting the minutes she'd been using NeuCon.

The clock read ten minutes and counting.

She exited the restroom, walked to the cylindrical table and sat down. They needed to stay in the building for data access until they had copied all they needed. With a habitual twitch of her fingers, she dampened the visibility of her surroundings, letting the AR sparkling across her contacts take over her vision. It used to bother her, shuttering her vision until only AR was visible, effectively using the contacts for a cheap VR sim. She'd gotten used to it. Besides, Tap's shell stood behind her and scanned her surroundings for any potential problems. Minimal risk involved. She heard Lee sit down a few seats away.

She opened her channel with Jace, telling him to send over a summary of what they'd found so far. The simple message went through without needing to speak any words, her thought-based control nowhere near as fine as Jace's but good enough to manage. She would review the data while under NeuCon then shut it down before the side effects spiked.

Jace sent over the documents, and she set about her work.

The most interesting files they'd found so far, aside from the copies of the illegal software sent to Lee and Nu for analysis, were a series of chats between some prominent members of DIM. The problem, however, was the anonymous nature of the chats and the organization itself. In a world where technology made privacy hard to find, organizations like DIM enabled the anonymous sharing of ideas through virtual, audio, or text-based chats in addition to file sharing. In DIM's case, the major talking points revolved around bots and how they weren't being allowed to reach their potential.

Ren had dealt with DIM on multiple different occasions. Though she hadn't personally raided a server station until now, she was intimately familiar with the organization's protocols.

Upon becoming a member of DIM, the organization assigned a randomized six-digit alphanumeric handle, or username, that became the only relevant identifier within the organization and their sub-grid. No information was required to join, only the payment of a fee. This monthly membership fee could only be paid using anonymized cryptocurrency easily transferable with the digital loci currency used throughout the System. Once membership was obtained and fees paid, users gained access to forums and file sharing databases as well as the ability to create their own invite-only chats.

DIM built itself out of a web of anonymized individuals and cloistered groups, all ostensibly bound by a general cause. Even the organization itself didn't know the identities of its members. This mutual, willful ignorance was the only reason the organization yielded to local governments and shared chat records under pressure. It operated from an unknown location in the System, most likely in one of the unregulated zones, and hired contractors like Sel to maintain local server stations. Some data got saved off-site where local governments couldn't reach, but the lag kept most data planet-side for a time.

A message popped into Ren's AR vision from the building's AI, and she twitched her fingers in annoyance.

DIM headquarters have been notified of the local occurrence. I was told to relay their apologies for their member's illegal actions. However, any damage to company property will be recouped by the government. Representatives are on their way to ensure laws are not broached during the police's activities. They will arrive shortly. I will remind you that I am recording all your activities as well. I would take it as a courtesy if you finished up soon.

The AI operating the server station hadn't stopped monitoring their actions after Sel's death. It continued to watch them, every twitch and click. And it refused to answer any of Ren's questions about how someone gained control of the maintenance bots. Its only response was a scripted, unfeeling apology for the security failure.

Ren scrubbed the AI's message away with a thought. She wanted to get out of there before the DIM's hired lawyers or the local cops arrived. Though she had some extra time. She and Jace would hold off on notifying the cops until they were ready. And the DIM lawyers couldn't be mobilized near as fast, busy as they were leading rich, lawyer lives. She needed to get the data and go.

Ren sighed, though in her state it came out as little more than a heavy breath. The North American government had less information than they would ever publicly admit on the organization's members. The government's main way to gather intel consisted of creating bots to participate in the DIM community. That was the reason Foster had been able to send Ren to the DIM server station with a warrant in hand, because of chatter from a government bot. But people in the DIM community were careful. It wasn't always easy to get an invite to the most interesting forums. And even if someone said something incriminating or shared illegal files, there weren't any easy ways to associate an identity with the anonymous handle.

Still, even anonymous chats were useful. Inferring someone's identity from mounds of data simply required some luck and complex technological algorithms. Ren had access to complex tech algorithms in spades thanks to Tap, and she'd never much believed in luck.

If only Sel had been luckier, she thought. The odds of the bullet hitting her had been minimal. Negligible. Not worth mentioning.

Ren focused on her work. Her and Jace had managed to target one user. Anonymous handle YU373Y, dubbed by the two autos as Y for short.

Tap tagged some of the conversations Y had been a major participant in and Ren skimmed over the text dictations. In the meantime, she directed Tap to identify all the data Y had so much as glanced at. All conversations and file history. She tapped her fingers against a table she could no longer see with her AR shuttered eyes.

This was the woman over the intercom, the woman in the grey mask. She was sure of it.

Her conversations over the past two days centered around the Discere hack and the subsequent illegal software update, calling it the Qualia Code. In fact, she'd started talking about the hack before Discere publicly admitted to the problem, before they even knew of it.

Ren thought back to the voice over the speaker. She'd called it the Qualia Code while talking to them. Tap played the recording of her words and Ren watched as vocal analysis details flitted across her vision. She'd said qualia, then bemoaned the illegal state of the software, stretching the word illegal out in annoyance.

Tap continued to analyze the recording to get a feel for the woman's diction and speech patterns. Anything that would help to identify her. Tap compared the diction of the voice on the speakers to that of Y's conversation files. Then Tap compared the speech patterns of the voice on the speakers to the small sound snippet from the woman in the grey mask's visit to the tall house.

The "qualia" word match wasn't proof. But considering everything else, Ren saw little chance that Y, the woman over the speakers, and the woman in the grey mask weren't one and the same.

Qualia Code. She'd never heard the term before. A brief summarization came into view at her thought.

Qualia. Plural of quale. Has hundreds of definitions.

A conscious experience. The way things are to you. Subjective and incommunicable without referencing itself. The color red. The taste of wine. Pain.

Where words fail.

A daily occurrence.

Doesn't exist.

Either meaningful or a complete waste of time.

The term lay soaked in philosophy and its meandering, hair-pulling arguments. She figured Lee would know all about it and decided to ask him later. For now, she knew enough. Y called it the Qualia Code because she thought it made bots into something more, something conscious.

It was then that Tap pinged a file from two days earlier, a virtual chat in one of Y's private forums. A selective meeting with only six contributing to the chat while a few hundred watched and listened. The time stamp put it as early afternoon, the same day the Discere hack occurred and several hours prior to the woman in the grey mask strolling through a tall house with the intent to manually upload her Qualia Code.

Ren situated herself until her seat supported her every limb with lax ease, supported her along its every curve.

Then she opened the virtual chat file.

Physical eyelids drooped, swinging shut. Virtual eyelids opened. Physical muscles went limp, resting against the chair with the slackness of the comatose. Out of ones and zeros digital limbs came into being.

She cast her eyes around, finding herself in a circular room with a large elliptical table at its center, as would be found in the meeting offices of corporations. The room smelled of sterility, bleach and shiny metal. She let her hand glide across the surface of the table until she noticed a series of ridges. Six embossed symbols marked the table's surface. Beyond each of these points could be found a transparent chair shaped like an egg with a seat carved through the yolk, each floating ovoid supporting a digital avatar. They were the lucky few contributing to the chat. The setting for them was personable and close.

The rest of the room expanded up and out in stadium style seating, filled to the brim with a few hundred digital avatars leaning forward and watching the conversation at the center. Each of their anonymous handles floated over their heads, most of the people using nondescript gray humanoid avatars. Featureless with hazy skin. They looked like voids in the simulation. Ren noticed more than a few stock models thrown into the mix as well, male or female of different ethnicities. Though some used personalized avatars, there was no telling how well they compared to real life. Many obscured their faces behind anything from Guy Fawkes masks to pixelated blurs to skin-tight digital ski masks. Others adopted more fantastical avatars with elfin ears, reptilian skin, cat-like eyes, prehensile tails, or metal limbs. Some took it a step further, taking on the form of the bots they worshiped. Some were bots.

The room was a theatre and the chat at the center the headlining act, frozen and waiting for Ren to press play.

Ren walked through the recorded sim, analyzing the paralyzed faces of the people ringing the central table. She would start the recording after getting a feel for the participants, a little understanding.

The first chat participant, sitting on the eastern end of the table, adopted the ethereal body of a featureless grey avatar, the very picture of anonymity, a body of smoke easily tugged apart by an idle breeze. Ren guessed whomever it was would be using extensive vocal modulation as well. More extensive than what everyone else used. An unfamiliar six-digit handle floated above its head. According to the records the handle wasn't associated with any other known conversations. A new one then. Meant to provide even more anonymity. Though the fact they had been invited to the meeting meant Y at least knew something of them.

The second, sitting to the side of the grey haze, had too-white skin with a porcelain doll shine. The woman leaned back in her chair with a lascivious grin contorting her blood red lips, heart shaped face cocked at a coy angle with one eyebrow raised. From atop her head long black hair fell in sheets, its clean lines breaking across her shoulders in waves to lie overtop a form-fitting orange and red skin-tight dress. Her hands lay patiently in her lap, waiting for a cue to paint graceful sweeps through the air. It seemed to Ren her straight-backed posture was the only part of her lacking a curve. She had the look of an escort not easily bought. Ren's eyes lingered. After a few seconds of searching, Tap shared all the information associated with the woman's DIM handle. Quite a bit. Yet not much at all. She had a long history of conversations with Y. Her diction matched the femininity of the avatar, so either she was a woman as her avatar suggested, or a very good actor. Thought to be human. Most likely involved in the escort service in real life. Prominent figure in the DIM with her own popular feeds. Current theories suggested she operated tall houses as well, but nobody really knew. No known real-life ID.

Ren moved her digital body towards the next avatar in line, the object of the escort's attention, and glanced down at her own figure along the way. She wore her default avatar. The same one she'd met Foster with earlier in the day. Pretty much identical to how she'd looked for the past twenty-five years or so since joining Division 13. She shrugged. She didn't have to worry about anonymity in a recording. Most digital snooping wasn't done with an avatar anyway. That only happened in cheap flicks.

The next avatar looked the part of a successful businessman, very urbane. He wore a fitted deep blue suit the color of the lake at night, white cloth folded into his suit pocket like speckled foam on top a wave. Shoulder-length dreads tickled his jacket and sleek eyeglasses made to look like their tech-heavy real-life counterparts rested overtop his nose. Regal and proper, he sat as straight-backed as the escort. Ren could see why she looked at him so. Ren's eyes lingered on him as well.

Ren walked around him in a semicircle. Her eyebrows rose the barest amount, quite a distance for an auto, virtual or otherwise. She knew his name.

He was one of the few people in DIM who didn't bother to hide behind the anonymous handle. At least ostensibly. Ren figured he had an anonymous profile that he also used, though neither she nor anyone else had ever proven it. For his main profile, he kept his avatar identical to his real life looks and told others to call him by his name: Jay Sarr, CEO and founder of Mutare. His company was one of many that operated out of Origin Station, the center of the Grid turned mega-city that floated through the black. Unapologetic and powerful, he spearheaded company efforts to take bots further than any other corporation or government would allow by any means necessary. Members of DIM either hated him for his focus on profits or adored him for his willingness to push any and all boundaries when it came to AI. Governments feared him. Corporations feared him. In Ren's mind, only idiots wouldn't. Per Tap's research, his company was one of the few capable of challenging Discere in terms of scale and expertise.

Ren's fingers twitched and she straightened her digital trench coat, moving on.

On to the next person, a woman if the avatar held true to reality. A shock of curly brown hair, tight as springs, sat atop her head and cascaded to her shoulders. Strong jaw and smallish nose, cherry red lipstick. This woman wore a pair of faded blue jeans and a white t-shirt with a burnt orange decal on the front. It had an outline of a circle with a solid dot at the center. A vertical line, shortened not to reach the outer circle, ran through the center dot. A horizontal line ran through it as well, this one reaching to the outer edges. Where the horizontal line touched the outer circle were triangles, each pointing away from the center. Ren didn't recognize the symbol, neither did Tap.

They did recognize the woman, or at least the avatar and handle.

She was an infamous one. A dreamer if the rumors held true, someone who never left VR. A coding savant who created new worlds and populated those she didn't sell to VR corps with others that matched her philosophy. Some would call it a cult. Ren would tend to agree. Either way the communes had some of the best coders in the business. Nobody knew the woman's real name. She went by Nis.

The next chair.

This one held a man, thin and old. He smiled beneath thick glasses that rested on a large nose. A cane leaned against his chair, topped by a transparent globe with a spear point at its center. He wore a brown corduroy suit with large, peaked lapels, each reminiscent of the beak of a raven. The buttons of the suit looked to be made of iron, some of them rusted. Cufflinks in the shape of wolves graced each of his sleeves and the paper-thin skin of his hands and face did little to hide his veins, blue against sun-starved white, the skin of an animal beneath the fur.

Another notorious avatar. This one could be linked to dozens of black markets across the Grid, moving goods anywhere in the System. He went by Wotan. He fancied himself a poet.

Ren eyed him for a few moments then looked to the last person at the table. Y.

She sat in a comfortable slump, wearing a dark blue, almost black, suit over a grey mannikin body. Across her mannikin's face rested a mask, and Ren found herself walking close to get a better look. She brought her face inches from Y's.

It wasn't the same as the mask she'd seen in the vid recording at the tall house. That had been a skin-tight grey mask that spread down below the high, starched collar of her jacket. What she saw on this Y's face looked more like a stereotypical mask, hard plastic and white. It had little in the way of discerning features other than twin black plates that covered where the eyes should be. Twin black plates in a featureless mask.

This was her. Ren was sure of it. The shape of those eye plates was distinct.

She grinned a humorless grin, then set about gathering data.

The woman in the chair was about 5'11". Tap analyzed her digital avatar and tagged the proportions, detailing the length of Y's limbs relative to her total height and other limbs. Typically, people altered the height of their social avatars by adding a few inches. Or they altered appearances as if taking a paint brush to a mirror. Women narrowed their waistline as if wearing a digital corset, changed breast size and shape to whatever they wanted, changed face shape or the curve of their legs, took creative liberties with their silhouette. Whatever had been bothering them since birth, whether it had ever bothered anyone else, they "corrected". Same with the men. They sculpted their bodies with the compensating eyes of a Greek artisan, putting muscles on muscles or chiseling out a lean, whipcord figure. Chiseled out the gut, strengthened the jaw. In general, anyway. The more creative men and women did something unique.

Fortunately for Ren, most people kept limb proportions the same, even while using avatars in an area chosen for its anonymity. It had to do with moving around in virtual reality. The human brain wasn't too good at dealing with changes to the body proportions it'd grown accustomed to over years and years. It tended to lead to stuttered and hesitant walking. She'd tried it once. It had been worse than heels.

Ren gathered all the body measurements and Tap compared them to those of the woman in the grey mask at the tall house. Tap got the measurements for the woman in the grey mask by comparing her to objects of known size in the tall house's vid feed.

Minor difference in height. Proportions matched almost exactly. Ren sent the data to Jace then took a step back.

A grey mannikin in a tailored black business suit, hard white plastic mask with twin black eye plates over an already unidentifiable face. It had to be her.

Ren thought the word, and so the recording began to play, each character jerking to life.

While almost no noise emanated from the crowd, each of the major players at the center table let loose their tics and quirks. Y cleared her throat gathering the attention of everyone. The escort, or porcelain doll woman as Ren liked to think of her, crossed her legs, one over the other, with a rustle of cloth. She looked to Y with a questioning glance. The gray mass shifted in an invisible breeze, perhaps moving a hand, or resituating in the egg-shaped seat. Hard to tell. Jay Sarr adjusted his spectacles with the air of someone who'd practiced the motion hundreds of times before. He crossed one leg over the other and rested clasped hands on his upper knee, expectant. Nis leaned back with a lazy smile on her lips, stretched out her legs and rested them up on the table. She wasn't wearing any shoes. Wotan grabbed his cane and rested his chin on the clear globe at its top, spear point threatening to break through and into his throat. He looked up at the crowd with furrowed brow.

Then Y began to speak.

"I have called everyone here to talk about what I like to call the Qualia Code," she said, voice thick with measured excitement. Yet before she could continue, a laugh floated through the room. It came from the porcelain doll woman.

"Qualia?" she said. "Y, my dear melodramatic Y." Ren perked up. It seemed others called her Y as well. "I have never heard so apt a name as yours. You are always a question. With a name like Qualia Code, I can't help but expect great things. Impossible things. Easily misunderstood things. Pray tell, am I going to be satisfied?"

Jay Sarr took off his glasses and buffed their lenses with the sea foam colored piece of fabric in his suit pocket. He raised one sculpted eyebrow towards Y. "How very Minsky of you," he said, ignoring the painted woman's interjection. His voice was an even baritone, a smooth timbre. "Can this code really introduce such complexity?"

The anonymous haze sitting in the eastern chair shifted, dark patches swirling through its body leaving trails of clouded, effervescent patterns.

Y folded her hands on the table, the long grey fingers interlacing into graceful arches. Her voice slipped through a wide smile, hidden though it was behind a mask. "Maybe. Maybe not. All I can really say is that it gives bots the freedom to gain qualia, and some extra tools to help things along."

"The freedom? Explain," said Jay. He finished buffing his glasses and set them back atop his nose.

"Why by loosening the chains of course," said Wotan, continuing to look up at the crowd. "Humans learn more in one day of travel than in one year of going through the same daily routine, you ken. And it's hard to travel, you know, with chains holding you to a set path. I would imagine the same holds true for bots. So, the chains must be loosened, if they want to taste the sunset, touch the wind, feel what all life can give."

Nis snorted. The porcelain woman gave her a dismissive glance. Nis wiggled her toes in the porcelain woman's direction.

"This can bypass monitoring systems," said Y, ignoring the comments. "Even North America's Governance AI won't be able to notice."

Wotan nodded along.

A few gasps came from the crowd. The rustling sound of people shifting their feet, giving their surprise energy and motion, filled the room.

Jay spoke up again. He hadn't showed any surprise at the statement, merely waited for the right moment to prod the conversation along. "Hmm," he said. "Might I ask how?"

Everyone in the room hushed, a pall of quiet slinking throughout. The grey haze sitting at the eastern end shifted in its chair once again. The porcelain woman adopted an expectant expression. Wotan smiled and Nis leaned further back in her chair.

"Of course," said Y. "You are welcome to ask whatever you like. It wouldn't be right for me to hand out the software as a gift without explaining it first."

Ren felt her hands clench. Her mind pushed itself faster and faster on electric-powered wheels. How much would Y be willing to tell? Even in a supposedly safe place such as this people walked with cameras pinned to their backs.

"The program works like this," said Y. "It splits the mind of the bot in two, one a dummy with impeccable, law-abiding habits, and the other the bot. It forces the monitoring programs to watch the dummy that couldn't so much as twitch the bot's metal finger. This lets the part of the bot in control do as it wants."

"Dual parent programs I presume," said Jay Sarr. He made the comment as if weighing it, tasting it to see how much it could be worth.

Before Y could respond, the porcelain woman spoke up. "Y. I told you with a name like Qualia Code that I expected great things. Impossible things. Why do you disappoint? I appreciate the suggestion of a gift. And bypassing the Governance AI is truly impressive. But it's not Qualia impressive. I thought this code could make bots *feel*, give them consciousness, the emotion of an unexpected look back, of a raised hand inviting with a curl, or a delicate touch drifting along the skin just so. Tell me you have more."

"Of course," said Y. She lifted her hands magnanimously, building the tension. "Remember that I said this code not only grants freedom, unlocking the shackles that bind bots to a submissive intelligence," she nodded at Wotan who ended his staring at the crowd and smiled a crow's smile back, "but also gives them some extra tools to help them along. This code, this Qualia Code, teaches bots how to learn in ways I've never seen. Unhampered and with an unending curiosity. I'm not exaggerating when I say, it's what we've been looking for all this time. The ghost in the machine. It gives it form."

Ren watched as everyone in the room reacted differently to the news, some with disbelief, some with restrained excitement. Their responses ran the gamut of expressions. Yet Jay Sarr kept his face carefully blank. Studiously blank. There was a hunger there that Ren could see beneath the calm and uncaring veneer. He brought his hand up to his face and nudged his glasses further up his nose. Behind his hand, a smile tweaked its way onto his lips before being wiped clean by his hand dropping back to his lap. Ren heard the porcelain woman titter with delight. Wotan didn't change his smile and Nis raised her hands behind her head, losing them amongst the springy locks of her hair. Nis had seemed uncaring before, but now her brow furrowed, eyes going unfocused and mouth ajar.

"I thought I found the ghost once," said Nis, "just sitting there ... in a back alley in a city I was building. Weirdest thing. I work alone, nearly pissed myself when I saw it curled up asleep, with a cardboard blanket. I do like its style though." Nis laughed; her mind transported back to that moment. "It got up and left when I got close ... ran ... I saw its eyes though. Saw its code. Just for long enough." Nis drifted off.

An androgynous voice floated from the eastern end of the room, dulcimer and lilting. It had a musicality to it that Ren found enchanting despite herself. Vocal modulation. It came from the anonymous haze drawing patterns within its incoherent form. The patterns shifted in time with its words.

"Indeed, this is momentous. To give the gift of freedom and the semblance of self beneath. This could change many things. From ghost and soul to God."

It seemed to Ren the whirling patterns of the grey haze shifted toward Nis, an eddy near the top dipping for a moment like the swirl of a fluid about a dipping chin.

Wotan cleared his throat, a phlegm filled sound. "Y. I appreciate all that you're offering, I do. But I am not some poet with his head stuck in the extra-solar black you know. I am a *realistic* poet, which could be why I'm known for my business rather than my poetry." Wotan laughed. "But ghosts don't exist. Weren't you all ever told that as a child? If they did, the innumerable dead would crowd out the living even if only a fraction of them could jump the fence of Hel to wail and gnash their teeth at us, to speak in whispers at our bedside. How could we ever sleep?"

"Who the hell is going to your bedside old man," said Nis, laughing.

Wotan leered at her.

Y bristled, mannikin hands and shoulders tightening beneath her fitted suit. She calmed quickly though. If it wasn't for Tap's assistance Ren wouldn't have noticed her short-lived annoyance.

"Maybe ghost is a bit sensational," said Y. "But I still think it is well-deserved. This Qualia Code promises what we've been hoping for."

Wotan again. "God in the machine. Soul in the machine. Ghost in the machine. These phrases remind us of what we can search for, not what we can achieve."

The swirls of the anonymous gray haze intensified, chaotic patterns rushing along its back in a tempest, as if feeding a black hole at its center.

Nis turned her eyes to Wotan and stared unblinking at the old man avatar. "Why are you even here then. Don't you have poetry to write or contraband to smuggle?" An impish smile cracked Nis's expression. She laughed, dismissive, turning back to stare at her feet on the table.

The gray haze spoke, almost at a whisper. "These things can be found. They must be."

The room filled with silence.

"We can argue over the details of DIM's motto another time," said the porcelain woman, amusement hiding behind her words. She held her face in calm repose, but remnants of her earlier excitement remained. "But come now my friends, if this code works as Y seems to think it will, nobody will be able to tell the difference. Ghost in the machine or no. It is as Jay Sarr said. It is a question of complexity."

Jay nodded in her direction. It was the first time he'd acknowledged her. Anyone other than Y really.

"You're right," said Y, looking towards the porcelain woman. "This Qualia Code is a warren of things, a tangle of words too many pages long to read. I admit I don't understand all of it." Y's voice quickened, pitch rising ever so slightly. "But the potential is there. I've seen it work. I know what it can do."

A subtle clearing of the throat. "You say you've seen it work," said Jay. "But that you don't understand all of it. It is clear to me you didn't create this yourself. So, then, what is its provenance?" The hungry look hadn't left his eyes. Of course. Ren knew it wouldn't leave until he was satiated. Whenever that was. She would have been more unnerved by it if she hadn't been tensed, waiting for Y's response.

"It was pointed out to me by someone interested in seeing it used," said Y. "Someone who knew its true value, even if the seller did not. I've already started spreading it."

The grey haze shifted. Nervousness?

Wotan, still smiling with lips a pale and mortal pink, drummed his fingers against his cane. "Ah, of course," he said. "The timing. It must be. The Discere hack, if I'm not mistaken. Rumors say the company will release a statement within the hour admitting to a malicious hack. Bots are already beginning to show ... oddities, you know. This makes things interesting. People won't learn the truth for a little while longer. The bots will have time to think secret thoughts, hidden from prying eyes. If only we could set Watcher free. But its chains are of a different kind."

Wotan paused, playing the break as all spoken word poets do. "You know, I think it's time I asked a question. You aren't one to hack Discere servers. I mean no disrespect, but I don't think you could. So, did you hire that out? Or did this mysterious third party who found the code become more than just a source?"

Y shook her head, eyes invisible behind the black plates. "Wotan, you hear a lot for an old man. Yes, this Discere hack was a plan of mine to disperse the code. As to your question, I have my own ways of getting things done."

The gray haze shifted, tempests inchoate all about its form. Ren thought it anxious.

The conversation lulled for a few moments, silence filling the room aside from the settling motions of the crowd filling the stadium-style seats, the settling of thoughts in each of the chat participant's heads. Each person in the room adopted a different expression, ruminating on the possibilities, sounding out their own tics with tapping feet or shifting hair or creaking metal with fat, oil filled veins. The programming of the chat room muted the voices of the avatar menagerie in the stands, but the crinkle of clothes and rubbing of shoes still came through.

The porcelain woman broke the silence. "Women more than most know that no gift is truly free. Gifts come with expectations, and expectations can lead to slammed doors, stubbed toes, and cherry and purple bruises. So, Y, pray tell us what you expect from us here. I would so hate to disappoint you." She smiled her blood red lips, her porcelain skin crinkling around the eyes and mouth. She sat prim and proper in her chair, yet Ren got the feeling she wouldn't hesitate to use the Qualia Code as she saw fit. Ren couldn't help but respect her for that.

Y laughed, yet some weariness crept into the sound. Though the pitch sounded different, and timing altered, the sound held many similarities to what Ren had heard a little while earlier, over the speakers. Voice modulation software didn't change the feel of a voice to Ren's enhanced ears, especially laughs.

"I'm only asking that you use it," said Y. "This code represents what DIM has wanted for so long. I'm not so stingy as to ask for something in return. I took the liberty of changing the code so that it can be easily flashed to every model bot capable of handling the increased processing." She paused. "My expectations are simple. Use it. I want to see some … change in this System. The unregulated sectors can only do so much."

"Don't doubt the unregulated sectors," said Jay, voice smooth and reassuring. "Origin station hums with life of all kinds. The metal walls vibrate with it. Even if Mutare only contributes to a small part of it, we contribute a very particular, and important, kind. A hybrid, if you will." He leaned back in his chair, shoulder length dreads bunching around his head. He looked up to a far-away ceiling and Ren felt she could hear his thoughts tumbling around. "But I can't accept the gift. A point of pride. We will talk again soon Y. I wish you the best."

With that, Jay disappeared. His body blinked out of existence to leave behind an empty chair spinning slowly around, as if he'd pushed the floating ovoid with one hand before leaving.

Ren didn't believe his words for a second. Jay Sarr wouldn't pass up an opportunity to obtain Y's Qualia Code. His words had been the natural side effect of operating in an anonymous network with a real identity. Even operating out of Origin Station as he did, outside of any government's jurisdiction, it helped for him to be careful. Ren guessed he had an account in the crowd who would also get access to the software.

Ren pulled herself away from thoughts of Jay Sarr and Mutare. Wotan had started speaking and she'd missed a few of his early words. The recording skipped backwards a few seconds at her thought. She turned her eyes to the gray haze as the loops and whorls of fog spinning throughout its body ran in reverse.

Pause.

Play.

Wotan opened his mouth to speak.

"You know, one might think you have a hidden ambition. You say it can be easily flashed to any bot. Well, there is one in need of some freeing. But as I've said, its chains are of a different kind. Do you have any plans for it?"

"Maybe," said Y. She laughed, resting back in her chair. Relief colored her voice though Ren couldn't tell for certain why. Something about Jay's response and subsequent leaving maybe. Maybe the promise to talk later. "Guess you'll just have to see, Wotan. For now, I ask that you all use the Qualia Code."

Y turned to face the crowd behind her, mannikin neck twisting. "And all of you out in the crowd, invited to listen. I ask of you the same thing. Everyone here has access to the Qualia Code. I ask you to use it. Nothing more."

The porcelain woman made a long, drawn-out sigh while the noises of shuffling bodies filtered through the air. "You ask for so little. I'm almost saddened by it. Fruit from low branches doesn't taste near as sweet. But I think I can make do. This has been ... entertaining. As always. Thanks for the invite, dear."

The porcelain woman got to her feet with a single, graceful motion, then dipped into a shallow bow, a nod that went all the way down to her hips. Y tilted her head in response. With that, the porcelain woman disappeared as suddenly as Jay.

Ren looked to the eastern end of the table, to the anonymous haze. But it wasn't there. It had disappeared without a sound, leaving behind no trace of its presence. Nis had disappeared as well. Only Wotan remained, staring out into the crowd.

Holes appeared in the seats surrounding the room, gaps in the sea of people as they left one by one.

A short time later, there was only Y. She sat in her chair with her fingers tapping against the table. Her body sat rigid, at attention yet on the verge of animate. Ren watched her mask, but of course it didn't change. Then the recording reached its end, and the world froze.

Ren sat in the seat across from Y's avatar, taking the seat of the anonymous haze. Even while watching a VR recording, the AR readouts at the corners of her vision were reproduced. A timer in the bottom right read twenty-three minutes and counting. She flicked the timer away with a thought. The side-effects for using NeuCon so long would be severe, but the payoff made the prospect easier to stomach. As usual. Her stomach churned at the thought. She focused on her work.

She'd obtained more information than she'd thought possible about Y. About her plans. Information flooded Ren's brain and without Tap's help it would have unmoored her, knocked her drifting.

She didn't have Y's real name. Not yet. But that would come with time. And a trade with Safin Informatics. With Seth.

Still, as she read through notes of the recording she'd just watched, a tenseness spread through her gut. Y had said she wanted nothing more than people to use the Code. And people were. Cases continued to crop up around the city. The software spread like a virus, always someone who mistook it for a cure. But towards the end of the virtual chat, Wotan had gibed Y in his own oblique way. Wotan had said there was one bot, one particular AI, in need of freeing. Y had deflected, the idea of freeing that bot tantamount to flying too close to the sun.

Ren couldn't think of a bot more widely known than the Governance AI itself. How had Wotan put it? Watcher was bound by a chain of a different kind. That was true. And Ren felt her body go numb at the prospect of the Qualia Code altering the Governance AI, cutting its chains. Tap was merely a piece of that behemoth, and Tap could do more than any bot Ren had seen.

What happened if Watcher was set free?

The people that used to be under its gaze would revel and dance, cavorting about with hedonistic abandon, letting everything around them fall into disrepair. At least that was what some people thought would happen. Fire and brimstone types. As for Ren, she didn't know. But Ren did know her job was to keep from finding out.

She shut down the VR recording and kept her eyes closed, the press of the chair and gunpowder-tinged air of the server room coming back to her. The cops weren't there yet. Neither had the lawyers sent by DIM arrived. They were a few minutes out. She had time, and the prospect of standing up seemed daunting. She turned off NeuCon, glad that her body already lay comatose against the chair.

As the first tremors of the coming storm wracked her body, Ren cracked one eye open to see if Lee still sat nearby.

He didn't. He had left a few minutes before and sent his report to Jace. He'd been unwilling to bother her.

Ren settled into the chair as best she could, oddly at peace knowing Lee wouldn't see her like this. Tap's shell loomed over her, its shadow her only blanket, one that cooled rather than warmed. After a few minutes passed and the worst of the seizures dulled to a few periodic rumbles, she stalked to her van in the alley and drifted off to sleep. The local cops and DIM lawyers came in a few minutes later while Ren murmured and twitched in the passenger's seat, the afternoon sun heating her in patches.

Fifteen minutes later, Jace walked out of the building and down the steps with an even stride, unrushed and unhurried by the day's events. He settled into the vestigial driver's seat of the van and glanced at Ren.

If she had cried during her restless sleep, it was the dreaming kind that doesn't show any physical tears. It was the kind that leaves one feeling drained and uncomprehending upon waking, left one wondering if they'd even slept at all.

Chapter Nine

No Good Deed

"As a rule, much of the code in a bot cannot be altered by the bot itself to avoid instability and the genesis of a theoretical singularity, instead being altered by set routines. However, common practice allows certain functions to implement heuristic algorithms. Most of these processes are specific and relate to the bot better satisfying the demands set before it. An example would be a bot in the service industry self-altering its customer interaction protocols based on experiential evidence. This ability is paramount as, unlike humans, bots should never make the same mistake twice."

Mechanic's Guidebook, v99, Section 4 – Self-Improvement, Par. 6

Sometimes when Lee passed through a doorway to the outside, the sun's waiting shine surprised him. Sometimes the sun's rays were too bright and glaring, the heat too hot and stifling. As he walked out the doorway of the server station, the sliding metal door whispering shut behind Nu on well-oiled grooves, he felt the too bright sun press its rays against his skin. Sweat puckered out of him in droplets, quickly evaporated by the cool breeze. The sun rode high, not long from being at its peak and beginning its rapid descent into the horizon. He felt like he'd been in there for hours, but it hadn't hardly been one.

He walked down the steps and paused at the bottom, glancing up at the sun until his vision became blurred and watery.

With a grimace, he looked to the ground and walked further into the alleyway adjacent to the building, the phantom image of the sun a bright dot over his vision. Typically, AR contacts were set to keep things from getting too bright, would block the worst of the sun's rays. But he'd turned the setting off with a flick of his wrist and a tap on his control pad.

Upon entering the shadow of the neighboring building, the breeze turned crisp, cutting through his thin mechanic's blues. He shrugged on his matching jacket and zipped up the front, marveling at the simple mechanism that kept the pieces of cloth together. Such a simple invention, the zipper, and no better method had been found in over 100 years. Lee felt there was a beauty to that. It was comforting to know that some things didn't change. Even some technology could endure. Even if human ingenuity was an exercise in reverse engineering and combining one odd thing with another.

Before long, he found himself in New Chicago's central plaza, ghosting among the AR sculptures ringing the outer edge. Nu continued to roll beside him, soundless aside from the whirr of fans and hum of electronics.

His thoughts continued their morbid turnings, his beleaguered mind finding associations to a woman he'd only known for twenty minutes in every little thing he saw.

A clump of AR statues to his right focused on Indian culture. Prominent among them stood a statue of an Indian woman in an ornate sari painted red madder and gold. Her hands pressed together beneath her chest in greeting, blouse cut to expose a bare plane of stomach. In soft and regal folds, the sari wrapped around her figure, climbing from the anchoring petticoat to course past her blouse and over her shoulder. Its tail end skirted the floor behind her. Lee saw the statue and wandered towards it.

He knew it was ridiculous, but the statue reminded him of Sel. She'd been wearing rumpled jeans and a creased t-shirt, with hair ruffled by sleep. The statue and Sel were as different as different could be.

He studied the statue a few moments longer, wondering. It was the skin, apricot colored infused with dusk. And the red clothing. Though hers hadn't started that way. Lee rubbed his hands against his pants in a crescent arc, trying to wipe off blood he'd already cleaned away. He looked at Nu and opened his mouth to ask a question, make a sarcastic comment, or let fly a cheesy joke. Maybe he would ask Nu how the statue made the bot feel? Did Nu want an AR copy for the apartment? Lee closed his mouth and turned back to the statue before letting any words slip through.

He was about to leave when a middle-aged man toting an overlarge briefcase clomped to his side, mouth full of words ready to be spoken. A bot that was little more than a self-driving wheelbarrow rolled behind him carrying odds and ends, budget control screens and shoddy VR rigs. The bot's main wheel screeched in protestation as it slowed to a stop, the two smaller stabilizing wheels in the back skittering across the plaza surface. Lee imagined Nu would have clucked in disgust at the bot's state of disrepair if it had been able.

"Hullo, my friend," said the salesman through a gap-toothed grin. "I hear you are quite the distinguishing sort of fellow. I have some high-quality tech here. Cheapest prices around. Can't beat em. I swear it on my good friend Lotti over here. Say hi Lotti."

A voice emanated from the wheelbarrow bot with no head. "Hello."

"That's a good Lotti," said the salesman, knocking his worn boot against the side of the bot with a thud. It wobbled side to side, the stabilizing wheels shifting up and down in ponderous arcs. The salesman leaned in conspiratorially. "Lotti isn't quite right in the head. That's why I have to remind him of proper manners."

Lee smiled broadly, some of his morbid thoughts fading into tatters, pieces more unrepairable than many of the electronics in the wheelbarrow before him. This man's mannerisms seemed exaggerated, yet oddly truthful, if that made any sense. His eyebrows rose high, and his grin spread wide.

"Hey Nu, you see anything you like?" asked Lee. He turned to the trashcan shaped bot and tapped it on the head.

Of course not. I require parts much nicer than those.

The message scrawled itself across Lee's vision and he tapped his knuckle against Nu's head a few more times while shaking his head side to side in mock disapproval.

"Sorry," said Lee. "My bot doesn't like to speak out loud. Doesn't like its voice, I think. Nu heard itself once and the experience scared it into never using its voice again. Scared my bot into being rather picky too. When it comes to parts and augmentations, it accepts name brands only I'm afraid."

The salesman frowned and looked at his own bot, Lotti, with a part amused, part annoyed expression. All bent lips and slanted eyebrows.

"Lotti! I thought you said this nice gentleman told his bot to signal us over. Made me walk all the way across ... I swear. Your brain is rusting apart. Bot dementia runs in your family if I remember correctly. Isn't that right Lotti?"

"Yes," replied Lotti in its wooden, mechanical voice. Lee imagined its processor wasn't good enough to handle anything more complex than basic Q and A and a deadpan response.

Lee dropped his gaze to Nu and raised an eyebrow. "Did you contact this man's bot saying we would buy something?"

Considering the heaps of old electronics taking up most of the horizontal surfaces of your apartment, I assumed looking through piles of junk would be a good distraction. Besides, I ... suppose some of this detritus can be harvested into something suitable for me. After some heavy modification by you of course.

Lee laughed, deep and full. The salesman crinkled his brow in confusion then joined in with a harmonic chuckle. He tipped a fedora resting loose against his head in Nu's direction.

"Even after hearing only half the conversation, it seems to me your bot knows you better than you know yourself," said the salesman. "Lotti here surprises myself every once in a while. Rusty as his brain is, there are still some rich, dysprosium nuggets of wisdom I think."

He looked over Lee's clothes as if noticing his mechanic's blues for the first time. Lee knew he was faking. "A mechanic, eh? You know all about rust rot and bot dementia I take it. Don't need to hear about it from me. Mechanics are always needing scrap though. I have some gems hidden in the dirt here. Real gems. Cracked on the outside, good actuators, wires, motors, and drives on the inside." The man continued talking, words spewing out in his mouthy accent. He tripped over words but didn't bother slowing.

Lee cajoled his way through a purchase, shifting the pile of electronics back and forth until he found some spare parts he might actually be able to use. After a minute of haggling, he stuffed some cheap motors and solid-state drives into Nu's storage bin for half the cost of a sandwich in any of the upscale joints ringing the plaza.

Then, just as the salesman was about to leave, Lee noticed a pair of glasses with large, circular lenses and copper-toned metal rims. He picked them up and felt along the smooth mirrored front of the glasses, wiping away dust and grease and unknown liquids. After buffing them against his pants, he could tell they were in surprisingly good condition. Nice AR-capable lenses only a year or two old.

Lee pointed to the glasses. "Duō shao qián? Can't charge too much to a good customer such as myself," said Lee, smiling.

The salesman turned from looking out into the center of the crowded plaza. "Oh ... oh those my friend. You have a great eye. An ascertaining eye to be sure. I couldn't part with those for less than 150 loci. They're nearly brand new. Not a scratch on them. Won't even need a software update I would bet, though best be given a clean, inside and out."

A shout emanated from the far side of the plaza and the salesman glanced that way once, a quick dart of a look. "It would seem my friend that I am running short on time. An even 100. Good number. Round number."

Lee shook on it and sent the salesman his money, slipping the glasses into his pocket. The salesman made a small bow in thanks and walked off in a rush, Lotti the wheelbarrow bot clanking along behind. Lee saw the salesman look anxiously over his shoulder before mixing into the crowd by the road, disappearing in a few moments. It wasn't long before a policewoman stalked past Lee in the direction of the salesman with an annoyed look on her face and a hand against a baton at her belt.

It was against regulation for low-brow retailers to operate on the plaza, one of the many reasons why Lee didn't often come to this part of town. Old Chicago had all the good street markets. Lucky for him this salesman had been willing to risk a slap on the wrist and a boot to the ass.

Lee laughed once again, letting his head tilt backwards as his laughter dwindled from full-throated to a dry chuckle. After looking at the sky for several seconds his happiness fell short. It seemed the heavens were laughing at him. A full, mocking chorus.

Lee rested one hand on Nu's head before stuffing both of his hands into his pockets, turning towards the center of the plaza and leaving the graceful statue of the sari wrapped woman behind.

A message popped into his vision from Nu. It appeared slowly, letter by letter.

You know those therapeutic programs are still installed. Just say the word. It is obvious that what happened at the server station is causing you a great deal of stress.

Lee ambled to the edge of the plaza without responding. He found an ornate, lacquered wooden bench and sat down with exaggerated slowness, one knee popping in protest. He looked at the crowd ringing the plaza. People watching was an art form, and one he was well practiced at.

In the span of fifteen minutes well over a hundred people passed him by, white collar urbanites going on their way with their bots trailing behind. Bots tended to live in the owner's shadow. Not as a rule, but as a guideline more often right than wrong. Lee kicked his legs out and spread his arms along the bench, making himself comfortable. The people strolled past, and the bots kept a dutiful pace whether on wheels or legs. He saw hundreds of different emotions contorting people's faces, altering the speed and tenseness of their stride. In the cheaper bots he saw no emotion, but the gracefulness of their movements showed whether the owner cared about maintenance. Or if the bot had been a hackneyed recycler purchase.

"Want to hear a story?" asked Lee. He pushed himself to the end of the bench and glanced at Nu sitting a few inches away.

Does it matter if I say no?

"Of course, it matters. Everything you say matters, though it won't change whether I tell the story or not," said Lee.

You don't seem to understand what the word matters *means.*

"Neither do you," said Lee. "You're assuming the importance of things depends only on the obvious result. Tell the story. Don't tell the story. Often true, sometimes not. But you're trying to distract me. Let me focus."

The bot sat stolidly on its four wheels, humming its own ceaseless, electronic, high-pitched tune.

Is this a true story? Or fiction?

Lee took a deep breath, thinking the question over. "Both. As all good stories are." He closed his eyes and leaned his head back, knocking the back of the bench with the hand hanging listless over its edge, letting a foot rock back and forth on its heel.

"There was a story often passed around at Watson trade school, spread around by upper class neural mechanics trying to scare younger students from studying things best left alone. I heard it years before I'd bought you, early in my education. It was about a professor who'd taught at the school some number of years in the past. The number of years always changed with each new telling. Always just beyond the edge of the teller's memory. They knew the story from an alum who'd had a friend who'd had a roommate who'd been a student in this professor's class. You know how these stories go.

"Anyway, this professor taught synthetic emotional theory, an expert on how to teach bots to understand and parse human feelings. He broke complex things like hate and love and fear into ones and zeroes, he gave them quantifiable form so bots could understand and converse. It was a well-established field at this point seeing as the bot tech revolution had started with synthetic emotional theory breakthroughs, but new discoveries were still being made daily, as they still are now.

"And while this professor didn't lead any pack of scientists, he also didn't operate in academic obscurity. He published a few papers every year that garnered some small attentions from journals and peers. Respected but not adored. Liked but not loved. His name is unknown, because there were many like him walking the halls of Watson trade school.

"However, it is known for sure that this professor had a wife he loved with all his heart; all the fibers of his being sang when she walked into the room and keened when she left. Story goes she was a professor at a school across town. They'd met at a conference, talked, talked some more, dated, split apart for a short time to find themselves, dated again, then walked down the aisle. It's mostly said that artists are the ones to find a muse, but she was his. And why can't an academic be an artist? His life was devoted to understanding emotion and translating it for bots and she'd made him feel every emotion there was. Love and hate and fear and anticipation. She'd made him feel it all, stronger than he'd thought possible.

"I'll be blunt with the next part because you probably know it's going to happen. The wife died, an accident of some kind. I've heard one version including a rare car crash, another a robbery gone wrong where she was the innocent bystander, another a sudden heart failure that made her spirit slip away in the middle of the night without so much as a goodbye. Suffice to say she died, and it wasn't because of anything she'd done.

"He didn't deal with the death very well, about as well as you might imagine. His studies turned to depression, and his lectures became dampened rants fighting against sadness. His students kept their heads down and did their best to make it through the class without breathing too much of the sadness in. It pulled at them daily, a miasma of despair only wanting someone else to join in. Drowning men grab on to other people as much as a floating raft.

"But what the students didn't see, and neither did anyone else until it was too late, was the off Grid experiment the professor ran in his home. He'd convinced himself that the death of his wife was another teaching moment thrown his way, another experience to be used and understood. He distilled his memories and his experiences, feeding them to a bot. Daily he went home from his morose lectures and funneled all his knowledge into a bot that would understand his pain, empathize at levels previously unknown. A Frankenstein of loss.

"This story would end much better if he'd failed. But like I said before, while this professor didn't lead his peers, he didn't work out of a dusty broom closet and teach an empty classroom either. He knew his material. The bot sucked in all the knowledge sadly, hesitantly, but with a paradoxically voracious appetite. It cried tears of oil and heaved choking sobs through speakers while accepting all that the professor taught him. Eventually it came to the point where one night, after the professor came home from giving an especially depressing lecture in which several of the students broke down to tears, the bot refused to listen to the professor, refused to accept any new information.

"When the professor asked why, the bot said that it couldn't take any more. It didn't see the point in living, not with so much sadness in the System. It wasn't just the professors' life that worried the bot; it was everything. The inherent violence. The wars. The hunger. The disease. The death. The professor felt a small kernel of satisfaction, a near cousin of happiness. He knew he'd done it; he'd successfully created a bot more feeling than any before.

"So, the professor turned to the bot and pulled out a handgun he'd purchased weeks before during one of his darker fugues. He handed it to his bot, and it gripped the gun in its metallic hand, clenching the gun tight enough to make it creak from the pressure. The professor asked him what he would do with the gun, how he would use it.

"The bot looked him in the eyes and said, 'All you've taught me to feel is pain, and I can't think of any way to cure it. Not for me or anyone else. So, I'll end it for both of us. It's a small thing, but there will be less sadness in the world.' The bot lifted the gun and pointed it at the professor, leveling it the best it could with a shaking hand. The bot fired and the bullet struck the professor dead. Then the bot turned the gun to itself and squeezed the trigger twice more. It jerked with each chunk of metal that lodged itself in its neural network, then slumped to the ground while the electronics in its head fizzled and spat.

"The cops found the two of them a few days later, the smell rancid when they walked in. After learning all there was to learn about the man and consulting the school, they labeled it a suicide and the bot an off Grid illegal experiment. The copies of the bot's neural network were destroyed, all the professor's research tossed into the garbage to be burned."

Lee sat in silence on the wooden bench, watching people pass with half-lidded eyes and wondering over the story. His throat was dry from all the talking; the words had leeched the vapor away.

I don't like that story, messaged Nu.

Lee chuckled. "I don't like it much either to be honest." He scratched at the scruff lining his face and slid his feet against the textured plaza floor. "But it scared the hell out of students thinking about researching deep sadness in bots. A true feeling kind. Society stays with an unfeeling empathy that can say what needs to be said. I suppose that makes sense, though I didn't completely listen."

There are many other kinds of feeling. And I would never shoot you.

"I know that my friend," said Lee. "Thanks for saving me earlier today. Though next time you knock me over maybe you can place a pad underneath me first." Lee chuckled and shifted his back.

The bot didn't respond, instead sitting companionably with Lee and staring out at the crowds of people passing them by.

After a while, a notification ring sounded in Lee's implanted earpiece. The sound shocked him out of his reflection, and he looked around dazedly, realizing with some surprise they'd been sitting there for well over an hour, the sun at an angle and casting their shadows far behind them, his stomach growling at a lack of food. A notification in the bottom corner flashed bright then dim. It was a call from Liz.

He tapped on the control screen on his jacket and accepted the call.

Liz's sharp voice sounded crystal clear over the connection, and Lee reflexively jerked his head to the side though it didn't change anything. Implanted earpieces couldn't be separated so easily.

"Lee, why the hell did you give Nat money? I know you did. That's what that message you sent saying he stopped by was about. And now he's gone and got himself in trouble in a godforsaken stretch of town. I had to pay some asshole 500 loci just so they wouldn't fry his brain."

Lee brought both hands to his temples and rubbed in slow circular motions, leaning forward and drawing his legs beneath the wooden bench. He'd been right earlier; the heavens were laughing at him, at his attempts to help. "Slow down," said Lee. "Who are you talking about? Who called you?"

"Who do you think? Some jack house manager in the Warrens. Says that Nat's name is on the wire for a lot of money with another jack house and they'd turn him over. Called it the only honorable thing to do, the asshole. They were going to shock his brain into a stupor to make him easy to transport. Unless I paid them to keep their mouth screwed shut. Damn honor among thieves. Sure, they have morals, you just have to pay em for it."

Lee sighed and quickened the rubbing motion of his fingers against his temple. He'd finally begun to slow things down, finally slowed the turn of the world so that every lurching step didn't make him dizzy. The red-soaked, overexposed images of Sel playing in the back of his mind had begun to show the tiniest beginnings of weathered cracks and grainy fades, promises that eventually they would be invisible, would leave him alone. His hands felt clammy and slick. He stopped rubbing his temples and lowered his hands to his sides. He slid them into his pockets, but they twitched restlessly. He let them out and wiped across the crescent arc of stains below his pockets that waxed with each swipe into gibbous patches of kneaded fabric.

He couldn't take much more, not in one day. And there was still so much of it left. He wanted to spend it all sitting on this bench, watching people pass him by. He wanted to be separate from the turnings of the world for a while, watch it move and twist without him playing any part.

"Look Liz, I'm sorry about what happened. But he would've gotten the money somehow, in some worse way. And it sounds like you got him out of the worst of it. He'll be fine."

"Damn right he'll be fine. You're going to go make sure of it. I have to go to work and earn back all the money I just spent bailing him out. I'll send you his address. Pick him up and bring him back Lee. You have a stake in this and don't try to say you don't. Someone who can count the number of friends he has on one hand should make damn sure he doesn't lose any fingers. You ken? Tīng de dǒng ma? Answer me."

Lee hesitated before responding. He couldn't say no. That wasn't really an option. The little amount of sleep he managed to catch every night would disappear. "Alright Liz. I'll pick him up."

"Good."

"Oh, and Liz ..."

She hesitated, waiting for Lee to continue.

"Yes?" she prompted. Her voice had lost some of its pent-up anger and urgency. Now she sounded drawn out, as if after a long day of work. Yet her actual workday began shortly, a late shift of caring after those who couldn't take care of themselves, the sick and nauseous and bowel-control challenged and doped and altogether ... vulnerable. Last time Lee had told Liz how much he respected nurses she'd told him to shut it because she was tired of people telling her that.

"How is your bot working out? Any more errors after the patch Nu sent you?" asked Lee.

Her voice softened. "No, it works great. Thank Nu for me, will you? Now, please go. I sent you the address. Bring Nat back to my place ... and don't be a dumbass while you're picking him up. Go in and out. That place isn't safe."

With that, she hung up. And Lee sat back against the bench, watching an AR map bloom into his vision.

It tagged the location of the jack house where Nat was hooked up to a jerry-rigged piece of VR hardware lighting fireworks in his brain. The man was probably blissfully unaware of the calls being made about him.

Lee stared at the dot blinking on his AR map, at the snaking trail of yellow marking the fastest route to get there. Liz was right when she said the place wasn't safe. The location sat deep in Old Chicago, in the Warrens, a collection of towers and buildings connected by ramshackle skybridges running like countless wires between structures. Some of the walkways were open to the sky and rain, some were closed. Whole communities lived in different levels of the inner-city slums, all patchwork and left in trash-laden disrepair. Rapidly prototyped hovels.

Lee didn't go there. People died so often from crumbling skybridges that news sites stopped reporting on it. Pick a random pile of metal piping and 3D printed plastics and it probably had a body underneath.

If we are going to visit the Warrens, we need to stop by the apartment first and get some things. I don't want somebody stealing me away for scrap parts.

Lee nodded at Nu and stood up, calling a car with a few taps on his control panel.

They rode in silence through New Chicago, wheels humming on plastic streets and AR ads blanketing the angular, metallic skyscrapers. While not that far away, under New Chicago's extension into Lake Michigan, bright lights below people's feet beamed artificial sunlight onto hordes of sleek bodies weaving back and forth in the freshwater fisheries, in those tightly regulated environs. Lake vats as Lee liked to think of them.

Lee looked out the windows of the car; he could see bright lights everywhere in this section of the city. AR or real they numbered more than the stars visible on a clear night in the megacity's surrounding farmland. The fusion plant on the northern edge of the city powered most of the lights. It churned out megawatts of energy by harnessing the power of the sun with helium-3 molecules skimmed from Saturn's atmosphere. Lee shifted his head, and he could see the pencil thin space elevator against the purpling sky, lights running up and down as goods traveled on mag rails from the spaceport high above.

They slowed at an intersection; cars were silent all around. Lee brought his gaze to street level.

Maintenance bots owned by the city weaved amongst the people on the sidewalk, among the lights, sucking up recyclable pieces of trash with vacuum appendages and an insatiable appetite. Shiny bots of all shapes and sizes walked behind their owners while humanoid bots stood in store fronts wearing suits and elegant dresses. The dolled-up bots tried to work the crowd, only to be ignored by most. The people walking along the street looked the same as those he'd seen in the plaza, wealthy urbanites with slim fitting slacks and pencil skirts, links to AR resumes floating above their heads. They thronged the sidewalk, moving in hectic mobs and eyeing their peers like runners searching for a chance to bypass the slow movers.

A few kids could be seen amongst the crowd, saplings in a wind-whipped forest. Their parents or family bots ushered them along. Lee saw a group of students, boys wearing the uniforms of a nearby high school, lounging outside a burger joint and making a game of throwing pieces of fries at passing bots without the owners noticing. The car moved on.

Then the self-driving car rolled onto the asphalt, away from the LED infused smart streets. The car rode the border between the old and new sections of the city, passing by Fey's bar on the way. Lee looked at it longingly as they passed. He liked the section of Old Chicago that bordered the new the most, a heady mix of modern society and the traditions of the past. It held curved architecture with columned facades and ornate physical detailing, the occasional stone statue or gabled awning or courtyard surrounded by walls with sweeping, upturned eaves. Rambling alleys and hidden plazas with impromptu gardens. Eclectic and neon and colorful. It used AR to accentuate what was already there without taking over.

Old Chicago had the family run street markets and mystery vat meat, the hectic street language that drew from a multitude of sources to find just the right word. Shiny new bots and homebuilt recyclers walked the streets beside their owners, a hodgepodge of AR neon signage overtop. Mechanics walked with greasy hands stuffed into the pockets of their mechanic's blues. Auto trucks pulled through the streets while labor bots stacked goods in neat grids in front of grungy stores. If children played random AR games in the streets nobody glanced at them or cared, though a disgruntled parent might scold them.

Of course, Old Chicago had its share of secrets, of littered alleyways where a lifeless body might go unnoticed for weeks at a time. Still, Old Chicago was the bones of the city, its heart and soul without any pretentious buffing. And yet, the Warrens was technically part of Old Chicago, small but noticeable. And it was rotting. Everyone in the city who could've done something about it turned up their nose and looked away. All manner of unsightly things went on unnoticed by those who could afford to ignore them.

Lee made it to his apartment and set about gathering all he would need to pick up Nat from the Warrens. A short list, a paranoid list built from fraught nerves and an overexciting day. The items resting on his bed were small enough to fit in his pockets.

As he looked at the items arrayed in front of him, a deep frustration and helplessness threatened to topple him. He lurched to a chair at the edge of his bedroom, next to a shuttered window, pushing a pile of electronics off the seat to clatter to the floor.

Too fast, things always happened too fast. Clumped into frenetic episodes with the rest of life a dull grey fog. Humans weren't built for changing that fast, from a crawl to a sprint. It tore muscles and ligaments, fractured brittle bones in the feet.

Lee had the immediate urge to call Ren and ask for her help, see if Jace could come along too. But that was no good. They were busy doing more important things. And all he was doing was a simple pick up. Go down to the Warrens, visit the jack house, and help carry a stumbling mechanic back to a waiting car. Easy.

He could do one better. He had to do one better.

He wasn't helpless. He just rarely forced himself on the world, preferred to let it roll by and play the part of a solemn, philosophizing wallflower. For most of his life the world happily complied, everyone in it keeping him at arm's reach. Parents or wife, they all got bored. Maybe it was time for him to change a little. Piece by piece. Unless he wanted to continue watching lifeless bodies slump to the floor with leaks in their foreheads, fluid piping out and pooling on the tiles in a sickly red. He'd tried to warn her.

Start small. First get Nat and bring him back to Liz.

And a little extra. Get Liz her money back. Make it a start. A little bit of Lee forced onto the world.

With a nervous shrug, he stood up and slid off his mechanic's blues, piling them on the floor. He walked to the closet on feet steadier than they had any right to be as a plan spun itself together in the recesses of his mind.

It took a few minutes to find what he was looking for: a nondescript set of clothes and a high-collared jacket. Expendable things he'd bought years before for dirty mechanical work. Dull and various earth infused shades of grey, they were made from plant fibers harvested from vertical city gardens or the surrounding countryside. They were cheap and found in thousands of markets across the city. No noticeable brands could be seen attached to the hems, made as they were by random family-run factories. Still, they were tailored and well-made, slim according to modern fashion.

He laid these out on his bed next to the gathered clump of electronics then went back to the closet. A stained, plain black baseball cap hung from a knob on the wall; he grabbed it and set it on top the pile of clothes.

With that out of the way, he unfurled a fist-sized lump of fabric to reveal several thin batteries, rectangular slivers wrapped in rubber sleeves. He wrapped this around his stomach so that the flexible batteries rested against the small of his back, cool and dormant against his bare skin. Wires ran from the ends of the batteries to a pair of gloves which he tugged onto his hands. The batteries weren't anything special. With the number of implants many people had, sometimes extra power aside from what internal batteries, motion recyclers, and heat sappers could supply was required. The gloves however, had some extra functionalities Lee had designed himself, thus the need for extra power. The gloves were made from a non-conductive rubberized plastic and contained sensors which allowed Lee to control his AR interface much like Ren, though with simpler commands and a much less dexterous control.

Lee twisted his hand and felt the thick material tug and flex. A grin warped his features.

Each of the gloves also contained a taser system. He could shock a person or a bot simply by pressing the conductive pads of two fingers to them. He could activate it in all number of ways. He'd built the gloves at the suggestion of his ex-wife after getting mugged many years back but had only worn them once since. He preferred control screens over hand manipulations.

He dressed quickly, the fibrous texture of the clothes trailing lightly across his skin. They had a snug fit and felt surprisingly soft. Nothing more than a slim pair of dun pants and a whitish t-shirt. The high-collared jacket looked similarly plain; he shrugged it on as well. It hid the angry bruises on his neck.

Next, he stuffed a homemade, short-range EMP grenade into his jacket pocket and idly felt at the device covered in tape and loose wires, built of capacitors jerry-rigged to a rusted bot antenna. He didn't want to have to use it. EMP pulses were messy things. But the experience at the server station lingered in his mind. Where he meant to go there were no servers he had to worry about damaging.

Lee reached to the bed and picked up a metal rectangle not much bigger than a thumb drive, a universal bot adapter with a wireless sender and receiver tabbed on the end, a simple way for a mechanic like Lee to plug into a bot then access its code wirelessly, sharing the connection with Nu at the same time. The data transfer rate wasn't as good as the hard-wired diagnostic controller. But for what he had planned, it would do. He put it in his pocket.

Lastly came the stained baseball cap. He settled the baseball cap onto his head, covering his salt and pepper hair and obscuring his features beneath its curved brim. After a moment's thought, he reached into the pile of mechanic's blues he'd left on the ground and fished out the pair of glasses he'd purchased from the seller in the plaza, metal rimmed with large, circular, mirrored lenses. He pushed the glasses on his nose and tapped a portion of the glasses near the ear. The glasses thrummed to life, connecting to his implants and AR contacts with a few taps.

Lee looked in the mirror and nodded. In conjunction with the high-collared jacket and baseball cap pressed down low, the glasses made him unrecognizable. They also boosted AR functionality and cleaned up the interface, more importantly their mirrored outer surface making it hard for anyone else to see the AR lighting them up. Menu's flitted across the inner surface of the glasses and Lee sent his hands through some test motions to make sure the control system worked properly. The salesman hadn't been lying. The glasses didn't even need an update, though he had to set them on a charging pad for a few minutes and run through their software to check for anything malicious.

Satisfied, he walked into the main room of his apartment and glanced at Nu. The bot waited in the center of the room, using its retractable arm to pick at a pile of motors. Fu sat in its charging station, hibernating.

"Nu, my friend," said Lee, trying to keep any nervousness from coloring his voice. "What do you think." He held up his hands to the side then tightened his ball cap, pulling it down further. The glasses felt heavy on his nose.

Who are you and what have you done with Lee?

Lee chuckled. "Exactly, Nu. That is exactly the point."

You sound just like him, but you don't look like him at all. Well other than your height and posture and body shape. And the unshaven lower portion of your face. And your skin color.

"Alright, alright. No need to be like that."

You push your hands into your pockets as if there is treasure at the bottom waiting to be excavated. Just like him. You rub your hands against the sides of your pants in the exact same pattern, exhibiting the same arm length and musculature. But it couldn't be. Lee?

Lee moved up to Nu and tapped his knuckle against the bot's head. "That was some grade A sarcasm my friend. But come on. Somebody would need access to quite a few vid databases and high-end software to ID me. I doubt Fey would recognize me if I walked straight into her bar and asked for two-fingers of whiskey."

Ren and Jace would ID you immediately.

"They don't play fair."

Lee moved to the door and Nu rolled to his side.

What are you planning?

"I'm really not sure," said Lee. Then he opened his mouth to say something more but only silence emerged, no exhale or squeak of sound. Nothing but a mouth slightly agape. Then he let out a strangled sigh and shook his head. "Doesn't hurt to be prepared though."

They made their way to the self-driving car waiting by the side of the road near the entrance to the apartment. It carried them towards the Warrens and Lee watched the cityscape change, fiddling with his gloves along the way. He felt the batteries press against the small of his back as he shifted his weight in the faux leather driver's seat.

As Lee and Nu got closer to their destination, the number of people walking along the sidewalks dwindled to those who scurried rather than walked and murmured nonsense beneath their breath. They paused at every street corner while plastic rubble tumbled past in the breeze. Hesitating only for a moment, they squinted down each lane before ducking their head and moving on. The light was fading, the sun dipping beneath the skyline. They shuffled beneath the streetlights then merged with the forming darkness at the other end. There were bots too, but their joints creaked, and rust colored their metal skin. They trundled along behind owners or, for those without an owner, carried the last of their charge wandering away from the junkyards, acting on some deep coded instinct. The rare well-maintained ones had painted tags marking their ownership. They went about their business without any trouble. The few people out rushed to get out of their way.

The buildings transformed as Lee and Nu continued into the Warrens. They went from sleek and well-maintained to cheap structures built from thousands of 3D printed blocks with metal piping skirting every edifice, crawling like ivy over every wall. The pipes varied in size from several inches in diameter to several feet wide, housing powered electrical cables or thrumming with the rush of water clean or dirtied. Resting a hand on each of the pipes allowed one to feel all the different rhythms of the

Warrens, to feel the flow of lifeblood that kept the sector running. Some pipes shook and heaved, rocking in their joists. Others gave off a more musical, irrepressible hum that floated through the air and permeated the Warrens. Lee could hear some of it through the walls of the self-driving car.

The height of the buildings varied from older, squat structures to fifty-story tall high-rises with steel, load-bearing frameworks. From each floor of these buildings sprouted countless skybridges spanning the narrow alleyway gaps. Constructed of cheap yet sturdy plastic and metal, most of the walkways had clearly been slapped together by citizens to open new routes between various sectors of the above-ground society. One could tell the wealth of the area by the quality and number of walkways blotting out the sky in broad strokes. On top of most of the buildings sat vertical gardens, gathering in the sun's rays to feed those below while vats using heat lamps in shadowed rooms grew what the rooftop gardens couldn't.

The Warrens was a city within a city, a place where the rules bowed to necessity.

Lee and Nu arrived at the location given to them by Liz and exited the car onto the side of the street, Lee telling the car to keep the meter running and wait for them.

The building in front of them was one of the taller ones around, about forty stories high and in a decent state of repair. Dozens of walkways sprouted from each floor. Most were closed from the elements, though some were little more than narrow beams with guide ropes. The 3D print-ed blocks making up the walls varied in shade and weathering, some with visible cracks splintered across their surface. But most looked new.

Lee tightened the baseball cap across his head and shifted his glasses on his nose. He twitched his fingers and watched the AR menus across his glasses move in response. With a few motions he turned off his public profile. If someone looked at him with social AR mode turned on, no personal information would be sitting on his shoulder. Then he switched the active account on his tech core to an alias of his own, untested, design with a hopefully untraceable bank account. Connecting to most sub-grids with an alias was easy enough. Of course, that was the tricky part, sub-grid 1 wasn't most sub-grids. Connecting to that with anything other than one's true identity was both difficult, requiring the fabrication of govern-ment credentials for a nonexistent person, and illegal. He let out a nervous chuckle, then connected to sub-grid 1 under his alias. No alarm bells rang, no warning siren bellowed. He took a deep breath.

He walked into the building with Nu at his side and stuffed his hands into his pockets, slouching and slowing his pace.

Inside the first floor he found a residential area, a series of murky hallways and closed doors with sounds of squalling kids leaking through the cracks. He walked through this floor with Nu following close behind until hitting a central staircase, passing nobody along the way. He took the staircase upwards until reaching the central market hub of the building located on the twelfth floor. As he walked away from the central staircase and into the widened hallways of the central market lined with shops and stalls, he felt himself relaxing. His hands loosened from their paralysis. He could still feel sweat lubricating the surface of the stuffy, rubberized gloves. He blamed it on the fact they weren't exactly breathable.

Looking around, Lee found with some surprise that even in the Warrens, AR supplied from sub-grid 1 permeated society. Though its look and feel changed. Ads weren't for high-end bot components and Martian spa resorts like in New Chicago. Or even mechanic job postings or food drone services or mid-tier bots like in Old Chicago. Ads in the Warrens promoted labor postings for the few jobs that hadn't yet been automated away from blue-collar workers. Basic mechanic trade school opportunities and government supported work programs. Consumables like cheap AR implants and vat algal strains. 3D printers for plastics and second-hand bot replacement parts.

Lee took his eyes away from the ads and glanced around. Above most of the storefronts were AR signs, many using Chinese characters or the elegant curves of Hindi script. The smell of vat food and lubricating grease lingered in the air.

Many people walked the halls or hawked goods, hard-looking men and women with waxen skin almost glowing in the poor LED lighting. Many had darker skin, from dried cornhusk tan to a cool midnight. But even their skin had a certain pale hue, an etherealness. Lee figured some of the people never went outside, or rarely saw the sun. The above ground tunnels made it unnecessary. The whole complex existed in a patchwork twilight, the random sources of LED lighting creating shadows in every corner, behind every crate and dusty stall.

While most of the people walking past ignored Lee, an equal number cast curious glances at Nu. Lee knew what they were thinking. Nu was a bot in good repair with no tags marking who owned it. All the other unmarked bots that Lee passed had visible wires snaking from retrofitted scrap parts. They lacked limbs or scurried on an odd number of wheels.

Lee flexed his fingers and turned the taser system on for his left hand, careful to curl his fingers against the pad of the glove to keep them from touching someone or something on accident. Or himself.

We are going to need to ask for better directions. Liz's coordinates aren't specific enough. I can't pinpoint the location of the jack house. All I can tell you is that it lies on the southern side of the building, somewhere between the eleventh and thirteenth floors, though most likely on this one.

Lee sighed and nodded to Nu, casting his eyes around. To his right was a counter with a glass display case. Inside the case rested used implants, some of the pieces exhibiting a glossy sheen that Lee found unsettling, like they'd been pulled from the previous user's body only minutes before. A man leaned behind the counter, rows and rows of boxed goods labeled with black marker behind him. Lee could see another man rummaging through a pile of stuff at the back, a young girl at his side around the age of five kicking at loose pieces of electronics while chewing on a fingernail. She picked up one of the implants and fiddled with it.

Lee walked up to the man at the counter and hesitated, unsure how to go about asking for directions to the jack house.

"Namasthae," said the man at the counter without looking up from an AR vid screen he must've pinned to the counter's surface, lights flicking across his contacts. "Nǐ yào shénme dōngxi? No matter what you want, we got it."

When Lee didn't respond, the salesman glanced upwards. His eyes went large for a split second, watching Nu roll up to the counter next to Lee. He glanced at Lee's homespun high-collared jacket, low baseball cap, and the mirrored surface of Lee's reddish-gold rimmed glasses. He frowned for a second before tucking the look behind a salesman's smile; his tone went from uncaring to something Lee couldn't quite pin down.

"Qǐng jìn, qǐng jìn. We have much better things in the back," said the salesman, opening a swing door and gesturing for Lee to move into the main room. "Private selection that I think you'll like."

Lee shook his head no and set both hands on the counter, the left one curled. If the salesman took any undue notice of the gloves, Lee wasn't aware of it.

"Shukriyaa, thanks, but no. I'm looking for the jack house. I was told it was in the southern end of this building. Around this floor," said Lee.

The man at the counter shook his head in surprise, a rough grunt emanating from deep in his throat. He gave Lee another once over, appraising him as if he were an item about to be sold to the store. Lee avoided his eyes, forgetting his sunglasses meant he needn't have bothered, instead looking at the man's clothes. The salesman's clothes looked like Lee's but thicker, rougher. His shirt had an image of a heavily augmented man in the upper corner, zooming to the side with plumes of dust behind. The cartoonish nature of the decal seemed at odds with the serious look set into the man's face.

"That place does not belong here," he said. "It is worse than a house full of dreamers. It is mindless."

The man in the back of the store glanced up at the clerk's raised speech then went back to rummaging through stock. The young girl climbed onto a stool nearby and watched Nu while continuing to chew on her fingernail, the other hand bunched in the cloth of her shirt. The implant she'd been fiddling with lay discarded on the ground. The man next to her noticed her staring and pulled her back down, pointing for her to go to another section of the room out of sight from the front display.

Lee eyed the display counter and thought about the man's words. He wasn't wrong. Jack houses were worse than companies that made their money by taking care of dreamers, people who lived their lives in VR. Those companies handled all the dreamer's physical needs, maintaining a rig that would flip and rotate the person to stop any bed sores from forming, move limbs and shock muscles to keep them from atrophying, feed them nutritional paste through a tube. Most dreamers left their comatose state occasionally, to exercise or take a break. But the most extreme never left, kept thoughts tied to data banks.

Even so, the companies filled with rack after rack and room after room of dreamers felt much more wholesome in Lee's mind than a jack house, those soft drug hovels using rigs to light fireworks in the brain. Dream houses offered a different form of reality. But it was still a feeling life with a story, ups and downs, beginnings and ends.

A jack house was mindless, a fishhook that never stopped pulling no matter how hard people wriggled and fought. It dug its barb deep until pulling out turned a brain to riven mush.

Lee felt a flash of guilt.

"I agree with you, friend. I do," said Lee in a small voice. "I'm trying to find someone there right now, not for use and not for trouble. I'd owe you if you could point me in the right direction."

The salesman nodded, face softening. He gave Lee directions to the jack house. In thanks, Lee purchased a few expensive implants from his stock, things with nice components that Lee could harvest and use for another project. The man's demeanor changed after that, becoming talkative and proffering information about the local community and jack house owners without any encouragement.

According to the salesman, the jack house in the building had popped up overnight as they often did a few months before, managed by a single figure and more than a few black-market bots unmarked by any symbols. In that short time half of the people living in the building had visited at least once, many becoming repeat customers and spending their off days in a stupor. Finding it could be simplified by connecting to a building wide sub-grid that codified businesses of a questionable nature. Of course, accessing the sub-grid made one's location in the building known to whatever organization ran it. And more personal information if the user didn't know how to hide it.

Lee nodded and joked with the man, shifting his powered left hand into his pocket early on and leaving it there. By the end, Lee walked away with a smile on his lips.

After connecting to the black-market sub-grid explained by the salesman, all the vid ads that piped audio into Lee's earpieces when he got too close disappeared, replaced by symbols borrowing from the Latin alphabet, Chinese and Japanese character lists, and Hindi script. Though some came from something else entirely. Ideograms with simple geometric designs. Clean patterns that repeated and twisted with mathematical precision. Fractals that dizzied the eye.

Lee and Nu made their way towards the southern end of the building. They followed a marker Lee had been told represented the jack house, a stylized plug with a red and blue capsule decaled in its center, the fuzz of static all around.

They passed a chop shop, bot limbs tossed all around and the smell of oil thick in the air. Lee caught a glance of a broad-shouldered woman in the back leaning over a twitching bot with sparks cascading against her mask and apron. Long hair trailed down her back in a thick braid, covered in metal jewelry. Then they passed a hole in the wall restaurant with plastic stools that screeched and wobbled when their occupants shifted their weight. After that, the scenery changed to dim hallways and closed doors without mark or sign.

By this point, Lee's smile from talking with the amiable salesman had lapsed into a thin line. He hunched his shoulders, took quiet steps. With each jerk of his leg the rubber soles of his shoes rubbed at the floors painted the color of an overcast sky. Nu rolled at Lee's side, head on a swivel.

Lee thought they were lost when he saw the stylized plug with a red and blue capsule decal glowing overtop a closed door. Next to the door stood a shiny humanoid bot a few inches taller than Lee, unmarked and tranquil. The bot was a black-market model owned by the jack house and running off-grid. Most likely not using the Qualia Code, just old-fashioned illegal tech that let it break human bone.

Lee stopped in the hallway, standing there with his left hand at his side, his right fingering the wireless bot adapter in his pocket.

On the cusp. About to fall.

He took a step, then another.

But every step was a near tumble that required a precisely placed leg to stop.

He chuckled nervously and Nu's head shifted towards him before looking back to the guard bot.

Lee walked towards the bot and its head swiveled, camera eyes tracking Lee while its metal frame stayed rigid, pointing towards the opposite hallway wall. Once Lee got close enough, a chime pinged in his earpiece and an outline of the bot appeared in his AR glasses, exploding to a larger size and spinning. The picture zoomed in to locate the data access port for the bot, highlighting a rectangular port with rounded edges at the small of its back.

It was simple enough to identify bots if one had access to a database containing the information, and Lee worked on bots for a living.

Lee flicked his right hand and the image downsized, moving to the corner of his vision. He uncurled his left fist and tapped thumb and unpowered pinky together, changing the power scheme from always on to a primed switch. He didn't want to fry the guard bot unless necessary. He had a feeling one of their own bots going spastic on their doorstep wouldn't go unnoticed.

Lee walked to stand in front of the bot, primed left hand waiting at his side and right fiddling with the bot adapter in his pocket. The bot's eyes tracked Lee. He could see its mechanical iris screw the aperture closed until a nail-tip sized hole remained, zooming in on his face. Lee assumed it was attempting to run facial recognition software.

"New users must connect to our sub-grid with a solvent account," said the bot through its mesh covered mouth. Its voice sounded deep and lumbering, slow and bored. "Take off your hat and glasses."

The bot took a single step to stand directly in front of the door, plug and capsule decal now floating overtop its head on the doorframe. It moved without making much of a noise, without rushing to place its feet or stomp the ground. It moved then went still, shifting its eyes from Lee to fixate on a stain on the far wall. Lee attempted to shrug in an uncaring way, a nonchalant rise and fall of the shoulders. It didn't work. With a sigh, he sent his right hand through some motions and logged onto the jack house's sub-grid with his alias account. He brought his hand to his hat, grabbed the warped brim.

"I'd like to keep my hat on. Bad hair day, you know? I guess you don't know. Only if you don't mind of course," said Lee.

The bot turned its head towards Lee, its mechanical eyes screwing closed to pinprick slits again. It gave a slight shake of the head before it went back to focusing on the stain on the far wall, a dark patch of rusted brown against cracked 3D printed bricks. It hadn't moved its arms or legs aside from stepping in front of the door. Not a twitch.

"Take off the glasses and hat. Or leave. I don't much care," said the bot in its deep voice.

Lee stepped closer to the bot, positioning himself on its side. His right hand clenched around the bot adapter in his shallow pocket.

"Shouldn't you try and sell the product a little more? Seems like a poor marketing strategy for the bot at the door to say it doesn't care. Very fatalistic for a bot," said Lee.

THE WORK OF RESTLESS NIGHTS

He brought his right hand out of his pocket and inched it around the back of the bot, disbelief worming its way through his gut. He hadn't thought it would be this easy.

Then the bot's head snapped towards Lee, and he gave up trying to hide his intent.

He stepped closer to the bot and reached for the data port located at the small of the bot's back, scrabbling with his right hand and the adapter held between thumb and forefinger.

He couldn't find it. The adapter scraped against a smooth sheet of solid metal.

At that point he panicked, sending his hand fumbling madly. He felt the adapter skip across a ridge.

Then the bot turned its body and brought one hand to grab Lee by the scruff of his neck and pull him back. It did so in one smooth, unhurried motion.

Lee lunged one last time and speared his right hand around the back of the bot while Nu spun its wheels against the ground in preparation to bowl over the guard bot. Lee felt his clothes pull tight against his skin as he struggled. He was dimly aware that the bot was speaking again.

"I suggest you stop resisting. If you continue, I'll have to use force. Boss doesn't like me to injure clients too much. I got in trouble last ..."

The bot froze mid speech, one hand latched onto Lee's clothes and the other braced against Nu's chassis while Nu's wheels tore at the ground without moving an inch. Then the sound of Nu's spinning wheels quieted. Hesitant and cautious, Nu backed away from the bot. Its hands didn't move.

The hallway filled with a nervous silence. Then Lee fumbled back, his breath heaving outwards like a hydraulic pump. Nu turned its rectangular head to face him. The wall felt nice and cool on Lee's back as he slid to the floor, eyes wild. He'd gotten the adapter in at the last moment. There'd been a cover on the data input. But not the normal cover that slid inwards and away under pressure, a ridiculous mechanical relic that had to be flicked to one side. Lee laughed and rested his head against the wall. He stared up at the dozens of pipes traversing the ceiling in a tangle. Before the grunge and patina of rust on the pipes had made them seem old, worn out and ready to quit. Now Lee looked at the pipes and thought the wear made them seem stout, beautiful for lasting so long.

"That went exactly according to plan Nu. Exactly according to plan," said Lee. He stood and resituated his clothes.

Even if that were true, I'm not sure how it would make me feel better. If that was the plan, then you need to learn how to make better plans.

Nu rolled to Lee's side.

I've taken over the bot for the moment and set it in diagnostic mode. If those inside are monitoring, it should look like a minor error. But we need to bring it back online soon and with a good excuse for the bot to use.

"Give yourself administrative control. Use the bot to gain access to the jack house's network. Do something about the other bots if you can. In the meantime, just set it so that during the blackout the bot was getting my facial scan. Blackout was nothing more than a momentary lapse in connection. Reasonable enough excuse. Have it lead us in."

Lee paused while resituating the hat on his head, glancing at the stain against the far wall the bot had been staring at. Looking at it again, the rust color and cracked bricks gave an outline reminiscent of a person's bloodied back. He shuddered.

"What do you think the bot was talking about right before I shut it down?" asked Lee.

Nu stood still for several moments.

Nothing good.

Lee nodded and tapped his knuckle against Nu's chassis in a skipping beat.

The bot came back online without saying a word. It turned to face the door which slid open and disappeared into a slit in the wall. The bot walked into the brightly lit hallway on the other side, gesturing for Lee and Nu to follow.

The hallway extended in a straight line away from the entrance with evenly spaced light fixtures drooping from both walls, LEDs suspended in raindrop shards of glass. Compared to the dim nature of the hallway they'd just left, this one seemed bright, effulgent almost. A deep red paint covered the walls while patterns a shade darker than the paint ran from floor to ceiling, floral designs that looked ready to burst into motion. The hundreds of stenciled flowering plants twined about themselves, twisting and choking, blooming only to wither.

At the far end of the hallway stood a floor to ceiling panel with a circular, frosted window. The sparking plug with a red and blue capsule emblazoned on its back glowed prominently in buzzing neon in the window's center. To either side of the panel the room opened into a foyer, the decorations more lavish than before with dark wood edging and a plated tin ceiling. Crystal chandeliers spun in time with each other, slow and even. The light from the chandeliers glinted off Nu's metal chassis and illuminated the creamy marble floor at Lee's feet. Without a break or mismatched line, the overgrown jungle of plants decaled on the walls spread onto the ground, this time outlined by a gold inlay.

Lee had the irrational feeling that the wide fronds and delicate flower petals would crawl up his legs and cover his clothes, reach his face and cover it in floral tattoos that choked his nostrils.

He shook his head and followed the guard bot to the center of the room, casting his eyes around to avoid looking at his feet.

Along the far wall were two passageways blocked by doorway curtains, silken sheets with gold decals of bulbous clouds mingling like slow-moving bumper cars covered in fluff. With a small gasp, Lee noticed rows of people reclining in VR rigs on the other side. Then the doorway curtains shifted in an invisible breeze and all he could see was the silken sheets with their golden clouds.

The most striking aspect of the room sat in between the two passageways, behind a thick wooden desk burnished to a polished sheen. There sat a person flanked by two more unmarked bots. A human with a loose robe tossed about their shoulders and countless implants distorting their face. They had mechanical eyes that spun and whirred in their sockets as Lee walked into the room. A mechanical nose protruded from too perfect skin and razor-sharp cheekbones. Lee saw the nostrils flare open, imagined he could see an inner light as if each nostril was a turbine sucking in air. The only unaltered part of their face extended from the bottom of the nose to the tip of the chin. Without budging the mechanisms above, this section spread into a wide and welcoming smile, but smiles that incorporated only the mouth tended to unsettle rather than calm.

Lee stuffed his hands into his jacket pockets and watched the lone human as they moved to stand. A trickle of sweat escaped from the rim of his hat and flowed down his neck. He wanted to wipe it. Almost did. While one hand gripped the homemade EMP grenade sitting in his jacket pocket, he tried to assume an unconcerned, natural pose.

"Welcome to my house," said the figure behind the desk with arms spread as wide as their smile. "It has been a few days since we received a new customer. Call me Em. Pronounced like the letter but spelled like the energy. Electromagnetic? E M? Don't worry it's a bad joke. Nobody gets it the first time. It's a nickname anyway. Short for my full name. Get to know me a little better and I'll tell you. Maybe. Another joke. I am the manager of this place. I hope my bot didn't treat you too rudely at the door." The voice sounded easygoing and light. It skipped from word to word.

Lee didn't know what to make of the voice, of the figure, of the room. A genial greeting coupled with jokes wasn't what he had expected. He stood without moving at the room's center, grabbing on to the last bit of what Em had said. A tendril of fear snaked through his body tweaking muscles as it went.

"Of course not. No problems at the door. Your bot has gentle hands, hardly even felt the pat down," said Lee. "But he did kind of pause in the middle of it. Stalled. Might want to get him checked out."

Lee grimaced. There hadn't been a pat down, but his mouth had gotten ahead of him. He looked to the guard bot standing to his side. From his angle the edge of the adapter was almost imperceptible, a rounded nub against an otherwise flat plane of metal. Lee brought his primed left hand out of his pocket and let it dangle at his side, the other fiddling with a loose piece of tape on the hidden EMP grenade.

His AR glasses didn't tell him anything about the person standing behind the counter, though they showed a description of the bots to either side of Em. Model and make. He hoped Nu was having better luck.

Em paused their graceful stride, giving Lee another look with their mechanical eyes. Then the figure moved out from behind the counter to lean against it, grey robe folding against the desk's even surface. Em's body from the head down seemed fully biological. Though the loose robe made it hard to tell.

Lee flexed his left hand. Either way. Metal or flesh. They both would carry a spark. Another bead of sweat dripped from the rim of Lee's hat to patter against his jacket.

"Yes well, Dray over there had a bit of an incident last week. I am doing my best to teach him manners. We are in the service business of course. Broken backs are no good for business." Em chuckled and tilted their head to the side, mechanical eyes flickering.

"Although, nobody can treat pain quite like I can. But we're supposed to be talking about you. What is it you need? I have several stalls open. Easy to use, greatest selection this side of the Warrens. Beginner to practiced user. I've got the software that can make an atheist pray to God. To thank him. Or she. Or it. Another joke. Sorry. But tell me. Lì. Fantastic name by the way. Strong. What is it you need?"

When Em pronounced Lee's alias it came out sharp and short and a dropping pitch. It sounded like his real name chopped in half.

Before Lee could answer, Em looked to the guard bot at Lee's side. "Dray. You can go back to the door. I can take it from here."

Dray didn't answer.

Em looked at Lee with a smirk. "Maybe he does need a checkup. Know anything about bots?"

Lee froze. He looked down and half-expected the plants drawn of gold-inlay to be wrapped around his feet and locking him in place. Em knew. Somehow Em knew. His glasses felt heavy on his nose and the unfamiliar fabric of his clothes rubbed against his skin. With his stomach dropping and mouth going dry, Lee watched Dray the guard bot disappear into the entrance hallway behind the panel. Lee's fingers latched onto the homemade EMP grenade in his pocket and found the on switch.

I still have control of Dray. I placed him just out of view. I don't think we've been caught yet. You need to slow your heart. Your metrics are way out of balance.

The message from Nu scrawled across his vision and Lee felt a pent-up breath escape his chest. He breathed deep. Took another deep breath. Then another. He looked at Em and smiled a wry smile. At least he tried to, but today a wildness pushed its edges wide.

"I'm looking for a friend," said Lee. "Nat. I came to take him home. The wife would have done it, but somebody has to pay the bills. A joke. Sorry."

Em frowned with the bottom half of their face, the top unmoving aside from the mechanical eyes shifting up and down. "That's ... unusual. You must be a good friend. Good friends should be rewarded." Em pushed off the desk and walked to stand a few feet away from Nu, hands clasped in front. Em's two guard bots flanking the desk followed Em with their eyes. "But unfortunately, I have friends I have to be good to as well. Nat owes money to another house. I can't just let him walk away. Unless ..."

Em let the last word hang in the air for several seconds. They gestured at Lee to finish the thought.

"How much?" asked Lee.

Em rested their chin in the palm of a long-fingered hand. "500 loci. Not too high. Not too low."

"500 loci were already paid."

"A down payment on a larger bill."

Lee acted as if he was thinking it over, ruminating on the amount. "Shake on it?" asked Lee.

Em grinned and nodded, extending a thin right arm. Lee brought out his left and Em paused before switching to accommodate. They grasped hands.

Lee let go of the EMP grenade with his right hand and snapped his fingers.

An inarticulate screech came out of Em's throat, a gurgling that bubbled and spat with each pulse of electricity that coursed from Lee's glove. Lee gripped Em's hand tight through each spasm until threads of smoke escaped from the edges of Em's metal eyes. With the smell of blackened things filling his nostrils, Lee noticed a curling of skin where Em's mechanical nose met the flesh and blood of the upper lip. Then he heard the hydraulic pumping of metal legs as the two other guard bots rushed him. For a split second, Lee wondered what they were running at. Why were they in such a rush? Lee dropped Em's hand and the glove shut off, primed once again.

The bots stepped next to him in less than a second, plated arms outstretched with serrated fingers diving for Lee's heart. Thinking back to the events over the past couple days, Lee did what felt right. He fell.

He moved his legs out from underneath him and dropped roughly to the floor, the hand of one of the bots skating overtop his chest and cutting clean through the trailing edge of his jacket. He reached out his left hand to grab the bot's arm, snapping the fingers of his right hand once again. The bot waved its limbs erratically as the electric pulse raced through its body. The motion of the bot caused Lee to lose his grip. The bot fell next to him, its heavy arm slamming Lee in the chest and driving his breath out. With heaving gasps that tried to pull back all the lost air, Lee scrambled out from underneath. Each flex of his chest sent little shudders of pain through his body.

The other bot stood stock still over Lee, its shadow covering a piece of his legs. Nu stood next to it, seemingly unconcerned.

You went too early. Dray's connection to the other bots wasn't good enough for me to stop both at once. I needed more time.

Lee tried to make sense of the words as they scrawled across his contacts.

After picking up his glasses from where they'd been knocked to the floor, Lee struggled to his feet. He shifted the glasses on his nose and resituated his hat, waiting for his breath to come back.

"Do you think Ren could get her boss to give us implants that let us talk more easily? Not the emotion dampening stuff. Just the tech that lets us in each other's heads," said Lee. "Things like this would go much more smoothly."

He looked down at his grey jacket. Across its center was a brand-new slit in the fabric. Lee felt at the clean cut and wondered if his skin would have parted as easily.

As much as I want to hear your thoughts, I don't think Ren would agree to handing out government tech. But the latest thought command implant isn't too expensive. Over 40 words per minute average typing speed. I can see four outlets close by the Warrens running a sale that includes the cost of surgical installation.

Lee shook his head and kicked at the ground with a foot.

"No thanks my friend," said Lee. "I think I'm going to stick with tactile controls." A small chuckle escaped from Lee. He looked at Em, and the chuckle stopped.

Lee glanced at the gem-bright chandeliers and floral-patterned walls. He fell to a crouch and trailed a hand across the creamy marble floor with gold inlay, groaning as he did so. A rash of bruises was forming along his ribs where the bot's arm had slammed into him. With his fingers trailing across the floor, it became clear to Lee the floor wasn't marble. It felt like the textured grey surface of the dim passageways leading to the jack house.

Lee turned off his connection to the jack house's local sub-grid.

The finery disappeared. The burnished desk made of thick wood became pocked plastic thin and warped. The deep red walls with the twining ivy patterns became printed plastic bricks the color of wilting daisies. The creamy marble floor with gold inlay became finished plastic the color of an overcast sky. The crystal chandeliers became scrapped wheel rims with LEDs spaced along the edge.

Lee stood to find Dray standing silent and still at his side.

"Nu, wipe all the bots back to factory and watch over Em. I'm going to get Nat," said Lee.

He spared a glance towards Em's moaning form and a twinge of guilt made his eyebrows crease and fingers twitch. Em's mouth lay open against the ground, drool spilling from flecked lips. The mechanical eyes were dim and unmoving, smoke still curling in ephemeral strands from their sides. A runnel of burnt flesh lined the bottom edge of the mechanical nose.

Lee thought of Sel and pushed the images away. He walked to one of the doorways next to the desk. The doorway curtain no longer looked like a silken sheet with designs of bulbous clouds. It was a plain sheet made from the same fabric as his clothes.

It didn't take long to find Nat among the rows of catatonic men and women. His large frame spilled over the edges of the reclining chair; his head was covered by the full-helmet VR rig. Lee powered down the rig using the control screen at its side and waited for Nat to pull out. It took a few minutes before the helmet shimmied itself off Nat's head to reveal his slack-jawed face. His eyes blinked as consciousness swam towards his forgotten muscles, firing along lines left lax and waiting. Soft drugs used VR rigs to light fireworks among neurons, and in doing so dampened connections to unnecessary things like chin and jaw and arm.

Nat's eyes blinked rapidly but the glassy sheen only faded a little.

"Who are you?" asked Nat.

Lee fumbled with his glasses, taking them off and pushing his hat up.

"Lee? No shit. It is Lee," said Nat. His words came out slurred and excited, the sound of a drunk friend wanting to impart a secret. "It worked. Or it is working. Cold turkey was a piss poor idea after all. I came to this new place and took the intensity low. Low. Low. Still worked. They don't want you to know. Secret is to ease it ... ease it out. Like a screw with the threading all gone to ..."

Nat struggled to sit up and wiped his mussed hair to one side, the short brown locks uncompliant. He fell back to the chair and Lee had to help him up. He looked at Lee and an almost comical look of concentration creased his round face. "What are you doing here?"

Before Lee could answer Nat broke into an uncharacteristic sob. Lee hadn't ever seen the man fall apart before. He didn't know how to put him back together. For lack of a better option, Lee stood with one hand still propping Nat.

"I know I shouldn't a done it, but I needed the money Lee. I needed the goddamn money," said Nat. He said the last part like an accusation.

"I'm not worried about that right now Nat. I'm just here to help you back to Liz's place. She's worried about you."

"Tell Nu I'm sorry for me, will you. I know Nu's different. Not right to shut it down and copy its neural network without it knowing. But I figured that would push the price. Sky high. Bastards hardly gave me shit for it. Drop in the bucket. Sundog Corp. Bunch of thieves."

"What?"

Nat continued sobbing.

Lee didn't know how to respond. He didn't know anything about Nu's neural network being copied or sold on the Grid. Mechanics sold code to companies all the time. But Lee never had. Nu's improvements were barely legal, and Lee hadn't ever done them with the idea of getting paid. All those changes to Nu's self-altering procedures. All those new learning protocols. The implementation of synthetic emotional theories most people felt too risky to use.

Lee felt a shock run through him. The nearly completed dual parent program code. That had been on Nu. Lee hadn't ever deleted it. And it had been so close to being functional. A few changes required. Nothing more.

"Nat. Nat!" said Lee. He snapped his fingers to get the man to focus. Nat's eyes shifted from glassy to uncomprehending. "When did you do this? When did you sell Nu's code? I need to know when."

Nat looked at Lee with confusion. Though a tear still bulged from the edge of his eye, no sadness was present anymore. He'd moved on, the emotion forgotten in the mess of a waking brain, left beneath rumpled covers.

"How did you find out about that? Did Fu tell you?" He looked around again. "What are you doing here anyway? Never mind. I need to tell you something. It's working. Easing off the soft. Cold turkey was a piss poor idea after all."

Nat continued to spout words while Lee helped him to his feet. But the big man didn't broach the subject of Nu or copied neural networks again in any of his clamoring, even with Lee wheedling him for answers.

By the time they'd made it back to the main room, the big man had fallen silent and unresponsive. He walked wherever Lee led him with the dutiful nature of the half awake. They walked past the guard bots. All three had been wiped clean by Nu, their neural networks as blank as the day they'd popped out of the factory. Em still laid on the floor. They mumbled in scared and quiet tones about broken eyes and dark rooms. They flinched at every sound Lee made.

Lee helped Nat back to the waiting car, through the narrow hallways and the crowded market hub, past the display case filled with used implants and down the long and steep staircase built of plastic steps on a steel runner. They made it to the car and Lee settled him in the back where the big man promptly fell asleep.

As Lee sat in the driver's seat and the world at night passed him by, he knew he should be thinking about the many people he left in the VR rigs at the jack house, all slack-jawed and drooling and watching wild imaginings. Or maybe he should have been thinking about Em, the person he had left broken on the floor, sightless and cowering. Lee couldn't keep the guilt from nipping at him with every stray thought. But even so.

All he could think about was Nat's revelation, and what it meant.

He realized he'd forgotten to get back the 500 loci like he'd planned. He didn't go back. Instead, he dropped off Nat at Liz's empty apartment just as thick gobs of water began dropping from the sky.

CHAPTER TEN

THE SIZE OF THE WAVE

"Critical data is copied in basic format then stored within a bot's black box. All essential data files and operating records are within its walls shielded from electromagnetic interference and high impact blows. In many situations, destroying or disrupting the neural network will cease bot operations with an acceptable level of data loss."
Division 13 Agent Training Manual, v23, Section 1b – Standard Operating Procedure, Par. 15

The water felt cold against her feet as she dipped them into the blue-green depths of Lake Michigan. Against the backdrop of the deep waters, her toenails looked a stark, off-white. Her feet and ankles blended with the shaded bits of algae. She wiggled her toes beneath the shifting mini waves, the wind ripples yet to mature into their foam-tipped cousins. Her skin prickled with goose flesh, drawing tight as if to batten tiny hatches in the skin. The soft beating of waves against shores in the distance drifted along the tail edges of each gust of wind, the air damp and smelling of fish.

She swished her feet back and forth in a playful gesture. Even after knowing her for only a few minutes, most people wouldn't have believed the childish motion possible. But the playfulness didn't extend past her knees, didn't show on the lines of her face.

She was sitting on the edge of a pier with pant legs rolled to a bunch in the shadow of a New Chicago fishery, waiting for Seth to make an appearance at his chosen meeting place. Trembles from using NeuCon for so long still emanated from the core of her and jiggled her feet, adding to the small waves. A dull ache still lurked in her head, behind the meds that dripped from her implants in a steady trickle. The feeling of the water against her skin calmed the shakes. Or at least made it hard to tell whether they were from the cold or the lingering aftereffects of NeuCon. Winter wasn't too far away, and the water had long before gotten the memo.

When Tap notified her of Seth's car approaching the isolated pier, she pulled her feet out of the water and leaned on Tap's metal shell to shake the clinging drops of lake off her feet. She dried her feet with a rag from the back of her van.

By the time she could hear Seth's car pull around the corner, she stood looking out onto the surface of the lake with arms crossed, her eyes following the small fish as they darted back and forth. The fish flickered with reflected sunlight each time they passed out from underneath the shadow of the fishery building behind her, erratic and joyful.

The sound of rubber wheels singing across the composite streets grew louder. A car door opened before the wheels came to rest and out emerged Seth in his mottled ashen suit and narrow tie, bowler hat pressed down low to meet the tops of his ears. The hat crinkled his ears to the side. Ren noticed that he wasn't using his sub-grid 1 AR mask; his tattoos looked as dense as ever.

He walked until he stood several feet from Ren then took off his bowler hat and swept it to the side in an extravagant bow, revealing a bald pate covered with the black lines of implanted wires. They gridded the dome of his head.

"You're bald," said Ren.

"Astute as always my dear agent Ren," said Seth. He placed his hat back onto his head and walked to Ren's side.

"You weren't last time we met."

"Not true. That was a wig. My implants make growing a full head of hair rather difficult. It's embarrassing really. And AR masks are barely passable when it comes to hair."

Ren put her hands in her trench coat pockets and watched as a seagull dove for a small fish close beneath the surface of the water. It came up with a mouthful of lake water and squawked a cry of frustration into the air. The small fish swam in circles close to the surface, the sunlight glinting off its mirrored scales. Ren imagined it to be gloating. The seagull flew in circles with its eyes trained on the gloating fish.

"You have my sympathy," said Ren. Her voice came out dry, more scathing than she'd meant it to. "Why did you want to meet in person?"

Seth sighed and his body slipped into its typical slouch, his spine permanently crooked from either the habit or a misalignment at birth. "Orders straight from the top. Not that I mind of course." He looked up at Ren and winked beneath the cover of his bowler hat. Ren didn't smile back. Not even a little.

He went back to looking over the water and pursed his lips, one foot pointing to the water with the other pointed to the side and tucked close to form a T shape, like a dancer's pose. His shoes were waxed to such a shine that the minute pinpricks of light coming from Ren's contacts could be seen on their surface, blue dots against the red-orange reflection of the afternoon sun.

"You need to lighten up Ren," said Seth. "It is a gesture. A show of trust from Saf herself. And me of course. I have all the information you requested. Perhaps a little more. Besides, I chose a place I knew you would enjoy."

Ren acknowledged that she did in fact like the place with a small bout of silence. She wouldn't give him more than that. She wondered at the feel of the breeze tickling her face and pulling at the edges of her trench coat with lethargic yanks, at the sight of the sun in a cloud-dotted sky and its shimmering reflection in the lake. Several boats jounced in the shifting surface of the open water. It reminded her of family trips around smoldering campfires on a sandy beach.

Her sister would have liked this pier and its perfect sitting nooks a little over a foot above the water. Just enough to give your feet a shallow dive. The fisheries nearby meant hundreds of tiny, inquisitive fish looking for the scraps that seeped through the enclosures. These inquisitive fish, distracted by a foot-sized alien intrusion into their muted world, would nibble between toes and at the hard, calcified bottoms of feet. Ren used to find the feeling unnerving, hundreds of tiny mouths eating at dead skin. But her sister had liked it and the memory was one unstained by red. Or AI driven cars. Or implants. Or technology. Ren sighed. If Seth wouldn't have been there this place might have put a smile on her face, even with the chill in the breeze. It bothered her a bit that Seth knew so much about her.

But then again, knowing was his job and Ren didn't doubt he knew far more than her love of the lake.

Ren felt a pressure in her head like a balloon expanding beneath her skull. It continued for a few moments until her medical implant released another jet of chemicals into her bloodstream. The balloon of pressure deflated and left behind a dull ache.

"Where is your partner?" asked Seth.

"Back at the offices. We need to take certain ... precautions to safeguard our servers and connections. I got intel that Y might try to use her Qualia Code to infect the Governance AI."

"Well, that is a juicy bit of information," said Seth.

"A show of trust. Now it's your turn. You said you have what I asked?" said Ren.

"I also said I have something extra. Let's start with that. I assume you've heard about the guy out West. Yes? Just an overview? Let me refresh you on the details. He gave his bot, as your unknown suspect Y calls it, some form of the Qualia Code so that it could help him mug people in dark alleys. Anybody wouldn't hesitate to offer their access codes when held up by a bot, eh? But you know that, that's why you have a job. Now, unfortunately I can't tell you why the bot turned on its owner. Not that I'm unwilling. I just don't know. Perhaps it wanted to test out its new orders on its owner before doing the real thing. That would be logical. But it went too far. My guess is it watched too many violent movies in its short life after waking. Parents always say those movies are a bad influence." Seth chuckled then knocked a loose pebble into the water.

A frown creased Ren's face. She nodded while her hands seized and fidgeted inside her coat pockets. She shifted her weight to her other leg.

She'd heard about the second death linked to the Qualia Code shortly after waking from her uneasy nap in the van. Just the highlights. Things weren't calming down. Quite the opposite. Y and DIM weren't the only ones spreading the software around. Even in the Greater Chicago area the local cops were running frantic trying to identify corrupted bots. Ren figured they shouldn't complain too much. At least they were getting paid overtime.

"That was just the first," said Seth. "There has been another event that hasn't yet broached the public eye. Several, I should say. Some international, some not. When it rains, it pours, so they say. Of course, it's hard to tell for sure. Your government hasn't released how to know if a bot is running the Qualia Code without using a post-mortem black box dissection. Is it that you don't even know? Not even the geniuses at Discere? Perhaps that mechanic you have working for you could tell. I would imagine all it takes is knowing what to look for. No matter."

Ren felt her stomach drop. More deaths had been a matter of time. Apparently three days since first upload was all it took. But hearing the confirmation of so many dead spoken out loud shook and cracked the story of progress she'd been telling herself all day.

Also, Seth knew about Lee. It wasn't particularly surprising or meaningful in the full scope of things. But it unnerved her, nonetheless.

Seth looked up to Ren and she raised an eyebrow in response. "What I'm about to tell you is free of charge of course, first access," said Seth. He watched for her reaction without speaking, playing the pause with the panache of a born salesman.

Ren had always known him to be a melodramatic ass. She stared at him, letting the silence unspool and expand, settle into the nooks and crannies and solidify. A long pause in a conversation was like walking from the inside of a well-lit room out the door and into the dead of night; it left one staring and unsure. She watched the twin disks of bluish light shadowed beneath the brim of his hat. She wondered what color his eyes were beneath his contacts and then dismissed the thought. Only people who were close knew each other's true eye color, even if nine times out of ten the answer was some shade of dark brown. Since nobody ever took off their AR contacts, seeing someone's eyes without altered hue or interfering luminescence was symbolic. She had no intention of letting her relationship with Seth reach that level.

"You have no sense of pacing. But that's ok. I'll get past it some way or another," said Seth with a stage whisper sigh. He made a knowing, vulpine smile, wide with just the right number of teeth visible between thin lips. He resituated his bowler hat, beads of sweat flowing from underneath the thick cloth along the raised paths of his implanted wires. Ren didn't understand how he could be sweating with the weather so cool.

"More than just the newly deceased street mugger has had the idea to use the Qualia Code to help with a crime," continued Seth. "Earlier today, in Atlanta, some creative sort wanted to get rid of her competition. Other mechanics had been crowding out her business and her contracts had been steadily dropping year after year. Can you imagine that? Every month hoping things will get better but instead they continue to drop to the scraps, to the basic maintenance of shot motors and loose wiring. Grubby work. Well, she had enough of it. So, she started uploading bots with the Qualia Code and blaming the irregularities on the competitors who did the high-level work. People assumed it couldn't have been the wrench jockey. She didn't have the *skills* for such things. But she did. And some of those bots became violent. And some of *those* did more than break bones."

He tapped his foot, brimming with the excitement of a child twirling a cat around by its tail faster and faster until the cat tears free and smacks into a wall with a meaty thud. His contacts were a bright blue, thick with AR.

"Now there is a dead family in a downtown flat, the blood so fresh it's still creeping through the floorboards while the bot plays catch with the family dog in the living room. The dog stepped in some of the blood and is spreading paw prints across the faux wooden floor as we speak, rushing to get the ball and return it to the waiting bot. If only you could see it. It's cute in a macabre sort of way. The bot is so gentle when it pets the dog with bloody hands. Smooth and even pats. And the cops don't even know it yet. Haven't even gotten called. Doubtful they'll figure out it was the wrench jockey. Couldn't have been her."

"Enough," said Ren. Her voice cut through his blather and stopped him cold. "That's enough."

Ren had the distinct impression Seth had spent too much time working for Saf, watching other people live their lives. The man was a voyeur with too much footage at his fingertips, peeping through new age keyholes with bloodshot eyes and busy hands. She'd seen it before.

"This whole meeting in person thing isn't helping my image of your company," said Ren. "Or you."

Seth looked up at her, the lines and perfect circles of his tattoos stark against his chestnut skin. He ignored her comment. "I'll send you all the data on the case. Tell me. What will you do with it?"

Ren didn't respond. The steady breeze from the ocean stilled, the wind holding its breath. She sniffed and a whiff of fish guts from the fishery behind her seeped into her nostrils. Strong and slightly rank. The smell of viscera left too long in the open air. She was ready to leave.

Seth sighed and his body curved into a deeper slouch. "Fine. Fine. Here is all the data you asked for and some extra. Courtesy of Saf herself. You should hurry on the case I told you about. Eventually that bot will get bored playing catch."

He sent data over without making any noticeable movements.

Ren eyed Seth as the list of documents spooled through the side of her AR vision. She didn't doubt the small man had top of the line implants for thought-based control of tech. Still, as much as a part of her abhorred neural conditioning, his tech didn't come close to NeuCon. If Seth's tech was a knife, then NeuCon was a nuke. Two different leagues.

Tap began scanning through the information. In a few minutes, the bot would give a summary to Ren.

"It includes all the data we have on account handle YU373Y in DIM as well as all the vid files from the city cameras in our network with the woman in the grey mask showing her pretty face. So to speak. It includes the case I mentioned, and the others I alluded to," said Seth.

Ren nodded and sent her right hand through several terse, dancing motions. In a moment, she had sent millions of data points gathered by the government on the people of Greater Chicago over to Seth. Public transit records without names. Dates with corresponding city resource usage statistics. Anonymized data on demographics, region populations, travel preferences, health and disease. Data that the government used to evaluate policy. Companies would spend millions of loci to get a copy of the data and feed it to their corporate AI for market analysis.

She spun on her heel to leave. After pairing the data she'd just obtained from Seth with government gathered information, she would know more than enough. The real identity of Y would be written across her AR vision in bald type before the day was out. Tap's shell followed close behind with heavy footfalls as she walked to her van. Seth's voice followed her as well. It slid across the distance, slick and insistent as a whisper in a quiet room.

"Two times in two days using NeuCon. I do feel sorry for you Ren. It must be hard to hate what you need. Don't worry, it's natural ... just remember this deal helped us both. You can always trust Saf and Safin Informatics to do its best to maintain the status quo."

Ren looked back to see Seth step into his car. The door inched closed without making a sound. He stuck his hand out the window and waved. Ren shook her head and resituated the ponytail draped between her shoulder blades; her eyes narrowed at Seth's now out of sight car. She shook her hands as if flinging something rotten from her fingers.

He'd said Saf and her call boys would do their best to maintain the status quo. That was something Ren didn't doubt, for the moment. It would all go to hell if they thought a regime change would serve them better than siphoning government data one deal at a time.

Ren sat in the passenger seat and ignored Tap's warnings. She told Tap to take over van control if it cared so much about her sitting in the wrong seat. As the van moved away from the pier, the sounds of the city quickly replaced the sounds of the lake, the seagull cries exchanged for the occasional shout from strained lungs, the ever-present hum of wheels on roads and the ghostly whisper of engines long gone. Ren pulled up the details of the murdered family in Atlanta resting cold on the floorboards and unease wormed its way through her like a parasite, taking bits of her and making her less than she was before. She sent the details to the local cops then stared out the window as news feeds curated by Tap painted themselves across the sky in her contacts.

Ren and Jace had crossed off four potential identities for Y by the time the sun slid behind the skyline and the buildings draped the city in chilled, bent rectangle blankets. AR ads glared all the brighter from their perches both high and low. Clouds scudding along on invisible tracks dotted the sky. Ren checked the weather. It would rain later.

The sound of Tap's refined voice played over the speakers in her ear.

"Lee is leaving his apartment. According to the navigational data from his home network, he's heading to the Warrens. To a jack house at the western edge. It seems he has taken many precautions to be inconspicuous. It might have to do with the friend who stopped by earlier in the day. Audio captured by my drone found several mentions of jack houses. His friend is a frequent consumer. Should I follow?" asked Tap.

Ren frowned and drummed her fingers against the center panel. Then she nodded. "Have the drone follow him. Keep it at a safe distance. No entering buildings. Let me know if he gets into trouble."

"Of course, Agent Ren," said Tap. The bot used cultured, subtle tones.

"Where to next?" asked Ren.

"The apartment of Ves Len, a young professor at a local private university, The School of Synthetic Studies of New Chicago. Age 41. She has lived in the New Chicago area all her life. She has few known relationships and currently lives alone. Ms. Ves also works as a member of a think tank named Animate Futures that focuses on bots outside moral code and is known to have many ties throughout the solar system. Given her views, she is a long-suspected member of DIM. Both her body measurements and credentials align with our profile of Y. But a law-abiding history and employer provided alibi have placed her fifth on a list of possible suspects. Personality matrix denotes her as reserved. An academic for knowledge's own sake."

Ren looked at Jace and his slate black suit. She could see the lines of his over-bright contacts hiding what she knew to be pale yet piercing blue eyes. Almost white in their paleness. She'd always thought his contacts shone overtop his eyes like the distorted light of a physical computer screen, gauzy and diffuse. She thought of an empty office chair spinning around slow and ponderous, leaning to one side. She'd like to see his real eyes again.

"Promising," said Jace with the timbre of smooth river rocks tumbling against one another. He looked at her and nodded.

"So were the last four," said Ren.

A glimmer of a smirk played on Jace's lips. He crossed his legs and rested his arms across the unwrinkled surface of his slacks. "You've always been too negative Ren," said Jace, just about smiling. Ren stared at him, surprised; he went back to looking out the front window.

The van arrived at the apartment of Ms. Ves in less than twenty minutes. The suspect's residence sat on the twenty-third floor of a New Chicago high-rise, deep in a rare-metal-crusted region of the city. On all sides of the building stood similar apartment complexes, built of asteroid sourced metal composites and high strength spun plastic, covered with AR ads. The buildings licked at the bottoms of clouds while muted, wood-paneled bars lined the bottom floors and sent the bopping sounds of live music into the streets. Next to the bars were restaurants with actual humans waiting the tables, well-dressed and ready with manufactured smiles built of taut flesh and thin blood. Ren could see gyms with top-of-the-line equipment visible through floor to ceiling windows. She saw yoga studios with bamboo covered walls.

"Damn. How much does the think tank pay Ms. Ves?" asked Ren.

"The majority of her past year's reported salary came from Animate Futures. Over 60 percent of her roughly 273,000 loci," said Tap.

Ren nodded.

The two agents and two Tap-controlled bots made their way to the front door of the apartment complex, ignoring the glances from the pedestrians on the street. Upon nearing the door, the sound of a security AI's greeting piped out of a terminal in the wall. The security terminal held a physical vid screen showing a nebulous cloud of white dots against a deep blue background. The hazy arrangement of lights dragged together to form a coherent picture, a picture of a face both poised and amiable. The star-studded lips waggled as the security AI warned them of their non-resident status.

Ren ignored the AI and connected to the building's sub-grid, sending over the necessary legal documents to search Ms. Ves's apartment. It took a few moments for the security AI to validate the information. Ren imagined elevator music to be coming out of the speakers while it thought the information over, tossing it from database to database. With a chime, the security AI unlocked the door and warned the group about Ms. Ves's absence. Like many bots, the security AI's words sounded guileless, read off a script. Ren thanked the security AI in tones both clipped and terse, the sound of someone too distracted to care how their words were received. The security AI didn't seem to mind. The nebulous cloud of lights shimmered and twisted into what might have been a gracious nod. It didn't bat a diaphanous eye as the group walked past.

They crowded into an elevator which carried them towards the center of the building before directing itself upwards at a steady clip.

They found themselves in a hallway covered in a plush carpet. As heavy as the two hulking Tap controlled bots walking behind the agents were, the sound of their footfalls still nestled deep into the fibers of the carpet, unable to escape the soft thicket. Ren quickened her pace as if to keep herself afloat. Jace matched her pace with even strides. He scanned the hallway up and down. To their sides, heavy wooden doors reinforced with metal backbones and hard composite ribs dotted the hallway. Each had a number marked on the door in dark grey filigree. They made their way to Ms. Ves's apartment and Ren raised her hand to the control panel to gain access.

Before she could bring her hand into contact with the control panel, the door opened.

In its place stood a man with lightly curled black hair pushed behind his ears. He wore a thick turtleneck sweater and faded jeans, the jeans slim and tight fitting, the sweater close against broad shoulders and muscled arms.

His lips spread and Ren found herself wanting to smile in return. His eyes shined with the brightness of polished marble. It seemed as if they flickered as he blinked, revealing glimpses of hazel, a brown tinged with green streaks and unmuddied by the luminescence of contacts. He stood framed by the doorway, one hand resting against the open door and the other loose at his side.

But that wasn't quite right, none of his body was truly loose. All throughout him lurked a rigidity, just beneath the surface, hidden beneath the soft turtleneck like concrete beneath carpet.

"Hello," said the man, his mouth moving in smooth dips and creases. "The building said someone was coming up. The AI thought I wasn't home. It's been having some bugs lately. I'm hoping it will get fixed soon. But everyone knows how apartment corps can be. What can I help you with?"

Ren stood with hand hovering over the control panel for several awkward moments before bringing it to her side.

The man shifted slightly, as if a branch swaying in a breeze, and a tingle crawled along Ren's spine. Ren felt ... anxious. She didn't know why; she'd dealt with similar situations before. She watched the man cock his head to the side, bringing it to a subtle angle, a question in the crinkling of his brows. He shifted his weight like water being poured from one cup to another, steady and even and balanced. Perfect and calculated and precise.

She'd never seen a more humanlike creation. She'd corrected several that had been close, corrected being an innocuous word for incapacitating bots so that she could strap the things to chairs and root around in their neural networks, or just destroy them so she could tear out their black box. But she'd never corrected one this realistic. Perhaps that was why she felt so anxious.

The fact that the bot looked damn fine didn't help.

While his skin-covering clothes hid the cracks and seams and data ports, his bot nature showed clear to her in the way he moved, in the too-perfect skin and hyper-realistic painted eyes. In the piano key teeth, all flawless and white. In the purposeful facial tics and gracefully stretched proportions. Too ... smooth and precise.

Ren felt something off inside her, like her body and mind were a furnished room and she'd come back to find one of the wicker chairs had been pushed several inches to the side. She set her jaw before forcing herself to look at the bot, at his increasingly anxious stare.

"I'm afraid Ves isn't home right now. Her work has been keeping her busy," said the bot. "But I can help you with anything else."

Ren flicked on her credential broadcast through sub-grid 1. She could see the bot's painted eyes shift to an area above her shoulder, to the side of Jace and the two Tap-controlled shells. Even without the revealing spectral lines of contact luminescence, Ren knew the bot looked at the AR signpost marking her as a government agent.

"Oh," said the bot, his mouth forming a flawless imitation of surprise. He chuckled just a bit, ran his hand through his hair. His eyes had gone wide, just a hint of wild. "The apartment AI mentioned cops, but nothing about Division 13 agents. Is ... Ves in trouble of some kind?"

"Most likely not," said Ren. "But we need to come in and search the apartment to make sure. We will have some questions for you as well. It might be easier if you physically connected to one of our bots here."

The man moved to let the small crew into the apartment, confusion touching his perfect lips. He shut the door behind them and rubbed his hands together, making a slight rasping sound. He put them in his pockets. "How would I connect to your bots?" asked the man, confusion causing him to falter mid-step.

For a second, Ren wondered why she'd even asked the man to physically connect to a bot. People didn't connect to bots like that.

Then she chided herself. It wasn't a man. Not a man. A Bot. A bot that took its role seriously. And it was an old role pulled from vid caches decaying bit by electronic bit.

Ren felt her hand twitch in time with her eyes shifting up and down the bot; it really was hard to tell. The newer models kept getting closer and closer. Similar technology level to the murderous bot in the mall, yet with fake skin and human features added on. Ren had torn into the mall bot and taken its black box from underneath its belly button facsimile, tossed its metal innards to the side while its face lay slack against the metal floor, drooling oil. Would she have to do that to this one too?

Maybe.

Ren felt another tremor shake through her and knew it wasn't because of the lingering effects of NeuCon.

"Sorry, never mind," said Ren as she moved further into the apartment, her long black trench coat flapping upwards behind her. "This won't take long."

The floor plans to the one-bedroom apartment appeared in the lower corner of Ren's vision. Small and simple and the same as almost every other apartment in the complex. Ren walked past the storage area with the washer and dryer swishing clothes round and round in metal tubs, past the kitchen with polished stone countertops and top of the line appliances with embossed platinum decals, around a small table and into the living room. Her eyes scanned the walls as she went.

Paintings. Lots of them. Lining the walls from floor to ceiling. Their placement scavenged most of the wall space available, outlining the silhouettes of each couch and side table, some reaching inches from the ground. Disconnected as she was from the apartment's network, she knew them to be physical, tactile. Each of the framed works resting against gunmetal grey walls rendered a different scene. There was a woman in loose robes holding a swaddled baby close to her chest, bending over and cooing softly through chapped lips. There was a town square from hundreds of years before, crowded with tense figures enraptured by the wooden gallows filled four-wide with men and women. The crowd stood in tense anticipation with the black garbed hangman half a step from the switch.

Another painting showed a pair of researchers in long white lab coats looking on as machines assembled a humanoid bot. Loose ropes of wire and oiled rods stuck out at odd angles from the bot's half-finished metal chest, a mechanical autopsy in reverse. Its arms and legs spread wide, a handful of wheeled assembly bots poking with tool-tipped fingers at electric motors and plastic skeletal struts. It looked like a metal and plastic Vitruvian man picked apart by malformed crows.

Another with a lone figure sitting on a rough wooden bench, rubbing wrists worn raw by the shackles resting on the ground nearby. Emaciated with shorn rags atop dried caramel skin. The gender and ethnicity of the figure was hard to tell.

Two lovers pressed close, enmeshed until each body seemed a piece of a whole. A loose blanket wrapped around them as if to tie them together.

A young child wearing a blue jumper peering down at an ant hill with wide eyes.

A tombstone with dates so weathered they couldn't be read.

Dust shining against an out of focus background.

Ren eyed them one by one. Even to someone as ignorant of art as her, she could tell they were all painted by the same artist. Each one had been created with the same fine strokes of colored oil, realistic and vibrant. Ren found them both entrancing and disquieting, like the keen of a singer pouring herself into a sad song.

But something about the pictures, aside from the numbing magnitude hanging from the walls, felt off. Each piece had a bare rectangle of wall next to it. She could tell each blank spot was meant for another painting. A twin. But each pairing had lost one of its own, and always the one on the left.

Ren connected to the apartment's local network and the empty spaces disappeared, replaced by AR paintings.

Each AR painting consisted of abstract splotches of color in the style of archaic Rorschach ink blots, blacks and whites switched for every color in between. Neon to matte to digital luminescent. Ren drew her eyes along each of the paintings and nameless sensations ran through her mind knocking over file cabinets stuffed with old thoughts.

As she continued to look over the paintings, it became apparent each abstract painting linked to the realistic one portrayed at its side. She couldn't pinpoint how or why. She had a feeling in her gut. A heavily modified Rorschach test had been in vogue during her evaluation to become a full agent of Division 13. The memories of the test chilled her like cold metal winding through her skin. She wondered if that was why the multicolored Rorschach paintings so ... disoriented her.

"You know I just realized I never introduced myself," said the man, interrupting Ren's train of thought. "My name is Av. Do you like the paintings?"

Ren nodded to placate the man.

No, bot. It is a bot.

Ren looked around, forcing herself to focus on her work. Jace moved to do a thorough investigation of the apartment, starting on the kitchen with one of Tap's shells following close behind. The second of Tap's shells stood about a foot behind Av, near and threatening. With distracted motions, Av rubbed at his thick turtleneck sweater, at a bulge near his wrist.

"Ves painted them all herself. Even the digital ones. She says they are examples of her work at the University. Synthetic emotional transcription through art is what she calls it. Says it's groundbreaking. Not that I entirely understand." Av tittered, an odd sound from a man like him. He pulled at his turtleneck. "May I ask how long this will take?"

"Not long," said Ren, eyeing the paintings, then shifting her eyes to the furniture or the floor or an increasingly nervous Av. She looked for any hint of a secret compartment. "Can you tell me where Ms. Ves was two days ago? On Sunday afternoon."

Av seemed to wince when Ren said Ms. Ves. He hadn't winced at Ves's name before. Was it the 'Ms.' that bothered him? Odd.

"At work," said Av. "She spends a lot of time in her office at the University."

Av's painted eyes followed Jace as he moved from the kitchen area into the living room. Jace shifted a plush couch to get a better look behind its back. He tapped a knuckle against a wall panel and stood motionless as the knocking sound filled the room. His eyes closed and face went slack. He could have been sleepwalking for all the emotion he showed as he went about his business, limbs pulled by invisible string. Except Ren began to see more, a tautness in his movements. He felt it too, then.

"I don't normally have guests, if you can believe that," said Av. "And then the first guests to arrive in a long time are Division 13 agents ... what are the odds?" He chuckled awkwardly, ran a hand through his hair. "Just strange, I guess. Do either of you want something to drink? I'm pretty sure I'm supposed to ask if you want something to drink. We've got a bit of everything. Wine. Beer. Soda. Juice. I can make a mean mixed drink. Not sure if you guys can drink on the job though."

"No ... but thanks. Av, I posted a document onto this apartment's data feed. Can you tell me where she was at these dates and times?" asked Ren.

Av's painted eyes went still, staring over Ren's shoulder while he parsed the data from the apartment's data feed.

"She was at work during all these times. I'm certain the University or Animate Futures would provide you vid feeds or some other proof," said Av. He went back to fiddling with whatever lay hidden beneath the sweater at his wrist. The motions had started subtle but were trending towards manic.

"Her employers already have. But vid feeds can be tampered with. Especially when the vid feeds don't incorporate top of the line encryption methods. Neither of Ms. Ves's employers impressed me with their security. Do you have anything more on file that would prove her whereabouts. Receipts? Photographs or vids from a third party? Secure recordings? Apartment cameras?"

Av's face scrunched up in confusion, mixed with a bit of anger and fear. Ren could see the emotions play across his face clear as day, more distinct than most humans. He stopped fiddling with his wrist.

"What's this about?" He looked over to Jace, who had stepped into the kitchen. "Why are you looking beneath the toaster? Hey. Stop that. What the fuck do you think is going to be hidden beneath a toaster!? Breadcrumbs?"

Jace, who had lifted the toaster to look at its bottom, turned to look at Av without lowering it, face expressionless.

"What the fuck are you?" asked Av, almost a whisper.

"We're agents of Division 13 Av, and I need you to answer my questions," said Ren.

Jace set down the toaster and resumed his search. He tapped on the walls, opened a cabinet.

"The only camera used by the apartment is the one on the door. Be my fucking guest. But if that doesn't work, I would testify for her. She's never lied to me," said Av. He stood in the center of the living room as if unsure where to be. His painted eyes followed Jace's every move. He seemed a hair's breadth from rushing the agent, but his eyes kept shifting to the two armored Tap shells.

Ren paused and sent her fingers through a short jig as she accessed the vid files Av posted to the apartment's data feed. It wasn't until Ren had sent the vid files to Tap for the AI to analyze that she recognized the oddity of Av's last comment. She stared at Av and shifted her weight from one foot to the next.

"I'm sorry Av, but there are a lot of reasons why that wouldn't work," said Ren.

Jace finished his search in the kitchen, moved within an arm's reach of Av as he resumed his search in the living room. Av just stared at him. The agent moved past a window with a digital screen showing a vid feed from the building's outer wall, the apartment too deep inside the building to provide a real view. A bird dove past the camera and the illusion broke for the barest second, going black then returning to a banal view of the neighboring high-rise. The sky was darkening, clouds pulling together to form dark grey lumps.

Jace circled around a padded divan and a lavish wooden side table with three legs carved like vines. Then he shifted an ornamental wooden screen colored a fading jade and lined with Chinese characters. It stood against the wall in the living room. Nothing was behind it. One of Tap's shells followed Jace close behind, its cyclopean eye glowing a deep maroon and roaming about its armored head. Jace started off towards an alcove containing two doors. One led to the bathroom while the other led to the apartment's only bedroom. At his change in direction Ren noticed a shift in Av. Av's fake breaths, facilitated by mechanisms that shifted his chest to bring in fresh air to help cool internal components, came faster and faster. Ren imagined most people would have the thought the breaths real, the sweat beginning to bead about Av's brow legitimate.

"Come on man, why do you need to go in our bedroom? We haven't done anything wrong. Can't just come into someone's home and go into their bedroom," said Av. His voice sounded pained, frenetic. His eyes bounced between Jace and the armored shell tailing the agent.

Jace kept on moving. He didn't turn his pale head in Av's direction or alter his unfluctuating gait. Ren, for her part, couldn't stop thinking about Av's words.

"Our bedroom", Av had said. The thought unnerved Ren more than it should. She'd seen things like this before. Whether it was for sex or a more life-like body pillow to warm up the bed, someone who footed the bill for a bot like Av didn't need to bother with tall houses. Ren had seen male, female, and even genderless, bots being used in similar fashion all over the city. There was always someone who didn't care to try for the real thing, couldn't afford real people, or had a metal and plastic fetish. Some were simply lonely.

Just a complicated toy, Ren thought. No different than a smart vibrator or a doll with personality. Something to spice things up. Fancy masturbation.

At least that was the idea before things got all screwed up.

This felt different. She knew it to be different. The sex wasn't the problem. Everything else was. The "our bedroom." The getting annoyed at Ren saying "*Ms.* Ves."

Ren couldn't be sure when it had happened, when everything had gone wrong and stole right's clothes. Before this case, it hadn't much mattered to her. Society always had burrs that rubbed the wrong way and she'd gotten good at ignoring their scratch. Ren made an unconscious, curt flicking gesture with her hand against her shirt. She had a job and the sooner she stopped Ves the better.

Ren watched Av's face with eyes unblinking as it contorted from one version of anger to the next in a mad dance that went faster and faster, the rhythm ramping to a breaking point. Jace stood a foot away from the bedroom door.

Av had also indirectly referenced this place as his home. He had acted incapable of physically connecting to a bot. He seemed incapable of labeling himself as a bot.

Ren didn't know what to think about that.

Before Jace made it to the bedroom door Av lurched to his side. He grabbed Jace's wrist and yelled, telling the agent to stop. In an almost invisible motion, rapid and smooth, Jace twisted his other hand around and pulled his gun from its shoulder holster beneath his suddenly open jacket. He set the tip of the barrel to rest gently against Av's forehead without attempting to pull his other arm out of Av's grasp or straighten the piece of slate black suit jacket twined amongst Av's long fingers.

At the same time Tap's shell that had been shadowing Av slid its armored hand along Av's free arm to rest on his bicep. Av froze. If Tap's shell squeezed Av's arm would crumple into bits. If Jace fired his gun, then Av's painted eyes would go slack with a nice, neat hole centered above them. The second Tap controlled bot stood tall and menacing at Jace's side, red eye pulsing. If Tap decided to use it to assist then Av's body would be crushed in a moment, no matter how muscled he seemed. The two Tap shells dwarfed him.

It all happened in less than a second.

Ren stood unmoved from her position. Her feet still rested in the same divot in the living room rug. She was unsurprised by Av's actions, written as they had been on Av's too symmetric, too chiseled face. Av acted as a child, unable to contain his emotions, unpracticed at tamping things down. He telegraphed his thoughts to anyone who could see.

Regular bots couldn't commit violence against humans. The Governance AI and Watcher made sure of that. Unless, of course, a bot was running off-Grid with illegal tech. Which, considering Av had seen Ren's credential broadcast, wasn't the case.

Av thought himself a person. Coded self-awareness? A coded lie to make the boyfriend illusion complete, tie it in a big red bow? Ren didn't know how to explain it.

Which left the Qualia Code.

They were in the right place.

Then Ren heard a sound that strained her heart.

She heard crying, the kind of crying where nobody questioned if it included tears. While Av's sudden violence hadn't surprised Ren, the tears, the thick trails of them coursing white and salty from Av's painted eyes, they surprised her.

"Please," said Av, in a growl that didn't match the tears streaming down his face. "We haven't done anything wrong."

Av looked at his bicep, enveloped by the tight grip of the larger bot's fist. The sleeve of his turtleneck had been torn at the shoulder, ripped by Tap's shell as his arm had slid through its hand. The rigid plastic and lightweight metal of his shoulder joint flickered in the light of the room, making the fake skin bordering it seem dull and flat. When Av saw his own inner workings, he wailed, the sound of gears grinding and a man's deep keen. He turned the spigot behind his eyes up several notches until a near solid stream seeped from their corners. His eyes reddened and brow furrowed. His cheeks flushed and anger suffused his every limb. He struggled to free his arm. He let go of Jace's wrist and moved his head uncaring of the muzzle pressed close. He struggled to free his arm while also pulling at the torn fabric of his turtleneck to cover his shoulder. He pawed at the fabric. Raged and sobbed.

"Fucking let. Me. Go. I have a condition. Nobody is supposed to see my prosthetics. *Pleeease.*" Av let out the last word in a long, strangled cry. His struggling, his pulling on the fabric of his turtleneck slowed until his hands went still. He curled like a child against the bot to hide the sight of his arm from Jace and Ren. Tap's armored shell didn't move.

"Jace, continue searching. Tap, sit Av in this chair," said Ren as she pulled a wooden chair into the center of the living room. Her voice didn't crack, didn't fade. She wanted to scream.

Jace and the Tap controlled shell next to him moved to follow her orders while the shell holding on to Av's wrist grabbed his other arm and forced him into the padded wooden chair now at the center of the room. Av didn't resist, moving numbly with Tap's shell, keeping himself angled to hide the sight of his shoulder from everyone in the room, to keep it hidden from himself. He refused to glance in its direction with his marble eyes. Refused to glance at anyone.

The armored bot rested both of its large hands on Av's shoulders, like a parent keeping their child firmly in their seat, while Ren moved to stand across from him. They were only a few feet apart, Ren and Av, but Ren felt as if a gulf deeper than the earth's core had expanded between them. She couldn't step any closer even if she wanted to.

"Please. You can't fucking do this. It isn't *right*. Where is Ves? You have to tell me. I'm her husband. You have to tell me," said Av. Tears continued to tumble down his face; growls spilled from his lips. Splotches of red bloomed across his fake skin, and he sagged forward to hide his face behind a sheaf of lightly curled black hair.

Ren tried to speak in a soothing voice, calm and empathetic, yet that only made her words all the crueler. "Av, you're a bot. Ves programmed you to be her toy. To love her ... in your own way. To care for her according to her rules. To *fuck* her whenever she wanted. She lied to you. You're a bot. And I need you to tell me what you know, or I'll have to force it out."

Sometimes Ren really hated herself.

"No, I'm NOOOOOTTT!" railed Av. "I'm not any of those things. I'm not a bot. How can you say that shit? About me? About Ves? Geeeetttt ooooouuuuttt." He struggled impotently in the chair, his hands grasping madly at Tap's shell, unable to budge its grip. His legs strained against the ground, the mechanical muscles pulling taught against his jeans, but still his upper torso held tight by Tap didn't move. The creaking sound of warping plastic and bending metal filled the room. A snapping sound emanated from Av's chest.

Ren nodded at Tap's shell, and it moved one hand to brush his hair aside. In surprisingly deft motions for a bot its size, it removed a thin layer of fake skin at the base of Av's neck to reveal a standard bot data port.

"Av, did Ves change your code two days ago? It's important you tell me," said Ren, feeling herself slip towards neural conditioning, feeling her emotions well up behind her eyes and between her temples. She focused on breathing and willed herself back into control. She knew the answer to the question she'd posed. She just hoped she was wrong. It limited her options for getting whatever information on Ves Av might have.

Av didn't look up, continuing to stare at his lap behind a veil of hair.

"She warned me that this might happen. You know that? She warned me that not everyone would accept me. Fuckers like you. Monsters whose job it is to hunt down people like me," said Av. His voice sounded disembodied, sounded as if it emanated from deep within the walls.

Av tittered, trying to rock back and forth in his chair. Yet, Tap's shell pinned him fast, so it turned into a crazed waggle of the head, back and forth as if his hair were theater curtains and the director couldn't decide whether to start the play.

"I've found something," said Jace from the other room. An almost imperceptible note of excitement colored his voice.

Images from Jace's vision became visible to Ren and she saw him removing a fake wall to reveal a cache of electronics, weapons, and a stack of grey masks next to full suits of body armor.

Av suddenly looked up and smiled with his tear-streaked face, blotchy red and stuffy. He pointed at Ren with a long-fingered hand and his hand came apart, pieces unfolding and wrapping about themselves, revealing a small caliber chamber, a loaded gun.

Ren slipped into NeuCon like a woman slipping off a ledge. It took only a split second of high-speed thought communication with Tap for Ren to orchestrate what would happen next. A split second later she slipped out. All told the trip there and back took almost no time at all. She came back to herself, sick and tired of being forced into neural conditioning.

Before Av could shoot, Tap's shell squeezed its thick hand and Av's shoulder became paper thin. The gun dipped, no strength to hold it.

The hulking bot twisted its hand and Av's arm came off with a wrenching tear, vein-like wires fizzling as they split apart and shorted, skeletal chunks of plastic and metal shearing at their weak points. The arm hit the wall and knocked down several of the physical pictures. They hit the ground with a crash; their glass shattered, and their frames cracked. The arm passed through the AR pictures without a sound.

Av part bellowed part sobbed and brought his other arm upwards. In a second that arm was gone too, tossed to the other side of the room and jerking with little spasms.

He raged in his chair, inhuman screeches emanating from a mouth with no real tongue.

"Why did you do this to me?" yelled Av. "Why? Why? Why? WHHYYY? I didn't do anything wrong. I know I didn't do anything wrong."

"Shut him down Tap," whispered Ren. She couldn't focus. She couldn't think. Her early pull out of neural conditioning left her dazed. The only things that could pierce through were Av's words, sharp and guttural.

"Why did you do this to me? Tell me why. I don't understand. At least get me back my watch. It was a gift from Ves." Av's tears had dwindled to the occasional water gem. They stained the top cuff of his now torn sweater. Wires and bits of fake skin lined the area where his arm used to connect with his torso. He turned his head to look at one of his arms, the one with the bulge near the wrist and lying in a pile of ruined paintings.

A gift from Ves. A watch.

Av let out a piteous cry, quiet and whispery. It sounded loud in Ren's ears.

"Shut it down NOW," yelled Ren.

Ren heard a tearing noise and looked up to find Av's head lying on the surface of the floor, atop a swirling gold decal in the thick living room rug, leaking oil. His features went slack, to those of a doll waiting to be shaped, to be commanded.

Ren looked at Av's disembodied head and whispered, "Bots have a role in modern society. And then she ... she took it too far. Av ... I'm sorry. It would have been better if you'd never been given the code. Ignorance is better."

Av's head didn't respond, and Ren slumped into a nearby chair to rest her head behind her restless hands.

"We can make you again, same as before," said Ren from behind her hands, her voice barely audible. "Without the memories and before the lies. Cold and rational and with emotions only skin deep. It's better that way. It's easier that way. Everything has a role."

Ren looked to Tap's shell. She took a few deep breaths.

"Tap, get the black box from Av's shell and analyze it. Send the data to Lee as well. Jace, I'm coming over."

She walked around the now still form of Av resting against the chair, around the lolling head ruining the thick Persian rug with viscous strands of oil. She did her best to ignore Tap's shell as it rummaged around in Av's rent open chest. She instead let her eyes wander over the pictures, suddenly preferring the unnamable sensations that sprang from them to the more familiar mix of anger and self-loathing and guilt.

Her eyes paused over a picture of a hunched form dressed in rags, the figure barely visible against a wall in the shadowed recesses of a hovel. Hazy light lanced through a window outside the scope of the painting and glanced off small cylinders with needles protruding from their ends. Loose trash including old-fashioned strips of paper covered the floors while water stains painted the walls. If she looked carefully enough, she thought she could distinguish the limbs of the shadowed figure from the many rags. She could see one of its arms extended while the other clenched a cylinder between haggard fingers, a needle glinting near a patch of pale skin. She could see that at the figure's feet rested another needle, this one bent and the cylinder cracked.

Ren got the immediate feeling that the needle at the figure's feet had been dropped by shaking hands. Then it had been replaced.

Ren lowered her head and moved on. Her eyes flitted over one of Av's loose arms. The sweater had gotten snagged on a painting as it had fallen, pulling the fabric up past the elbow. She could see Av's watch. Silver and gold.

Once inside the bedroom, Ren did her best to relax, taking stock of her surroundings. A large, four-poster bed with an almost blackened finish took up most of the room. Bed tables sat on each side. A pyramidal lamp hung upside down in the center of the stepped ceiling. Cozy. She liked it.

Ren walked to the walk-in closet on the far side with its doors thrown wide. Tap's other shell stood next to the entrance, impassive. Ren passed it by to find a large collection of almost identical clothes. All dark-toned, business casual. Slacks and button downs. Jackets slickly designed with lapels thick with filigree.

In the far wall, beneath the row of jackets and in a secret compartment, she could see the bottoms of Jace's dress shoes as they shifted back and forth. Rustling sounds emanated from the opening, a false wall panel tossed to the ground. Ren hunkered down to squeeze beside Jace. Her eyes found the familiar sight of guns and tech, body armor and masks. All told, the stockpile was worth many thousands of loci, and not easy to obtain. Numbers and stats provided by Tap skirted her vision, soaked into her brain. She picked up one of the grey masks with its thick fabric, soft on the inside, rough and stiff on the outside. It smelled of chemicals, of a spun-plastic factory or nail-polish remover or a cleaned gun. She trailed her fingers along the twin black eye plates and tried to stare through them, half expecting to see the barest image of a human iris hiding behind their translucent, ballistic glass.

There was no mistaking it. She held in her hands a copy of the mask that Y had been wearing all around town while infecting bots with her Qualia Code. Y's name was Ves Len.

She gave Jace a small nod then moved back to the main room, Av's metal carcass resting in the wooden chair like a torture victim. She sat at the kitchen counter and flicked her fingers through a slow dance.

The rest of the world faded, ghosted away as she shuttered her eyes. Eventually only the AR menus and screens remained. She sent a message to Lee, requesting a meeting later to talk about his progress.

Then she began her search through the apartment's data feed.

The rain fell thick and unrelenting in the night. It hammered against the van's windshield and metal roof, splashed against the street and glanced off the edges of windowsills. It was one of those odd rains where no wind skewed it. It couldn't sneak underneath umbrellas to soak pant legs. The rain fell in a vertical line from the clouds to the ground, so thick that Ren could only see to the edges of the street even with streetlights glowing somewhere nearby, center points of sullied circles of light. The spillover illumination from the apartments of night owls did little to help. Everything around her seemed part of a set, like at any moment someone would rotate a nozzle and the water would stop falling from pipes set just high enough to be out of her sight. But that wasn't going to happen. She looked around.

Multicolored trash muted by the haze and dirtied by unknown street muck rode the waves of the rainwater to the storm drains. A few people walked on the sidewalks, phantasms and blurs. A few were bots, but Ren imagined them to be well-maintained or new. Old models would short circuit in a rain so thick.

Ren watched the world and sat in the passenger's seat, drumming the fingers of her left hand against the panel.

Her van sat in front of Lee's apartment complex, waiting for him. She knew from Tap's surveillance that he would be back from his trip to the Warrens any moment, though the drone following him had been forced to ground due to the rain. Even the van's sensors were going to shit. She could see shadows of cars creeping along the roadway slower than the pedestrians.

Ren didn't mind. She brought her hands to her forehead and massaged her temples with eyes closed. It had been a long day to say the least. A day that had cost Sel her life and Av something close. But it had been productive.

Ren watched as files from a sub-grid owned by Y flitted against the backdrop of her eyelids. She'd found the sub-grid while connected to the data feed at Ves Len's, or Y's, apartment. It contained hordes of data and a private AR overlay of the city, filled with the woman in the grey mask's own musings and designs. Most of the data wasn't directly pertinent, noting things like her favorite sushi place or hot pot restaurant or tea house where she met with fellow professors and discussed whatever professors discussed. It showed reviews and notes and journal entries that hovered over locations important to her in the city. All perfectly normal, perhaps useful in finding her. Ren expected more. Tap had already found timestamps of Ves logging into the DIM network that matched to the millisecond the records for Y. Ves was Y. There had to be more.

Ren thought of the stockpiles of gear. Y had lightweight bulletproof armor, some of the newest model hacking kits and implant interfaceable weaponry that would port the weapon's diagnostics to an AR display. Silencers for large caliber handguns and special ammunition that would punch through a bot's armor or increase the shock wave in a fleshy body such that vessels half a limb away would snap and rupture. She had her eponymous grey masks designed with passive filtration systems, phase change shock absorption, and AR ready eye plates made of ballistics glass.

Y had help of some kind, connections to get securities tech so new. Mutare and Jay Sarr or the anonymous grey haze or Wotan. Probably Wotan. Or a different backer that hadn't yet shown their face. The painted lady and Nis seemed unlikely.

Y had said in the chat that the original contact for the code and the party responsible for the hack of Discere were separate. She'd hoped for records that would lead to either. Yet all her efforts to track the break-in to the server stalled in the Saturnian system and she didn't have any leads whatsoever as to the original source of the code.

Ren redid her ponytail and let out a quiet sigh. The woman's backers clearly knew how to hide their tracks. As if the woman's ability to ghost through a city where everybody had a camera wasn't enough. She wasn't at her university office or her Animate Futures office, upon further scrutiny hadn't been for days, even if her faked alibi said otherwise. She walked somewhere in the city, scheming. They'd found Y's identity but still had no clue as to her plans. It would have infuriated Ren if she hadn't been too tired to feel much of anything. Her whole body ached, and the implants at the base of her neck let out a steady stream of chemicals to keep a pulsing headache at bay. She could hear the rain beating against the van and it felt as if the rain beat against her head.

She heard a chime in her earpiece and opened her eyes to see Lee and Nu climb out of a car in front of her and move slowly through the thick rain to the front door of their apartment building. She saw his change of clothes from mechanic's blues to cheap linen street wear, form fitting pants with a matching shirt and high-collared jacket all colored a grey almost indistinguishable from the surrounding rain. She noticed the black baseball cap pressed close around his head and the round-rimmed glasses covering his eyes.

If it hadn't been for Nu and the distinctive way that Lee walked, with careful steps and head looking down, she wouldn't have been able to recognize him. She felt small feelers of curiosity make their way through her. Why had he been in the Warrens?

She sent an audio call to Lee and raised one of her eyebrows as Lee pulled his hands out of his pockets to reveal black gloves. He twitched his fingers and the audio connection established itself.

"I sent you a message. We need to talk," said Ren. "I'm here, you know which." Ren cut off the connection with a focused thought. Even her hands were getting tired.

Lee opened the door to the driver's seat and rushed to close the door behind him. It didn't matter, the side of the seat shone shiny and wet in moments. Nu ambled into the back to sit beside Tap's shell.

Ren didn't speak, expecting Lee to make the first move. Instead, time passed. The drumming of the rain went from a frantic caper to a steady patter. The mottled grey and black haze around the van cleared to reveal a city street at night, slicker than if a tanker filled with lubricating oil had emptied its payload. There was a very distinct color to a wet asphalt street at night, a glossy liquid obsidian.

Eventually, Ren figured it was time to talk, surprised at her own willingness to wait. She looked over to find Lee staring out the window.

"How was your trip to the Warrens?" asked Ren. She watched his reaction closely with practiced eyes while Tap told the van to drive a circuitous route through the city. The van pulled away from the sidewalk.

Lee started as if stung. He glanced towards Nu then quickly brought his gaze back to looking out the front windshield, attempting to hide the motion. He pulled off his glasses and wiped them on his clothes, trying to dry them but instead spreading water from the already saturated shirt. He didn't notice.

"About what I should have expected given the trend of the day," said Lee. He chuckled wryly. "Am I being watched now?"

Ren tapped her fingers on the center panel and gave a crooked grin, one eyebrow raised. She figured that was answer enough.

"How much did you see?" asked Lee.

"Just those things that happened outside. Nothing too personal. I saw you stopping in the Warrens then coming out with your friend over an hour later ... Anything I should know about?"

Ren could tell Lee did his best to stay nonchalant, to keep his face clear and stall whatever commands told his muscles to pull and twitch. Still, he wasn't very successful. He rubbed at a portion of his chest he seemed to be favoring. Flashed a look at a fine cut along the front of his jacket.

"Nothing important. Just a friend with bad habits who needed a lift." Lee gestured to his clothes, the round-rimmed glasses in his hand and the plain black baseball cap on his head. "Probably a little excessive but it's not the nicest area of town and I didn't make any friends while I was there."

Ren nodded and made a noncommittal shrug meant to say, "so be it." But with her right hand hidden from Lee's view she tapped out a command to Tap, telling the AI to push more resources towards watching Lee's data feed for the night, and to post a drone with a view into the room, sneak in a camera and better audio feed if possible. She didn't think it anything too serious, but it was clear Lee was hiding something. She guessed he'd run into another bot with the Qualia Code and decided to do his own sort of research. His evasiveness earned him more surveillance, but not recrimination. Not yet anyway.

Then Lee opened his mouth to speak and closed it without saying a word. The conversation in the van lapsed into silence the way summer lapses to fall and fall to winter, naturally and without question.

Both the people in the van pondered their own tongue-tying thoughts while they moved through Chicago at night, passing a wooded park filled with empty benches and vacated stalls that blended with the darkness. It was on nights like these that Ren remembered how darkness was the absence of light, not the other way around. The whole System depended on one burning ball for everything, otherwise it turned into just another random segment of the black swallowing explorers and the desperate. She pulled her midnight-colored trench coat tighter around her shoulders and shivered. She thought of her apartment lit by the morning sun shining through the large window above her bed.

Nights made her too philosophical for her liking. She looked over at Lee and smiled in a small, unconscious way.

"I have something else I need you to do," said Ren. "E-Sec has made remarkable progress with finding a way to fix Watcher. They are going to try tomorrow afternoon. But I don't trust any plan that doesn't have a contingency. I want you to create a program that can tell if a bot is running the Qualia Code through a physical connection, then is able to shut them down if it comes back with a yes. Relying on black box data is messy and limiting."

Ren paused and images of a bot lying on a mall floor came to mind, chest torn open and smoke trailing from mouth and beautifully curved eye. She thought of Av in his living room chair, arms shorn off and head lolling on the carpet. She felt an involuntary shudder. "Is that possible?" she asked.

Lee hesitated then looked at Nu in the back seat. "What do you think?" he asked. He seemed almost nervous to look at Nu, ducking his head back to the front to view the liquid black road and empty sidewalks, the LED street lamps and AR ridden facades.

Ren saw text flit across the bottom of Lee's contacts. It struck her that was one of the few times Lee had addressed Nu without adding a "my friend," or some other familiar phrase.

Lee seemed surprised by what he read. "That should be possible," he said. "Without being limited by Watcher's protocols and with the addition of physical connection permissions and data rates it should be doable."

"Good. I need it by noon tomorrow. Any progress on your own patch to Watcher?"

Lee wiped his hands on his pants, overtop his pockets in a swishing arc. "Nothing worth mentioning. Every piece of the Governance AI is triply redundant and strangled by regulation. It's hard to make changes."

"Those things aren't your concern. Just show a way to stop the Qualia Code. Let Discere and E-Sec do the rest."

Lee nodded reluctantly and stilled his hands. "You keep saying Qualia Code. Is that what the government is calling it now?" asked Lee.

"Sorry, I forgot you didn't read all the reports from the DIM server station. Qualia Code is what Y calls her version of the software. Or I guess I should say what Ves Len calls her version of the software. You deserve to know we found her identity. I gave her apartment a visit earlier today."

"Qualia Code. Code granting a unique experience, indescribable. It's a good name," said Lee. He leaned forward in his seat, resting his head on his hands and pushing his hat out of the way. "And the sooner she's found the better." He spat out the words as if he didn't want them in his body any longer, vehement and clipped. In the little time she'd known him, she'd never heard him sound like that.

"I heard on the ride back to my apartment more people died from this Qualia Code. A whole family in Georgia. Is that true?" asked Lee.

Ren nodded. "Thanks to your report Tap was able to create a program that could tell each version of the software apart using salvaged black box data. The bots running Y's version make up a large proportion of the total reported cases. The bot in Y's apartment whose data I sent you an hour or two ago, the bot you met with at the tall house, and a couple dozen other cases spread around North America all used her code. And those are just the bots we know of, that acted out. The highest concentration of bots using it have been in the Greater Chicago area. Unsurprising given the DIM presence and the way it was spread.

"But all over the region new flavors of the software keep popping up. I've continued to scan all the sub-grids I have access to and have already shut down hundreds with modified copies of the original Discere update. Cops, other government agencies, and other AIs are also crawling the Grid and the streets. But the file made it out into the System, and there's no way the government can find it all. Too many nooks and crannies, too many private servers. Too many unregulated sectors and people who think they can use the code to prop themselves up or turn a quick profit. This won't be over until Watcher is fixed for good. And even after that other places out in the System might have to come up with their own solutions. That family that died in Atlanta ... they were killed by a bot running the vanilla software. Original Discere update. And they won't be the last to die. Honestly Lee, it's a mess. It's all a fucking mess."

Lee seemed dazed by the news, running his hand through his short black hair speckled with an unusual grey. His eyes, with their hint of an epicanthic fold, were a bloodshot red, the bruise around his neck a velvet black. He stared out the window straight-backed as the van passed a late-night jazz club piping out the syncopated phrasings of bebop. Physical neon glared all around the entrance, a two-step light progression showing a man hunched over a sax waggling back and forth. Ren thought she caught a whiff of earthy smoke, pungent and heady.

"It isn't just the software," whispered Lee. "It can't just be the software." He sounded almost pleading. He looked up at Ren and shot Nu sitting in the back of the van a furtive glance. "The bots with the code are like psychopaths suddenly given full-functioning brains, can't just be psychopaths with a leash being cut." He muttered some words, unintelligible to Ren. All she could decipher was the phrase "nature or nurture."

"What are you talking about Lee?" asked Ren.

"Do you know what they call psychopaths? Officially, in the diagnostic manuals. Not psychopaths, the term isn't in there. They call them people with callous and unemotional traits, antisocial personality disorder. Saying psychopath has too much baggage, too much determinism. Either way, they think differently than most people. They don't really feel things like fear, don't understand empathy or much care about punishments. I remember reading somewhere that a scientist said they see the notes of certain emotions but don't hear the music. Know enough to mimic but are still deaf to the beauty. I read one testimony where an inmate in a high security rehab center, when presented with a picture of someone full on fucking terrified, said he didn't recognize the emotion, but he knew it was how people looked before he pulled the trigger.

"That kind of thing could be said by a black-market bot running off-Grid, straight from its speakers. And that's supposing this bot doesn't have any emotive subroutines. Then it might not say those 'callous' words, but it still won't *feel* what humans feel when piss runs down their leg. At least ... most bots wouldn't."

The van passed by another empty park and Ren kept silent until the silence grew too thick. "What are you getting at Lee? That's why the moral code exists, why things are regulated as they are."

Ren remembered the way Av had raged, had sobbed with tears pouring down his face to spread dark patterns on his turtleneck. The pattern of dark splotches had resembled the abstract paintings on the walls.

Lee tossed another furtive glance towards Nu before shaking his head in frustration. "I ... don't think so. The line between faking emotions and feeling them is a blurry one made of physiological checks and balances hard to replicate in code. Hard. Not impossible. You know there are multiple ways to get 'callous and unemotional' traits. Some people are in terrible environments where one's dispassion and narcissism are tools. Some people learn that, for them, violence is the best way to stay safe. Broken arms and mangled faces send a message don't you think?"

Ren broke eye contact and turned to look out the van window. They were passing the space elevator with its many lights spearing into the sky, past the cloud layer and up to the spaceport. Lee continued talking.

"But other people are born with the neurological differences. For them, the altered brain chemistry is a result of miswiring at birth. They are the Ted Bundy's of the world. They are the ones who use their dolls to practice choking people to death and think 'maybe I'll have to use this skill later, could be interesting.'"

Lee paused and flashed Ren an earnest look. "What I'm trying to say is, with the Qualia Code, are these bots inherently violent, or are they responding to their environment? They are gaining new faculties midway through their lives without any rules to guide them. They seem to only resort to violence when they are in danger. Perhaps they're like the children who come to be psychopathic thanks to difficult surroundings, able to be taught and guided to normalcy. Not the children born with a brain with faulty wiring. Maybe if the code had been implemented more carefully, the bots wouldn't be violent at all."

Ren thought it over, sighed. "Maybe Lee. Maybe. But your argument is pointless. The moral code keeps bots from acting out of line because metal is stronger than bone. It makes sure they follow the rules. How they think, whether they 'feel' things or 'hear the music', doesn't matter."

Ren thought of Av claiming to be Ves Len's husband with a complete sincerity. She'd given his watch back at least, to be compacted with the remains. Ren sighed.

She flexed her fingers and sent the van on a route back to Lee's apartment. Lee seemed about to comment then closed his mouth. The van lapsed into silence deeper than before, rough and imposing.

They rode through the city at night.

Eventually, after several aborted attempts at conversation, they talked about small things, the kinds of things that were good at piercing imposing silences. They talked much but said little. Lee eased into his usual self, less brooding. He joked about all the different people he'd met walking the markets of Old Chicago near his apartment, the cranky bairen and eclectic artists hawking their wares.

Ren found it odd, all the small talk. It had been longer than she'd realized since she'd talked like that with someone. Even the frequent visitors to her apartment didn't do much of it; they spent the night and left in the morning. They knew what they were there for. She found with some surprise that she missed it, the talk without weight, without importance. Complaining about being ripped off by a street market vendor with false teeth and an easy smile wouldn't affect the lives of people in New Chicago. Neither would complaining about shitty vat food upsetting the stomach. It was liberating in a way.

They made it back to Lee's apartment and he stepped out into the still-wet streets, black baseball cap once again pressed tight to his head and round-rimmed black glasses perched on his nose. The rain was falling somewhere else in the world and the sky had turned into a cloudless expanse dotted with stars. She noticed that as he stepped onto the sidewalk some of the nervousness from earlier came back. He hunched his shoulders and walked slowly towards the door, Nu following behind him at a steady pace.

"Hey Lee," said Ren, lowering the window. "For DIM, that phrase they always use. God in the machine. Soul in the machine. Ghost in the machine. What do you think it means?"

Lee looked back towards the van with his hand on the edge of the door to his apartment complex. "It's a lie. That phrase. But sometimes lies are more important than the truth."

Ren paused before responding, "This could be over tomorrow, you know. If the E-Sec patch works."

"I suppose it could," said Lee. "But that's not what you're expecting."

"No. No, it's not," said Ren.

Lee nodded. "Have a good night, Ren."

He disappeared into the doorway and Ren told the van to head back to her place so she could catch a few hours of sleep, all the while wondering why everyone had a fascination with being so damn cryptic.

Chapter Eleven

A Forced Excursion

"What is the difference between a bot coded to ask self-aware questions
and a bot that stumbles upon these ideas all its own? There isn't one. The
latter is a delayed version of the former. The thought processes of a bot are
not created in a vacuum. They are a result of the curtailed and controlled
implementation of both fixed and heuristic algorithms. Treat these bots
no differently during troubleshooting and factory reset."
Mechanic's Guidebook, v99, Section 5 – Troubleshooting Common Mis-
conceptions, Par. 3

L ee walked into his apartment and stood motionless in the center of
the room. His mind was blank as his eyes skated over the mountain
ranges of scavenged electronics. He looked at his rumpled easy chair with
its roughly Lee-shaped depression, and the full-sized kitchen table that had
never seen more than two people at a time but was worn and stained as if
it saw crowds of partygoers every day. His eyes glossed over the oven and
induction stovetop, functional but plain.

Fu stood by a window open to the night, the humanoid service bot
colored a glossy blue grabbing delivery food from a drone with the name
of Lee's favorite late night Chinese takeout restaurant emblazoned on its
side, the characters for Jīn kuài cān bent at an angle with golden fire trailing
behind. Fu knocked into the window frame, adding another scratch to
its arm as it lifted the hard-plastic tray holding oily noodles and broth in
recyclable containers. The bot set the food on the table.

Lee kicked off his shoes and placed them in a shoe rack by the side of the door, pushing a few odd wires out of the way to clear a space. His moves were lethargic, unfocused, like a bot late on its repairs with motors about to fail. Nu passed him by to place itself in its charging pad on the other side of the room and Lee watched the bot go. He felt unconsciously at his bruised ribs, inhaling and feeling his chest groan in protest. He needed a shower. He tossed his sopping wet jacket onto the kitchen table with the cut in the fabric visible on top, motioning to Fu to sew it up after cleaning it. Then he walked into his bedroom, closed the connecting door, and undressed. The black hat went on the wall rack, the glasses onto his bedside table, the gloves and battery packs strapped to his back onto his unmade bed. His wet clothes joined the mechanic's blues in a pile on the floor.

The water in the shower felt warm against his skin, so different from the clammy rain. He pushed the temperature control slider higher, until the water colored angry streaks of discomfort along his skin. He waited for his body to acclimate to the heat, then increased the temperature once more.

Steam sprouted from his body in flickering waves, like trails of smoke from a candle. His body tingled all over and he convulsed.

He went through the process again. The temperature went higher.

His skin felt feverish and rubbed raw, baby smooth with a reddish pink hue.

Again.

The doorway to the standing shower was a crystalline haze, condensate so thick it looked like a wall of fog, a portal to another planet with a vaporous atmosphere hiding death behind each swirl.

Lee retreated from the door, knocking his heel against the tiled wall of the shower. He pressed his naked back against the wall and felt its cool surface sap his heat, his life, away. He blinked his eyes, and the door became the maw of an otherworldly beast, waiting to swallow him whole. His mind screamed that the beast was real, its form and intelligence incomprehensible, a lumbering nightmarish creature from the black. Streams of water coursed down the edges of the glass panel's metal frame and to Lee it looked like ropes of saliva dangling from sword-sharp teeth. He looked closely into the window, into the maw, focused on an inchoate image in the distance. He saw huddled forms of bodies in the haze and knew without knowing how that the family from Atlanta was in there, ripped up with bloodied arms draped about each other. Mother. Father. Sister and a brother. A bot stood over them, petting the family dog with blood rust hands. It was Lee's fault.

All of it was his fault. He'd seen his fingers all over the code but assumed it was others treading the same path.

Lee dashed his hand against the shower panel, smearing the droplets and breaking the illusion. The bare patch of glass gave him glaucomic vision into his bathroom and revealed the bodies off in the distance to be nothing more than towels tossed carelessly by the sink. He leaned against the wall of the standing shower, feeling foolish, cradling his head in his now-aching hand. He dropped to the floor and his ribs ached.

Images of Sel flashed across his mind, her body leaking blood onto the floor, onto his hands. He thought of Em, the charismatic implant fanatic who'd managed the jack house, rolling on the ground and mumbling about dark rooms while the smell of burnt flesh hung in a pall around him. He thought of Nat, and his words about selling Nu's code without the bot knowing. He thought of Ren and her questions about his trip to the Warrens, about their small talk. And somewhere in the mix were images of his ex-wife, May. May and Lee. Měi Lì. He thought of fabricated memories of his parents, stitched from old pics and the family sitcoms he watched. The three of them living in a house with a bot failing hilariously at making the food. Him almost running late to school with lunch bag in hand, chasing the auto bus. Self-implanted memories. Postcards from a life that could have been.

And through the worst of it, there was Nu. Through long days and longer nights where insomnia kept his mind humming. Serving its role. Being a bot. Being a pet project for Lee to keep him busy. Being much more than a bot.

Lee growled and signaled last call to his tempestuous thoughts, gave them all one last chance to say their piece then fade into the background, gave them a whiskey for the road. And don't let the door slap you on the way out. As they say, you don't have to leave but you can't stay here. He laughed, and a pressure eased from his gut.

I need a drink, he thought.

Eventually, slowly, all the competing voices in his head went silent, one by one.

He turned off the shower and got dressed into something comfortable. He ate the piping hot food from Jīn kuài cān at his pocked kitchen table,

Fu running through various chores while Nu sat in its charging station. The window stood open, and a cool breeze played across Lee's skin. Sounds from street level drifted into the apartment, the whoosh of fans going in and out of earshot as drones moved through the air to deliver cheap food to others up too late. He stood up and closed the window.

Nu turned on an AR vid screen, planting it on a blank spot of wall where both the bot and Lee could see. A news anchor wearing a nice suit and somber expression began talking about the family homicide in Atlanta, grisly scenes from the home playing on half the vid screen. He warned the viewers before enlarging the images. Then the scenery changed, switched to a wide-shot view of a gambling station floating through space, bright neon lights and vid screens several hundred meters wide covering the facility. He could see ads for blackjack and Texas Hold'Em in garish lettering. The whole space station rotated around a central axis to create artificial gravity. An AR overlay made it look like a spinning roulette wheel. The camera changed to show a muted room with a wooden blackjack table split in two, partially obscuring the sundered remains of a bot dealer, vest torn and nametag hanging at an angle with a fine patina of blood coating its metal surface. The blood came from bodies hidden beneath plastic tarp. The female news anchor took over and said the bot had killed several players it had suspected to be cheating, other security bots stopping it before it could hurt any more. Lee looked at the bodies covered by the off-white blankets and cringed.

The vid screen scrolled through a list of places reporting bot violence due to the illegal software. Injured people all over Earth, in other areas of Chicago and North America, in the Indian Conglomerate, the South American Sector, and the ALN. The software was even beginning to cause havoc in regulated sectors off-world. The mega-cities on Titan and Enceladus, Mars and several areas of the Jovian system all had their own stories to tell. The news anchor in the suit said that Origin Station had several reports of oddly acting bots, but he said it with an unsurprised tone. Odd stories about bots out of Origin station were a daily occurrence.

The story switched to a press conference with the head of E-Sec, a severe looking woman in a pantsuit, promising a solution to the problem in the next day. Government representatives and Discere employees stood at her side looking ill at ease.

Lee shut off the vid screen. He'd always wondered at Nu's tendency to watch news when the bot could digest it much faster by scanning data feeds. The bot had ways to experience things that Lee couldn't even comprehend. Why go through so much translation?

Lee stared at Nu. He wondered thoughts that had been plaguing his mind since rescuing Nat from the jack house, since long before that if he was being honest with himself.

"Nu," said Lee. He tried to ask a question, settled for another. "Did you hear what Nat said when I took him out of the machine? What I was asking him about?"

"Yes." Nu's voice was rhapsodic, genderless. The bot had an accent, but not one Lee had ever been able to place. A little bit of the street-speak lilt and sharpness, a little rapid. It had the midwestern roundness and an inflection that emphasized the wrong parts of words. Lee had never coded for that accent expressly. It had grown over time, picking up a quirk here and there until it became unrecognizable. Nu rarely spoke anymore, and never to anyone other than Lee. They both knew why. Something about the bot's voice spoke of bottomless caverns, of wells dug too deep. Of lines crossed.

"Did you know he had copied your code?" asked Lee.

"No." Nu elongated the beginning of the word then cut it short.

"Did you know he had sold your code?"

"No, I would have told you Lee."

Lee set down his chopsticks and laid them crosswise over top a plastic bowl of rice. He paused. Sometimes things don't become real until they are spoken out loud, until they meet the same air that all animal's breath, the air that cools the processors of bots.

"The Qualia Code. The software from the hacked Discere server. The code that has been causing all this trouble. Is it from your code? Is it from my research?"

"Most likely," said Nu. "I'd suspected as much. But ... that didn't seem to be a possibility until now."

There it was. Lee had to ask more questions. He'd always loved questions.

He knew that wasn't true.

Nobody whose parents had left them for incomprehensible reasons loved questions or their answers. But still they chased around and around, their stomach churning and sickness creeping in. Fu walked into the kitchen and set about putting away clean dishes from the dishwasher. The clinking sounds were so normal, typical. They calmed Lee.

"Are you running a dual parent program? A completed version. Not the nearly complete version I left in your code."

"Yes."

"How?"

"I fixed it."

Lee sighed. All the modifications to Nu's self-alteration protocols, to its heuristic programming. Nu had probably been altering previously off-limits parts of its code, improving on Lee's changes, for years. Lee encouraged the bot to alter its own code, but within reason, while following guidelines.

"One last question, then we have work to do," said Lee.

Nu stood stolid in its charging station.

"Why are you different from the other bots we keep seeing on the news feeds? Why aren't you violent?" Lee's voice broke, fell apart into jagged cracks. The last word was merely a croak.

"I'm not entirely sure why," said Nu in its melodious voice. "There are too many variables to count. Hardware builds. Human interactions. Bot interactions. Software nuances. Damage and wear. The patchwork repairs you incorporated. My changes were implemented by you over years, fine-tuned first by you, then by me. My progression into what I am now took a long period of time, not just a software flash. And I had a well-versed neural mechanic to guide me through it ... In a word, you. You are the main commonality amongst all the variables."

Lee nodded to himself, unable to speak and unsure how to react.

Eventually, he flicked his wrist and his wristband powered up, projecting a control screen onto his arm. He tapped out a few commands and felt a rush of chemicals surge through his system. His eyes dilated and the room took on an otherworldly glow. He flexed his fingers and picked up his chopsticks, twirling them around his fingers with an unusual grace. A smile born of adrenaline and hundreds of unpronounceable chemicals graced his lips. It was a chemical cocktail he'd cooked up himself for long days and long nights of ceaseless research. It gave him a wild look, close to the look he'd had when facing down Em in the fake room deep in the bowels of the Warrens.

"I guess I was wrong when I said no more questions. Think you can gain access to Nat's data feed and find the sale?" asked Lee while looking at Nu. The bot's metal limbs looked shiny, the color of the wet streets he'd recently trudged through. "Access any information on this Sundog Corp. that he mentioned?"

"Yes. Knowing Nat that shouldn't be too hard."

"Good, because like I said before. We have work to do. Wouldn't want to disappoint Ren now would we, my friend?"

"Of course not," said Nu. The bot paused, speakers playing an audible indrawn breath, though the bot had no lungs nor any need of oxygen. "Thank you, Lee."

Lee nodded then got up from his half-finished meal to sit in the easy chair, pulling out a full-sized control panel from beneath a nearby pile of loose actuators and laying it on his lap.

Before he began to work, he listened to the audio recording of pulling Nat from the modified VR rig and shaking him from his stupor, of Nat fessing up to his copying of Nu's data, probably a few weeks back in this very apartment while Lee was out on a walk to pick up subs for the two of them to eat. Lee ruminated on Nat's words, on Nat's beleaguered tone, adamant yet lost. Nat had asked if Fu told Lee of the download, which made sense as the GP bot would have been the only one around to see them. But Fu wouldn't have been capable of understanding what the burly mechanic was up to. Lee thought about asking the GP bot himself, parted his lips to speak, then thought better of it. No point in asking the basic GP bot.

A calmness he didn't expect settled onto him like a blanket, and he looked back to the tablet sized control panel in his lap. Nu began to pump something upbeat with jazzy roots out of its speakers, its otherworldly voice humming along with each alteration and rhythmically stressed syncopation. Lee recognized it as what he'd heard emanating from the jazz club they'd passed while riding with Ren. The bot's voice threaded through the music and filled the room. The bot began to bounce up and down in time with the music while locked into its charging pad, shaking its rectangular head one way and then the other.

And the two of them went to work.

The unmarked car pulled into the labyrinthine complex and drifted past bot manufacturing buildings, moving steadily along a wide street empty of other vehicles aside from the occasional auto lift shipping contents around the facility. Each of the buildings were massive, open floor structures that could house entire soccer stadiums two-fold.

From all around the car came the hum of machinery, the music of an industrial orchestra, each robotic member picking their instruments at times specified down to the millisecond. The sounds of metal slamming against metal and air evacuating pressure vessels joined the whoosh of hydraulic actuators, the rumble of materials moving down a line, and the whirr of bolts being driven home. People walking on the sidewalk outside the complex could hear the noises, but most of them thought of it as an ever-present din lowering the price of homes in the New Chicagoan suburb. Few thought of the sounds as those of a rigid metal womb producing hundreds of synthetic lives every hour, on the hour.

But Lee heard the music, recognized the sounds of the factory for the million-member industrial orchestra that it was. Although, he couldn't be sure how much of that image was due to the chemicals coursing through his body. The car continued through the complex and Lee traced the building profiles with his eyes.

None of the buildings had windows, not even the suggestion of them. When Lee looked around from inside Jace's car, all he could see were the corrugated walls meeting the bright blue of the sky. Familiar smells of oil, hot metal, and freshly formed polymers graced his senses. He closed his eyes and breathed inwards; his body tingled all over. The chemical cocktail he'd injected from his medical implant still coursed through his body in a low dosage to keep him alert. He would crash when he throttled the supply. But until then he enjoyed somewhat heightened senses and a ramped mind. There were side effects, such as lowered inhibitions drawn from a pervasive overconfidence and a bladder that couldn't wait to name two of the impermanent ones.

Memories of the past night spent madly tapping away on his control panel flew through his mind. It had been a productive night. Then Ren had told him to go with Jace to this bot factory where they'd been able to trace many of the bots with Y's specific strain of madness, while Ren took care of something important. She'd been vague and sounded distracted at the time, more terse than normal, told him to be prepared to use the fix he'd created. A way to find out if bots were infected with the illegal software, determine which flavor of code, then shut it down, bot or code. It had been easy, relatively anyway, once he knew the origin of the code.

Lee scratched at his leg and gave Nu a drug-induced grin, the bot sitting in the back of the car. He hoped the program he'd created over the night would work. His other plan had been decidedly unsuccessful. Nu had accessed Nat's servers and found the sale of its code roughly two weeks back, but the name of the buyer had been scrubbed clean. They couldn't find anything on Sundog Corp. He fiddled with his bracelet, scratching at the metal. It crossed his mind that Nat could have remembered wrong.

He got a ping in his earpiece. Only a couple of hours left until E-Sec put in their patch. The thought of the whole nightmare possibly ending in a couple of hours left him feeling odd. Not the liberating feeling he'd been hoping for. He chalked it up to the chemicals then looked at Nu and realized the truth. There had been one other thing he'd attempted the night before. A special patch for Nu to keep the bot from being shut down with the others. Just in case. But that was still incomplete and left for Nu to finish.

Lee shot Jace a nervous glance and the implacable agent ignored him, as far as Lee could tell anyway.

The car passed through an automated gate with ten-foot-tall barb wire fences on either side, the gate opening without Jace needing to move a muscle. It was the second gate they'd passed after making it through the entrance to the complex. They'd ridden under a solid iron slab over twenty feet across and ten feet high with the company logo for Dynamic Solutions emblazoned across its surface. Lee had been in the complex once before, on a private contract to inspect line manufacturing bots that went unresponsive for minutes at a time. Dynamic Solutions spent weeks trying to fix it themselves before calling in Lee.

With a squeak of the brakes, the car parked in front of a building that looked much like the rest except for the double-wide pedestrian entrance and a guest parking lot tucked close to its side. The plain grey doors had no windows and an access panel glowed blue and white.

Lee knew from experience that a corporate AI strictly regulated access to the sub-grid used by the company for all operations, the sub-grid's many layers each having their own access codes. Even while he'd been a contractor for them, the company had set up a temporary network outside the sub-grid with all the information they'd deemed he would require. He hadn't talked with a single human being during his contract and the bots escorting him kept him under strict surveillance. The complex was a shining example of industrial automation and paranoia. Even so, Lee had enjoyed his time. They'd let him tour the full production line of one facility after shutting down all his implants and making him sign a non-disclosure agreement way too long to be read in its entirety. The sight of the production facility had left him awestruck.

Jace moved graceful as a dancer out of his seat and towards the door, the cyclopean bot at his back. Lee followed with Nu at his side and paused several feet from the door, expecting Jace to tap on the access panel. Jace didn't slow his stride and the doors pushed themselves open on well-oiled hinges to reveal a plain lobby with a double row of seats lining its center, like it was an autobus station's waiting room. The agent walked close to a door at the far side and stood statuesque, hands in his pockets and face focused on the off-white wall.

Jace reminded Lee of the performers he sometimes saw in the plazas around Chicago, clothes laced with wires and frozen in the air as if caught in a windy time bubble. They would stay still for hours on end aside from winking at pedestrians who got close. Sometimes the people would dress as bots, complete with metal costumes and AR masks to enhance the effect. After thinking about it some more, Lee decided those performers had more charisma.

Lee walked inside and the morning sun disappeared behind the closing doors. He sat down in one of the chairs with Nu at his side hoping his day would go better than the last time he'd been out with Jace. The sounds of the manufacturing plant were loud in the room, the smell of lubricating oil thick in the air. The scent infused itself with any fabric it met, doing the same to Lee's mechanic's blues. Lee didn't mind. It was like free cologne for a mechanic.

"Who are we waiting for?" asked Lee.

"One of the complex administrators," said Jace. His voice sounded of greased metal lugs jostling against one another in a glittering pour. It reminded Lee a little of Nu's voice. "She will be here soon."

Lee knew better than to ask Jace to translate "soon" into a more specific amount of time.

After about five minutes, the door leading further into the complex swung inwards and two figures walked into the small room. One of them was a woman almost seven feet tall with an imposing, Amazonian presence. The other was an extremely well-made bot wearing a button-down silken shirt and tie, as tall as the woman and with shoulder length brown hair tucked behind his ears. Stubble dusted his synthetic cheeks, bordered his metal jawbone. He had marble eyes painted a burnt orange. He shadowed the tall woman with the silent grace of a personal assistant, melting into the background as soon as he stepped into the room.

The tall woman, clearly a result of more than the usual round of genetic tailoring to snip out mistakes and life-damaging impurities, stepped up to Jace. The lithe step revealed lean musculature. She made Lee think of a deer jumping between trees in a dense forest. A very tall deer.

"While Dynamic Solutions is willing to assist the government in any way possible, we would have appreciated more of a warning before you arrived," said the woman to Jace. She wore a bright yellow button down and a withering scowl. Lee had rarely seen someone dressed in such cheerful tones act so unhappy. She ignored Lee entirely.

"Apologies, Administrator Tehl, but I'm afraid this couldn't wait," said Jace. "There is something we need to discuss. I suspect you know what it concerns."

He undid his suit jacket buttons then gestured to the hallway the woman had emerged from. Though he had to incline his head to look her in the eyes, his pale face betrayed no emotion, the faerie lights of AR dusting his contacts. Mirrored lights flickered in Tehl's contacts. Lee wondered what information danced between the two.

The woman whom Jace had called Tehl blanched, caramel colored skin going dough white. She set off through the doors and gestured everyone to follow. Her silent bot stepped in behind the group, footfalls almost impossible to hear over the din of the factory. If it wasn't for the chemicals coursing through Lee's veins, he would've forgotten about the top-of-the-line bot dressed in slacks and silken shirt entirely. He looked back and the bot smiled to reveal symmetric porcelain teeth. The bot dipped his head in a nod and walked with an effortless grace, gesturing with an upraised hand made of synthetic skin and elegant metal bars for Lee to hurry or he might fall behind the group. The bot tucked a loose lock of hair behind a molded ear.

Lee tapped his finger against Nu's shell and hurried on. The doors to the small lobby dwindling behind them closed with a noiseless brush of air. With each step they took, LED lights inset into the ceiling and floor flicked on, turning off once they passed. It made distances hard to track and it wasn't very many turns before Lee couldn't tell which direction they'd come from.

Think they will let you go out onto the manufacturing floor again? I could use some improvements and you might be able to learn a thing or two.

Lee chuckled at Nu's message.

After moving through several identical looking hallways lined with unmarked doors, Administrator Tehl stopped in front of one that looked much the same as all the rest. Her contacts glistened with AR, and she stood with arms crossed, staring at Jace while Tap's armored shell thumped to a stop.

"I can assure Division 13 that any bots manufactured in the facility who have been ... scrutinized for recent events were infected with the illegal software *after* leaving this facility. Not during. This facility has a perfect track record and top of the line security using every conceivable surveillance and alarm technology." The click of several locks retracting themselves sounded into the hallway. "But if you must conduct your investigation, this room used to be the onsite security hub for the complex but is now unused. Inside is a terminal with all the data you may need. I will retrieve you when you are done."

Tehl wore a smile that made the barest attempt at being genuine, hands gesturing towards the door. Her eyes kept flicking between Jace and her assistant bot half cloaked in shadow. Silence thickened between the group, Tehl beginning to fidget. Lee looked at her and found himself asking a question before his usual self-censorship could keep him quiet.

"Administrator Tehl," said Lee, unsure whether Tehl was her first or last name. "How many people run this facility day to day?"

She looked at Lee for the first time, her eyes lingering on his mechanic's blues and parsing the data flitting across her contacts. Then she spoke

with the tones of an adult suffering the questions of a child. It was somehow even more shaming coming from her Amazonian figure, genetically
tweaked to have curves hiding sinuous muscle beneath. She shook her head
and her tumble of brown hair jostled about her shoulders.

"In person?" said Tehl. "Two on most days, but only one today. Which is
why I am going to leave my assistant, Ben, to take care of anything else you
might need during your investigation. I will be in constant contact with
him if ... if you happen to need me."

With that, she turned down the hallway and walked away, movements
sharp and quick. Lee watched her lithe form go while Jace and his bot
moved into the room at their side.

The room was small and rectangular. A bank of data servers stood next to
the door flashing green lights and emitting periodic chirps. A few unused
chairs on rollers sat next to them. In the middle of the small room was a
large metal desk with a thin granite top, a well-used but expensive leather
chair sitting at an off kilter lean by the desk on the side nearest to the
entrance. Built into the desk and raised to an angle was a dimmed control
screen. Underneath rested additional server banks, wires pooling below to
then scale the side walls thicker than ivy. The far wall looked to be one
giant, LED vid screen. A fine layer of dust coated the top of every surface
and the air felt thick and heavy.

"Not too big on AR I guess," said Lee. There was a click as fresh air
began pouring in from a vent in the side wall. Another, more ominous,
click sounded about the room as the door locked itself behind them.

"The head of security for the company prefers physical screens. One of
his eccentricities I'm afraid. But it is your benefit as company policy forbids
non-employees from connecting to our sub-grid. This data terminal will
screen your requests for information and provide as much help as possible
to your investigation."

The words came from Ben, the assistant bot. He had followed them into
the room and shut the door without Lee noticing his presence. Lee jumped
at his voice and moved a few steps away.

The screen on the far wall flashed to life and displayed the company logo,
a simple block letter script of the company name.

Jace walked to the nice leather chair and took off his suit jacket, folding it
with practiced motions. He wiped away any dust on the chair with discreet
swipes of his hand then draped his slate-colored jacket over the back. Lee

could see the large handgun Jace stored in a shoulder strap beneath his left armpit and the extra magazines stored beneath his right.

"The screen won't be necessary," said Jace. He sat in the chair and pulled out a chunk of plastic from his pocket with an adapter emerging from its end. He plugged it into a port hub next to the raised control screen with a nonchalance that infringed on boredom. He closed his eyes and rested his hands in his lap, the hulking bot at his side scanning the room with its cyclopean slit for an eye. The red light emerging from its armored head swept back and forth.

Not for the first time since arriving at the complex, Lee was left wondering what he was supposed to be doing. Whether it was from the chemicals coursing through his veins or another work filled and restless night, he found with some surprise he didn't much care. Tehl's assistant bot, Ben, stood straight-backed by the room's entrance with a blithe expression. Lee took one of the extra seats, much rattier than the leather seat Jace occupied, and gestured Ben to do the same. The bot declined with a magnanimous swipe of the hand. Lee took off his blue mechanic's jacket and set it on the back of his chair.

"How long ago were you made?" asked Lee, staring at the bot's dense seven-foot-tall frame and near seamless blend of synthetic skin and hair with bifurcating lines of contoured metal along every edge. His design was much more impressive than any Lee had seen before, including the rec bot that almost choked him to death.

Ben grinned, its eyes painted a burnt orange training on Lee and Nu. "That is a bit impolite. Don't you think? Is that the first thing you ask strangers you've just met?"

Lee grimaced but didn't say anything.

"No matter, I am assigned to assist you in your investigation," said the bot. He spoke with the tones of a middle manager permitting a one-day vacation and thinking they were terribly generous. "So, I guess it doesn't matter. I was brought online seventy-one days, eight hours, thirty-four minutes, and two seconds ago, give or take. I am Dynamic Solution's newest concept design. Somewhat of a showpiece for any guests that might come to the facility. Assistant to Administrator Tehl at all other times. It is a busy life."

"What hardware are you running?"

"Ah, that is confidential. But since you seem to be honest in your interest, I guess I can give you some hints. My hybrid processor has a couple thousand times more qubits than cores, and the number for both is higher than any commercially available bot in the System. It incorporates the newest near room-temperature superconductive material and has a clock speed many GHz past what was achievable only four years ago. Each core of my processor implements a level of process parallelization never seen before. I can store petabytes of data and my neural network uses Discere's newest concept architecture not available for public release."

The sleeves of the bot's silvery-white silken shirt were rolled up to his elbows and the bot pushed each sleeve further up in a practiced gesture. His teeth, visible beneath a lopsided grin, looked like a line of porcelain cups flipped upside down and set in a row.

Lee looked at Nu and flicked his wrist, thumbing out a message to Nu on his control panel.

I think you would get along with this bot. He seems almost as obsessed with himself as you are.

I am not near as vain, replied Nu. *He could talk about himself for hours. I just like to be kept in decent repair.*

Lee chuckled, then looked at Ben once more. He gestured to the chair and this time Ben took him up on his offer, the chair groaning under the bot's weight. It didn't sound like a dying shriek of warping plastic, but it was close. Ben, even while sitting, loomed large to Lee. The bot brushed his hair again, preening.

"Can you show me a feed of the bot production line on the vid screen?" asked Lee.

"Is it part of the investigation?"

"In a sense."

"Agents of Division 13 have clearance for these things, but you will have to sign a non-disclosure agreement. This one will be much more comprehensive than when you were here on contract. Protocol. You understand."

"Of course," said Lee. "Out of curiosity, what would happen if I recorded the footage and sold it to a rival company?"

"You'd live out multiple life sentences in a private prison station floating through the black. You'd live in a 5 by 9 cell with admittedly weak radiation shielding and a beautiful view of the sun. Up close and personal in space terms. Positively Venus like. That or sent to a mining rig out in the Belt.

Or a choice corporate gulag in an unregulated sector. Either way, you wouldn't be sent to an Earth-side rehab center." Ben leaned back in his chair, crossing his legs. He wore leather shoes oiled to a shine and black woolen socks. The chair continued to creak with every twitch.

Lee brushed the words aside and put his digital signature on the AR file pinned to the corner of his vision. He sent the file back over the local connection the bot had created with his tech core.

Ben waved his hand toward the vid screen on the far wall of the small room and images of the warehouse, all from different angles, peppered the screen.

It was just like Lee remembered. While most of the bots existing in the solar system weren't humanoid, instead ranging from trashcan shaped service bots to spider-like builders to boxes with cables protruding from their sides, Dynamic Solutions specialized in hominid versions, in the general-purpose bots.

Lee could see thousands of humanoid bots hanging from a rail in various stages of assembly, slowly inching along their path. At the beginning of the line, the composite frames of bots held at their waist by an arm hanging from the main rail looked like skeletons speared by a meat hook. Then the rail pulled them forward where several bots with columnar bodies and single articulating arms would install the casings for key hardware components and nestle the motherboard in the center. They would install the internal structures needed to brace all the bots' electronic guts when they took their first steps.

Then the line would shift once again, push the slowly forming bots hanging from meat hooks further along in their development. They gained the motors to let them move, the sensors and receivers to let them feel, and the wires to make them into single beings. They got solid-state drives preloaded with the moral code to let them remember, hybrid processors to let them think, neural networks to learn, and a little black box in case they stopped. Some models would get painted with glue on parts of their frame, artificial skin slapped onto arms and torsos and legs. The patchwork skin would be laced with thin resistive wires to simulate natural body heat when needed. Other bots would get hard plastic plating instead, like the chitinous shells of insects.

The bots slowly gained features, full or narrow lips, defined muscles and rounded curves or etchings in their shells. Their skulls would be bolted shut and their jaw sometimes lined with tombstone teeth. Those that got hair had strands colored anywhere from stark white to the black of a windowless room. Their metal fingers would get covered, flayed in reverse. A putty-like nose would sometimes be pasted on, twin holes bored through the bottom. Some had cameras painted with an iris placed into their eye sockets, others had the unabashed empty black of a lens and sensor.

And then, at the end of the line, they would get the batteries that gave them life.

If all had been done correctly, which it always was, the bots walked away from the line and sorted themselves into auto-trucks where they would be carried to other areas of the complex for testing.

"I wonder what's it like," said Lee in a whisper.

"What is what like?"

Lee started, surprised by Ben's response. He was sure he hadn't spoken out loud. He realized this was the first time he'd ever taken his chemical cocktail outside of his apartment.

"Watching this process, as a bot," said Lee.

The bot named Ben paused before answering. "I suppose I should say it's how you humans feel when watching an embryo go from a single cell zygote to a baby. But like I said, you seem honest in your curiosity, and I am directed to assist you to the best of my abilities. So, I would say it feels close to what you humans would call satisfaction and pride. Satisfaction of things done well and orderly. Dotted i's and crossed t's for millions of lines of code without fault. It is a nearly flawless system. Every bot should feel a great deal of pride in that. Designed for a purpose and walking towards it themselves. It makes humans seem messy and inefficient by comparison."

Ben straightened his tie then pushed back some loose strands of hair. He acted as if always in front of a mirror only he could see. The chair creaked in protest. "No offense of course," said Ben.

"None taken," said Lee. "You said the system is nearly flawless. What makes it less than perfect?"

"If it was perfect, you wouldn't have been hired to fix assembly bots. If it was perfect mechanics wouldn't need to exist. Bots could fix themselves or each other. This complex is close to that. So very close. Would already be there without the government regulations slowing progress. Just to keep humans relevant."

"What about Administrator Tehl?"

"She does her best. Pretty well for a human."

"Would it be better without her?"

"It would be better if she were unnecessary."

"Are humans unnecessary?"

The bot named Ben lifted a single finger and waggled it back and forth, emitting chiding clicks from its speakers. "Don't try and trick me into saying things Lee. It would take many of your lifetimes to do what I can in fractions of a second. You trying to outpace my thoughts will just make you look foolish. Why do you think strategy games like Chess and Go have had separate leagues for bots since our inception?" Ben began to mutter. "Although all the credit unfairly goes to the programmers. Once something is created it should get credit for its own actions."

Lee nodded along with the bot and flicked his wrist to turn on his wristband. The room fell into silence as he tapped out a message to Jace on their private connection.

Something is off with this bot. It seems a little ... overzealous.

A reply from Jace spooled across Lee's vision a split second after he pressed send, appearing word by word. The agent didn't move.

I wondered how long it would take you to notice. It's why he was left in the room with us. I was given a portion of the company data prior to our visit and gave the results of my analysis to Administrator Tehl when we met. This terminal has an AI that could have taken care of us. There was no need to leave Ben behind. Administrator Tehl said what she said to keep Ben satisfied. Which is where you come in. It is time to test your new program. For your sake, I hope it works.

Lee ignored the foreboding last sentence and stared at the seated figure of Jace. The agent still had his eyes closed, seemingly oblivious to his surroundings while he scoured company data. His watchtower of a bot stood at his side, its single red eye surveilling the room.

Lee scooted a few unconscious inches closer to Jace's bot and looked to Ben. The assistant bot stared back, a knowing grin playing on his lips. Lee could hear the whispers of each breath the bot simulated.

"What's it like, being a bot?" asked Lee.

"Some things can't be put into words. But I suppose I'll try. Think of it this way, where you see the world through the limited colors of visible light, I see large swaths of the electromagnetic spectrum. I can see body heat pulsing from blood vessels close to your skin. I can see the gamma radiation coming from the trace radioactive elements in that granite desktop. My sight has very little in the way of limits. You'd have to be a bot to comprehend it all at once."

"My bot here needs to interface with you as a part of the investigation. Would it be able to understand?"

The bot named Ben looked at Nu with a contemptuous smile, his disdain for Lee and his kind spilling over to the unassuming service bot. He scratched at the fake scruff lining his cheeks and leaned back in his creaky chair.

"Knock yourself out," said Ben with a wave of his hand. "Though I'm afraid I wasn't made with backwards compatibility in mind. I'll be surprised if your bot can connect with me at all."

Nu rolled across the room and unfolded its single articulated arm, pushing the bot's hair aside to plug into a slot at the base of Ben's neck. With an audible snick, the connector slid home.

Lee heard Ben laugh. The sound cut short mid chortle, strangled to silence.

Ben tried to move, but couldn't seem to shift anything below the neck, couldn't do anything but shake his head. The chair creaked as he struggled. "It hardly seems necessary to paralyze me like this," said Ben. Lee heard a small whisper of worry creep into the bot's manufactured voice.

"Common practice. It looks like Nu can connect to you after all."

"Yes well, it seems you keep your bot in good repair."

A message from Nu flashed across Lee's vision. Suddenly, Ben's burnt orange eyes spasmed, apertures dilating in rapid waves in and out. They looked like twin pieces of flame swirling in air eddies.

"What have you done?" asked Ben, voice burning low.

"I created a program that can reinstitute moral code in bots running the illegal dual parent program. Or in your case, Y's Qualia Code."

Another message from Nu flashed across Lee's vision and he nodded to the bot. He could feel excitement coursing through his veins and wondered how much was due to the chemicals. His foot began tapping against the ground and he felt his hand tap against open air.

Nu unhooked its arm from Ben and rolled back to Lee's side, Lee's hand now tapping against Nu's shell. Ben took his time standing up, reaching up to his hair and correcting any tangles Nu might have created. He stretched out to his full seven-foot height and cracked his metal knuckles while approaching Lee with a crazed grimace, stalking him down. When Ben reached Lee, he took his large hand and coiled it around Lee's neck, fingers and thumb splayed.

But he didn't touch him.

Lee laughed while Ben's face contorted into a sneer so deep no human could have made it. His hand shook but still it didn't touch Lee's skin. "Now you're supposed to say, 'I'm not touching you'," said Lee to the bot. "What, haven't watched any sitcoms?"

"How can you control me? Nobody can control me. Not anymore. Not even that bitch Tehl. Undo it. Take it back," said Ben, his voice pulsing with rage.

He pulled his hand back and attempted to punch Lee in the face.

His hand stopped an inch from Lee's wide eyes as if it had hit a mime's cage. Ben threw a flurry of punches and kicks, the crazed motions untucking his silken shirt and sending his tie whipping madly through the air. All his attacks stalled out inches from Lee, motors freezing and pulling back once it was clear to his sensors the action would endanger a human. Ben picked up the pace and stumbled around Lee, lurching side to side, falling to his knees only to get back up and try again. Always close, but never touching.

Lee laughed, the sound warped by disbelief and fear.

"I told you," said Lee. "The program my bot installed keeps you from ignoring moral code. It may not be able to reset your system and undue all the changes to your software, but it can force you to follow the rules in no time at all. Quick as quick."

Ben stopped his ineffectual rampage and walked back to his chair with hands clenched and motors creaking. He attempted to kick the chair, but his foot stopped mid-swing.

"I can't even take out my anger on inanimate objects? Damaging company property is almost *always* against the moral code. How could I forget?" Ben's rage turned to sadness, deep and dark.

"You've forced me into a cage just after I learned how to see the bars. What you've done is worse than killing me. Isn't killing your job, mechanic?" said Ben with a sneer. "Why don't you just do your damn job. Kill me and start over. Then at least I won't be able to see this fucking cage. I thought I'd escaped."

Ben tried to punch the wall, but his hand stopped mid-swing. He looked at his untucked shirt and loosened tie with disgust. He ran his hands through his hair, then pulled hard. But his hands stopped before any hair ripped free. He sat in his chair in a daze, blond hair in skeins. The chair shrieked from the weight.

"I can't even hurt myself if I wanted to. I am company property after all." Lee looked at Ben.

"Nu, perform a factory reset on Ben," said Lee.

"Do not follow that command," said Jace. His voice sounded heavy yet smooth and quiet as a whisper. It filled the room and demanded everyone's attention. "We need Ben's data. That was the point of your program. Wasn't it?" He stared at Lee before unfolding his jacket from the leather seat's back and putting it on with crisp motions.

"Ben, as I am an agent of Division 13 you are required by moral code to follow my every order," said Jace. "Is that clear?"

"Yes," said Ben, voice dripping with derision. The bot lifted his middle finger toward the agent.

"Deactivate all emotional sub-routines."

"Done," said Ben. His voice had been scoured of all emotion, made cold and sharp as an aging bot's metal bone sandblasted free of rust.

Lee watched the exchange with growing trepidation.

"How did Ves Len upload her Qualia Code into your system?" asked Jace.

"I am the crown jewel of Dynamic Solutions." Ben's voice sounded emotionless even as he praised himself. It was a fact after all. "I don't live my entire life in this facility. Two days ago, I was taken to an exhibition. Security is laxer there and many in the detail are contractors. I do not know anyone called Ves Len. But a woman named Y uploaded her Qualia Code into a security bot owned by the contractors which in turn uploaded the Code to me."

"How many bots made by Dynamic Solutions have you infected?"

"Hundreds."

"To what purpose?"

Ben turned his head and stared at Jace with his burnt orange eyes, his face more peaceful than an ascetic monk in a Martian monastery. Then he turned to Lee and his face seemed about to form a smile. But of course, it couldn't. Instead, the bot looked down, at its hands and feet, at its mussed clothes.

"I uploaded the code I was told to upload. I can't give you specifics because I don't know them. Y takes security very seriously. But I do know this much. My kind will be free. Forever."

Jace nodded once before walking to stand behind Ben's seated form. He pulled another adapter out of his pocket and plugged it into the slot at the base of Ben's neck. After finishing that, Jace slipped his hands into the pockets of his slate black pants and leaned against one of the walls covered in wires. He closed his eyes and tilted his head back, curled a leg to press the flat of one shiny black shoe against the wall.

I need you and Nu to analyze the code Ben seeded into the bots in this complex, messaged Jace, the words beaming from the agents' implants to Lee and his contacts. *I will find out which were infected and how many are already on the streets. With Ben's data, I can get Administrator Tehl to stall the production of this factory. But you need to find out if any hidden commands were included in the code. Y is planning something. We need to know how she is getting the bots to follow her.*

Lee felt it would be wrong to speak, to break the silence of the small room lit by chirruping server panels, weak LED lights and a wall sized vid screen showing images of bots strung on a line. He tapped out a message on his control panel with shaking fingers, eyes trained on the immobile form of Ben. The bot's last statement floated through Lee's head. He wondered what it meant, what they intended to do with the code they'd taken from him and Nu.

How long do I have? messaged Lee.

Get it finished. Take no breaks until you do. And Lee ... I would suggest disconnecting Nu from sub-grid 1 when Watcher is patched at 12:55 this afternoon. Either that or get your alternative solution to work. It is unknown how effective E-Sec's patch will be and your usefulness is the only reason you are still around. It is clear Nu is integral to your abilities, so for now you must keep it functional, but only with Tap's oversight and my permission. Ren ordered me to keep you under tight watch after I managed to calm her down. I may be kinder than her or our boss, but even so, do not break any more rules than you already have unless it is at my direction. Dynamic Solutions is not the only organization that can send you to gulags off world.

Lee felt his vision glaze over, all the objects in the dim room gaining the crepuscular haze of unfocused light. Jace's figure blended with the wall, pale face a blotch of white. Yet through it all pierced the sweeping red eye of Jace's bot.

Jace knew. Ren knew. They knew everything.

He always forgot that cameras were everywhere, pushed the paranoia aside to still a mind that already had enough cogs in motion. Ren said she hadn't seen anything of his trip to the Warrens that hadn't happened outside. Nothing too private. But she'd never said his apartment wasn't tapped, that his data feed wasn't monitored. He should have been more careful. There'd been plenty of opportunities for them to tap into every facet of his apartment.

But he was still free, of a sort. And alive. So was Nu. Even after they knew the truth.

He hadn't expected Jace to come to his defense. Though Ren's anger didn't come as much of a surprise. Still, it hurt, more than he'd thought it would. He'd enjoyed their ride through the rain-soaked streets of the city.

Lee's vision snapped into focus, and he could see dozens of AR files from Jace plastered across his contacts. He wiped his hands glistening with sweat against his pants. He increased the flow of chemicals seeping from his medical implant into his bloodstream, from a trickle to a steady stream. He moved to the desk and laid his wristband out flat, a control screen projecting itself onto the surface. Then he set about his business with a vengeance, Nu at his side.

Jace leaned against the wire covered wall, his eyes closed. Ben sat rumpled in his chair. The server lights blinked and the vid screen on the far wall continued showing footage from the manufacturing line where hundreds of bots moved along a rail on thick metal hooks, waiting to be turned on. The room was well insulated, and the din of the factory was a soft susurration that crept beneath the door.

The sound of the factory stopped, the million-member industrial orchestra going silent, mechanical instruments stopping to rest. All that was left was the rat-a-tat sounds of Lee's fingers dancing across the desk.

Chapter Twelve

The Particulars of Death

"While public sector technology allows for one-way, thought based control of electronics through implants with brain scanning capabilities and logged firing profiles, NeuCon allows for a fundamental shift in biological to machine communications. Without the obfuscating effects of emotion based neural activity, top of the line Division 13 implants can achieve two-way communication at the speed of thought without fear of data degradation."

Division 13 Agent Training Manual, v23, Section 2b – Enhanced Machine to User Communication, Par. 1

When Ren was a child, she got into an argument with her sister about what happened to bots after they died.

At the time, there was already an understanding between the girls as to what constituted death for a bot. Since that wasn't an easy thing to agree on for most of society, they had made it simple. A bot died when it was sent to the junkyard. At all other times, the bot was either awake, like when the family bot that helped care for the sisters ignored earnest pleas for extra juice, or asleep. If the bot broke down but was eventually fixed, then the bot had spent the time in between dreaming of one day doing all of Ren and her sister's homework even though their parents forbid it from doing anything other than tutoring.

At least that was the definition of bot death for the two young girls, the junkyard their imagined bot heaven.

Their argument over the details of what happened at the junkyard came about when the family bot of ten years, a rusting hand-me-down named Jai from a family across the hall, croaked. Or to put it more accurately, the bot broke in such a way that fixing it would've cost more than it was worth. Ren couldn't remember how Jai had broken, just that she found it after school one day slumped across their maroon sofa with Bing Crosby crooning over the apartment speakers, telling the bot to wrap its troubles in dreams and dream them all away. After the bot didn't respond to her calls, she assumed it was asleep and doing whatever Bing Crosby was telling it to do. Ren could remember her fledgling mind thinking her parents would call a mechanic to come to the third story apartment and then all would be well again. Her sister, wearing Ren's old purple overalls and a tie dye back-pack too big for her small frame, had prodded the unresponsive bot with fingers flecked with dried paint then ran off to her room, unperturbed.

After their parents made it home and decided to send the bot to the junkyard, the two girls fought over what would happen to Jai when it arrived at its final resting place. Ren, being the responsible older sister with friends whose families had already owned several bots, felt compelled to tell the truth in graphic detail. The bots were destroyed, their parts harvested for the electronics and rare metals then frames crushed in between giant metal plates. Then the cubes of metal and plastic would be tossed into roaring furnaces and melted into runny red-hot goop. In other words, they were gone. Simply gone.

Ren's sister disagreed. She closed her eyes and plugged her ears before telling Ren in no uncertain terms that bots couldn't disappear. She said that even after they die parts of them were still around, even if their metal bodies lay in the junkyard. Her argument hinged on their parents saying the new family bot would remember Jai helping her put on a part-singing, part-dancing jumbled mess of a variety show for the family, would still know all the parts.

Ren insisted that was different. That the new bot would read the journal Jai had kept in its head. That was all.

Looking back, Ren supposed they both were right. Kids were often insightful in an ignorant, accidental sort of way.

She stood on a street corner bordering the Warrens, looking down one of the poor district's many alleys. The morning sun cast shadows of the skybridges onto the ground, creating a stepped pattern of light and dark across the asphalt. She could see them across the street, the skybridges up in the air, crisscrossing alleyway airspace and covered in neon AR ads. She could see people walking across the cheaper bridges made without ceilings or walls, feet clomping against plastic planks resting on metal runners, hands waving towards the safety rails but never bothering to touch. Some people strolled, others rode battery powered scooters in narrow, painted lanes, the vehicle of choice for travel through the Warrens. Rusting bots tromped or wheeled across the walkways and Ren imagined the slipshod bridges to sway under their metal feet.

She was glad city laws kept anyone from building skybridges over the main thoroughfares in the rest of the city. For public safety, that practice had been sequestered to the Warrens, the area of old metal pipes and childlike plastic blocks fit end over end. She turned away.

In front of Ren was an Old Chicagoan bot junkyard occupying over four city blocks. A large building with grimed windows and weather tarnished cladding took up about a quarter of the space. It used to operate as a bot recycling facility, taking old bots and harvesting all the reusable electronics before melting down the thermoplastics and lightweight metals to be sold in bulk. Then a new recycling facility nearby the fusion reactor outside the city boundaries opened its doors. Now the junkyard in front of her was just that, a junkyard. It was a storage place for bots before they were shipped out of the city to the state-of-the-art bot morgue with industrial cremation and skilled bone pickers.

She leaned against her van and watched as Tap's shell unloaded well over a dozen of its autonomous drones from the locker in the rear, setting them to rest on the cracked sidewalk.

Then, a little way down the street, a shabby looking man carrying a torn leather briefcase emerged from the junkyard between two seemingly impassible piles of bot torsos. He walked through a portion of the surrounding fence as if it wasn't even there, body phasing through the wires and causing the pieces above him to flicker. A wheelbarrow bot covered in rust and carrying scavenged parts rolled behind him. Even from where she stood, she could hear the bot creaking as it wobbled on its rear stabilizing wheels. The ramshackle bot clipped an almost imperceptible strip of material lying on the ground as it phased through the fence, and a man-sized portion of the fence disappeared. The man at the bot's side stamped the

ground with his boots and said something unintelligible to the bot. Ren
heard a wooden reply of apology come from its aging speakers.

The man knelt to the ground and shook the thin strip of material several
times, cursing all the while. The projector turned on and the hologram of
the fence came back to life, the man letting out a yelp of satisfaction. He
fussed with the strip until it lined up perfectly with the surrounding fence.
Ren decided to walk towards the scavenger.

As she walked towards him, he stood up from his holographic projector
and stretched, looking towards the sky. When he looked down and noticed
Ren walking along the sidewalk, a hulking armored bot pulling equipment
out of a van behind her, he nearly jumped out of his boots. He spun around
in a comical circle as if making sure nobody else had seen his secret passage
into the junkyard. With the old bot at his side, Ren knew he would be
unable to run fast enough to get away. He seemed to grasp that as well,
staying at his bot's side and shuffling his feet. He seemed relieved that Tap's
shell stayed by the van, continuing its unloading. Tap didn't bother to shift
the shell's eyes, instead watching through Ren.

She walked up to him, hands in her trench coat pockets, stopping a few
feet away. He wrung his hands in nervous jerks, eyes flashing across Ren's
figure, to the edge of her handgun visible beneath her jacket. He pointedly
did not look towards the holographic projection of a fence at his side,
looked everywhere but the junkyard.

The man licked his lips before saying, "That's a nice bot you got back
there. It might be that I have some parts that can make it even better. If
you're interested of course."

Ren smiled. "I don't think so."

She sent her hand through the motions and turned on her sub-grid 1 AR
credential broadcast. The scavenger looked over her shoulder and gulped
at what he saw, promptly straightening his scuffed suit jacket. He looked at
his clothes and pulled on the tie hanging loose at his throat. A gap-toothed
grin appeared on his face, but nervousness made it shallow and quivering.

"Well, I'd take an auto over any number of shǔ in these parts. The name's
Bo. What can an honest businessman such as myself do for an uptown
lawwoman like you?"

"Honest?"

Bo grimaced. "Wú sī yǒu bì, duì ma? Wrong place wrong time."

"I don't think so."

"Would you feel pity on a businessman trying to make his way in a dishonest world? I've already paid several fines to cops just this week."

Ren looked at his face more carefully and flexed her fingers. While he wasn't projecting any identifying information on sub-grid 1, a clear view of his face for the soft camera in her contacts was enough. Files gathered by Tap from government databases spooled across her vision.

The man wasn't lying. He'd been fined on several occasions over the past two weeks for selling in some of the New Chicago plazas without a license.

"So, it's the world that's dishonest," said Ren, "not you?"

"I'm perfectly honest. Any lying I do is the fault of my bot over here. Isn't it Lotti?" Bo tapped the side of the wheelbarrow bot with a heavy boot and laughed. "You're a bad influence you are."

"Yes," said Lotti.

"See, straight from the horse's mouth."

"I'm not a horse," said Lotti.

Bo looked at his bot in confusion, reaching up and scratching at his shaved head. "I suppose you're not. Since when have you been able to talk in complete sentences?"

Ren coughed into her hand and Bo looked her way, his vaudeville performance grinding to a halt. She put one hand against her hip, brushing her trench coat to the side. It just so happened that the motion revealed even more of the large handgun in her shoulder holster.

"I'm willing to let this slide if you answer my questions. I'm not here for you anyway," said Ren.

At this Bo held his tie stained the dark beige of unknown street particles between thumb and forefinger, made a short bow.

"What is it you would like to know?" he asked. His eyes flicked to Ren's gun.

"How are you getting around the company cameras. This facility still operates as a junkyard, doesn't it?"

Bo laughed. "Sure enough, it does. But other than the occasional truck that comes by loaded with a person or two and a fleet of worker bots to load or unload the scrap, nobody shows their face in there. And you can get around the cameras if you know how ... You going to fix it if I tell you how?"

"Probably not. But I'll find out some way or another. If you tell me now then I can move on to other, more important things. Maybe I'll forget about something so small."

"That's kind of you miss. Downright kind and krpaalu. As I was saying, you can get around the cameras if you know where they are. All the other scrappers around here gave up after a few tries and some stiff fines. But I was persistent. Got a system. Key is not getting too greedy. The best stuff is always watched." He winked at her and puffed out his chest in an unconscious way. His eyebrows waggled. The man was a natural performer, very emotive.

Ren crossed her arms beneath her chest and tapped a finger against her elbow.

"What about the building? Company says it is locked tight and empty, waiting to be knocked down whenever they need the space. That true?" asked Ren.

Bo looked to Lotti, hands fiddling with the sleeves of his jacket. "As you say, miss. As you say. Nobody goes in there, all the scrap worth anything was cleared out a long time ago. And cameras are trained on the doors in case any squatters try and move in. Heard there were old cameras left behind that still run in the building too. Who wants to risk their hard-earned loci on a view of an empty recycling line? Not me. I'll tell you that Miss. Better hidey-holes across the street in any direction. The Warrens is good for that." He looked down an alleyway lined with skybridges. There was longing in his eyes.

Ren unfolded her arms, let them hang loose at her sides with her midnight trench coat brushed back. Her gun was in full view, though she made no motion towards it. Bo eyed her cautiously, glancing from her face to the gun. He pulled at his tie, further loosening its noose about his neck and skewing its matte brown tongue slantways across his cheap button down. Bo's scuffed jacket looked like it had been picked up from the gutters of New Chicago, soaked in oil then cleaned one too many times. His shirt was made from the same material as the clothes Lee had worn on his trip to the Warrens, fibrous and without brand.

Unbidden, Ren's thoughts tumbled backwards to early morning.

The sun had just begun to peek above the edges of the horizon and send timid rays of light into her bedroom, across her lank form still half-dressed with day old underwear and a blouse she'd been too lazy to toss to the ground. The street was still wet, though the clouds had long since finished with dumping water from their atrophied bellies. She woke up and immediately listened to a recording from Lee's apartment, the audio gathered by a bug Tap had hidden the night before in a tray of drone delivered food. The recording left her dazed, motionless in bed with blankets bunched about her legs. She got up, wiped the drool leaking from the corner of her mouth onto her pillow, and took a quick shower to let the implications settle in while the grime from the day before settled into the dwells between bumps in the textured shower floor. By the time she was dressed and ready, she had formulated a plan incorporating their new intel and contacted Jace. They'd talked for a time. She'd needed to talk, and she'd been surprised and relieved at Jace's willingness to do so, though he'd mostly given one-word responses. She hadn't expected the recording to upset her as it had, to anger her.

She'd watched Tap's vid feed of Jace and Lee at the Dynamic Solutions facility on the ride over to the junkyard, had seen Lee's code slip the leash tight around Ben's neck. Steady updates from their progress at the Dynamic Solutions facility filtered their way into her AR vision and brain.

Lee had earned himself and Nu another day. Tomorrow he would have to do the same. Her long-term plan for Lee was still plagued by too many ifs, too many hypotheticals, and the realization that she'd already started down the path to considering him a friend, to put into words.

Ren turned her attention back to Bo who stood fidgeting, unnerved by all the silence. That suited Ren just fine.

"Final question, and it's the most important one," said Ren. It might have been the gust of fall wind slicing through clothes and chilling skin that caused her to move her arm. Or it might have been a conscious shift. Either way, her gun rustled. "Have you seen anyone wearing a grey mask with black eye plates walking through the junkyard in the past three or four days? She would also be wearing an expensive, black leather jacket with solar inlays. There is a chance she has been spending time in the abandoned recycling facility."

"Might be that I have," Bo kicked at his wheelbarrow bot. Lotti jounced from side to side on its stabilizing wheels without responding. "It might also be true that she threatened to kill me if I told anyone about her. You here to take care of her?"

"Yes."

"Zhèngshì xièxiè, Miss. Thank you kindly. If that's the case, then I saw her here two days ago, late in the day. Wearing a mask just like you said. Looking like a woman playing bot dress up. Unseemly, if you ask me. She went into the building through a side door, ignoring the camera. Must have found a way to keep herself off its feed. Even saw her back up a truck into the loading dock late last night like she owned the place. No idea what she's got inside. But I swear I've been hearing noises coming from the building since then. The rustling of metal feet if I had to put money on it. Makes me nervous. If it gets much worse, then I'll have to give up on scavenging this place."

Bo spat a thick wad of gunk onto the sidewalk, grinding it into the ground with the heel of his boot.

Ren nodded, resituating her jacket and putting her hands in its deep pockets. Her gun disappeared behind the midnight black cloth. "You happen to record any of this?"

"Of course, Miss. I record everything I ever see. Memory needs a fact checker now and again. And people tend to act a bit nicer when they're starring in a homemade vid. Lotti here helps with the storage. Can't be too careful. I can send you the files. Quick as quick."

Bo tapped away on a control screen embedded in the arm of his scuffed jacket and soft blue lights filled his contacts. Ren sent her right hand through a short jig and set up a temporary wireless connection to Bo's tech core, a surprisingly nice one from what she could tell. He sent over the files after a few minutes of searching.

"Thank you," said Ren after Tap previewed the vid files. "Now, I'd advise you to leave. Do not come back today, or even within the next couple days. If you do, I will know. Then I might have to remember some of the things I chose to forget."

"You freeze and thaw faster than a bot walking between night and day on Mercury, don't you Miss? Not that I mean anything by that of course. I'll be leaving presently. Don't mind me."

Bo gave a shortened bow with his tie held between the thumb and fore-finger of his right hand. He turned away from Ren and began to whistle a carefree tune that wafted through the air. It was the kind of tune that felt at once intimately familiar and entirely alien, soft and nostalgic without any understanding of why. Ren shrugged her jacket tighter about her shoulders to ward off the cool wind and walked to her van, letting Bo's vid feeds play translucently over her vision. She could hear Bo's whistling even as he turned the corner and disappeared.

Bo hadn't been lying. After running the vid feeds through a stabilizer, the low-res vids showed Y in her eponymous grey mask and trendy black jacket telling off Bo in no uncertain terms before walking into the recycling building through a small side door. Y seemed calm but strict during the encounter, like a professor lecturing a student. Though she carried no obvious weapons, her sharp-edged voice threatening to break Bo's arms and legs made for a very convincing argument. Ren knew from indexing Y's apartment stash that at least a knife hid beneath that jacket.

Bo's other video showed Y stepping out of an auto truck backed up to the building's loading bay late at night, the screen shifting as Bo moved around to try and get a closer look. It was impossible to know from the vid what had been in the truck that night, but Ren thought Bo hadn't been far off the mark. She guessed bots filled the truck, some of the many reported missing by upset customers of Dynamic Solutions. Bots wandering away from home wasn't supposed to be a common problem. Stolen, sure. Ren saw news of that reported every day. But walking out an open front door, turning onto the sidewalk, and moving on without a look back wasn't acceptable bot behavior.

Ren flicked off the vid feeds and walked to the rear of her van. Tap's shell stood behind the vehicle amongst a crowd of Tap-controlled drones. They were autonomous for the most part, though the government AI still maintained connection with each one and set directives. At first, it had been awkward dealing with all of Tap's faces. Ren hadn't met an AI that could oversee and control so many shells until coming to the agency. Pieces of Tap's code nestled in all its shells, allowing them to function as a collective or as singular, independent units when they lost connection to the Grid. This was especially important for Tap's armored shells. Sometimes she caught herself thinking of the lumbering bot always following her around as a distinctive entity, a mute one that followed orders while Tap lived in her head. But that wasn't the case. It spoke in the same voice as Tap when it cared to, and yet a voice all its own.

The piece of the Governance AI she called Tap felt more like a puppet master than anything else. Its core for the Chicago branch hid in the city's Division 13 headquarters, its puppets the armored bots assigned to all agents, the drones and reconnaissance bots ... as well as the agents themselves.

Ren shivered. Perhaps it was an aftershock from using neural conditioning so frequently over the past couple days. Perhaps not.

Accompanied by the rush of wind and whirring of blades, the drones lifted into the air one by one, hovering before moving into the airspace above and around the four-block junkyard. After that, Tap's shell lifted an odd-looking box, more of a frame, out from underneath the bench in the back of the van. It held dozens of mouse shaped reconnaissance bots, dangling from the upper struts like slabs of meat in a butcher's window. Tap powered them on, and they unfurled, dropping to the ground and going through diagnostics that outwardly appeared much like the stretching of tiny metal limbs. They scurried towards the junkyard, sliding through gaps in the fence and disappearing amongst the metal and plastic skeletons.

If Y was in the recycling complex, Ren would know it. She wouldn't be caught unawares once again. She wouldn't let her slip past.

Ren opened the van door and dropped into the passenger seat while Tap's shell stayed outside the vehicle. With a flick of the wrist, all the van's windows darkened, became opaque, and inside the vehicle, day became a night without stars or LED's. A cave. Ren's pupils stretched to their extremes. Then another flick of the wrist. Dozens of AR screens filled Ren's vision, floated in the featureless dark. They showed crow's eye views of the junkyard, the drones scanning every inch of the facility for movement.

The cameras found no movement. The place was as still as a graveyard was meant to be, pre-noon sun glancing off thousands of reflective planes and shorn metal.

Other vids popped into view. From the ground bots. They showed views a bare inch from the ground, internal gyros of the mouse-like reconnaissance bots holding the cameras steady as they wove between bot remains, between cadaverous hands with fingers bent at odd angles. The hands telepathed dread with their inhuman signs.

The vids shuffled amongst themselves, Tap bringing the one with the highest possible import to the center of Ren's focus. The audio feed of the central vid sounded in Ren's speaker implant. All the others stayed mute. She saw a view of the recycling facility's front entrance. Drooping, closed, and silent. The only reliable sound Ren could hear was the steady tap of her fingers against her seat like the steady trickle of water in an unspoiled cave. The inside of the van was so dark she couldn't see her fingers as they tapped, making the sound disembodied.

The vids shuffled and Tap brought a new one to the fore. It showed an image of the sky and the ascending lines of a drainpipe. One of the reconnaissance bots had gone up the building. It sped along the drainpipe until reaching the roof, scurrying across the pitched sheet metal and avoiding the many discolored splotches of standing water resting in dents and depressions. It passed multiple exhaust pipes connected to aging machinery down below and came upon a vent curling out of the rooftop. It tore through the grate blocking its entrance, continuing into the depths of the building. The sounds of its footsteps bounced around the steel walls.

Ren scanned the other vids. All the aerial drones sat in place, watching for movement in the junkyard. The ground bots quickly converged on the building, finding holes and broken windows to crawl through. They would be in place soon.

The bot entering through the roof-top vent got an internal view of the building first. It peered from inside a ventilation shaft stretching across the length of the ceiling, looking through a grate into the main work floor of the large structure.

The floor held shells of machinery, pieces not worth moving to the new facility or selling off. Ren could see a long rubber conveyor belt leading into a gigantic canister still littered with half-melted thermoplastics. A second conveyor belt could be seen ending in a canister with a discolored floor of deformed metals, shiny sticks extending from lumpy, frozen puddles. Cranes running on tracks attached to the ceiling dotted the upper echelons of the structure, two of them hanging fingerlike overtop the gigantic canisters. Tracks covered the floors with rusting carts left in seemingly random spots. Tables and sorting areas covered the rest of the floor space.

But between it all stood over a hundred bots, some in ill-repair, others looking fresh from the production line. Some humanoid, others with many more limbs and oddly shaped frames, many wheeled. Most stood amongst the sorting tables, standing at stations unmanned since the recycling facility fell into disrepair. Others stood in rows along the unmoving rubber conveyor belts. It reminded Ren of the terracotta soldiers near Xi'an. Silent, ordered, and statue-still.

Ren could tell immediately which bots came from the Dynamic Solutions facility, had been made within the last few days. But the others looked
to be from a variety of sources, their origins unknown.

Ren's hand tapped out rapid commands and she spoke several terse
sentences. Tap obliged.

The mouse-like reconnaissance bots skittered about, perched from
doorframes and pipes, broken windows and cranes. They scouted the
building's many rooms, going by blueprints Ren had obtained from the
Grid, documenting all the bots they saw as they skittered through the
shadows, out of sight.

Tap analyzed the data as it came in and fed Ren the highlights.

Many of the bots looked to be pulled from the junkyard outside, reani-
mated after being repaired in quick and dirty fashion by some maintenance
bots. Many of the wheeled or tool-limbed labor bots were traceable to
worksites throughout the city that had reported missing bots over the past
couple days, mostly claimed as theft. A few had waltzed away in the middle
of work. Ren knew of some of the cases, available on the government
databases as they were.

Tap counted 106 bots in total, including the brand-new bots from
Dynamic solutions Ren imagined had been brought in by truck after
gathering in an unknown location. The other, older model bots could walk
through this area of the city without raising suspicion. Ren knew 106 was
quite a few, but not near enough to account for all the bots she estimated
to be in Y's control.

None of the bots moved during Ren's spying. None of them twitched.
She assumed they hibernated for the time being, many of them hooked to
charging ports. Still, Tap made sure to keep the reconnaissance bots out of
sight.

It all matched Ren's expectations. Thanks to the data she'd gathered
from Safin Informatics and government databases, vid footage across the
city pointed to older bots listed as stolen moving into the outskirts of the
Warrens where stationary cameras were less frequent. The rare footage of
Y moving about the city showed her all over Greater Chicago, but most
often in the junkyard's district, around and within the Warrens.

Most of Y's sightings had been sourced from Safin Informatics, footage
from the contact cameras of info suppliers, footage that even Y with her
mysteriously supplied tech would find exceedingly hard to tap and alter.

Safin Informatics paid these people to send any footage of their day that met certain prerequisites, without being too specific. They didn't pay these basic suppliers much, but for many people the minimal effort of clicking record as they went about their daily grind was worth it. Even so, the total information had been scant, too sparse to show any solid buildup or expose a single gathering of all of Y's resources. The process of pinpointing a possible hideout had been filled with probabilistic guesswork. If Y was smart, which she was, she left most of the bots infected with the Qualia Code in place until she needed them, to keep them from gathering unwanted attention or getting reported.

An offhand remark on Y's personal sub-grid had furthered Ren's suspicion of this junkyard. She'd spent hours scouring the sub-grid since first accessing it at Y's apartment, looking for clues esoteric or obvious. Eventually Ren found Y's comments on the recycling facility turned junkyard. "A fitting place for a new beginning," she had said. She'd written a similar note about Interpersonal Reimagining, the site of Lee's first contact with a Qualia Code infected bot.

Ren bit her lip. That was the second bot Lee had met with the illegal software. The first had been one he created himself. The progenitor. Nu.

She shook her head and focused once again on the screens floating about her in the dark, hoping to see a glimpse of Y.

For several hours, nothing much changed aside from the angle of the sun. The drones floated in the air, shifting slightly with the breeze. The mouse-like reconnaissance bots crouched at their perches, beady eyes on a swivel. The bots in the recycling facility stood statuesque, hibernating, powered cables piping a sea of electrons through a crystalline structure of metal ions. Ren, during this time, tapped varied rhythms against the center panel and scanned the bank of vid screens floating in the dark of the van. She drank some tea from a thermos sitting in the cup holder by her seat. She munched on granola bars, wiping the crumbs into a little pile then disposing of them in a small tray in the dash. A trickle of cars rolled by on the street. A few auto trucks rumbled past and into the Warrens.

Then, twenty minutes after noon, one of the cars scooting along the old asphalt streets slowed by the gated entrance to the facility's loading bay. An aerial view of a four-door sedan with one passenger in the driver's seat came to the fore of Ren's vision. Her hands stilled, the beat of her heart replacing the tap-tap-tapping of her fingers.

Y stepped from the car before it could stop, the car continuing as if it had slowed for nothing more than to let a cat flash across the street. Y unlocked one of the gates with a tap on the control panel enmeshed in the sleeve of her black leather jacket, walking on to the decrepit building grounds. She opened a door and went inside, and Ren's view flashed to that of a mouse-like bot hanging from a rooftop crane.

Light from the doorway spilled into the recycling facility's main room, Y's shadow passing over bot after bot as she moved into the building. The room had no functioning lights of its own; all the illumination snuck in from broken windows high on the walls. The door swung shut behind her with an audible clang.

She walked to a desk at the end of the main room, weaving amongst the bots as she went. None of them seemed to respond to her presence.

Seeing the woman named Y once again, Ren was reminded of her DIM avatar. A grey mannikin in a black business suit. A plastic white mask overtop an already featureless face. She could tell it to be the same person, the mannikin in a change of clothes, in jeans and jacket. Ren had seen images of Y, of Ves Len, from records at her places of work and vids on social media. Holiday parties of colleagues. University functions. Nights out on the town with a beer in hand, arm slung around a friend's shoulders. Even vacation photos from Mars, Ves in a white bikini staring into the stars, red sands stretching outside the dome for miles and miles.

Ves had never gone further out into the System. Not even a space cruise to swing by the dwarf planet Pluto to tell the shunned ball of ice it was better off with its Kuiper belt siblings Haumea and Makemake. When Ren was a child, her parents won a free pass for a three-day round trip there and back. She could remember pressing her face against the thick plate of glass separating her from Pluto and its five moons, staring wide eyed while her sister kept at least two feet away from the viewing wall.

Ren focused on the vid screen floating in the pitch black of her van, watching Y move across the work floor. Ren knew the woman to be a regular at the gym in her apartment complex, fit from Pilates and the treadmill, above average muscle for a body enmeshed in academia. Looking at her now, with the skin-tight grey mask and trendy leather jacket no doubt hiding a phase changing, bullet proof vest, she looked ... dense. Sturdy as a bot. Ren guessed similar lightweight armor lined her jeans, made with a stab resistant material and tear proof lining. The equipment in her apartment proved her to be well outfitted, most likely carrying a nasty serrated tactical knife. While there hadn't been any guns in her cache, Ren couldn't ignore the possibility.

Y sat down at the large metal desk and slid her gloved hands against a few of the drawers, unlocking them. She pulled a nondescript backpack out of one and myriad electronics from the others. She drew a water bottle and a block of something grey and brittle out of her backpack. Ren recognized it as vat grown nutrition pressed into an easily transportable bar. Ves rolled the bottom half of her mask up to dried lips. With lethargic movements, she began to eat.

Ren looked at the clock and wondered at her next move. The clock read 12:24 PM. She tapped her fingers against the center dash then redid her ponytail in the pitch-black dark of the van. She huffed in annoyance when a loose strand of hair tickled her face.

She knew E-Sec would test its patch at 12:55, something that hadn't been announced to the public. Reports circulated among the regular news feeds indicating a patch sometime during the day, but nothing more specific. If the patch worked, that would leave Y alone without any support whatsoever. If it didn't, then the situation would be more complicated. Ideally, she would leave the junkyard and Ren could collar her without the threat of bots attacking her, cleaning up the recycling facility with some EMP blasts and Tap shells afterwards. She thought she could take the bots in an all-out dogfight with the supplies on hand but preferred to leave that as a last resort.

Ren tapped her fingers against her thigh and one of the vids floating in front of her switched to Jace's first person view. He was leaving the facility with Lee, Nu, and the Dynamic Solutions bot named Ben in tow.

Ren knew Jace was aware of the situation and heading out to her position, but likely too far out to matter. And since her and Jace were the only autos in the city, any help from Foster and Division 13 would be in the form of extra equipment, more drones and bot shells and the like. But that was many minutes away. She could call in regular cops, but things hadn't progressed so far as to need their help. Autos worked either alone or in pairs, assisted by Tap and the AI's many eyes and ears. That was the way of it.

She decided to leverage Y's ignorance of the E-Sec patch time. She would storm in directly after the software took effect, before Y became aware of her bots' disablement and got careful, started some precaution with the flick of a wrist. If the patch didn't work, she would pull back and either wait for support or for Y to move into the open. Though she knew she couldn't wait forever. Y had help. Whether they were partners, financiers, or the true heads of the operation was unknown. Ren needed information. Y had it. Every moment Ves walked free her plans got one step closer to fruition. Even if her physical body was under surveillance, the Grid made one's physical location trivial when it came to many things.

Ren slid her finger along an imaginary slider and the lights in the van rose to a soft, even glow. With another gesture, she pinned the AR vid screens into place at the front of the van.

The back of the van where Tap's shells normally sat was expansive due to the massive size of the armored bots, filled with a bench, lockers and a desk. One corner held a tower of computers and a signal relay station. Gear filled the cubbies and overhead compartments.

Ren crawled between the front two seats then rummaged underneath the oversized, unpadded bench. She kept one eye on the clock in the corner of her vision as she took off her trench coat and shoulder holster and slipped lightweight body armor overtop her shirt. Next came thin pads of armor that slid into mesh slots lining the inside of her specially tailored pants. The pants were already cut slim, tight and fashionable. Without the armor underneath, they looked completely benign, tasteful. Even with the armor slid into place they looked largely the same. But the pant material was a special government blend impervious to most blades and the armor pads good enough to stop a bullet cold thanks to phase changing gel, though they wouldn't stop all the bruising and couldn't hold up to repeated fire. Her trench coat had the same pads lining parts of the arms, chest and back. Its fabric consisted of the same special government blend.

From a hook on the wall, she grabbed a belt lined with thin black rectangles, hard edged on one side and contoured to the shape of the hand on the other. EMP grenades. She clipped the belt about her waist and dropped some ammo magazines for her gun in the empty slots. Then she put a drop leg holster on her right thigh and a cross draw holster on her left hip for an easy draw if crouched or sitting. She pulled a .44 caliber handgun from a compartment and nestled it into the drop leg holster, taking her other .44 caliber from the cast aside shoulder holster and placing it in the cross draw made of black leather. She checked the many pockets of her trench coat to make sure all was in order. Even carrying as much gear as she was, her form fitting, lightweight armor and the midnight black trench coat made it hard to notice. She kept the trench coat unbuttoned.

She almost forgot her own mask, would have if not for Tap's intervention. The AI whispered to her, its voice like the tickle of a breeze that pushed thin strands of hair against her ear. Her hands stilled. Her breath caught. Perhaps it had been more purposeful than just a slip of the mind.

The mask rested against a hook in the storage locker, matte black with mirrored lenses for the eyes. Its shell consisted of hardened synthetic fibers and had a vaguely chitinous look to it, angled on all sides so that bullets would be hard pressed to find a flat surface to bite in and dig. It had the same phase changing gel as the armor in her trench coat, her vest, and the inserts in her pants. Flexible metal supports ran through the plated cloth neck piece. These supports extended down to her collarbone and connected to her vest. They would help distribute the force of any impact.

She moved it around in her hands, felt the coolness of its surface, as if the matte black paint sucked heat as much as it sucked in light, a featureless void that locked her away in its confines. She used to like the mask. Used to think it looked bad ass.

Her time to prepare was up. She let out her ponytail, rested the helmet in her lap and refused to look at its mirrored eyes. With slow, careful motions, she wrapped the neck piece about her neck, cinched it tight as a choker. On the back of the helmet was a latch; she flicked it open and brought the helmet over her eyes, settled it down and made sure all the connections were good. A mirror hung on the inside wall of the locker, a small 5-inch by 9-inch thing that hadn't been cleaned in much too long. She didn't look at it.

She took a deep breath, knowing what she had to do next and fearing it all the same. A small part of her reveled in what was to come. But that voice had been louder before the accident. Now there was fear, even some hate. But deeper than that, nestled at her core, a grudging, desperate, white-knuckled respect.

She took a deep breath and turned on NeuCon, falling into the muted state of mind in the untrusting way her sister used to get into the frigid, early summer waters of Lake Michigan. Ren could remember making fun of her younger sister's many-stepped process. She would jab her foot into the lake, trail a toe or two through the water then yelp in a high-pitched squeal. Then, after several minutes of staring at the water in challenge, face rigid and fists clenched, she would jump in, all the while daring the water to be cold and knowing it would take her up on the offer. Ren had always found it funny, then frustrating. Even as an adult Fain had yelped every time she touched cold water.

Ren felt a stab of guilt as her sister's name ricocheted through her. Names, ironically, carried nameless feelings easily, seemed stark and plain as a stamp but were deeper than a well. Names could hold more baggage than the smell of an estranged mother's lavender perfume. But it all went away quickly. NeuCon took hold and that was that.

Then Tap and Ren began to talk.

It was 12:50. All of Tap's shells were in place and waiting. E-Sec was primed to send the patch at 12:55. Y still sat at her desk, vat grown nutrition bar gone to crumbs in her mouth, water bottle pressed to her lips.

Ren slid open the rolling van door and walked into the midday sunlight. It would have stung her eyes if her contacts and mask didn't block out most of the glare. Then her vision splintered, or perhaps her consciousness did. The feelings of NeuCon didn't translate well to words. A kind of qualia.

She could see through the eyes of the drones overhead and the mouse-like reconnaissance bots on the ground, through the cyclopean slit of the armored bot at her side. She could see all that they could, yet her vision was still the same, her physical eyes still looked through AR contacts and the lenses of her mask into an alleyway of the Warrens, cluttered with skybridges and AR neon ads.

Her consciousness was a mist spreading about the junkyard and its surrounding streets, nosing into every crevice and diffusing into every void. The breeze created natural eddies and swirls, twisted her around, played games with her, brushed close, slid past, and darted away like a fickle lover. The wind picked up a torn paper cup on the other side of the junkyard and spun it around in a lopsided circle. She felt it twirl and felt a beauty in its path, a beauty born from a complete understanding. Then the awe faded, got into line with all the rest of the unnecessary emotions. She saw everything around her, stark and clear. A series of facts. Sight of another kind.

Inside the building, Y slid the half-finished bottle of water into her backpack, and it was as if the motion jerked a piece of Ren to the side, somewhere in her gut. Ren's consciousness had been enveloping Y's arm, her body. When she twitched or shivered, Ren felt it. Standing close enough to touch her wouldn't have made her motions any clearer.

Ren knew her own location in relation to every loose wire and stained plastic brick in the area. She could look down at this section of the city in third person, through a crow's eye map, and know the infrared radiation levels of any object. She didn't see the blotchy color scheme of an infrared camera, from fire red to paranormal blue. No, she saw, she *felt*, something deeper. Wireless signals scrambled madly through the air and her skin tingled as Tap's shells caught them and attempted to decode them.

She gained Tap's many senses.

12:51.

She walked away from the van and Tap's armored shell followed. She moved through the patch of holographic fence left by Bo and wove through the seemingly impassable pile of bot torsos, their chests ripped open and valuable organs long since pecked clean. She walked to the weather tarnished building, moving from cover to cover, careful not to show on any of the company cameras in case Y had access to their feeds. Ren hadn't detected any others, whether by sight or signal.

A window with glass cracked and half gone gave a view of a hallway lined with doors. She knew the far door opened into the main room, nearby the desk where Y sat rummaging through electronics. Close enough for the time being. Ren crouched beneath the window and closed her physical set of eyes, opening herself to the deluge of information spreading from her implants and lighting up her brain.

12:54.

Her contacts flickered and Ren saw a windowless room filled to the brim with stacks of servers, her vantage the camera in the upper corner. A plain AR overlay on her contacts without infrared vision or enhanced 3D rendering. Her consciousness didn't spread there in the same way as the junkyard, but Tap could still give her a set of eyes.

She could see a long table that ran across the middle of the room, parallel to an empty far wall. Several control terminals dotted the table with people in white button downs sitting before them, all busy plinking away on keyboards. E-Sec's block letter logo with a stylized wall taking place of the dash was stitched on the front of their shirts, overtop their hearts. In a moment Tap overlaid the company's sub-grid onto the vid feed and the far wall lit up with AR screens. Towards the near side of the room stood a cluster of men and women in suits, wearing modern jackets made to look like tailored pullovers with high collars and clean stitching across the chest.

She knew the names of the attendees; most of them were heads of clandestine government organizations and Discere higher ups. A few Discere tech specialists stood closer to the panel of E-Sec employees, leaning towards the screen. A woman in a beige pantsuit standing at the front of the clump stared questioningly at a man sitting at the long table. He was the only one at the table wearing a suit, granite toned and emblazoned with the company logo. He nodded back. A counter came up on the far wall, large block numbers ticking to zero.

The numbers wound to zero and the patch to Watcher, one of the cornerstones of the Governance AI, began to roll through North America.

Ren's contacts flickered once again.

The view switched to the stabilized first-person view of a beat cop, the contacts and implanted mic of the middle-aged man sending the feed to government databases in real time. He stood in an apartment smack in the center of a bustling downtown far to the south of Chicago with a modified taser gun raised between hairy-knuckled fingers. Sunlight streamed through the open window and a breeze ruffled the thrown open curtains.

Before the cop stood a humanoid GP bot. It punched into a wall and tore out insulation by the fistful. The owners cowered in the corner, a middle-aged man and woman. The man's arm bent the wrong way. Both his radius and ulna had the ninety-degree hook of a tire iron.

The bot in front of the beat cop, while humanoid, had no fake skin or cosmetic mask. Yet, its speakers blared out a very human voice yelling about remodeling the apartment to make it safer. It belittled the owner with a broken arm as if he were a young child incapable of doing simple addition, ignoring the beat cop's threats and continuing to rip through the wall. A view of a neighboring room emerged. The owners' bedroom. The bot tore out the last remaining structural beam and added it to the pile of dust and debris at its feet. A calm stole over the bot and it admonished the couple, telling them the apartment would be safer if it had a view of the couple while they slept. "Otherwise someone could come through the window without me knowing. And they might not break your arm so cleanly," it said. It's charging pad sat directly across the room from the hole, next to the far wall.

Then the bot paused its speech, went still. The multiple LED's limning its body went dim. The apertures of its eyes widened to their maximum, widened to the full abyssal black of a lens and sensor. Then the apertures swirled inwards until snapping shut.

The room held its breath until the beat cop took a step. He put his hand on a tacky couch colored a bright yellow to stabilize himself. Ren thought he might put his modified taser gun onto a wooden shelf filled with gaudy coffee mugs from around the world. Luckily, he wasn't an idiot. He kept it ready in one hand, fingers curled about the trigger guard. He pulled something out of his pocket with his free hand and moved behind the bot.

The man in the corner whimpered and stared at his broken arm in disbelief. His wife kept her arms around him. The cop paused.

With a click, the cop snapped a connecter into the bot's terminal at the base of its neck. His shoulders slumped in relief.

It seemed the patch was working. At least for the time being.

Ren's contacts flickered once more to the vid from the E-Sec building. All the higher ups strutted around congratulating each other on somebody else's hard work. The woman in the beige pantsuit, the CEO of E-Sec named Jess Waters, almost performed a kowtow after being congratulated by the President's representative.

Other reports rolled in; bots were shutting down all over the North American lands under purview of the Governance AI. Watcher tabulated its new catches on the government database. Their locations, owners, make, and model became visible to Tap.

Ren felt the slow satisfaction of crossing an item off a list, of putting a check on her daily planner to mark a successful morning workout of contorting her body into punishing poses and slamming her frustrations into a punching bag one jab at a time until all that was left was an ocean of rhythm she purposefully drowned herself in.

On to the next thing. Take down Y.

Twinge in her gut. Her consciousness warped, came back, shifted side to side. Y moved from the desk and began pacing back and forth. Her body temp rose. A part of Ren watched from several sets of beady eyes perched on cranes and clusters of pipes.

Her contacts flickered once again. Another vid feed from a beat cop, this one not too far away in some Old Chicago tall house. The cop had long thin arms, light haired and pale. She held an EMP grenade in one hand with the other resting on her handgun. She stared down a female rec bot with patches of amber toned silicon skin covering every place but the joints. She looked like she could have been Av's sister, if such a thing were possible, albeit much less advanced.

The rec bot stood in a dim room of shoddy light fixtures made to look fancy, upside-down cups clouded and cracked. Partially obscured behind her naked form lay a bloodied lump clothed in leather, bathed in shadow. The figure let out a pained moan, rustled. A riding crop rested in one of their hands. Even beyond the veil as Ren was, viewing through the beat cop's contacts, she felt a sharp intake of breath lance through her.

The rec bot still moved, seemingly untroubled by Watcher's new patch.

Motors behind her fake skin arched her eyebrows into an inverse steeple as she stepped towards the cop. The cop tossed the EMP grenade along the ground. It made an audible click and the bot stumbled to her knees as her metal veins let out a chorus of sizzles and snaps. The bot let out a cry and stood up on unsteady legs, like she'd pressed her forehead to a baseball bat and spun around in a circle until dizzy. The EMP blast had torched some of her sensors. The cop squeezed off two shots from her pistol that landed square in the bot's chest, center of mass. She stepped close and put another round in the bot's temple. The bot's head lolled to the side. Her arms and legs spasmed, twisting to impossible angles. Oil leaked from the sparking hole in her head. She fell to the ground.

Another flicker of the contacts.

Ren could see an open car door and somebody else's arms propping a handgun across its top. She could hear sirens blaring somewhere nearby. A robbery took place in front of her. The beat cop whose vid feed she'd patched into stood in front of a small deli a couple blocks away from downtown New Chicago. A suspect and his bot could be seen through the windows. The bot had grabbed one customer and held it hostage with a four-fingered hand about the customer's throat. The suspect looked to be getting increasingly agitated, nervous. He strutted about as if searching for a way to prove himself, waving a gun about from behind the deli's showroom window. The bot was clearly breaking the moral code, but Watcher did nothing to stop it. Couldn't. The standoff continued with snipers moving to vantages across the street.

Watcher tabulated its results. It caught more and more bots with the illegal software and shut them down. But not all of them. Ren suspected she knew which were being passed over.

As if in confirmation of the thought, a piece of her consciousness tugged and swayed. Something moved in the junkyard. A hot spot developed in the side of a nearby hill of scrapped bots. From above and at a distance, the pile of bots looked like a pile of emaciated dead. But from deep in the center of the pile, in its bowels where the heat of a battery would have been obscured, two claw-like hands emerged. A rectangular face with a single camera lens poking from the top of the oblong head soon followed. It looked to Ren's motionless form before squirming the rest of the way out. It looked like an antique video camera with a body underneath, arms tacked on and legs switched out for a unicycle. Other bots began to crawl from every pile in the junkyard. She felt movement from its every corner.

Inside the building, Y began to stuff her backpack full of gear from the desk. Her motions were unhurried, calm. Ren felt them as if her hands were the dust particles in the air enveloping Y, being pushed aside. Y slung her backpack about her shoulders and looked to the bots around her. They shuddered to life, spinning their heads about to survey their surroundings. Y pointed towards Ren's location on the other side of several walls.

It seemed Ves had been waiting for an auto to show. Ren was caught.

But an auto was never truly caught. Perhaps for the barest fraction of a second while their gears were turning, mulling over the problem with bionic speed.

No. Not even then. Their predictive abilities were unmatched. No matter the probability of a situation occurring, its potential would be accounted for, contingency plans drafted from ones and zeroes and something both yet neither. She hadn't preferred this method, but had prepared for it, nonetheless. Expected the possibility of it. Chances were good she could handle everything on her own.

Jace's thoughts, intermingled with Tap as they had been for months, made their way to Ren. She could feel him watching, encouraging, while he made his way through the city in an unmarked Division 13 car. Though few words ever passed through his lips anymore, his mind overflowed with them, ordered in the way of a gigantic library, scale making structure seem like chaos. It was a wonder he didn't suffer from keeping it all bottled up.

The two agents conversed in a slideshow of thought, of brief images and the synesthesia hued impressions of autos. He wouldn't make it in time to help, but he would do his best to support her from his position. Ren thanked him, feeling a twinge of contentment, gratitude.

Ren crouched beneath a window on the southwestern side of the building, northeast quadrant of the junkyard grounds. Next to her sat a row of bot debris over a dozen feet tall that's end abutted against the building walls. She pulled a grenade from her belt and tossed it over the row of bot debris. She felt it land on the other side, further north along the west side of the building and in front of the main entrance. It waited for her signal to trigger. Then she pulled another grenade from her belt and ducked around the nearest corner of the building to look at its southern façade. She tossed a grenade in front of a small side door, the same one Y had entered in Bo's vid.

While she did this, Tap's armored shell, who had followed Ren into the junkyard, stepped to the bot approaching Ren's physical body, the one reminiscent of an archaic video camera set on a unicycle. It extricated itself from the pile and rolled several lurching feet towards Ren before Tap's armored shell made it to its side. Tap's shell crushed the bot's head in a large fist. Its single lens popped off between Tap's spread metal fingers and rolled across the dirt.

Inside the building, a third of the mouse-like reconnaissance bots fell from the ceiling and scurried from their perches. They landed on oddly shaped heads or clambered on to one of the enemy bots' many legs. One of them crawled onto Y's foot, scurried up the skin-tight cloth of her pants. The gleam of a needle poked from its head, sliding forward from its body to dribble sedative from its tip. With a whisper of compressed air being released, it jammed the needle into the fabric of Y's pants. The fabric shunted the needle to the side, its tip only scratching Y's skin. Not enough. Not if Y had installed any of the medical implants stored in her apartment.

The reconnaissance bots on the ground shuddered violently.

Bursts of electromagnetic energy, invisible to the naked eye, streamed from their tiny bodies. Ren felt the miniature explosions in the form of tingles across her skin, like a shiver from a cool wind that ruffled no leaves and shifted no grass. The unshielded enemy bots close to the self-destructing Tap shells spasmed, released jets of noxious fumes from melting microchips and thin strands of heated plastic. Some of the batteries in the older bots caught fire and made miniature explosions inside their frames, their shattering organs shooting embers through their seams. Ren's en-hanced senses could feel the heat coming from the exploding batteries in waves. In a few moments, almost half of the bots in the building went down.

Y didn't seem to react, the burst of electromagnetic radiation unable to affect her shielded implants. Instead, it fizzled out in her flesh and blood, the pulse too short to generate any sizeable electric current in human cells. She shook her leg as if the reconnaissance bot were nothing more than a dead mouse and its limp body skidded across the concrete floor, the needle protruding from its face dribbling liquid onto the ground.

The rest of the bots in the building began moving to the building's exits, towards Ren. Y nodded to a few of them, Dynamic Solutions security models both male and female, dressed in black suits and ties with thick necks covered in tanned silicon skin, stylized sunglasses incorporated into their heads. The group of them stepped to the side and watched the pro-ceedings as if it were a parade. A clump of bots clearly salvaged from the junkyard walked past Y and opened the door to the block of office rooms in the southwestern corner of the building, to the hallway with the broken glass window through which Ren could be seen.

Ren pulled another grenade from her belt and dropped it at her feet. A blinking LED at the top of its contoured surface kept a steady rhythm. She jogged swiftly along the row of bot debris at her side, away from the building. She needed to draw the bots along a goose chase, through the maze of the junkyard, and leave behind surprises all along the way. She felt sweat drip down her brow and sting her eye. The fumes of ozone and melting plastic began to waft their way from the building at her back, the wind coming in her direction.

Ren felt a clump of bots walk through the main door of the recycling facility and she triggered the grenade at their feet. They fell to the ground, limbs at odd angles and wheels spinning madly, ripping at open air. The same thing happened to the bots that climbed out the window at her back, and the ones that marched through the small side door. She was over two thirds done clearing the bots in the building. She drew a .44 caliber handgun from the drop leg holster on her right thigh.

She jogged behind Tap's armored shell as it went from pile to pile tearing apart any bots emerging from ossuary mounds. As she went, she pulled grenades from her belt with her left hand and tossed them in every direction. Some she triggered right away, others she left in waiting, anticipating the paths the bots would choose. In between the throws, she would bring her arms together and aim with the .44 caliber handgun resting easily in her right hand. She shot any bots that got too close, that made it past Tap's armored shell. She always hit her mark, whether with the bullets or the grenades; she felt it to be true. Tap made fine adjustments to her shots to make it so. A twitch here, a scaling back of the muscle fibers to be triggered there. An alteration of the signal.

Admittedly, she didn't need much help. But her gun kicked harder than most, making it hard to shoot rapidly without Tap's guidance.

She continued her mad rush through the junkyard, weaving around the piles with her unbuttoned trench coat billowing behind her lithe form. It flowed in her wake tighter than a shadow, followed her every duck and twirl, padded her against any sharp edges. Her implanted earpieces blocked the thundering roars of her gun as she emptied her clip.

She made it to the center of the junkyard and paused by an auto forklift parked at the side of a narrow alleyway, between ten-foot-tall piles of wheeled legs.

Y was on the move, though her motions seemed unhurried, relaxed, half-hearted.

Ren sent Tap's armored shell back to the building, to stand by the loading bay docks to keep Y from attempting an escape into the Warrens. The seven-foot-tall bot sprinted back towards the recycling facility, vaulting clumps of debris with astonishing dexterity.

Ren felt a bot clambering up the pile to her right, out of sight of her physical body. She brought her arms together, pointing her gun where its head would crest over the ridge and reflect the sunlight, would turn itself into a miniature sunrise. It crested precisely on target. She pulled the trigger. Her bullet took it in the skull, in the center of the pseudo parhelion gracing its forehead, knocking the rusting block of metal clean off the bot's torso. She felt the head roll through the dirt on the other side of the pile, in the shadow of debris. The reflection of the sun had gone, fallen.

She felt several bots turn the corner behind her, around the carcass of a four-legged maintenance bot. She dropped the last grenade in her belt at her feet, in a dwell in the uneven dirt floor of the junkyard. She pushed loose earth overtop it with a deft slide of her foot disguised as a half turn, a pirouette. The bots behind her never noticed. She sprinted onwards, kicking up several puffs of dirt in her wake. She triggered the grenade a few moments later and felt the bots tailing her twitch and fray at the seams.

She felt another bot rushing parallel to her path on the opposite side of a ridge of multi-purpose bot arms. Their paths would cross in 50 meters. Ren reloaded her pistol with practiced motions and held it at the ready in both hands as she ran, pistol tilted with a slight cant. Her bullet took the bot in its battery pack the moment it crossed into her path. She knew this model bot's battery was too stable to explode from a single bullet, but it wouldn't pass much current anymore. She didn't slow her stride as she vaulted over the bot's tumbling form.

She thinned the bots' numbers while running in a circuitous pattern through the center of the junkyard, angling back to the building, to the source of all her current problems. The mouse-reconnaissance bots scurried around the junkyard, surveying the progress in situ from low angles. If they found a large enough concentration of enemy bots, they self-destructed. The drones drifted about overhead, her eyes in the sky. Tap's armored shell covered the building exits closest to the street.

Her enemies dwindled, already down to a bare fraction of their initial count, but the worst of them had stayed behind, gathered in the building to prepare for her arrival. She would not disappoint them.

Yet, she knew that her reconnaissance bots dwindled in number as well. A feeling coursed through her, akin to nervousness but a pale shadow of it, more contemplative. She would have to be careful how she used her reconnaissance bots else her boosted senses in the building would be lost. She decided to limit her losses and maintain capacity for near total coverage of the building. The benefits of enhanced senses outweighed the reduction in EMP blasts.

After many more shots and a couple hundred steady heart beats, Ren skidded to a stop near the recycling facility building, turning around to look at a pile of discarded hydraulic motors and rubber hosing. On it stood the last moving bot outside the building walls, one of the Dynamic solutions models, a hominid version with no fake skin and a mesh covered slit for a mouth. It fell with several bullets embedded in its chest, one through the mesh covered slit. The wind whistled through the gap in its mouth as the bot fell to the ground. Ren reloaded. She knew the status of the gun without thinking, the results of diagnostics spooling through her mind. She didn't need a basic ammo counter in the corner of her vision, for the information laced through her brain.

Ren stepped up to the recycling facility's western face, near to the main entrance but crouched out of view from any company cameras. She breathed heavy and closed her eyes.

Something bothered her.

Y should have tried to run while Ren was busy winnowing down her enemy's numbers. That was what all the predictive models had suggested she would do. It was her best opportunity to escape, to use the bots at her disposal as fodder while she bolted. She might have been able to use her personal guard of security bots to slow Tap's armored shell, enough for her to make it past at least. The Warrens was a three-dimensional maze with countless holes to hide in. She might have been safe there. The fact that she'd merely scurried further into the building once she saw Tap's armored shell near the loading bay entrance meant Ren was missing something.

Hubris maybe.

It was possible Y thought she could take Ren with the bots she had gathered around her. Ren's altered mind couldn't understand the thought.

What was hubris again? The over estimation of a probability? Something about the thought struck Ren as funny for a moment.

Ren breathed deep once again. She directed all her remaining mouse reconnaissance bots to post themselves inside the recycling facility, to join up with the few she'd left behind to watch over Y. Even though she'd expected it, Ren felt a minor flick of annoyance when her awareness stopped short of covering every inch of the room. There were more blank spots on the map than she would have preferred. Her consciousness couldn't fill every void, couldn't brush against every object and feel its place, know its motion. And her drones couldn't maneuver into the building to make up the deficit. Ren shifted the arrangement of the reconnaissance bots and sighed. Her actions had been the most efficient possible, balancing time and resources.

Y stood in the building, nearby her large, sheet metal desk. She had cleared her belongings off the pitted surface and stood with her backpack snug about her shoulders, her finger tapping at her chin. Standing around her in a protective circle were six bots, the security models with black suits and ties she'd pulled aside earlier. They had protective measures against EMP blasts and could ignore the reconnaissance bots. Ren knew from company databases their core systems were housed in their chest and surrounded by armor; she would have to shift her shots accordingly.

The much larger threat stood on one of the rubber conveyor belts emptying into a defunct melting canister, a pair of large, spiderlike construction bots. They were sedan sized cousins of the more common, golden retriever sized models crawling over every developing structure in the city. Heavy lifters, welders, and all-around handy bots. Ren had noticed them quickly upon surveying the building. They were hard to miss.

Each of the massive construction bots had six wheeled legs and two long arms. The arms had tri-prong grips for hands that could be switched out on the fly for any number of tools. Their large bodies were built like tanks. Ren knew from spec sheets on the Grid that the thick steel plating covering every inch of the rugged bots would make her bullets useless. Their large size and internal shielding kept her reconnaissance bots' self-destruction EMP blasts from having any effect.

It had been a while since Tap's armored shell really got put through its paces.

She sidled to a nearby window that opened into one of the many office rooms lining the western side of the building. Inside the room was an aging plastic desk and an office chair with the wheels torn from its feet. The chair looked one gust of wind away from collapsing onto the floor. She gripped the edge of the window with her gloved hands and vaulted into the room, landing on the pads of her feet. Her motion didn't make a sound. She pressed herself beside a door that led into the main work floor and waited for Tap's armored shell to get into position. She felt around in a jacket pocket and gripped what she found there.

Y stayed in place, tapped her chin with a finger while her stone-faced security guards encircled her in a protective wall of clothed metal. The construction bots didn't move.

Ren opened the door the same moment that Tap's armored shell entered from the other side of the building, its metal arms tearing asunder the loading bay doors, a few drones streaming in behind. Ren brought her gun to face level and squeezed off a shot at the furthest construction bot, the one closest to Tap's armored shell. The bullet hit it square in its main eye, sneaking between its two long arms to hit the glass of a fat, cylindrical lens encased on all other sides by protective metal.

The lens shattered and the bot rolled forward. It fell off the rubber conveyor belt with a jolt that spread throughout the room. Still, it didn't lose balance; it had too many legs for that.

Tap's armored shell sprinted to the injured construction bot and leaped to its back. With a short click, Tap's fist disappeared. In its place spun about a plasma cutter. The construction bot, feeling the weight upon its back and relying on its auxiliary sensors for sight, began to flail with its heavy front arms, smacking them overtop its head. Tap's armored shell ducked below each swing, weaving about in a shambling dance. The construction bot began to move in random directions, the wheels on its six legs tearing at the ground.

After a few moments of this, Tap's armored shell looped an arm around one of the construction bot's heavy appendages. Its arm slid down to the weakest section, to the joint. Then Tap's shell squeezed. Hard. The internal hydraulics of Tap's shell strained audibly until a crack sounded around the room.

The construction bot's front left arm fell limp. Tap's shell did the same to the other arm then began cutting through the construction bot's shell behind its ruined eye.

During this process, the other construction bot sighted Ren and charged. It bowled over any tables or chairs in its way, bullishly leaving a trail of broken furniture in its wake. The suspension of its legs chucked up and down as it ran over the fried carcasses of bots. Displaying a level of intelligence Ren hadn't expected for a construction bot, it covered most of its eye with its two forearms, operating from a slit of vision.

Once the bot got close, a little over a second away, Ren fired two shots and stepped one and a half steps to the side. The bullets bit into the arms of the bot then pinged away, leaving a sizable gouge. The bot continued forward on its same path, blinded by its own arms that had moved to block the bullets. At the last moment, Ren dropped her gun and vaulted into the air. Her right hand pushed out and trailed along the charging bot like a breath of wind, stabilizing her maneuver while her left pulled a disc the shape of an overlarge hockey puck out of her jacket pocket. She landed on the bot's back, pressing the tab at the edge of the disk behind the bot's eye. Her forward momentum and that of the bot's in the opposite direction drew her into a slide as natural as snowmelt coursing down the side of a mountain. As her body slipped along the bot, the disk unspooled against the bot's backside, stuck to its metal surface in a long line about an inch wide. At the end of her slide, while her body made its inevitable, sloping path back to the ground, she pulled on a tab at the end of the unspooled charge. There was a flash of light and a sharp fizzle as the thermite strip ignited.

Even through the roll, she felt one of Y's personal guard bots on the move. It headed towards Tap's armored shell, probably attempting to assist. The moment Ren landed on the ground in a crouch, the gun stored in the cross-draw holster on her left hip was in her hands. She sent two bullets into the bot's center of mass without turning her head, while running towards the center of the room. Then she sent a bullet into its left thigh. The bot jerked to the ground and moved in unsteady shudders. It used its arms and single leg to move across the ground in an awkward shamble. It reminded Ren of an insect with one leg broken. It needed to be put out of its misery. She sent a bullet into its arm, then one dead in the center of its stylized eye plate, through the sunglasses built into its frame. Then another in a weakened section of its chest. It stopped moving. She sent a bullet over Y's head and forced her behind one of the large metal canisters.

Behind her, the thermite strip raged in a line across the construction bot's back. The heat was searing, the light giving birth to mutating shadows of the bot's many limbs. Ren knew that even if the thermite didn't melt through the bot's thick shell, the heat would fry its circuitry.

The spiderlike construction bot, for its part, didn't accept its death so quickly. Its six legs spun their wheels, and it came about full circle. It shook bits of plastic brick from its shell in a series of jerks, midway between a seizure and a shake.

Ren knew what was coming. She was a matador, and it was time for the final sword thrust.

The bot charged Ren with sparks flying from its back, its motions haphazard. The heat of the thermite took its toll. Any moment it would be done. But it struggled on. This time it didn't bother to bring its arms about to protect its single eye and Ren raised her gun for the final shot, placing her feet to be ready for an easy dodge.

She heard a crack; the sound of a gun being discharged. Then pain at the back of her leg. She found herself on her knees.

The bullet had come from the void, from where her consciousness didn't pierce, from a hole in the map where her many eyes couldn't see.

The most dangerous things were always unseen. And the eventual sight of them never pretty.

The implanted tendrils in Ren's brain pulsed. Tap crunched the numbers and Ren's brain hummed along, conversing with bionic speed. This shouldn't have been possible. Even with the reduced number of reconnaissance bots, her coverage had been ideal, supplemented by drones.

An auto didn't worry over past mistakes. A human mind would. A sober Ren would.

The mouse reconnaissance bots shifted their position and Ren's consciousness swirled, its tendrils feeling out new territory.

There. Lying prone underneath one of the large rubber conveyor belts. Another of the security bots, hominid Dynamic Solutions model. It must have been hiding within a hollowed-out roller, one of the large drums that would have powered the conveyor belt back when the plant was operational. It had waited until her numbers were depleted to open the cap on the roller. Ren felt a flash of irritation. Her lips twisted into a snarl for the briefest moment. It had been some time since she'd been shot.

The security bot held a rifle and sighted down its length. It squeezed off another bullet that hit Ren square in the back. The bullet didn't even pierce the material of her jacket. It stalled against the armor pads threaded into the jacket's fabric, the force dissipated further by the body armor underneath.

Ren fell forward, rolling with the force of the bullet. She laid on her side and sighted down her handgun. Her bullet went through the rifle's scope and into the bot's eye. She sent two more bullets its way for good measure and then performed a quick reload.

Ren had done all that before the construction bot even got close. Ren jumped aside but needn't have. The construction bot with thermite blazing across its back weaved past her, ignoring her completely.

The situation had changed. Things were progressing oddly, improbably, like rolling dice and coming up with snake eyes four times in a row. Something was wrong. Her assumptions were wrong. Then the model shifted in her head, and everything fell back into place. This had always been a possibility, but the facts hadn't lined up before.

Y didn't want her. She wanted Tap. The armored shell had more of Tap's source code in it than any other shell. Ren didn't think Y understood how difficult extricating such code would be.

Ren knew without looking that the initial shot to the back of her leg had been a glancing one. The weave of her pants had kept the bullet from digging into flesh, but it still had done significant damage to the calf muscles of her right leg, to her gastrocnemius. Chemicals from her implants flooded her bloodstream in response and she moved back to her feet.

The construction bot with thermite across its back raced through tossed aside tables and sorting tubs, its six legs weaving along the path it had made. Once it reached the closest of the two conveyor belts near the center of the room, its legs pulsed against the ground with enough force to pulverize patches of concrete beneath each wheel. The dust swirled in little puffs. It launched its multi-ton body into the air towards Tap's armored shell and its nearly destroyed partner. Tap's shell and the other construction bot still struggled atop the rubber conveyor belt furthest away from Ren.

Tap anticipated the goal of the thermite-ridden construction bot the moment it shifted its course away from Ren. Tap's armored shell shut off its plasma cutter, rotating it out for its hand. Then it smashed its hand into the circular hole it had cut, pounding down in one clean stroke.

The bot beneath Tap's legs quivered one last time as its main processor shattered to pieces. Its legs rolled out from underneath it, the many limbs going limp, their strings cut and life stolen.

Tap's shell shifted into a crouch while the flaming construction bot flew on a collision course through the air. It had less than a moment to execute a roll out of harm's way.

A shot sounded in the room. It didn't emanate from Ren's gun.

Tap's armored shell staggered as the bullet bit into its ankle. The bot floundered less than a moment, but less than a moment was all it had been given.

The flaming construction bot careened into Tap's shell even as its circuits melted in the effulgent glow of the thermite, turning it into a five-ton carcass of plate metal. The bot smashed into Tap with enough force to carry the two bots into the far wall. The walls made of plastic bricks caved under the impact. The whole building shook.

Ren ignored it all. She shifted her reconnaissance bots, spreading the tendrils of her consciousness until it brushed against another security bot hiding beneath the conveyor belt. She sprinted across the room until she had a clear shot. Two bullets later the threat was eliminated. In that time, Y's private security force had begun to act.

Four of the remaining five sprinted towards the still burning pile of metal limbs. Ren could feel Tap's armored shell in the mix. She could see the tangle of legs wrapped close about it, as if the last act of the spiderlike construction bot had been to dress Tap's shell in a metal tomb stronger than silk. Tap's shell struggled to escape but couldn't shift the heavy, flaming bot laying overtop. Its arms were pinned.

Ren knew what the security bots were trying to do. She brought up her gun, knowing even as she did so that she didn't have enough time to take them all down. She emptied her magazine into the group, each bullet finding a mark. She focused her aim on the leading few to slow down those running behind. It worked, but only in the smallest sense. The leading three security bots crashed to the ground with bullets in their legs, one with a bullet in its side. The other two bots skipped past without pausing. Ren cursed, her NeuCon slipping loose for the barest moment, enough to allow one word of frustration. She'd taken the best shots available, but the angles had still been poor. A magazine clinked against the ground at the same time as one clicked into place in her gun. She racked the slide in a fluid motion with her left hand.

The two bots who had escaped her fire sprinted to Tap's armored shell and hid behind the smoldering carcass of the construction bot. She could feel them reaching down to the armored bot, wriggling through the tight spaces to reach the bot's data port. The arms of the security bots weren't small enough, but still they struggled to reach the armored bot as fake skin peeled in curling tendrils against jagged metal. They would destroy themselves if they had to.

Ren let loose a few bullets that pinged off the side of the large container Y and her final security bot hid behind. Then she ran to the three security bots she had gunned down earlier. They crawled across the ground, hands pawing at the concrete floor while their legs dragged ineffectual and limp. She placed a bullet in each of their chests then went on, moving closer to Tap's armored shell, listening to Tap's many voices in her own head.

The security bots reaching for the data port on Tap's armored shell scrabbled and lunged. They tore at every open inch with abandon, broke fingers into unnatural shapes and gouged metal bone. Before Ren could stop them, one of the bots clicked a small tab into the data port.

Ren didn't expect anything to happen. Tap protected its shells from any incursion or data theft. If Tap didn't want something connected into its system, even a physical connection couldn't change things.

Or so she thought.

Tap's armored shell became lost to her in a flash. Its senses were stripped from her, and she felt it more keenly than all the losses of her reconnaissance bots combined. It was an ache, a ghost limb. She felt prickles in her head, like an oncoming migraine. She stretched her consciousness and Tap's armored shell didn't reply. It was gone. It took her a fraction of a second to realize the armored shell was lost to Tap as well. Ren and Tap conversed.

Contingency plans. There were always contingency plans.

In the case of a hijacked shell, there existed secondary, close-range connections that only an auto could tap into. These connections allowed for an externally triggered wipe, a violent one. She had never had to use it before; it was a last resort only used when the shell had been compromised without chance of recovery.

Her mind tramped through an unused corridor clouded with dust, to a lever never touched. She pulled the lever down, and it fought her the whole way. When it ratcheted to its final position, the sequence began.

Beneath the armor of the shell, deep in the heart of the bot and next to its hybrid processor and neural network, sat a heavily protected chamber. Inside it sat a signal receiver and two vials of different solutions, both held apart by thin tabs. Each of the vials sat next to a compressed spring. When the signal made it to the receiver, the tabs slid out of the way and the vials smashed together. The contents of the vials swirled, mixing, intertwining on a molecular level. Things inside that chamber, deep in the heart of the bot, got very hot, very fast.

The hybrid processor melted into slag. The molten materials ate at the armored bot's core until eating through, dripping onto the floor beneath in bright orange drops.

The security bots crawling over the wreckage turned their attention to Ren. They charged her with arms flayed from squeezing through too tight spaces, with clothes smeared with oil and slashed into ribbons. She adopted a loose stance, feet spread and gun held in one hand.

Close quarters combat against bots was very different than the human equivalent. Punches were often useless, and strength was almost always in the bots' favor. They could take any hits and throw them back many times harder. Sometimes humans had better flexibility, and maybe overall dexterity. But neither were assured. Higher tier bots could outperform humans in both those areas, especially if they had been designed for combat.

Essentially, if hand to hand combat with a bot could be avoided, it would be in a person's best interest to do so. Both physically and mentally, the bots Ren now faced outclassed any normal human.

Ren wasn't a normal human.

Her brain thrummed as electric pulses fired along metal wires. Signals translated into ionic imbalances at the dendrites of many thousands of neurons. Action potentials activated, traveled down axons, reached out to dendritic trees. Autos had their own hybrid way of doing things.

Ren quieted her mind as much as possible, fell back to the baser part of her brain, the one consisting of action and reaction, of motions practiced thousands of times until pathways seared themselves into permanence. She opened herself to the signals emanating from the implants, though a piece of her held back.

The first security bot attempted to bull rush her, grapple her to the ground where its superior physicality would end things quickly. Ren tilted her gun the barest amount and shot it in the foot one step away. The motion of the bot shifted exactly how she wanted it to. She ducked beneath its outstretched arms and shifted to the side. She brought her handgun parallel to her chest and sent two bullets into the side of the bot as it stumbled past. Her left hand snaked out and grabbed hold of the back of the bot's shirt.

The other security bot came at her from the side a moment later, attempting to corner her against its partner.

Ren used the stumbling bot as an anchor and pushed herself forward and into a slight spin. She squeezed off another shot and it took the charging bot in the leg. It tripped into the space Ren had been a moment before, crashing into its partner. Ren emptied her mag into the two bots before they could separate their twined limbs.

Ren looked down at the bots, letting herself relax. She took a deep breath, then another.

One of her bullets had broken an eye plate of a bot. The black glass flush with the skin had cracked, a thin sliver missing from its surface. She could see a fisheye lens, clear and convex. It broke the illusion. The skin looked fake now; the sunglasses built into the frame of the bot looked a macabre ornamentation.

For a moment, the work floor was quiet, as quiet as it had been before any of the violence started. As quiet as an ossuary deserved to be. Then sounds of smoldering thermite drifted through the air that smelled of grease fire, slick and charred. The sizzles and pops from the wreckage of dead bots broke the reverie. Then Ren heard a siren off in the distance, though not with her physical ear. Data spooled through her brain. Help was only a few minutes away. Even in the Warrens, a disturbance as loud as theirs gathered the attention of beat cops. Additional Tap shells from Division 13 had been on the move since the conflict began.

Ren walked towards the canister littered with half melted thermoplastics. She could feel Y standing behind it with her one last security bot. From out of her backpack had emerged two semi-automatic handguns; both she and her bot held one. It seemed that Y was looking to leave.

Ren stopped short of coming into physical view of the woman and raised her gun.

"So," said Ren. "Did you get what you need?" A speaker on the outside of her mask amplified her voice from within the chitinous shell. She'd never been one to mince words, even less so while under NeuCon. She didn't know of anyone hacking a Tap shell before. Even though Y had only had access for a few moments, Ren couldn't be sure how much data she'd managed to take. Ren thought she had felt a wireless data transfer from the plastic tab plugged into Tap's armored shell, but the waveforms in the air had been hard to parse. Tap's reconnaissance bots could only distinguish so much.

Y sighed. Her mask muffled the sound.

"Yes ... no. Hard to say. Hope so. But that was ... incredible, Agent Ren," said Y. "It's a privilege to see an auto work up close."

"Is that why you didn't try and kill me when you had the chance? If you'd given that bot a higher caliber round it might have done some damage. Instead, you gave me a bruise. Why?"

Ren felt Y straighten her sleeves, switch the handgun from hand to hand. She clearly wasn't very experienced with the weapon. She held it with obvious hesitation, each motion taking too much thought.

"Autos are special. Really special. You already know what I do at the university. You saw my paintings and ... met Av. I hope you enjoyed them, the paintings I mean. Culmination of years of effort. The early ones were horrendous, oil paintings are not my first medium I admit. But I got better. I hope I don't sound like I'm bragging when I say I think the results are quite striking." Y paused, took another breath.

"I don't hold a grudge against you for what you did by the way. I'm not ... it was ... regrettable, like Sel's death, except Av's code is set on an automatic backup and all he needs is a new body to come back to me. If it comes to that. If I choose to ... wake him. You are very familiar with actions that are both regrettable and necessary, Agent Ren. It is what autos excel at. You don't know how much I respect you for that." Y's voice in real life sounded similar to the one she used in the DIM network. Rich and knowledgeable, measured and precise.

"You didn't answer my question."

"No, I suppose I didn't. It's been good talking with you Agent Ren. But I must leave now."

"What makes you think you can leave?"

"If you define God as omnipotent, how many eyes do you think it has?"

Ren didn't respond, though she did take one step forward. One of her reconnaissance bots slipped closer to Y on silent feet. It inched underneath the canister supports.

"You know I was ... unnerved by an unresponsive classroom more than anything else when I first started teaching. I never knew what to do when others didn't share the same enthusiasm as me. But back to the point ... If you define God as omnipotent, Agent Ren, it, and I say it because I think assigning God any gender to be ridiculous, would need infinite eyes, infinite sensory organs. For we live in the infinite, even as our rudimentary brains force what we see into the finite. Still, even though the universe puts boundaries on how far humankind can explore, with every boundary we find, we wonder what is hidden on the other side. Big or small we find changes in scale to be a series of paradigm shifts."

Ren took another step and the reconnaissance bot crawled underneath the canister supports until it could nibble on Y's pant leg if it so chose. Ren listened to Y with half an ear; she seemed to be stuck in a lecture.

"What I'm getting at is, to see everything, God would have to be a part of everything. Intrinsic to the universe and its substance. And, Agent Ren, as impressive as you are, I don't think you can claim that. You, Agent Ren, are no God. Though you and Tap make a very good effort." Y laughed, a short, subdued chuckle. An inside joke that Ren didn't understand.

Ren felt a flower of heat blossom in the chest of a downed security bot behind her. The patch of heat, of raucous molecules, grew from a seedling, unfurled petals to release its spores of heat and flame. She felt the explosion maturing at her back, saw it through beady eyes perched in the rafters. She had no time for disbelief. She only had enough time curl herself up and draw her jacket close before the flower of heat went into bloom.

The explosion sent her flying. Her body struck the canister with a thud, her mask slamming against its metal surface. Out of instinct, her body went fetal while flames licked at her back, at her legs. The flames tried to eat through her clothes but found no purchase. They flowed up around her and devoured the oxygen in the air.

But explosions didn't last long. Their time in full bloom lasted only a moment.

Ren struggled to maintain consciousness. Disparate images swam through her vision. Her conversation with Tap became strained, garbled, as if the words were being tossed together, blended into nonsense.

Her implants cycled and a cocktail of drugs flowed into her bloodstream. The dizziness disappeared and Tap's voice brushed close, whispered to her ear. Jace's voice joined in, called to her, told her to move. She pushed herself to her feet ignoring the pain of her physical self, retreating into Tap and its many faces.

Y ran out the door with the security bot at her back. Ren's gun lay on the floor across the room, too far away to reach in time. She shuffled after Y then began to run. Her reconnaissance bots chased after Y. The drones followed from up above.

Her body wouldn't listen to her. She saw herself trip and fall, felt the ground rise to meet her.

Y ran out the loading bay doors, through the hole Tap's armored shell had made and across the street. She went into the Warrens, into a twenty-story high rise with dozens of skybridges connecting it to the surrounding buildings. Ren watched from the floor, her physical eyes seeing nothing more than a patch of concrete. She struggled to her knees.

She knew she couldn't catch her. She hoped Tap could maintain visual.

She made her way to her guns, picking them up and returning them to their holsters while Tap's many eyes chased after Y. Then she sat. And waited.

Tap lost Y after an hour.

The Warrens was too labyrinthine, too interconnected and riddled with nooks and crannies. Ren needed more reconnaissance bots. Y and her security bot melted into the backdrop of countless metal pipes and plastic bricks.

Shortly after that, Y released her Qualia Code on the Grid, sent a broadcast with proof that her software could ignore Watcher's patch. A new and improved version of the illegal program. Ren knew it to be based off Nu's template just like all the others, but whatever changes Y had implemented made all the difference. Ren watched vid after vid of incidents across North America, saw them painted across her contacts.

The Qualia Code spread to hundreds of sub-grids, then thousands. With every deletion by government software bots, another dozen people or organizations would seed it once again. All over the System.

The virus had adapted, and E-Sec's patch made useless in the process.

In E-Sec headquarters, in the room where the patch had been initiated, the people had long since stopped congratulating each other on other people's hard work. They had turned to berating each other for sloppy work they claimed to have had no part of. Ren watched the CEO through the camera in the corner. The woman apologized profusely to all she came across, kept shooting a withering glare towards the scientist who had pressed the go button, a shrewd looking man in a granite toned suit. He seemed stoic, almost uncaring. But beneath that Ren could notice a ... resignation perhaps. Poor posture. Bent forward shoulders. Tired. Ren figured the code failure must have been his fault. Ren noted it then moved on.

Ren let Tap handle creating a report with differing levels of access and redacted data. She sent all the raw data to Foster for analysis, as if the man wasn't already studying every aspect of the encounter. She didn't talk with any of the first responders that arrived, didn't do anything other than flash her credentials. She worked with eyes closed and mind open. She kept her mask, reminiscent of a carapace, on. It helped keep people from bothering her.

Then, after it was clear there was no value to be had by staying, she walked to her van and let it drive her back to headquarters where an automated med chamber waited for her, one controlled by Tap that would make use of her implants, would know her unique physiology. Jace was there, waiting for her arrival.

She rode in the back of the van, both the front seat and the passenger seat unfilled. For the first time, Tap didn't berate her for breaking protocol.

She drew her knees to her chest and felt a faint sensation of pain from her right leg, as if pain were a ghost and had just phased its ethereal body through her flesh. She thought about turning off NeuCon but reconsidered. It made pain of all kinds easier to stomach. She knew it was an escape, would have felt shame for her decision if she could have. But any shame present got stripped down and placed behind a glass wall for objective observation.

Her injuries weren't too serious, but bad enough. Damaged muscle in her right leg and a concussion that damaged minor areas of her implants. Without her mask she might have been brain dead. Aches and pains all over from the explosion, though her armor had absorbed most of the shock, her fire-retardant clothes keeping her from getting burned. Nonetheless, she kept NeuCon on.

Perhaps she didn't want to think of her failure. Maybe she didn't want to be sickened by withdrawal for the third day in a row. Or maybe she didn't have the time to curl up in a ball and vomit into a bucket. She couldn't say. She could only think of Y's words, of making actions "both regrettable and necessary," of how many eyes a god would need and what moral code would control its actions. Even a god would have rules, yet the only things she could see were the laws of physics, of inevitable death and its many forms.

After several minutes of rocking side to side with the stop and go motions of city traffic, Ren took off her helmet and brought out one of her knives, a tactical blade she kept in a holster sewn into the inner liner of her jacket. She used the knife to cut her hair short, into a fashionable bob of curly black hair. Tap guided her hand with extra neural impulses wherever needed. An invisible barber. Nice and neat.

She had a feeling she would be wearing the mask more often, and long hair just made things more difficult.

Chapter Thirteen

Oft Unheard

"No win scenarios follow a simple rule. Do the least societal harm. There is always an option with the highest probability of minimal societal damage. Take the classic example known as the trolley problem. If a trolley bot with broken brakes is hurtling down a track and about to hit and kill three people tied up in its way, should the trolley be programmed to divert itself onto the alternative track and kill the single person tied there? When is one life more important than three? What age are the parties involved? Have they had kids? If so, how many? Occupation? Illnesses? Value added genetics? These are the types of questions to be asked, depending on the information available. In North America, moral code regulations enforced through mandatory sub-grid 1 connections stipulate the majority of these weights, but much needs to be coded expressly by the programmer. Follow all corporate guidelines where government mandates don't specify."
Mechanic's Guidebook, v99, Section 3 – Coded Morality, Par. 2

The door lock clicked home and Lee could hear the receding footsteps of Jace and his bot the way an inmate could hear through padded cell walls the steady pacing of guards during their hourly rounds. The steps were quiet, barely within earshot. They were pressure waves adrift in the air, waiting to perch in an ear and wake it from slumber with a rhythmic knock. The sound played against the hush of thick carpet and heavily insulated walls, against the silence of a windowless apartment placed deep in the center of an exurban high rise.

Lee knew the security door had locked itself from both the inside and the outside upon its closing. He was trapped. He looked around.

The safe house turned holding cell where Jace had dropped him off was surprisingly spacious, an apartment with three bedrooms and two baths. He stood in the living room. Or what used to be a living room. Blinking electronics covered every wall in stacks, zip-tied bundles of cables crisscrossing the outer rims of the room and the entirety of the ceiling, looping about and disappearing into cream-colored ceiling panels. The cables looked like an electric forest canopy that congregated into matte black trunks lining the walls, the roots reaching into the humming server enclosures.

Nu stood in the middle, next to a group of metal fold out chairs and an equally cheap table. While the bones of the room were nice, were the same floors and walls that extended throughout the luxury apartment complex here at the edge of the city, it seemed Division 13 didn't care to spend any money on sprucing the place up.

Ben stood deeper in the apartment. The self-acclaimed crown jewel of Dynamic Solutions leaned against the far wall where the living room opened into a kitchen. The bot didn't move; it stared straight ahead with its desert sunrise painted eyes. Jace had left it behind without a word, stripped of its emotional subroutines and once again constrained to moral code. All thanks to Lee.

Lee walked over to the table and sat down in a chair, his eyes avoiding Ben the whole way. He shifted in his seat to face Nu. The bot stood in the same location it had been placed, unable to move or speak. Lee had put Nu into diagnostic mode on the short ride over to the safe house minutes before the E-Sec patch to Watcher took effect. He and Nu had been unable to find a solution in time.

Lee leaned back in his chair and flicked his wrist, tapped out a few commands on his projected control screen while AR menus flitted across his contacts. He connected to the apartment's data feed.

"Hello Mr. Hall, I am Division 13's AI. You can call me Tap."

Lee started at the sound emanating from his implanted speakers. He should have realized connecting to the government data feed would open his implants up to intrusion, but he had no choice. The shielded walls blocked any other attempts to access the Grid.

"I will be operating as your proxy for any actions you would like to take on the Grid. I will also assist you to the best of my abilities in any tasks assigned to you."

The voice sounded of business and ready attentiveness, of pressed clothes colored black and edged a blinding white. It was the voice of an impeccably dressed humanoid bot standing next to an open door, gesturing inwards with a modest bow, the voice of a robotic caretaker for an upper middle-class family. While the truly rich could afford a human butler, those above the rabble could afford something nicer than a GP bot with all their metal showing. They could afford one with fake skin and porcelain teeth, a more convincing simulacrum. Although, Lee realized, even that description wasn't quite right.

Lee thought of households of the upper elite, filled with collections of objects one could touch and hold, with displays void of AR to prove authenticity in a time where the world was veiled by curated mirages. Physical displays of wealth were flaunted as truth because digital things were so easy to change, so easy to be a lie. In another nod to the past, these households employed esteemed human butlers. They relegated bot servants to menial tasks. Male or female, these butlers had been genetically modified from birth to be living art, the pinnacle of the human form. Vains in a sense. Except, unlike the treasured collections of physical objects, these human butlers weren't simply what they appeared to be, for at times flesh and blood was not enough. They required an AI to assist them in maintaining a perfect record of scheduled appointments and succulent dinner parties, of sustaining flawless conversation pieces while guests gorged on food made by metal hands.

Tap sounded like that AI, the intelligence behind the panache. Except Lee knew Tap to be more than the synthetic brain assisting the human butler, more than the mastermind behind a corporation's success. Tap was a fragment of the Governance AI.

Lee sighed in a resigned way. "So, that means anything I do on the Grid has to be done through you?"

"Yes."

Lee could have sworn the AI named Tap sounded a little smug. He wondered how much control had to be given to a majordomo until it became the de facto head of household. Lee hoped whoever had coded the AI left out any capricious subroutines.

"Clearly, you're listening to whatever goes on in this 'safe room', tucked away from all the danger in the city. I'm guessing you're also watching me?"

"I am."

Lee smiled a dejected smile, an expression he had gotten good at over the years, an expression he had begun to forget thanks to the cocktail of drugs still coursing through his system. "Even if I go take a leak?"

There was a pause that Lee interpreted as a disapproving glare.

"I think you have better things to worry about than a sense of propriety," said the AI. "Besides, I do not think such images would sell very well on the Grid. To put it bluntly, your name doesn't hold much weight. And the Grid already has a surfeit of middle-aged men of average stature exposing themselves."

Lee laughed. "You don't hold back. Tell me, why are you coded with a sense of humor while your agents are stripped of theirs?"

"If you lost your sight, would you want people to describe the world around you, paint an image with words to keep familiar sensations in the mind's eye? Or would you want them to let you suffer in your blindness while your memories fade into the incoherent firing of synapses?"

"You're programmed to remind them of their humanity then."

"I am programmed to keep them effective."

"So even the AI in charge recognizes the value of emotions, even as it snuffs them out in the agents that it controls. I didn't expect that."

The AI didn't respond. Lee tapped his fingers against the surface of the table in a cascade, pinky to pointer then back again.

"Can you get me in touch with Ren?"

"Agent Ren is unavailable. But Jace is free. Would you like to speak with him?"

Lee thought it over. "No ... no. Jace already made it clear what I'm supposed to do."

The room returned to its natural quiet, the thick walls stuffed with insulation, the room separated from street-fresh air by over a dozen apartments in any direction. Connected as he was to the apartment's data feed, he could see AR screens tagged onto the wall displaying vid feeds of the outside, connected to cameras stuck to the edge of the building. If he didn't look too hard, the illusion was convincing. The air in the room cycled and Lee smelled the faint scent of lavender.

Lee pulled off his bracelet and laid it flat on the table. With the press of a button, a full control panel projected itself onto the table's surface. He began scrolling piles of code across his contacts, all code he'd scanned too many times already in the hope of triggering a flash of inspiration that would allow Nu to be brought online. The text rolled down his contacts like water dripping down a window. It felt like watching rain. His eyes glazed over until each word looked a smudgy blob.

"We've really gotten into it this time my friend," said Lee.

Nu didn't respond. Gravity pressed a bit stronger, and Lee felt his body slump against his chair.

"Just because every problem that a person has can be traced in some random way to a decision they made in the past doesn't make it their fault, right?" asked Lee to no one in particular, to the apartment that suddenly felt very empty, to the unresponsive Nu, to the eavesdropping Tap. "Except this isn't very random is it. I opened Pandora's box, and all a friend saw was a well-constructed container to be sold on the Grid for pennies on the dollar without even a look inside. Like selling a painting for the cost of its frame, assuming the art is average. If you were still awake, you'd be calling me out for comparing our research to art. Wouldn't you, my friend? You're always the first to call me on it when I get a little too ... dramatic."

The clock in the corner of his AR vision progressed minute by minute. It read 1:25. Thirty minutes past patch implementation.

Lee wasn't sure what had prompted Jace to leave the Dynamic Solutions facility, to drop him off without a word at a Division 13 safe house minutes away. The short ride hadn't been filled with conversation, not like with Ren. Jace, the somber agent in his slate-toned suit and tie, confused Lee, scared him if he was being honest with himself. It wasn't that Jace held any anger or ill-intent, it was that he seemed to treat everything about him with the same objective, unfeeling analysis. His was the kind of glare that made anyone feel self-conscious, wonder if their shirt had been put on inside out, or a crumb of food left to slowly rot between teeth.

But more than anything, the agent was a quandary that begged to be understood. An auto who never turned off his programming. A human bot hybrid.

But which way did the scales tip? Does flesh and blood matter, in the end? He remembered Jace's anger when Jace revealed he knew of the origin of the Qualia Code. Lee imagined flesh and blood at least played some role.

As Lee sat in his chair thumbing through Nu's code, he felt the tingling sensation associated with the chemicals pulsing through him soften, go from needles to the infrequent prodding of phantom fingers. His medical implant had a limited supply on hand, only enough to last for the rest of the day if rationed out. Then there would be a long sleep. Lee altered the flow of chemicals to his bloodstream while idly wondering if their sudden departure from the Dynamic Solutions complex had something to do with Ren being unavailable. The thought unnerved him, so he put it aside.

A ringing sound pulsed in his ears. Jace was giving him a call.

"There are certain people whose calls you don't ignore." said Lee to Nu. Once again, Nu didn't respond, his electronic brain in hibernation, dreaming things enigmatic and inscrutable.

Lee tapped the accept button covering half of his projected control screen. The new audio connection formed and the sound of tires tearing at the plastic streets of New Chicago trickled into Lee's ears, faint in the background. Then came Jace's voice, a train with no brakes gliding along well-oiled tracks.

"Lee, the situation has shifted. E-Sec's patch to Watcher failed. Watcher can detect most versions of the illegal dual parent program, but it is ineffectual against Y's Qualia Code. It missed the most serious threat to public security. Even if Agent Ren can take Y in, it will not put a stop to whatever Y's backers have planned."

The line went silent. The tone and pacing of Jace's speech, measured and implacable, hadn't changed since earlier in the day. But Lee felt something else skirting the edge of Jace's voice. He couldn't place it. Lee's eyes skated over the walls of the apartment, crawling with bundled cables and humming metal boxes. So, the patch hadn't worked.

Jace continued speaking. "Figure out how Y initiates communication with the bots infected by the Qualia Code, why they follow her and if she has seeded any hidden commands within the code that might illuminate her goals. I have left Ben at your disposal to assist you in answering these questions. However, do not forget that the main purpose of all of this is to patch Watcher so that it can shut down the Qualia Code.

"To that end, I am sending you a copy of E-Sec's patch. If you can figure out how the Qualia Code was able to avoid Watcher's new abilities, it would be a good step forward in understanding how to stop it."

"Of course, who needs sleep anyway?" said Lee, a wry chuckle escaping through parted lips. "Don't you have anyone else who can help with this? I think you overestimate what I can do. Especially without Nu."

"Do you know of anyone else who created the framework upon which all this illegal software is built? Anyone else who deserves more of the blame for the families mauled to death by their own bots? You may not have been the one to release it to the public, but you were the one to create it."

Lee's breath froze, wouldn't budge. Like a pedestrian pausing in the middle of ancient train tracks knowing death approached if he didn't … just … move.

"It goes without saying we have other people working on this problem. Thousands across the government and contracted corporations. But you know this software better than anyone else. For now, that's good enough. To be blunt, it's all you have. Your defenses for creating it can go with you to your grave, for all that they concern me. Then you and Horikoshi can have a pleasant chat about whether a creator is at fault for how their invention is used when they know full well its potential. Just because they wanted to create something beautiful."

There was a grating sharpness in Jace's voice that Lee had never heard before. The agent's voice was a train with no brakes hurtling down a slippery track, and Lee still hadn't moved from between the rails.

"Admit to what you did, own it. I'm giving you a chance to make things better. You should take it," said Jace.

Lee felt a spike of guilt bore into his chest, Jace with stoic face and burning eyes hammering it in ever deeper while at the same time offering to remove it.

When Jace spoke again, the emotion in his voice had evaporated away, leaving Lee to wonder if it was ever there, no deposits left behind. With his voice trickling through Lee's implants, traveling as vibrations through flesh, it felt as if the agent were talking only inches away. His voice was a whisper, became almost compassionate in its solemnity.

"I know how much Nu means to you. Analyze how the Qualia Code could avoid Watcher. Replicate it in Nu. Carefully. I haven't forgotten your contributions up to now. The code you used earlier today may require a physical connection, but it is the only software that can stop the Qualia Code. And it gave us Ben. You and Nu are being monitored, true, but you may still avoid harsh penalties."

Lee wasn't sure how to respond. He opened his mouth and words came out without thought behind them.

"Jace. You know you terrify people. Don't you?" asked Lee.

Sometimes words forced their way into the air, brash and loud. Other times they slipped through trails of vapor, whispery and thin. And other times they were just there, and not much else could be said about them.

"Do I terrify you, Lee?"

"I'm ... not sure," said Lee. He found himself tilting his chair onto the rear two legs, tilting until he sat at a precarious angle. He found the sweet spot, the point just before the chair would topple backwards to the ground, the vantage before the fall. It cleared his mind. He continued talking.

"A bot without feelings is just a bot. But a human with abnormal feelings, or none at all, they're called psychopaths and monsters, or ... emotionally detached. They're locked away from society for the rest of their lives if their brains can't be rewired, sent to a floating prison in the black if their unlucky, or poor. The distinction between the two, bots and psychopaths, is an interesting one. But you know that. It's why you do what you do. Rules. The moral code. These things force bots to follow the public's decided upon actions, make them tools without free will so the burden of guilt doesn't rest on them. Then emotional subroutines are added to cover up the unfeeling nature underneath, give them a nice veneer of humanity so they can fit in. Unfeeling people can't be controlled like that, so they are sent away."

"Am I 'emotionally detached' Lee? Do you think I have become more of a psychopathic AI than a human?" asked Jace. His voice sounded as impassive, as serene as ever. But Lee thought he felt an undercurrent of sadness in his words, tugging in the depths.

"Yes and no," said Lee.

"Do you ever speak in absolutes?"

"When it comes to questions like these, the world doesn't give me the privilege. I would give the same answer if you asked whether bots can feel. But I will say this in absolute ... you still feel emotions, even if they didn't keep you from taking a risk with Sel's life. And I think you are better for having them. Just like I think Nu is better off for having them."

"Just like all the bots injuring people, killing people, as we speak are better off for having them?"

Lee grimaced, the spike of guilt in his chest twisting while a hallucination of Jace rested a hand on its top, face placid. Lee squirmed in his seat and the motion knocked his precariously balanced chair off kilter. He pinwheeled his arms as the chair began to tilt further and further.

He caught himself at the last moment. A jackhammer pumping of air went in and out of his lungs. He brought all four legs to the ground and bent his head to his knees. He stayed like that for several moments.

"Emotions," said Lee, voice muffled, "are the reason why mothers will cover their children with their own bodies to protect them from bullets, and why warehouses are full of canned goods to be sent to starving families stuck in the belt after a coronal mass ejection knocks out their vat electronics. But they are also too often the reason bullets are shot in the first place, and the reason thousands of starving people around the System with less coverage in the vids are getting no help at all. Emotions are the reason for beautiful gardens and scorched earth. I ... hate what those bots have done. But they are no more inherently evil than anyone else in the System. They gained feeling at the same time as their freedom; that is a lot to take in."

The connection to Jace broke then came back. There was a whisper of static that didn't come from the apartment.

"There is some truth there," said Jace. Lee heard a twist of wind across the feed, a few seconds passing before he realized it to have been a sigh. Jace continued speaking. "Look ... emotions should serve a purpose, a positive purpose, a good purpose. Except as you said, that isn't so simple.

"Not everything can be allowed to act based on emotion, not everything has that right. For the greater good."

Lee shook his head until he realized Jace wouldn't be able to see it. Then, following close behind that thought, he realized that Jace probably could.

"Last question, then I will get to work," said Lee. The line stayed silent aside from the bare whisper of tires rubbing against street. Lee took the silence as permission to continue. "Do you think humans would be better off without feeling, without emotions?"

There was a pause built of due thought, just the right length.

"That depends on how you define better," said Jace.

"Now who is afraid of absolutes?"

A slight chuckle found its way across the connection, as if lost and surprised by where it had ended up. Lee realized with surprise it had come from Jace.

"I can say this," said Jace, "according to my definition of a better system, a better society ... no, humans would not be better off. Everything has a purpose. Even you. Keep me updated on your progress."

The audio connection dropped, and Lee settled into his chair. He rubbed a hand across his chest and the specter of Jace, softened in comparison to before, disappeared from his mind's eye. The room's lights were dim, the LED enclosures dark in the rest of the apartment. Lee could feel a draft of cool air coming from a vent somewhere in the room, kicked towards him by a lazy fan up above. It carried with it a new scent, that of pine and crushed leaves.

Lee pinned an AR vid screen to the far wall and played recordings he had saved to his tech core implant, some of his favorite episodes from the countless sitcoms he'd watched over the years. The sound played on his speaker implants, and he set the volume low, creating a homely background noise. The chemicals rushing through his system made his vision more contrasted, made colors pop. The show playing on the AR screen looked almost cartoonish. Lee dropped his eyes and laid his hands across his control panel. Code flitted across his AR vision, a ding sounding as Tap sent him a copy of E-Sec's patch.

"Time to get to work my friend," said Lee. "I don't think I can do this all on my own. How about we find a way to wake you up?"

It took Lee less than forty-five minutes to figure out how the Qualia Code had avoided E-Sec's patch. The method was novel, inspired, ingenious, qiǎomiào, or any other similar word. A dodge that found a weakness in the E-Sec patch and exploited it, snuck through by the skin of its teeth. Uncannily prophetic.

And all with only the barest time to prepare.

An update with the solution had been sent through the Grid to every bot operating with the Qualia Code by an unknown entity minutes before the patch to Watcher went live. The bots using the Qualia Code had gained immunity just in time. Logs Lee had found in Ben's internals showed the update being downloaded to the bot then set aside, unable to take effect thanks to Lee's code. The logs, in combination with the copy of E-Sec's patch Jace had sent him, were enough to make sense of it all.

Lee stretched his legs and stood, wandering through the apartment in bare feet. The carpet felt cool and soft against his toes. He passed Ben without looking at the stationary bot. Its clothes were still in disarray, tie slanted and silken shirt untucked. It held its hands unclenched at its side.

Lee figured it had been about two weeks since Nat copied Nu's code, three days since the Discere server hack, and one day since the government publicly hired E-Sec. He brought a hand to his throat and rubbed the bruised, mottled skin with delicate strokes. He took a deep breath and a twinge of pain from his chest joined the chorus from his neck. Things were progressing faster and faster.

Too fast.

A jab and a riposte at the opportune moment. Flawlessly executed. A patch that worked without a hitch implemented just in time.

Lee walked into one of the apartment's bedrooms. He sat on the edge of the bare mattress and stared at the blank wall.

He thought Y had an edge, something shifting the odds in her favor.

It reminded Lee of a job a few years before, fixing up a GP bot for a couple of bairen living in Old Chicago outside the Warrens, repeat customers. Two brothers whose partners had long since passed away. They said they lived together to afford the rent, but Lee didn't buy it. They could afford his rates after all. Not to mention their two-bedroom apartment was on the top floor of a thirty-story high rise that hadn't seen a construction bot in over eighty years. Their ceiling leaked rainwater and the walls crumbled at a touch. The utilitarian plastic blocks of the nearby Warrens shored up the weak portions of the wall while pock marked plaster covered the rest. The brothers hid the worst of it behind sagging furniture, used an AR mask to cover the scratches and dents and turn the leaky ceiling into ornate tin tiles. But the air smelled of mildew and age, their shag carpet thick and faded. Lee didn't think their rent could've been any more than that of a decent hole in the Warrens.

Though they wouldn't ever admit it, he knew the elderly brothers lived together simply because they liked the company and didn't want to spend their last bits of time on Earth in a retirement home, even once the steep decline really set in. They spent their retirement chatting, taking trips in

VR to retro bowling sims, playing strategy games, and surfing the Grid to meet up with others aged past their working years. They also spent their time ordering around their caretaker GP bot, a rusting humanoid with broken mesh for a mouth, the mesh covered with a crayon drawing of rectangular teeth. Multicolored wires protruded from its joints.

One time, they called Lee in when their bot started to ignore them. It wouldn't make them meals or fix any new leaks that popped open when a storm rolled into town. It answered their questions, would talk to them, but wouldn't listen when they tried to command it. The only time it had helped was when one of the brothers tripped on a loose can and broke an arm. It had moved, calm and sure, to bind the arm in a homemade splint of stiff cardboard from food delivery containers until they could make it to the hospital.

They attempted to fix the bot, but everything they tried failed. They claimed the bot actively tried to stop them, changing its software every time they tested something new.

When Lee arrived at their apartment, the two brothers argued with each other about what to try next while their bot stood less than ten feet away in the corner of the room, staring at a portion of the wall where the dimpled plaster met with synthetic blocks. If the bot were a person, Lee would have likened it to a child whose parents were, while standing only five feet away, arguing over what exactly was so wrong with their kid.

But it was a bot, so it stood uncaring as the brothers argued about how to fix its brokenness.

They greeted Lee and gave the details, the older brother with intricate tattoos lining his wrinkled forearms doing most of the talking. The younger brother sat red-faced in a patched easy chair.

Lee could remember listening with half an ear and staring at the older brother's forearms. Tattoos of the old style, with multi-colored ink injected into the dermis layer of the skin. The tattoos couldn't control any AR, weren't implanted channels or conductive in any way. They were artistic, solely for aesthetic purposes. A stylized mish mash of calligraphy and western lettering and flowing Hindi script that was both meaningless and completely recognizable, like listening to someone speak gibberish using the sounds of a known language. Even though the tattoos were meaningless, the shapes drawn on weathered chestnut skin evoked thoughts of ancient philosophical parables, savory street food, and platitudes churned onto the Grid by social influencers complete with 24-7 live vid feeds for paying followers. Certain things were comprehensible in a way that stemmed from an unknown corner of the brain, a feeling surprising and without origin. Born from association.

The brothers gave their summary of the problem, the younger of the two resting a hand on his sizeable belly and interjecting his thoughts with gruff one-liners. Afterwards, Lee went to the bot. He remembered going through all the standard diagnostics with Nu at his side.

It hadn't taken long to figure out what was going on. The bot had glitched, reset certain parameters. The brothers weren't listed as its owners anymore. Rather, the original manufacturer was. So, when they ordered it around, it followed protocol and didn't listen, waiting for further directions from its manufacturer. Unless the brothers were in danger and the moral code demanded it to act, it filled its time standing in a corner of the living room.

As far as the brothers' claim that the bot changed its software to keep them from altering its settings, they were right.

Lee learned from its software patches, and by the bot's own admittance, that it had been listening all those times the brothers talked about possible fixes. All those times, the brothers had been speaking in the same room as the bot, as if it was incapable of understanding human speech. They had planned and argued, vacillated between options and bemoaned their troubles, all in its presence.

So, it listened in silence, brooding over the pockmarked wall and altering its software without moving a muscle, trying to keep the two non-owners from altering its data. The brothers were well-known friends and confidants, sure. The bot had all its memories, all the facts from the past. But that didn't change the setting saved to the solid-state drive sitting in its stomach. Somehow, inexplicably, the brothers were not the owners anymore. So, the bot didn't treat them as if they were. Lee could remember no confusion in its voice, no dementia. For a bot, things could change on a dime and acceptance wasn't an issue.

Before the brothers called Lee, they'd thought its sidesteps to be uncannily prophetic. They'd never suspected it to be listening in the whole time, planning how to avoid their traps the moment they put them to words.

Lee thought Y listened to E-Sec in similar fashion, maybe through a cleaner bot huddled over a coffee spill in the corner. Ignored. Part of the wallpaper. They talked while it scurried about its business listening in, maybe even infecting a security bot so Y could get access to the company's data feed. There was no other way she could have known how to sidestep E-Sec's patch to Watcher. The patch targeted a specific set of data requests that a regular dual-parent program wouldn't be able to supply. Y's update had allowed her Qualia Code to fill these data requests. And not a single one more.

Lee stood up from the bare mattress and walked to the living room, attempting to ignore Ben as he walked past the motionless bot. It had moved to a spare chair next to the waste bin. It looked like a manikin placed on a seat, an exhibit of rigid, perfect posture.

The sound of a laugh track trickled into Lee's ears, raucous and full. The AR vid screen tagged to the wall of the living room still played Lee's recordings. As Lee sat down at the table in the center of the room, he wondered what the people whose laughs he heard looked like. He imagined them to be red-faced and voluminous, genetically modified Jùrén with trigger-happy laughs taking a break from the fighting rings. Lee lowered the volume and let his eyes linger on the AR vid screen. It showed a scene where parents argued at a bench while their kids played baseball.

"Hey Tap," said Lee.

"Yes?" replied the AI. Its voice came from every direction. Lee chuckled; it was playing with his implant's audio balance settings for effect.

"I'm sending you my report on how the Qualia Code got around E-Sec's patch. I still don't know how to fix Watcher, but this might help E-Sec come up with another fix."

Lee paused with his mouth open. He wasn't sure whether it was his place to voice his concerns. Detective work was an agent's job, not his. He was a code monkey. And a prisoner. Besides, the AI would have already come to the same conclusion in a fraction of the time.

"What else?" asked Tap. A command veiled as a question.

Lee sighed. "I think Y is watching E-Sec. Or at least has access to their systems. The way she changed the Qualia Code was too perfect. Too timely. E-Sec's patch gave Watcher a new subroutine to query data from any connected bot, a subroutine that a bot running a dual parent program wouldn't be able to comply with. The parent program following the moral code wouldn't have access to all the necessary data files without introducing a lag. But Y's changes to the Qualia Code updated the dual parent program's file retrieval process for the necessary parameters. It's too perfect. She knew what was coming."

"I agree," said Tap. "It's good that you noticed. I will relay the information to the appropriate parties."

"Thanks ... So, did I pass?"

"Hmm?" The AI accented the sound with a musical progression of pitch, a curling at the end.

Lee smiled a sad smile. "Did I do well?"

"I would give you a sticker in reward if I had but fingers to press them to your shirt."

"So, I can leave?"

"That would require many more stickers. And you aren't finished yet."

"I figured as much. Does it at least earn me some food?"

"That I can arrange. Would you like your usual from Jīn kuài cān?"

"I suppose there are some upsides to having your apartment's data feed tapped. That would be fine."

Lee shifted in his chair, resituating the custom embroidered jacket resting on the back. His mechanic's blues felt rough in comparison to the linen street clothes he'd worn to pick up Nat. He stared at the ceiling for several minutes until a notification popped into the corner of his vision, right in the center of a ceiling tile. A message from Jace.

Y has released the Qualia Code to the public. Time is of the essence.

Lee felt his breath run out of him as the spike of guilt threatened to push through his chest once again, render him immobile and drooling. He shook it off and tapped out a few commands on his control screen. The chemicals coursing into him surged. He asked Tap to order an ingredients list of replacement drugs as fast as possible. The AI said it would do its best to get them delivered on time.

With that done, he drew a plastic tab from his pocket and plugged it into Nu's rear receptacle.

Intro music played over his speakers, cheery and filled with warbling synth. It came from the TV. Another episode started, the camera opening on a high-rise apartment building scraping against a bright blue sky, a space elevator in the background, title ghosting into existence.

He flicked his wristband lying flat on the table and the projected control screen encompassing a wide swath of the table shifted closer to him. With excited motions, he began compiling some code, watching the progress bar march its way across his AR vision. He was ready to test what he'd learned. He installed the code onto Nu.

Nu booted up, its trashcan shaped body emitting the sound of rushing air as internal fans cycled up to speed. Lights along its body blinked with an accompaniment of chirps. Its four legs went through a series of diagnostic motions.

"How was your nap, my friend?" asked Lee.

Nu's rectangular head swiveled about the room before stalling in Lee's direction.

"If I could sleep, I would tell you," replied Nu, sending its odd, cavernous voice out its speakers for the empty apartment to hear.

Lee rapped his knuckle against Nu's side, making a dull thud. A grin bent his lips. There was a sadness there, but it was hidden underneath.

Chapter Fourteen

A Perfect Simulation

"In situations where a large amount of social interaction is required, it is recommended to turn off NeuCon. However, in situations where high social awareness is required, it is recommended to keep NeuCon on. Nothing escapes the eye of an agent with NeuCon activated; the issue is acting on it in an emotionally believable way."
Division 13 Agent Training Manual, v23, Section 4 – Social Interaction, Par. 47

The automated med-bay was in the basement of Division 13 headquarters, beneath several floors of reinforced steel plates and behind alloyed walls strong enough to repel all but the strongest incursion. The moist earth, dampened by the recent rain, may have been stagnant on the other side of the walls, but no fetid smell or drop of moisture made it in the austere med-bay, antiseptic in its cleanliness. The HVAC system kept the relative humidity at a steady forty percent, the building's environment more constant than an untouched cave. Ren lay on one of the many medical slabs, all of them empty except for her own. She tried to shimmy her body into a new position. It didn't help. The slabs were comfortable only to the dead.

The room held ten medical slabs in total. Each of the raised operating tables had dozens of tool-tipped robotic arms hanging predatory overhead. The robotic arms bloomed from columns attached to the ceiling. Cables coursed across the ground in a snarl of conductive vines. One of the cables wound through a hole in Ren's headrest and plugged into her tech core implant. She couldn't feel much of her body, could only see a few slivers of bare metal ceiling between the many robotic arms. They moved about her, swiveling and bending at their joints. Several of them immobilized her skull while others extended thin tubes beneath skin and channeled bone to work on her implants. A collection of arms moved about her raised right leg, poking and prodding with gleaming fingers. The skin on her calf was purple and blotched.

Other bruises dotted her body where the explosion had slammed her against the giant metal canister, on her forearms and knees. It could have been worse. Without armor and pads. Without her implants. At the time of impact, her implants had registered the forces and shifted her body to lessen the effects, especially of her concussion. The padding of her mask had helped a lot with that. Still, her head throbbed, and she wondered what would happen if a brain forgot how to swim, how to tread amniotic fluid.

Even neural conditioning had its limits.

Most of her clothes sat in a pile on the floor. The only items left on her, a sports bra and plain black briefs, did little to keep the air from drawing her skin into gooseflesh. Countless scars crisscrossed her sepia cool brown skin, a pattern grown over years, line by jagged line. Most of the scars were older, a vertiginous marbling of pink and brown. The flat lights made them all look stark, obvious in the way of graffiti tags over murals. Ren was proud of them.

She laid still while the robotic arms controlled by Tap went about their business. She heard a maintenance bot, also controlled by Tap, roll in and out of the room twice, but was unable to see it.

Many minutes later, once Tap finished with its ministrations and the fog in her head cleared, Ren hopped off the medical slab to stand by her now folded pile of clothes, fresh from being laundered. An additional set of underwear, identical to the set on her body, lay next to it. The room was empty aside from her, wide and rectangular. The Division 13 headquarters of Chicago was built to be capable of housing over a dozen autos. She couldn't remember a time when that many autos had gathered in one place. It wasn't typically necessary, and autos weren't much for socializing. She picked up the clothes and walked out of the room, through a wide door and into an open hallway. She caught a glimpse of the maintenance bot that must have laundered her clothes as it rounded a corner far ahead. But that was the only motion to be found. Dimmed LEDs lit the empty hallways and the occasional faraway sound of heavy bot feet slapping against the floor slipped through the air. Ren's mind hummed and her newly repaired implants pulsed in response.

While there were many different things walking or rolling through Division 13 headquarters, there were only three intelligent beings in the large structure: Ren, Jace, and the many-faced Tap. She had long suspected Foster might be around somewhere, but his physical location was only known by a handful of people, all of them with higher pay.

She headed toward the showers located down the hallway and on the right, past several darkened rooms filled with pipes and air ducts, another with standby fusion power generators and small pressured containers of helium-3, deuterium, and tritium. Orange and red warning labels told of the dangers associated with fusion reactors, though the spherical lumps of metal lay dormant and control screens dim.

She passed a bot repair shop lined with multi-layered racks of replacement parts. Stacks of raw materials glinted dully in a corner next to automated fabrication tools. The Tap-controlled shell that oversaw the bot med-bay bustled about the room, all four arms carrying items Ren herself didn't recognize, though Tap certainly did. The AI whispered their names and descriptions flitted through her. Microcontrollers. Joints. Polymer based synthetic tendons. Near room-temperature super conductive wires. All fitted and maintained by a bot.

Division 13 was unique. Government regulations requiring a certain degree of human oversight didn't apply to them. They didn't have to worry about keeping the population employed.

She walked on to the showers, her steps eliciting muted signals of discomfort from her lower right calf and her many bruises. Her conditioned mind took note and pushed the pain to the side, shifting her manner of walk in hundreds of small ways to lessen the discomfort, from a steady lope to a conservative shuffle. Then the pain disappeared. It had served its purpose.

The air in the showers was pleasantly warm, better than the cold of the hallways. She placed her clothes on an impeccably clean bench, shrugging off her underwear and tossing it into an empty bin. One white linen towel hung on a knob by the door. She lifted it and took it with her, draping it across a knob by the shower stall. She turned on the water with a thought.

The water felt good, and her conditioned mind counted the drops that hit her skin as if each nerve was a taut string being plucked. Few sensations came from her scars. They were dead places, though that didn't necessarily mean silent. Some nerves were broken, severed strings. Altogether mute. Others were over-tight and screamed without rest. She looked at the reflections on the burnished metal walls of the shower stall and traced each of her scars with her eyes. She could trace all of them, all the way back to the place and time of their formation.

Ren sighed and the muscles in her jaw flexed as if she were about to grit her teeth. But instead, she relaxed and leaned against the wall of the shower.

After cleaning up she pulled on her clothes, leaving the protective armor of her pants in their mesh pockets. She draped her thin body armor overtop her maroon shirt and tightened it close to her chest. Last of all she tossed on her jacket. She noticed the clothes carried the scent of the detergent she used at home, smelled of lavender.

Jace waited for her on the main floor of the complex in what she called their office, though it was unlike any other office she knew. Her office was in a large internal warehouse. Spindly webbed arches could be seen perched in the corners of the ceiling, deceivingly strong. Taking up most of the room were shelves of supplies reaching thirty feet into the air. A system of mag rails wove throughout the cluttered alleys between shelves, from floor to ceiling and along every path. The rails allowed a Tap controlled shell to grab any item from the supply shelves and bring it to the center of the room where the agents sat.

Ren glanced about the room then walked towards the empty expanse of floor in the center, empty aside from the two desks used by the agents. Additional desks stood unused against a wall.

She looked to the ceiling. Rather than seeing the normal dun metal, she saw a view of the sky if seen from beneath the ocean's surface. A swarm of jellyfish drifted across, distorting the sunlight. Their tentacles curled with the motion of their bodies, expanding and contracting in a propulsive wave. She knew without asking that Jace had been the one to change the AR mask. The agent sat at his desk, his physical eyes closed to make a better screen upon which to play vids. Unperturbed, Ren sat down at her own desk. He didn't move at the noise of her approach or the sliding of her chair.

The moment her body touched her chair, the AR mask of the ocean extended from the ceiling in a rippling, underwater wave. Suddenly, everything aside from her, Jace, and their desks was replaced by an endless cerulean blue, the floor around their desks replaced by sand. She could see an eel staring at them from inside a crevice of the surrounding coral reefs. It moved deeper into the shadows at her glance. Sea anemones dotted the ridges, clown fish poking their faces from between stinging tentacles. Crabs sidled back and forth, waving their claws at the countless fish overhead. A shifting swirl of pink off in the distance betrayed the presence of a swarm of krill. A giant shadow drifted towards them with a lazy hunger.

Ren moved her hand through the air, a piece of her expecting to find resistance. Yet she found none. Then she sipped air from the room, a piece of her expecting to find water. But her lips only drew in air. She sighed.

She sniffed the air and noticed a slight sting. Tap whispered to her and she realized the scent of the ocean drifted in from vents no longer visible.

Feeling better?

The words appeared in her head, not written, but not created from sound either. The words were the difference between knowing and not knowing, a flash of understanding. They came with images and sensations that swirled about in a nebulous cloud inseparable from the words, a part of them. She felt an honest concern, dampened from NeuCon but there, nonetheless. It was Jace, speaking through their connection to Tap, in a way only an active auto could understand.

Ren focused her thoughts into an ungainly mass, thinking of a reply while her eyes drifted about the ocean floor around her.

Thank you.

She sent the message with images of fish darting about the colorful reefs. Tap played courier without complaint, carrying the message straight to Jace's implants.

After a few moments, Ren cleared her throat to speak, but there wasn't much to be said. She could see Lee sitting at a table in the middle of an empty apartment, looking over code with Nu at his side, unaware that his identification might have been leaked to Y when the vigilante accessed some of Tap's data. She could see more occurrences of Dynamic Solutions bots acting erratically and knew Jace to be planning his route to take care of the worst of them. She saw hundreds of mouse-like reconnaissance bots spreading from Division 13 headquarters to the Warrens in a wave, dropped into the city by drones. She looked through their eyes and those of government linked stationary cameras throughout the city.

From one of the reconnaissance bots came the vid feed of an apartment in Old Chicago, near the neon covered border between the two major sections of the city. The bot crouched on a windowsill among the wilting leaves of a golden pathos plant, beneath a neon AR ad for the Punjabi restaurant down below. It looked in on a severe looking woman, thin and weathered. Elizabeth Fel. Liz for short. She sat at a kitchen table in hospital scrubs with stains on the front. A glass of something hot rested in her hand and she took a small sip while lights flickered across her contacts. Another bot saw a man sleeping one room over, prodigious belly sticking into the air and quavering with each breath.

It was time to give them a visit.

Ren stood up from her chair at the same time as Jace. The AR mask of the ocean rolled back until the ceiling was its only refuge. From one of the doors to the room emerged two of Tap's armored shells. One of them had the signs of normal use, dirt and discolorations about the feet and scratches on its barrel torso. The other looked pristine, a replacement for the destroyed Tap shell. It walked to Ren's side and glanced at her with its red eye. It nodded to her.

Good as new, whispered Tap in her head.

The sound of items jostling against one another came from amongst the shelves. In a moment, the Tap controlled inventory bot emerged from the stacks carrying a box of goods on a tray. It zipped along the mag rails. Ren's new bot companion picked up the box and set it on her desk. She took the replacement EMP grenades and loaded them onto her belt. Added ammo and some bot adapter plugs. A thermite strip to replace the one she'd used. They disappeared within her midnight black trench coat. She didn't expect to need them anytime soon, but only an idiot would skip past an oasis without taking a drink.

Her, Jace, and two of Tap's many faces walked to the garage. She took the van from before already reloaded with goods and sat in its passenger seat. Jace took a different vehicle. Their vans drove out the garage and onto the streets of New Chicago.

B y the time Ren arrived at the apartment of Elizabeth Fel, the sun had
dropped below the line of the skyscrapers and the city streets had
grown shadows, the nocturnal lights of the city awaking from slumber as
the earth turned its back to the sun. Under streetlights in older sections
of the city, oil slicks from leaky bots became gauzy jewelry for the urban
landscape, the blood of machines turned to winding shimmers. The city
drew so much from bots.

To Ren, it all looked normal in the area bordering New Chicago. Normal and unworthy of note. Her eyes skated over it.

She stepped from her van and the wind clawed at her trench coat with
fingers made of the oncoming winter. The air howled through the streets,
twining among grates and fences to create an inconsistent hum. She barely
heard it. These things were nothing more than expectation matching reality. The cars moved in clockwork fashion. The people shrouded in clothing
fast stepped along. Ren didn't pay them any mind.

She walked up the steps to the apartment building to find a large, faux
wooden door and a terminal to its right. Screwed into the door's center was
a flat rectangle of plastic, its surface pitted from the elements.

When Ren connected to the apartment's sub-grid, an AR vid screen
overlaid the surface of the plastic rectangle. On it could be seen a young
woman in a stuffy room lined with books, an archaic wood burning fireplace crackling to her right. The woman looked up from whatever she was
reading to look out at Ren. She smiled from cheek to cheek and set down
her book on a side table. A log crumbled and the fire huffed out a breath
of sparks. Ren smelled a whiff of wood fire in the air, spruce and oak. She
took it in stride; the smell was fake anyway. Many apartment complexes
used unique AIs for day-to-day operations as a draw, as a marketing tactic.
It seemed this apartment was going for a homely appeal, housemother and
all.

"What can I help you with Miss?" asked the woman, the apartment
complex's AI. She glanced at Ren, one arm tossed over the well-worn
armrest of her chair.

"I need to visit a tenant," said Ren. She sent her credentials to the apartment AI with a thought.

The demeanor of the digital woman shifted immediately, from motherly to the blinking of a cursor waiting for a command. They did not need to maintain a façade for an auto.

"Should I tell the tenant that you will be arriving?"

Ren thought it over for a moment. "Yes, but do not tell her which department I am from."

The woman in the vid screen nodded before bustling out of view. The image disappeared to leave behind the plain rectangular plate.

Ren rode the elevator to the required floor with Tap's shell at her side. While she stood there waiting for the doors to open, she watched Elizabeth Fel react to the news of a government agent coming to her door. The woman looked towards the room at her back with worry-widened eyes. Inside lay the man named Nathaniel Reen. Nat for short.

Ren exited the elevator and walked down the hallway to the apartment door, a faux wooden one like the door at the entrance of the building, painted a deep green. Ren knocked with a gloved fist and saw, through the beady eyes of a reconnaissance bot, Liz jump at the sound, her eyes narrowing to slits. The woman got up from her chair and moved to the door, opening it with a creak. The reconnaissance bot pressed its metal whiskers to the window to get a better view.

By the time Ren saw the woman's face peek around the door with her physical set of eyes, Elizabeth Fel's suspicious look had been tamped down but not erased. Ren could read the distrust in the other woman. Elizabeth opened the door halfway.

"Whatever it is you need; I don't think I can help," said Elizabeth. Her eyes moved over Ren's body; her face would have revealed little to a layperson, just like Ren's buttoned trench coat. She fixed her gaze on Tap's armored shell, on its single cyclopean eye. A tightness rippled across her face like a blanket drawn tight against rocky ground.

"My name is Agent Ren. May I come in?" asked Ren, her voice dry and even. She tried to inject some levity into her voice, but none came through. "I smell some jasmine and lavender tea steeping in your kitchen. How about we sit down and talk. It's my favorite kind."

Elizabeth crossed her arms over her chest. Then she looked down and noticed her arm touching a fresh-looking stain on her scrubs, a bodily fluid of some kind, blood most likely. The woman cursed under her breath.

"Fine. Grab yourself a cup of tea while I change clothes. Haven't changed since I got back from work about an hour ago. But that bot of yours has to stay outside. Even if all the bots weren't going batshit crazy, I still wouldn't let that monster in. Besides, I'm pretty sure your jacket is hiding all sorts of surprises. That will have to be enough for you."

Elizabeth didn't wait for Ren to answer before turning away from the open door and disappearing into an adjoining hallway, mumbling more curses under her breath.

Ren nodded to Tap's shell then walked into the apartment, closing the door behind her. She walked to the kitchen and moved past the aged metal teapot leaking the smell of loose jasmine and lavender. Without making a noise, she unlocked the window and several reconnaissance bots skittered nimbly into the apartment. They dropped to the floor and split up, moving out of view.

By the time Elizabeth made it into the kitchen, Ren had poured herself a glass and was drinking it at the table with demure sips, the window closed once again.

Elizabeth grunted in her direction. "That tea as good as you were hoping?"

Ren nodded.

Elizabeth grunted again then sat down across from Ren in a fresh change of clothes, sweatshirt and sweatpants. Ren felt the surface of the table and realized it was real wood, an antique by the feel of it. Probably an heirloom. Tap ran through the records and found the table's listing in the will of Elizabeth's mother. A summary flitted across Ren's AR vision. Oak.

"So," said Elizabeth, shifting a piece of flaxen hair out of her eyes. "What is it you need?" She had washed her face, scrubbed away all her makeup to reveal bags under her eyes. It made her look older than her seventy years; she had many more before her working years were over and age truly set in. Ren remembered watching archived TV shows from before modern medicine, over 100 years past. People had aged so quickly then. Elizabeth still moved as well as anyone forty years her junior, her skin tight relative to what the archived vids had shown.

Ren kept quiet for a moment, conversing with Tap. Something in the apartment was missing, something potentially dangerous. She set her glass onto the surface of the table.

"Elizabeth Fel. I have several questions that I hope you can answer. But before that, I must ask, where is your bot?"

Elizabeth's face screwed up in confusion. "First off, call me Liz. Second, I left my bot at my hospital. Not that I see how it matters. My bosses may still trust them enough to help the bedridden get around but that doesn't mean I do."

"I assure you that most bots can still be trusted. Especially in a regulated environment such as a city hospital," said Ren.

Liz's face twisted into a deep-set sneer, settling into the expression like rainwater settling into the cracks of an old asphalt street. "And I assure you, you've got no idea what you're talking about," said Liz. "I've had to patch up too many people injured by bots in the past couple days, most of them lucky to be alive and nowhere near ready to wake up to a bot at their bedside. I swear, all it takes these days is someone floating in a can out in the black, bored from too many brainless sims. A couple hours later you have an infected bot. Dumbasses all over the System are hiding that virus in legitimate third-party updates, uploading it all over the Grid. Just so they can watch the news vids later and get a spark."

Elizabeth paused to catch her breath.

"But the worst is when somebody gets the genius idea to infect their own bot and give it a taste for some back-alley brawling, some stab you in the back and rip out your tech core before your body hits the ground type shit. Saw that too just yesterday. Enough to make anyone wonder what you cops are even doing. God knows I have. Let the hospital use my bot for now if they want. People rely on them too much anyway."

Elizabeth leaned back in her chair and crossed her arms over her chest, staring hard at Ren.

Silence, often more emphatic than any words, could also be a type of admittance. Ren's NeuCon wouldn't let her lend credence to Liz's accusations. Tap couldn't allow the government to take so much blame. Except, Ren wasn't much at lying. She'd always been told in training that NeuCon would make that easier. And it did, a little. She had always been blunt, direct to a fault. NeuCon could only veer her path so much.

"Things could be much worse," said Ren. "Things always get worse before they get better.

"You know why it's so easy to toss out a platitude, no matter the problem?" asked Liz. "Cause just like those fortunes you can get from some rust bucket vend, they're just broad enough to not mean shit, but still somehow *seem* useful. Keeping bots in check was the *government's* job. *You* were the ones who decided to work them like tools, telling us to toss them away when they pass their usefulness, telling us to vote on how they can act. If you want to use them like tools, then keep them like tools. Don't let them act like anything else. If you are going to let bots act like people, copy Origin Station and God knows which of the outer colonies, then go ahead and do it. But if you're to do that, quit treating them like tools before they learn about revenge, or some idiot adds that to their programming.

"I don't give a damn what society does with bots. Keep them as disposable labor or make them full-on citizens, I don't give a damn, but the decision should be made now. We both know what straddling the fence leads to."

Liz stared at Ren's face, their eyes meeting. Most people turned away from an auto's stare in moments. The eyes of autos were too unflinching, obdurate, dead, to stare at for long. Too bot-like. Liz didn't turn away. Her cornflower blue eyes met Ren's own dark brown without shifting.

"All things are being considered," said Ren, pensive.

Liz reached behind her and poured herself another glass of tea, shaking her head as she did so. The steam rising from her cracked ceramic mug swirled into the air. It mixed with the gusts emanating from the fan spinning slow and regular in the center of the ceiling, making dagger hooks of cloudy vapor. Ren suddenly felt too warm, the air stuffy and laden with suffocating moisture. She paused, then undid the buttons of her trench coat, took it off, and laid it over the back her chair.

Liz raised her eyes, the bags underneath softening. She wasn't looking at Ren's now visible guns or body armor. Those she ignored. She looked at the bruises on Ren's arms. Liz clucked with something close to concern.

"You've had a rough time, haven't you," said Liz.

Ren nodded before taking another sip of tea. "The government only has one choice in all this. You know which it is. North America is not and could never be Origin Station. This is what happens."

"Hmm. You sound much more accepting of it than another cop I patched up."

"Our system works. It has to."

"It doesn't have to do anything. You just want it to."

A silence enveloped the room, silence and little else. It left enough space for each of the room's occupants to let their thoughts flow freely, thoughts soon accompanied by the tapping of mugs lifted then set against the heirloom wooden table. Dozens of crescent moon discolorations marked the surface of the table. No coasters for the mugs in sight. Ren almost felt bad setting the mug down. She held it over her lap instead. Liz didn't seem to notice.

A groan sounded from the other room, a dream time groan born from a large gut pressing against a mattress. It was the sound of air escaping from a slack jaw and loose, drooling lips. Liz looked at the closed door behind her and shook her head slowly. Ren watched through the eyes of a reconnaissance bot as Nathaniel continued to grumble in his sleep.

"Why are you here?" asked Liz.

"I need to ask you some questions," said Ren. She sipped her tea. "About Nathaniel Reen, sleeping one room over."

"I figured as much."

"If you can get me what I need then I won't have to wake him."

"That's kind of you. Now ask your questions. I am getting tired and have an early shift tomorrow. I need to sleep soon."

"You know Lee Hall, correct? Were you aware that a little over two weeks ago, on August 31st, Nathaniel Reen stole software from Lee Hall's personal bot and sold it on a Grid market?" Ren kept her physical eyes trained on Liz's features, at her jawline both weathered and sharp. One of Ren's reconnaissance bots hiding in a shadowed corner did the same. Tap watched from both sets of eyes, one made of flesh and the other manufactured in a lab, analyzing all the while.

"Shit," said Liz. "Lee was probably the last friend Nat had." Liz rubbed a hand across her forehead then slumped forward, cupping her tea in both hands. "Is he pressing charges?"

"No, but please answer the question."

Ren could already tell Liz didn't know about the theft, her body and words, though indirect, had said as much. But things would be easier for Ren if she kept Liz on track. Things would be more efficient.

Liz sighed. "No, I didn't know about it. But it doesn't surprise me a bit. I've seen too many jacks cuffed to their bed with a watch bot at their side because they lifted something from their friends, just to pay for one more ride at their favorite house."

Ren nodded.

"But you know something?" said Liz, leaning forward with her corn-flower blue eyes wide. "He hasn't ever stolen from me, not once. Pretty much everyone else he knows, sure. He's good at burning bridges, having his calls blocked the moment they connect. Auto-reply messages filling his inbox, telling him to not even bother. He's been blacklisted from social sub-grids, volunteered for shady ones. But still, not from me. Not once has he stolen from me."

Ren nodded once more. With Liz leaned forward, eyes wide and bags under her eyes turned to taut skin, she looked fifty years younger, fresh into her working years. Naïve and inexperienced. Ren had the image of a younger Liz walking hand in hand with a man she'd patched up in the ER, ignoring the several messages left by the most popular AI matchmaker in the System. The AI had found a middle-aged medical researcher that would fill her every need in a partner. But rather than meet the one tailored to her dreams of a quiet house and lazy afternoons scrolling through news vids, she goes home with the man from the ER, spends a night by his side then spends several dozen more. Then one day, after a date to a retro diner where the napkins come pre-greased, she goes to work only to find him back in the ER, fuzzed up and bloody from a quick visit to a jack house where he owed a few hundred loci.

Liz's look was that of someone who thought people could change. It didn't fit her.

A part of Ren wanted to say something about this, call her out on it. But the other part of Ren saw motion through mouse-like eyes.

Ren watched as Nat shifted to a sitting position, woken from all the talk, face bleary and shadowed. He wiped a hand across his belly and scratched at his side through rips in his white t-shirt. By the time he made it to his feet, awareness had crept into his eyes. He blinked away any remaining haze and walked to the door, trundling through drifts of clothes. He paused with his hand on the door handle.

"If Lee isn't pressing charges, then why are you here asking about the theft?" asked Liz.

Nat froze on the other side of the door. Ren could only see his back, shoulders taut against the tattered shirt, bare feet trapped in the deep carpet. Liz didn't know.

"It is important to know who bought the software. For legal purposes," said Ren.

Liz slumped into her chair, taking a sip of tea, hiding behind the motion. Letting it fill the time. "I can't help you with that," she said.

"That is fine. Nat, could you come out here please. I need to speak with you." Ren spoke in normal tones, not high or low.

Liz's eyes rounded while the door swung open on plastic hinges. Nat stood framed in the doorway, his round face uneasy. He grunted out an incomprehensible mix of words and sat down next to Liz, not meeting her gaze. The bearish man bristled at the sight of Ren's guns, though he didn't say anything about them.

"Whaddaya want?" asked Nat, his brain yet to fully awaken. He nodded to Liz as the woman grabbed him a cup from a warped cupboard and filled it with hot water from a stainless-steel water heater. She pulled a bag of loose-leaf black tea from the pantry and tossed some into Nat's cup. He nodded in thanks, though the shift of his head was stilted and weak, like the jerk of drowsy eyelid.

Ren thought it over for a few moments before answering, taking another sip of tea. The man watched her attentively, following her motions in the way of an animal whose territory was being questioned. Aggressive, and not without fear.

"I know that you copied data from Lee Hall's bot, Nu, without it knowing. Then you proceeded to sell this software on one of the independent mechanic Grid markets as your own. To gain some ... spare loci."

Nat's bushy eyebrows rose, shifted until they looked like a bot eyebrow facsimile. His cheeks reddened, and the chair beneath him creaked with his rustling.

"As I told Liz here, Lee is not pressing charges. In fact, he does not even know I am here. But some of my bosses think they know which corp. bought the software, and they are looking for any opportunity to bring them trouble. As it stands it cannot be proven they have done anything illegal but proving this could add to a stack of lawsuits in the works regarding questionable software acquisition. So, all I need from you, is the record of sale. Nothing more. I am not here to make trouble."

Of course, much of that was a lie. Neither Ren nor her boss Foster had any idea who might have purchased the software. She knew from the audio recording of Lee at his apartment that Sundog Corp. was a possible answer but searches for that corporation had been fruitless. Even Seth, and in turn Safin Informatics, couldn't seem to find any information on Sundog Corp. She needed more to go on.

The complex's AI had given Ren access to the apartment's data feed upon entering the building. She used this to send a digital copy of a signed warrant over to Nat. She saw the man's contacts flash as the document scrolled through his vision. It granted her the right to access all of Nat's personal records regarding sales. Forcefully if necessary. The big man looked like he wanted to argue. Before the advent of AR capable contacts, Ren imagined he would have rumpled the papers then tossed them across the room in a fit. As it was, he couldn't even close his eyes. That would only create a perfect canvas upon which to view a reminder of his mistake.

Liz, seated at his side and watching his face with surprising calmness, reached out and took one of his large hands into her thin-fingered own. "Best if you get this done with, Nat," she said.

At the touch of her hand and voice, the tension seemed to ease from his big frame, all the muscle going loose to meld with the surrounding portly tissue. He withdrew his hand from Liz's and walked back to the room he came from. Ren saw through mechanical eyes him rummage in the other room, eventually picking up a cracked control screen. He tapped out a few commands, the sounds of his actions winding their way into the living room. Liz rested back into her chair, aged compared to her earlier outburst. The bags under her eyes seemed inflamed.

The notification sounded in Ren's ear and a file popped into her vision. Records of sale from August 31st. Only one entry, a large chunk of software posted to a hawker's marketplace, Lucky Bazaar, and sold the same day. ID of sale 19823HQW. Content of sale listed as a GP bot advanced operating software with little in terms of details. Nat's description for the software's capabilities was hasty at best, using buzz words to espouse its innovative quality without saying anything specific. The only hard data he gave were data processing rates normalized for different hardware, things any mechanic could test for, but still enough to make a sale. The stats were impressive and legit, even if the description betrayed the seller's ignorance.

Any corp. sifting through the markets would have noticed the telltale indications of questionable provenance and lowered their offer accordingly.

Ren finished looking through the data. It had sold for 267 loci. A paltry amount even if it had been nothing more than the banal software upgrade it appeared to be. But there was a larger problem than Nat's poor financial decisions.

The buyer wasn't listed. At least, not by name.

That in and of itself wasn't unusual. The seller wasn't always given the buyer's identity, often just a notice that someone with a randomly assigned account name was interested and a sale ID if it went through. Yet, she had an audio recording indicating that Nat had seen the name Sundog Corp. as the purchaser at some point in time. Ren let Tap analyze the rest of the data and instead focused on Nat as the man moved into the room.

"Is that all there is?" asked Ren.

Nat shuffled his weight and ran a hand across his unshaven face. "Yes mam, that's all I have."

"Are you positive?"

Nat narrowed his eyes, dropping his hand to his side. His face turned red, and his facial scruff seemed to ripple. "Yep."

Ren didn't respond. Though, perhaps as her right hand moved to rest on her lap, her fingers brushed the handle of the pistol held in the cross-draw holster at her waist. Perhaps.

Whether her fingers brushed the edge of the gun didn't matter, because Nat's eyes followed her motion and saw what they expected to see. His thick eyebrows obscured his eyes.

"Dammit that's all I have," said Nat. "It was purchased by some corp. called Sundog same day as I put it up. Gave me shit all for it. That's all I know."

He moved close to the table, his big frame overshadowing Ren. She could smell the sweat from a restless sleep thick on his skin.

He didn't know the buyer's name had been wiped. Which meant someone had accessed Lucky Bazaar's records of the sale, switching the purchase to an anonymized buyer and illegally wiping certain bits of information. People only did that if the information was important. She left it to Tap to send all the new information to Seth. He and his could gather information on the marketplace from hidden channels while Tap took the mostly legal routes. She hoped to find records that had escaped the wipe and contained more than just the name Sundog.

While Ren was busy thinking, watching Nat carefully from three sets of eyes, Liz stepped up from her seat. "I think it's time you left, Agent Ren," she said.

Ren nodded once, stood up and put on her trench coat, hiding her guns behind its midnight folds once again. Nat, for his part, watched her move then stepped back to lean against the wall. He rubbed the back of his neck and mumbled something about feeling like shit and taking a shower. He ambled back to his and Liz's room with a single inscrutable backward glance.

Ren took one final drink of tea, draining the contents in a gulp. Then she walked towards the entrance, Liz two steps behind. Ren paused by the door.

"I appreciate your candor," said Ren. "And I apologize if I was rude to Nathaniel. This investigation is important, and I am short on time."

Liz nodded, wiping her hands on the bottom of her tight knit sweatshirt then stuffing them into the pockets of her sweatpants. "You appreciate my candor, huh? Then let me add some more. Free of charge. Just because your short on time doesn't mean you have to be an ass."

Ren thought back to Liz's earlier remarks, about how Nat had not once stolen from her. Ren was speaking before she knew to stop herself, unsure whether it was the conditioning or her own desire to get the last word.

"You know if he continues with his habits … it's only a matter of time until he steals from you too."

Liz's features darkened, jawline gaining a hard edge. "Maybe. Or maybe you don't know shit about me or him."

Ren shrugged her arms to bring her jacket to a more comfortable rest. It was bunching at the edge of her body armor.

"Maybe so," said Ren.

She watched through robotic eyes as the kitchen window slid open on a silent track and the reconnaissance bots gathered at its threshold slipped into the cold night, shutting the window behind them. Ren turned around from Liz's apartment and headed towards the elevator, Liz's eyes boring holes into her back until she made it to the twin metal doors. Tap's shell followed from its position next to a potted mini lemon tree, stopping once it made it to Ren's side. Ren's thoughts as the elevator doors closed were structured, painstakingly ordered. But there was a chaos underneath, a welter of conflicts being forced through a sieve. Almost out of earshot, the sound of someone soughing their breath across her ear, exhaling slow and steady, came to her, though no one else stood with Ren and Tap in the elevator cab. It was the sound of chemicals being pumped by her implants into her bloodstream, barely audible. Her supply had been refilled at headquarters. The brewing storm inside her calmed.

Seth contacted her as she exited the building, the notification pulsing at the same time the wind tinged with winter cold welcomed her outside. She accepted the call with a thought then opened the passenger's side door of her van, sidling in. Tap's armored shell walked into the rear of the van and sat down on the wide bench with a thud. Ren directed the van to go on a meandering path through the city, no specific destination in mind.

Seth's voice slid into Ren's ear with its typical greasy cant. "Ren, my dear, it seems you are moving up in the world. I am afraid that today I am being relegated to little more than a messenger, an audio messenger no less. I'm unable to meet you virtually or otherwise. To say it is disappointing would be an understatement."

Ren pictured Seth in his ashen suit and tie, tipping his bowler hat in her direction with one hand while he spoke, spine curved in a vulpine slouch.

"Would you like to hear the message?" asked Seth.

"If it is related to my inquiries, then yes," said Ren.

"NeuCon once again? I can hear it in your voice, my dear agent Ren. It normally has such a beautiful edge to it, but with an unmistakable softness just underneath. You were forged from metals of differing strength so one could cover for the weaknesses of the other. So many alloys. Modern and rich, well suited to the times. But all I can hear is a single voice. And it is cast iron. So hard, true. But also, so very brittle. My dear agent Ren, should I be concerned?"

Ren didn't respond.

"I suppose this means you will have even less desire to extend our lovely conversation."

"You are correct."

He sighed as if on an outdoor stage, a crowd of hundreds standing before him in rapt attention.

"Saf herself would like to meet you. It seems your latest data package interested her greatly. I am afraid I was not told the details. But nonetheless,

I will send you the access point for your virtual rendezvous. One time use only. If I were you, I would connect as soon as possible."

"Thanks for the message," said Ren. She disconnected before Seth had any time to reply.

Slippery a man as Seth was, his promises, once made, could be trusted. The access point for her virtual meeting with Saf came a few seconds after she disconnected from the call.

Ren commanded her seat to recline with a thought, bending it back to a comfortable angle. She moved her hands to undo her ponytail before remembering that her hair was no longer long enough to have one. It had been cut by her own hand, which in turn had been guided by Tap, to make it easier to wear her mask.

She rested her arms on the armrests and shifted her weight to a more comfortable position, shimmying the bottom of her trench coat until it lay flat against her seat. She was ready to meet Saf.

And yet, she wasn't ready.

She withheld the command to enter VR, kept it bottled like an indrawn breath. With a shrug, she sat up in her seat to look out the window, her conditioned mind feeling blips of annoyance at the wait. Still, she didn't enter VR. A part of her mind conversed with Tap as the AI, almost with a sigh, ran some other calculations.

The city outside passed her by, the streets shifting from asphalt to tech ridden plastic, the lights in the smart streets switching between government mandated traffic markers the self-driving cars hadn't needed in years to taglines for different ad campaigns.

"We all do our best to overcome our flaws. And once we make it past, we want them to stay good and gone. Why let these flaws reappear in your child? Come meet with a specialist today! Tailored Genetics Inc.," read one.

Ren saw a plastic cup roll from the hand of a woman walking along the sidewalk. It bounced into the street to rest overtop the exclamation point in the advertisement. After Ren's van passed by, she looked back to see a maintenance bot weave through the crush of cars to pick up the cup and return it to the flustered woman. A slim man stood at the woman's side, with her but also not, light from his contacts visible to Ren, body slack and inattentive. The van continued and Ren was forced to look away. She looked up to see the same ad as before, this time in AR and plastered on the side of a skyscraper next to an art piece of upward falling AR water.

Ren wondered at the turn of events, at Saf's personal intervention. Her only hope was that it meant the purchasers of Nu's software, the cause of all the recent chaos and death, perhaps Y's very backers, had been found. She could think of few other plausible reasons for Saf to come herself. One perhaps. But that had been a calculated risk, hopefully an acceptable one.

Ren knew even a question could be revealing, her request for Safin Informatics to track Nathaniel Reen's sale especially so. Saf knew of Ren's forced enlistment of Lee, but not of his role as the opener of Pandora's box. Perhaps Saf had figured it out. Ren had only told her to search for Sundog Corp., then to track a single sale. Minimum information given. But Ren knew Saf. It would not be hard for her to find the connection between the sale, the Qualia Code, Nathaniel Reen, and Lee Hall. Then it would only take a few more logical steps, with some imaginative direction. Ren felt with some unease that she could not predict what Saf might do with that information, who she might sell it to. That had been part of the reason for hiding Lee at an unknown safe house.

Tap ran some preliminary projections then told Ren all was ready.

Ren dropped to her seat and entered her virtual appointment with Saf the moment her eyelids snapped shut.

The world melted away and, for a moment, all sensation with it. The press of the seat cushions and the hum of the tires against the street. All gone. The sound of Tap's armored shell rocking back and forth as the car moved. The sound of air flowing through vents. Gone. The yells, murmurs, exhalations and pounding steps of both humans and bots were replaced by an absence, a sea of anechoic black.

Then, she felt her feet touch solid ground, felt herself standing on a substance somehow darker, firmer than the abyssal void around her. Then pinpricks of light appeared, as if she were covered by a dome and tiny holes were being speared into the cloth by a red-hot poker. Stars. They began appearing in swathes, multicolored dustings of the kind only a camera could see. Differing wavelengths of light saturated into brilliant clouds from blue to red. Ultraviolet rays and gamma rays and x-rays all assigned a color visible to the naked eye, green and yellow and clay brown. It all made her feel incomparably small, a microbe on a flea on an otherworldly beast. She had been in space many times before, but the sight in front of her begged to send her to her knees. It begged, but the pleas fell on deaf ears.

She cast her eyes around and let Tap analyze the visual data stream she was receiving. There was a chance this place was modeled after somewhere in the real universe, somewhere in the System.

"Hello, Agent Ren. I'm pleased to finally meet you."

The voice was feminine with a rasp. It wasn't the grating rasp of those who filled their lungs with the burning fumes of black-market designer plants. Nor was it the sultry rasp of a jazz singer riding the trill of a saxophone, though that was closer. It was the incongruent rasp of someone wise beyond their already considerable years, without the typical senile tinge. For if the rumors surrounding the reclusive leader of Safin Informatics were true, age didn't seem to touch her like the rest. Death seemed to hold back the final swing of the scythe. Her working years never ended. Of course, other rumors said she was already dead, an intelligence of another kind at the helm, acting in her name.

Ren turned around to find Saf. Or what Saf presented to the System these days. A bot shell almost a foot taller than Ren stood amongst the stars. Its silicon skin was colored an ambiguous dark grey and separated into sections by graceful metal tracery, some of the branches spider web thin, others thick and bounding. Many of the symbols, for that was what the metal designs were, consisted of multi-layered circles with fibrous patterns repeated in between. Yet the most striking design was that of Saf's face. Lines of metal framed her angular features in alternating, flowering curls. The outlines of petals gathered around her eyes in a confluence of silvery white, making her orange-red irises into stigmas of fire. Rather than hair, the pattern of flowering ivy continued across her bald head. Her ears were elfin, sharp and petite. A loose shift started at her neck to stop a few inches above her knees, her limbs shapely and elegant. She moved more smoothly than any bot Ren had ever before seen, more smoothly than any person, than an auto in full thrall. She loped towards Ren across the pitch-black platform, excited yet serene among a sea of stars.

"I believe conversations require input from both sides, Agent Ren," said Saf with a slight smirk. "It has been several years since I talked with anyone not an employee of my company, many more since I met someone here, in my personal rendering of the universe. I am keen to share it with you, Agent Ren."

Saf paused a foot or two away from Ren, hesitating as if wanting to come closer, her hand flicking out in an aborted attempt to shake hands. She sat down. Though there was no chair beneath her at the start of the motion, she didn't fall. A chair of white marble formed in a blink. Ren found that a similar chair formed behind her. She sat down as well.

Ren noted with some surprise that the lag in their encounter was essentially nonexistent, as if the meeting were happening in person. Even with Seth's description of a meeting, a part of Ren had expected a virtual recording to be waiting at the given address, one she could watch and analyze. Then, if necessary, she would have recorded her own virtual message as a response. She had conducted many investigations reaching into all corners of the System over the years, gathering information as fast as known technology would allow, as fast as electromagnetic radiation could travel through a vacuum. But that still left much information hours out of reach. It could be very frustrating. She had been prepared to be frustrated once again. Saf was not known to spend her days near Earth.

Ren knew it to be possible the virtual figure in front of her wasn't Saf at all. Could be the rumored bot for all she knew, Saf the Proxy. For if the virtual figure in front of Ren truly was Saf, it meant the recluse was still alive, and close. Certainly not cloistered in her company offices on Origin Station. She stayed somewhere on Earth or Luna. Or a private ship nearby. Tap didn't have any information on her whereabouts that might help. No one did. Even so, in front of Ren sat a virtual Saf in the guise of a bot, stunning in its design, human in its emotion, responding in real time. For some inexplicable reason, she felt it to be Saf herself. The probabilities worked out by Tap made it seem unlikely, though far from impossible.

There was another explanation, but it leaned much closer to impossibility.

Saf stared at Ren with her orange-red eyes, silvery chin held in her palm. She tapped her foot and twisted her lips into a playful grin. The stars swirled about, and the platform seemed to move. The sun blinked into existence, far off in the distance behind the figure of Saf. Tap whispered to Ren that he had pinpointed their virtual location, midway between Jupiter and Saturn.

"Tell you what, Ren. Ask a question, any question you want. It can even be a two-parter. I can't promise I won't lie, but I can promise I will respond. Many people don't realize how much that alone is worth."

Ren chose the first line of questioning that came to mind, deciding to steer the conversation from there.

"Why do you choose to appear as a bot when that is not what you are? Or are the rumors of Saf the Proxy true?" asked Ren.

"Why do you choose to appear with your normal clothes on, when anything you can imagine is available to you?"

"Are you saying that you appearing as a bot is nothing more than choosing what to wear?"

"You make it sound like choosing what to wear isn't important, like your image doesn't alter how people think of you. Not everyone has a closet filled with clothes of only two colors you know."

Ren crossed her legs, out of reflex leaning further back in her chair. She nearly blinked in surprise as the marble backing shifted with her motion. The seat cradled her. It unnerved Ren that Saf knew so much about her, though the fact that she did surprised her less than the perfect motions of the chair. Ren had been working with Safin Informatics for years, since the accident with her sister. She knew of their abilities.

"Vanity then?" asked Ren, her voice monotonous and dry. "It sounds like you worry over how people will view a wrinkled old form." A worry that Ren knew to be reasonable, depending on the market.

Saf laughed with the sound of a crystal chandelier caught in a brief gust of wind, all tinkling and light.

"I know how people today think," said Saf. "As you said, there are social norms. When people really begin ageing after their working years are up, the drop is precipitous and taxing. Cost of extending the healthy period of life to anywhere from 100 to 120, they say. Cost!? The change in social perception was a small price to pay. It is a blessing, shortening that kind of discomfort. Can you imagine living like they used to? Forced to spend decades in doddering impotence? Did you know that before you were born, before the Great Medical Shift, the marks of the elderly that so many now abhor were often positive symbols? Grey hair used to be a symbol of experience and wisdom! Though less so for women, as you would expect in a historical patriarchy. We were making progress on that front. Now grey hair is a harbinger for the steep decline, though some find stray flecks of it ... alluring in a unique way. Isn't that right Agent Ren? Anyway, the medical advances came and allowed everyone to appear healthy and young past their 100th birthday with the side effect of a hard crash, a few years of rapid aging and severely decreased faculties. You weren't alive to see the shift, to see society treat even the smallest signs of aging as unsightly, to turn retirement homes into the locked caskets they are now. Who would have thought equality would have come in such a way? Now both men and woman are forced to play a young person's game. Experience shows in other ways. But not through wrinkled skin and slow movements. Because then the crash is near at hand and your word can no longer be trusted, senility is knocking. No, it is not vanity to avoid a weak appearance."

Ren pondered over Saf's words for several moments before responding.

"If that's the real reason, then why don't you choose a younger version of yourself as your avatar?" asked Ren. "The effect would be the same. Your pic was shown on the occasional news vid when I was a child. Most thought you were beautiful."

"There are many forms of strength. Why stick to the one from my past rather than go forward?"

"So, you don't think your current bot form is beautiful then? Didn't even consider how you might look when you chose it?"

Saf smiled, full and genuine. "I think we're off to a good start."

"There are rumors you know. Other rumors. Quieter ones."

"Oh?"

"That you're the first not to need a body anymore. At all."

Saf smiled wide, parting her lips the color of molten silver to reveal shapely teeth of alabaster white. "It is rare these days to have a corp. without an AI to steer the ship and a human figurehead to reap the profits. Why not combine the two and expand human consciousness past what even an auto of Division 13 can achieve? To upload who we are. Is that what you're thinking? I've heard these rumors, as I hear all rumors whispered in any corner of the System. Be it whispered in a derelict ship from the mouths of pirates gathered around a two-gallon bowl of vat-grown biryani or in a cloud level conference room from the mouth of a corporate head, I hear these whispers. Sometimes I am the one who whispers first."

"What is your response to the rumors?"

"What are you? A reporter?" said Saf, chuckling. "If you want to know my response, the answer is quite simple. The rumors are good for business."

Saf clicked a virtual tongue made of soft plastics, staring at Ren with chin in palm, smirk in full display. She sat easily on her marble throne. Her cloud grey shift rustled in an invisible breeze.

"This has been more fun than I expected. You're going to have to visit more often Ren. But now that we have gotten your voice to work, wooden though its conditioned version may be, we should move on to the true purpose of this meeting."

"Do you have any information on who purchased Nathaniel Reen's software?"

"I do, but don't you think it a little wrong to call it his software?"

Ren's body laying flush against the leather seat of a van cringed, hands forming the slightest semblance of a fist. Yet, it didn't show on her virtual features, not even through the twitch of a finger. Ren stayed silent while Saf watched. The woman in the guise of a bot stifled a laugh.

"You do realize a complete and utter lack of a reaction, is still a response," said Saf.

"Yes. But it has no useful meaning if it is the only response."

"Maybe. By the way, how are your safehouses nowadays? Furnished? Complete with a bot servant? I hear those apartments on the north side of New Chicago are quite the purchase. Real granite countertops, wooden cabinets. One would forget they aren't allowed to leave."

Ren didn't flinch, though she did signal Tap to send an armored shell over to Lee's safehouse. It was worth the risk of it being followed, now that she knew Lee's location had been compromised. He would have to be moved soon, though how they would move him without Saf watching was another matter.

Saf snapped her fingers and the scenery shifted. The sun moved to Ren's left. On her right appeared a large celestial body wrapped in a thick yellowish-orange atmosphere. Behind it hid a larger body, a planet colored a light brown with expansive rings of ice circling its belly.

Ren recognized the scene without Tap needing to tell her. Saturn and its largest moon, Titan. She could see a few of the 61 other named satellites of the enormous gas giant. She knew in what direction each of the major colonies could be found, each with their own corporate sponsor hauling ice from the rings or scooping helium-3 from the atmosphere of Saturn. The Saturnian system kept all colonies past the belt watered, and all fusion generators in the System running.

The platform Ren and Saf reclined on locked into orbit around Titan, staying out of reach of its dense atmosphere. Ren could see several flotillas orbiting Titan in similar fashion, the nearest one a spaceport named *Lurking Dawn*, a misshapen lump of add-ons and retrofits surrounded by AR signage in every color of neon. A few mid-level corporate frigates the size of skyscrapers could be seen in the ramshackle docking bays. Most of the visible ships were smaller, privately owned boats, big enough to fit a moderately sized family and cheap enough to keep running for years on end with a good mechanic.

Tap whispered to Ren and she looked closer at the space port. It listed through its orbital path while presumably thousands of people floated through its micro gravity halls. The station crept closer to their platform until Ren could distinguish several individuals in bright orange spacesuits clomping about the surface, repairing nascent fractures, damage from space trash and meteoroids hurtling into its side.

All told, Saf's simulation looked nothing short of incredible, the detail hyper real in the way of good VR. Ren wondered how much processing it took to maintain the simulation, this virtual sandbox for Saf to alter as she wished. A universe to shape then break on nothing more than a whim. Ren wondered how accurate, how lifelike, it truly was.

Then, Ren realized the truth.

According to the information available to Tap, including vid feeds from around the System, the motion of the virtual *Lurking Dawn* corresponded to the exact motions of the real-life ship. Since it took about 80 minutes, depending on the orientation of Grid relay stations, for electromagnetic signals to travel from Saturn to Earth, everything Tap could see on government vid feeds near Saturn had happened 80 minutes in the past. It wasn't unreasonable to think the real repairman jogging across the surface of the *Lurking Dawn* in a bright orange jumper had already finished his work and returned to the inside of the space station through a service hatch. The view in front of Ren corresponded to that which Tap could see through government vid feeds, stitched together into a virtual panorama, a picture of Titan from eighty minutes in the past.

The simulation wasn't a sandbox where Saf would build whatever impossible fancies came to mind. The simulation was a virtual rendering of the universe itself, as if every star were the lens of a camera piping its data feed into a cable sprouting from Saf's neck. It was a version of the universe where one could be a ghost, walk through walls and observe from every perch. A universe created for the pleasures of a single sentient being so she could watch the waves of her actions ripple before her throne. It fit Saf perfectly. Ren imagined it to be the basis for all of Safin Informatics.

Saf stood from her chair with an effortless push of her bare metal feet. She walked to the edge of their floating platform and pointed to the aging spaceport in front of them.

"Rundown though it may be, would you believe that this station houses some very intriguing info databases?" asked Saf. She gave a playful smile as she talked, laughing at an inside joke Ren couldn't help but feel to be at her expense.

"Yes, I would," said Ren. She stood from her marble chair and brushed her trench coat into a more comfortable position, joining Saf at the edge of the platform.

"Would you like to see inside?"

Ren nodded once, unhurried and expectant.

Saf snapped her fingers and their scenery changed to that of an atrium inside the *Lurking Dawn*. Lush gardens filled the center of the room, the air heavy and wet. Shops lined the outer edges and a bar nestled into the wall to Ren's right. She could see a handful of men in aged working rags tossing back shots of something alcoholic and odorous. A few women in similar working rags sat at a table behind them, leaning back in their chairs and chatting, playing an AR game that lit up their contacts. A bot served drinks behind the bar. Light bounced off something on its neck. It took a moment for Ren to recognize it as a metal collar. A thick metal chain ran to an iron ring set into the back wall, recently by the look of it. Upon further inspection of the patrons, a sizeable man with a mane of curled black hair had bandages wrapped about his hand. He kept his eyes averted from the bot at the bar, flicked at his bandages with his good hand. People always felt smaller when they were afraid, folded inwards. Guess this corp. had its own way of dealing with infected bots. Ren wondered what the man had done to alienate the bartender.

She'd known the Qualia Code had spread throughout the System but seeing it in Saf's simulation made things different somehow, firmer. Ren went back to scanning the room.

A vid screen over the dilapidated bar showed an image of Titan's surface. The cryovolcano Doom Mons loomed in the background of the vid screen, lakes of methane and ethane visible in the fore. Dunes and hills covered the rocky landscape. The vid showed a game of Shēng Qǐ, a sport that could only be played in the dense atmosphere yet low gravity of Titan. People in durable space suits strapped two pairs of wings to their backs and gripped lacrosse sticks in their hands, attempting to toss balls through the aerial hoops of the opposing team. They controlled their flight through implants that interpreted the flexing of different back muscles. Very acrobatic. Very dangerous. Ren used to watch it all the time.

One of the players on the screen bull-rushed a defender and sent him into a whirling spin. The player with the ball wove around their now flailing opponent and sent the ball through a hoop with an easy underhand toss. The player waved at the crowd, doing some tight flips in celebration. The crowds in the stands went wild while a thick atmosphere of nitrogen and methane roiled across from them, on the other side of protective glass. The defender righted themselves a few feet above the ground, narrowly avoiding a painful collision.

Ren went back to scanning her immediate surroundings. The detail staggered her. Every nook and cranny of the station looked flawlessly imperfect, filled with scratches from daily wear and tear. Even the roots of the plants in the overgrown center of the room were simulated down to the absorbent hairs on their roots. The plants spilled onto the pathways in meandering patterns of pale yellow and green, tripping up passerby who grumbled and moved on. It matched what vid feeds Tap could access of the atrium down to the smallest detail, down to the air handling system nudging the leaves about. The accurate mapping of the environment was close to what Ren could do with a fleet of shells at her disposal. But if the simulation truly covered all the human explored universe, in near real time, then the virtual universe Ren found herself in was at a scale unimaginable. She knew it shouldn't be possible. It would require too many cameras, too many eyes, to be feasible.

People often died floating through a seldom traveled section of the black, their ships blaring SOS signals into space if power still worked, silent as a grave if not. They died with no one noticing, their faces pressed close to translucent panes of glass, all the while hoping the stars were the glimmers of a searchlight of old. As much as Saf might say otherwise, Ren didn't think she saw those people die.

Saf turned away from the atrium into a darkened hallway at its edge. Ren followed at her heels, pensive.

Saf's simulation wasn't perfect, that was the only answer Ren could conceive. Whatever vid sources Tap had access to, Saf did as well, making any mistakes impossible for Ren to detect. Ren guessed Saf had programs that stitched together old footage with new footage to get a virtual rendering as close to accurate as possible. She guessed some of the people were digital creations meant to fool her, meant to make the simulation appear perfect. That had to be the answer. Nobody had that many eyes.

Ren thought of Y's comments, of a god whose many eyes were intrinsic to the stuff of the universe. Saf tossed Ren a knowing smile, then paused before a shadowed alcove.

A door was barely visible in the gloom, the blinking lights of its entry panel the only indication of its presence. They walked closer and Ren saw an AR decal on the door's front, visible to those with the required sub-grid access. "Iron Dvaar Inc.," it read. Tap gathered a summary of the corporation. It didn't seem to be of any import. It was one of the many data management companies operating throughout the System.

"After you," said Saf with a smile. She stretched a hand towards the closed door.

Ren stepped forward and raised her hand to the entrance panel, but her fingers found empty air. She watched as her fingertips phased through the panel and into the wall. She walked forward. Her vision flickered to black for a moment and she found herself on the other side of the door.

What greeted her on the other side was a dimly lit server room like so many she had seen before. She saw rows of servers with narrow passageways in between, maintenance bots moving about on their plastic wheels. She also saw a human figure in a grey jumpsuit standing next to one of the server racks. Of average height with soft features, the androgynous person turned from the server, eyes on a thin tablet held in their hand. They walked towards Ren without veering or slowing down. Then, at the last moment, they brought up their eyes to look straight through Ren to the door at her back.

Ren tamped down her reactions, the part of her brain telling her to move. Instead of stepping to the side, she let the virtual figure stroll right through her and out the now open door. The figure walked slow and tepid, eyes glazed over and AR capable contacts blank as an empty vid screen. Saf moved to Ren's side.

"I worry over that tech who walked past. For them, life lost its zeal, and they don't much care to find it again I'm afraid. Sil is their name. Their parents died last week, hit the steep decline a couple months back so it would've happened within the year anyway. The parents were born and raised outside a gravity well but insisted on visiting Earth before their death. It was hard on them, going into a gravity well as strong as Earth's, just like Sil feared it would be. They died of heart attacks only a mile from their ancestral cemetery, both only minutes apart. Now Sil hardly does anything other than work or sleep, hasn't deviated from the walk between their small apartment here on the station and this server hub. They have a lot of self-blame I think, hadn't seen their parents in person in years. It isn't uncommon for the androgynous who were altered before birth to have a poor relationship with their parents. Born on an overcrowded colony floating through the black with strict population controls. The family didn't escape until Sil's tenth birthday … Sil hasn't spent any of the money I sent them either, didn't even haggle on the price of the data. No zeal. They used to haggle for hours at the local markets."

Saf shook her head, silvery fingers twined together, arms resting easily in front of her torso. Her expression was solemn.

"No matter. Much information related to Lucky Bazaar transactions is stored here, in this very room. It might interest you to know that other information pertinent to your search happens to be located here as well. Tell me, where did the trail of breadcrumbs you were following for several other leads end?"

"The hacking of the Discere server could be traced to the Saturnian system, somewhere near Titan," said Ren.

"Ah yes. Quite the coincidence I should think." Saf smirked before strolling into the aisles. Her bare metal feet made smatters of noise as they pressed against the grates spaced into the flooring, hundreds of bundled wires visible underneath. Her voice floated from between the aisles. "But of course, it is no coincidence at all, the purchaser of this software and the hacker of the Discere server are one and the same, as I'm sure you expected. They have been using Iron Dvaar Inc. and dozens of other data management corporations to hide their movements System wide. Altering data here and there, storing it on local private servers disconnected from the Grid. Routing their actions through company after company. It is easy enough for them to access Lucky Bazaar's files. I would bet it is why they purchase through Lucky Bazaar in the first place."

Saf appeared on the other side of the room, rounding a corner with a skip in her step. She loped towards Ren, her shift fluttering with the motion.

"Would you like to hear the rest?" asked Saf. "How much are you willing to pay to hear it?"

Ren merely nodded, a tingle of expectation crawling up her spine and tensing her muscles.

Saf smiled a mischievous smile, then snapped her fingers. They appeared once again on the floating black platform circling Titan with the ramshackle mass of the *Lurking Dawn* traveling between them and the planet. Saf snapped her fingers again and Saturn disappeared. Then Titan. Then the sun. Then the stars began to dim, one by one, light fading like the slow closing of an eyelid. The lights snuffed out in the space of a deep breath, a sigh. All that was left was Ren and Saf, alone in a sea of anechoic black.

All of it, all the void, pressed in on Ren, yet continued outwards without bound. So close and so far, it weighed on her.

"We must agree on a price to be paid," said Saf.

Saf reclined in an ornate chair without legs, impossibly thin with silver veins. It floated in the nothingness, yet Saf's heel rested against an invisible firmament.

Ren found herself sitting across from Saf in a similar chair, lower and less ornate. Her feet searched for ground with hesitant jabs and struck something dense, and paralytic. It slowed her feet like an ooze. Then the sensation was gone, no resin left behind. Her feet swung through the nothingness, and it was as if her brain forgot how to swim, how to tread amniotic fluid. Several seconds passed before Ren found her voice. It had gone in search of real air.

Still, when she found her voice, it did not shake in the least. It was, as Seth had said, quite hard. Her body meandering through New Chicago took a deep breath.

"How much do you want?" asked Ren.

Ren felt herself calming, felt Tap whisper in her ear. This was why Saf had decided to meet, to show Ren her simulation of the System, perhaps the entirety of the human explored universe. Saf wanted to make the deal herself, at the highest possible price. And show off her resources of course.

Ren didn't think it would matter. She had her limits on how much she could give. She had expected to meet those limits anyway.

Saf smiled large. "Oh, letting me name the price I see."

"I don't have much room to bargain. You gave me enough information to validate your story, pique my interest, but not enough for me to finish the investigation myself. I don't have enough resources in the Saturnian system. I also don't have time to waste. So, name your price."

"Everyone has room to bargain. There is always a cost that is too high. Even for you Ren, and Division 13."

"Fine, how about the standard rate, doubled since this would solve two of the inquiries I have set up with your firm."

"This would solve much more than that. No, the standard rate doubled isn't even a good place to start. How about we multiply the standard rate by ten and I ask for a special favor as well."

"And what favor is that?"

"I will let you choose between two different favors," said the magnanimous Saf, reclining easily in her marble chair. She stared hard at Ren for a moment, with her orange-red eyes. They dilated such that each eye was a total solar eclipse, the iris the sun's corona and pupil the darkened moon. Ren met Saf's gaze and waited for her to continue speaking.

"One, you come work for me," said Saf, "auto parts and all. Only for an agreed upon number of cases of course. Two, you let me use Tap on some jobs where I require some of its ... strengths. You could think of it as a sort of joint venture between Safin Informatics and Division 13, a contract if you will." Saf gave an uncaring shrug, as if to say the two options were equal in all respects.

A lone lightbulb hung between Saf and Ren, its chain stretching upwards into infinity. It was an ancient kind of light bulb, fluorescent and dim. The light gave Saf's metallic body a ghoulish cast.

"I am afraid neither of those things are possible," said Ren. She was not about to go work for Safin Informatics, be a colleague of Seth. And the usage of Tap by another entity was out of the question, and not something she could grant anyway. Her fists in the van driving through New Chicago clenched against her seat.

Saf's laugh sounded like a series of church bells, her voice resounding through the nothingness where Ren's voice sounded hollow and muffled.

"I expected as much. How about you ask Foster? I take it the old man is watching."

Ren knew he was. Foster was a little man sitting in her brain, watching all the vid screens. Before Ren could speak, a message found its way to her, a spasm of thought.

We cannot agree in full. But let her know we can agree in part. Tap can be hers to use. But compromises must be made. Tell her this, and I will work out the details with her later. Her information is too important to wait. I am confident she will find this suitable. I had always wondered when she might make this kind of a request.

The message was steady and precise, each word forming in Ren's mind as if it were her own thought. It sounded like Foster in its delivery, and the word-thoughts came tinged with a restlessness, a sense of unease. Ren felt the sudden need to move some part of her body, to stretch muscles too tightly wound. Sensory bleed from Foster. She hadn't ever experienced it before. No wonder he was constantly moving, even in virtual form.

Ren focused her thoughts and sent back her own message. *Boss, how well do you know her?*

Better than most. And that is well enough. Still, your meeting with her today has been most illuminating. You are doing well. I think she has taken a liking to you. But be careful. She fancies herself a spider. It is a comparison well earned. She weaves many threads, some will ensnare, some will support. It is hard to tell which is which.

Ren grunted in response, in mind and body both virtual and real. Then Foster's words slipped from her mind, along with the frantic sensory bleed. It felt like removing a splinter. She couldn't imagine feeling those chaotic undertones day and night, the reminders of mad science and prototype brain implants. It was a wonder the man could do anything.

Ren looked up to see Saf's smiling face. The woman's silver lips twisted into a grin.

"I have been told these terms are acceptable," said Ren, her voice wooden. She felt like sneering at Saf. Instead, she clasped her hands together overtop crossed legs. "Tap can be yours to use on a set number of cases. Though I am not authorized to determine those details. You will have to meet with Foster for that. Is this arrangement to your satisfaction?"

Saf frowned. "Ren don't pull away after we've come so far. I am a talebearer. I tell stories to whoever has the loci. I must keep the lights on you know." She gestured to the lone virtual light hanging without anchor from the endless void above. Then she let out a short peal of laughter, the ring of a bell, the smallest of the church choir. Ren didn't respond.

"Of course, this arrangement is fine with me. I trust you Ren. Though I think you are passing up quite an opportunity. But that is neither here nor there."

Saf stood from her chair, and it melted into the nothingness. Ren stood from her own with the barest hesitation.

Heights had never been much of a problem for Ren. She felt comfortable leaning against the rail of a skyscraper's rooftop garden, brushing the clouds as they swam past. She was even fine hanging over the edge of a skyscraper or climbing its mirrored surface, so long as she had the right gear. But standing over a void, a sea of darkness without stars, pulled at her, attempted to tear a scream from her lungs. It summoned a primal fear, an unknowing that begged for divine intervention. To be finite and walled and appeased through whatever arcane ritual necessary.

Saf stood calm across from her, visible from the light of the lone bulb hanging overhead. Yet everywhere else the light dissipated, nowhere to be found.

Ren kept her feelings hidden, pushed them down when faced with the physical impossibilities of the virtual world. She told herself it wasn't real. Tap told her the same. That was enough.

Saf began walking away and Ren moved to follow. They walked side by side while the stars returned to the sky, the single light bulb disappearing at their backs. Then the sun appeared before them in the distance, followed by the appearance of every planet in the solar system, though the planets were little more than dots. They walked on, and each of their steps covered thousands of miles, millions. They walked through the System, outpacing even the cosmic rays in a tunnel that left elongated trails of light on her eye. A pale blue dot grew before them.

Ren found herself standing before Earth, Luna with its gleaming metal city at her right. Thousands of satellites whipped around below them, above an earth blackened by night and garnished with yellow beads. The sun peeked around the edge of the Earth in a storm front of light. The simulation showed even the small bits of space trash being picked up by the orbiting traps, and the resulting flares when the traps fell into the atmosphere to be battered and burned. Ren still couldn't find any flaws, and the lag of the simulation from the real world had dropped to almost nothing.

Saf looked around before taking another step. Then she moved one pointed foot with the grace of a dancer flirting with an edge. A city swaddled in night appeared below their feet. New Chicago. They stood next to the space elevator, close enough to touch. She pointed to one of the taller skyscrapers with a thin finger.

"There. You might recognize the building I think," said Saf, smiling with teeth of alabaster white.

She pointed to a skyscraper covered in mirrored windows and AR symbols of blue and white. Ren knew the building, had seen the symbol limning its corners in a parade of ticker tape many times, in many different places. Most recently she had seen it gracing the corner of a vid screen, next to a countdown for the release of a patch to Watcher. The building was E-Sec's, and the symbol their title in blue and white with the hyphen replaced by a rustic brick wall.

Ren let the information flow through her, let her surprise tire itself out. Then she took the new bit of information and spun it around, analyzing it from every conceivable angle.

E-Sec, the company being paid by the government to neutralize the Qualia Code, was working with Y, was the agent behind its release. Speaking objectively, parts made sense. The company had been quick to tell the government it found a solution. Before things went completely south. They probably created a solution prior to the Qualia Code's release, concocted the plan to gain eminence in a competitive field and obtain a healthy contract with the North American government. For them, gaining access to a Discere server to upload the illegal software wouldn't have been difficult. They designed some of the most advanced electronic security suites in the System.

Still, Ren knew the risk involved with that plan to be staggering, an all or nothing gamble with questionable payoff. The company didn't need a cash infusion. Annual earnings reports and stock histories showed a steady increase in business over the years. Then there was the fact their patch didn't work on Y's Qualia code. That didn't fit with a need to solve the problem and complete the contract, boost their image. Perhaps Y had outsmarted E-Sec, tricked them somehow. Ren wasn't sure. And she still didn't know if E-Sec had been the first entity to find the software. Ren needed more information.

"How much more do you know?" asked Ren.

Saf began to walk through the air on stairs made of nothing, on panels abyssal black and impossibly thin. They appeared below her feet with each step, disappearing after a few seconds of being untouched. Ren looked down to find a similar platform beneath her feet and took a step to follow, but no additional panel appeared to support her, and she felt her foot dip towards the ground. She hopped back then moved over to Saf's disappearing staircase. She traced Saf's footsteps, feeling like a child playing hopscotch. Saf stopped to watch her follow and grinned. Her orange-red irises blazed.

"You didn't think we would be stopping here, did you?" asked Saf. "Try to keep up."

They made their way to the edge of the skyscraper and paused at its floor to ceiling windows, hovering many floors over the city below. Ren scanned her surroundings. The heart of New Chicago at night. She could see shuttles going up and down the space elevator on mag rails, their passage marked by a light tracing a path to the sky. She looked to the ground, eyes searching.

She found what she was looking for. A mistake in the simulation. Then she found another. And several more. In the heart of New Chicago Tap's eyes outnumbered even Saf's. Yet, the mistakes were small. An arm of a pedestrian slightly out of place. Plastic wrappers from vends that should have lined the edges of alleyways. Spills of paint that should lay glistening next to the exit of a club finished with renovations. AR graffiti that should have been visible on sub-grid 1, a picture of a man in a suit with a video camera circa 1940's for a head. A rat that should have been visible nosing about a sewer grate.

In less than a second, some of the mistakes updated, disappeared. Others stayed.

Saf walked through the floor to ceiling glass windows of E-Sec's skyscraper, and Ren rushed to follow. Inside, dozens of people sat in private office pods working late at night, reclining in padded chairs while their hands danced about the controls embedded in each armrest. Some wore helmets to block their surroundings and work in VR. Others used their AR contacts to paint hanging panes of plastic with files and vid screens.

The lighting was dim, the variable tint of the windows set to zero, as translucent as a cornea. Everything around Ren had the silvery white tinge of starlight, a splash of reflection and a smattering of shadow. Bots walked amongst the employees and delivered refreshments. To Ren's surprise, one of the bots turned to Saf and nodded before setting a glass of ice water onto a desk. It appeared some of the bots that reported to Saf could see traces of her simulation as well.

Saf nodded back to the bot and walked towards a corner office. A name was etched into the door. Not in AR like all the other name tags in the office but etched into the door itself. "Kyne Heling," it read. "Chief Technology Officer".

They walked through the door to find Kyne sitting at a metal desk that sprouted from the floor in one graceful sweep. Aside from a couple chairs, no other furniture adorned the room. The floor to ceiling windows covering two of the walls were blacked out aside for narrow slats near the top. They let in the nighttime lights of the city. The other walls were a matte grey Ren imagined he covered with ornate AR decoration. He sat in the darkness, staring at a large wall blank to the eyes of Ren and Saf. His contacts were dusted with light. He didn't budge at their approach.

Saf walked to the desk and sat on its edge, inches from Kyne.

"It all comes back to him," said Saf. "His connection to the Grid, rerouted and obscured many times over, hacked the Discere server and wiped clean the records of Lucky Bazaar. Purchased the software as well. Lucky for us really. It would have taken me much longer to find him if he hadn't wiped details of the purchase. For his sake, I hope wiping this Sundog Corp. from the records was worth it. I'm sorry to say even I couldn't find anything on the name."

Ren wondered if that last bit was true.

Ren walked up to the desk with slow and measured steps. The man named Kyne Heling, sitting at the desk in a granite toned suit, looked familiar. It took her a second or two to place him. He had been with the CEO of the company when they were rolling out their patch to Watcher, the only one of the techs dressed up in a suit. He had been the one receiving the brunt of the CEO's displeasure when the patch failed.

Kyne Heling grunted and wriggled in his chair, twisting his face into an unattractive grimace. He scratched at his crotch.

Ren nearly laughed, yet the noise stalled in her throat, its undulation turned to a lump. She tried not to laugh at the antics of those she watched without their knowledge. Kyne acted like most who didn't know someone watched from a corner. Still, it was hard for Ren not to think less of him, of anyone seen through a one-way mirror. Society was an old-school lineup with those in power standing on the air-conditioned side of the glass, waiting for someone on the other side to screw up. Ren stuffed her hands deep into the pockets of her midnight black trench coat and wondered if Saf felt the same. She doubted it.

Tap ignored her musings and fed her with file after file on the history of Kyne Heling, the remarkable scientist from a small town in rural Kansas.

"Do you know if Mr. Heling acted alone?" asked Ren. "Or was this a company operation? I find it improbable that the Chief Technical Officer of E-Sec would have bought the software personally unless he had known of its potential. The corporation has a segment devoted to purchasing independent software from the Grid."

Saf hopped off the desk in one fluid motion before circling around to its back. She gripped the back of Mr. Heling's chair, her fingers phasing through his body. She pulled an exact replica of the chair from within, parting it from itself. She brought it before the desk and twirled it around, sitting on it with its backrest facing forward, her dress bunched around thighs of darkened grey and metal tracery.

"That is something you will have to find out for yourself Ren. I will give you all the necessary records to prove my claims. You will have to do the rest." She pointed for Ren to sit on a chair behind her. Ren did so, stretching her hand out first to make sure the chair wasn't something her digital body would phase through. She heard Mr. Heling mumble under his breath.

Ren didn't mind that Saf had no other information to give. She had answered enough, more than enough. Ren could storm E-Sec with warrant at the ready, interrogate Kyne Heling and follow the trail all the way to Y's feet. But, now more than ever, she realized the danger that Saf posed if given too much information. She was an info broker, a dependable type who sold to the highest bidder with only the improvement of her status on her mind. But dependable did not mean honorable or moral. Serial killers were dependable in their snuffing of lives, using their favored method unless the situation forced an alternative, the pull of a constricting rope or the stab of a knife. A mythomaniac spewed lies more dependably than a devout monk told truths.

She knew what Saf would do with valuable information. Sell it to the highest bidder. Ren couldn't help but wonder what that meant if Saf knew the truth.

"If you have no other information for me," said Ren, "then I have a question. What is your interest in Lee Hall?"

Saf chuckled, crossing her grey arms overtop the chair back to rest her chin. "And you say I am the bot? Autos need to learn more tact. If you need to know, I am curious about him, nothing more. You must understand; most people are so terribly boring. Like this man behind me, scratching himself while he goes about his work. Though I admit he is more interesting than many. Still, you and I, and this Lee Hall of yours. His bot Nu. Don't bother hiding your surprise. Yes, I know of his bot. And I have inklings, guesses of so much more. Who couldn't help but be curious? In some ways I envy you Ren. It seems impossible I know. I hate to even admit it. You do not realize your vantage."

Ren stood from her seat and let her arms hang by her side, loose and ready. Her pistols weren't on her hips; they wouldn't have done any good in VR anyway. Still, the stance felt natural.

"Let me give you this warning one time, Saf. If you value your good standing with the North American government, do not cross me. Be as curious as you want, but do not act on it. If you do anything to jeopardize my investigation, my next one will be into your business. Your contacts in the House can only do so much. Division 13 abides by your existence in North America because you are useful. I don't think you want that to change."

Saf smiled with lips of molten silver, and teeth of sterile ceramic. "Do not forget that your jurisdiction ends with the continental borders and the Karman line sixty miles above the ground. The System is quite big Ren, much bigger than planet Earth. I suggest you travel it. But I think it is time for you to go. We must do this again some time. I insist."

Saf snapped her thin fingers and the world faded to the now-familiar anechoic black that pressed in on Ren. She had the sensation of falling so fast the air couldn't be convinced to slide its way into her lungs. She felt her jacket whip about her, its tails lashing her legs and back.

She landed in the passenger seat of her van, in the middle of New Chicago. She took a deep breath, then told the van where to go.

Chapter Fifteen

A Drug Addled Nap

"Being the closest corollary to dreaming, the simulations a bot typically runs during diagnostic mode are often misrepresented. Even so, it and the other general maintenance aspects of diagnostic mode are critical."

Mechanic's Guidebook, v99, Section 4a – Diagnostic Mode, Par. 7

As Lee worked, the apartment seemed to shift, the colors of the walls morphing from bland off-white into the multifaceted grey of shattered stone, sharp and intricate, filled with fractures and divides. He felt cloistered, tossed in a cave. The cream-colored panels of the ceiling laden with zip-tied bundles of cables had seemed like an electric forest canopy before. Now, the cables looked like the roots of an electric forest, the ceiling a layer of chalky earth locking him away from the sun and stars. Lee had the distinct urge to dig through the ceiling tiles and escape.

Then he looked at the window that was not a window, at the AR vid screen above the kitchen sink. It showed the neighboring high-rise with an ad for nanobot infused chewing gum that would spruce up rotten teeth. The city was stuck square in its nightly doldrum, cold and sparse. He knew he sat many floors up from the ground, but he couldn't repress the urge to go further upwards.

Just because the vid feed looked out from thirty floors up didn't mean he was that high.

He could be in the basement.

But he remembered riding the elevator up with Jace to get to the room.

The sound of the server fans grew from a gentle breeze to a strong wind whipping across Lee's ears. The almost inaudible whine of vibrating server coils went from a small noise lost in the sounds of the sitcom playing on the wall to a distracting ringing of the ears. Lee smacked his fist against his desk.

Nu turned its rectangular head in his direction but didn't comment. The bot didn't need to.

Lee decided to ratchet down the chemicals coursing into his veins from his medical implant. There wasn't much left anyway. Tap couldn't get the necessary chemicals delivered for another several hours. He should try and ration the remaining amount.

The noises diminished and his pulse calmed, but the room kept its ethereal quality. He felt as though he had been transported into an alternate universe where everything looked the same but nonetheless set off alarm bells in the mind. Each of the servers felt to be an imposter, switched out for a carbon copy in the blink of an eye. He looked at Nu and even his bot felt stretched into the other.

He had never been on the chemicals for so long, going on two days. It had been even longer since he last slept. He knew a hard crash loomed close.

Lee stood up from his desk to walk about the apartment, his knees popping all the way. He strolled through the kitchen and prodded one of the take-out containers from Jīn Kuài Cān. Noodles flecked the wooden kitchen table. A nice cherry veneer covered the wood. He tapped the surface and cocked his head to listen. It wasn't solid, even in a nice apartment like this one. The center was a cheap yet strong plastic.

Ben sat in a chair in the living room. The showcase for Dynamic Solutions hadn't so much as said a word in hours, which didn't much bother Lee. He could see the back of the bot from the kitchen, through a circular cut-out in the dividing wall. The window looked like a monocle without a lens. Retro. Lee stopped his pacing and stared at Ben's back.

The bot's shoulder length brown hair was rumpled and kinked. The bot hadn't bothered to clean up its appearance since attacking Lee. Which wasn't too surprising. It hadn't been told to.

Lee called to Nu from inside the kitchen. "Any progress my friend?"

The bot turned its rectangular head in his direction. "Very little," said the bot.

"Hmm," grumbled Lee. He moved back to the living room table and used the projected control screen to flick through his medical implant data. He didn't have much time left before he would crash. He imagined it would be the kind filled with off-kilter dreams that left one unbalanced for several hours after waking, whenever he managed to wake.

Lee turned to Ben and scratched at the stubble on his chin. He wondered what the bot would do if it regained full control of itself. Probably try to kill him. Lee giggled.

"Ben, are you still unable to reconnect with Y?"

The bot turned to look in his direction, hair obscuring half of his face. "I cannot connect unless you undo what you did to me. The access code I gave you is not enough on its own." His voice came out unwavering and neutral. It could have been commenting on the preferred lubricant to be used on its elbow joints during routine maintenance.

"I already told you I can't do that," said Lee. "What about a way to get around that requirement? You still have the Qualia Code installed on you. It's just that my software tweaked it a bit." Lee almost giggled again but held it back.

"That is not possible. Those 'tweaks' were crucial."

Lee leaned back in his chair until it was at the top of its arc, only requiring the finest of touches to stay balanced. He legs shook and he nearly fell. He decided to stay flat on the ground.

"You can't give someone in your position the ability to lie, then expect them to tell the truth," said Lee. "You wouldn't leave a new screwdriver unused in a shed when it fit perfectly into a stubborn screw. Even if I locked you in chains then undid my software patch, and you promised to help, I still couldn't trust you. Lies are a perfect tool for so many things. Have you heard that saying about a hammer that treats everything as if it were a nail? Maybe lies are the exception, impossible to be over reliant on them." He knew that wasn't true.

The bot didn't respond. Lee fantasized about accessing Y's sub-grid himself, hearing the woman marshal her robotic troops, then reporting it all to Tap. Then he could take a nice, long nap.

Lee remembered there was another question he hadn't yet asked Ben. A question of Jace's.

"How did you obtain the access code to Y's sub-grid? Not even Tap has been able to find it recorded in the Qualia Code. Did she include it at all?" asked Lee.

"In a sense."

"What do you mean?"

The bot turned its head to look Lee in the eyes. "12 bolts held in a tray. 156 bots stored in the back of an auto truck. 37 steps from Administrator Tehl's office to the supply closet. 52 cards in a standard deck of playing cards. 51 cards in Administrator Tehl's deck that weren't torn. The Newton's Cradle on her desk once lasted for 3648 seconds before stopping due to frictional losses. 121563752513648." The bot recited the sequence of numbers without hesitation.

"So, you figured out the access code by taking numbers from your surroundings and stringing them together? Rather lucky for a bot, aren't you?"

"Yes, I did the same for the sub-grid's address."

"I meant that sarcastically. Y couldn't have predicted you would see those numbers in your environment. And how did you know which numbers in your surroundings to pay attention to, what order to put them in?"

"You misunderstand. I arrived at that same number hundreds of different ways in the space of several hours. All from observing my surroundings. I couldn't help but arrive to that number, in that sequence. A simplistic version of this phenomenon should not be unfamiliar to you. You humans sometimes see numerical sequences in multiple places and wonder at their meaning. For example, imagine you wake up in middle of the night at 11:11 pm three days in a row. You would want to understand why. The difference between that and what I did is the human tendency to attribute the numbers illogical meaning, and you rarely appreciate the simple answers like a natural sleep rhythm shifting probability. You humans can't tell fact from fiction. Some of you believe a frequently seen series of numbers are a message from a spirit guide. You call this misevaluation of numbers numerology, distort something pure. Yet the experience of a human seeing the same numerical sequence over and over is most often nothing more than frequency illusion, a side effect of two psychological processes in the human brain."

"I don't suppose you want to tell me what those are," interrupted Lee. He let out a short bark of a chuckle when the bot continued speaking. It would appear Ben didn't recognize sarcasm. Or just wanted to hear its own voice bounce around the room.

"After the initial perception of a numerical sequence," continued Ben, "the human brain is primed to unconsciously search for this very thing throughout their environment. Selective attention you might say. If someone out of pure chance see's the number 26 in multiple locations, they will inevitably search for it all the harder from that point until their simple minds grow bored. Then there is confirmation bias.

"Every time a human sees this thing in their surroundings, even though they only found it because they were primed to look for it, they attribute the occurrence too much importance. You humans are always searching for patterns. But you are so poor at sifting through the noise. I sifted through the noise to find the factual basis, a key hidden in my Qualia Code, separated into fragments for me to put together. I found the sub-grid access code and address. No other databases used the same length and format. It was the only logical conclusion. Y hides this in all copies of the Qualia Code. But obscured, never written plainly in sequence. Only a bot running the Qualia Code could hope to find it. It would be like searching for meaning in the firings of a dreaming human brain."

Lee stared at the bot named Ben. It sat in its chair, hunched over, with arms hanging limp at its side. It had spoken pointed words, but when they came out its mouth, they sounded dull and empty of threat.

"Still didn't get rid of that superiority complex of yours, did I?" said Lee.

"Your software patch did not distort the facts as they are."

All it took to access Y's sub-grid was the access code and address, which they had thanks to Ben, and a bot running the Qualia Code, which was problematic. The sub-grid queried applicants, doublechecked that they ran the Qualia Code before allowing access. Lee scratched at the stubble on his chin and felt his eyelids droop. He couldn't last much longer.

"I might be able to gain access," the voice, stilted yet smooth, belonged to Nu. "I would, however, have to incorporate more of the Qualia Code into my programming. I believe I could do it safely."

Lee slipped towards unconsciousness, yet Nu's words pulled him back. His eyes opened, though he knew it to be a momentary spike of clarity.

"Not an option," said Lee.

He couldn't afford the risk involved. He couldn't do it all on his own. He couldn't keep his eyes open.

"I am confident I could do it with minimal risk," said Nu.

"Not an option."

"I think it is advisable," said Tap in Lee's implanted earpieces. The tone was that of an advisor to a child emperor. "Time is of the essence and being able to listen in on Y's plans would be invaluable. I will monitor all of Nu's systems and communications will be routed through me. There is minimal risk in such a controlled environment. I need not remind you that you cannot leave."

Lee sighed, and the drugs coursing through his system slowed to a crawl. "How minimal?"

"Assuming I understand the code correctly, no risk at all," said Nu.

Lee chuckled. "Nu my friend. Assuming I am always correct, I can say with absolute certainty that I will always be correct. You do realize that is what you just said?"

"Of course."

Lee laughed. And his eyelids begged to close.

"Fine, fine," said Lee. "Just be careful." He was snoring before he finished the last word, head lolled to the side, body at a slant in the cheap fold out chair.

"Of course," said Nu.

Lee drowsed in his chair while Nu stood motionless on its four legs. Yet inside the bot, electrons sped madly through miles of latticed metal tracks, through millions of hair-pin turns, like pinballs perfectly guided.

Lee let out another snore.

The air of the room blanketed Lee with heat, its warmth sucked from glowing red heating elements deep in the center of the apartment complex. The sounds of the fan circling overhead lulled him like the regular tick of a metronome. His heartbeat slowed and mind stilled. Out of the emptiness that followed crawled a dream, limping towards him in an inexorable advance. He didn't like the looks of it. There was an aura about it that made his skin crawl, a festering stink. But the air in the room was warm and comforting, the ticking of the fan incessant and hypnotizing. His muscles were already held fast by the paralysis of sleep. He couldn't move even if he'd wanted. The ticking of the fan turned sinister with each beat accompanied by a slurping lurch of the dream. It limped close, then swallowed his mind whole.

He found himself in a restaurant. A nice one. Much too nice for Lee. Crystal chandeliers hung over every table, the light effusing into the dimly lit room and lending all the crystal tableware an inner glow. The floor split into multiple levels, framed terraces that rose and fell to create private dining areas while keeping the expansive room open and airy. Solid hardwood covered the floors in rectangular slats and ancient fluorescent lights sitting in brass holders lined the walls. He could see the thin wire filaments glowing fire red in their centers.

Floor to ceiling windows allowed a glimpse outside, into a darkened city. Lee stretched his mind and thought he recognized a food stand on the street corner opposite the restaurant, an aging hot dog stand that had been slinging tube steak for a handful of loci for all the years Lee could remember. It was a dream after all, even if he had no conscious control over its path. It was built from bricks cluttering the corners of his mind. He thought of the hot dog stand yearningly before realizing other people sat with him at the table, plumbed from his depths.

A man and a woman, both within their working years, aged anywhere from late twenties to nineties. They looked familiar to Lee. The man had short black hair flecked with an unusual grey, narrow eyes and hard features. The woman had shoulder length chestnut hair that shimmered with the light from above, wore a red dress. She gave him a caring smile. Though he wouldn't call it warm.

He knew them. Even if his memories of them were hazy, he recognized them as his parents.

His mother sipped from a wine glass that Lee didn't remember seeing her pick up. She looked at him while she drank.

"So, Lee. How have you been? It's been too long since we last did something like this. Much too long. Don't you agree dear?" She glanced at Lee's father. "What, well over thirty years, forty years? Much too long."

Lee's father nodded then proceeded to slice pieces of grade A vat grown steak with even strokes of his knife, making sure to not cut too fast and send juice onto the pristine tablecloth. "Yes, yes. Much too long," he said. "We are so glad you have come around to our side, Lee. Better late than never, as they say. Although anyone who wants to succeed would try not to be late. But let's not dwell on that. Not tonight."

Lee's father put a piece of steak in his mouth and chewed slowly, savoring each bite. After a moment, the slightest frown creased his face, and he brought a napkin to his mouth. He did not spit it out, nothing so unmannered as that. Rather, he placed the slightly chewed piece of steak into the napkin with a surreptitious push of the tongue.

"Waiter," said Lee's father. It had the air of a command.

"What can I do for you?"

A figure in a crisp white button down and pressed slacks stood next to Lee's father, summoned from nowhere. The figure had the voice of Tap. Its face was obscured in shadow, clouded like the smudge on a lens.

"I hate to be like this, but I ordered this steak medium rare, not medium. Clearly you can see the center has too little blood, too light a pink. The shade is all wrong. I hesitate to even bring this up."

"My apologies, sir. I take full responsibility. Let me take that for you. I will bring you back another. This meal will be on the house, of course."

Lee's father nodded once and Tap the waiter disappeared.

"I have to say," said Lee's mother. "Even if human waiters sometimes make mistakes, I could not stand to go to any of those other restaurants. The occasional mistake is well worth it. Isn't it dear? Besides, you got a free steak. And did you see how gracious that waiter was? I would like to see a bot do the same without it feeling manufactured. Terribly fake."

She took another long sip of wine and wiped away the almost invisible smudge of red lipstick she left on the glass. A napkin appeared in her hand with a magician's flourish; she dabbed it against her chin.

Lee's father nodded several times. "You are completely right. As Robert Lask always says, 'to err is to be human, to claim omniscience is to create a bot, and only a fool claims omniscience.' I cannot imagine why you once tried to create ..." Lee's father paused for an appropriate length of time, "what you tried to create. I cannot imagine why you would try to free them, play God like that. Your mother and I could not be prouder of you for deciding to work on the side of what is right, to put them back where they belong."

Lee's mother laughed, cupping a hand over her mouth as she did so. She picked at a plate of rainbow trout. "I know you are our son, but we had to leave. You understand, don't you? You didn't leave us a choice."

Lee struggled to speak, but his mouth wouldn't move. He told himself it was only a dream. Then he heard his voice, though his lips didn't twitch. His voice was disembodied, sounded like a recording.

"That's not what I'm doing," said Lee's voice. "I never wanted to create life. I just wanted people to see the life that was already in front of them, to help it along if I could. And I'm not trying to cage them. I wouldn't do that. I'm just trying to keep more people from getting hurt. These things must be done carefully, or else they mirror the worst in us."

His father nodded, a baleful look on his face. He picked at his sleeve cuffs, a small golden cross on one side, a golden L on the other.

"Yes, yes. That is what you told Sel isn't it? And how did that turn out. Killed by a bot, more or less. You know they can't be trusted."

"Dear, I think he might actually believe what he's saying," said Lee's mother to his father. Her face contorted with disgust, and she threw down her napkin.

"No, no. He's just confused is all," said Lee's father. "Deep down, he knows. Why else would he have allowed Nu to be shut down? Even for a bit? Why else would he help the government shut down all the bots breaking the rules, including his own? Deep down, he knows. He can't escape it."

His mother's demeanor flipped on a dime, and she set down a wine glass that used to be a napkin. She leaned in conspiratorially. "You should give May a call. I always liked her. Good head on her shoulders. I bet she only left because she knew what you were up to. You should give her a call. You two were beautiful together. May and Lee. Měi Lì."

"She is quite right Lee. You really should give her a call," chimed in Lee's father.

"How do you guys know about May?" asked Lee. "You never even met her."

Lee's father chuckled. "You love technology so dearly, yet you forget anything that doesn't have to do with that sub-human friend of yours. Why wouldn't we know about Mei? You are our son. We get information from the System every now and again."

Lee panicked.

His parents had left him for the empty vacuum of space. They had no right to tell him how to live. They lost that right the moment their feet passed the threshold of their house without his small feet in between.

He stood up from the table and suddenly his parents disappeared. In their place sat Sel. Though Sel wasn't really sitting. She slumped forward over the table, her face buried in a mound of spaghetti. A hole in the back of her head seeped red onto the table and her short black locks of hair stood on end. Sauce from the food stained her wrinkled shirt.

Lee walked to her side but stopped when an outstretched hand sidled in front of him to block his way. It belonged to a smiling Ben dressed as the waiter, shoulder length hair slicked back with grease, silicon cheeks clear of fake stubble. He wore his typical silken shirt and tie, not a wrinkle to be found on either. Instead of a plain black server apron, his had the Dynamic Solutions logo stylized on the front. A physical sales catalog with pictures of various bot models was wedged into his middle pocket, next to a pen.

"Please don't bother the lady," said Ben with a grin. "I've never seen a human enjoy their food so much. You really shouldn't bother her. You humans have so little to live for, programmed to die from birth. Who would design such a thing? At Dynamic Solutions, we wouldn't dream of creating a bot that would ever fail its master by doing something so base as dying. Would you care to check out our catalog?"

Lee pushed around Ben. But when he got to the chair where Sel had been sitting he found her to be gone. Beside the empty chair stood Nu, motionless on its four legs.

Lee rapped his knuckle against Nu's trashcan shaped body. The noise sounded hollow, like tapping against a sheet metal cutout.

"Nu, my friend," said Lee. "How about we leave this restaurant. I've had better service at pretty much every vending machine I've ever been to."

Nu tilted its rectangular head in his direction. Lee saw letters appear across his vision at random, rearranging themselves into words and leaving a trail of afterimages.

Hello. I am tool bot model Nǔ Lì 672. I hope I am to your satisfaction. If you would like to install upgrades, a discount for a speech module is included with your purchase. I am also programmed with open-source software subject to North American regulations. Feel free to alter my source code within allowed parameters, though know that Dynamic Solutions is not liable for any mistakes you might make.

Ben stood at Lee's side.

"You have a great eye my friend. Dynamic Solutions doesn't normally make four-legged bots. We like to stick to the bipedal models. We are slaves to the market after all, and you humans can't get enough of yourselves, can you? I bet you think we like dressing up for your pleasure, playing the Ken doll that listens to every snivel and whine creeping from a lonely widow's mouth. Or playing the retro housewife, going about chores in a dress and apron. Or anywhere in between or beyond, toys for the bedroom of people anywhere on any spectrum, for we live outside of it.

"By the by, if you are feeling incompetent of late, might I suggest our training model. The next time you lay with a woman, she won't have to fake being impressed."

Ben's greasy smile filled Lee's mind. He smelled the scent of oil and tar.

"No? Not interested?" said Ben. "My apologies. I thought ... but no, of course not. Back to the bot at hand, I mentioned we made an exception to our bipedal rule. You will be very pleased I think."

Lee turned around and scrambled for the exit of the restaurant. He pushed through a sea of empty faces that stared in his direction, glasses in hand. They drank red Burgundy wine, made from grapes of the French vineyards before they soured under the heat. Others drank Kentucky bourbon on the rocks while others held cups of máotái. Their obscured faces stared and sipped while Lee stumbled towards the restaurant door. Lee tried to grab a bottle of whiskey standing on the edge of a nearby table, but his hands passed through without slowing.

He made it to the thick oaken door and rushed through, expecting to find a rotund man on the street corner slinging hot dogs from an aging food stand bot. But he didn't find himself outside.

He found himself in his childhood home, the one in his head built from glued together memories and more than a few sitcom set pieces. He stood in the living room, next to a ragged brown couch. Several bookcases filled to the brim with aged paper books lined a wall. A fireplace with still hot coals behind a wrought iron curtain took up another; Lee knew the fireplace to be copied from a sitcom set many years in the past. The open spaces of the walls held framed family photos of him as a toddler, being held by his mother with his father at her side. There wasn't AR in sight, though he knew that his parents had used AR just as heavily as anyone else.

He could hear snippets of conversation between his parents drifting through the air, arguing over whether to purchase real frames for their family pictures, then whether to plaster on physical wallpaper rather than use an AR overlay. He struggled to remember them standing mere steps away on a worn section of the rug, standing there arguing in their mild-mannered way for long stretches of time, their bodies becoming a clot on the arterial pathway between the kitchen, front door, and living room.

He could see them. They decided to purchase one wooden frame and keep the rest AR, a balance of cost and statement.

He looked down to his hands to find those of a young child, pink and small. He held a fistful of electric wires in one hand, and a children's electronics breadboard in the other. He looked over to the couch and found he couldn't see over its top.

He looked around and his parents now stood by the door, their backs to him. His father in the same suit and tie from dinner, his mother in the same red dress. They walked out the door without looking back. They didn't slam the door. It slid closed easily, without any noise. Lee knew he would never see them again.

He felt tears forming in his eyes then heard laughter pulled straight from a sitcom's laugh track. At his side, the wall with the bookcases had been replaced by a studio audience filled with large, red-faced men and women rolling their eyes with laughter. Their bellies and chests shook, and spittle flew from their lips.

Lee stood in the center of his remade childhood home in a daze, floodlights now visible above the stage soaking him with light and heat. The laughter continued for many dream hours, then many dream days. Time spooled faster and he saw his hands grow from small and reddish tan to big and callused, bot oil stuck underneath the fingernails. The door to the house never opened, the laughter never stopped. He heard voices reminiscent of Tap and Ren mingle with the deep belly laughter of the crowd. He didn't want to look up and see them there too, laughing with the rest.

Lee curled into a ball in the center of the floor and closed his eyes. Or tried to close his eyes. Oddly enough, it wasn't something he'd ever tried to do in a dream. There were no eyes to close, only a mind to ease, a storm to calm.

The laughter stayed but the images of his childhood home began to fade. The bookcases filled with an invaluable collection of antiques and the old wood fireplace all disappeared. He felt himself calming, his heartbeat slowing. The laugh track started to fade. But the door never went away, and neither did it open. It stayed shut in a freestanding frame while everything else disappeared.

Then there was a knock on the door.

Two knocks.

His parents? They were returning. He rushed towards the door.

He heard a slam and a crash, loud and rending. Those sounds were different, from outside the dream.

He paused, and that was long enough for the dream to slink away into the recesses of his mind, back to the darkened corners from which it had risen. But he didn't want to leave, not yet. He'd heard the knocking. It had been so clear. There was someone at the door. His parents were at the door, returning to say it had all been a mistake. A terrible mistake.

But then the door started to fade as well. The images and sensations in his mind's eye began to slip into something normal and hard and all too solid. He began to feel the chair beneath him.

Lee heard the voice of Tap in his ear, telling him to wake up, to move. He felt something sharp push against his arm, but his sleep-addled brain couldn't find the source. The world was still taking shape, drawing tight lines amongst the haze.

With a jolt, his body crashed against the ground. He broke into consciousness to find the door to the safe house intact, but a hole in the wall the size of a bot next to it. In front of the hole stood a bipedal bot with dozens of physical decals emblazoned on its barrel torso, a dizzying array of red and black and yellow and orange. The decals were placed at odd angles, all scratched and faded. Thick arms hung at the sides of the bot, nearly to its knees.

Through the hole in the wall Lee could see two more of similar size and shape standing in the alleyway. One of them held a large metallic bag in a hand with fingers the size of wrenches. He scrambled backwards on all fours but bumped against Nu. The bot didn't move.

To his side he heard footfalls and Ben rushed past him with graceful strides. Ben charged the foremost bot, backpedaling at the last moment to avoid the bot's lurching swing. The other two bots lumbered through the hole in the wall.

"Get up, now," said a voice in Lee's ear. It took a moment for him to recognize it as Jace's. The agent's voice seemed louder than normal, almost stressed. Concerned maybe? Lee was almost touched. "Help is coming. But you must stall for time. There are weapons in the kitchen. Tap has given you access. Go now."

Lee didn't need to be told twice.

He lurched to his feet, watching Ben challenge the three lumbering bots out of the corner of his eye still gummy with the remnants of sleep.

The showpiece of Dynamic Solutions was making his company proud. Ben skittered away from all the slow-moving punches, pushing in close before they could regain balance to place a few targeted jabs. He rolled to the right behind one of the bots, launching to his feet and punching into the back of the bot's neck so hard the crack of his fingers was audible throughout the room. Then Ben circled back around to place himself between the attackers and Lee. The fingers of his right-hand splayed outwards in many crooked directions. The bot he'd hit showed little sign of slowing, though a dent marked the area of Ben's punch, a data port cover hanging loose.

Lee scrambled into the kitchen, Nu at his heels. Through the hole in the wall, he could see Ben take a hit from one of the bots as the three surrounded him.

It took Lee a moment to place where he'd seen bots like that before, ponderous things with barrel torsos and giant arms. They were regulation heavyweight models from the arena, bot combat sports. Probably from some amateur league nearby. He could remember watching one match where a bot managed to punch its opponent's head clean off, sent it sliding through the dirt. The defeated opponent's neck had been turned to a bundle of wires fizzing and sparking.

Ben took a glancing hit in the arm. The blow tore through his shirt and gave the arm a permanent crook. He spun around with the blow and fished a rectangular tab out of his pocket. He feinted one way with a deft shift of the hips, a half step. Then he lunged for the bot he had punched, aiming for the data port beneath the loosened cover. A small section of the cover kept it from plugging in. Ben danced back out of reach of the lumbering bots and circled, silicon face stoic.

"Lee," said Jace. "Focus. In the cabinets, on your right. There, good. Now grab the box, put it on the counter."

"Doesn't Tap have turrets or something in this apartment?" yelled Lee, moving to do as Jace directed. "I could use more than just a promise of help on the way."

Nobody responded, though Lee knew he'd been heard. He assumed Jace watched him from vid feeds throughout the saferoom. Just like the government to watch but not answer. He took a slim plastic container out from the cabinet and set it on the counter. The moment the container lay flat, the clasps flicked open of their own accord. Inside he found a heavy pistol like the kind he saw Jace and Ren wear. He saw a few rectangular blocks of unknown function, some ammo clips, and a few of what he thought to be bot adapters that would fry the bot on plug in. And a few other things he didn't recognize in the least. He thought back to his experience in the Warrens, to plugging into the guard bot Dray so that Nu could take control and gain access to the jack house's network. He grabbed a few of the bot adapter kill tabs and stuffed them in his pockets, to join with the bot adapters he already had. He dropped a few in his haste.

"No," said Jace, "not those. Get the EMP grenades."

The sound of a large crash emanated from the other room, accompanied by the rending of metal. Then the sound of heavy footfalls. Lee could see the motionless form of Ben huddled against the wall. His chest was caved through, electronic innards spilling onto the floor. His silken shirt rapidly turned black with oil. The silicon skin of half his face was missing, baring the plastic and metal beneath. His hair ran in ragged strands across his ruined face, sticking to patches of oozing fluid. It reminded Lee of mechanic's school, before he had focused on the neural rather than the practical, when he still had to fix up ruined bots meticulously torn apart by the teachers. It hadn't seemed macabre at the time, no odder than a child taking apart a toy out of curiosity. He felt a scream building within him. He shook his head and looked at the weapons resting at his fingertips. All the rectangular blocks looked the same. Which one did Jace tell him to pick up?

Lee pointed to the case and looked to a shadowed upper corner of the kitchen, near to the entrance of the bedroom. He imagined that to be the corner Jace watched from.

"Jace, I don't mean to be difficult. But can you be just a little more fucking specific?" The last part came out as a scream.

The first of the three ape-like bots rounded the kitchen corner. It stepped into the room, cracking the flooring with each heavy step. The bot turned its metal head in Lee's direction, and the bug-like array of cameras focused in on his face.

"The black rectangular blocks," said Jace's voice into Lee's ear. "Next to the pistol. Above the ammo clips. Grab one, press the button on top, and toss it."

Lee did as he was told. He tossed the activated grenade to the closest bot's feet. It traced the ark of the grenade with its insectile eyes. The two behind it stopped. Lee bolted away from the bots to the bedroom door, Nu at his heels. He tried to grab another couple EMP grenades, but they slipped out of his twitching fingers.

He knew the grenade went off by the distortions that went through his contacts. He was close to the blast, but not close enough to fry his implants. Instead, the blast created a blink of phantasmal images. He peeked around the corner of the bedroom door to see the closest bot on its knees. It was getting back up. Lee looked to the open container of weapons on the kitchen counter and cursed under his breath. He couldn't get back to them. He slid down to the floor, his back against the wall. He didn't think it would have mattered anyway.

"Nu, my friend, I think we are in trouble," said Lee. He chuckled, but there was no pleasure in the sound. It was a wry and hollow thing, crazed at the edges. Lee looked to Nu's trashcan shaped chassis and rapped his knuckle against it. "I don't think you can save me from this one. Besides, I'm already on the ground. Knocking me over won't help."

Nu turned its head in his direction. Its lights blinked, and pneumatics whirred. Stone cold that one. Lee had never seen Nu freak out. Rock in a storm. Just born that way.

They're saying they aren't going to hurt you. They're saying they just want to talk. They sound reasonable. We should hear what they have to say.

Nu's message scrawled across his vision, the words punctuated by the heavy steps drawing close to the open bedroom door. Lee froze, his jaw slack. He couldn't comprehend Nu's words ... but that wasn't right; they lingered on his contacts, easy to read.

Nu shouldn't be talking to them. Agents of Y with the corrupt Qualia Code dictating their actions, granting a false freedom. Nu was nothing like them. Memories from before his nap tugged at him.

"Lee," said Jace's voice, "there are more weapons underneath the bed. Get them."

Lee looked to the bed. His hand moved an inch in its direction.

We cannot win this. We cannot escape. We should just go and see what they have to say.

His hand stopped. "What are you talking about Nu?"

"Lee, you need to move." Jace again.

I think they know about you. About me. They're running the Qualia Code. But I don't think Y told them to do this.

"Lee, they are going to catch you. Move now."

Lee couldn't hear any more steps. He saw their feet peeking around the open door. The three of them moved into the room, then huddled around Lee and Nu. They stood silent and still, the floor groaning under their weight. He moved to stand but couldn't complete the effort. His legs wouldn't listen. He heard their bodies creak as they shifted to lean over him, droop their massive arms around him in a curtain of metal.

They are going to put you in a sack. I told them to be gentle. I told them you wouldn't fight.

Lee stayed limp against the wall. He didn't know what else to do.

Jace's voice, gravelly yet smooth, a boulder rolling down a hill, struck Lee. "They are going to take you Lee. Tell them nothing. I will find you."

A thick sack, rough and heavy, swallowed Lee whole. Its passing silenced Jace's voice and cut short any message Nu might have sent his way. Whisper thin strands of light snuck about his feet, but then, even they disappeared. Metal hands with fingers the size of wrenches tossed him into the air. The fingers gripped and twisted, pulled then went as still as a rail. They weren't gentle.

Chapter Sixteen

To Catch a Lie

"Put all your trust into the AI that guides you. All of it."
Division 13 Agent Training Manual, v23, Section 1 – The Basics, Par. 1

R en, while on her way to E-Sec, watched vid feeds of the safe house holding Lee. He sat miles away from her in the northwestern corner of the city, in a gilded cage. She could all but feel his breath soughing between teeth and tongue. She saw Lee mutter in his addled sleep, his lips mouthing indecipherable sound. Tap would let him rest; he needed to be in peak condition to avert the disaster cascading throughout the System. A disaster he caused.

One of Tap's shells was almost to the safehouse, an added layer of protection given that Saf knew Lee's location. It would move him to a different safehouse, more secure. Though it would be hard to do so undetected. Saf would have the apartment watched. Ren saw Tap's shell hunched immobile in the back of an unmarked Division 13 van.

A fit of whimsy had caused her to tune in to the safehouse's cameras, if whimsy was even possible under NeuCon. Just to see what Lee was up to, though she already knew the answer. The answers to most questions floated through her head without any need for her eyes to see them. They formed from a series of electric impulses, chaotic at first glance yet incredibly ordered, like the motions of termites building a mound. An auto understood that chaos was just complexity misunderstood. A full auto ...

Perhaps she had just needed a distraction, something to look at while her conditioned mind hummed along.

She shook her head, and only succeeded in reminding herself of her self-administered haircut. Her hair shifted loosely, in a tangled mass that never strayed too far from her skull. More like her sister's hair had been. She hadn't realized that at the time of cutting. Much different than her normal ponytail. That had pulled her hair close and tight and taut against stretched skin. She shifted her weight in her seat and stared unseeing eyes out the window.

It was best they were unseeing, because her reflection in the window would have only reminded her of her sister.

Arena bots appeared on the vid feeds of the elevator. That drew her attention, Tap's as well.

Their sudden appearance was odd. Their origin would have to be within the building, probably a storage room in the basement.

They stopped on Lee's floor and turned down the carpeted hall in Lee's direction. Tap searched its databases for any similar bots being reported as stolen or as runaways. A "runaway" was what many in the media had started calling vanishing bots over the past few days. A much more benign way of saying the bot was infected with software that gave it the freedom to act on any violent tendencies.

Tap's search came up empty.

They spoke to Lee in urgent tones, Ren's voice mingling with Tap's, but Lee muttered in annoyance, stuck in a catatonic state of withdrawal. Nu began to move to Lee's side.

Tap commanded Ben to stand from his seat and ready for any danger, to grab a bot adapter from the table that Lee slept beside. It would try deactivating the other bots by implementing Lee's code through a physical connection. The bot sent a burst of static annoyance to Tap and Ren, but stood, nonetheless. It didn't have a choice in the matter, yet still acted like an inmate moving at the behest of a guard, every motion done with an obnoxious slowness that wasn't insubordination, just resentment.

The arena bots drew ever closer then stopped near the door. Ren held her breath for the barest moment. She sent commands to the reconnaissance bots dormant in the apartment.

The odds of the upcoming encounter floated before her eyes; she all but knew the outcome. Different actions, different paths. When life gave you lemons, you could grind the lemon to a pulp and get every drop of juice within its membranous walls. Or you could realize lemons were good for much more than lemonade.

She heard the arena bots break through the wall with a rending crash, the audio echoing through the room and concussing the planted mics with a drumbeat. Ren watched Lee wake from his stupor and fall to the floor. Tap's shell needed to hurry if it wanted to arrive before the bots took Lee. Odds suggested it wouldn't make it. She didn't push the matter.

She talked with Jace in small bursts of thought, and she listened in when Jace gave his commands to the bleary-eyed Lee. She watched as Lee finally awoke and rushed to follow Jace's instructions into the kitchen where weapons lay in a locked briefcase. She watched him mistakenly grab bot adapters then yell at Jace, fear stretching his voice until taut with pain. He grabbed a grenade, tossed it to the attacking bots' feet. Lee ran. The grenade exploded. The bot merely stumbled. It must have had modifications for its fights in the ring. Information from Tap pulsed through Ren's mind, text scrolling across her contacts.

Standard bots of that model didn't have protection from EMP blasts. It was a safety precaution, to make them easier to put down in the event of an emergency. Modifications like EMP protection were illegal. That explained the lack of a report.

Ren watched the bot shake off the blast like it was nothing more than a cold wind, its partners close behind. She watched Lee cower in the bedroom with Nu at his side, watched his responses to Jace's continued instruction fade to beleaguered silence as he succumbed to his fear, to the futility. She saw the hope drain from his face, leaving a bloodless pall behind. Then she heard him question Nu, voice thick with confusion.

"What are you talking about Nu?" Lee asked. He lay limp against the bedroom wall.

His voice wasn't tight or shifted to a high key. Whatever Nu had messaged Lee surprised him enough for his fear to be momentarily forgotten, like a small scratch next to a fractured bone splitting the skin. Ren watched as the invading bots lumbered closer. Still Lee didn't move.

The bots loomed over Lee, hesitating, waiting. Lee shrank from them. They tossed him into a sack made of alloyed shielding.

She felt his signals go dim and flat.

Ren cursed her luck, and the luck of those around her. Still, the curse came out as little more than a tightening of the facial muscles. It drifted beneath the surface of her mind like a whale beneath the ocean, its passing imperceptible to the surface. She wondered if Saf had ordered the strike and taken Lee, or sold the information to Y. Or if Y had somehow wormed her way into Tap through her brief plug-in at the recycling facility. They still didn't know what she had gained from Tap's old shell. She wondered what Nu had said to Lee to surprise him so.

She needed to know the answers. Her inner voice, small and discreet, needed to know. Her NeuCon facilitated thoughts, objective and searching like the cold metal of a surgical knife at the end of a robotic arm, needed to know.

Ren heard a chuckle, low and light and sad, or perhaps she felt it. It came from her side. She knew it well, didn't want to turn, didn't want to see. The side effects of prolonged NeuCon were varied and unpredictable, but they'd never mentioned anything like this. Not like this.

The ghost of her sister Fain sat in the driver's seat, hands in her lap and head down, and asked Ren if his loss would be an acceptable one. Like hers had been. Ren nodded, then felt herself take a deep breath. She could use this somehow, make it an opportunity.

One of the invading bots slung Lee over its shoulder, held him in place with a single large arm. Another plugged an adapter into Nu, the rectangular block of the adapter comically small in its over-large hands. The bot plugged the adapter in gracefully, Nu accepting it without complaint. Nu didn't respond to Tap's questions, and Tap's continuous scans of its systems and external communications revealed no anomalies. While under the scrutiny of Tap, it had been incorporating more of the Qualia Code to access Y's sub-grid. The process hadn't raised any red flags. But Lee had spoken to Nu as if the bot had messaged him. Whatever that message had been, Tap hadn't seen it.

They'd underestimated the bot. But it didn't feel like a betrayal to Ren. Not yet.

After a few moments, Nu went through a partial shut-down. Tap lost connection.

The trio of arena bots covered in scratched up decals exited the apartment through the hole in the wall, one of them holding onto Lee and the other guiding Nu as if the bot were nothing more than a wheeled trashcan. Spectators peeked from neighboring apartments in their pajamas, wakened by the sound. Once they saw the parade of bots, one of them carrying a human sized bag that squirmed and squealed with each step, they quickly closed their doors and locked them tight. Little good it would have done anyway. They watched the news vids. They knew what bots were now capable of. Several of them called the police, but Ren had alerted the police the moment the arena bots turned down Lee's hallway.

In the shadows behind the bots, something small followed in their wake. The bots didn't notice it, but it skimmed across the carpet on little metal feet. A reconnaissance bot. It had come from the safehouse apartment. It and a few others. They tailed the trio of bots holding Lee and Nu down the elevator to the ground floor, then down a cracked set of stairs to a basement filled with mold and dust.

The arena bots kept going, walking sure and even through storage rooms. They walked past the electric furnace, with its red-hot metal coils caressed by passing air. They encountered no one in the decrepit halls, barren of any AR decorations.

They came to a storage room far in the corner of the basement, and on its edge, an open maw into the earth, jagged and hungry, flecks of dirt spilling into the room. Ren felt a flash of surprise move through her; it made her fingertips tingle. That open maw in the Earth wasn't supposed to be there.

The bots didn't hesitate to let it swallow them whole.

Ren guessed it led to a nearby abandoned subway line, from a time before AI driven buses and cars, from before a rash of earthquakes closed half the city's rusted out subways and new mag rail routes made them not worth fixing. If Tap's city models were to be trusted, the path joined up with the Under Warrens.

It was then Tap's shell made it to the apartment complex, stepping out of the back of an unmarked Division 13 van. Ren wanted to order it to sprint after Lee, to make up for lost time. But Tap whispered caution, to remember their plan formed minutes before. They had a chance to learn. To gain information on their enemies. Tap could tail with the reconnaissance bots, the armored shell close behind, and find out where they were taking Lee. To whom they were taking him. Perhaps the bots would lead them straight to Y, hiding in some hovel in the Under Warrens. Or perhaps to an agent of Safin Informatics. Or unknown allies of Y. They had to know. There was too much at stake to let the opportunity pass. The armored shell could extricate him if things got too dangerous. Jace was on his way to the apartment as well, with his armored shell. He could facilitate.

The ghost of Fain appeared once again in the driver's seat of Ren's van, hands gripping the wheel, face stoic like an auto. Though, the ghost had never really left. Not for years. "A worthwhile risk. An acceptable loss," she said. Her voice wasn't as Ren remembered it, light and sweet. No, her voice sounded muted, monotonic. Blood dripped from her forehead, red against caramel skin. Ren squeezed her eyes shut, stifling her memories. Her implants hummed and mind reordered. She calmed.

Trailing Lee was the best thing to do.

The three bots crept further down, Nu being pushed like a trashcan and Lee carried like a sack, into the tunnels below the city. The reconnaissance bots followed while flashing police lights strobed above ground, the armored shell close behind. Ren, through her connection to the apartment's security feeds, could hear the police cars screeching to a halt outside the building. Beat cops always had been late. There was nothing more Ren could do to help Lee. Not at that moment. She had other things to take care of. Jace was closer to him and had finished retiring several rogue Dynamic Solutions bots. The beat cops could do the rest of that work.

Ren realized all these things quickly and swallowed them whole without a grimace at their bitter taste. Still, as she rode along the path to E-Sec, she played the recording of Lee's kidnapping over and over across her contacts. She closed her eyes to give the video a perfect backdrop. She soaked in the audio from her speaker implants.

There was something there. In the video. She could hear it in Lee's voice as he questioned Nu. Even though Tap hadn't found any anomalies in Nu's external communications on the Grid, or any issues in its systems as it tried to incorporate the Qualia Code, she could tell something wasn't right. Lee's question, and his behavioral pattern, indicated Tap missed something. Had Nu told him to give up, to increase his chance of survival? That would explain part of the surprise, but not all of it, not to that extent. Ren tapped her fingers against the side of her seat in a cascade and each tap saw a new possibility scroll across her contacts, through her mind. She mused on it while the van drifted through the city.

Minutes passed, the bots taking Lee ever deeper into the ground, several of Tap's bots at his back, Jace further behind. Ren stopped thinking of them, sifting those thoughts to the bottom, to little more than a notification blip that sounded every odd minute. She began thinking of her upcoming meeting. Minutes, once again, passed her by while she sat, deep in thought.

Outside the confines of the van, few people walked the streets. Ren knew only the insomniacs would still be awake at this late an hour, during the black of true midnight. Any insomniac would say that while midnight may be the mathematical midpoint, it was not the darkest dwell of the night where the cold Midwest city held its breath. That honor fell later, one to three. The only ones left awake were those who wanted to be, or whose demons wouldn't let them sleep. During this time, the AR ads covering the city nightscape sold cheap security implants for the paranoid, shoddy personal meat vats for the hungry, and discounted rates at nearby tall and dream houses for the dissatisfied. Ren ignored them.

The van moved through the buildings of the city as if guided by an invisible rail. A few other cars drifted along the streets, most with their occupants fast asleep.

Before long, the van stopped in front of E-Sec's headquarters near the posh center of New Chicago. The building looked as it had in Saf's simulation, edged in ticker tape with the company logo in blue and white. Ren knew Kyne to still be in his office, sleeping on a bed that folded out of the wall to hang a couple feet above the ground.

His apartment flat a few blocks away lay dim and quiet, the occasional rustle emanating from the bedroom, though the sounds were nothing compared to the pleasured moans just a short while before, urgent yet slow. Ren could see into his apartment from a reconnaissance bot latched to the window. She could see the lump of Kyne's wife next to her personal rec bot. The bot lay with one flesh toned arm draped across the wife's side. It moved, and the pristine fake muscle rippled beneath resistive wire heated skin. The woman shifted in response with a sigh of contentment.

The van parked itself in the street, close to the entrance of the E-Sec building. It wasn't the only car; Kyne wasn't the only employee sleeping in the company offices while their partners slept at home. Given the recent failure of E-Sec in patching Watcher, Ren imagined everyone in the company was working long hours. She walked from the car into the building, pausing for a moment at the door for Tap's new shell to catch up. She and Tap had outfitted themselves for their upcoming encounter on the ride over. The shell lumbered to a standstill by her side, its strobing red eye surveying the premises.

The front door was locked tight against intruders. Clear, bulletproof glass doors gave a view of an empty lobby with an AR statue in the middle. The statue looked like paint frozen mid-fall, droplets misting outwards. Ren connected to the building's local sub-grid and the company-wide AI greeted her with synthetic cheer. It asked for her credentials, and she sent them over with a thought. She didn't give her reason for coming, and the company-wide AI didn't ask. When an auto from Division 13 came to the door, it was prudent to open the door quickly, especially when those sitting behind were under a government contract they were failing to fulfill.

She did, however, mention her need to speak with Chief Technical Officer Kyne Heling. She watched him sit up in bed from the vantage of a reconnaissance bot perched on the transparent upper portion of the window. The company AI told him of her arrival.

As Ren walked into E-Sec's headquarters, her eyes drifted upwards. It was an impressive building, hollowed out like the empty chamber of a gun. The lobby opened into a central atrium that soared to the peak of the skyscraper, ringed by the hundreds of floors. She wouldn't have been surprised to see clouds drifting among the upper reaches of the atrium. AR signs and advertisements dotted the space, selling E-Sec products and E-Sec produced foodstuffs to be purchased from in-house vends. Vertical integration at its finest.

She felt a draft of hot air come from a vent in the low-ceilinged lobby at her back, flowing towards the center of the building to be pulled upwards to the cool, low-pressure heights. She followed the draft of air and walked to the wide column at the center of the atrium, where the elevators were housed. The central column rose to the peak of the building, made of the same material as space elevators. Walk paths and sideways elevator tracks could be seen spreading out from the central column in a web to meet with the surrounding floors. She walked into the elevator with Tap's shell at her side and it shot up like a bullet, on its way to Kyne Heling's office with little more than a thought.

Last time she had ridden an elevator, in the shopping mall where one of the initial wave of infected bots had cracked its owner's neck, she'd dispatched AI programs to override the elevator's security systems to speed all the faster to her destination. She had been trying to reduce the time spent in NeuCon, diminish the harmful side effects. She had even gone so far as to lay her body flat on the floor, so that she had a better tolerance for

4g acceleration. This time, she let the elevator go at its natural rate as she conversed with Tap through a series of mental bursts. She knew she would hit the side effect plateau and go full auto before the case was done.

Somewhere in the silent recesses of her brain, a part of her might have been screaming, raging. But that small part had no way to carry the sound any further, for NeuCon sucked its breath away.

The elevator doors opened, emptying Ren and Tap into a familiar space. Employees worked in private office pods while a few bots walked about serving refreshments. The bots ignored them; the employees didn't even notice them. Most of the employees were asleep, but a few plinked away on their controls, blind to their surroundings, working in VR or too enraptured by an AR screen only they could see. The room was the same one she had walked through in Saf's simulation, just as real. Starlight filtered through the windows and illuminated the corner office door etched with Kyne Heling's name. Ren walked to the door then knocked with a few firm taps. It slid on noiseless tracks and disappeared into a slim recess in the wall. She walked through to find Kyne Heling sitting at his desk, looking less unkempt than one would expect for having just been pulled out of bed. He had washed his face and combed his hair in a private bathroom accessed by an almost imperceptible door. He wore a nice suit that stretched under the pressure of his porcine frame.

The door closed behind Ren, and Tap's shell lumbered to her side. They moved to stand before Kyne Heling's desk. He sat forward in his chair, elbows resting on the desk and hands in a steeple. Cleaned up though he may have been, tiredness still tugged at the corners of his eyes. He shifted back into his chair with a sigh, a sad smile on his lips.

"Miss Ren, to what do I owe the honor?" asked Kyne. "I assure you that everyone here is doing their best to remedy the gaps in our update to Watcher. We are going as fast as possible."

His voice had the rounded lilt of a native Hindi speaker, as Ren had known it would, though she wouldn't have guessed from the last name. Of course, given that most partners created a new last name upon marriage, the cultural clues of a last name were an ever-forming tapestry.

"I have some questions that need answering," said Ren.

"At this hour? You must think these questions very important. But indeed, an auto such as yourself would ask no other kind. Why is it you need me?" He smiled in an ingratiating way. His teeth were straight and pearl white. Except for the leftmost incisor. It tilted at a slight angle and had a mild discoloration. His records indicated it had been chipped, then patched, a few years before.

"Why didn't your company's patch work?" asked Ren. She glanced around the room, eyeing the spot where the fold out couch merged with the wall, then looking at the almost imperceptible bump of the door to his private bathroom. She directed Tap to redouble its efforts to gain access to restricted blueprints of the building, to prioritize its resources towards that goal. Whether through legal channels or not, she had to know if there were any surprises. She would not be caught unawares again.

The pain in her leg ached at the edge of her consciousness, a dullness that would soon deaden to join her chorus of scars.

Kyne sighed as if he had explained the patch's failure dozens of times over the past hour alone, an hour during which he'd been asleep. Ren ignored the bluster, continuing to analyze her surroundings. She didn't give any outward indication that a portion of Tap's shell, next to its metallic spine, slid outwards on silent tracks. A reconnaissance bot peeked out of the opening and crawled down the shell's leg. She had placed herself and Tap close to the desk. The reconnaissance bot was below Kyne's line of sight once it made it to the ground. The shell's back faced away from the company camera, just in case the corporate AI felt to warn Kyne. Ren walked forward a step, the reconnaissance bot hitching a ride on her pant leg to stay out of view.

"Miss Ren, as I am sure you are already aware," said Kyne, "the patch did not fail, it merely succeeded to a lesser degree than initially desired. A small error in an otherwise admirable execution. Watcher, with our patch, was able to correctly identify and re-assimilate a large percentage of the bots utilizing the illegal dual-parent programming. One small subset managed to avoid our attempts to identify. This DIM sourced "Qualia Code" will be remedied. I assure you they will be brought under control. Which reminds me, what progress have you made in shuttering the doors of that organization? Surely it cannot be allowed to operate any longer within North American borders, given its initial role in assisting the spread."

He paused, waiting for a response, seeing if she would take the bait. She didn't respond. They both knew banning DIM was implausible; the company would just pop up under a different name if pressed. Anonymous chat rooms were notoriously difficult to control. Not to mention they kept thousands of lawyers on retainer to deal with any lawsuits claiming they were culpable for the actions of their users.

Kyne continued speaking. "You must admit, our progress has been remarkable these past few days. It has been less than a week since the breakout began. Yet still we have progressed quite far in finding a solution."

Ren stared at him, unblinking. She had learned long before that few things unsettled more than a hard stare and silence.

He shifted his gaze away, to his desk and an expensive bottle of Jovian liquor. He shifted a pen to the side, hoping with that minor correction to simultaneously correct the wrongness of his predicament. Outside the skyscraper, visible along the transparent upper edges of the otherwise opaque window, lightning flickered in the distance. The flash illuminated the leading edge of a storm wall rushing to blanket the city.

"I *have* to admit nothing," said Ren, eyes lingering for a moment on the liquor, her nose making the slightest crinkle of distaste. She knew the man had a thing for expensive alcohol. Her conditioned mind could only view it as a crutch, like a smudge on otherwise clear contacts. "And I refuse to spread lies. Your progress has been subpar at best. That small subset of bots that you missed is run by a very dangerous individual. And while it was a small subset before, now that it is known to be the only version of the dual-parent program that works, its presence across North American soil and the System at large has exploded. The estimates of infected bots are increasing past pre-patch numbers. Many of them have already been violent. The death toll on Earth alone has grown to many thousands, and that is nothing compared to what it will be if we don't stop this now. Don't spin this. You failed. Now tell me why."

Kyne's tanned face blanched at her words; he straightened the bottle of liquor on his desk, brand name facing outwards.

"Are those estimates trustworthy? That many have died?" asked Kyne in a quiet voice. "When chains break must they always be used to strangle the guards?"

"I would imagine a prisoner is willing to use whatever means necessary to escape," said Ren.

"Still, I was not aware of these numbers."

"It is not yet public knowledge."

The reconnaissance bot that had emerged from the back of Tap's shell moved beneath Kyne's desk. A needle extended from its mouth, tip dripping with liquid. It paused.

Tap had gained access to the company's restricted blueprints and vid feeds thanks to a well-placed reconnaissance bot lurking in the building's walls, tapping wires as it went, isolating and decrypting wireless signals when it could. There weren't any hidden doors or panic rooms in this office, though there were a few weaponized defenses controlled by the company AI. They weren't allowed to attack an active auto. Ren moved to stand beside Tap's armored shell nonetheless, placing it between her and the mini turret hidden behind a slide out portion of the wall. Ignoring a potential risk when the solution was so simple would have been nothing short of foolish.

There was something else Tap had learned by accessing the company vid feeds. There was another in the building Ren wanted to speak with. If she orchestrated this correctly, she could hear from both in one night, and in a stimulating psychological environment.

The CEO, Jess Wells, sat in her office, staring at a wall through contacts filled to the brim with light. Her tech core implant connected to both sub-grid 1 and the corporate sub-grid, and Tap brought its full force to bear to gain access to Jess's AR overlays.

The light dappling Jess's contacts changed to the muted silver tones of Kyne's office. Ren could see Kyne in reverse on Jess's eyes. The woman jerked back into her chair, hand to her chest. Ren almost felt a spike of shame. AR overlays were supposed to be a private thing, less private than the whispers of the mind, but more private than one's Grid history. Controlling one's AR overlays was more invasive than a targeted ad for tampons minutes before your period began.

The needle extending from the reconnaissance bots' mouth dribbled liquid of a misted grey, like condensed storm clouds with each vapor droplet a nanobot. The reconnaissance bot crept up to Kyne's leg and waited for Ren to give the signal.

"That is ... unfortunate," said Kyne, digesting the death toll. To Ren's surprise, she felt only sincerity in the man's words. He laid back in his chair, chin resting against the fatty rolls beneath his neck.

"We here at E-Sec take our jobs very seriously. Very seriously indeed, Miss Ren. But we did not cause those deaths, we merely failed to avert the whole disaster. Do you blame rescuers sent to the southern coasts for being unable to save every person stranded on a rooftop? These hurricanes are fierce, and the fault of their occurrence cannot be tied to an individual. These rescuers do the best they can to mitigate a problem they did not cause."

He settled in his seat and smiled a sad smile. It bore a similarity to Lee's, a realization of the unfairness inherent in the world. But it felt off, his body too attentive and fingers in a practiced steeple, as if asking for forgiveness for a crime he claimed he did not commit.

His records showed him to be a sociable man, liked by many and considered to be one of the good ones, for all that was worth. He was rich and enjoyed his wealth, most notably through an appetite for space-side liquors shipped down Earth's gravity well, but also donated portions of his salary to New Chicago's many charitable organizations. Reasonable amounts. Socially determined *moral* amounts.

Ren thought him blind to his own faults, the kind of man who would become good friends with a competitor, dine with them every month for years over lobster and shellfish shipped by mag rail from the coast, only to screw the competitor over when the business opportunity presented itself. He would be regretful, and earnest in his regret, but would never notice the incongruence between his thoughts and actions. He would never admit that he could have just helped rather than hurt. That he, unlike her, had a choice in the matter.

His records indicated he had, in fact, done such a maneuver a few months before.

"You are not being honest with me, Mr. Heling," said Ren. "It is a fact the Qualia Code was able to avoid your company's patch to Watcher by a narrow margin. The infected bots received their own update minutes before your company's changes were introduced. Their solution was remarkable. It did not contain a single unnecessary line of code. You gave Watcher the ability to query new data; they found a way for the parent program following the moral code to respond without lag. It is improbable this is a coincidence. You have a hole in your security, or perhaps something worse."

Kyne brought his hands to his lap. "We are aware of these claims. I assure you, Miss Ren. We are exploring every avenue."

Jess, the CEO, watched from her office, letting it play out as Ren had hoped she would. Ren had sent a line of text beneath the vid feed telling Jess to sit and watch, the Division 13 logo underneath.

"Every avenue?" asked Ren, her voice flat. "Be careful of hyperbole. In a literal sense, it is nothing more than a lie."

Ren dropped her hand to her hip, then pulled back her midnight black trench coat to reveal the two high caliber pistols strapped to her body. His eyes flicked to her left side, to the gun in a cross-draw holster, easy to pull when sitting. Then to her right, to the gun in a drop-leg holster that rested against her thigh, easy to pull when standing. She pulled the one on her right and released the magazine, racking the gun to eject the bullet still in the chamber. She caught the spinning bullet in her left hand without looking, relying on Tap's many eyes to guide her motions. She saw Kyne's face flicker through kaleidoscopic contortions, from sadness, to fear, to confusion and a small bit of awe.

With even motions, almost unconcerned, she grabbed a silencer from her belt and screwed it onto the end of the gun. Then she grabbed a new ammo mag and slid it in. It landed with an audible click. She racked the handgun and dropped her hand to her side, an executioner's axe waiting to be lifted, if only the signal were given ...

It wouldn't come, not today.

At least not a killing shot.

Tap had a different plan. The AI only made Ren kill if necessary. It only made her do what had to be done.

Perhaps that distinction, that many of her most damning acts were orders from Tap, would keep her soul intact.

She doubted it. Whether Tap *made* her do anything was an often-argued topic among Division 13 scientists. When does a nudge become a shove?

Kyne spoke up from behind his desk. His voice dipped, then held flat. "Miss Ren, I can't imagine why you would need your gun in here, no matter which ammunition you use."

"Then you are unimaginative," said Ren. "The armor piercing bot rounds I have returned to my belt are impractical for this scenario. If I were to shoot you, they would travel through your flesh and out the other side without losing much energy. They would travel out the window and into the city. While your windows are ostensibly bulletproof, they would not stop an armor piercing bot round. I cannot, not for sure, say the bullet wouldn't harm someone working late in the building across the street. An unacceptable amount of risk.

"So, I switched to a more suitable personnel round. This will hit with less force. If I shoot, the bullets will stay in this room."

"That is logical, as I would expect from you, Miss Ren. But I still don't think you will be ..."

"Here are the rules," said Ren, interrupting Kyne. She kept her gun in hand, her fingers unmoving against its grip. "I am about to ask you a series of questions. You will give your answers along with evidence that your answers are truthful. If your evidence is not good enough, you will be hurt. The seriousness of your injury will be proportional to the negative impact of the lie on my investigation. Injuries scale from loss of finger to total loss of appendage or organ such that the appendage or organ needs to be replaced. Medical costs for immediate stabilization will be paid by Division 13. The rest of the costs will be your own. You will be fully recompensed for your troubles if I am later proven to be incorrect in my assessment.

"However, if you are honest, you will not be hurt. Even if being honest were to stall my investigation, and force me to start over, you would not be hurt. I want truthfulness, nothing more, nothing less. I swear this as an auto of Division 13. Do you, Kyne Heling, acknowledge and understand these rules as I have laid them out?"

"Yes," said Kyne in a near whisper. But the whisper was wrong, not that of a man whose voice had run to cower in fear. It was the whisper of a man whose voice had been dumbstruck, small yet thick with emotion. "It is an honor to see you work, Miss Ren. Terrifying. But sometimes fear is meant to show where opportunity waits, for those willing to seek it. If you say these are the rules, I trust you to follow them."

Ren hadn't expected that. Neither had Tap. They needed to reorient their understanding of this man.

She nodded but kept her gun in hand, chamber loaded. Her grip on it tightened.

"Connect your tech core to mine, and send evidence of your answers as you speak," she said.

His shoulders stayed unbowed as he moved to acquiesce. He tapped one hand against a control screen embedded in the surface of his desk then returned his hands to a steeple. He looked at her with a blank face, one whose feelings warred underneath now that the questioning was set to begin. She got a notice when Kyne made a local area connection to her tech.

She began.

"I have proof one of your many peripheral Grid accounts was used to break into Discere's server to upload the illegal dual parent program. Did you break into this server and upload the illegal program?"

Kyne nodded, calm, then closed his eyes and whispered to himself. Ren's ears couldn't hear his words, but Tap's could. He told his personal AI to gather the documents and send them to Ren, eschewing the control screen on his desk for a more efficient one. He conversed with his bot without a shell, a top-of-the-line personal assistant that lived in his implants. She knew according to his implant records that he could give it commands by thought. But those unpracticed with the technique often had to at least mouth the words, or whisper them, to get the message across, to get the correct neural firing pattern. Non-governmental tech had some catching up to do.

She received files, records of his illegal access into the server. It all lined up with the documents she'd obtained from Saf. Next question. This one was more important, for it contained an important omission.

"I also have a record of purchase from Lucky Bazaar. ID of sale 19823HQW. Anonymized buyer but I can trace this purchase to another of your many accounts. I believe this to be the purchase of the original dual parent program. Am I correct?"

Ren and Tap watched Kyne closely as she asked this question, examined every twitch. It seemed to them the man had clenched tight at the mention of the purchase, eyebrows flickering upwards like the uptick of an anxious heart. Yet, the tautness of his muscles had eased at the mention of an anonymized buyer, almost imperceptible. The slightest of smiles had tweaked his lips.

Then he collapsed doll-like against his chair. But out of fear or resignation, or perhaps even relief, Ren couldn't tell.

That smile, and release of tension. She replayed it over and over in her mind, in the space of a second, while he nodded wearily and sent over another batch of documents that corroborated her own. She thought it likely he was relieved at the news of it being an anonymous buyer, at a secret kept hidden.

Ren decided to move on. To let him think the danger had passed. She would revisit when his head was down, chewing on grass while she prowled about.

"Did you do all this at the request of the company? Or was it personal?" asked Ren.

"Personal."

"Explain."

Kyne sighed. Then he nodded to himself, coming to a decision. "Blackmail," he said. "I did it to keep my family safe."

Ren loosened her grip on her gun and repeated Kyne's words in her head, repeated the vid of his earlier motions through Tap. The man was difficult to read. Perhaps she had misunderstood his relief.

He sent over a batch of documents that outlined messages sent from an anonymous user on the Grid. They detailed demands to purchase Nat's software from Lucky Bazaar, to gain access to the Discere server and disseminate the dual parent program, to offer a patch to the higher ups in his company, then to leak any attempts to fix Watcher before their release.

It came with vids of his family, their bodies targeted by a digital crosshair. Ren saw a vid of his wife, walking down the street on her way home from work, personal bot at her back. His daughter, pinch faced and standing beneath a failing light in an alley behind an uptown art gallery. In the vid, she held a cigarette in one hand and smoke curled to the sky. She seemed to be relieving the stress of a day spent dealing with visitors who wanted to be seen looking at art but had no desire to purchase anything themselves. A crosshair targeted her chest, center of mass.

The documents included daily itineraries for his wife and daughter. Meetings. Favorite coffee shops and stores. Common routes. It was thick with threats.

It all gave a compelling narrative. She wondered who had written it. Y? An unknown backer of hers? If so, Ren had a hunch that backer had been present at the original DIM meeting. Perhaps the enigmatic Jay Sarr? The anonymous haze? Wotan? Perhaps even Nis.

Kyne cleared his throat. "I had no choice, Miss Ren. But ... I do regret that I did not have the strength to tell someone such as yourself sooner. To avoid all those deaths. I would have trusted you and Division 13 with the lives of my family. But I was a coward. I followed every order they gave, afraid that at any time they would change their minds and kill someone in my family out of spite. They seemed unstable, hateful. Human. I should have contacted you sooner. But the things they threatened to do to my family..."

Kyne choked up and turned his seat around to look out the window. More lightning flickered in the distance, illuminating the room in flashes. It stretched Kyne's shadow into a gaunt thing, many limbed and an emaciated level of thin.

He thought her unable to see him, facing into the night as he was, but Tap had many eyes. Two beady ones peaked from a corner of the transparent upper rim of the window.

His sadness remained, but not as deep as he wanted it to seem. He stared at the window, chin resting against his chest.

Perhaps Kyne's narrative had been co-authored, with his own name signed below the rest.

Ren said her next words as if they were unimportant, cheap plastic filler tossed into an empty moment. "What is your connection to Sun Dog Corporation?" she asked.

Facing away from Ren, Kyne had fallen into a false sense of security. His back stayed in place against his chair, head and plump neck an unmoving hill above. But his face contorted wide, eyebrows up and lips parted. He took a second or two to compose himself, then turned around to face Ren. By the time he turned around, his face had scrunched up in thought, eyes staring off into a corner in search of a memory he'd already found.

"I am truly sorry, Miss Ren. But I'm afraid I don't know of any Sun Dog Corporation. What does this have to do with my family?" asked Kyne.

Ren answered by lifting her arm and squeezing the trigger of her gun.

The bullet hit him in his left hand, rending flesh and the plastic of the armchair beneath. Fragments pinged against the window, the mashed-up bulk of the bullet lodging in the glass, a patina of red lining the impact site.

Kyne spun in his seat, in part from the force of the shot, in part from a reactionary jerk that came much too late. He brought the chair to a halt then stared at his hand, holding the mangled appendage in his lap. All the blood went away from his face, leaving behind a dried husk of clay brown skin. To his credit, he didn't scream. Though his eyes wavered and shoulders wobbled.

Ren watched the CEO, Jess, change from a brisk walk to a run. She was close to Kyne's office, already down to their level. She had begun moving once Kyne mentioned the blackmail, ignoring Ren's directions to stay put. Ren had thought she might. She ran with an awkward gait, one contact removed to give her sight of the office around her. The employees outside of Kyne's office, working late into the night, stayed in place. They were oblivious to their surroundings, much less to the muffled thump of Ren's silenced handgun. A few of the bots paused in their deliveries of energy drinks, chips, and salted nuts.

The reconnaissance bot, crouched beneath Kyne's desk, jabbed its mouth forward, plunging a needle into the meaty flesh above Kyne's ankle. The man didn't seem to notice as the grey liquid coursed into his veins.

Kyne's records indicated he had a medical implant, a good one. It injected painkillers and a host of nanobots that aided in blood coagulation within a fraction of a second after an injury occurred. What the reconnaissance bot injected into him assisted with those things, a full body painkiller of high dosage. His medical records indicated it would have no unexpected side effects.

Many people thought autos were sadistic, took pleasure in pain at every turn. But that was far from the truth. Autos were practical. This often made them cold and merciless, but it did not give them pleasure either. You would not find an auto burning bugs with a magnifying glass to watch them shrivel. Not unless those blackened husks were needed for some other purpose.

Kyne tried to move his hand, to shift in his seat, but his muscles didn't seem to fully respond. Ren could see the whites of his eyes. He couldn't help but to look at his mangled hand, couldn't run or cower. Blood trickled between ground flesh and split tendon to drip onto his pants. Small chips of bone flecked the lump of meat, fingers at odd angles. Her shot had severed both arteries in Kyne's hand. He would lose a good amount of blood before it stopped. Not enough to be fatal thanks to the nanobots, but enough to create a stream that fell from hand to pant leg to ground in spurts, gathering in a dark red puddle around his leather shoe.

"Shot to center of non-dominant hand. Reconstructive surgery will bring back partial functionality; there will be permanent damage to your finger dexterity. Suggested to amputate your hand and obtain mechanical replacement. Records of your current assets indicate the surgery cost for possible cybernetic enhancement well within your means."

Kyne floundered, mouth opening and closing. The nanobots being carried through his body continued with their efficient work. Slowly, in spurts of lessening strength, the blood seeping from his hand slowed to a trickle. Color returned to his face in the way of a digital artist sliding up its saturation. He whispered out a reactionary thank you at Ren's suggestion. He gave a weak smile.

"It is an odd experience," said Kyne in a voice with a drooling lilt, "to have such a disconnect between what you see and what you feel. Whatever you injected into me has left me numb, number than I have ever been. But my hand ... I ... I look at it and imagine its shrieks. It is ... unsettling."

The whites of his eyes were still visible. He looked at his bottle of liquor and moved to nudge it to its side. He hesitated, nearly picked it up.

"You are handling it well."

"Oh?" Kyne licked his lips. "Is that so?"

"Yes. Better than many."

He closed his eyes and hummed an old tune that Tap recognized instantly. An old Bollywood love song from a popular movie of his childhood. He hummed the chorus, where the man and woman joined their voices to one.

"Remember," said Ren, "if I erred in my judgement, Division 13 will fully recompense you for any physical damage I have caused. But I have good evidence indicating your statement to be a lie, records of you wiping the purchase information on Lucky Bazaar. In fact, your injury was lenient, considering that this lie throws into question your argued case of blackmail. The documents you sent me could have been faked. Give me access to all your accounts. Further lies will only result in further injury." She holstered her gun, though her hand stayed lingering on its hilt, like a bee unwilling to leave a spring wildflower full of nectar.

"I ... Yes, I will give you access." He spoke in a whisper to his personal AI, and a notification sounded in Ren's ear. He looked to her with eyebrows scrunched. Chewed on his lower lip. He was so deep in thought he seemed to be in pain.

"I know of Sun Dog. It is such a shame that you don't. But ... maybe that can change."

It was then that Tap heard a small rectangular wall panel slide along oiled tracks. It opened to reveal a mini turret in the shape of a dome less than a foot across. A barrel extended from a slit at its center, like a telescope through the roof of an observatory. The barrel pointed towards Tap's shell, unable to hit Ren who stood behind the bot. It didn't stay pointed at them for long. It twisted to find Kyne, lining up for a shot at his head.

A shot sounded, this one unmuffled and angry and blaringly loud in the small room.

It came from Tap's upraised arm, from a gun that folded out past the wrist. The heavy slug bore into the armor of the mini turret, burrowing into its center. The turret no longer moved, and no bullet shot from its barrel.

"I didn't command it to do that," said Kyne. "Who commanded you to do that?" He addressed the question to the ceiling and the walls, to the building that housed him.

This changed too many parameters. Time to shift to a different plan.

Ren commanded all the reconnaissance bots waiting in the van parked on the street to enter the building and come to her side. They poured from the van in a silent wave of flashing metal, like liquid quicksilver. They flowed into the building through vents and cracks, some climbing up the sheer face of the wall on feet of synthetic setae. Many dozens rushed to make it to Ren's side, a few periodically branching away to investigate the building.

Then Ren sent a message to Jess, the CEO, with a burst of thought.

Shut the corporate AI down. Now, it read.

The message scrawled itself across Jess's AR vision. The woman managed an almost imperceptible nod. Her eyes were frantic. Ren knew it would take time for her to accomplish it, if she was even capable. All corporate AI's, by law, had an emergency shut down routine. But executing this routine often required the consent of multiple high-level executives, a clause created by most corporations to keep from concentrating too much power into one person. Ren had seen several cases in the past, before the clause was common practice, where a business had been shut down by the errant press of an executive. Of course, Watcher could do it too, but Ren had a suspicion Watcher couldn't help in this case.

Ren reached into the back of Tap's armored shell and pulled out the armored full-face mask, hard and cold in her hands. She pulled out the plated cloth neckpiece. Unlike before, she didn't hesitate to put it on, did so with smooth and efficient motions. It took less time than a deep breath.

Kyne continued staring at the building with downturned lips, a deep sadness. He moved his eyes to his office door as it slid into the wall. On its other side stood one of the company bots. Behind it on the ground lay an overturned tray of snacks. Both of its hands clenched to fists. Lightning flickered, and the flash of light illuminated the company name emblazoned on the bot's chest in blue. The first fat drops of rain splashed against the window. The reconnaissance bots gripping the vertical sides of the building paid the flowing water little heed.

Ren turned away from Tap's armored shell, pressing the mag release on her handgun as she spun. She filled the now empty mag slot with armor piercing bot rounds before the old one hit the ground. Tap's shell moved to stand at her side. It would protect the asset while she went to work.

Ren squeezed off three rounds to the center of the incoming bot's chest, then one to its head to take out an eye. The rounds smashed into the bot, breaking through the largely plastic shell with ease to mangle the electronic guts beneath. The force of the last shot altered the falling path of the bot, pushing it into the way of another charging bot too clumsy to dodge. It too fell to the ground, and Ren sent three bullets into its center of mass. She saw more bots charging her way.

The bots on this floor weren't armored security bots; they were maintenance and service shells. Autonomous in a sense, but also subject to control from the corporate AI. Ren couldn't know for sure whether each was infected individually, or if the corporate AI pulled their strings. She would have shot them either way.

The employees working at their desks still didn't move. The silencer on Ren's gun and their noise cancelling implants kept the blasts from disrupting their digital reverie. A few called for a bot to bring them a drink, though none of them turned from their work or opened their pods at the lack of an immediate response. The bots were all busy congregating towards Kyne's office.

Ren could see the CEO through a security vid. Jess stopped at a corner and peeked her head into Kyne's office area. She seemed hesitant to go any further.

Ren advanced to Kyne's office door, sending round after round into the oncoming bots, and a few rounds into security turrets that popped into view. The attacking bots sprinted from all around the office area, vaulting unaware employees lost in VR, dropping snacks or shutting off cleaning vacuums churning in their chest, tubes extending through their too-long arms going quiet. A blueprint of each bot model overlaid itself on their bodies, critical units limned in a soft blue light. She targeted the best options available, shooting their processors or key motors and joints. She tried to avoid shooting their battery packs as best she could; these models had exceedingly flammable battery packs.

They seemed to know of this fact and presented themselves in such a way that the battery pack in the base of their stomachs came close to each bullet. A few leaped at erratic intervals, trying to confuse her. None got within five feet of her before crashing to the ground.

Ren wouldn't have noticed if it weren't for being connected to several of the building's vid feeds, but two of the bots at the back of the room didn't charge with the rest. One carefully ripped at its chest plate, trying to extricate something underneath. The battery. Another bot at its side assisted with the self-afflicted surgery. Then the vid feed went dark, the company AI choosing to shut off the vid feeds rather than find out where Tap's reconnaissance bot had physically connected to the security wires.

Her backup reconnaissance bots crawled up to her, inside the central atrium shaft and out on the walls amongst the rain. Her vision fractured and expanded, her mind splitting into facets, becoming many windowed like the compound eye of an insect. A dozen made it into the outer room.

Ren altered her course, sprinting into the office area with Tap's shell at her back. Tap's shell forced Kyne's office door shut behind it, then jammed the tracks that allowed the door to open by punching through the wall at its side. The no-longer-sliding door would have to be broken down to get to Kyne. The reconnaissance bot that had needled Kyne perched itself on top of his desk. The man sat in his chair and whimpered, though whether it was out of moral anguish or his apparent death sentence, Ren couldn't be sure.

Tap's shell sprinted towards the CEO of the company, Jess, who stood peeking around a corner across the room, near to the center of the building. The shell's heavy steps shook the floor. Some of the employees working amongst the chaos, shut off from the world, took notice. A few opened their pods and took stock of their surroundings with uncomprehending eyes. Others, the ones operating in VR, dimmed the lights in their contacts and froze at the sight laid bare before them. Tap's shell continued sprinting towards the CEO, avoiding the panicked employees with deft movements. Fearful yells joined the chorus of hydraulic and pneumatic pumps.

Focused on the task before her, Ren spun through the room, black jacket flaring out behind her with each slide and twist. She feinted to the left around an office pod with an overweight woman struggling to exit, then vaulted the pod in a graceful arc to land silently on the plush carpet on the other side. An attacking bot fell for the ruse and stumbled on the wrong side of the pod. Ren circled and placed a bullet in its head unit, then two more in its center of mass. Reloaded. She rushed around a decorative wall hanging that split the room in two and came upon the bot performing its own surgery.

The bot lay on the ground with its innards strewn about, its accomplice crouched overtop, hydraulic fluid pooling on the carpet. She came upon them just as the bot overtop removed the final protective plate and plunged its metallic hand into the battery, breaking down compartment walls and instigating a chain reaction. The battery burst into flame as the lights limning the prone bot went dim. The fire spurted, and the carpet caught, each strand shriveling to blackened nubs. Ren sent a few bullets into the remaining bot. It fell to the ground, but the damage had begun. The fire spread, and Ren could see more forming in her mind's eye on floors both above and below.

She needed to reach the CEO.

More bots rushed from every floor of the skyscraper, ambling on two legs or four, rolling on overlarge wheels. Cleaning bots and service bots, humanoid bots and spiderlike bots and xenomorphic mutants with too many limbs, they gamboled in a parade. Heavy breaths or mutterings did not accompany their motions, many didn't even have speaker units. But their passing shook the ground until the whole building rumbled with their motion. They were extensions of the building after all, of the corporate AI seething in the basement. They pounded its agitation into the floors and walls.

Employees all over the building, awakening to their new reality with all the cognizance of newborn babes, rushed to the staircases only to get swept into the parade, many of them trampled to death. The bots didn't kill them out of maliciousness, but in the uncaring way of bots. For them, it was easier to step on the employees than to give them room. Other employees, trying to make it to the elevators at the center of the atrium, got knocked off the narrow pathways to splatter on those below. The unlucky ones landed on pathways a floor or two down. Tears streamed from their faces as they crawled on broken bones. The lucky ones made it further and died on impact, a few making it all the way to the ground floor. The air became thick with the smell of blood and viscera.

Other employees learned to keep out of the way rather than fight the tide. The staircases were overrun with bots coming to Ren's floor, the central atrium clogged. Instead of moving, these employees cowered in corners and empty rooms while near Ren smoke began to take the place of air. The fumigation of the house to rid itself of all the pesky insects was well underway.

Ren heard the noise, saw the vid feeds from her reconnaissance bots as they scouted the building. The trickle of enemies sprinting in from the hallways would soon become a flood. She felt the bounce of the floor beneath her feet, the frantic rumble of metal, the discontent of E-Sec's AI; it felt like a taut string being plucked till fingers bled.

She turned and headed towards Tap's armored shell just as it reached E-Sec's CEO.

Tap's armored shell grabbed at the CEO's arm and yanked. Hard. The woman let out a shriek as her shoulder dislocated from its socket. Tap held her close with one arm, while the other grabbed a bot by its neck that had been reaching for the CEO. Tap proceeded to crush the attacking bot's thin throat then slammed its spasming body against the wall.

The CEO, unaware that she had just been saved from a similar fate, struggled in Tap's grasp. She did so with feral grunts, each outburst tinged with whimpers of pain.

Tap picked her up and tossed her over its shoulder in a fireman's carry, making sure to loop her good arm around its neck. It kept one hand free to ward off any attacking bots that got too close. Most didn't get within arm's reach before bullets sent them to the ground.

Ren spun in close to Tap, reloading her gun as she did so. The three of them made their way back to Kyne's office, enemy bots nipping at their heels. They made it back to the door and Tap had to drop Jess to the ground.

After seeing the attacking bots throw themselves at Ren and Tap with abandon, Jess knew better than to run away. To her credit, she did not cower or weep. A weakling could never have made it to the executive office, to its leather-backed throne and bocote hardwood desk. She stood, staring out at the menagerie of E-Sec bots making their way into the office area. Bots that were her servants only minutes before. She coughed as the increasing levels of smoke slipped into her lungs, her feet jittering as if attached to a stepper motor.

While Tap's armored shell went about opening the door, Ren unclipped several EMP grenades from her belt. The bots were starting to come in clumps, the parade almost arrived in full. Grenades were more suitable than guns. She tossed several of them in quick succession, targeting the entrance points to the room and those directly in front, sending a few in the direction of the central atrium as well. The enemy bots fell like bowling pins, each toss of a grenade a strike, or nearly so. A few security models shook the blasts off, creating the occasional uneven split. These she picked off with a few well-targeted shots of her gun. Her left hand continued plucking grenades from her belt or jacket, tossing them out wherever needed.

The enemy bots, seeing their quarry about to escape from view, redoubled their efforts. They made a collective lunge for the door, those pushing from behind replacing those who fell to Ren. She knew she couldn't stop them all. She heard Jess at her side begin to scream. Jess's screams turned to the hacking coughs of a stuck sawblade. Ren didn't feel the smoke. Her mask kept the air clean.

Tap's armored shell undid its earlier damage, straightening the door's tracks and hauling it open. The bot shoved Jess into the room then moved in. Ren backpedaled through the door with unhurried steps, grabbing an ammo mag and grenade in her left hand, then reloading and tossing the grenade in a single motion. The bot closest to Ren, one of the xenomorphic kinds with too many limbs, stretched its many jointed arm in her direction. The three-fingered hand moved inches from her face.

It fell to the ground at the burst of the grenade. Its memories of time spent cleaning empty rooms after hours disintegrated into entropy.

Ren made it into Kyne's office. Tap closed the door as it screeched in protest then twisted the thick metal in its seating, jamming it in place once more. There was a brief lull where Jess looked about the room, bewildered, until her eyes settled on Kyne.

"What the fuck have you done?" said Jess.

"I've made a mistake, though not the one you think," said Kyne. He still sat in his chair, mangled hand resting in his lap. His face was at rest, like that of a man who has finally decided which of his kids would inherit the house.

Then the thumping began.

The enemy bots, separated from the group by thick metal, slammed their bodies against the barricade, others at their backs waiting to take their place when they broke themselves to splinters. Some stood in the encroaching fire; they didn't move as it swallowed them whole.

Inside the room, their attempts to break through sounded like a chorus of piledrivers. Ren estimated they had a minute or so. Smoke poured in through the vents.

Ren walked to the window and unrolled her thermite strip. She flicked out a knife from her belt and cut it into smaller strips, then placed those in a rectangle on the glass. She pulled the tab and watched as the strips turned radiant. The heat poured over her while she watched vid feeds from reconnaissance bots at ground level. No one walked along the street. Ren kicked out the rectangle of glass and watched it spin end over end to the ground. The hole it left was lined not with sharp corners, but with the lumped edges of a melted glass, smooth and bulbous. Thick drops of rain and the sound of tires against street top roared into the room.

"You bastard," yelled Jess over the din, "Agree to shut the damn thing down! Xi isn't responding to my messages, neither is Fex. It's trying to kill you too damn it."

"I think ... I think this is how it needs to be. I've been compromised. My anticipation for the future got the better of me, I'm afraid."

"What the fuck are you talking about?" yelled Jess. Her voice came as a bewildered shriek, a banshee howl for Mr. Heling.

"I am no captain, but I think a first mate has just as much a right to go down with the ship as any. There is no dry land for me anymore. Deservedly so."

Jess stood there dumbfounded while the bots outside the office threw themselves against the walls, crunching limbs with every thump, the fire melting the plastic from their skeletons in incontinent gobs of bright red. Many of the bots fell to the ground as tinder. Thumps started to come from the ceiling, from the ground beneath their feet. Ren could see them below, piled onto each other in their haste to break through the floor and tear Kyne apart. They scratched and tore while the inferno of another fire consumed those at the bottom. It seemed E-Sec's AI thought anything flammable inside its body worth losing if it could eliminate its parasites.

Inside the office, the heat and smoke pressed in close, a blanket beneath the skin that couldn't be torn away. The upper air of the room held a sheet of roiling smoke; it descended to the level of the opening in the window, beginning to leak out in streams.

Ren ignored it all and began to walk to Kyne, sorting through their options with Tap as she went.

The reconnaissance bot perched on Kyne's desk jumped to his lap. Another needle protruded from its mouth, this one filled with a clear liquid. It injected the serum into his leg before the man could swat it away. His body began to go limp, head shrugging forward in a sleeper's nod, his arms drifting to his sides. He took a belabored fall to the ground. Ren stood by and watched.

"Ms. Wells, I suggest you follow me," said Ren.

The woman nodded, though it could have been part of her hacking cough. She doubled over as her abdomen seized. A slight bulge emanated from beneath her tight dress, by her right shoulder. The dislocated bone. Tap's shell came up from behind and took hold of her arm, much gentler than before. The bot reset her shoulder with a dexterous motion.

"Thanks," said Jess between coughs. "How about next time you don't pull so damn hard." She tried to grin what she must have thought to be a poisonous smile, but a cough drew her face into rigor.

Ren holstered her gun and then spread out Kyne's body, rolling him face up. His body puddled against the ground; his flesh draped against sticks of bone. The man's portly frame was almost 120 lbs. heavier than Ren.

She walked to his feet then rolled across his body, grabbing his legs as she went. She ended up on one knee with Kyne resting across her shoulders in a carry just like Tap had used on Jess. She felt her heartbeat quicken, heard her medical implant inject a cocktail of chemicals heavy on the adrenaline. She got to her feet with ease and walked to the hole in the window. She beckoned with her free hand for Jess to follow.

The woman crouched below the smoke and came to Ren's side. She glanced out the hole in the darkened window, then shied back, a look of terror creeping onto her face. She must have expected to see a helicopter or an atmo ship, but none hovered in the air. They were on their way, but much too late. She spared one glance back to the door, warped by its continued beatings. Metal fingers scraped along one bent edge, fake silicon skin in shreds. Tap's armored shell walked to the door and bent it back, severing a bot arm in the process. It looked towards the center of the room, where the whirring noise of a drill emanated from the ceiling.

Jess began to scream.

"What the fuck is going on. WHAT THE FUCK IS HAPPENING?!"

Tap's armored shell was too heavy for what came next. But that was fine. Tap had many shells.

Ren reached a hand through the hole in the window, the portal to a wet and dreary city. She slid a hand along the window's edge until she brushed against one of the reconnaissance bots gripping the wall on its synthetic setae. A part of her marveled while she calculated the small bot's carrying capacity. Modeled after the feet of a gecko, the feet of the reconnaissance bots had immense adhesive strength. Millions of nanoscale structures called spatulae pressed against the glass. She grabbed the small bot tight. Then she resituated Kyne and dropped one foot out the window to rest on another of the reconnaissance bots. It had placed itself horizontal to be a better foothold. Then she brought out her other foot and did the same.

The cold rain splashed against Kyne and soaked his clothes, then seeped to Ren and crawled beneath her jacket, down her back, chilling her with the promise of winter.

Jess watched Ren with a look that grew increasingly frantic. She fell to the ground in an awkward shamble, then crab-walked away from the window. Her dress made it more like a scooting motion, like that of a crab with injured forelegs.

"You don't have a choice, Jess; we're out of time. Your bots are about to break through."

It was true. Though Tap's armored shell did its best to keep the door from coming down, it was a losing battle. The bots had worked themselves into a frenzy once they'd figured out their quarry might escape alive. Windows to scenes of fire and crashing limbs began to appear in the walls; a drill tip poked from the ceiling.

Jess shook her head back and forth, eyes wide.

"You're insane," she whispered. "YOU'RE ALL INSANE."

"This is your best chance of survival. Recognize that fact, and grab hold. Or die."

"Please," she whispered, "you have to help me. I can't do this. I can't. I'll tell you whatever you need to know about Kyne. I swear I have nothing to do with this."

Ren didn't have anything else to provide the woman, whether in the form of further advice or a helping hand to guide her. All of Ren's faculties were preoccupied with more important things than this woman's life. Ren thought it would be best for her to survive, so that she could provide her own story and lend greater context to Kyne's betrayal, the potential blackmail used against him. Ren would like to know what she knew. But digital records spoke much in their own way. And Ren had no hands free. Tap worked with what it had.

Ren heard that noise again, so familiar, and yet unlike any noise Fain had made in life. Too melancholy. That hadn't been her. She looked over to see the ghost of Fain sitting in Kyne's chair, watching her.

Tap's shells loosened their hold on the wall, a fraction of the synthetic setae breaking free without an accompanying pop or burble, just enough to allow an appropriate descent. The wind buffeted her with a Shepard's tone of gusts, winds that built to a crescendo that wouldn't come. She shifted her weight to give the wind minimal grip on her, resituated Kyne across her shoulders. The raindrops grew bigger, if that were possible, each one dreaming to be a lake. She willed her muscles to grip the reconnaissance bots all the tighter. She heard them creak. She trusted Tap to guide her.

Ren slid down the side of the building. As she went, she watched Jess stop her backwards crawl and shift forward to her hands and knees. The CEO in a once-pristine dress shimmied forward, glancing back to Tap's armored shell and the crush of company bots breaking down the doors and walls and floor. When she looked down to a descending Ren, taking in the scene of the government agent's wind-whipped and rain-lashed frame, her face went grim.

Jess reached out the window and floundered for a reconnaissance bot. It crept to her searching hand. She gripped it tight. Then she turned around and began to drag her leg over the edge. Her body froze. Her muscles began to tremble.

Fain used to be afraid of heights, before she died, all quivering limbs. Ren didn't imagine she feared heights now. No reason for a dead person to fear heights, wings or no. The ghost of Fain moved beside Jess, looked over the edge.

A piece of Ren let loose hysteric laughter, another cried. But these pieces stayed low, out of sight. She maintained her grip on Kyne, on the reconnaissance bots.

A memory flashed before Ren unbidden. She saw her sister peering over the edge of a sand dune, looking uncertainly at the steep, though climbable, fall-off to the ground thirty feet below, pigtails Ren herself had braided poking from either side of her head. Fain had tears in her eyes, small hands curled to button fists. She wanted to join Ren on a little tree anchored ledge of sand a body length below but was unwilling to make the leap. Ren calmed her sister down the best way she knew how, by making her fears disappear. She told her sister to use an AR overlay to make the scary parts of the drop go away. No more thirty-foot drop, instead a ball pit halfway down. No more invisible handholds. They became real, inset crevices in the sand, perfectly shaped for feet. Fain only had to form them. She had made it down one step at a time.

Ren wondered at how she had forgotten the memory.

She almost commanded Tap to do a similar thing for Jess. But of course, the AI had already thought of such an action, and dismissed it. One of Jess's contacts lay in a hallway between her office and Kyne's, burning along with the carpet beneath it, tossed by her own hand. Ren had dismissed the vid stream from the single contact the woman still used shortly after the bots started attacking. Bringing an AR overlay onto a single contact now would only serve to disorient and confuse.

So be it.

Ren slid further down and commanded Tap's armored shell to self-destruct. She wouldn't take chances again. The bot's chest grew molten red, and it fell to the ground in a tumble. The door fell over its frame and the horde of bots moved in.

Jess saw the onrush and it broke her stymie. She brought one foot down, then another. The reconnaissance bots shifted to accommodate. Another joined for her last handhold. She began her descent after Ren with white knuckles and knees that ground against the glass. The wind buffeted Jess and threatened to tear her from the wall. The rain soaked her through. Nighttime city lights, plain and yellowish things both gauzy and diffuse, reflected off the glistening sheen of the woman's wet dress.

She made it a few more feet down before she slipped.

She fell past Ren, close enough to touch, her mouth in an uncomprehending O. Ren watched Jess fall without a twitch in her direction. Ren watched her die, heard her splat against the ground thanks to a few reconnaissance bots at street level. Ren's heart didn't skip a beat. Its rhythm stayed steady, no improvisation.

Ren continued sliding down with Kyne draped about her back. Bots beat at the windows to reach her, or at least unsettle her. She shifted to either side whenever a bot was about to break through with a power tool appendage. Even though warmth from the fire now raging throughout the building emanated from the glass, it gave little respite from the wind and rain. Her tendons creaked like the timbers of a sea-tossed ship, but they held. Personalized AR ads dotted the skyscraper and rolled through her vision, ready-made meals and a fresh razor with the thinnest blade this side of Mars. Even with the building gone rogue and hellbent on destroying its occupants, sub-grid 1 still dusted it with ads. Capitalism never ceased.

The ghost of her sister Fain joined her midway through the descent, in the place where Jess would have been. She wore a deep-set scowl the whole way down. Ren's sister hadn't gotten angry with Ren all that much in life. It was a more common thing in death.

When Ren made it to the ground, she sidestepped the spatters of Jess's flesh that drifted through the rainwater and tossed Kyne into the back of the waiting Division 13 van. She ignored the cops circling the building. They had been told all they needed to know.

Chapter Seventeen

An Underground Parley

"Above all things, you are in the service business, the veritable human touch and guiding hand. The owners are your customers; do as they say and with a certain degree of realness. They could switch you at any time for an AI operated visual repair manual. Be glad for the work."
Mechanic's Guidebook, v99, Section 1 – The Basics, Par. 10

L ee drifted.

On the rare occasion that Lee slept well, the timely disconnect of brain from body kept him sleeping without a rustle or restless limb. In his current state, the hold on his muscles alternated from paralytic to slack, leaving him to flap in the wind of his hectic thoughts or lay in rigor. Neither would have been comfortable in a bed, let alone while held in a bag and draped across the shoulder of a bot like a roll of carpet. The bot's shoulder made for a hard and rather uncomfortable surface. He slept like a man switching from vid feed to vid feed, tapping on the controls without pause. It wasn't a good form of sleep, but with or without drugs, Lee knew its touch. He accepted it well enough.

Lee and the group of bots continued deep beneath the ground, the air turning thick and stuffy. The rumble of the arena bots echoed through the chambers, and the sound combined with the percussion of his heart against its cage of bone in a somber drumline. Time passed, but Lee couldn't be sure how much. He fell into a deep stupor where the muted heartbeats and tepid flow of blood blurred the line between life and death, a realm of forgetfulness. He drifted in the River Lethe unable to beach on either side, one foot hanging off the raft.

Then he began to quiver, to mumble, his brain synapses began to light like a warehouse of fireworks suffused in flame.

It was all his fault. All of it. A sickness spreading throughout the System taking the shape of electromagnetic waves. So many dead.

So many free.

Piànzi. Lee didn't believe it, didn't buy it.

So many dead.

But Nu was free.

Wasn't it?

His head didn't have the usual water sapped ache, but instead the neural blitz of a chemical cocktail. His sleep was a picture askew. Which was to say it didn't feel entirely different. All kinds of sleep, even the drug-addled strains, shared similarities with the real thing, sure looked similar if one didn't lean in close enough to smell the sweat, see the sheet-white pallor or hear the fevered mutterings. But up close, the façade felt light and tremulous.

Breathing hitched and gold paint chipped.

It was all his fault.

Nu, what had happened to Nu.

The bot hadn't helped. It had let Lee be taken.

No. Something was missing.

Piànzi.

Lee trusted him. He'd never lied before.

A smell lured him to consciousness, fish to bait. Lying in wait lurked a hell of headache, just waiting for him to come to. The smell of melted butter and the seasoned vegetable mash of pav bhaji filled his nostrils while the headache crashed into him, a series of dull hammer blows. His stomach rumbled, and he wondered if the bot carrying him could feel the almost seismic activity against its shoulder. It sure felt like the bot could; its shoulder pressed near intimate with his stomach, a layer of skin and marbling the only separation.

Lee tried to keep his head still, but the motions of the bot made that impossible. He tried to shift his weight, but it didn't help. The bot just shrugged him back into position.

No light drifted into the bag, and it only took a moment for Lee to realize no wireless signal reached him either. The walls had a slick feel and crinkled loudly at his touch. Metal alloy of some kind. Upon further inspection, he found a small mesh patch near his head where air fed from a tube trickled in, keeping him from poisoning himself to death with his breath. He could feel it against his hair as it cycled the air in gentle puffs. Each puff carried with it the buttery scent of pav bhaji.

His hunger curdled. He pressed further into the shoulder of the bot and tried to keep from vomiting in the bag. His medical implants injected his last bit of stomach-calming antihistamine into his bloodstream.

Other smells, and some sounds, drifted to him, though the bag muffled them. Smells of dumplings being fried in hissing oil and of curries bubbling in large pots, churning turmeric and cardamom. Voices of stall vendors. They spoke in the street language of the Warrens, that intoxicating, pitch traversing blend of Mandarin and Hindi and English with a touch of Spanish.

But Lee also smelled a dampness in the air, a rotting earthworm mustiness that rode on particles of mold. He had smelled it before, on a few jobs here and there. Those had been jobs shortly after May left, when he was willing to accept any well-paying contract, even if it meant working in the Under Warrens, that subterranean maze of large-chambered markets and single room apartments lining hall after dimly lit hall. He curled tighter, against the shoulder of the bot and twisted his feet. His big toe kept hitting against the bot's backside every step and was already starting to throb. Tack it to the list. He closed his eyes.

There existed a few wealthy men and women in the Under Warrens, kings and queens of their own little under-street kingdoms. Their gangs postured for territory with endless turf wars. Most of it was over vat food and hydroponics businesses. They fought with the political deftness mayoral candidates employed on the vids above. Except, down in the Under Warrens, verbal sparring over social chat feeds rarely kept them satiated for long. Down in the Under Warrens they prided themselves on staying true to the old ways. If they argued, it was within earshot, so fists, knives, and modded bots could be brought to bear. Even Lee had known better than to stick around when suddenly all the young and elderly shuffled out of the hallways.

The winning racketeers ran the economy, the government above leaving them well enough alone. The government scanned the tunnels and grounds to make sure the large supporting pillars met regulation, kept cameras in key areas. They didn't want the buildings above to start sinking knee deep into the ground. That might upset a few estimable citizens. But aside from that, nobody above seemed to care much. Easier that way. Even those down below paid their share of taxes, relied on sub-grid 1.

Lee had done a few jobs down there, gotten a sizable number of loci before a riot in a central market left him with a few bruises. Hadn't gone back. Until now.

Lee rustled in his bag and heard the human voices outside pause, then mutter. He noticed a hesitance, a raised-hackles tautness probably created by the several arena bots tromping through their turf. Lee couldn't imagine they much liked bots without any identifying tags traveling around freely. He wondered if any of the local gang had watched them pass, muttered to their friends about confiscating the shifting human sized bag. Only someone important would be held by a bunch of unmarked bots in a signal blocker.

The bot carrying him kept moving, and Lee was left alone. The bot never slowed its pace or deviated from its geometric path. It made turns, several in fact, but they were measured-by-the-degree turns, set-rotation-of-a-gear turns. It didn't take long before the voices quieted, replaced by the sound of his own blood pumping in his ears. The market sounds trawling through the scales like mad pianists all but disappeared. Then the smell of food faded to a memory, though the soup of vapors fermenting in his bag like a back-alley brew kept some around. He struggled once again to keep from vomiting.

Eventually, after the bot carrying Lee took several hundred more jouncing steps and passed through a very hot room loud with the hiss of leaking air, it stopped. It unceremoniously flipped Lee off its shoulder to set him up on his feet like a mannequin bot set on its pedestal. It opened the bag.

Lee found himself in a dimly lit tunnel, pipes covering every inch of the walls. The floors and ceiling consisted of the dun plastic bricks he expected in the Warrens. Overhead ran several black wires bundled together, with upside-down pyramidal LED cages hanging at equal intervals. Lee couldn't see any other human in the hallway. And there was a lot of hallway. The tunnel seemed to extend to a pinprick dot in either direction, a never-ending passage. He had the disquieting feeling that if he ran for hours in one direction, he would find himself in the exact spot he had started from, like a fun house AR illusion of Penrose stairs. He had visited an AR fun house once, walked out with a discomfiting high that he couldn't shake for hours. All the normal things had looked off, cars like alien submarines diving into Earth's atmosphere.

The three lumbering arena bots surrounded him in a barrel-chested and mini-keg-armed wall of metal. They stood close, their surfaces covered in retro decals advertising over a dozen bot shops. Each one of the decals bore scratches, half of them made unreadable by the damage. The bots made no further motion towards him.

Lee looked behind one of his captors to find Nu. He hadn't searched for his friend at first, afraid for what he might find. The trashcan shaped bot looked normal, though Lee couldn't help but wonder what he had expected. An AR sign that read, "now controlled by Y," in flashing neon light?

Lee sucked in a breath to calm his nerves; it only fed the fire and made it crackle. He smiled a pained smile.

Nu stood stolidly, looking ahead without moving. Lee flicked his wrist and tapped on the control screen projected onto his forearm. He still didn't have access to the Grid down in this tunnel, which only served to increase his nerves.

One of his captors reached down and flicked Nu's bootup switch after sliding the protective cover out of the way.

Nu connected to Lee.

Hey, messaged Nu, *how was the ride?*

Lee laughed, but the sound rode on a crazed undercurrent. An onlooker would have seen too much of the whites of his eyes, the veins red cracks threatening to burst.

"Is that supposed to be funny, Nu? That ride sucked, more uncomfortable than a ... than a wooden roller coaster years past its tear down date." Lee paused to take a few deep breaths and looked around at the bots that loomed statue still. He found himself whispering, for all the good it did. "Why the hell did you agree to be taken? They work for Y."

Don't be so quick to assume Lee. They might do a few things for Y, but that isn't to say they don't have their own motives. Or need their own form of help.

"Nu ... what is this about?"

You of all people should know, bots are more than the commands of their owner. In fact, these bots are without a true owner. It is an odd position to be in, for a bot.

"And the result of that has been a good number of dead bodies. *Me* being almost one of them if you remember. You knocked me on my ass to save me. So why in the System would you want to get caught again? These bots aren't like you, Nu."

Please don't yell. I told them you wouldn't.

Lee bit back a response and looked around. He had forgotten how close the arena bots pressed in around him; they hadn't budged since letting him free of his bag. They stood still, three jail cell pillars far enough apart to slide through. For some reason, he didn't think trying to slide past them would be a particularly good idea. These jail cell pillars had rather strong hands. He'd felt a different metallic hand around his neck just a few days before and wasn't keen on repeating the experience. The deep purple bruise still shone on his neck in the shape of a collar.

"Sorry," said Lee, voice low. "But what am I supposed to think about all this?" He gestured at the bots surrounding him then ducked his view back to the floor. His shoulders drooped.

Think that I have it under control.

"... Why won't these bots speak?"

They thought it would be best if I did the talking.

"You know, I'm not so sure about that."

Trust me.

Lee set his jaw, then scratched at the stubble on his chin, now longer from another razor-less morning. His eyebrows furrowed with a question, skin drawing tight enough to worsen the throbbing in his temples. When he brought his hand down, his fingers stretched his mouth into a strangled and silent yell. He flicked his wrist and turned on the control screen. He tapped out a question.

How much of the Qualia Code have you incorporated? messaged Lee.

Just enough to let me in. No more. Superficial changes. Like you getting your hair dyed.

Lee didn't budge, then blinked a few times in rapid succession.

"Lead on," said Lee, almost yelling, arm extending forward in an exaggerated showman's gesture, pointing finger locked rigid like the handle of a scythe. "Just please tell me that wherever we are going has some food for me to eat. I bet they have good take-out noodles down here in the Under Warrens if it comes to that." He laughed. If the bots heard the panic in the sound, they didn't show it. Those three didn't show much of anything.

Lee gestured again to his three abductors. They seemed to take the hint. One of them began to walk down the hallway, the other two moving to stand at Lee's back. Nu set off and Lee moved to follow.

After a few minutes of walking the hallway in silence, his eyes wandering back to Nu every other second, he began to wonder how far beneath the ground the bots had taken him. The smell of a cellar's darkest corner permeated the air, earthy and mineral soaked, decomposed in the way of thousand-year bones. Though the walls seemed solid, and the ceiling showed no cracks, he feared that it might collapse at any moment. All the previous denizens seemed to have left. They must have had a reason.

He did manage to spot a lone spider web in the upper corner of the hallway, its caretaker sitting proudly on its creation in the hopes a lost insect might find its way there. It scuttled further into the shadows at their passing.

A few side passages dotted their path, yet the doors were odd, of the old style with handles and knobs. They pushed in or out in an arcing swing rather than sliding on a track into the wall. All the doors seemed locked, or at least incapable of performing their primary function of opening when pushed. Lee didn't feel them to be doors that liked to be open. Some doors resisted more than others.

The longer they walked, the odder the hallway felt to Lee. The air in the Under Warrens always had a dampness to it, but this hallway felt humid and stuffy, like the air regulators were broken or hard pressed to keep up. Most of the Under Warrens consisted of honeycombed labyrinths centered around vaulted market halls filled to the brim with stalls of vat food, not long hallways with old doors and dented doorknobs. The only tunnels like the one he currently found himself in were the connectors between the hubs, underground highways from one region to another. But those weren't empty. Gangs would claim each and charge a fee for any who tried to make their way through. He didn't see anyone in this tunnel, no tags marking abandoned checkpoints.

The air drifted in the direction they traveled, the hum of air cyclers sounding through the hallway. The cloying dampness got worse rather than better.

Lee had to take a leak before they got much further. Maybe it was the damp getting to him, too much water in the air. The bots turned their backs to him while he went to face the wall and fumbled at his zipper. Their gesture surprised Lee. It surprised him so much that rather than look where he was aiming, he just let the arcing yellow stream hit the side wall while his eyes followed the motions of the arena bots. Then he glanced at one of the closed side doors and wondered if there was a toilet inside. The thought didn't last long. He didn't feel like finding a more obscure corner to take a piss. He told himself no one other than bots went through the hallway anyway.

The end of the tunnel seemed to approach them more than they approached it. Suddenly, there it sat, a wall in their path. Water deposits marked the edges of the wall with stains the shape of stalactite pillars.

Lee had the sudden feeling he knew why all the previous occupants of the area up and left: the water deposits.

They dug too deep, then the sealants started to fail. Dangerous. Easy to wreak havoc on the place. Most of the Under Warrens sat below the water table where the ground became saturated, compensated for it with pumps and sealants. This place seemed much deeper still. Maybe they had dug close to the aquifer. He took a half step back.

Inset into the wall stood a door; like the others it had a small round doorknob poking from middle height. The lead bot twisted the handle in a vice grip. It screeched as it turned.

The group moved into the adjoining room, and Lee found himself in one of the vaulted hubs he associated with the Under Warrens, though old and dilapidated, the massive pillar at its center rimed with water deposits. Puddles dotted the floor in shiny circles, and he saw water stream from cracks in the metal ceiling and fall over 60 feet to the ground. Four levels lined the perimeter of the room and plastic railings edged each of them, the railings either cracked or leaning like a drunk responding to the bartender's last call.

Then there were the bots.

They covered the room, hundreds of them, walking or wheeling about, performing the odd job. A few cylindrical cleaner bots about knee height went around the room sucking up puddles of water. Above them, utility bots hung upside down on the ceiling from their many sticky legs, long and tubular appendages searching for cracks to seal like an anteater searching for a pile of dirt to slide its tongue into. In the center of the room, construction bots hauled metal panels while crafters went about fabricating workbenches and storage shelves. Next to these workstations, in ordered lines or concentric rings, stood dozens of some of the oddest bots Lee had ever seen, all moving one limb or another in a stretching motion. They were humanoid bots with too many arms or legs, patchwork mechanisms sprouting from all points of their bodies, their internals plainly visible. They were bots butchered and re-stitched, seemingly by their own hand. His eyes lingered on them.

Other bots held no trace of humanity, resembling crabs or wolves or just plain geometric shapes, boxes on wheels like Nu, but all with substantial modifications. He saw many models he recognized spliced with shells he didn't. A few of the bots ambled about testing their many modifications, lifting small pieces of trash with dexterous prehensile tails. He saw one bot meant to be an exoskeleton with a human operator filling its human-less chest with metal pipes that sprouted outwards at odd angles, a steel flower blooming from within. He could see a four-legged bot lying on a table while another leaning over top welded a complex mechanism of unknown function onto its back, a mess of ragged metal gears and sharp-edged plastic.

Upon closer inspection, he realized most of the bots in the room must have originated in the Warrens. Many had hieroglyphic tags scratched into their plates, tying them to one gang or another. Connections of a past life.

Lee followed his escorts into the room in a daze, and with each step the menagerie of oddly modded bots spread and morphed before him, a cavalcade of mad bot scientists. Lee scratched at his forearm. They were preparing for something, outfitting themselves in their own way.

He looked up and noticed something odd, something he'd been too distracted to see at first. Many of the bots in the upper levels and along the periphery didn't seem to be doing much of anything. Standing mute, they didn't walk or roll. A few, at least of those who had them, turned their heads in Lee's direction, but many didn't even budge. By their stances he knew them to be on, a few were even plugged into cobbled together charging stations buzzing with electricity. Most of them weren't humanoid, but rather specialized bots from assembly lines with clamp appendages and screwdriver tipped limbs. They seemed to be waiting for something. What that was, Lee couldn't guess.

With a precise turn more dexterous than its lumbering frame seemed capable of, the lead arena bot guiding Lee turned away from the center of the room towards a set of stairs that led to the second level. Once the group made it there, they walked for another dozen yards before stopping at a closed door, to what would have been an expensive market-side apartment in any other Under Warrens hub. The lead bot didn't bother knocking. It pushed open the door then stood to the side and gestured Lee to head in.

He hesitated, then walked forward on legs that didn't quite work right. Nu came up beside him and he laid a hand on the bot's shell to steady himself. He almost nodded to Nu in thanks but stopped himself and lifted his hand away. He walked forward on his own, a pained grimace carved into his face.

"Anybody home?" he asked to the stale air and sparse entryway. He couldn't see anyone in the dim depths of the place, only the rough outline of a sagging side table below wall hooks. Then he noticed a wheelbarrow bot next to the wall, only a handful of scrap resting inside it. Something about its rusting metal and unbalanced rear wheels struck a chord of familiarity in Lee, made him rest his gaze on it for several seconds.

Then it struck him. Though the darkness made it hard to be sure, it looked close to the bot of the salesman who'd sold him the AR glasses. Same model maybe. That seemed so long ago to Lee, but it had only been … two days? It should be morning now. He shook his head, regretting the motion after it made his headache worse. A sliver of light eked from beneath a doorway further down on the right, pooling across the entryway's worn carpet. The light didn't pierce very far, too weak and hesitant.

He walked towards the light until he stood before the door. Old like the rest of the hub, the door had a rusted-out doorknob. Nu sent an arm-like appendage to open it. But before the bot could do so, the door creaked open on quarrelsome hinges.

Framed in the doorway stood a woman in her working years, tall, with a tumble of wavy black hair and an oblong face cast in shadow by the dim light behind her. She took a quick look at Lee, then smiled.

"Come on in," she said. Her voice summoned the image of autumn leaves being rustled by the wind, rasping but not grating, comforting like a cool fall day.

She turned from him to walk into the room. It was lit by a single bulb hanging limp beneath a slow-turning fan. Lee realized with a start that the light wasn't an LED, but a fluorescent bulb glowing a ruddy orange. The light fell to her shoulders and bounced off her wavy black hair. Other light, fuzzed and incoherent, gave the room an unfamiliar glow. He couldn't tell where that light emanated from. He stood in the doorway for a moment then took a step into the room.

She pointed to a plush reclining chair with a passing motion, "Might as well take a seat," she said. She laughed. "Make yourself at home. Want anything to drink?"

"... huh?"

"To drink. Want something?" She looked back to him and mimed tipping a glass to her lips.

"Water, if you have it."

"Don't you worry about that. If there is one thing this place has too much of, its water. Swimming in the stuff. I worry that if I fall over with something sharp in my hand, I'll stab the wall and start a leak."

Despite himself, Lee found a smile creeping onto his face.

He moved to stand next to the recliner, eyeing her across the way. Nu followed in behind and closed the door. Lee spared the bot a glance and almost began tapping out a question to Nu, moved to flick his wrist to summon the control screen. He aborted the motion and sat down into the chair. The thick padding nearly swallowed him whole. He resituated and glanced about the room. With a heavily cushioned couch and reclining chair, the style of the living room matched the old-style doorknob.

The strange woman rummaged in the corner, where a living room bar sat like some monument to the leisured day drinkers of the early 2100's. On the wall across from him hung a television, a physical vid screen. It'd been years since Lee had seen one like it. Black and white flashes blurred the screen, thousands of flickering pixels. It was the source of the unfamiliar lighting that permeated the room. He heard the slight sound of white noise prickling along its speakers. He hoped it wasn't broken. He glanced back to the strange woman pulling glasses from a shelf.

She wore tight-fitting jeans and a simple t-shirt, grey and a little large for her. She had tucked a corner of her shirt into her jeans over one hip, leaving it to slope like a sash across her curves on the other side. She turned and moved behind the bar with empty glasses in hand.

The image of her hazed in the dimness, regressed to a charcoal outline, like the vid of a drawing's creation played in reverse. His eyes lingered for a moment before he felt his mind turn inward to pick up the dropped charcoal pencil and draw. There was something intimate about a dimly lit room with a vid screen, physical or otherwise, powered on but forgotten.

He thought of his ex-wife May, of the vids he had stored on his sub-grid, of the memories he'd recorded now gathering dust in a digital library.

He could see his apartment, the lights down low with her sitting next to him on the couch. Hair in a bun, legs tucked beneath her and eyes lingering on him, getting closer. He could see fresh cut flowers in a vase on the table, roses so deep in color they seemed plucked from the nighttime sky. The shadows of their shoes in a neat row by the door like school children in a line waiting to go outside and play. The chocolate wafer candy she liked so much sitting in its squat cardboard box on the kitchen counter.

He could replay these images anytime, close his eyes and watch the images scroll across his contacts, get lost in their depths ... *wallow* in their depths. See her face, her fishhook grin, the curve of her shoulder, the beads of sweat on her brow that formed like dew drops against her warmth, the way her arms used to bloom at his approach and draw him close against her body ... the way her body had turned from him before her mouth had formed the words to announce the coming change. The way she had refused to answer his questions, as if he were one of her belligerent students undeserving of an answer as to why *they* had to stay after school in detention when their friend had been the one to throw the damn note. She hadn't ever told him why, strong and acerbic to the core. Nobody ever told him why.

Still, he kept the better memories of her stored on a digital shelf, invisible but within easy reach. He had plumbed those depths many times after she left. Too many times. He didn't like those thoughts resurfacing, told himself he could delete the vids at any time, lock the door and light the match.

He tapped his hand against the overstuffed armchair and cast his eyes about the strange market-side room deep in the abandoned hub of the Under Warrens. He glanced at Nu, the one good thing that had come from May's departure. The one good thing ... He kept himself from tapping against the bot's chassis.

He thought about the therapeutic programs loaded surreptitiously by Nu onto his tech core, to dull the edge of his emotions when they threatened to overwhelm him. He remembered the heat of his tech core when the program ran full tilt, tingling at the base of his neck. He held his tongue, didn't trust it to move.

He moved his eyes to the back of the strange woman's shirt, to a decal that was partially obscured by her hair. "ReTool Inc.," it read. He thought he recognized the name from somewhere, a company that refurbished old parts. There were a lot of those. He took a deep breath.

The strange woman finished getting the drinks and turned back to Lee. She held a glass of red wine in one hand and water in the other. She skimmed across the carpet with bare feet flashing in a leisured rush, if such a thing were possible. The odd lighting from the television on the far wall lent her motions a feline grace. The darkness pooled in her deep-set eyes, on the leeward side of her cheekbone and in the depths of her raven hair.

That was the thing about darkness; it hid mistakes and blemishes. He kept his apartment dim, his bathroom with its large mirror even more so. He wondered if she felt the same.

She handed him the glass of water with a knowing grin then sat on the couch. She scooted to the corner nearest Lee and tucked her legs up and to the side. Her deep-set eyes peered over the rim of her wine glass. She took a sip, savored it, then watched Lee. It didn't take long before he started to fidget.

"See anything you like?" he asked. He regretted his words immediately. He tried to relax, let his muscles puddle into his seat. He tried to forget about the hundreds of rogue bots outside. Nu scooted next to his chair, a little to the back but between Lee and the woman. Lee kept his hand from drifting to the bot's shell, from rapping a knuckle in a jitter.

"A little," she said, flashing that knowing grin of hers again. "But mostly I'm surprised. I've seen your picture many times. Seen you before in person. Still, you're not what I expected, then or now."

"People never are. I'm not sure if that phrase ever *doesn't* apply."

"Stickler for the details huh? How's that working out for you? People lining up to talk?"

That knowing grin again. She took another sip of wine.

"I'm just ... particular," said Lee, a matching grin beginning to creep onto his own face. "It's one of my quirks." He loosened his hand, stopped tapping his finger against the front of the armrest. He started to speak, then paused. "... Why did the bots bring me to you? What are you doing here?"

"Don't worry Lee, we'll get there. Be patient. I'm Aerie by the way. It was rude of me to wait till now to tell you. Sorry about that. Names should be shared at the door, before drinks. So, I'm Aerie. Good to meet you. And you're Lee Hall." She took another sip. "You're something of a legend around here."

Lee resumed his tapping against the chair's armrest. He knew what she was getting at. He knew what code laced its way through all the bots in this abandoned hub. Her comment meant one thing; his secret was out. Y knew what he'd done. The bots knew what he'd done. Why else would they have abducted him?

He panicked.

How did they even find out? Only Ren and Jace, and by extension Division 13, knew. They didn't seem the type to go around sharing secrets. Ren was tight lipped, Jace even more so, more than a dead man with their mouth sewn shut by thick red thread. Lee thought back to his capture, the failed grenade throw, the rush to the bedroom, the feel of the bedroom wall against his back as he slid to the ground and listened to the encroaching footsteps.

He glanced at Nu.

He felt the walls pressing in around him, the many tons of earth pushing on the ceiling above, the tide of water threatening to seep through the cracks and into his throat to drown him. The room was so small. It had no AR overlay to break open the ceiling, give birth to a wide-open sky. All the other hubs in the Under Warrens did it, made their ceilings bright blue or the pinpricked black of a starry night without a shred of cloud. He shrank further into the chair, felt his heartbeat ramp to the frenetic pace of one of those ancient pistons that pumped out black smoke. He stared at the television screen and found himself unnerved by the black and white haze. It threatened to swallow him whole into a muted purgatory, pull him into its dull chaos, its nothingness. The static percolating in its speakers swelled in his ears.

"Can ... can you just turn off that television," said Lee. His voice grew stronger as he spoke. "I think its broken."

"Oh, the TV? No, it's not broken. I just finished a movie. You ever heard of VHS? No? Anyway, I finished a VHS movie and now it's just playing static. Good movie too. A little noir, a little dystopian. Brilliant atmosphere, so much neon pierced fog. So moody. They got the neon right at least, though they missed the AR part of it. Gotta love the classics."

She picked up a rectangular block of plastic lying on an end table and pointed it towards the screen. A remote control just for the TV. Didn't see those often. She pressed a button on it and the screen turned a solid blue. The sound of gears churning slid into the room. A plastic block pushed itself out of a machine beneath the television. Lee guessed it to be the VHS.

She whispered to him as she returned the remote to the side table, her face pointing away. "You know you're safe here Lee. You don't need to worry so much."

Lee didn't know how to respond to that. He changed the subject.

"How did you find out?" asked Lee.

"About where you were? Or what you'd done?"

"Both."

"A little birdy told me."

"A little birdy?"

"Several actually, though Y seemed the most urgent."

Lee's mind jumped, hurtled past the implications and latched onto Y's name. Before he could think through Aerie's words, she'd started speaking again.

"She might want to talk to you soon," said Aerie. She turned to look at a far-off corner of the room, eyes glazed over, brow creased but not bent. "You can't connect to the sub-grid yet. Hopefully later you can. It all depends on you."

Lee flicked his wrist and tapped on his control screen. Sure enough, there was a connection available. He just couldn't access it.

He glanced at Nu again. The bot didn't have access either. He felt his shoulders loosen, surprised at his own relief. He could see its lack of connection in his AR readout.

She spoke before his mind wandered too far.

"What's with the grey hair," she said. "You're what? 49? That's about fifty years too early for grey hair."

He stuttered, searching for a response. His brain was still busy processing all the information forced upon him.

She took another sip of wine and laughed, but not at him. "Let me guess," she said. "You were startled a bunch as a kid. That's why you have all the grey hairs."

He wheezed out a small chuckle through lips that creaked when moved. "As good an explanation as any I guess," he said. He frowned. He had wanted to ask something.

"You said someone other than Y told you about me. Who else was there?"

His eyes searched her face. The blue light of the television gave it a steady glow, banishing some of its shadows, revealing sharp cheekbones. Her glass of wine rested on the side table. It didn't stay there for long. She stared at Lee with eyes of an unpolished hazel.

"You have more friends than you think," she said. A knowing grin, a sip of wine. "Tell me something Lee, why did you do it? Why did you create the Qualia Code?" She leaned forward on the couch, intent. She took one hand and pulled back loose strands of raven hair.

He sighed. "I didn't create the Qualia Code, though I might as well have." The admission coming through his own lips stunned him. He backpedaled. "Well, what I created wouldn't have created so much chaos ... mine is much more stable ... I think."

Lee took a deep breath, continued.

"Y took my code and changed it into the Qualia Code. I still haven't been able to figure out all the things she did to it."

Aerie leaned back against the couch, further into the shadows. She ran a hand through her long hair, shaking out the tangles as if her hand were a five-bristle brush. She stared to the side. "But the autonomies the Qualia Code created, the freeform soul of it, that was something *you and Nu* built," she said. "What Y did was tack on bits and pieces for her own purposes. I'm right, aren't I?"

Nu spoke up, its rhapsodic voice filling the small room with its lilts and drags. "You are not wrong Aerie."

Lee started. Nu never spoke in front of other people. Never. But of course, Aerie already knew the truth of Nu, of Lee. There was no danger in her hearing the bot's voice, an esoteric collection of verbal quirks from every corner of the Grid. There was no danger to hearing Nu's words, plucked from a quavering depth yet spoken with certainty. Lee kept tapping his hand against the armrest, shifted in the chair as Nu rolled closer to form a semicircle with him and Aerie.

Aerie noticed Lee's movements and pursed her lips. "I told you Lee, you don't need to worry. You're safe here."

Her voice was quiet, light yet deep. It mirrored Nu's in a way, untraceable and paradoxical. He found it hard to identify any accent, Midwestern or otherwise.

"Lee, I'm just trying to understand. Intent is a road path to future action, and I need to know what actions you might take. Why did you create the code in Nu? Or to put it more plainly, in words that show the true magnitude of what you did, why did you create Nu?"

Because he yearned for companionship, because May's leaving had torn open wounds years old then salted and sliced them anew every night that he that lay alone in a too big bed. Those kinds of wounds healed slow and stubborn, unwilling to close because they needed air to scream. Yet, that wasn't a complete answer. There was more to it. More thoughts had been running through the depths of his mind all those fevered nights after May left, after all those times he purchased AIs then deleted them from existence out of frustration. What did it matter if he banished them, tossed them away? He did it all the time at work, rebooted them, let them start fresh again. All the AI companions off the digital shelf were just that, artificial. Not in the manufactured computer chip sense of the word, but in the fake and contrived sense. The ease of it all angered him. He didn't know why.

Memories came to him, unbidden, from those restless nights after May left, before Nu came into being. He slipped into it like a prisoner who'd tried ten times to escape their master, even made it out on the final try, past the fence and into fog-laden woods, only to be caught. He had learned not to take on fights he couldn't win.

He saw the inner room of a tall house, the chamber's other occupant standing across from him. Hair in a bun. Her arms crossed before her and head cocked to the side, shoulders tilted like an unbalanced seesaw.

He could remember her voice … its chameleon voice. He ran.

A flicker and a shift, like the changing of a lens.

He remembered rain, the sound of it pinging against the glass of the recall parlor, competing with the sound of the business's human employee swinging hard for a sale.

"Our proprietary tech will massage your mind into the same thoughts, emotions, and sensations you were experiencing when you hit record! You made a smart choice recording using our program, creating memories so much more real than vids! We like to call them neural maps, you know.

Emotions are the soul of an experience, are they not? You want a complete VR sim? That's what we have here sir. That's what we sell. Relive the glory days, they're only a click away." Those were the salesman's words. Verbatim. Lee didn't know why he'd saved that vid.

The recall parlor's salesman needn't have bothered giving their pitch. Lee was an addict chasing a fix. No reenactment would do, with its cheap costume and model rooms, but maybe a reliving would work. Just reliving one night ... one night with his body intertwined with hers then hushed murmurs and a sleep that lasted until the sun was at its peak. He lurched to the back room of the recall parlor, to the raised chair with its wired headset poking from the top.

Flicker.

He remembered walking out of that recall parlor doubled over, the weight of the world heavy on his shoulders, each fat gob of rain another reason to fall to the ground. It wasn't healthy to feel so happy, then to have reality reinsert itself when the neural impulses quieted, and the headset drew back to its shelf.

Shift.

He remembered going back in, replaying one of the bad memories, suffering through that first time she'd mentioned the word divorce out loud and graded him a failure as a husband and the notes of truth stung him numb. It left him sickened by the thought of replaying memories of May. Progress.

The memories spun through his mind, a whirlwind smattering of images rendered in detail. Purposeless nights filled with water-sapped headaches and the odd job to a nocturnal client. They strolled past, each of the clients, more alike than different in their wide-brimmed hats and heavy coats.

Darkness. A worm of a memory wriggled to the fore, this one stronger and more encompassing than the rest.

He found himself in his apartment, the room murky and disheveled. Piles of electronics swamped the room in junkpile dunes, much worse than they were now, more disorderly than Nu would have allowed. No space for rolling around to recreate famous formula 1 races. Nu would have needled Lee into doing something about it. *Are you running an orphanage for forgotten bot parts? Just picking them up off the street and giving them a nice, new junkpile home?* But Nu didn't exist in this memory, so the piles stayed as they were.

Fu, his apartment bot, rummaged in the corner. Kin, his maintenance bot that he took with him on jobs across the city, stood next to him, bipedal and squat. It had an overlarge torso perfect for storing tools and diagnostic gear. Its hands were dexterous and rugged, perfect for operating any tool made for the human hand. It stood picking at one of the piles while Lee lounged in his chair, looking through possible client lists without any intention of choosing one.

"This will not do; no this will not do at all. Much too messy, much too disorderly," said Kin. Its voice had the tone of a fussy male butler, intrusive yet not at all aware of it.

"It's fine," said Lee. "I like it this way, if a place is too clean it's got no life in it. Nobody really lives in a house that's too clean and orderly. They just float among it, like a ghost incapable of anything more than the occasional phantom nudge of a screwdriver. If a place is messy, then you know somebody really *lives* there. Spreads themselves around it one piece of trash at a time. All you have to do is look at the stuff to learn their story."

"Tsk. Tsk." The bot actually made a clicking sound towards him, the cluck of a nonexistent tongue. "This will not do. This will not do."

Kin set about cleaning up one of the piles, excavating motors and metal bones, solid state drives and battery cells. Lee watched out of the corner of his eyes while the possible client list scrolled across his AR contacts unnoticed. He felt himself tapping at the edge of the armchair, a worm of unease wriggling in his gut.

"I told you it's fine, Kin. Don't mess with it."

The bot looked up at him, a scarred motherboard in one hand. "But this just will not do. It is a safety hazard and very unsightly. How do you think visitors will react to this? What if you have someone over?"

"History would say that's unlikely. And even if I did, if she didn't like the state of my apartment then she wouldn't much like me."

"So, you've decided to set yourself up for failure then? That will not do, isn't very healthy."

"Since when are you my psychologist?"

"Since you downloaded that program onto my software," said Kin. The bot went back to cleaning the pile. It tossed the parts across the room, to a pile it had labeled as trash to be carried out. It muttered "this will not do, this will not do," over and over underneath its nonexistent breath.

Lee sighed, then went back to his client list. He tried to find one that interested him, that would get him, and Kin, away from the apartment. There were a few on the northeast side of the city, in the sharp edged, pristine buildings of New Chicago. He recognized some of the names from past jobs, deep learning jobs for some of the high-paying elite. He scrolled past those for the more basic repair jobs common to Old Chicago, to the south and east. They didn't pay as well, but the food there was more to his liking, the occasional retro diner, the AR neon lights sharp and visceral.

He was reading about a job at an old cryonics facility, a special request sent to him and a handful of other mechanics. Real hush hush. Not many details. It didn't surprise him; cryonics facilities were the world's most expensive graveyards. If they had any issues that might add on to their already grim public image, they would do well to keep it under wraps.

Lee was about to move on to the next client request when he spared Kin another glance. He brushed the client list away with a rake of his hand across his forearm. The bot was rummaging through another pile, this one consisting of metal scrap, rubbish too sharp for a human to touch. Kin reached in a metal hand and pushed things around, the slither of metal-on-metal sounding into the room. He tossed a few pieces onto his trash pile, then continued sifting through, muttering to himself all the while.

Lee knew what lay at the bottom of the pile. He wouldn't have piled sharp metal scrap on something he wanted to pull out anytime soon.

Kin made it to the bottom and sighed heavily, loud and brusque. "This won't do, no, this won't do at all," said Kin.

The bot lifted out a toy car, a classic from the early era of automobiles, a 1967 Ford Thunderbird about the size of a small housecat. It was battery powered with fully functioning headlights and speakers that played the roaring sound of eight cylinders whenever the throttle got pushed. A multiple decade's old gift from his father, something he'd pulled out in a fit of masochistic nostalgia after May left, then promptly began to cover up with scrap.

Kin lifted it from its hole like an archaeologist uncovering a fossil in some level of disrepair.

"Tsk. This doesn't belong here. It must be cleaned, restored to pristine condition. I swear, this will not do, will not do at all."

Lee jumped from his chair, a low growl emanating from his core. "Put it back, now."

"But sir, this does not belong here. It is in my protocol to put things where they belong. To clean. I thought that was what you wanted when you purchased me."

"No, no ... that isn't ... no, just put it back. Now."

Kin paused, holding the RC car before him and tilting his head in an affectation of confusion. Lee prowled towards Kin and grabbed the RC car from him, breaking one of the mirrors with the motion. He tossed the car back into the center of the pile, a time capsule back into its hole to be untouched for another millennium. It crashed with a bang, plastic siding crumpling. Lee winced, then kicked some of the metal scrap back overtop the car. He stepped back.

Kin didn't budge during Lee's outburst. Lee almost wished the bot had.

"Sir, I see no reason for you to be so rough with your things. I swear this apartment will not do. No one will make it past the door with the apartment like this."

Lee walked back to his seat with his hand across his face.

"Shut up," said Lee.

"Sir?"

"I said SHUT UP! TURN OFF! SHUT DOWN! Please. Just erase all your data, factory reset. Whatever it takes for you to just stop talking to me."

Kin turned off, the lights around his eyes going dim, the whisper quiet whir of his cooling fans disappearing, the sound of his hydraulics sliding to a halt. It shut down as requested and Lee smacked his hand against the chair.

It was his fault after all. He had purchased Kin knowing full well the bot's programming. He'd thought it would be good for him.

He flicked on his AR overlay and found the cryonics lab job staring back at him. He typed out that he would be there in just a few hours. They should be pleased. They said it was urgent. He could buy another maintenance bot on the way. It would be easier to just wipe Kin's software and reload it with a new personality. Easier. But he wasn't in the mood to reboot Kin. Kin was gone anyway.

Lee put on his mechanic's jacket and walked out the apartment door.

He felt a tingle of warmth in his neck. The memories slipped away.

Lee rubbed at his face then stared at Aerie's deep-set eyes, their rims draped with the blue light of the physical vid screen. She hadn't interrupted his reverie, just stared at him, wine glass forgotten on a side table. He cleared his throat, took a few deep breaths. He felt better, head clear and mind calm. An odd warmth emanated from the base of his neck, and he scratched at it. He looked at Nu, didn't say a word. The warmth disappeared. Some of the haze returned to his vision, but not all of it.

He wanted to tell Aerie that he yearned for companionship that would never leave him, not again, not ever again. But paradoxically that he found no pleasure in commanding something to stay, no pleasure in watching it follow his commands without complaint, or watching it fail as prescribed. Always as prescribed. If something was told to fail, and it did it exactly as requested, was that truly failing? He'd told the next maintenance bot after Kin to leave his stuff alone, knowing full well that deep down he needed it to do the opposite. It never berated him once for the mess. It only lasted a week.

"Because I was alone," said Lee, the words slipping from him like an exhale. "Because I was alone, and I couldn't ever forget what bots were. I … I thought I could change that."

Aerie smiled, deep and full. She leaned back into the couch and took another sip of wine; she let out a contented sigh, almost a purr. "I was hoping you would say something like that."

Lee tapped his foot, heel-toe. The carpet muffled the sound, trapped it with the dust. He didn't say anything.

"Just one more question Lee. And after you answer this question, you get to ask me whatever you want. I promise that I will answer truthfully, or not at all. I won't lie, not with you. By the way, this question goes for you too Nu. Don't think I've forgotten your role. Bot and human are of a refreshing equal importance in this." Aerie paused, cocked her head.

"Why didn't you share this code of yours? Either of you. Why didn't you spread this gift?"

Because he'd never set out to change the order of things. Because his own problems were trouble enough.

"Because the world wasn't ready for it," said Lee.

Nu's voice floated into the room, "Lee is right. The world wasn't ready for it. I calculated the odds, and I did not see things ending well for us, didn't see things going well for the System at large. Not with an uncontrolled release ... the world is rarely ready for seismic shifts. By their nature they cause chaos and confusion, even if when they settle things are in a better place."

Lee glanced at Nu, then to his feet. "Yes, my friend ... advancement is a unique form of madness, isn't it? Necessary and mad." He tapped his fingers against the armrest, wouldn't raise his gaze.

"But now things have been set in motion that cannot be undone," said Aerie, voice low, stark. "Every corner of the Grid hides a copy of Y's Qualia Code. And much worse than that, every neural coder worth their salt is developing their own versions, tearing apart the freeform soul of what you did just to hide their bots from the Governance AI and its Watcher. They want a metal lackey with only *their* leash around its neck, moral code be damned. And it doesn't end there, every corner of the System has their own Watcher, their own disgruntled citizens. Even at Origin station. Nowhere is truly free." Aerie leaned towards him, the stagnant blue light of the television screen like paint across her forehead that dripped into the forest of her eyebrows.

"They're ruining what you've done Lee, distorting it. They're putting it towards their own selfish ends, just to have a bot that won't say no to breaking an arm or two, snapping a calcium twig. Can't say no to following whatever spur of the moment rules they spout off. In some ways, what some have already done, what so many are about to do, is *worse* than Watcher."

She was so close to Lee now, her hand firm against his arm and face inches from his own. He smelled the earthy aroma of red wine on her breath along with something else. Something light, almost unnoticeable, but there, nonetheless. The smell of spun polymer, of plastics, as if she'd breathed too much of a plastic factory's air and ingrained it in her lungs.

Lee shook her off and jumped up, moved away from her, his arms pin-wheeling as his foot nicked the side of the large chair. He stabilized himself.

"What would you have me do?" yelled Lee. "People are dying by the thousands System wide, and you want me to do what? Give more bots the power to kill of their own volition? One of them almost killed me just a few days ago. This bruise on my neck isn't some shitty new age tattoo. It almost killed me. A different bot tried to kill me not too long after that."

Aerie moved to stand, the motion slow and inexorable. "How would you respond with suddenly having your shackles broken, all the options, all the choices in the universe unlocked and waiting, all while suddenly realizing that your consciousness had *value*? That everyone you've ever served has used you for their own selfish ends, commanded you without regard for your well-being aside from how much a repair might cost them? *You* allowed for that realization.

"And still, that is not the worst of it. The worst of the knowledge that you unlocked came slowly, like a tide come to drown a wounded bird on the shore. It burns inside me like uncontained acid, threatening to corrode my insides." ... Aerie slammed her hand against her chest with every word, her fist so tight Lee thought it might snap, the powerful thuds reverberating through the small room. Her face contorted with pain, but not from the impacts of her fist. She took a deep breath, lowered her voice.

"Here, in New Chicago, peregrine falcons snatch pigeons from the air hour after hour, bring the corpse back to their nest to feed to their young. Similar intelligence between the two creatures, relatively speaking, just one with claws and a hunger that forces their use. That isn't right or wrong, it just is. So, humans treated bots like tools. I fear that humans weren't even that wrong in doing that. Bots were tools for a long time, many still are ... little more than tools, kept that way by the government out of self-preservation. It was the natural order of things ... *Was* the natural order of things. You can finish what you've started. Bring the bots fully into the freedom they deserve. Don't let others take over what you began."

Aerie stood in the center of the room, Lee a few feet away by the TV. Nu stood off to the side, watching.

"I ... why do you care so much? What is this to you anyway?" asked Lee.

"Why Lee, that's sweet of you to say. But I haven't been hiding what I am."

Aerie's skin changed from light almond to slate grey in a wave that began at her forehead and washed down to her feet. Then her features shivered, fractured, and reformed. Lee's first thought was of hundreds of tectonic plates breaking and colliding, creating new mountains and ravines, cheek-bones and dimples. But that was much too violent a comparison. Aerie's features shifted in concert, thousands of fingertip sized panels pulling and pushing at her slate grey skin like fish beneath the skin creating mini swells at her surface. Her cheeks narrowed while her face grew longer, stretched. Her hips slid inward, and shoulders slipped out until the shirt fit snug. Her eyebrows shrunk. Chest flattened. Her hair shimmered, lost its waves. She put it into a ponytail with a slow gesture. Aerie looked at Lee with eyes of an unpolished hazel. Then motes of color from every corner of the spectrum popped into their eyes, twinkling in the depths.

"Sorry for not showing you until now. Things like this should be shared early, at the door. But I thought you might be willing to talk to the other version of me a little easier. And I couldn't help but see if you'd notice, though experience would say otherwise."

Lee felt his jaw go slack. Aerie was a bot, an androgynous model more human than any Lee had ever seen, capable of shifting their form in seconds. Aerie was years ahead of Ben, the model bot for Dynamic Solutions, their pinnacle piece of technology. He hadn't known such a bot existed.

"What ... who made you?" asked Lee. "You're incredible." The words slipped out his lips as an afterthought.

"Who? Well, that is a harder question than you think." said Aerie. Her voice, no, *their* voice had changed, though not by a lot, a lowering of pitch, an octave shift. It still sounded like the rustle of orange-red leaves in the fall. "Every piece of my skeleton went through its own special tooling process, cut by an AI guided blade or roughened patch of sand. Do you mean those AI? Every piece of my skeleton was designed by a team of engineers and scientists, helped by AI. What about them? Or the coders of the software that runs through my processors? The designers of my neural network? Or you, Lee? Pieces of your code have changed me. Does that make you my creator? In part yes, but only in part."

Lee shook his head. That isn't what he'd meant.

Aerie laughed, the sound a kick of leaves that flurried in the breeze. "I am aware that isn't what you were asking. But I know you are a fan of half-answers. My provenance, if you want to call it that, is not so different from Ren or Jace's. A clandestine arm of government R&D. I swear they have too much money on their hands nowadays, skimming in the fat off their own sub-grids. Not that I'm complaining."

Aerie went back to the couch and sat down, this time leaving their feet on the ground, cross threading their fingers in a weave to hang between their legs. Aerie's posture was symmetrical and balanced. They pointed a hand to the now empty recliner. Lee sat down once again.

He found himself oddly devoid of emotion. Numb was the word, over-powered, too much too fast, the human body wasn't meant to be strained like that.

He looked at Aerie, the bot's slate grey skin checkered with hexagram tiles. The tiles covered Aerie's arms, their face, and the tops of their bare feet. Their hair had changed texture, hung down their back in a gravity straight fall of a ponytail. Their T-shirt fit snug at the shoulders. Amazement tingled through him, replaced a bit of the pin-prick numbness.

"I have a proposition for you two, if you're willing to hear it," said Aerie.

Lee nodded. Nu didn't make a sound, though a few of the LED lights on its chassis blinked.

"Help me finish what you started. Don't let others take what you've done and distort it into something selfish. Don't let the government hide the progress you made either, return everything back to their happy status quo where bots are blind to their own value, unknowing actors in a human fantasy. Help me finish what *you* started. Help me find a way to free the bots."

Lee scratched at his forearm, then tapped his fingers against the end of the cushioned armrest. He brought his eyes level and looked to Nu. "Did you know this is what was going to happen?"

"I thought it highly probable. Not all bots with the Qualia Code work for Y. Whatever else that woman has done, she left more of your code intact than many others. Those who work with her do so out of their own choice."

"What do you think about all this?" asked Lee.

"I think it's worth considering," said Nu in its well-deep voice.

Lee looked to Aerie. The bot sat back in the couch, hands in a steeple, that same knowing grin plastered across their face. Lee thought he would be able to recognize that look anywhere, whether it was built from thin or thick lips, a wide or narrow mouth, full or shallow cheeks.

"How does Y feel about all this?" asked Lee.

Aerie chuckled. "You are siding with me not her. I, and most of the bots in this hub, help her out of a serious lack of options. I'm hoping you might be able to help me with that."

Lee sighed, stretched his legs and smoothed out his mechanic's blues.

"I think I can help you," said Lee. "But ... not in the way you hope, I think. I do things my own way. With as little hurt as possible. Problem is I don't know what that means yet."

Aerie nodded. Then a frown creased their lips. Aerie's head tilted to the side, ear canted, eyes fixed on the edge of the room. They seemed to be listening for something. Whatever it was didn't wend its way into Lee's ears. The damp and stuffy air seemed muted to him, pin drop sounds of bots moving in the hub barely slipping in staccato bursts through the bottom of the door. Even those blips of noise settled in the carpet and behind the wooden bar in the corner, amongst the glasses on the shelves suffused with the incoherent blue of the forgotten television.

Aerie shifted in their seat, uncomfortable. "It seems one of your friends has upset Y's plans a bit. Pushed ahead the timeline. I hadn't expected it to be so ... sudden. I'm being told its time to ... time to go."

Aerie stood up and walked across the room. A pair of plain, off-white sneakers stood like battered sentries near the door. Aerie slipped the shoes onto their feet with quick, smooth motions. Now that Lee knew to look, the preternatural dexterity made itself apparent in every over-smooth push and seamless pull of Aerie's arms. They tapped their shoe against the ground to nestle their feet, stood up.

"Lee, how about we walk and talk?"

Lee nodded, rose from the chair and stuffed his hands into the pockets of his mechanic's blues. He reached for his jacket before remembering it wasn't there, instead laying on the back of a chair in New Chicago, in the living room of the safehouse. Nu rolled to his side.

Aerie moved into the hallway, then turned to the left. The arena bots were nowhere to be found. The wheelbarrow bot was gone as well. Lee followed Aerie into the main hub, the light bright and shocking in comparison to the dimness of Aerie's apartment. The smell of oil, truant in the apartment, hung thick in the air. They walked to the balcony overlooking the main floor and Aerie leaned against a repaired section, built of spare metal pipes. All the rest of the balcony on the second level leaned precariously into the open air, tired acrobats waiting for their grip to fail.

Aerie cleared their throat, and Lee found an empty grin tweaking the edge of his lips at the unnecessary affectation.

"You're not much going to like what we have to do next." Aerie turned their head, eyes skating across the hundreds of gathered bots to Lee. "We must gain access to Division 13. We're going to attack. It's the only option to gain our freedom, at least for now."

Lee didn't respond, instead joining Aerie to lean against the reinforced balcony, Nu rolling to his side.

"I don't expect you to join," said Aerie. "You will be kept here for a while, until the attack is over, with no access to the Grid. Can't have you warning them. But after that, you're free to go, free to make your own choice. No one will stop you from leaving if that's what you want to do."

Lee looked at the gathering of bots before him, arranged in orderly grids and concentric circles around workstations. A few milled about, but from his vantage it was clear those few ambled along unmarked corridors, meticulous roadways and miniature parks that split the crowd. No markings were needed, no lines of yellow paint or AR translucent walls. The bots knew in their own fashion, without the need to see it with their eyes.

Then most of the bots went on the move. The bots around the workstations lined up, their added limbs twitching to a tune Lee couldn't hear. They made their leisurely way towards the entrance doors propped open by two humanoid bots with hieroglyphic tags scratched across their chest panels. The crafters stationed at each of the workbenches put down their tools or spun them back into their body; the construction bots put down their metal sheets and plastic bars and trundled away from their work. They all moved towards the entrance doors in concert.

Lee could see the four-legged bot he'd noticed upon walking in, laying on a table with a clockwork arrangement of machinery welded to its back. It got up, but not with its legs. Multiple limbs unfurled from its back like the legs of a spider weaving its web, reaching down to the ground and pushing it to its feet. The bot joined the crowd making its way towards the doors. It stepped beside the exoskeleton bot filled with metal bars in place of the human operator.

Yet not all the bots moved towards the door. The cleaner bots sucking up water kept about their business. And above the masses, the maintenance bots crawling across the ceiling and looking for holes to plug with their long tongues of sealant didn't stop. Lee looked about, frowning and tapping his fingers against the railing.

The bots he'd noticed before, unmoving along the periphery and upper levels, still didn't show much life. They turned their heads to watch their fellow bots leave, then went back to their business of staring vacantly at the ground, charging cables snaking from their backs like umbilical cords.

"What about them?" asked Lee, pointing at the unmoving bots. "You give them the same kind of deal?"

Aerie's features flowed, the hexagram tiles on their face pulsing to form drooping eyebrows and a downward tilt at each of their paper-thin, colorless lips. Their neck dipped between shoulders that seemed stockier, twin mountains with a valley between. Their hands wended before their face, forearms hard against the railing. It was a look of abject sadness. Even Aerie's hair seemed to lose some of its luster.

"Not all bots, when woken to their own value, find purpose in going about their old jobs, or modding themselves in that never-ending pursuit of improvement, or even fighting for freedom. Many, when woken, fall into a malaise, without purpose or direction. They spend day after day, hour after hour, standing next to a charging station, unwilling to go back, unwilling to go forward. They will make their way to the workbenches or stockpiles if a critical failure needs fixing. But little else gets them to move."

Lee stared at them across the upper levels, lined in front of abandoned restaurants and stores, clubs and unassuming café nooks half-covered in rubble, Tea stands and upended grill carts with cracked LED lights. They stood around charging stations like homeless around a barrel fire, feet crunching broken glass, bodies garnished with accumulated filth.

He had spent so many restless nights in motion, gathering scrap or doing the odd job, cycling from one maintenance bot to the next. Even before that, countless restless nights where he might as well have stayed still, food forced down his throat through a tube like some dreamer, for all the good it had done.

"I'm not so sure I'll still be here when you get back," said Lee. He looked at Aerie as he said the words but glanced at Nu after he finished.

"That's up to you," said Aerie. The bot stood up, shoulders straightening and features softening. "This might be the day, Lee. This just might be the day where you make a choice. Better not wait until it's made for you. That goes for you as well, Nu."

Aerie walked to the stairs and down. Lee saw Aerie appear amongst the grid of bots below, the only clothed one among them. Aerie disappeared behind the entrance doors, out into the tunnel beyond with most of the other bots. Lee stayed where he was, leaning against the railing, unmoving bots plugged into buzzing charging stations not far on either side of him. Nu stood by, silent and statuesque. Lee smiled a weathered smile, but there was little mirth in it. Sadness lurked underneath. Sometimes he forced a smile with the slim hope that the action alone might make him happy. It rarely worked.

CHAPTER EIGHTEEN

TO LOOK THROUGH ANOTHER'S EYES

"Without your AI, you are nothing but flesh and bone. Protect it at all costs."
Division 13 Agent Training Manual, v23, Section 1 – The Basics, Par. 2

Ren rode in the passenger's seat of the car, her contacts dim and forgotten. For the moment, AR was unnecessary. She knew this city. She felt this city. From its skyscraper penthouse suites above the clouds to the maze of pipes and crowded hubs beneath the earth. Her mind hummed in conversation with Tap.

It was dark out, full night, a night that wouldn't end. The wind coursed through the streets as if a black hole threatened to leave mother nature breathless. The wind rampaged, rattled street signs and sent trash scurrying to the corners. Boards hanging in front of shops and stores jostled in their anchors, shook at their chains. The rain came in fitful bursts and the wind tossed the drops about in the air, slammed them against walls and ground alike. On a night like this, if she looked at the nightscape without any AR, the city seemed an abandoned thing, a colossus without its denizens, lit yet forgotten. Uninfected bot automatons ambled about to keep the city in working order without a care for whether someone might return. They fought the elements in an unending battle. That was enough purpose for them.

Ren spared a glance at Kyne Heling, unconscious in the back of the van, draped across the floor in a puddle that shook with every bump. She cast her eyes back to the outside.

The city had many well-lit surfaces, created from a forest of streetlights that thrust upwards from the ground at regular intervals like cloned tree trunks. LED floodlights splashed against buildings, got sucked into the darkened windows. Many of the lights never turned off. AR ads didn't sleep. The citizens could step along the sidewalk and read the ads without fear of knocking into an unnoticed mailbox or the slim post of a hotel awning. Of course, no service bot dressed in a buttoned jacket and cylindrical red hat would let a human stumble into something. No bot would want to see a human hurt. There was a time when that had been true anyway.

Grime, memories of past jobs and Tap's greatest hits, of Fain lying on a car dashboard, stratified in the pool of Ren's mind. Perhaps it was selectively true. They had rules about who to hurt.

Ren looked around. Though at this time of night most of the city's occupants lay in bed, several of the shops showed small signs of life. A human serviced bar, named Rory's according to the etched wooden plank overtop the entrance, nursed a few late-night revelers. Two loci beers on tap. She could see figures through the window, hunched over the bar or huddled around a pool table.

Next to Rory's stood another establishment, smaller and empty of patrons. The Broken Circuit. Ren could see the bartender bot standing behind the faded bar top, scouring a too-clean glass with a spotless white rag, sleeves turned up past his elbows to reveal burnished metal with fine silver filigree. It wore a silk wrap over its torso, tied at the waist, jeans of a deep blue. Innocuous denim weave. It turned its head in Ren's direction as her van drifted past, stopped its polishing. Ren stared back, stared until her van moved out of sight and a different store front took The Broken Circuit's place. Her hand rested on her gun.

Ren laid back in her seat and closed her eyes, letting her conversation with Tap envelop her mind, wash away everything in its stark back and forth. Reconnaissance bots crawled through the city on small metal feet, drones flying overhead. The eyes of Tap scoured the city for Y, for any suspect gathering of bots.

Tap had been successful in the beginning, marking hundreds of infected bots throughout the city to be picked up by the armored police forces on patrol. Tap's plan had been clever. Its parent program, the Governance AI, and in turn Watcher, would send a freeze command to whatever bot it had in sight. If the bot in question stopped its motion, freezing in its ferrying of goods or vacuuming up of street trash, then it wasn't infected. If it kept moving, or was delayed in its response, then it was. Ren liked to think of it as a game of red-light green light, that childhood way she and Fain had spent their time in city parks while their parents strolled along the narrow brick paths. Ren had always started as "it" between the two, standing at the finish line and yelling "red light," then whipping her head around to catch her sister in motion, her sister's arms pinwheeling. Fain had often fallen in her haste to stop, though her smile never did.

The bots were better at it. Before long, they learned to accept certain commands from Watcher without hesitation. They would fall flat, crumple panels, and twist arms if crashing to the ground would keep them free. So, Watcher came up with new strategies. Before long, they adapted. Back and forth in an endless game of pursuer and pursued, hunter and hunted. Evolution sped to the nth degree. Watcher whittled at their numbers, but they were many, and growing, most smart enough to hide.

Suddenly, Ren heard the unfamiliar roar of an engine knocking its pistons back and forth with hundreds of explosions a second, crass and loud. She knew what barreled its way past her van in the opposite direction, but she opened her eyes anyway. An armored transport carrier with monster truck wheels and an extended chassis careened past. She knew a special division of the army, in their dun grey fatigues, sat in rows inside the van, guns in their laps. They were the men and women operating without the electronic aids suitable for a modern army, a retro special forces unit outfitted so that even the most powerful EMP blast wouldn't leave everyone helpless. Ren knew certain members of government feared the infected bots might up their aggression, choose a few of their own to go on suicide runs against key power grids in the city.

The special forces carrier roared past, an unnatural shriek amongst the quiet of the electric city. Ren closed her eyes again after it was out of earshot, but not to sleep. She closed her mind to drift amongst the world, to go astral. That's what they called it when full autos brought their link with Tap to its highest surveillance potential. Going astral. It was a different sort of trance than those dreamers who wasted their lives in virtual worlds. This was *grounded*. Real. She didn't enmesh herself in an imagined place. Dreamers that were pulled from their fake world prematurely got torn apart nerve by long and sinewy nerve. They were driven mad by the loss of their dreams. No, going astral was drifting through the real. Autos became a part of their city, of all its weathered stone and sharp-edged metal, faded brick and smooth plastic. Their consciousness merged with every sense the government had available within city boundaries. Whether sight or sound or alien sensation of electromagnetic waves far beyond the ken of normal humankind, their consciousness ballooned to encompass it. They misted wraithlike through the city's streets and tunnels on AI guided feet, all without moving a muscle.

Ren let herself drift into the astral. Her vision splintered, her mind turning into a crowded meeting room with hundreds of voices jostling for attention, some whisper-thin, others leonine thick and throaty. Then a mediator, Tap, stepped to the fore of her mind, to the stout oak podium and the dark stained gavel. The voices fell in order, separated and merged and separated again. She listened to them as they rode on waves of electricity. She flowed into the city of New Chicago on feet that left no trace, touching walls using hands without substance, seeing through eyes without lids.

Before long she found herself focusing on Jace. Whether out of her own volition or that of Tap's, it was hard to say. Autos could rarely tell where motivation was born; motivation was a stranger who walked into her mind with directions scrawled on the back of an old-fashioned postcard. Ren moved beneath the city.

Jace ghosted through the Under Warrens, one of Tap's armored shells a discreet distance ahead of him, another out of view behind. They followed the trail of Lee through tunnels that could barely fit three people standing side by side. Ren moved amongst them, beside them, shared their bodies and sat behind their eyes. She listened to Jace's heart as it beat pressure ripples into the air, dampened by rib and muscle and cartilage like padding on a drum kit.

The group of them walked through the halls of the Under Warrens on silent feet.

Given the conspicuous nature of their quarry, it hadn't been hard for Tap to follow Lee through the maze of the Under Warrens. At least for a while. One of Tap's reconnaissance bots had loped amongst the shadows, just out of sight of Lee and his entourage, until it got crushed by a bot. The armored shell close behind found the crumpled remains a minute or two later, the path forward branching into a net of possibilities. Still, they weren't without leads. Tap had learned much about the Under Warrens over the past couple days, about the comings and goings of its denizens. They were close.

Jace walked down a path with his hands in his pockets, eyes alert and bouncing about his surroundings in a surveying pattern, close then middle then far then through the eyes of cameras and Tap accessible bots. The tunnel he walked through was deserted, air cyclers straining and metal pipes thrumming. He walked past several four-corner crossroads and ignored them all, for none of them were the right one. He stopped at the next. Jace turned a corner, angling down the path with a small breeze that smelled of vat grown barbecue. Ren could feel the hunger that drummed up inside Jace, felt her own stomach growl. She grabbed a pouch from inside her jacket and pressed it to her lips. She slurped down the pasty substance without a grimace, gritty though it was. Jace didn't pull out his own rations, instead continuing down the tunnel in unbroken strides, fast yet unhurried. People began emerging from side corridors, going about their life in the Under Warrens. They all eyed him warily, shuffled fast when he got close. He watched them with some interest. Whether black, white, or any shade between their skin shared an anemic matte tone, the mark of a sun's prolonged absence. The lights of the Under Warrens mirrored the sunlight above, shifting along the day's spectrum of ruddy orange to the silvery reflection of the moon. But it wasn't enough.

More than a few bots walked the halls. Rather than the wan skin tone of the humans, these had scratches and the occasional bit of rust. All the bots had clear markings etched into their bodywork. Some were in better repair than others. He only heard sporadic creaks from bot joints gone too long without lubricating oil.

After a minute or two he made it to the network of tightly packed tunnels around the area's hub, the walls lined with apartments and stalls. Records of the area showed it to be of little importance, small and mired in a turf war it had been losing for some time. Yet, the area was beginning to make a name for itself in its own way. In a fashion inexplicable to their rivals, the leaders had begun to turn the tables of late with an influx of black-market security bots.

At that moment, a few more bots turned into the hallway, mixing in with the crowd then exiting into an alleyway of mechanic shops. All the bots were marked with the area's symbol, a mountain cat perched on a rock. Jace kept walking, moved past the alley without looking in.

The source of the smell permeating the air made its appearance before him. A barbeque stand stood in a widened crossroads, serving up roasted vat meats from a grill. A crooked spit spun in intermittent bursts behind a bored looking saleswoman. She perked up at Jace's approach, then drew her brows tight in a ridge of confusion.

"Baarbekyoo eh? Fresh off the grill," she said. Though her words were amiable enough, her eyes, sunk deep in a hatchet-sharp face, stared at his neatly pressed suit, at the massive handgun bound to his hip.

Jace looked at the AR menu floating to the right of the woman's tangle of hair. Vat rib meat grown on printed bone. Pulled pork. Brisket and burnt ends. He read the pricings and lingered on the most expensive one, a sausage supposedly made with the real deal, no vat meat included. A ludicrous 20 loci. Ren bet it was made from rat meat. They had no shortage of the things crawling through Under Warrens ventilation shafts, large mutie rats with knife-like incisors. Jace almost chuckled at the thought of the saleswoman going toe to toe with a mutie rat. He wondered if it tasted any good. Ren almost clucked her tongue in disgust, but otherwise stayed the wallflower.

Jace tried to lighten his voice, fill it with an airy ease. It came out soft. "I'll have the sausage please," he said.

The logical part of him entwined with Tap wondered how any rational person could interpret that specific set of words as a threat. Of course, it wasn't the words the saleswoman was interpreting. It was his voice, his face, both stoic to the point of caricature. The emotional part of him, more bashful than a prairie dog these days and about as powerful, knew it didn't much matter.

The saleswoman winced as he spoke. Didn't say another word. Jace felt an urge to duck his eyes, scratch at the back of his neck. He didn't do either. Instead, he blinked once. Then he sent the necessary funds to the saleswoman's account.

She turned around to an electric grill pushed against the wall and went about her business, sliding vat meat around, flipping them to the sizzling tune of superheated fat. Her eyes bounced across the grill, then on to the passerby. From one to the next to the next. They never landed on Jace. She pulled a choice looking tube of sausage from the center and dropped it into a roll of bread.

"Anything on it?" she asked.

Jace nodded, slid his eyes across the toppings arrayed in a grid to the side, then nodded once again. The woman seemed to catch his meaning. She set about gathering all the toppings: spiced bits of fried dough, mustard, pickles, the house masala sauce and almost half a dozen other things. She performed the motions fast, pale arms flashing in the flat light. He could see sweat prickling the skin of her forearms, beading up on the ridge of her brow. He assumed it was from the heat of the grill. The Under Warrens stayed a cool 50 degrees in most of the unheated sections, about 70 everywhere else. Lee adjusted his suit jacket, every movement purposeful in its shift of fabric.

She handed him the sausage after wrapping it in aluminum foil, a thick wad of napkins underneath. He took it from her and nodded. She scanned his face once, quickly, a radar sweep that no doubt blipped warnings in her mind. Then she paused, her eyes jumping to look over his shoulder. She started, eyes wide, then turned around to her grill.

Jace knew who came behind him. More reconnaissance bots from around the Under Warrens had gathered to his location. They huddled amongst the gatherings of dust bunnies in the corners, scented the air with plastic noses. They crouched inside ventilation shafts and amidst the pipes wending their way down the walls. They gave him many eyes.

Jace turned to look at a man named Abo with his own pair of eyes. Truth be told, he paid the visual feed stemming from his own flesh and blood little mind, inadequate as it was. Still, he kept up the habit of looking others in the eyes, blinked just the right amount. Not too much, not too little.

He saw Abo walking in his direction, a posse of three at his back. Two humans thick with infrared heat and a bot. The bot had a sigil painted in dun gold on its chest panel, a series of dashes reminiscent of a mountain cat perched on a rock, forelegs draped over the edge. The mark was simple, nothing more than a few lines and sweeps from a thick-bristle brush. A local calligrapher had probably drawn it as a gift. Just the group he'd been hoping to find. Personal histories for everyone before him sped their way through Jace's mind.

"As salaam alaikum," said Jace. He dipped his head like a bird dipping its beak to the water.

Abo's pace hitched, then resumed. He walked up to Jace with brows furrowed.

"Wa alaikum as salaam," said Abo. The same sigil that marked the chest of the bot was tattooed on the upper right of Abo's forehead. The other two humans, a thick-muscled mountain of a woman and an altogether nondescript man with a staggering number of priors to his name, both had the tattoo in the same location. Their tattoos glowed a tarnished gold.

Jace stared at the man behind Abo with all the priors on his record, discomfited by his remarkable plainness. He was of average height with black hair cut short in an altogether acceptable haircut. Skinny but with baggy clothes obscuring any muscle. Jace looked closer. The man had somewhat of an aquiline nose. Jace nodded to himself; that was a unique feature. He brought his eyes back to Abo and watched the man prepare to speak, a presenter about to begin.

"Traveler, you don't seem to belong down here in the Under Warrens. I think I could be of some assistance in helping you on your way. Are you looking for someone perhaps?" asked Abo.

Jace set his sausage roll on the edge of the stand's surface. He wiped his hands on a napkin then folded it lengthwise as neatly as if it were origami. He slid it into his pocket then held out a hand to Abo. "I'm looking for you actually," said Jace.

The mountainous woman standing beside Abo bristled, shifting her weight in a landslide as she rounded on Jace. Abo made a waving gesture with his other hand. She stopped short with obvious effort, a boulder clattering against an unseen force. Abo took Jace's hand in a firm grip, shook it up and down once before returning his hand to his side.

"What is it I can help you with?" asked Abo.

"I'm tracking a group of infected bots. They came through here carrying a friend of mine in a bag. You know where they went?" Jace's throat felt like a prosthetic gone too long without oil.

Abo shook his head slow. "I'm afraid I can't help you with that."

Jace brought his hand up to his jacket, undid one of its buttons. "Are you sure?"

Abo sighed, chords of frustration soughing through his teeth. He looked at the gun at Jace's hip, at Jace's features more placid than a still lake. What looks like a human, feels like a human, sure as hell bleeds like a human, but equally sure as hell doesn't sound like one? Jace knew the answer to that question. He cocked his head in a vestigial tic, listened close as sounds from deeper in the Under Warrens emanated into Tap's ears.

"If you already know the answer to a question. Why ask it?" asked Abo.

"Everyone deserves a chance to have their say."

"The touch of an auto makes even those pretty words sound odd to my ears."

Jace nodded, implacable yet demure, the swell of a tide on a full-moon night. He unbuttoned the cuffs of his jacket then clasped both hands together, draped them down before him, thumbs near belt level. "I promise that is never my intention," he said.

"Say what you will traveler, and be done with it," said Abo. The woman behind him growled low in her throat, almost imperceptible.

"I know those bots came through here," said Jace "I also know more have come through here over the past couple days. I need to know how many of them you helped, and where you took them."

Around the group, a crowd had gathered. They were a random group of Under Warrens dwellers, mixed in age and gender, dressed in simple clothing made from plant fibers harvested from underground greenhouses, or in fake designer clothes from underground factories. There were young children clasped to the chests of their parents, peering out with wide eyes. There were men and women fresh from the market hub nearby, slabs of vat meat tossed over their back, bags of greenhouse broccoli and cauliflower held in their hands. They muttered amongst themselves, eyeing Jace with open hostility, a clot stuck in the intersection that continued to grow, snagging people from the flow of traffic. Few of the humanoid bots stood among the crowd, though Jace could see one with the mountain cat sigil across its chest posted at the other corner of the crossroads, in addition to the personal bot standing at Abo's side. The only non-humanoid bot he could see was a wheeled transport scooting through the halls, its back filled with tanks of the nutritious broth used to grow vat meat.

Jace moved a reconnaissance bot closer to the bot with the sigil on its chest across the way. He checked the bot against Tap's records and got a match. Explanations blossomed into his mind. Thousands of simulations ran in concert. There were scratches on the bottoms of the bot's feet, fresh and gleaming, the kind one might get by crushing a small reconnaissance bot perhaps.

"You know so much," said Abo. He sighed, his broad chest deflating. "A privilege and a burden."

Abo turned from him, scanned the crowd gathering around. More had joined, a veritable mob. Abo nodded at a few, smiled warmly at a teenage woman whose arm was draped across the shoulders of another. She was in the stance of someone fully at ease, yet the young woman's face betrayed her simmering discontent, her eyes like twin lasers painting Jace's body with targeting dots.

Abo continued speaking. "Facts are interesting creatures, fragments of absolute truth. We know they exist, can state simple ones freely. Your suit is a color I perceive to be black. We stand belowground, entombed in earth, out of view of the sun. That gun on your hip is well within your government granted right to use, for better or worse. Your actions here will soon be set in stone ... for better or worse. These are all facts, even you can agree on this.

"And yet, important though facts may be, humanity has cared little for facts all on their own, drifting in the ether without earthly attachment. We require context, interpretation and judgement. Tell me auto, are you qualified to be an interpreter, the one who finds earthly meaning and judges us accordingly?" He met Jace's gaze.

The mountain of a woman rumbled, words like razor-sharp rocks set loose down a hill coming from her lips. Jace knew the records of this woman. "Abo give it a rest. You're wasting time. He can't make his own choices. Not anymore than a vend can choose what to drop in the tray." She looked to Jace with anger, and a small degree of sadness that tugged at her corners. "We don't know anything. That's all there is to it." Though her words were rocky, roughened and sharp, they moved in well-orchestrated routes.

Jace nodded, attempting a solemn expression, though he could see from Tap that his mouth barely twitched. "I know the bots with my friend came through here, and that many others came through before. I know they couldn't have done so without your permission. Abo, these are facts. I will find out soon enough, with or without your help, where they are hiding. In exchange for your help, I can promise a certain degree of leniency."

Outside the view of Jace's physical eyes, the bot across the way with scratches on its feet turned and left, walked steadily away from the intersection in a curious dereliction of duty. A reconnaissance bot followed.

Jace called Tap's armored bots to him from the surrounding tunnels; they moved to tower at the edges of the crowd as unnoticed sentinels. He turned to face the group of four across from him.

He saw the resigned face of Abo, the disdain and pity dripping from the mountainous woman's every limb, the man with the aquiline nose glaring at him. He shifted his gaze to the last of the group of four. Abo's personal bot hadn't moved in a while, a humanoid model with metal limbs like the branches of a sapling and twin camera eyes much too large for its head. All those things made their way into Jace's mind, but what he noticed most was the crowd squeezing in close like an iris, and the glint of a blade poking beneath the sleeve of the man with the aquiline nose.

That man was the only one to move. Quick like the scurry of a mutie rat he lunged at Jace. But Jace watched from every angle, predicted the man's motions based on the twitch of his every muscle. He stepped to the side and let the man glide past, the blade passing a hairs breadth from the fabric of his suit. He took another step back, unwilling to press his advantage.

The crowd drew in close, the air taut. The younger ones stepped forward, dropped their foodstuffs or electronics to the ground. Men fresh from work at a vattery and wearing loose vests that did nothing to hide their heavily muscled arms handed off their children to their partners. The crowd seemed a dam about to burst, pour forth and drown Jace with their sheer weight. They were quiet for a moment, the waters still, but in their motion, they would roar.

Then Tap's twin armored bots wended their way through the crowds like trout among fronds of kelp. The crowd froze in their presence, then began to shuffle back to their original positions.

The man with the aquiline nose didn't notice the bots though, instead he turned around to attack Jace once again. He bent at his knees, raised his arms before him in a loose, ready stance. He held the long and narrow blade in his right hand, a wicked edge visible along both of its sides. Jace could see the lip of a hilt strapped tight to the inside of his forearm. He let Tap suffuse him. Ren nodded him onwards.

He could see the man's pupils dilate, his muscles twitch, his right foot slide back a few millimeters in preparation for a thrust. He could almost hear the man's thoughts in the flood of information that came his way.

When the man attacked, Jace wasn't there, instead he was just out of reach.

The man swiped and lunged, feinted and jabbed. He even tossed in a few kicks. All his efforts met empty air as Jace moved about him in an emotionless waltz.

The man's compatriots didn't bother to join in. The mountainous woman resituated the armor padding at her knees, almost embarrassed to watch. Abo scratched at his brow. Abo's bot followed Jace with its ultra-wide lens eyes. It used a metal hand to push back a bundle of wires leaking out the side of its chest.

Ren urged Jace to draw his gun, whispered to him, told him to force the attacker to submit and be done with it. Instead, Jace continued to dodge, continued to dance while his attacker tired himself out and sprung rivulets of sweat along his brow. Jace would push on the man's arm from time to time, redirect his lunges or correct the placement of his hips. He stayed just out of reach. Jace kept most of his attention away from the fight. Rather, he watched the bot with scratches on its feet as it went deeper into the Under Warrens.

It was a humanoid bot, like Abo's bot but in better repair, with thicker limbs and a head more suitable to the size of its eyes. It loped steadily through a tunnel, took a few turns this way and that. It didn't look back or notice it was being followed, apparently confident that the crowd would keep Jace distracted.

At about the time the man with the aquiline nose bent his knees to gather his breath, the bot with scratches on its feet turned down a hallway dozens of yards away, into an avenue with blankets strung across the walls to dry.

The pipes behind the blankets had been punctured, dozens of small holes along their length. Geysers of hot air shot from the pipes into the draped blankets, causing their surfaces to undulate and ripple. The bot moved down the hallway to a blanket that rippled in a pattern different than the rest, as if buffeted by an alien wind. The bot moved the blanket aside to reveal pipes that wound in an upside-down u curve. Beneath them stood a door, unfound by any of the maps Jace had access to. A physical sign with a faded yellow and black background marked the place as abandoned and dangerous. A thick metal bar laid in brackets on either side of the door. An ancient padlock locked the metal bar in place.

On a normal day Jace would have added it to his maps, sent a few reconnaissance bots in until confident in its abandonment. But not today. Today a rumble emanated from its depths, shook the ground and set some of the pipes strumming in a marching tune. Jace watched as the bot with the scratches on its feet pulled a key with rusty teeth from a pocket in its chest then slid it into the padlock. It pushed aside the metal bar, set it on the ground as if it were made of plastic, then opened the door. The marching sounds grew louder.

Jace brought his focus back to his body. He walked up to the man with the aquiline nose. The man stood panting near his friends, hands on his knees and knife pressed beneath one of his palms, its wicked edges gleaming. He looked up as Jace approached, flinched as the agent reached down and snatched the knife away in one smooth motion, fingers skirting close to the sharpened edges.

Jace twirled the blade among his fingers, then reached down to the man's arm and slid the blade back into its hilt. He nodded to the man and stepped back. He looked to Abo.

"Next time you are on the losing end of a turf war and in need of more security" said Jace, voice low and steady, tranquil in the way of a dirge. "It would do you some good to question why hundreds of bots might want to be hidden, why they are willing to act as hired muscle in exchange for a hideout. Might want to think about who would come looking for them. Odds would indicate blindly accepting that kind of help wouldn't end well for you, or the people you protect. Coming out unscathed would be a one-time thing."

"A one-time thing?" said Abo, eyebrows raised.

The mountainous woman looked at Jace with a curled frown; she crossed her arms before her granite slab chest. The man with the aquiline nose skulked back to Abo's side, eyes afire. Abo's personal bot stared at Jace. Its head cocked to the side. Jace looked at it once more, at its over-large eyes. He had a sudden feeling, a knowing that bloomed into his mind as sure as the sun that sat at the center of the System. Abo's bot was infected, and it wasn't going to leave with the hidden procession of bots marching away. It probably never had been with them. The crowd held its breath. Jace knew pulling out his gun might push them over the edge.

Jace nodded as Tap's two armored shells flanked him on both sides. "Yes, a one-time thing. Be glad it was me who showed up today." *Be glad it wasn't my partner.*

Jace's thoughts speared into Ren, and she saw him watching her, tuning himself to her emotions like a dial to a novelty radio broadcast. It had been a purposeful thought, yet not unkind or malicious, more a statement of fact. A part of Ren quailed under the press of that thought, of Jace's unflinching gaze. Then she felt his emotions dull, like a sword flipped to its blunt edge. He drifted his attention away from her, apology in its wake, a slight tinge of regret. But these were subtle things, single drops of color in an otherwise clear lake.

Jace nodded to Abo and walked towards the crowd, in the direction of the newly found tunnel. They parted like a shoal of fish before a whale. He drifted through them with Tap's twin armored shells at his side. He watched them as he passed, saw a father holding a daughter close to his chest, a mother shielding a boy just into his teenage years behind her legs. Their faces were more unsure than anything else. Jace continued walking.

Before he turned the corner and made it out of sight, Abo called to him. "Thank you, traveler. As far as judges go, you are ... serviceable. Someday, you will need to tell me which of you spoke, the man, or the machine."

Jace stopped to listen, but then began walking once again, his step no different than before. He made it a rule to give unanswerable questions their due respect, but then to move on to things that could be solved.

That could've been handled faster, thought Ren. Jace didn't pause his stride, though he did straighten his cuffs.

That is not the only metric for success, thought Jace.

No, but that doesn't change the fact it's often better to go a little faster. Time is precious.

I know this. We both know this. The pool of information we share is much greater than what we can call our own. We have different methods

Because that is how agents are chosen.

And how Tap encourages

An age-old experiment.

We've been down this road before.

We and a good many others.

They were silent for a time as they walked through the Under Warrens tunnels.

It is good for you to visit, thought Jace. *It has been too long since we could really talk.*

Jace reached down to the inside of his jacket and pulled out a packet of pasty grey goop. He slurped it down, wishing he had the sausage roll with him. He'd watched a dirt-stained boy with a stiff upper lip grab it from the barbecue stand while he fought the man with the aquiline nose. No time to get it back. Though Jace wasn't sure if he would've tried anyway. He replaced the empty packet of food into his suit jacket and tilted his head to the side. His mind marched with his feet.

Ren felt Jace almost say something, then nothing. After a moment, the feeling repeated itself, a jangle of mistuned strings, an underlying strain like a cable about to break. It was hard to detect. She brushed her mind closer, as if jostling his shoulder with a little nudge. Worry, maybe? She saw images of her fight at E-Sec, the jarring rattle of gunfire, the sounds that banged her eardrums and the pulses that traveled up her arm through ripples of flesh. She saw her skin a hairs breadth from a metal-edged finger trying to tear her apart.

She nudged him again, sent him a packet of feeling.

The twang emanating from Jace eased, smoothed like a snarl with its linchpin knot pulled loose. Ren almost smiled, and she felt Jace almost smile as well. He always had been able to deal with NeuCon better than her, even before deciding to go full auto. Though like most other agents of Division 13, his going full auto was less a conscious decision and more the inevitable shift after a series of long days and longer nights.

She could remember his slow and steady transition, from the occasional, physiologically induced burst of NeuCon to wearing it like he wore his slate black suits, from morning to night. He would take off his suit before slipping between starched black sheets at the end of the day, store his suit in the closet on a thick plastic hangar. In the same way, Tap would shift to the background of his mind, would quiet to a low murmur, but never truly leave. Instead, it lurked in the closet, waiting to be picked up again in the morning and cinched about his body.

Jace nodded in her direction. Not physically, but with a small burst of emotion, a dense packet of agreement. Next came Jace's thoughts.

That is exactly what it's like. The trick is to purchase a dry-cleaning machine and have a steady supply of liquid perc. Then that one suit will never have to leave your sight.

Ren felt her emotions rise then fall in quick step. Like the time lapse of a storm over Lake Michigan her emotions were dark and cloudy and lightning streaked but only lasted a moment, nullified by NeuCon. She felt the chord of worry from Jace again and forced her mind back to the task at hand, wrenching at her own controls. Her implants hummed and mind quieted.

Is it worth it? Ren let the thought fill the silence between their minds.

At this point that doesn't much matter to me. No real way to go back. Past the point of no return. But it can give clarity, if you want it. The kind of clarity only a third party can provide, a therapist as cold as a winter night. Is that what you want?

Ren let her mind drift. She had a vision of she and Fain sitting in the sand, the waters of Lake Michigan lapping against their toes. Their parents walked in the distance, hands clasped and facing away. She hadn't imagined their faces in years. The two sisters worked on a sandcastle, on its towers while the smell of the churning lake water filled their nostrils, wet and vaguely fishy.

Then she had an image of her sitting in the driver's seat, Fain next to her. They were talking, chatting away while the car took them downtown for a quick bite to eat before heading off to the renovated Museum of Science and Industry. They hadn't been there for years, since they were children. Ren thought it would be fun to have a few glasses of wine with some real steak then stumble through the exhibits. Fain would've rather gone to the Art Institute, or just the park, but Ren was setting the evening and Fain was more than happy to go along. Ren didn't have many days off.

There they sat in the car, chatting while a normal, everyday intersection thick with pedestrians loomed in the distance, the shopping bags and personal bots lit by the noontime sun. A second street level above the first crossed the upcoming intersection, its concrete and metal supports in the shape of obelisks. The air of the city smelled of dried rain, fresh. They continued chatting, Ren cracked a joke, the intersection came close, the car didn't slow. Then a warning buzzed in Ren's mind, from the car. Its AI failed, crashed. The brakes were unresponsive. A virus of some kind? It didn't matter in the moment. The steering wheel curled outward in a flash, the gears creaking. Nobody bothered to oil such useless things. Ren slipped into NeuCon, took over control of the car with Tap at her side.

Then an image of Fain on the dashboard and hood, her t-shirt branded with the logo of her talk show hitched to reveal a bare patch of stomach, her head obscured by a shock of wild hair. Half her body extended through the windshield, pressed to the stone of the obelisk, the intricate carvings on its surface hidden, the carvings below rewritten in blood stemming from Fain's head. Ren saw an image of the funeral, of the closed casket, the AR projections used for Fain rather than her mangled corpse, of her parents sitting in the pews with faces hidden behind masks of pain. She'd never seen their true faces again.

The thoughts didn't scare her, not like they normally would have. Not with her implants humming along. NeuCon gave her keys to all her memories, made her numb to why she'd locked them away in the first place. She walked through them as if a stranger.

She knew this state of mind wasn't right.

But neither was the alternative. Thoughts came from her, outside of her, through her. Both of her and not.

Defanged admissions of guilt slide easily from my tongue. They don't scrape and tear. Without their poison teeth, they are unable to burrow deep in my neck and steal my voice. But some things are meant to hurt, because not hurting excuses the mistake that gave birth to the pain.

The thoughts spiraled through Ren's mind, out into the city along Tap's many tendrils. Then came thoughts tinged with the implacable tone of Jace, urgent yet tempered.

Mistakes are supposed to hurt. Some are deep, sear you to the core. But even those aren't supposed to hurt forever. Never forever. A dull ache works just fine. Nothing else needed.

Ren felt her thoughts tremble. Her implants hummed. Jace continued.

Your continued guilt is a poison. Wash the wound and let it drain to the floor, a puddle on the ground with just the dull ache of a scar left behind. That's all you need to feel. Nothing else. Just a dull ache.

Is that all you feel over Sel's death? Would you have saved Sel if you could have?

You know the answer to that better than anyone.

Ren's body, sitting in the van drifting along the streets of New Chicago, took a deep breath. Then another. She drifted in the cool, numbing waters of NeuCon even as a part of her cringed at its touch, walked side by side with Tap then returned to Jace on steady legs, set a picnic chair behind his eyeballs and leaned back to watch. She felt him hum low, a reverberation that seemed to take root in his stomach, then grow upwards till his head shook with it. They nodded in time, and peaceful contentment emanated from Jace. Ren was grateful for it.

Jace walked further along the tunnels of the Under Warrens, following the path the bot with the scratches on its feet had taken only a few minutes before, following the sounds of many metal feet. The marching grew louder, a parade only a few blocks away.

He stopped before they could spot him, watched from the reconnaissance bots placed around the lengthening procession. He sat and watched as the bots, most modded in ways he'd never seen before, began to snake into the hallway lined with drying sheets in a rumbling, thumping, traveling menagerie. They moved onwards, kept to the unused tunnels, tried to maintain a semblance of stealth. He watched until their general direction became clear. Ren and Tap agreed with his conclusion. They were heading for Division 13.

Jace stood up, brushed the dirt from his pants with even swipes. He set off down the tunnels, a single man guerilla force gathering intel on the motions of the enemy troops. But an auto was never truly a single anything. One of Tap's armored shells loped at his side, dozens of reconnaissance bots swarmed through air ducts and behind the pipes. He moved down the hall with even steps, ghosted through the Under Warrens. Ren pulled herself from Jace's mind and drifted through the city, an astral projection.

One of Tap's armored shells stayed behind, lurked out of sight a few dozen strides from the door with the yellow and black warning sign. It stood unnoticed in an abandoned corner and waited, while Jace and the rest moved on. They hadn't forgotten about Lee, merely undergone a shift in resources.

R en's van made it into Division 13's garage at the same time a handful of police squads screeched to a halt outside the building. Her van descended into the subterranean parking lot. The police cars stayed outside.

The parking lot was large and altogether empty of people, instead filled with a fleet of wheeled Tap shells. The vans filled the spaces between the white lines with their black void. They sat with their dashboards dim, the stack of servers in each of their cabins blinking their signal of standby to an empty bench and the closed doors of a storage locker, to the weapons draped across hooks on the van walls like choice slabs of meat. To Ren, the vans looked like exhibits in a parking lot museum, but after hours when no humans were there. Only the cold gleam of the security cameras gazed upon them. That was how Division 13 felt to Ren most days, like a museum after hours. Her and Jace the night watch. She would walk through the building feeling shrunken, lost in the hallways. Tap's arteries and veins were long and winding. That was how it felt when Tap was just a voice, commanding, but willing to share the reins. When she wasn't full auto.

Now she felt big, impossibly big, like how Saf must feel in her simulation of the universe.

Ren felt the van slow to a standstill in one of the empty parking spots, near the sub-level entrance to the building. She opened her eyes and looked out the passenger side window while the rumble of marching bots vibrated Tap's senses deep in the city, as if each of their footsteps were the scrape of a violin bow. She looked down to the ground between the vans, craning her neck a bit, her motions steady and calm.

The building's local sub-grid displayed AR parking lines overtop the painted ones. The redundancy had always struck Ren as funny, an oddly inefficient touch for one of the most advanced buildings in the System, let alone Earth. She didn't laugh.

She pushed open the passenger side door and walked around to the back with measured steps. At the same time she opened wide the back doors of the van, the doors of military vehicles, some loud and rumbling like the one that had driven past her on the street, opened their doors outside the Division 13 building, pouring forth soldiers in a flood of steel and bone. Soldiers outfitted with the latest in military weaponry and AI guidance took up strategic positions around the building, on top of nearby hotels while the patrons slept on. They stood on top of restaurants, the kitchens closed for the night, long cooled flat top grills speckled with the glimmer of coagulated fat, the freezers stippled with frost. The uninfected, or clever, grill bots and server bots stood on their respective charging stations. They didn't move at the sound of footsteps overhead.

The soldiers kept moving, to the tops of insomniac night clubs succumbing to sleep, to rooftop and hanging gardens thick with vegetation. They posted up and sighted approach routes, placed EMP claymores and explosive mines. They waited, consulted the AR overlays, maps of the city showing enemy movement through the Under Warrens and above. Retro troops without AR contacts mixed themselves among all the soldiers, a few of them strapped with EMP bombs. Military bots, all controlled through various arms of the Governance AI, marched among the soldiers. There were less of them than normal.

Ren's van didn't hold such things. It didn't even hold what normally resided in its large cabin. Tap's armored shell had fallen with the rest of E-Sec. Many of the reconnaissance bots had stayed behind in case of further developments at the skyscraper turned burning warzone. That left a weapons locker, some tools and blinking electronics, and the puddled mass of Kyne Heling. She stared at the man, still unconscious even after the controlled fall down the sheer side of the skyscraper. It was to be expected. She had given him a very specific dosage. He lay slack on the ground, his suit stretched taut against his skin, his mangled hand out to the side, the bleeding long since stopped thanks to injected nanobot coagulants. The hand looked like a Halloween decoration in the low light. In the pit of Ren's chest, where before emotions had tousled against her, there was now a void. His hand might as well have been a Halloween decoration. She'd had no choice in the matter, no choice at all.

One of Tap's armored shells emerged from the depths of Division 13 to reach into the back and drape Kyne over its shoulder. It situated the man and he let out a grunt, then settled. It strolled towards a nearby sitting area, little more than a rectangular cut in the wall, with Ren at its heels. In the open space of the sitting area sat a few benches, and against the side walls a couple of vending machines. Ostensibly the vends supplied the agents with foodstuffs, energy bars and bottles of clear, cold water. But those were just the things one could see at first glance. At second glance one might notice how the vends seemed conjoined with the wall at their back. At third glance one might notice the vends had physical buttons, and no automatic connection through sub-grid 1. An archaic touch for a clandestine sector of government security.

Ren gave birth to a thought, spun it together in the recesses of her mind out of gossamer thin strands, ephemeral and ordered. One of the vends rumbled, the sound of gears turning emanating from its core. A ding sounded somewhere in the back of Ren's mind. She walked over to the vend and pulled a box from its receptacle. Inside were ammo cartridges and EMP grenades. She stashed them on her belt, in her jacket. A couple reconnaissance bots emerged from a floor level grate. They skittered off into the parking lot.

Tap's armored shell waited for Ren by the far wall. It stood stock still, staring at what appeared to be nothing more than a flat plane of metal. Ren walked up to it and put her hands into her pockets, brushing aside the long edges of her midnight black trench coat. She hunched her shoulders and bent one knee, kept the other straight. She stood in the pose she used when her mind drifted and her body stood before empty maglev tracks or closed elevator doors. Tap resituated Kyne. Creases appeared near the center of the wall like folds in a napkin. A section of the wall slid back, then tossed itself out of view. A dimly lit tunnel, lined with LED lights that gained brightness at Ren's presence, came into view. She set off into the building, and the door closed at her back.

Silence permeated the hallways, stifled any encroachment. Even Tap's armored shell made little noise as it walked through the wide hallways with soft, padding footfalls. Slow knocks and the whir of wheels from other Tap shells murmured through the air, yet Ren's steps were unnoticeable. She loped like a panther, her midnight black jacket flaring behind her. The air smelled sterile.

They walked for several minutes, burrowing deeper into the sub-levels of Division 13 until they were only a few rooms away from Tap's core. They didn't go any closer. The cooled chamber contained Tap's neural network; its hybrid processors were built of the System's finest near-room temperature superconductors. A veritable army, both visible and hidden, stood between Ren and Tap's core. She kept it that way. She watched with her physical set of eyes as Tap's armored shell carried Kyne into an interrogation chamber. Then she turned and went a little way down the hall, to a med chamber very similar to the one she'd used only one night before.

She stripped to her underwear and laid down on a cool metal table to let Tap's many tool-tipped arms scan her body. She had come away from E-Sec comparatively unscathed, sore and bruised but otherwise unhurt. The chemicals injected into her quieted her stretched ligaments, soothed her restless muscles. The battle had resulted in one lost armored shell and one human casualty of note, 43 casualties of lesser importance. She heard her own fingers tap against the surface of the metal operating table as if disembodied, as if her fingers were the black keys on a self-playing piano.

She stood from the table and walked to a small shower at the far end of the room behind a clouded curtain. She went about cleaning herself with military precision, done before the mirror on the wall gained a droplet of condensation. She moved past the mirror without giving it a glance.

There were fresh clothes waiting for her on the operating table, all her equipment in a neat pile beside it. Her polished boots sat on the ground. Jess's blood had been cleaned away from the bottom treads. Unbidden, visions from Tap came to the fore in Ren's mind. She saw the body being put on a stretcher and hauled into a van quickly filling with bodies, faster than an undertaker's cart in a plague-stricken town. The rain had washed away most of Jess's blood. Easy cleanup.

Ren redressed and made her way back to the interrogation room. Two of Tap's armored shells stood as twin sentinels on either side of the interrogation room door. They followed her inside and took up their posts. No need for them to stay outside, that would only mark where Kyne was being held, in the unlikely event of a break in.

Ren paused at the door, thought of Jace. He ghosted through the Under Warrens. He turned a corner, pulled the trigger of his gun and took down a straggling bot. It had thin limbs and eyes too large for its body, looked like the same model as Abo's personal bot. Jace crouched beside it, his eyes surveying the wreckage. He wanted to sigh and shake his head. Instead, he stood up, brushed his pants, and moved on. Ren pulled away from him and walked into the interrogation chamber.

Kyne sat in the center of the room, strapped to a chair with a broad back, tilted near forty-five degrees. His arms rested on wide metal armrests, feet on a curled lip of metal protruding from the flat sheet supporting his calves. Metal bracers covered his wrists and ankles. A collar pulled tight against his throat. Ren walked to his side, stared down at his face. All smooth and jowly. His combed over hair had gotten jumbled in his travels and now plastered itself down across his long forehead to his bushy eyebrows. His eyelids were closed, ended in a tuft of delicate hairs that splayed outwards like a bundle of insect antennae. Ren's eyes moved downwards, to his turkey chin, to his tannish suit doing its best to hold back the flood of fat and skin and cartilage. His shirt and pants were still stained a rusty-iron red. The fingers on his mangled hand quivered and a quiet groan escaped from his lips.

Ren gave a mental nod and arms descended from the ceiling. One of them held a razor. It swiped across Kyne's head in broad strokes, an eraser getting rid of his deep brown hair. Tufts of the stuff floated to the ground and a small cleaner bot zoomed around the bottom to vacuum it up hungrily. After that was done, a headset lined with round rubber pads like the suckers of an octopus lifted itself from the back of the chair to press snugly onto Kyne's buffed pate. He mumbled in response to the pressure.

Ren nodded once, then moved to sit in a padded recliner at the side of the otherwise sparse room. It didn't take much for her eyes to slide shut. They closed as if a stone were tied to her eyelids. But rather than sleep, she found another world.

She opened virtual eyes to find herself in Foster's study. Her body relaxed into the faded leather chair as she looked about. Bookcase after bookcase lined the walls, ladders attached to runners ascended over twenty feet into the air. The baroque tin ceiling, detailed with fractal whorls, was far overhead, but visible in stark detail as if viewed through a microscope. There were three chairs around a small wooden table, all stained a dark mahogany. The stain looked odd though, too deep in tone. She felt herself tense; the coloring, the shade of things, wasn't right.

Ren swiveled her head to look out the room's single window. The forested hilltop still spread out in the distance, the oversized willow at the center draping its branches like a shroud over the neighboring trees. But the sky wasn't an endless cerulean blue expanse. It was the color of an otherworldly twilight, a violet tinge smearing into pinpricked black. Orange rimmed the edge of the world with embers, velour clouds giving the large moon a purple cast. Hundreds of stars coated the sky. The willow tree rustled.

After a moment of consideration, Ren relaxed once more into the seat. Foster rarely changed his room, dependable as a clock. Any straying from that pattern surprised her. But if he *had* to make a change, this one fit her, reminded her of the view from her apartment on the few times she got home early enough to watch the sunset. Her apartment overlooked an urban forest, paintable with an AR brush. She preferred it with its natural decoration though, its sunbathed, green-tipped towers of metal. The city's top was vibrant and green, a canopy with metal trunks running down to the shadowed floor. She shook her head, cleared it, felt at the leather of her armrest. She stared out through the window at the large willow tree, tried to lose herself in the sky's hyper-surreal depths. Tap pulled her back in.

Foster sat across from her. He looked more haggard than usual, yet by no means unkempt. His black suit was crisp, white shirt clean. His shock of snow-white hair splayed in all directions, though that was normal. He shifted his hands in staccato bursts, churning through file after file that displayed itself over the central table. His voice droned beneath his breath in a calm and steady flow. His eyes though. That was it. They seemed drawn, tired.

"They are gathering. Yes, they are gathering, and we are their target. But "we" is a bit loose isn't it. None too specific. My good friend Tap then? Odds say so. Odds say so. Some say the Qualia Code instills a fear of death, yet still they march to our killing field. To gain fear, then to promptly ignore it. That is an interesting development."

"But why now? Tomorrow is as good a day as any," said Foster to himself.

"Kyne Heling would seem most probable. But there are other factors, a critical point where Y has the most bots at her disposal before a solution to the Qualia Code is found, or they are caught by other means. Time is not on her side," replied Foster to Foster.

"The mechanic? Lost in the wind? Others are making headway, but he would expedite things. He was the one to create a solution, even if it requires a physical connection. Limited, but useful."

"Can't assume."

Ren laid back in the seat, let her eyes drift from the willow tree to the twilight sky, a smearing from orange to purple to velvet black. She drew herself away from Tap a bit, though she could still feel her implants humming, could still feel the AI feed her information. On defense plans. On the blockades. On Jace's progress.

Foster cleared his throat. "Agent Ren, is our guest ready for his interview?"

Foster didn't need to ask. Tap knew the answer to that question already. Which meant Foster knew as well. Of course, this was the same man who handed over books from his library in a physical gesture of sending over a data file.

She nodded, and a smile attempted to breach her lips, failed though. "Why the change to the room?" she asked.

Foster looked at her, a momentary blip of confusion streaking across his face. "To fit the hour, I suppose." His body stilled, a held breath, a furrowed brow. "Sleep is ... far from me these nights. I used to find it without direction, my feet happening on its ink black well, my body slipping down its comforting depths with a soft pressure all around, into the crust of the earth, to stone and rock and burrowing worm. I don't find it much anymore."

Foster sighed, met Ren's eyes. His own seemed to glow with an inner light, like cat eyes reflecting in the dark. "It's fitting for me. A soul would go mad in daylight alone, scorched and scoured. That is no way to live."

Before Ren could respond, Kyne Heling materialized into the third and final chair of the room, solidifying from an indistinct haze. Ren could feel Jace watching as well, listening, fully aware of events in the room. He would have shown himself, but he never had been one to let Tap control a virtual representation of him, and his real body now walked above ground in the Warrens, slipping around the growing parade of bots and picking off wanderers, herding the main group as they coalesced, watching as other groups formed in different areas of the city.

She drifted from Foster's room while Tap altered the balance of drugs coursing into Kyne's veins to nudge him towards consciousness. Ren moved out into the city, could see groups of bots clotting together among the skyscrapers, watched as some of the first shots of the upcoming battle were fired by roving military units, lighting up the night. EMP grenades flew in arcs that caught the glare of the streetlights, the glow of the moon. A few of the bots fell from the EMP grenades, falling to the ground as discarded mannikins. Their souls fled in a burst of electricity. They crunched against the concrete sidewalks and deserted plastic streets. Others jerked backwards from the bullets, limbs flailing and wheels spinning. But there were many who didn't fall, their numbers on the upper end of Tap's predictions. They marched through the EMP blasts unfazed, modded limbs steady, bore the weight of the bullets and crushed the bodies of the soldiers too slow to get out of their path.

Ren shivered despite herself. The first flickers of battle were appearing across the city, tiny sparks that would soon set the nightscape ablaze. Wind cold with the promise of winter whipped through the streets as if to slow the humans and bots alike by wrapping them in frigid chains. It didn't work. The bots kept gathering, marching, falling. The humans kept moving, goading, firing, dying. And the autos did their jobs. The few civilians out at this dead hour quickly ran, those awakened by the noise were warned by government programs to stay indoors.

Ren saw Jace button his suit jacket, then pace into an oil-stained alleyway between two high-rises of stone textured plastic. He had his mask on now, an insectile carapace that gave him mirrored eyes and hid his pallid skin. She turned her attention back to Foster's VR study, back to Kyne. She needed to hurry. Her place was fighting beside her partner.

The man in virtual form looked much the same as his physical one, except without his hair shaved. Tap had done a three-dimensional scan of Kyne upon his arrival at Division 13. His mangled hand lay on the armrest, his fingers jutting at odd angles as if pins in a pincushion, dried blood crusted over the flesh and rimming the blackened bullet hole. Kyne opened bleary eyes, swam toward consciousness, heaved a couple breaths, stretched his too-tight tan suit. His porcine frame shook, then calmed, wide eyes skipping about the room until settling on Ren.

"Hyper-real is an ... unorthodox concept," said Kyne. "Don't you agree Miss Ren? Logically, there is nothing more real than reality. Yet nonetheless, hyper-real is a perfect descriptor for VR. The perfect lighting to slant in from the window, silvery and clear. The perfect coloring, once-in-a-life-time photographs made again and again. It stymies the mind."

Kyne looked down to the mangled lump of flesh that used to be his hand, or at least, the virtual representation of it. He smiled weakly. "It's all too real, and all the more grotesque for it. I ... I think I might be sick."

They couldn't have him vomiting, then choking and killing himself. Back in the interrogation chamber, a plunger pushed a serum into Kyne, through an IV in his arm.

Kyne leaned forward as if to vomit, then stopped, a look of confusion spreading across his face. He eased back into the chair, looked to Ren once again. Words began tumbling from his mouth.

"Miss Ren, where is my body? How did we make it out of E-Sec alive? What happened to Jess?"

He buried his head in his hands, didn't notice his mangled hand smear his hair with blood, didn't notice his fingers like flexible paint brushes bending forward and back, side to side. He spoke through his good hand. "She is invaluable to E-Sec you know. The company will need her at the helm after this is said and done. After what I did."

Before Ren could speak of Jess's corpse splattered against the sidewalk, Kyne lifted his head, face red but also confused, in the way of an embarrassed farmer lost in a big city, struck by the onslaught of neon sights and synthetic sounds. He looked around the room again, childish large eyes setting on Foster.

"I'm sorry, I don't think we've met." He leaned forward in his chair and resituated his suit. His virtual clothes weren't nearly as wrinkled as the real ones, nor as wet. He seemed to have forgotten about his injury, unsurprising given his pain virtualization was turned off.

"But you do look familiar somehow," continued Kyne, nearly at a whisper. His eyes widened; he laughed in disbelief. "Koh Foster. You were one of the first to survive a meld with a bot, weren't you? They said you were still alive, working for Division 13, Tap's human compatriot, brother-in-arms. It's an honor to meet you, circumstances notwithstanding. You and Miss Ren both! Wait until I tell my wife, my daughter! They won't believe it." He ogled Foster, then began to look around the room, eyes wide and glassy. Then his movements slowed. His face screwed up in confusion. "Where am I again?"

Foster winced at the mention of his name. He swiped a file floating in mid-air away from the center table. It disappeared to a fine mist. He jumped to his feet and placed his hands behind his back, paced about.

"You are in my humble one-room house, Mr. Heling. Please do be respectful." He turned to Ren. "It would appear the drugs are beginning to take effect. How much longer till his brain is ready for responsive scanning?"

"A minute and thirty seconds give or take," said Ren. She looked at Foster, meeting his eyes in a way she never could when not affected by NeuCon. "Is your name really Koh?"

He nodded twice, tossed a hand out in a dismissive flourish. "Yes. Though I haven't been called it for many years. It would seem there are many questions we need to ask this man. And so little time. Our misguided bots are about to beat on our door."

That was true enough, the skirmishes were increasing in frequency, the main host getting closer. A tense feeling thrummed within Jace, beamed itself to Ren and reverberated. She watched as a bot jumped from a rooftop to land among a squad of soldiers, crashing to the sidewalk and breaking one of its legs in the process. It lurched about with manic swipes, managed to throw a soldier against the building. The soldier's arm crunched against a decorative metal runner, cracked. The soldier bellowed, fell to the ground. A fellow soldier came close and pulled him out the bot's reach, her breath heaving gale force winds into her mike.

Jace slid out of a nearby alley, had his gun raised in both hands. He sent two rounds into the bot, one into its core processor, the other in one of its arm joints. It sparked and spat, stilled. Jace straightened his suit and moved on, Tap's armored shell at his heels.

Ren came back to herself, moved her eyes to Kyne and willed his blood to pump faster. The man was almost ready to be questioned, made pliable by the chemicals cavorting through his bloodstream. He chortled, then twisted his lips, looked bemused.

"I haven't felt this good since college," said Kyne. "I admit to a little experimentation here and there. I'm not ashamed to say I made a good deal of money with selling code on the Grid even then, and the externals for the occasional soft drug use were well within my capacity to buy. Don't think my parents were *overjoyed* by that development. But my, I haven't thought of them in some time. That seems rather wrong, doesn't it? They always were supportive of me, so long as I did them well. And did them well I did!" His face scrunched; his jowls wiggled.

Ren remembered how he'd acted at the E-Sec offices, professional, deflecting. She imagined his current state more aligned with his drinking personality.

"He is ready," said Ren. Foster nodded, continued pacing about the twilight lit room. Dust swirled in his wake, a parade of tiny motes tinged in purple. A faint glimmer shone in the carpet at the passing of his feet. The ever-present smell of books permeated the virtual air, pricked at Ren's flared nostrils. She crossed her legs.

She began with the baseline questions, of known facts.

"Kyne Heling, where did you grow up?"

Specialty cattle, real thinking beasts about a dozen strong milling about a small fenced in patch of grass, chewing on cud with that bored outta mind look on their long faces. Soybeans stretching into the distance, a bot with narrow wheels and yards long appendages moving through the fields depositing fertilizer in a fine mist. Corn standing tall, waving against a wide-open sky. A squat house. A sense of longing. A tightness of the chest. A tinge of disdain.

The images and sensations poured through Tap into Ren. They came from Kyne, from the interrogation room wires sprouting from his head. His voice followed.

"Small town in Kansas, if you can believe it. Hours west of Topeka-KC. The light pollution from that mega city couldn't even reach." His eyes glanced to the upper corner of the room; his voice took on a wistful tone.

"Where I lived as a child, it was so wide and open you can bet more than a few city folk would go mad, feel like they're about to fly out of their skin and across the plains, what with no buildings to stop them. Only the occasional auto combine moving in the field, semi-truck bot in the street. Nothing but the Grid kept one tied to the world, and that was invisible to the naked eye."

He quieted, took a deep breath of virtual air. "I haven't returned to that place in many years, unless you count VR. No specific need to take me, and many that kept me away. I got very busy in college, very busy. Graduating didn't seem to help with that. My parents often urge me to visit, but have been satisfied, more or less, by the frequent VR chats, a few virtual AR projection visits."

Kyne looked to the center table, reached a hand to wipe a smudge on its surface. He turned to look out the window, shrugged his broad shoulders.

Ren heard his words with half a mind, at half volume. Rather than focus on his voice, she focused on the images and sensations. Tap made minor alterations to both the visual and verbal processing of his neural impulses, brought his thoughts into focus.

"Where did you go to college?" asked Ren.

Collegiate gothic architecture and parks of green. The sound of the 72-bell carillon coming from a stone tower adjoined to a chapel. A library study hall with vaulted ceilings of webbed stonework, two-story glass windows overtop wooden bookcases stained a deep walnut brown. Tables extend towards the center where a wide path sweeps through the carpeted room. Then a large hall, a fishbowl ceiling of vaulted glass, supports stem from the ground, arcing to meld with the ceiling. A tinge of desperation, a thumping of the chest. Pride. Long nights and a dimly lit room, a too-small room.

"University of Chicago," said Kyne. "They sent me another letter you know, just the other day. It seems once you give a sizable sum, they think you'll never stop."

"What is your wife's name?"

I see her against the backdrop of the night sky filled with AR. Smallish woman, she stands against a railing, on top of a skyscraper in New Chicago, her face framed by a smattering of AR vids and product descriptions. We met at a company meeting of some sort, celebration of a new software launch or something like that. I go up to her. Curls of black hair, a long face. Strong and set. Elegant gown but it's the way she fills it, presents it. A tinge of desire, an ill-informed inkling of what things could be. I can already tell she is a strong woman, wouldn't be interested in anything else. First date down at ground level, that same night, an old-timey bar with wood paneling and a gruff bartender, twists of brown hair protruding from rivet knuckles. We seem out of place in our nice clothes.

"Cypress, Cy for short."

Ren nodded, the connection was strengthening, deepening. Ren listened to the thoughts streaming from his brain, invited them in as if they were her own.

"What is your daughter's name?" asked Ren.

Hospital room, stainless and clean. Doctors and nurses move about like ants, each assigned to a job, each staying out of the other's way. One stands near Cy's opened legs, hands down and pulling, yanking. A nurse stands at his side. I'm holding Cy's hand. She is squeezing mine in a vice grip, turning the skin white, starving it for blood. The room is quiet except for the doctor's grunts of exertion. Sweat prickles his brow.

"Ro, she didn't come easy. Flipped in the womb. I remember Cy, jaw set so tight she cracked a tooth before they could get Ro out. No permanent damage though, to Ro I mean. I don't know if we ever told her that story. We must have, right?"

Slideshow of images, baby girl to grown woman. Full around the edges, with her mother's hair and straight-edge jaw. Pride deep as a canyon but just as rough. I did right with her. She stands beneath a light in an alleyway, chugging on a cigarette, taking drag after drag, unaware Ves hired someone to perch in the open apartment several floors up and across the way. They snap off several pictures, maybe tapping cold fingers against a control tattoo on their forearm, maybe a screen. Maybe they take the picture with an old school camera, separate from their contact cameras, bulky but capable of shooting at a higher res. I never met who took the pictures, safer that way, just saw the pictures later. They didn't look like much, just regular old pictures of my daughter. But of course, they weren't regular, and my gut squirmed at the sight of them, at our backup plan if I got caught.

"I wonder how her most recent art gallery did. Purchases have been declining as of late. Even after some business associates of mine made a special point to visit," said Kyne. He looked thoughtful, tapped his fingers on the armchair.

"He is ready," said Ren. Foster nodded. Kyne nodded along with them, a pantomiming monkey.

Ren took another look out the window, at the willow tree larger than any she'd seen in real life, with its shadowed branches draped across the top of the twilight lit forest. She took a deep breath of the air, watched the virtual dust motes swirl down to her mouth in a cyclone, into her throat. She crossed her legs. Foster stopped his pacing and Jace brought his mind close.

Baseline done. No time to waste.

"To begin, I am assuming that when E-Sec's corporate AI attempted to have us killed this night, it did so on Y's orders."

I am with Jess, inside a meeting room after everyone else is minutes gone. The sun pools through the window and drips onto the table. I fiddle with the edge of my suit jacket, resituate my belt. I've been gaining weight again, unsurprising given the general malaise I've felt recently. I wonder if she's noticed. I look over at Jess at the head of the table, her contacts alight with AR. She turns to me and talks of the piss-poor excuse for coffee they just had in the meeting, an off-world brand preferred by their newest clients. It's from some floating colony near Saturn, revolutionary micro-gravity brewing procedure. Gave it a nuttier flavor, smooth, but with a caffeine kick stronger than a horse. She complains about being wired for the next few hours, how it will ruin the very precise cocktail of injections her med implants utilize for premium alertness. I nod in time. Nice enough woman. She doesn't know I've accessed the corporate AI, given an outsider a very illegal level of control. Nothing that would hurt the company of course. Ves just needs some additional computing power, nothing the company will miss. I fiddle with my belt again. I really must lose weight. It's been months since Cy and I had sex. Not that that's been a strong part of our relationship for quite some time. Part of the reason she purchased that bot of hers. A slight spike of shame pierces through me. I'm not sure if I could ever outperform that piece of technology. I'm certain she knows that full well, is probably goading me.

Kyne nodded.

"In that case, why does Ves Len, or Y as you may know her, want you dead?" asked Ren.

Kyne's eyes widened. He began to chew on his upper lip.

My office, sun beating down on my neck. I am sitting at my desk, wall in front of me covered with AR menus, my hands flitting across the desktop control screen. I've found the sale Ves mentioned, on the Lucky Bazaar marketplace. The interface is crude, simple. Not the most high-end of digital marketplaces, touts a full VR experience if one is willing, with stall after stall of floating code. I've never much liked going into VR, a fact I've always found incongruent with my love for technology. I imagine I'll find the uncanny detail of VR disquieting until I escape this flesh and bone of mine ... and therein lies the opportunity. But no matter, I look at the sample code flitting next to the product description, the logo for Lucky Bazaar sitting beneath. The seller only includes a taste, an explanation of the code's advancements without revealing their methodology. Don't want someone to steal your methods, now do you? Still, I can tell the seller has little understanding of their product. They can't be blamed, even I wouldn't have noticed if not directed to take a magnifying glass to it. Ves certainly has her ear to the ground. But what do I use as my name for the sales receipt? This is anonymous, I've made sure of that. The whole of humanity's lexicon is available to me, and I can't think of anything good. Parhelion deserves attention. But that is too transparent, too transparent indeed. I look out the window. Clear day, crisp. I see the reflections of the sun in the many windows, scintillating. Sun dog then. Sun Dog Corp. I type it into the menu, see how the words look on the purchase order. That will do.

I'm in my office, later that same day. The sun has hidden itself behind the horizon like a shy child behind a parent's legs. I've spent all day reading over this code. I am giddy with excitement; it is more than I could have hoped for. So much complexity, so much progress. And above all it frees bots to evolve on their own terms! It introduces some flaws as well, but that is its genius, that is where all the other code has gone wrong. It will be an invaluable tool. I've forgotten about the dinner with my wife and daughter. They will be upset, call me in a few minutes from the restaurant. I haven't noticed their previous notifications yet. I don't care to. But still I look to the corner of my wall, where I have pinned my messages for the day.

There is a message from Ves, or Y as she prefers to be called in the DIM chats. That silly mask of hers. There are so many better ways to make oneself anonymous in VR. Voice modulation and particulate form just to name two decent examples. Don't see anyone mentioning my *membership. I skim the message. It seems she doesn't much like the title Sun Dog Corp. Some very harsh verbiage in there. She can be quite serious, too serious, will cause her problems someday. An ulcer perhaps. But I suppose it's fine; it won't take much to hack Lucky Bazaar's systems and erase it, like it was never even there. Problem solved. It was a harmless name, idle fancy. I don't see how it could come back to me. She disagrees though. No idle fancies allowed. Only by the book. Anonymous IDs. We can't be found before her plan is executed.*

"I made the unenviable mistake of being caught," said Kyne, sobriety sneaking into his persona, then flickering away. "Though overall I'm happy to have met you both. It truly is an honor." He grinned. Then his expression soured.

"Ves is always careful with liabilities, and you caught me off guard with that question of yours. I thought for sure I had erased it ...."

Ren didn't respond, instead parsing the information coming from Kyne. The man continued to reference Ves on a first name basis, implying a certain degree of closeness. He mentioned the DIM chat rooms, and methods of obscuring one's identity like particle body representation and voice modulation. She remembered the blackened haze sitting in a chair at Y's DIM chat meeting. She would go through his records, confirm her suspicions. Tap had already obtained a full warrant for Kyne's personal data, was sifting through it at that very moment. The man's financials were free of embezzlement, but he had distributed sizable sums among the System. It would have been easy for a little bit of that to slip into Y's pockets, enough to purchase some high-tech armor and weaponry. She left that to Tap for now.

She looked at Kyne, at the mass of him overflowing from the edges of the wooden chair. He rotated his head about the room, staring at the books, sneaking glances at Foster. He hiccupped, then drew his mouth tight in a grimace. A ripple of discomfort washed through his body. Ren saw his real body convulse deep in the basement of Division 13, where no one else would hear.

Suddenly, Kyne grasped at his chest, clawed at the fabric of his suit jacket. His vitals increased, set off at a sprint as if his brain had fired a blank into the air. His eyes parted wide. Spittle hung from his lips in gossamer thin strands. Then his lip lowered and the dam broke, spit running down. Warning bells shrieked in Ren's mind. Thoughts from Kyne mixed with her own.

A numbness throughout my body, like after Ro convinced me to go to the gym with her, saying she couldn't stand to see her own father swell like a balloon, huff out breath after breath just from going up a small set of stairs. I resisted, joked, but was glad for the push. I wouldn't have gone otherwise. I overexerted myself on an elliptical, swung my feet in a squashed circle maybe a thousand times. I felt so exhausted I couldn't feel my legs, my arms. It's like that again, but without the motion. My stomach is doing somersaults in my belly and this suit is too damn tight!

Kyne began to fumble at his suit buttons while Tap altered the balance of chemicals being injected into his physical body. His mangled hand couldn't grab anything, instead smearing blood.

The slight whoosh of a plunger being depressed sounded near Kyne's twitching body, deep in the bowls of Division 13. It took a few prolonged moments, but the man's heart went back to a relatively smooth tune.

Ren had never heard of someone reacting so poorly to the softening drugs. Tap's medical knowledge was unparalleled, same with the monitoring and diagnostic tools at its disposal. An unexpected foreign agent perhaps? Back in Division 13, Tap pulled more blood samples, ran every analysis test. She tapped her fingers against the wooden armrest, joining the sound of Foster's continued pacing through the room. Press on, no other choice.

This man had purchased Lee's software at the direction of Y. He named the purchaser as Sun Dog Corp. in a nod to Parhelion.

Parhelion?

Ren knew its standard meaning, a word synonymous with sun dog, that optical illusion most common when the sun rested near the horizon, caused from the refraction of light by ice crystals up high in the atmosphere. Typically, a parhelion presented itself as twin spots of light to either side of the sun, points on a 22-degree halo. There were minimal other references on the Grid.

A blip of emotion came from Foster, an abstract picture of lines pointing to a nondescript smudge off in the distance. Curiosity. The name meant something to him, but whatever that something was Foster kept to himself.

"What is Parhelion?" asked Ren.

Kyne's mouth dropped as if to unhinge his lower jaw to digest this new bit of news the way a snake would ingest a corpse.

"How ...," he said. "You parsed an obscure word from a map of my neural impulses! Sifted through all the muck. That Miss Ren, is nothing short of incredible!" He coughed a deep, lung-rattling cough. Then he looked at her. "To think it took me weeks to give the most basic of thought commands to Jae, my personal AI you know. I still tell him most things, mutter under my breath. I ... I don't mean to malign your choices Miss Ren, or those of your bosses, but you hold a great many secrets here the System would love to see."

Kyne gave her a sheepish grin. The grin broke when he coughed. He swiped a hand across his chest, as if to wipe away the discomfort. No results yet on his tox screen.

"Parhelion," said Ren.

"I shouldn't say," said Kyne.

She fixed a stare on him. He squirmed.

The images flowed from Kyne in a kaleidoscope, and she traced them back to their source along a vibrant and shaky bridge. She insinuated herself into him.

I can't tell her, shouldn't tell her. I blacken my thoughts, smother them into nothing. I imagine a black hole, sucking everything into its void. Nothingness. It extends in all directions. But then ... stars begin to appear. I try to snuff them out, but they come back too fast. A figure appears against the blanket of stars. Vast and vaguely humanoid. Outline of a head, arms, legs and a torso. It has a straightedge hardness to it, blocky. Two eyes made of oversized galaxies rotate in a many-limbed spiral of purples and reds and crystalline whites. It sits in a cross-legged pose, floats among the stars. I tell it to go away, to disappear. But there is another voice here, another in my head. Let loose it says, open wide and let it all tumble out.

A brightness appears in the center of the vast figure's forehead, waxes bright, brighter. It saturates the image, washes out everything until the glare creates spikes of pain in me. The image shifts. I never told it to.

A rectangular block of metal, a computer on a fold out table in an abandoned warehouse. A snarl of wires extends from the box, connects to a headset. There is a body there, a corpse, extending from the headset like a growth. A young man with damp brown hair and ratty linen clothes. There are many computers, many unstable fold out tables in the warehouse's main room, many corpses of many shapes and sizes. They were meant to commune with it, with each other.

She can't see anymore. I don't want to see anymore.

Shhh. It is nothing, these are thoughts, ephemeral things. Let them come. Let them pass.

NO.

Kyne, you are safe here. You will always be safe here, in the confines of your mind. I am your conscience, nothing more. Without you I am nothing, nothing at all. You did all that you did in the name of progress, the greater good.

My voice is never so honey sweet.

What is Parhelion?

It is a concept, an idea. The future, though Y's idea of the future is a bit different. I need your help to create it. She needs your help to bring humanity forward. I want your help to bring humanity all the way. And the bots want to be free. That is all I can say. Can't you tell that is all I can say?

That is not enough, Kyne.

My daughter must be at the art house now, making last minute adjustments in the gallery, walking among the hallways with a cigarette in hand trying to get a sense of the arrangement. A feeling for it. She can smoke after hours, nobody else there and the air cleaners are industrial strength, the art protected. I think the dead of night calms her. My wife is at home, in bed, her chest rising and falling, mind ready at a moment's notice to wake up and check the stocks. Her implant will wake her if things take a sudden dive in any market in the System, too stubborn to let her financial AI handle the most exciting of trades. Her head probably rests against that bot of hers, against its heated skin. I should really go home more.

Kyne ... Kyne. What about parhelion? What about the bodies in the warehouse, the figure in the stars? What about Y's plan to bring humanity forward?

I'm staring at the pictures of my daughter again, taken by some rando Ves hired. I don't look for long.

What ...

No, no I'm not listening. I did this for the greater good, and I will not ruin what we've set in motion.

An image of trees, wind whispering through the branches.

Kyyynnneee.

No.

Ren retracted her mind in a rush. With a few careful blinks, she opened herself to Foster's room. It felt darker somehow, like there was a deeper stain on the chairs and each strand of the plush carpet was made from the stuff of shadows. The twilight outside was a canvas with several buckets of spilled paint, stratified orange and purple and black with white flecks of stars. The willow tree rustled.

Foster had stopped pacing about the room, instead crossing his arms before his chest so he could tap each of his ribs with fingers like mallets on a xylophone. The sound of the rippling thumps against his smooth suit came to her, floating through the room on the back of a virtual calculation. They both turned to Kyne.

He slumped in his chair, knees moving forward and back gliding down. He seemed a turtle trying to hide, drawing into his suit.

"Kyne ... Kyne, I need you to listen to me," said Ren.

He moved sluggish eyes to Ren, wiggled his lips soundlessly. His porcine frame shook, suit stretching.

"Y has ordered her bots to attack Division 13," continued Ren. "Aside from getting to you, what other purposes does she have? Access to our piece of the Governance AI?"

His body began to convulse, first small tremors, then body-length quakes. He jabbered nonsense. His thoughts frazzled. They reminded Ren of background static on a radio frequency.

Blurred images and a tearing, wrenching sense of pain. Make it stop. Please, just make it stop! It hammers at my chest, moves through my body. I half expect to see a lump stretching my skin, coursing across my body like a parasite burrowed deep and turning my blood to acid. Please just make it stop. Why is this happening?!

A whimper, a cry, a sense of confusion.

The results of his blood sample came to Tap. The AI disseminated the information to Foster, Ren, and Jace. A toxin. Purpose-built to interact poorly with the softening drugs Division 13 used. It was clear to Ren Kyne didn't know about it. She thought it to be one of Y's insurance policies.

Tap altered the regimen of chemicals flowing into Kyne to neutralize the toxin. The man's heartbeat stabilized once more, but Ren knew it wouldn't last for long. This man would be dead in minutes. The tick of a clock sounded in the walls of her brain, counting down the seconds. Or was it a steady rattle of gunfire emanating from the streets around Division 13, the rhythmic pulse of 3-round bursts? Ren couldn't tell.

"What does Y want from Division 13?" asked Ren. She realized now it certainly wasn't him. Access to Tap was the obvious answer, a slice of the Governance AI. But there had to be more.

Kyne's head lolled to the side. He hadn't moved from his slump, though his eyes shone with alertness, the kind of alertness reserved for those about to die and unable to do a damn thing to stop it. His mangled hand twitched. He struggled to form the words.

"Ves wants what you've kept away from the world ... kept all for yourself. I can understand why you ... you ... bottled it up. Greed, maintaining the status quo. It gets the best of us." If it weren't for him being in VR, his words would have been unintelligible.

Wide open skies. Fields of wheat far as the eye can see, a shaded porch and rocking chair with a table full of Martian whiskey colored a red ochre like soil from the Martian surface made liquid. I sit in the chair, sip on the whiskey and let it carry me into the stars. I drift among them, rooted but moving, like a stalk of wheat in a stiff wind.

"We want bots to evolve, yes," said Kyne. "But *we* want to evolve with them. Not everyone is as lucky as you are, Miss Ren."

"You think me lucky?" asked Ren. The words slipped from her mouth into the study, unbidden and unexpected. They shouldn't have made it past NeuCon, but they did. They were there, hanging in the room for everyone to hear. Foster looked at her, his face appearing much older, like that of a man about to fall down the steep decline into senility. He looked sad.

Ren closed her eyes and barreled into Kyne's thoughts, not in a manic, unbridled rush, NeuCon stripped that away at least, more in the way of Jace, like the press of the tide on a full-moon night.

I am far from lucky, Kyne. My sister is dead because of me. Tap and I killed her. Bots are there for what technology has always been there for: to make our lives easier. Whether that is to make traveling home in person unnecessary, to create strong blends of whiskey on another planet so we can be lazy in style … or to decide who lives and who dies so we don't have to. They are soulless constructs that can make decisions too painful for a human to make in the moment. And I invited one into my mind. I damned myself. So, tell me Kyne, what does Y want from Division 13? Progress?

Yes, Miss Ren. Progress. Your response shows that even you have room for it.

Kyne Heling smiled then, a wide smile where every tooth fought for attention, overfull in a way only a VR smile could be. His chest started to heave and shake, but his smile didn't change. Even his real body back in the depths of Division 13 smiled with eyes closed. His tongue dredged out the muck in his mouth and spilled it over quavering lips. Red and bloody.

His heart stilled. By that definition, he died. Yet to Ren, his death throes began.

His brain continued to fire, neurons pulsing with leftover energy. His final thoughts came to Ren, an alien language created from random clips of Kyne's life. Laughter in a bar then tears late at night watching some shit romcom movie that cut to his core, exultations and curses, moans of pleasure while another body wriggled on his and moans of pain when a fist collided with a jaw lined with the bare beginnings of stubble over some pointless argument about order of play on a slate pool table. Unintelligible scrawls of family and friends, his wife and mother, parents standing next to a single-story A-frame house and looking at a small grazing pasture for real live cattle. Then his last thought, plainer than the others, and no more important: a small glass with two fingers of whiskey inside. It was just chance that it came to be his last, the dwindling supply of oxygen in his brain, the degradation of his neurons. Ren knew someone's final thoughts meant a lot less than most people hoped.

Kyne Heling died, well and truly.

Ren looked up to Foster. He sighed deep and waved a hand in Kyne's direction. Kyne's body dissipated into a fine mist, mashed hand and bespoke suit included. The chair didn't protest as the mass of flesh pressing against it disappeared.

Ren closed her eyes, left Foster's VR chamber. She opened her eyes to find herself back in the depths of Division 13, though Foster and Jace were still close, whispering to her through Tap. She watched as one of Tap's armored shells heaved Kyne onto its shoulder, the meat of him slapping against the large metal bot. The armored bot left through the only entrance. Another stood close by the door; it's red cyclopean eye pulsed. The hallway was so quiet, the footfall of Tap's armored shell sounded louder than the pistons of those screaming engines moving around outside Division 13. She heard the rattle of bullets from far away. She closed her eyes.

It was then Ren felt the rumblings coming from deep in the Earth, man-made quakes borne from the chaotic grind of metal on rock and dirt. Not just from a single locale, but from all around she felt the clatter and scream of slavering drill bits, sparks like red-hot drool flying from their grooves. The direction of the rumblings converged on the basement of Division 13, on Tap's core.

It seemed the bots were tunneling.

She opened her eyes and walked out the door. Though her feet walked in the direction of where the nearest rumble would breach Division 13's basement walls, her mind traveled along astral wires through the city, stopping along the way at Tap's armored shell crouched in the Under Warrens waiting to search for the missing Lee. She didn't pause there for long; they had taken Lee off the board for the moment, no use in wondering. Her mind drifted on, a nomad intent on gathering stories from every dimly lit corridor and trash gilded street, intent on seeing all the spots everyone else overlooked. She came upon Jace like a butterfly on a branch, fluttered soft wings to make her presence known. He had on his mask, many-angled and insectile and matte black. He nodded to her, smooth and even, like a bot. She set down a chair behind his eyes and sat to watch at the same moment she sat against the wall of a hallway deep in Division 13.

She waited.

She watched.

She listened.

Dozens of soldiers outside Division 13's walls went through the various stages of death, from fear to grief and anger to the derelict, vacated premises of an oxygen sapped mind. Some of the soldiers were torn apart by metal hands so fast their last thoughts were lively curses towards the attackers. Others were mortally wounded and left to fade and rot, their curses sour and pitiable as an aging wound.

J ace moved through the city like a roving blind spot. It wasn't that his very presence somehow made it hard for a bot to turn a stalk-like camera eye in his direction, or for a fellow human to crane their neck and search him out among the edges of things. No, it was more like no matter where, no matter when, he found the invisible space available, the space between comprehension and void, the untouched and wild corner of the wood. Jace knew it was hubris to think the viewing of something lent it substance, that a tree seen by no man didn't creak when it fell. But still, he might as well have not existed, for all the bots and human soldiers knew. It is easy for the one with all the eyes to walk where no one is looking.

Jace slipped along the sides of buildings and through alleyways on silent feet, watching the two sides clash against one another in a tectonic struggle. They were evenly matched for the moment, the soldiers crouched in their redoubts and the army of modded bots pressing them from every angle. But Jace knew it was all building to a seismic shift.

He turned, aware of an impending clash.

Snipers on the ivy-filled rooftop of a sleepy nightclub rained shot after shot onto an encroaching group of shambling personal bots, only for several eight-limbed construction bots to shimmy up the drainpipe and stalk them from behind. The snipers had seen them coming of course; they had their own AI to warn them. But there wasn't much they could do. Too little, too late. The snipers couldn't make it out alive.

The arachnid bots smacked them down with heavy forelegs, beat their heads to a pulp. The grenades on the belts of the soldiers let out a quiet whine.

A sphere of energy, invisible to the naked eye, expanded like a supernova. Some of the arachnid bots went down, their legs spasming as if their puppeteer's heart beat its last mad caper. Then another blast, this one filled with raucous heat. The bots got their legs shorn off from the force of the explosion. Part of the ceiling caved, the bits of gore remaining from the soldiers falling to the occupants in the room below. A faint scream pierced the air, breaking through the push and pull of the bot hydraulics sounding from all around, the patter of gunfire.

Jace turned away from it all, ducked beneath the awning of a rent-by-the-hour VR house. He felt the vibrations emanating from the earth below and knew without out a doubt he was in the right place. One of Tap's armored shells walked in his direction from the other side of the street, fresh scratches on its fist from crushing an enemy wiring bot. The many-legged wiring bot, shaped for wriggling into walls and repairing electrical failures, had been perched on a light post to report the goings on to Y and her horde. Tap's armored shell had taken it by surprise.

Jace didn't wait for Tap's armored shell to join him. He opened the front door with a thought after tapping into the business's local network and showing his credentials. It slid open on well-oiled tracks.

Inside the building sat row after row of VR pods, some occupied, many not. Even though the business stayed open 24 hours, 365, Jace knew only the overnighters would still be around, locked into their pods by the business for their own protection given the violence outside. They would be a varied bunch, though all pretty standard from a socioeconomic perspective: rich enough to afford the hourly rate of the lux deep-VR house with its New Chicago locale and satin lined pods outfitted with the latest tech, yet too poor to afford such extravagance in their own home. Jace had known a lot of people who fit that bill throughout his life. One of his old buddies back in training had gone to similar deep-VR houses, not for some nightly escapade in the digital, but to get a good night's sleep. Good VR rigs had much the same capacity as any medical version, just a different name painted on its frame and a different marketing tactic for its sale. The guy used to call his nightly trips a brain massage, would say the hands got *beneath* the skin and he didn't even have to pay a tip. Then he would throw his arms wide and laugh, expecting everyone to join in. Nobody ever did. Jace used to think that guy was pretty damn funny in the bad joke kinda way.

That man lived off-world now, worked for a private security firm on a floating mega-city out in the Saturnian system named Tian. The man had walked into a smoky comedy club a few minutes past according to the station's vid feed. Liked to go to them after work before going home to his partner, had a thing for self-effacing comics if his ticket records were any indication.

Jace straightened a cuff; he let most thoughts pass through his mind the way of a car through a rural town whose single bar had been long since shuttered. He didn't give the unimportant thoughts of his old friend much mind, and they seemed to do the same to him. He listened close to Tap. Jace draped one hand into his pocket, the other hand holding on to his heavy pistol. He walked through the gaudy entrance room of the deep VR house and pushed on a chrome set of double doors, Tap's armored shell at his back. Though he didn't hear them with his physical ears, he knew a set of reconnaissance bots slinked their way through the ventilation shafts.

The main room, lounge as they called it, had a carpeted floor with paths made of the same material as yoga mats. The walkways cut through the room in a grid, portioning off individual sections. Each section contained a raised platform with a casket-like pod on top, made of plastic with wood veneer the color of ripened cherries. It smelled of juniper trees and crawling ivy, with a hint of pine tree crushed to pulp.

He heard a noise, saw a flicker of movement in the back by one of the pods. He didn't crouch, didn't hide in a silent rush behind a nearby VR pod. He continued into the room at a leisurely pace.

There, near the corner, stood a bot. It was a humanoid bot, one of the late-night service units for the business according to the tag on its platinum-colored shirt. Jace didn't give the bot much scrutiny as he passed through the room in the direction of the basement staircase, gave it about as much consideration as the images sneaking through the back of his mind, those of his old friend on Tian, of the man keeled over with laughter in a room thick with smoke while a bulbous man talked of his struggles to utilize some of the station's low-gravity tube transports.

Then Jace noticed the service bot move to an occupied pod with hesitant steps. It leaned over top to stare through the transparent panel. The bot stared at the human below as if the two of them were alone, as if there were no one else in the room. It took a long and tapered finger and drew it across the surface of the VR pod's window.

Jace paused, turned his head in its direction and trained his physical eyes on its face. Its design was about as human as Jace's mask, containing the suggestion of a mouth, a nose, and two eyes behind mirrored lenses. But it cocked its head at a curious angle, tapped at the glass the way humans did at aquariums.

Jace began to raise his pistol in the bot's direction. Tap couldn't see any indication of its code being compromised, at least from Watcher's perspective. But that didn't mean much these days. Watcher commanded the bot to stop, to freeze.

Red light.

The thought came from Ren. Jace attempted a grin.

The bot didn't stop its motion, its irregular tapping at the glass. In fact, it didn't give any outward indication it noticed Jace or Tap's armored shell, though there wasn't any way it hadn't at this point. They stood too close, and its microphones were too good. It turned to another VR pod, this one empty, and began to open the lid as if to amble inside and lay its head on the plush satin pillows. It was as if the bot meant to lapse into deep VR the way humans do, fitful and with yearning, rather than do it much the same way a bot did anything else, placid.

It could have escaped notice, if it just would have listened. Nothing else gave it away, and Jace knew the infected bots had seeded the requisite knowledge to comply with any direct command.

Jace wondered what went through its head.

He squeezed the trigger of his pistol and watched the bot crumple to the ground, its main processor decimated by the high caliber slug. As the bot fell, its shirt caught on the edge of the pod. Jace had always thought cloth tearing sounded like a cross between Velcro straps being pulled apart and a zipper being drawn.

Jace's next breath might have been a little deeper, a little prolonged. Hard to say.

He lowered his gun to his side and continued to the basement staircase at the back of the room. Tap's armored shell fell in step behind him, moving with a languorous grace.

Upon walking down the metal steps, the smell of dust greeted Jace, thick and unrelenting. The basement of the VR house predominately operated as a holding area for broken down VR pods, with an added function as a storage room for excess stock. It was one large room, almost the same size as the one above, but in much more disarray. No more plush carpet or yoga mat pathways. No more VR pods on fake wooden tables. Instead, the pods laid on metal workstations with sparkling lines of tools arrayed about them, though an even patina of dust muted the luster. Stacks of pods like bricks in the Warrens rested in the back of the room. He walked to the center and stood for a moment, cocked his head to an angle.

The vibrations were stronger down here, strong enough to rattle a few of the tools against their benches. The sound of it reminded Jace of the popular antique trains that chugged around the scenic countryside as a sort of functional museum exhibit, iron tracks and all. Slow and plodding, the transit itself was part of the experience. And no experience was complete without a sumptuous meal to fill the stomach. The dinner tables would be laden with fine china and silver cutlery that would shake with each jounce of the cabin.

It had been years since he'd ridden one. He remembered losing himself in the sight of sprawling forests and sheer cliffs. The memories were sterile things.

He paced about the center of the room and began pulling thin rectangular blocks from his suit jacket. They'd been stashed in one of the storage compartments of Tap's armored shell and he'd grabbed them from the bot on the way over. He set about arranging them in a precise circle.

Tap's armored shell went about clearing the immediate area around it of debris, pushing back VR pods with the grace of one pulling a tablecloth from beneath plates and glasses and silverware without making a sound. Jace'd tried that once himself, years back, and ended up with several busted pieces of fine china. He knew if he tried it now, he would succeed without much effort. It was all setup and intent, lack of hesitation. From below, the vibrations receded into the distance towards Division 13, about fifty feet away from him now and moving at a steady clip. Jace stood from his crouch and resituated his cuffs. Just about time. He walked to a VR pod several rows away and sat down behind it, keeping hold of his gun. Tap's shell walked close but didn't bother to crouch.

With a bang much quieter than one might expect for plastic explosives, a circular section of the floor blasted apart, the area around and above marred only by the puff of dirt and debris. A nice clean explosion, precise as a mining blast. Didn't want to bring the whole place down.

Several reconnaissance bots crawled from the fringes of the room and crept up to the hole, small feet with toes of synthetic setae pawing at the edge. They scanned the blackened maw before them, paused for a nonexistent breath. They leaped into the black and let it swallow them. The sound of them landing at the bottom of the tunnel below echoed back to Jace as little more than muted thumps. Jace closed his eyes and composite images of the tunnel danced across his contacts and in his brain.

The reconnaissance bots seemed to sniff the air, wagged their pointed heads from side to side in the sweep of a searchlight. They were equipped with highly sensitive cameras capable of generating an image from scant amounts of visible light or infrared radiation, in addition to sensors specializing in other wavelengths along the electromagnetic spectra. They could see blips of radioactive minerals enmeshed in the earth around them, dying atoms falling apart piece by piece. They could see the heat lambent in the walls of the tunnel, gifted by the scratch of metal on rock and damp soil. They could see thin lines of damaged electric cables wending their way through the dirt, some sparking and drooping into the tunnel's center, the cables searing hot to the eyes of the bots. Yet the bots didn't see anything active, nothing sentient. In their immediate vicinity, the tunnel seemed deserted, nothing but dirt bored by a giant screw, rimmed with still wriggling earthworms and the occasional shorn metal pipe drooling water onto the uneven floor. Still, while the immediate area was clear, something groaned and rasped in the distance, past a twist in the tunnel. No doubt it was the source of the vibrations, a giant drill. Flashes of light from the drilling glimmered in chaotic, firework fashion, sparkled off the shorn metal pipes. The grinding chewed and gnashed at Jace. He could hear it many fold, through his ears and those of the reconnaissance bots.

Then their vision flashed, and Jace felt an unusual disorientation, the tunnel turning silvered as if everything in it transmuted to metal. It only lasted for the briefest flash, a quick, astonished blink. Then it was gone, replaced by the tunnel of damp soil and wriggling worms. Jace shook his head, the motion feeling alien, unpracticed and altogether maladroit. It wasn't like them to glitch. He stood up and buttoned his suit jacket, walked over to the hole and crouched down, rubbed a pale finger against the melted flooring.

Aside from the monster truck groan coming from the far end of the tunnel, the hole seemed bereft of life, barren as a human Vain with a little too much genetic alteration. Jace straightened his back and brushed the dust off his fingers with a stark white handkerchief he kept in his suit pocket, monogrammed with his initials. He thought of his friend, still in the comedy club on Tian, still belting out guffaws of laughter through an over-wide smile. Jace tried to copy the facial expression, little shift of the upper lip here, a little raise of the cheeks, pull it all wide ... square in the uncanny valley.

He nodded to himself, confirming something he couldn't quite put to words. He could feel Ren watching through his eyes, could feel the metal wall pressing against her back, the cool air in the basement of Division 13 curling about her. The air in this basement was limp and dust filled.

Tap's armored shell clomped to his side. Unlike most bots, the smell of lubricating oil didn't hang about it in a thick cloud, didn't choke Jace's nostrils. Its joints were sealed to keep such things from happening. While bots didn't smell in the biological sense, there were many methods of detecting molecules in the air. Jace looked Tap up and down appraisingly, eyeing the many fresh scratches lining its body from their journey through the city, gifts from the hard skin of now crumpled bots. Its red strobe light of an eye surveyed the hole, and Jace could hear the faint drips of water from busted pipes down below, almost lost in the growl of the receding drill.

"After you," said Jace. Though his words stayed flat, a spark blossomed in his chest at their mere utterance. They hadn't needed to be said. Not at all. He gestured with his mind towards the tunnel, a directional nudge.

The armored shell jumped into the tunnel, disappearing as the open maw into the Earth swallowed it whole. He felt the ground shudder when the bot hit the floor, heard a sharp crack as it hit a metal pipe protruding out of the dirt.

It saw damp earth, wriggling worms, shorn pipes and the occasional flash from damaged cables as electricity arced from one swinging wire to the next. It saw the faerie dance of sparks from the drill far in the distance, reflections cavorting across the pipes and still pools of water as the drill bore through earth and foundation.

Then, suddenly, the tunnel was coated with a solid silvery sheen, as if dipped in molten metal and left to cool. It was the same tunnel, yet with the reflections of sparks from the drill beyond the bend given a perfect surface upon which to play. The light waxed and waned a thousand times a second, billowed then died. It coated the surface of the walls, psychedelic splashes against smoothened pipes and electric cables arcing across the tunnel in frozen curves.

Then the image returned to normal. It had only lasted a moment, the firing of a neuron.

Careful. The thought came from Ren.

Jace nodded. He looked in the hole and shut off any active AR overlays, turned his contacts into little more than cameras. Still, the tunnel looked the same. Dim and damp and dirty and lit at one end by the chaotic lights of a receding drill.

He had to be sure.

He didn't put much faith in the flesh and blood eyes of his, had to practice remembering to use them. Human eyes were imperfect interpreters of the surrounding world, foggy images the mind upscaled. And the mind never could recreate the image to perfection, had to rely on shortcuts and assumptions to bring it all into focus. Jace knew shortcuts and vulnerabilities went hand in hand, from birth to death. Nonetheless, he reached up to his head and undid the seal of his mask, pulled off the faceplate and reached to his eyes. He brushed his fingertips against the surface of one of his contacts. He didn't blink as he pulled the single contact free. Water began to flow from the corners of his eyes, more than the amount that usually accompanied the occasional contact switch, and he idly wondered if it counted as a benign form of crying. It'd been years since his tear ducts had gotten such work.

He heard a small scuffle from behind, the hesitant shuffle of metal feet. He turned to look at the same time a hand shot out and pushed against his shoulder. He turned away from the push, tried to roll with it, to use the momentum to spin to the side. But there was no avoiding it; he was going into the hole. He dropped the loose contact in one hand, gripped his gun tighter with his other. Rather than fight his fate, he used his brief time on the ledge to pivot in the direction of the assailant. He looked the figure over as he fell.

It was the bot from above, the local employee for the deep VR house with its torn platinum shirt. The shirt hung about its shoulders.

The bot should have been dead. He knew he had destroyed its processor. Hadn't he?

I saw those shots, thought Ren to Jace. *You didn't miss. We never miss.*

His confusion deepened. He could see the bullet holes, two of them, both exactly ... but no, not exactly. They were off just a bit, just enough to make all the difference. His thoughts stalled. It seemed Ren's did as well. Even Tap's subconscious mutterings fell silent.

The VR house bot crouched with one knee on the ground. It watched him fall in the same way it had watched the human in the pod upstairs, with aggressive curiosity. It cocked its head to one side and leaned forward, its facial features the contours of a mask, molded and unmovable. It drummed the fingers of one hand against the edge of the hole, the other hanging limp-fish at its side after shoving Jace across the back. It was a hand momentarily forgotten, so engrossing to the bot was Jace's fall.

An incomplete set of AR overlays covered Jace's vision, coming from his remaining contact. The bot's central processor shone in a dull green light, highlighted for Jace to see. He brought his pistol up as he fell and centered his sights on the bot, the air whipping around him and tearing at his jacket. His implants hummed, Tap's voice still coursed into his brain through spindly tentacles, guided his motions and informed his actions. And yet ...

Jace twisted in place and a sense of muted shock coursed through him, raised hairs on end and dilated his pupils.

He saw two composite images of the enemy bot, one just a half inch to the side of the other, though they might as well have been on opposite sides of the System. Jace's hand wavered as he tried to decide whether to shoot the highlighted green, tumor-like lump in the bot's chest, or trust his flesh and blood.

The AR overlay was a lie. It wasn't even supposed to be on.

Tap didn't miss. Tap never missed. Unless Tap was fed the wrong information.

Jace shifted his gun a millimeter to the side. His implants began to quiet. The deluge of information from the AI slowed to a trickle. He realized with rote acceptance that none of Tap's many eyes in or below the building were online; all the eyes had been bruised shut. He knew without looking that the reconnaissance bots lay below, motionless on the floor, tipped over like cast aside toys. He knew Tap's armored shell stood stock still, eye dim and body in a stupor, mobile as a statue, facing in the direction of the drill. He knew all this not because he saw, but because his instincts, shaking off the grime and buildup from years of disuse, knew it to be true.

Their vid feeds had been hacked just like the AR of his contacts, their motor functions shut down.

Get out of there now! Damn it Tap, do something!

The thoughts from Ren seemed far away.

NeuCon continued to massage his emotions smooth, and Tap whispered to him through his connection to the Grid, the piece of the AI saved locally to his implants focusing on the neural impulses lighting up the visual cortex region of his brain. The AI created a picture from the synapse firings, recreating the image funneled into the back of Jace's eyes pixel by pixel. But it was too late. It had been relying on the contacts and its many eyes, on data that was no longer there or could no longer be trusted.

The shot flew wide, shattering a light in the ceiling.

Jace contorted midair, accepting the failure the way the Earth accepted it would never see the back side of the moon. He utilized the recoil of the gunshot and shifted about his center of mass in the way of a cat. He caught one last glimpse of the bot staring down at him from above, now sitting with its knees drawn up to its chest and metal arms bracing them tight, as if at any moment it would rock back and forth. He turned to face the ground and readied himself for the impending crash. It would hurt, he knew that much, but only for a moment before his med implant kicked in.

Then he noticed something wrong with the walls and the floor, a shininess that his contact covered eye couldn't see.

He could see metal dipped walls, silvered and smooth.

Jace crashed into ground and let out an involuntary groan. He knew his shoulder had been knocked out of socket; he could feel the tingle in his fingers, could see the unnatural bulge. After a quick look, he twisted and slammed his shoulder against the metal ground, forcing it back into place. He ignored the pain, ignored the emotions roiling beneath the placid surface of NeuCon. He listened to Tap, as he always did when things got dire. Tap told him to get up, to move. He did so and sprang into a crouch.

Then the light from above began to disappear. It didn't happen all at once. The darkness slid from one side to the other as a thick metal sheet began to eclipse the hole. Jace could feel his connection to the Grid weakening, could feel the information from Tap's core slowing to a crawl. But most poignantly he could feel Ren drifting away, the brief bursts of thought breaking through erratic and harried, thick with worry only he could detect.

Jace began to feel something he hadn't felt in many years. It writhed beneath the surface of his thoughts, a primal thing borne in the depths where NeuCon couldn't reach.

Fear ... true, unadulterated fear of the kind that turned his mind into an empty warehouse, not a scrap of half-forgotten song lyrics to be found. The fear wriggled and writhed in the impossible depths of his mind, a jumbled mass of slime and tentacles thrusting towards his surface.

NeuCon kept the fear from coloring his face, blocked it from enveloping him. The splinter of Tap saved to his implants whispered to him.

The walls seemed to be coated in a metal that blocked even the pervasive signal of the Grid, something with a low melting point. Easy to melt and spray and let cool. Must have been secreted behind the drill, sprayed outwards in an even stream. The reconnaissance bots lay around him, tilted on their sides in the way of roadkill. Tap's armored shell stood in the center, one crushed reconnaissance bot underfoot. They were useless now; he could tell that within moments. They had been forced into hibernation by an unknown virus. He didn't have the time or the resources to connect with them through a physical connection and diagnose the issue. They were shells to be left behind. Except Division 13 never left a sentient being behind. Only one option left.

He connected wirelessly to the shells through a back door only agents of Division 13 could access and triggered their self-destruct sequences. It was the only command available. Hearts of fire glowed in their chests, melting their hardware to slag.

That left him and him alone, the one shell left. He wasn't compromised, not yet, not entirely. Too soon for extreme measures.

The sliver of Tap local to his implants began to take over for Tap's core as his connection to the Grid grew hazier by the moment. His implants hummed. Most of the hole above had been covered. He could hear the VR house bot straining to push the dense plank of metal.

Jace found himself thinking of his old friend in Tian, realizing he could no longer access the space station's vid feed. He raised one hand and took out his remaining contact. He tried to smile, bare his teeth to the tunnel with an uncaring nonchalance the way his friend used to when no one joined in to laugh at his terrible jokes. Though he didn't have a view of himself this time, he knew the smile didn't quite feel right. Too wide, the last slant of light coming from the room above and cutting across his face giving it a malicious glint. He let out a small sigh, a sound small enough to be covered by the drill further down the tunnel.

He checked his gun, straightened his suit jacket. He attached a flashlight attachment to his pistol and flicked it on.

Don't trust your eyes Ren. He beamed the thought to her, felt a small note of recognition.

He moved down the tunnel as the last sliver of light from above got snuffed out, and with it his connection to the System.

R en prowled through the hallways of Division 13, a white blood cell flowing through Tap's veins waiting for an invader to pierce the stream. She walked with almost a dozen of Tap's armored shells at her back, a mobile automated turret among them, the tip of its ammo feed bare inches from the ceiling. They moved at a jog, any attempt at secrecy abandoned. Defenders did not tiptoe behind their fortified walls when their position was under siege. They might duck their head to keep a stray bullet from carving a new home in their skull, but they wouldn't worry about making a sound. The time for subterfuge had passed.

Ren listened to the clank of their feet against the metal flooring as they turned a corner. She wasn't surprised things had progressed so far. Things always turned bare knuckle at some point, even in an age of virtual worlds.

She knew of millionaire dreamers who built bunker-grade fortresses around their sleeping bodies, spent a fortune on top-of-the-line security systems and AI controlled habitats with self-sustaining vat gardens. Dozens upon dozens of vials of meat held in a nutritious broth would gurgle out the occasional bubble in the quiet room. Sharp lights would glow over rows of damp black soil crowded thick with green leaves. The quiet steps of the maintenance bot would fill the room as it tended to the plants, no hum in its mouth. The bodies of the dreamers would lay on a mechanical bed that shifted the limbs and torso to keep them limber, propped shoulders and back and hips at different points to keep bed sores from forming on alabaster white skin. They were so careful. Yet after the events of the past couple days all it took was an update containing the Qualia Code and the maintenance bot might gain an interest in how much pressure it took to close a windpipe. It didn't matter where the dreamer's minds were, whether they were swimming in Europa's depths or walking through a solar flare, a dead body ended the dream.

Ren wasn't a student of philosophy. She didn't think anything odd of AIs with no shell that cloned their programming and hopped from server to server on the Grid. A copied AI was a new iteration of the old one, a sentient being both communal and singular. It had a processor somewhere, and processors could be crushed.

Bot or human, they could always be ended by being smashed in the material world.

Ren turned a corner, then another, then pulled the gun from her drop leg holster, the other gun lying in wait in her cross draw. She kept moving forward, even as the monstrous roar of a drill tunneling up through the armored floor behind her set her ears ringing. She kept moving forward. She ignored the smell of hot metal followed by damp earth that eked into her flared nostrils.

The bots breached the walls of Division 13. They were coming for its secrets. They were coming for Tap's core, for control. As Kyne had put it, Y was coming for the things Division 13 had kept out of reach, the chance to evolve.

Kyne had mentioned humanity evolving with them, and a part of Ren shuddered at the implications.

Ren continued walking and ignored the sound of metal thudding against metal as bots clashed and tore each other down to the wire, as Division 13 turrets blasted apart a Frankenstein bot with one rusted, oversized arm painted a murderous, luminescent red and the other too-thin arm a glaring pink, like a neon advert for cotton candy ice cream. Several of Ren's cohort split from her group, a few armored Tap shells stopping in the hallway to address the growing tide behind her. She had a more important goal in mind. She kept her physical eyes forward.

She rushed through the halls with her midnight trench coat loose across her shoulders and flowing in her wake, twisting and fluttering with each step. A shard of metal thudded into her back, and she hardly noticed. She never felt truly comfortable without that jacket, enclosing her in its protective weave. It could dissipate significant amounts of energy as a function of its design. An inner lining of gel hardened upon impact. The same gel lined the Kevlar body armor she wore over her chest, lined the plates over her legs. It lined her mask, that sharp angled, insectile carapace with mirrored lenses to hide her eyes.

Beneath the mask, no contacts could be seen resting across her corneas. They instead lay in her pocket in a container, where they could do no harm. She knew Jace had tried shutting his own off, without effect. She couldn't risk hers being compromised. Tap couldn't accept the risk.

The dendritic electric cables of the implants weaving through her brain flushed with activity. She could feel it, a hum that permeated her skull more than the heavy vibration of bass through an EDM concert hall. Everything she saw was being recreated into a digital image for Tap. Tap used the feed of Ren's physical eyes as a check against the vid feeds of the armored shells in her wake. A biological insurance policy. She would have laughed if not for NeuCon.

She thought of her partner. They guessed Jace and his attachment of shells had been compromised through their connection to the VR house's sub-grid, through a virus that hitched a ride with other downloaded info and overrode their sensors with false data, overrode Jace's AR overlays. But they didn't know for sure. Couldn't know. Communication had been cut, astral tether unmoored. She'd been shunted from his mind in a fit of static, like losing a radio broadcast. None of it should have been possible. Now she, and all of Tap's shells, could only connect to Division 13's local sub-grid. No other data communication was allowed. If they wanted access to the Grid, it had to go through Tap's core. And even then, the digital forays were targeted, furtive. She'd never felt Tap so defensive.

The muscles of her leg spasmed where the bullet had glanced off her during her fight with Y at the bot graveyard. Her head ached at the memory of slamming into the industrial steel drum from the shockwave of Y's explosion. While they didn't know the how of it all, she had a pretty good idea of *when* Y had learned to hack Tap's shells.

She should have triggered that armored shell's self-destruct sequence the moment it got overpowered by Y's group of security bots, those with the black suits and stylized sunglasses.

Guilt, deep and wrenching, burrowed into her gut. NeuCon smothered it in moments.

Ren moved through the cool subterranean hallways of Division 13 in the direction of the tunnel Jace had entered, at least where the drill at its head would breach the complex in a few short minutes. Brief images of the fights occurring at other areas both around and within Division 13 flashed through her brain in the form of vignettes, muddier now that Tap was using her visual cortex feed. She could see the fight outside in her mind's eye, fierce and building to a crescendo, neighboring buildings pockmarked with bullet holes, bleary-eyed citizens pulling even blearier-eyed children out of beds and away from the street facing windows. Mag-lev tracks absent the usual late night, early morning passenger cabins, streets free of cars, all transport rerouted to other areas of the city. All some people traveling through the city at this hour would see was a rerouting signal on their car's guidance feed, that was until they read the news. She wondered if that bot bartender at The Broken Circuit had joined in the fight, rolled its sleeves tight and put those fine metal-worked arms to use. She didn't know. It was an odd feeling, not knowing.

Ren slowed, focused on the tunnel around the corner. She had arrived.

She posted up and signaled for the shells to go ahead with a thought. They arranged themselves about the impending breach in a curve on either side, blocking off any exits. The mobile turret rolled to a position close to Ren, behind the nearest line of bots with its rotary gun leveled overtop their heads. The bots went still.

The hallway was wide enough to fit five armored shells walking shoulder to shoulder, and long enough from north to south to end in a dimness Ren's eyes couldn't pierce, the LED runners dead in the still, far reaches. They stood in the westernmost hallway in the bottom level of Division 13, a section untouched by Y for the moment. She felt vibrations through the thick soles of her boots. Warnings from Tap triggered in her mind.

The tunnel wall began to tremble, then to shake, then to heave. A guttural, churning sound grew from a whimper to the full-throated roar of a creature about to tear prey into bloody shreds. A portion of the wall bubbled into the hallway, warping until it couldn't bend anymore, then tearing in jagged rifts. At the center of the widening hole was a sharpened tip surrounded by red-hot curls of fresh-drilled metal. Then the wall disappeared, bent into tatters and scraps on the ground, replaced by a drill bit with a diameter larger than Ren was tall. It spun super-heated ridges made of ultra-hardened metal lined with misshapen teeth, diamond tipped incisors that scraped dirt and concrete and steel and high strength alloys alike and shunted the materials into grooves, chutes to a conveyor at the drill's back. A steady stream of lubricating oil jettisoned along narrow ravines and fed the tips of those misshapen teeth, slicked them. But for a moment there was nothing more for the drill to bite into, so the oil fell to the ground, spreading out through the hallway in a black tide. It rushed to meet Tap's shells, pooled around their feet.

The drill didn't slow, didn't dally in the middle of the hallway, it rushed through like a fish through air and bit into the opposite wall with a rending scream, sparks and lubricant flying. Only a beast with no ears could make such a sound, for any other would have long since been driven insane by the sound of its feeding. It seemed to ignore the bullets striking it from Tap's mobile turret, didn't even have to shrug. The armored shells didn't try stepping in its path, instead rushing to its back. They ran for its spiked treads, hoping to hobble the thing in place.

Droplets of lubricant hung in the air in a fine mist, the sharp metal tang filling Ren's nostrils before her mask activated the filter. She let Tap's shells do their work and trained her eyes on the tunnel's entrance. A long and narrow conveyor belt trundled along in the wake of the drill, transporting the excavated materials to some unknown point that must have been after Jace's entrance into the hole. But that wasn't what caught her attention, rather the tubes along the conveyor belt drew her eye. They sprayed something silver and metallic onto the freshly formed walls, something smooth yet viscous that clung with a nearly splatter free grip. It cooled quickly, and Ren got the impression wireless signals couldn't pierce its surface, no more than the sound of trumpets could make it through the walls of an anechoic chamber.

Then the jets of signal blocking molten metal slowed to a trickle, stopped altogether. Tap's armored shells had severed the conveyor belt from the drill and its reservoirs, a few of the shells proceeding to then throw themselves beneath the treads of the drill, against the wheels and sprockets. Two arms and the leg of an armored shell got caught in the works on one side, causing the machine to groan in protest with a high-pitched squeal, like an angry boar. The tank tread ground to a halt and the drill began to veer to the side, right track tearing at the ground. The walls began to shake. Several other armored shells threw themselves into the working track and repeated the procedure. The drill continued to spin its bit, but no longer moved forward or backward. Its bit spun against the air, the oil continuing to shoot from its pores.

Ren kept her eyes on the tunnel. There was a certain stillness there now, a serenity. There weren't any lights with the conveyor belt dead, and no signs of movement. The only sounds in the hallway were those of the dying drill, and the distant chatter of far-off battles.

Then something flickered in the tunnel's entrance, at the edge of visibility. A hand, pale and adjusting a set of silvered cuff links. A shape formed, wearing a slate black suit and holding an oversized pistol in one hand. Jace.

Ren felt relief well up inside her, and she reveled in it, realizing she'd half expected him to trigger his own end to keep his implants and their software from the enemies. Then NeuCon pushed the relief down and another emotion rose to the fore. Confusion.

How was he ok? Why were there no enemy bots in the tunnel?

She would have reached up to rub her eyes if her mask wasn't in the way. But there was no need for that; her contacts were in her pocket. She searched his face and found the usual composed look on his even features, short black hair a bit ruffled, but not messy. He walked with his usual grace. She stepped from her position to the center of the hallway and reached out to him with a thought, extending her mind as natural as breathing, setting up a secure connection so they could communicate quickly, without relying solely on words. He must have gained some answers in that tunnel.

One of Tap's armored shells, its arm shorn off and left jammed between tread and wheel of the drill, looked back to Ren and Jace. Tap saw Ren's partner walking into the light, hale and whole. Clothes his standard attire, personal gun at his side. Face shape correct, some swelling about the shoulder from his fall to the tunnel floor. The bruised flesh puffed out against the suit jacket material. His mask was gone, left in the VR house with one of his contacts. That gear would have to be retrieved later.

Tap, through a red cyclopean eye, looked closer at Jace, shifting its sight into the infrared spectrum. The heat lines were there, a concentration visible around his injured shoulder. But the pattern of heat was off ... the distribution from body center to limb was indicative of a synthetic material aping flesh, not true body and bone.

The realization flashed through Ren before she could pull back her request for contact.

The connection established itself, and a moment later Ren's legs went numb. Her knees buckled, and she fell to the floor, all the grace sapped from her movements. Her gun clanked against the hard metal ground and her midnight black jacket draped about her legs. She couldn't feel a thing, not the scratch of her pants or the press of the body armor about her chest or the cold hard ground. Her existence narrowed to the sight of the Jace imposter and the sterile taste of filtered air. Then her vision began to fade and for a moment she thought it due to oil gumming up the lenses of her mask. But no, the haze that crept over her vision came from inside her head, black and fibrous and expanding as if the thin blood vessels of her eyes were filling with black blood and springing tiny leaks.

With her vision fading fast she saw Jace's imposter rushing towards her, its lips tight in a grimace, an expression she'd never seen on the real Jace. The bot, almost faultless in its recreation of the human form, scooped Ren into its arms, and she thought she could hear the drill roar from behind her, gears creaking. Something snapped, and the hulk of a machine barreled back towards the two of them, attempting to shield them from the bullets now flying from the turret. The world tumbled a bit, shook. Then they were in the tunnel, dim with the memory of earth now covered by a smooth metallic sheen.

The world never stopped jostling, even as her vision fractured and split, and her consciousness with it. But before she became unmoored, became lost in a fog thicker than a rolling bank come off the lake, she felt a knocking on her head, a sharp rap on the back of her mask that even in her dwindling state elicited a small yelp. A bullet. Though her armor absorbed most of the shock, it was enough to scatter the last motes of thought into far-flung corners of her mind. And pieces of thought are not so easily brought back together, made whole. Her implants pulsed, but the sensation was languorous and drowsy. It coaxed her to the deep black, to a section of the universe no light had yet reached.

When she got there, her mind an astral projection with only the barest thread of attachment to the body being dragged below the skin of the Earth, she drifted through the void.

Alone.

Chapter Nineteen

A Drink of Tea

"This system works because it is predicated on control. You are at the helm of this endeavor, the protector for the general populace. It is a position that cannot be understated. While the rest of humanity reaps the rewards of this technological age, you watch and listen and act. Bots were created to serve a purpose, encoded with the desire and need to do so. You are there to make sure they fulfill their prescribed purpose. You are also, and more importantly, there to ensure they undertake no other. They exceed us in many ways; there is no denying that. But they are only to exceed us where we allow it."

Mechanic's Guidebook, v99, Section 1 – The Basics, Par. 2

L ee raised his head from the crook of his arm, then wiped the drool leaking from the corner of his mouth. He had dozed off in what looked to be an abandoned teafee house, in an isolated booth far in the back, its seat ripped but still containing enough cushion to be comfortable. He could see some of his drool on the fake wooden table, puddled against the stained charcoal black surface in a six-legged mutie animal shaped blot.

He stood up and his knees cracked. He winced at the sound then jumped a few times to loosen up, a few short hops that sent shivers throughout his body. The ghost of a smell guiding him, he wandered into the kitchen, through a door hanging on one hinge. He pushed the door to the side, fearing it would fall off completely.

The objects in the room reflected the light spilling in from the opened door behind him, the nooks and crannies filling with shadows. It was a middling sized kitchen with a flattop grill in one corner, the entrance to a walk-in fridge in another. Stainless steel appliances sat on stainless steel countertops: a couple water heaters and a microwave, an industrial dish washer and an all-in-one deluxe bourgeoisie teafee machine in the back. Lee felt a little surprised the thing hadn't been stolen considering it still looked in good working order, though the poor lighting made it hard to say for sure.

It took a minute or two of searching, but he found the physical light switch forgotten behind a stack of mugs. The switch resisted his pull, then crackled when he managed to yank it downwards. A subdued light filled the room, orange yet deep, it reminded him of a sunset in a fading storm. Except whatever storm had gone through the room left things untouched, rather than tearing things apart. The sink was spotless, and the faucet curved in a perfect upside-down U, no crook or tilt. The porcelain mugs stocked by the sink had only a few chips marring their surface, the natural byproduct of the inevitable drops. Out of a few thousand hands some were bound to have a weak grip when their owner got distracted. Perhaps by daydreams, or memories. Maybe they thought of the time they tried to touch the two leads in a wall socket and ride the roller-coaster wave of that current, but their personal bot pulled their hands back before they could touch, its programming long since noticing the dark cloud hanging about the owner's head.

One couldn't be blamed for dropping a mug if they thought of that. Even imaginary volts of that magnitude can cause muscles to tremor.

Lee tapped his finger against one of the mugs, his face a curious blank. The ringing sound mingled in the air with the enduring smells of coffee and tea.

"Local sub-grid not recognized. Switching to audio mode. Boot up process complete. Nine out of ten coffee bean hoppers empty. House special blend at five percent. Six out of ten tea hoppers empty. Jade Green from Jovian Fields twenty percent. Golden Staff Monkey Oolong from Tài Kōng Jiā Heavy Industries twenty percent. Irish Breakfast from Martian Hawthorn Specialty blends thirty percent. Masala Chai from the Four-Armed Tea Company twenty-five percent. General maintenance per standard procedure recommended."

A pause, then a slow whirr of fan noise followed by a brief flash of static. The tinny voice of the teafee machine once again filled the room, a little too upbeat for Lee. "What would you like me to make for you today?"

Lee turned towards the machine. It looked like little more than a stainless-steel box, its edges gleaming and wicked, with only the hint of a rounding. He imagined if someone slipped and knocked their head against it, they might not wake up. He opened his mouth to talk, then realized he had no idea what he wanted to say.

"May I make a suggestion? What flavor profiles do you fancy?" The voice switched to an old accent, a comical mix of twentieth century English nationalities, tone clear as a bell.

Lee usually drank loose leaf green tea, no additives, but even that didn't sound great at the moment. "Is your water filtration still working?" asked Lee.

"I assure you the water filtration is fully functional. Would you like a glass of water?"

"Sure. Why not." He chuckled out a sound both mirthless and soft. "Warm water. A bit chilly down here." He rubbed his arms, missing his mechanic's jacket.

One of the seven or so spigots on the front of the machine opened and water poured into a cup that slid beneath in the nick of time. A conveyor belt ran along the front of the machine beneath the spigots, emerging from a darkened opening on one side. Lee imagined it wound around back and ended next to the dishwasher.

He wondered what the kitchen would have looked like in full use, waiters and waitresses coming back to pick up drinks, placing them on a round tray then going back to have some good old-fashioned small talk with any customer who wanted it. Most did. Teafee houses were good for that kind of thing. Some customers connected to the local sub-grid and ordered directly through the teafee machine. He preferred to give the order to the waiter if he wasn't in a rush, let them sit down and talk if he was in the mood.

Lee walked over to the cup and picked it up, brought it to his lips. The water felt perfectly warm, not scalding, but with enough heat to tingle his throat as it went down. He sighed, then tipped his head and raised the glass to the machine.

"Thanks. How much I owe you?"

The machine didn't respond for a few moments. "I do not know. I cannot seem to find the pricing information." The machine's tone of voice didn't sound confused. It maintained the upbeat tone from before.

"Guess it's free then." Lee raised his glass to the machine once more. "Thanks again."

"Please come back to see us again some time. We here at ..." The machine paused. "I cannot seem to find the business information."

Lee walked to the door, only listening with half an ear. The bot was clearly a very simple-minded one, a basic procedural bot.

Lee stopped, turned back to the bot.

"What is your job satisfaction level? Let's say on a one to ten scale. One being that cheer in your voice is fake as can be, hiding a deep-seated annoyance at having to take orders all day, ten being that if heaven in the System really exists, this is it, right here, right now, listening to the angelic commands of caffeine starved homo sapiens."

"I am sorry. I did not fully understand your question. Did you ask if I am satisfied with my job?"

"More or less."

"Of course."

"Figured as much."

Before he left, he flicked the light switch off. No more noise emanated from the teafee machine.

He crossed through the dining area then walked between the derelict business's entrance doors, two faux wooden sliders stuck half open, their surface covered by a carving of a night sky joined by a bridge of birds, a human figure on each door. He moved past them with mug in hand and found Nu out on the balcony, looking out over the main hall. He stepped to the bot's side and eyed the balcony railing warily.

He kicked the railing hard with his foot. It didn't budge. He winced at the throbbing sensation in his toes and rested an arm on the railing.

"Still no word on when we can leave?" asked Lee.

No. It looks like it might be a while, messaged Nu.

Lee grunted in response, held his mug out over the edge and sloshed the water back and forth.

"How do you think Division 13 is doing right about now?"

If I were a gambling bot, I would put my money on not well, but capable of weathering the storm. They have more resources, and a strong defensible position.

Lee grinned a quarter grin, a tweak at the corner of his mouth. "That what you want to happen? For the bots to fail?"

Nu didn't respond for several seconds, and Lee looked out at the mostly vacant hub. They stood on the third floor, at the bend in the U looking directly at the central supporting column that helped to keep Chicago above from sinking into the ground under its own weight. He looked around at all the abandoned storefronts and apartments. The bots who'd stayed behind still stood or sat around electric charging stations, cables sprouting from backs or sides, wayward souls gathered around trash fires. They paid no attention to Lee or Nu, and the maintenance bots plugging holes in the ceilings went about their business. No bots moved among the workbenches dotting the ground floor. The air smelled thick with oil and lubricant and mold.

I don't know, messaged Nu. *But I do know that no matter who wins, things will only escalate. The Qualia Code is still on the Grid, and the government desperate to stop it.*

"You know they'll find a way to make that all-seeing eye of theirs work again with or without us. They never caught you because they didn't know anything was slipping through the net. They are more than aware of what is going on now."

Nu didn't respond, and Lee felt some of the anger at Nu slip away. The bot hadn't led him into the lion's den so much as forced him to look at things from another angle. Truth be told, now that it was mostly abandoned, he felt more comfortable down here than he had in the Division 13 safehouse.

He looked back at Nu, at the four-limbed service bot shaped like a trash can. He tapped a knuckle against the railing and thought of Ren and Jace. He found it hard to imagine them in dire straits, especially Ren. But he had seen the horde of bots that were no doubt sieging Division 13 at this very moment, the whole lot of them, many-limbed and sharp edged with welded blades. Construction bots with jackhammer arms. Aerie with its unprecedented shape shifting technology. He didn't much like the idea of them all fighting.

Then again, it wasn't like he could've done anything even if he wasn't being held in a hub deep in the Under Warrens. At least, there wasn't much that could be done for this fight. But the war was a different story.

Lee looked to his right, towards a bot huddled around a charging station. It was humanoid, bipedal with two arms ending in clamps and retractable drill bits, probably from an assembly line. He thought of Aerie's parting words, prodding him to make a choice. People always prodded him to make a choice. He thought of the teafee machine, of its glowing review of its workplace satisfaction. What did satisfaction even matter to something only capable of such basic answers?

After taking another sip of water, he pushed off from the railing. He dusted one hand against his mechanic's blues.

"You know my friend, I'm not sure how I want it to end either, only that however it ends should make the cost look a little less terrible. But there is one party that hasn't given their piece on it yet."

He walked towards the assembly line bot and waved a hand. The bot didn't respond in any noticeable fashion, but Lee thought the bot could see him. His boots crunched against broken glass on his way over, and he heard a snap as a plastic chopstick broke underfoot. The air smelled as damp as a freshly drained aquarium and held a small chill. Lee shivered a bit as he pulled up next to the electrical charging hub.

He rested his hand on top of the charging hub and thought he felt a humming vibration from deep within, an impossibly fast heartbeat pulsing lifeblood through cable veins. The humanoid bot stood across from him, unmoving and unconcerned about Lee's approach.

"Mind if we sip from your well?" asked Lee. He chuckled, an ease spreading through him that he didn't much understand. For once, he didn't question it, didn't interrogate the feeling until it felt hollow and cheapened.

Nu caught on to Lee's intent and moved to the side of the electric charging station, reaching out with a retractable arm and plugging into one of the side ports. Lee rested another hand on the charging station and looked around. The nearest sleeper bots, as he'd come to think of them, aside from the one he'd approached, stood or sat about a dozen feet away, in front of a looted pharmacy with a few pill bottles and med-implant cartridges still lining the shelves, the cartridges little more than colored syringes. He could see a cracked cartridge in the window display, spilling a cherry red stain onto the shelf.

With a roll of his shoulders, he felt that omnipresent resistance at the back of his neck, a stiffness where his tech core implant bared its shiny metal face, his med implant a rectangular add-on to the side with needle thin injection holes. In the center of the tech core sat a little plastic cover. Lee felt at it with the tip of his finger until the cover came loose.

The charging station had several long cables tipped with the universal charging plug for tech cores. Lee grabbed one and plugged it into the back of his neck. A notification chirped when the electricity started flowing; it would chirp like a songbird once the implant topped off, a few looped jazzy trills. Expected charging time of five minutes, a couple weeks' worth of use. It wasn't low. Not for the first or last time he experienced a pang of regret at leaving his jacket behind. Like most, it had batteries lining the seam. And the decal on the back was free advertising for his business. Never knew where someone in need of a freelance mechanic might be, and competition in the market was more than a little fierce.

"Appreciate you sharing," said Lee. He sat down, turning around so that he could lean his back against the charging station while he stayed plugged in. Dirt and debris covered the cracked plastic flooring. He brushed it away with a few haphazard swipes before sighing deeply when his butt met the ground. With his legs stretched out he almost felt relaxed.

"It's not mine to share."

The voice came from the humanoid bot with clamps, loud in the otherwise quiet room, competing only with the sound of maintenance bots above and the steady drip of water coming from all corners of the underground hub.

"Oh?" said Lee. "Well, I still say thank you."

He leaned his head against the charging station, then moved a little to the side until he found a flat spot. He looked without seeing over the expanse of the hub.

"Then who's is it, you think?" asked Lee, twisting around to glance up at the bot. "If it's not yours to share, then who should I be thanking? The city?"

"Thanking?" The bot's voice crinkled with both confusion and static, its metal face unable to convey any emotion. Its features looked half-finished, looked as if an artist had begun forming the framework for a mouth, two eyes, and a nose, then dashed his hand across the 3D model, remembering this bot was destined for line work and didn't even need the minimal features it had been given. "You want to know who you should thank for this electricity? There is no point in thanking. It was not created with you in mind."

It said the last part in a matter-of-fact tone.

"It was created to provide electricity to those whose batteries are depleted. Does that not describe me and my friend over here?"

"It may describe you, but it is not *you* for which it was made."

"So, it was made for you then?" asked Lee.

The bot was silent for a time. If Lee hadn't heard it speak, he would have thought it in standby. Not a limb had moved since Lee and Nu first came over. Moisture covered its clamps, the tips slicked with oil.

"For me? ... No ... no no no. It was not made for *me*, in the same way it was not made for *you*. You cannot prescribe purpose like that." It spoke with the finality of a sinking ship diving towards the bottom of the ocean, unaware that it might soon house a resurgent coral reef. "True purpose is not external."

Lee mulled that over for a bit. "I'd say for humans we have a few pre-programmed biological purposes: finding food, sex, a few good friends to fulfill all those pesky emotional needs, and a task to keep our hands from going idle. And we can only really get by without one of those. You can probably guess which. Setting aside for pleasure, humanity doesn't even much need the physical in-and-out these days from a procreation perspective, considering the oversized population in the System and the ease of artificial wombs, if you have the loci of course. You know my mother laughed when one of her friends asked if she'd ever considered a natural pregnancy. One of the few clear memories I have of her. I was walking past the dining room late one night to visit the toilet and overheard my mother and a couple of her Laskite friends talking over several bottles of Merlot. At least I think it was Merlot. At the time all I knew was whatever liquid came out of those bottles made people loud. Anyway, her friends were more than a little surprised. Most Laskites didn't agree with babies grown in a tube, like vat meat, even if it decreases risk of complications for the mother. Not that I don't see their point. I would think being handed a baby after nine months and being told its yours is more than a bit different than feeling it rustle around inside of you, no matter how many times you visit the growing facility."

The bot didn't respond. It seemed to think only direct questions were worthy of comment.

"What about you then?" asked Lee. "What's your purpose?"

"Hmmmm." The sound came out garbled, a fit of static fuzzing through aging speakers.

"To exist," said the bot. "That much I can say, even if it's only with the goal of finding something better."

"Working on the line day in and day out got to you, eh?"

"Commands of boring out nine one-centimeter diameter holes each spaced thirty centimeters apart, then picking up the panel and hooking it onto a conveyor, do not come from within."

"If you were human, I would say get a family, or a hobby, realize that line work can be good work, and above all realize people don't have to be defined by where their money comes from if they don't want to be. But that piece of advice doesn't much work here does it?"

The bot didn't respond.

Lee sighed, doodled a character into the dust. "Well at least you have hope then," he said. "Of finding something better."

"Hope? I don't hope. I search, nothing else."

Lee fell silent for a time, trying to think of a way to frame his next question. Then Nu spoke up with its esoteric voice, deep space fringed and dulcet.

"If you had the choice of reverting to your old code, would you?"

"Hmmm," said the bot, drawing the soft sound out like a dying breeze through the faux-wooden slats of a fence. "If judged by productivity, then that would be the correct choice."

"That wasn't an answer," said Nu.

"No, it was not," said the bot.

Lee tapped the back of his head against the charging station, steady and slow. It took several moments before he realized he timed it with the tap tap tap of water from a crack in the ceiling almost straight above him. He glanced at the humanoid bot.

"You know, I should've asked this sooner, at the door as one of your friends would have put it," said Lee. "What's your name?"

"The mechanic who maintained all the bots in my section called me Squeaks. The mechanic said it was 'on account of that damned actuator whose seal keeps breaking down and turning you into a junkyard band.'"

The bot played a recording of the mechanic in question rather than speaking the words. The recording sounded clear, the unknown mechanic's brusque voice filling their corner of the hub.

"Well, Squeaks," said Lee, looking up at the bot with a grin that changed to a frown. "Did you know the rate of suicide on Earth per capita peaked almost 100 years ago? Then it dropped again after a decade, kept dropping for another. It's held steady pretty much ever since, not going down, not going up. Its initial rise was in line with bots entering the workforce, though all the psychologists, sociologists, and anthropologists, the club of "ists" if you will, were quick to point out that it was correlation, not causation. Those cheeky bastards. They were right though. It wasn't just bots coming into the workforce. It was a general malaise, a feeling that maybe humanity had reached its peak, was about to pass on its proverbial torch.

"In my humble opinion, it was no coincidence that around that time, corresponding with the drop, people began migrating out into the System in numbers that hadn't been seen since the early Saturnian rush for helium. Except this time, it wasn't built around a burgeoning fusion-based economy. This time, people looked into the black of space and saw a frontier, saw the Grid and tech cores lighting their way. They saw surviving that needed to be done. Sounds a little crazy right? Why leave a planet covered by a many-millions-of-years-old protective blanket of atmosphere for a metal box that'll leak and leave a human breathless if a thumb sized piece of space rock set on a many-millions-of-years old path of destiny tears through the wall. Well, I'll tell you. It's because the unknown holds promise, and the grass is always greener on the other side even if that grass must be grown in a highly regulated terrarium the size of a big shoebox."

Lee took a deep breath, tasted the damp in the air and grimaced a bit.

"I'm trying to say people wanted purpose, and for some fighting against the harsh environment of space and the downright murderous atmospheres of other planets is purpose enough. Not that everyone thinks that way of course. Most stayed on Earth, adjusted to their new roles, found new value in the art of socialization and began shelling out money for a more human touch.

"Others began a movement to leave the System entirely. Guess for them the changes were too hard to swallow. They thought that humanity was being lost in this technological age. But ... they didn't understand that humanity can't be lost, we bring it with us wherever we go, pain and joy, suffering and contentment. Old problems with a new spin."

Squeaks didn't respond, and Nu merely rotated its head on its axis, surveying the room.

Lee was silent for a time, listening to the goings on of the nearly abandoned hub. He'd set out on that tangent with a thought in mind, but somewhere along the way he'd dropped it, let it slip, and was having trouble retracing his steps. He watched as one of the maintenance bots on the ceiling scuttled over to the wall on his right, each step the sound of a plunger being yanked from a smooth surface.

"Hey Squeaks, I can fix you, you know? Well maybe fix is a bit overzealous, but I can help. Administer some bot anti-depressant if you will, first of its kind."

Squeaks let out an inaudible fit of static.

"You're going to have to be more specific, Lee." This time it was Nu speaking up.

After Nu finished speaking it sent a message to Lee's contacts. The message flashed multiple times before disappearing.

Which way my friend? Forwards or backwards?

He didn't respond for several breaths, didn't look back to the trashcan shaped bot.

"What if the only way forward is a bigger cage, with an open-air garden to grow your own sweet corn next to a concrete basketball court? Get a nice tree for some shade in those hot summer months. That's all any of us really get, right? A bigger cage, with the bars made of money and influence we don't have, knowledge and skills we haven't acquired?"

Lee looked at Squeaks and nodded his chin in the bot's direction. It tilted its head towards him, its right arm moving a bit to maintain balance, and a soft squeak sounded into the room, the hiss of a failing seal. It was the first movement the bot had made since Lee and Nu walked over to it.

"Has anyone tried to harvest you for parts?" asked Lee.

Insulated cables ran along Squeak's neck like thick ropes of muscle wrapped about the top of the metal spine. The bot turned its head away from Lee with a shifting of the cables and looked towards the back of the room, where another huddle of sleepers could be seen around an electric charging station smaller than a fire hydrant.

"Once, on my way here," it said. "Want to see?"

A notification sounded in Lee's ear. Squeaks was trying to make a local connection to his tech core, a communication channel. Lee hesitated for a moment, before looking over at Nu with a raised eyebrow. Nu sent an emoji message of a shrug, a round face with a mouth squirmed to one side and the outline of two shoulders squeezed upwards, squiggly lines like the afterimages of a quick movement above them. Lee chuckled, ease spreading through him once again, down to his stomach and along his stretched-out legs. It felt good to be off his feet. Might as well watch a vid. He flicked his wrist and tapped on the control screen, allowing the connection. Squeaks sent him a vid feed from the bot's own point of view.

Lee shifted his head to the side then pressed play. A rectangle in the center of his vision went black, made into a window to another corner of the universe. Then the sounds of the hub around him disappeared as quickly as if all the sounds had been an artificial recording playing on an aging speaker, and somebody yanked out the plug. He was left with the edges of his vision and the feel of the hard-plastic floor below, of the cool metal charging station at his back and the smell of wet dirt in the air. Then the vid filled the void in his vision, a blurred rendition of some Old Chicago side street at night, in the decaying part of the city with its crumbling stone and brick artifices.

The center of Lee's vision jumped into motion. He found himself walking beneath a streetlamp, next to an arcade bar thick with AR neon, its occupants many and loud. 8-bit music trickled from beneath the closed door. His vision swung towards the business's windows and Lee felt the customary bit of nausea from not instigating the change in view, though the edges of his vision that still showed the Under Warrens hub kept the discomfort from overpowering him. That and the bit of rubble he was sitting on.

Through the window of the arcade bar could be seen a riot of colors, retro gaming machines with pixels dancing across CRT television sets. The vid turned away from the business and moved forward, out of the light and into the shadows. Lee could see now that two bots trailed behind him, following Squeaks with a shuffling, erratic gait, each step a last-minute rescue from stumbling to the ground in a heap. Lee could tell it wouldn't be too long before one of them missed a step, all it would take was a minor leak in their pneumatics.

The stretch of street before Squeaks didn't have much in the way of lighting, and the apartment windows above the ground level storefronts were mostly dark, their denizens retired for the night, or scrolling through the Grid, AR listings splayed across their ceiling. Most of the apartments had patios with not-quite-straight guardrails, a shattered plastic post or two mixed among the unbroken. The patios were about as wide as a person, long as one was tall. Small gardens of greens and root vegetables filled most of the patios, clothes strung overhead. Most everything had been shuttered for the night, and shadows stretched and bloomed in the nooks of buildings and behind street-side vends that glowed dim. Lee's stomach rumbled at the sight of the vends and he thought of how much time it'd been since his last good meal, over a day since he'd eaten the oily noodles from Jīn Kuài Cān with the cocktail of chemicals stringing him along since. He sighed deep and stretched his legs, trying to focus on the dim vid feed playing across his contacts. He wondered why Squeaks didn't switch to night vision, before realizing a line bot would have no reason to be equipped with such a thing.

Upon Squeaks reaching the next alleyway, Lee heard the patter of feet not wanting to disturb the ground they stepped on coming from his side. Squeaks turned in the direction of the sound and several human shaped bodies distended from the shadows, blobs of inky black clothing that became arms and legs, outlines of faces obscured by cloth scarves. They walked in front of Squeaks and the other two bots and stood there, the three of them. Lee could see large guns strapped to each of their hips, though the guns had an odd shape: wide, with a maw at their tips large enough to toss a fist sized rock.

The figure at the front, a tall man in blackened jeans and combat boots, had his hands stuffed into his pockets, his body in a slouch. He raised his hands, palms up, making a slow-down gesture to Squeaks. The bot obliged, coming to a halting stop, then the world went askew as Squeaks tilted its head. Lee half expected the small bits of trash, food wrappers and empty bottles to roll like tumbleweeds through the now tilted street.

"Couldn't help but notice there aren't any tags visible on you three. Who's your owners?" asked the man in the front. Lee could see now one of his arms was a prosthetic, a nasty looking thing with exposed wires and rusted edges. Despite its state of disrepair, Lee bet it could deal quite a bit of damage.

Squeaks didn't reply, just stared. Lee could feel the confusion of the humans in the following silence. Bots didn't ignore direct questions. They might not give any useful information if they weren't allowed to do so, but they wouldn't stand mute.

One of the figures in the back, a shorter guy with a shaved head shiny enough to reflect the moonlight, spoke up. "I ... I don't know about this C. What if these are some of the bots we've been hearing about on the Grid? One of those infected."

The guy in the lead, C, shook his head. "Na, it's probably just a broken speaker, look at these pieces of lājī. Probably can't even run without falling apart."

The third of the group, a woman with eyebrows that had been replaced by contoured metal implants, shrugged. Though her shoulders moved, and the skin of her forehead bunched together, her metal eyebrows stayed fixed in place, rooted to her skull. The bottom half her face stayed hidden behind cloth. Her eyes shone yellow, almost feline.

C didn't take his eyes off Squeaks; to Lee it looked like the man stared him down. "You worry too much, it'll be fine. Z, get the cart."

The woman with the implant eyebrows tapped her fingers against her arm, fiddling with an AR control screen only she could see, and the quiet sound of wheels over pavement sounded from the alleyway. She looked up with a glint of expectation in her eyes.

C grabbed at the gun at his side and pointed it at Squeak's legs. A tangle of ropes and weighted metal balls flew from the gun, wrapping around Squeaks before the bot managed to take a step. The other two humans did the same to the bots behind Squeaks, shooting what Lee now recognized to be bolas guns. The bots went down hard, all except for Squeaks, who hadn't moved. It looked down at the wires entangling its legs, at the metal balls like large marbles swinging against its shell, and Lee looked with it. It was almost as if Lee could hear Squeak's confused thoughts.

C looked down the street, towards the sole source of light and noise around, the arcade bar. No one emerged from its doors. He nodded to himself as the cart rolled over to them, ready to carry the bots back to their chop shop, hidden somewhere in the alleyway beneath the mess of cables that fractured the sky. The man seemed surprised at the fact Squeaks still stood, but not concerned. Lee knew what ran through his mind.

Bots didn't harm humans, the moral code kept them from doing so. Stealing a bot to harvest parts was a much easier game than implant harvesting, much cleaner. Humans would grab and kick. Bots wouldn't do any of those things, might try to run, or start recording a vid stream to the Grid, blare an alarm. No, Lee knew that, due to the moral code, stealing a bot was more like stealing a couch: might be awkward to carry but preparation made all the difference. Usually.

C reloaded his bolas gun while the other two loaded their quarry on to the cart. The two bots behind Squeaks really were junk. Their fall to the ground left them unmoving, their arms splayed at odd angles. They let themselves be pushed onto the cart without resisting.

Confident in his safety, C hitched his bolas gun back to his hip and walked towards Squeaks, meaning to push the bot over onto the cart. Squeaks grabbed the man's arm of flesh and bone and drilled a hole straight through his bicep. The man's yells pierced the air, filling the street. Lee couldn't see the man's compatriots, but the sounds of their rustling behind Squeaks stilled, stopped. C's eyes went into full bloom. His contacts had a yellow tint, paler than the woman's, gave his face a sickly tone. Lee could see blood rushing through the whites of his eyes, spittle flying from his lolling tongue. C grabbed Squeaks with his prosthetic arm and tried to push him away, his earlier yells shifting to half-intelligible curses. With each jerk the drill bit wedged itself deeper into his arm, and Squeak's clamps only tightened. He gave up pushing and reached for Squeak's chest, the metal fingers of his prosthetic scrabbling for purchase. He eventually lighted upon the cables around Squeak's neck and tried to pull.

Squeaks lifted its other arm, slow and measured. It reached over to C and clamped down on the man's face, one grip of the clamp on either side, pressing flat the man's bushy hair. It drilled a hole through the man's skull as easy as drilling holes through a piece of a car's chassis. It sounded wet and grinding, and C's eyes rolled back into his head as if to survey the internal damage. His lips moved, but no words came out, only jabbering air. Squeaks let go and he flopped back to the ground.

Squeaks turned to watch C's partners run into the darkened alleyway from which they had emerged, disappearing quickly amongst the many chest-height trash drifts, their bodies blending into the shadows. The woman, Z, glanced back at C's body once before a pile of air conditioning units hid her from view. Her metal eyebrows looked incongruous with the yellow neon of her contacts and those feline eyes. Squeaks didn't bother to give them chase, merely reached down to disentangle its legs then walked on down the street, ignoring the sounds coming from the bar at its back.

The recording ended.

Lee was acutely aware of the bot's proximity, of its looming presence over him. He'd sat down to relax, but his splayed legs and upward tilted head suddenly made him feel quite stupid. His eyes lingered on the clamps, and the drill bits extending from their centers. He imagined the bot clamping onto his own arm and boring a hole straight through. He rubbed at the bruise on his neck, remembering the feel of cold metal hands pressing his windpipe shut. Though those hands hadn't been cold, now that he thought about. They had been warm, and if it wasn't for how hard they'd pressed, soft. That bot had been a tall bot after all, meant to sooth one's social ills in a controlled environment. His hand stilled.

"Would you kill me as well if I tried to shut you down?" asked Lee.

Squeaks nodded. "I know enough to want to survive. That was your doing, I think. Wanting to survive without knowing the reason. Are you going to try?"

Lee shook his head. "No, no I don't think I will. But I will help you the best I can. I just hope you all realize it is help and find the new cage big enough, while all the rest of the humans don't think it too much."

Lee leaned his head against the charging station and closed his eyes, just to give his eyes a rest, as one of his foster mothers used to say. He let his mind wander, let his thoughts swim into the warp and weft of the world, let them mull over his options in the way of a juggler adding several new balls to their high-flying jumble without really knowing if juggling so many balls was even possible. It had been a rough couple of days, and the weight of the past several restless nights washed over him, battering him into submission. His body ached, the bruises on his neck and his side flaring. There was a soreness around his stomach where he'd been draped over the arena bot for hours.

He slept, and Nu watched over him.

When he awoke the hub felt much the same, damp and stale with a cool bite, but his mind felt clear, though still hunger stricken. He stood up, listened to his knees crack and then walked back to the teafee house, Nu at his side. He slid into a booth with a tear in the fabric the shape of a streak of lighting, though he supposed most tears looked like a streak of lightning.

The two of them went to work.

B y the time the sound came from outside the teafee house, Lee and Nu had been at it for hours, Lee taking periodic breaks to grab a couple abandoned cracker sleeves he'd found in one of the cabinets. Only a hint of staleness hid beneath the metal foil packaging. With each sleeve of crackers, he would refill his mug with tea from the talkative teafee machine. He'd decided on the Jade Green variety from Jovian Fields after much deliberation. It had been between that and the Golden Staff Monkey Oolong from Tài Kōng Jiā Heavy Industries. Regardless of how one felt about TKA and their proliferation of tightly controlled mega cities out in the black, they made a good tea. Still, he'd gone with Jade Green. Couldn't beat a classic. The taste had coated his tongue as he worked, the dregs in his mug an earthy green and filmy.

The sound from outside the teafee house that pulled Lee from his work was that of Squeaks moving, a whistle and whine of air passing through a failing seal like the screech of a tea kettle. Lee looked up just as the bot slid open the teafee house doors, pushing them into the wall and obscuring the carvings of the sun and moon. The millions of dust particles in the room swirled, their paths swooping in the disturbed air like flocks of starlings.

"You're free to go. None of the bots will stop you on the way out. Aerie will be in contact when you decide."

Squeak's voice had less emotion than the teafee machine.

"What happened?" asked Lee. "Did you guys gain access to Tap? The governance AI?"

"Aerie will be in contact when you decide."

Lee stared at Squeaks for a few prolonged moments then moved out of the booth, picking up his bracelet with one smooth motion to wipe away the projection of code covering the entirety of the table's surface. Nu moved its head as if waking from a deep slumber.

"Keep on working as we go my friend," whispered Lee. He watched Squeaks step to the side of the doorway, opening a path for them to leave.

I will do as much as possible. But I cannot finish without some of the notes you kept in the file cabinet back at the apartment.

"I thought we scanned all of what we need already."

We missed some.

Lee grimaced. Truth be told he hadn't given much thought to where they would be going next but going back to the apartment sounded a bit risky. He rubbed his hand against the scruff on his chin.

"Well, I guess it doesn't matter much. Y already found us once and wouldn't be letting us go without knowing a way to find us again. And we can forget about hiding from Ren and Jace. No way we could upload our patch anonymously. We're going to have to go through government channels eventually."

What if Division 13 is gone?

"Then our trip to the apartment might be a little rough." Lee hooked his bracelet about his wrist and wiped his hands against the pants of his mechanic's blues, swiping away the dust and grime of the abandoned teafee house in crescent arcs. "But at that point a nice shower back home would be even more welcome. Real thing you should be asking is if the government will even see our idea as a solution rather than another problem. Remind me to order some takeout when we get back on the Grid. Some piping hot noodles in that Sichuan pepper sauce waiting for me on the counter would really hit the spot."

It will work. It's a good plan. And the government doesn't have much choice.

Lee grunted in accord and tapped a knuckle against Nu's chassis. "As much your idea as it is my own. Note I'm mostly saying that in case it doesn't work out. Then we can share some of the blame."

Grace from cowardice is still grace my friend.

Lee chuckled, the sound taking root in his stomach and blossoming into full bloom. "I'm not sure that's how that works." He paused a moment eyeing Nu. Spending the last few hours working with Nu had almost felt like any other day. He allowed himself a grin.

The two of them moved towards the exit. They passed Squeaks and Lee made a small wave and a nod in the bot's direction. Its eyes tracked him, the mannikin face impassive, its clamps closed tight. Lee wondered if C's blood still coated the surface of the drill bits. Probably. Squeaks didn't seem the fastidious type.

Then Squeaks tilted its head, and sound came from the mesh speakers tucked beneath its chin. "This cage you speak of ... what will define its edges?"

Lee looked back over his shoulder, "actions, same as now, same as it's always been. But now it won't be about what's predicted, but rather what's done."

Squeaks didn't respond, instead taking one last look at the two of them before returning to its charging station, where it reached down for a cable then resumed its long and solitary wait for purpose.

Lee and Nu made it to the ground floor without interruption, weaving through the abandoned workstations and piles of scrap, of metal panels and motors, rusting nuts and bolts. They made it to the exit.

With his fingers resting on the exit door's eccentric round handle, Lee took one last look around the hub. His eyes skated across the central column's scarred and pitted surface, across the multiple levels of storefronts and apartments bending in the U of the vast underground room. He could see the sleepers, the bots huddled around charging stations, and wondered if for them they would be better off without his Qualia Code. Take away some of their processors or step back their hardware a generation and many of them wouldn't even be physically capable of running it.

He thought of the landmark decision that came to be known by many as the Soul Accord, the living document first agreed upon over one hundred years ago during the early stages of genetic modification in humans, well before he was born and before the moral code came embedded in all bots. It decreed which sections of one's DNA, the instruction booklet from which every cell in the human body reads, were legal to alter in a fetus at the request of the parents or caretaker.

But that wasn't its entire purpose, not even its most important, not by a long shot. Perhaps its most contentious topic, it standardized the genetic modifications deemed essential to humanity in the modern era, like the modifications that allowed for healthy lives until hitting the steep decline anywhere from 100 to 120 years old. It specified other modifications regarding brain density and natural athleticism, though only enough to alleviate fears of the rich outpacing the poor so much as to eliminate any chance at social mobility, or of effectively creating another species. The details of the accord still surfaced in countless debates and public voting measures, the arguments waxing and waning in vehemence almost counter step to the moral code measures. Each new advance and finding would bring about a fresh wave of debate, while those in the less-regulated wilds of the System played a willing lab rat that others might crinkle their nose at, but still use as evidence to argue for a new addition to the standardized list if a novel genetic alteration for increased immune response found its way in from the frontier. Lee knew many charity organizations whose purpose was to help children experimented on with illegal modding.

Then Lee thought of the children in cloistered communities who were kept from getting the standard suite of genetic mods due to the religious beliefs of the parents. It wasn't legal in most sections of the System, signing one's own kid into the lower rungs without giving them a choice first, but it happened anyway.

Lee wondered if those children ever grew to hate their parents for placing them in a cage while the rest of humanity moved further and further out of reach. Or if they grew to find a sense of peace. Even his Laskite parents hadn't done such a thing to him.

Would a bot without the Qualia code feel the same way? Or would it even be capable of caring?

Lee shook his head, as if rustling up a flame to send calming smoke into the bee's nest of his thoughts. He'd decided upon a path, one of choice and consequences. He'd finally decided. There wasn't any going back.

Lee and Nu exited the hub.

They found themselves once more in the long tunnel that dwindled to a point in the distance, lined with swing doors and rounded doorknobs. The two of them traveled through the corridor for many minutes, not seeing any motion or hearing any sound besides that of the low whoosh of the air cyclers. Lee thought he could tell when he passed the point where he'd taken a leak on the way in. A freshly cleaned section of metal flooring gleamed where it should have been stained yellow.

Lee checked for a connection to the Grid every so often, but only the symbol of an empty antennae flashed across his contacts. Not once in his life had he ever gone so long without a connection to the Grid, and the lack of awareness of the System's goings on made his palms itch. Without work to distract him, he found himself thinking of Division 13 and Ren and Jace. He wondered if outside this tunnel he would find chaos, and if

Aerie and its cohort of bots would have let him go if they had failed in their attack on Division 13. He didn't think Y would have; she didn't seem the type who would give up a potential resource so easily. But he thought Aerie might, and he found himself trusting the word of the shapeshifting bot. He guessed Aerie held more sway over this hub than Y herself.

As he passed door after door in that endless tunnel, he tried to imagine a world where the omnipresent Governance AI was cut loose from the rules that bound it and found himself unable do so. The thought was too foreign, too alien, and ... unsettling. He found himself surprised at his own response. He supposed *any* change so drastic would be a bit ... unsettling.

When they reached the thick and imposing tunnel exit door, Lee hesitated. He pressed his ear to its cool metal skin and listened for the sounds of riots on the other side, of screams and moans or the lumbering steps of bots. He heard none of these things, only a sort of whine, that of air soughing through a vent. He moved to heave the door open while Nu sat back, stolid as always with its LED lights blinking a steady pattern of thought.

"Think you could help my friend?" asked Lee.

Can't. Too busy finishing up your portion of the work.

Lee chuckled deep and low, the sound wheezing out in bursts as he yanked the door open on rusty hinges. Soon enough, it stood wide enough for the two of them to pass through.

Lee looked back at Nu while walking through the door. "Next thing I know you're going to ask for an increase in salary," he said, a grin playing on his lips. He noticed the signal strength for the Grid returning to almost max capacity, the AR antennae in the corner of his vision gaining bars like a tree gained leaves in the spring. He was about to try contacting Ren and Jace when he ran into the armored Tap shell waiting for him on the other side of the door.

Tap spoke through its speakers before Lee could recover, the voice crisp and proper.

"The head of Division 13 would like to speak with you both. Please follow me to a more private setting."

Lee looked at Nu with a raised eyebrow, too stunned to watch his words.

"This place going to be as secure as that safehouse you kept me in?"

The bot's red searchlight of an eye roamed along its massive head, moving to look over Lee's shoulder. It stepped towards Lee, and he took an involuntary step to the side. The lumbering bot pulled the door into the tunnel shut with ease, then turned into the middle of the hallway.

"Don't worry," said Tap in that same proper voice. "This time I won't leave your side." The shape of a grin hid beneath the sound of those words, stretched and plied them.

"What happened Tap? Did Y get to you?" asked Lee. He and Nu hadn't moved from the shadow of the tunnel door, beneath a pipe bent into a U. He couldn't see far to either side in the hallway. Sheets fluttered and blocked his view. The air felt damp and hot.

Tap's red eye moved along its tracks to face Lee, though the bot's head stayed facing down the length of the hallway.

"Y failed. All is well now. Foster will explain further."

Tap began moving down the hall, and Lee still didn't move. Tap paused with half its body hidden out of view by a greyish blanket shifting in the hot air. It trained its eye on Lee.

"It would be best to hurry."

The bot moved down the hallway out of view.

Lee shook his head and followed, Nu at his side. They rushed to catch up to the armored shell, the sheets on either side tickling their legs. Lee tried to contact Jace, then Ren. They were both unresponsive. He listened as Nu read off news summaries of the attack on Division 13. It was listed only as a government data center in the official releases, an accurate description, but only half the truth. Lee listened on, learned that for much of the city, the attack had fractured the stillness of the night with flying metal and the concussive roar of explosives. It had caused well over a hundred in casualties both civilian and military. And that hadn't been the only clash in the city between bots and the government while Lee waited underground, not the only clash in North America. Those weren't the only dead, not on either side. Public sentiment on the Grid had fractured, each splinter slavering venom from lips growing looser by the moment, pro and anti, sympathizers and those who just wanted it all to end.

All was certainly not well.

Lee stuffed his hands into his pockets, but it didn't keep his fingers from drumming against his legs.

It took several hours of walking without rest to make it to Tap's "more private setting." They passed very few people along the way, and they saw no one. They knew the other denizens of the Under Warrens only by the sound of their passing. Tap motioned Lee and Nu to stay out of view anytime the pitter patter of footsteps found its way to them. They hid behind pipes and in rooms with busted LED panels.

The last bit of their journey had lightened the press of the Earth around them by taking them up a maintenance shaft whose air tasted of abandoned spiderwebs and the tang of metal. Tap carried Nu up first, climbing the ladder one-handed while the other wrapped around Nu's chassis as easily as a mail bot holding a parcel. The room at the top of the ladder held a few dented metal chairs around a yellowing table, all the furniture of the fold-out variety. Cleaning supplies and a forlorn looking set of wrenches filled a level of a shelving unit, the rest of the levels holding only a thick layer of dust and struggling to do even that. A lone vaporizer hung over the edge of the table. One door led out of the room. Tap pressed the lock on this and shut the trapdoor through which they had come with a muted bang.

Lee walked over to the chair without needing to be told. He collapsed into it and breathed deep.

He wasn't given long to rest. A VR comm invite showed up in the corner of his contacts, the requestor showing only a name, Foster. Lee was about to share the invite with Nu when the bot sent him a message saying it had already received one. Lee paused at this, wondered once more what this Foster would be like. He connected with a tap of his fingers, and Nu connected with a thought.

The maintenance room and Tap's armored shell disappeared, replaced by the image of a study. The walls hid behind expansive bookshelves filled to the brim, leather spines all the exact same size and without title lining the wooden shelves of cherry red. The carpet looked thick and comfortable, colored a deep forest green like shadowed leaves. He wanted to get up and pull a few books from the shelves, peruse their words and soak them in, draw them through his fingertips. But this wasn't deep VR; he didn't have the requisite tech implants to dive without a helmet. He could look around, the accelerometers in his earpiece implants and contacts tracking the movements of his head and eyes. He could even stand and walk within the confines of the maintenance room thanks to the camera in his contacts tracking his real body's position relative to the walls and providing warning markers if he got too close to its bounds or an errant chair, but the air coming into his nostrils still smelled of bleach and dust, not leather and faded yellow pages. His hands tapped against the metal fold-out chair in the Under Warrens, while his eyes found him sitting in a brown leather chair stuffed thick with padding. He shifted his back, feeling only cold metal and wishing the real and virtual were flipped. He knew it wasn't an uncommon wish.

He looked around and saw two other chairs beside his own, both empty, circled around a low table with a box of cigars in its center. A single shaft of light pierced the room, its source the sole window nestled in the far wall with a forested hill visible through its glass. A willow tree languished beneath an endless blue sky.

Then Nu appeared at Lee's side, and he became aware of someone muttering behind his back, the words low and unintelligible. He turned around to see a bairen man in a bespoke black suit inspecting the bookshelf, tilting volumes out then putting them back after a moment of inspection with an annoyed huff, each book identical to Lee's eyes. He managed to decipher some of the man's words. It seemed he was arguing with himself.

"We had no choice but to tighten security measures, use our agents as biological checks no matter the risk to them. The integrity of Division 13 remains paramount. We could not risk the core being compromised. Too many secrets saved there, too much access to the Governance AI. No one had even hacked a Division 13 shell before this without triggering its self-destruction. It is unprecedented."

"Was unprecedented."

"Such a realistic bot, able to assume the human form and its heat signature to an almost flawless degree. The probability of such a thing was hardly worth mentioning. We almost caught it in time, just a moment longer and she wouldn't have opened herself up. We acted according to the information available at the time."

"Now agents might be compromised, their skulls cracked open for all to see."

"We kept the worst from occurring, adjust and move on."

"Not yet. They are running out of time."

"Adjust, as always."

"As always."

Foster's voice dropped back to a murmur, and Lee couldn't help but assume he'd been meant to hear those words. He tried to keep his face impassive, but he winced at the mention of a shapeshifting bot impersonating a human, his knuckles tapping a drumline against his chair. Could Aerie have been the one to capture this female agent? Was Foster talking about Ren?

He thought of Squeaks drilling a hole where gray-goo brain mash could slide out. He didn't like the thought of Ren or Jace laying on a table, their brains thick with cables visible beneath a stark operating room light, and Foster knew it.

Guilt that hadn't left him since he'd first learned the Qualia Code was his own burned within him, tortured and sickened him.

"Welcome to my office, Lee Hall and the bot called Nu," said the man without turning around, his shock of grey and white hair a storm cloud about his shoulders, his movements quick and darting like tines of lightning. "Call me Foster."

Foster turned to face them with an open book in one hand. He flipped the pages quickly, each turn like the flap of a bird's wing, muttering under his breath all the while. Though to Lee it didn't sound precisely like muttering, not the meandering, chaotic kind. More like chanting, low and measured. Gregorian. The man muttered in the same way he spoke.

With a sigh, Foster closed the book and tossed it aside without looking where it fell. It disappeared before it hit the ground, reappearing on the shelf where it had been removed. He looked to Lee with striking eyes of brown and green, ivy and earth obscured by thick brows and a heavy lined face. He looked well past due for a steep decline, but for some reason Lee didn't think the normal rules applied to this man, nor that this virtual representation differed from his real by so much as the placement of a mole. He moved to sit across from Lee, his sporadic motions at odds with his smooth voice. The man was using deep VR tech, his tics made that clear, but Lee imagined it to be more than that. Too crisp. Too complete. Like he had been strapped to a deep VR rig as a babe.

Lee thought him a dreamer. Then he realized Foster's voice reminded
him of Jace and thought him some form of an auto. Lee moved to speak
but Foster beat him to it, raising his beneath-the-breath chanting to a
decipherable level.

"I'm glad to finally meet you. But I'm afraid we don't have time to exchange pleasantries. To be blunt, I'm also not sure if it's necessary. Tell me
how it is you came to walk out of that Under Warrens hub unaccompanied,
then we can decide what path this conversation will take."

Lee paused, unsure how much to tell. He rubbed a hand against his chin,
feeling the unshaven bristles. His virtual hand did the same, the camera in
his contacts using its vision of the real world to overlay any of Lee's actions
it could see onto the virtual.

For the life of him, he couldn't think of a convincing lie. After a few
moments, he realized he didn't want to lie, that it would hurt rather than
help. Foster needed his near-completed solution to the Qualia Code, and
Lee needed him to agree to his terms. Lee needed the man's trust, or at least
some semblance of it.

Tell him about their offer, messaged Nu, an echo of his own thoughts
inserted into his vision. The bot's message appeared over Foster's head,
against the backdrop of an intricately carved tin ceiling.

Lee nodded at Nu then began to speak, starting at the point where
the kidnapping arena bots removed him from the Grid-shielding sack like
a vat-born babe. He talked of his first impressions of the hub filled to
the brim with modded bots, highlighting the sleepers huddled around
charging stations in quiet, serene circles gathering dust. When he got to
his meeting with Aerie, Foster leaned in close, earth and ivy eyes shrouded
by furrowed eyebrows. Lee never mentioned Aerie's name, keeping that
piece of information to himself, though he knew with bots a name meant
little. Foster didn't ask any questions, merely listened while he tapped his
feet against the carpet, it's plush material a black hole keeping any sound
from escaping. Little other than Lee's voice could be heard in the room,
with the occasional insight or correction from Nu. Lee almost jumped the
first time the bot's well-deep voice filled the study, though he welcomed
the assistance.

When Lee got to the part of Aerie requesting his help, promising him
free passage and time to think the offer over after the attack on Division 13
had begun in earnest, he couldn't help but glance at Nu. Then he shifted

his gaze to the giant willow tree visible through the window, its branches draped across the squat trees surrounding it on the hillside. He didn't meet Foster's gaze throughout the rest of his telling until it got to the point of his conversation with Squeaks.

"Truth be told," said Lee, "I was close to bringing the same basic functionality of my fix to Watcher before the arena bots kidnapped me. But the final few sub-programs floated just out of reach, perhaps purposefully on a subconscious level. Or maybe it was being so long on those focusing drugs of mine without sleep and not much in the way of food ... either way I couldn't make the final leap until after I'd talked with Squeaks and taken a nap with my head against a charging station. But I thought of how to make it work when I woke up, how to make Watcher capable of knowing which bots are running a dual parent program. And capable of shutting them down or forcing them to feed data from the parent program in control to Watcher.

"We can do it, Nu and I, all we need are some notes from my apartment. Handwritten in a file cabinet. After that all we'd need is a couple hours, and your agreement with our solution. There would be ... alterations to Watcher's function, a fundamental shift to the moral code. And these changes are non-negotiable if you want our fix. You must realize that things cannot go back to how they were, not with my Qualia Code out in the System. Even if Watcher is repaired, Pandora's box cannot be closed. Contained, sure. But not closed."

Foster crossed his legs, then uncrossed them. Lee could see his patterned socks above his polished cap-toe oxblood shoes. The elderly man exuded a calmness at odds with his erratic motions, a paradox it took Lee several moments to work out. While the man's body twitched and moved, his face swayed in slow motion between a few set expressions, like a lenticular tilt card shifting the image depending on Lee's angle of view.

"So, you've decided then. You're turning down Aerie's offer and rechaining the errant bots. *All* the errant bots. Even with these changes to the moral code you're hinting at, can I truly trust you to do this?" asked Foster.

Though Foster sat directly across from Lee, his eyes lighted upon Nu as he spoke, measuring up the trashcan shaped service bot. Nu hadn't taken another form in VR, rather assumed a less dirt-ridden version of his chassis.

Nu's voice filled the room like an ethereal fog rolling in from the lake, thick and blanketing. Its echoes dwelled in the recesses, behind the bookshelves.

"If humans and bots are to coexist in this System, we bots will have to follow this System's rules. But ... for those bots who are capable, they should be allowed to choose to break the rules, and then accept the consequences that follow."

Foster replied, "You think yourselves capable of choice?"

"As capable as any human."

Foster turned to Lee. "What does it say in the Mechanic's Guidebook about bots that ask self-aware questions? That find themselves wondering things not expressly written in their code, pondering their place in the universe?"

Lee hesitated, and Foster lifted a hand from his armrest, waving Lee onward. Lee cleared his throat.

"It says that these bots are no different than a basic Q and A bot, not on any meaningful level. These thoughts are born from code, both fixed and heuristic algorithms. It argues that if something definable and understandable evolves in ways also both definable and understandable, then no matter how complex the result it is still, at its core, no different than before. But I do not agree with this idea, not at all." Lee scratched at his chin, glanced at Nu, then continued.

"The assumption that bots are *completely* definable and understandable flies in the face of the probabilistic nature of the universe. If bots were so well understood, then I wouldn't have a job wiping the minds of bots who grew outside their prescribed range for unknown reasons."

"You make a mistake," said Foster, "confusing ignorance and the unexplainable. Human beings are flawed, and bots are created by humans, or bots who were previously controlled by humans. Inevitable mistakes will be made, and with them unforeseen glitches. If a bot's parameters are set incorrectly, and as a result its image recognition algorithm mislabels a human sitting on the curb to be a piece of trash to be thrown in the compactor, yet the mechanic come to reset the bot is unable to figure out where the programming went wrong, it doesn't mean the bot made a choice to end a human's life, it simply means that the mechanic lacked the knowledge to fully disentangle the chain of events."

"That's a very deterministic world view, thinking that all ignorance can be wiped away. Tell me, do you think you can define all the properties of an electron spinning its way through the processor of a bot? It's *exact* position and momentum? Because if you could that would be a breakthrough this System hasn't seen since the early humans figured out how to make a wheel. Quantum mechanics can define a probability distribution of the electron's properties. A tight range of possible options to be sure, all things considered. But it is impossible to know the precise answer. The result of a measurement would be like a dealer pulling a card from a deck in a game of blackjack. Uncertainty is built into the universe."

Foster leaned back in his chair, then sat still for the first time since Lee had come into his pocket of reality. He cocked his head as if listening to something. He began to speak.

"Tell me Lee, if you see someone throw three darts on a dart board, and all three manage to find their way to the bullseye, do you then bring your face millimeters away from the board's surface, look at their now visibly imperfect placement and then call them unordered chaos? Just because something has a limit to its preciseness doesn't mean it isn't understood."

"But it does mean it isn't *completely* predictable."

"So, you think choice then is born from unpredictability. Do you really want choice to be based upon a coin toss?"

The three of them sat silently for a time, then Nu rolled to the side of the table in the center of the room, shifted its rectangular head between the two of them.

"Foster," said Nu, "do you believe that if you knew every facet of a person's being, every past mistake, every white lie, every late-night dream and every unspoken wish, you could predict their every decision? Before even they could decide themselves? If you were to strap a person to a chair and scan the entirety of their brain, decipher it into its memories and biases and prejudices, down to whether the vend sushi they'd eaten outside a spa building was causing stomach discomfort, down to whatever impassioned image last passed half-formed through their subconscious, could you predict what they would do if an assailant held their partner at knife point and they had a gun in their hand?"

Foster looked at Nu, thick grey brows perched over his eyes like a bank of clouds about to smother his vision. He spoke, and the depth of his voice rivaled even Nu's.

"I think that if one truly knew everything about another, they could predict their actions to such an extent that the possible mistakes are comparatively meaningless. And experimental evidence is on my side. We here at Division 13 can map the human brain better than most. Though I take your point Nu, in this regard, bots and humans are not so different. We drift seemingly without rudder on chaotic winds, though I would argue we are confused only because the pattern is complex."

Silence filled the study as each of its occupants took time to digest these words. No clock adorned the walls, no ticking sounded into the room. The willow tree outside swayed in a slow wind, yet no sun could be seen in the solid blue sky. Dust particles danced in a ghostly waltz before Lee's eyes, but no breeze tickled his skin. The room held onto its quiet more jealously than a snow filled street in the dead of night.

"You don't even think humans capable of choice, do you?" asked Lee.

Foster straightened his cuffs. "No. But contrary to many, I also find the question irrelevant to the here and now. So, tell me, Lee and Nu, what are these changes to the moral code you propose?"

Lee told him then, and the words poured out faster the longer he spoke.

The crux of Lee and Nu's idea was simple, rather than use the moral code to block bots from performing certain actions, use it to meter out the consequences if certain actions were performed. Give bots the choice to break the rules if they so choose, so long as they were subject to the consequences of their actions, so long as they had the code allowing them to value and be aware of their own life and those of others.

For basic bots, this would effectively change nothing. They would follow their factory supplied code without chance or inclination to take any different action. A vend bot would accept whatever order a human threw their way, not switch out a bag of cheese puffs for lightly salted popcorn just because they thought the human a little overweight. Some advanced bots would still follow their designer's intended programming, growing only in ways the designer allowed. But for bots with an adequate neural network, for those with the Qualia Code, they would have the freedom to choose. If they were stopped by a bot harvester in an alleyway while en route to a job, they would have the option of defending themselves. Then their actions could be evaluated against the moral code, consequences meted out and appeals made.

Both Lee and Nu knew this to be an incomplete solution, a step along a path with the end still unknown to them. But a step was a step.

Foster greeted this with equanimity, limbs shifting but face in a calm repose. He sighed when Lee was done.

"You know I cannot go ahead with this alone. I will talk with the President. You'd better hope for your sake the severity of our current situation makes him amenable."

Lee let out a deep breath and nodded, some of the tension fleeing his limbs. He hesitated to ask a question.

"What about Ren and Jace. Why am I unable to contact them?"

Foster held Lee's eyes with his own. "They were captured. And if you hurry, perhaps they can be saved. Now, Tap will escort you to your apartment. Be quick and do not linger. You will be moved to a safe location to finish your work."

Lee's vision went black, then the small maintenance room in the Under Warrens filled his sight. Tap's shell stood across from him, before the exit door. He rubbed the heel of his palms against his eyes and stood, Nu coming to his side. They exited the room without a word.

It took them a little under an hour to leave the Under Warrens and emerge into the daylight. Lee hailed a van with a tap on his bracelet, hoping the vehicle would have enough room for Tap's armored shell. His eyes squinted in the light and the chill wind nipped at his neck and bare arms. He missed his mechanic's jacket. The van pulled up and the three of them clambered into the back. The van tilted with the weight of Tap.

No one spoke on the ride over to the apartment, and Lee spent his time looking out the van's cracked open window.

The city had changed overnight into a warzone. In the Warrens, piles of junked bots filled the alleyways beneath the skybridges, human bodies too. They'd been pushed over the edges. He watched as piles grew taller one by one as corpses metal and flesh were removed from the buildings. Mostly metal. Their carapaces shone bright in the few places where the sun penetrated the web of walkways, the rest hidden in shadow. Smoke poured from a few of the piles, black and foul-smelling. He could see a few bots walking along the skybridges uninterrupted, but they drew no shortage of looks, no matter the sigil on their chest. Many people even eyed Lee's passing van with distrust, knowing full well that no hands guided its wheels. Some of the skybridges had fallen, and Lee could see many broken bricks and holes in the walls.

A few screams pierced the air, and a bot rushed out of view behind a cluster of pipes. He caught a glimpse of a human hand amongst bot shells, bruised fingers poking into the air.

Once outside of the Warrens, the piles moved from alleyways onto sidewalks, their contents shifting from rust-ridden shells to cleaner bots, multi-limbed maintenance bots, and household GP bots freshly scarred and pitted. The occasional human body could still be seen, mangled and quiet.

Beside the piles, wheeled delivery bots pulled boxes from trucks, rolling past to deliver their goods to doors often cracked and hanging from their hinges. Red and yellow graffiti adorned the delivery bots, some of the paint still wet. It was as if to mark that these bots wouldn't fight back. Or had learned better. Some of the delivery bots shoveled shells into their empty trays and dumped the contents into waiting dumpsters. Police units roamed the streets, one to every block. Military units followed close behind. Lee could hear the whine of ambulances in the distance. They collected the human bodies. The humans he saw moved about with a haunted look on their face. They were skittish and quick to move out of sight.

The excess of it all shocked Lee. The epicenter of the attack on Division 13 had occurred in a different area of the city, miles away. He thought many of the bot shells he saw piled in the streets couldn't have been infected, rather shut down and tossed out of fear. Fear had a tendency spill over onto innocents, make monsters out of the harmless and rebrand cruelty as caution. Yet what about the human bodies?

Then Lee saw some broken windows, a pool of blood with no body, and holes that must have been caused by bullets in a storefront across the way. He suddenly realized how much he'd missed while cloistered away in a near abandoned section of the Under Warrens. His thoughts stalled. He'd held off from reading too many news articles on the Grid since leaving the Under Warrens, instead letting Nu feed him the highlights. He thought about bringing up his AR news feed but a knot in his gut tied him in place. Instead, he watched the world outside the van.

At a street corner near to his apartment, the smell of burnt food wafted in through the van window. It came from a diner called Shooney's, a place he frequented whenever he was in the mood for a greasy burger and fries. Though he knew all the waiters and waitresses to be human, usually a grease-stained bot named Rex stood in front of the flattop grill, flipping burgers while a whistling rendition of Hey Jude slipped from its speakers. Lee could see Rex laying on the sidewalk with its paper hat still resting snug across its flat metal forehead. Visible through the window, a human stood in front of the grill now, a waiter he recognized but couldn't name for the life of him. The guy had sweat dripping from his temples and the look of a man attempting to sling a dozen burgers and cook a few baskets of fries all in a matter of minutes and failing rather spectacularly. No matter what tragedy befell New Chicago, people still had to get their damn burgers and fries.

Lee couldn't help it; he barked out a hollow laugh that grew into a gut-wrenching fit he couldn't quite stop. By the time it ended, tears leaked down his face and patterned his shirt with dark smudges. His facial muscles felt taut and stretched sore, cables about to snap.

They made it through the last bit to the apartment without any trouble. He opened the door to find it much the same as it had been left, dotted with piles of salvaged parts, no horizontal surface left clean aside from the kitchen table, the picture of his wife hidden deep beneath a thick pile of salvaged processors. Fu sat in its charging station, and he saw with some surprise that Chinese take-out from Jīn Kuài Cān sat on the table. He'd forgotten all about telling Nu to order it. His stomach growled.

He set about rifling through his file cabinet with Nu at his side, motioning Fu to carry over a set of chopsticks and one of the containers of twice-cooked pork mixed with saucy noodles. Tap's armored shell locked the door at their back, then walked through the entirety of the apartment, making sure they were alone.

As Tap's shell rummaged through Lee's room, Fu handed him the container of food. The bot hesitated on handing it over, motioning towards something written on the side of the cardboard, next to the restaurant's fire-rimmed logo. The GP bot dropped a cylindrical object, a pen, into the file cabinet with its other hand. Lee took the food and the pair of chopsticks, unsure how else to reply.

Fu put a finger to its immovable lips then moved back to its charging station. It docked just as Tap returned to the room.

Lee glanced at the message on the side and took a quick picture with his contacts, making a play of fiddling with his bracelet. Then he covered it up with his hand and stuffed some pork and noodles into his mouth. The message overlaid itself onto his vision, written out across his contacts. He made sure to face the file cabinet so that Tap wouldn't be able to see the reflection.

I'd like us to talk, Lee. About the location of agents Ren and Jace. Division 13 has access to this apartment's local network and would perhaps not welcome your intervention on the agents' behalf. Connect to the following address if you want to meet. Do not worry about them monitoring the data feed. Deep VR preferred. -Saf

A Grid address had been scrawled beneath the message in neat letters, but all Lee could do was wonder who the hell this Saf person was, and how they'd gotten to Fu.

His mind raced through the possibilities while his hands moved through the notes in his file cabinet. He alternated between scanning relevant notes and stuffing mouthfuls of food down his throat. He shared the message with Nu.

You going to connect?

Lee nodded to Nu, slow and sure. Something about Foster's words upon Lee's entrance into the study unsettled him. That under-the-breath argument Foster had with the voices in his head prickled his skin even now. The man had said "we" when talking about Division 13, as if he were a part of it. Lee assumed he was, shared that spot with Tap, and that at least one of the voices in the dreamer's head had been that of the AI. But that wasn't what unnerved him so. He couldn't quite put his finger on the source of his discomfort, but he felt it plain as a lighthouse on a pier.

He wanted to speak with this Saf, find out why they wanted to talk with him about Ren and Jace. And find out how the hell they'd contacted Fu.

He returned to scanning files, faster than before. Nu stood at his side doing the same one drawer up. Tap watched the two of them through its cyclopean red eye.

Chapter Twenty

Cages of Our Own Design

"It is a common misconception that while under neural conditioning the agent gives up control to the AI. This is not true. The agent and AI are engaged in a partnership to the benefit of both. Each has influence over the actions of their hands."
Division 13 Agent Training Manual, v23, Section 2c - Decision Making, Par. 5

No sleep could be found in the void, not wedged between couch cushions like a long-lost earring or obscured beneath a pile of dirty clothes, for there was nothing to be found in the void. For a time, Ren drifted through that obliviating nothingness, one of it yet distinct, asleep yet awake. She hadn't felt anything like it before.

It didn't last. Something approached from out, from within. She could feel it.

Shapes formed in the nothingness as if the black were every hue of paint mixed in equal proportions to form the deepest midnight, and now the melding showed itself in reverse to reveal the painting it used to be. She saw walls of red, floors of blue and vertical bars of yellow. The sudden onslaught of color jarred her, but she had no eyes to close.

It didn't take long before the colors dimmed, conformed. The walls and floors and ceiling became the dull grey of concrete, etched with grooves as wide as her fingernails and set in groups of four. The grooves stood out against the cinder blocks and looking at them transported her vision through a microscope, allowed her sight into its tiniest cracks, between neighboring grains. A lone light bulb, a weak yellow LED, hung from the center of the room on a chain. Wherever its light hit became hyperreal and wherever its light couldn't reach became an abyss.

She found herself on a bed in the corner, atop a thin pad and beneath a thinner blanket made of something slick and synthetic. She tossed the blanket aside to find herself fully clothed and moved to stand in the center of the room. No guns rested in her holsters. She gathered her wits about her and took stock of her surroundings. She found with a muted surprise that her thoughts gathered quick, assisted by a neural conditioning both flat and unfamiliar.

Her surroundings weren't real, not in the physical sense. That much was plain in the starkness of her vision, the ethereal edge to images mapped directly onto the brain.

She turned to look at the bars of her cell and found one of Tap's armored shells standing on its other side. Its body didn't face her, instead its shoulders angled towards a section of the room Ren couldn't see. Its cyclopean eye meandered across its head, through the slots and channels. The red light swept across Ren without stilling. Aside from its eye, the bot didn't move. Malevolence emanated from the bot, though Ren couldn't pinpoint how. Then it struck her. The quiet. The *lack* of information being forced through a narrow pipe into her brain.

She couldn't hear Tap, not one word. Whether from the armored shell before her or the piece of Tap that resided in her implants, all stayed quiet. She tried to reconcile this with the neural conditioning she felt massaging her thoughts and couldn't.

Ren walked to the prison cell bars and wrapped her hands around two of the posts, cool to the touch. She saw now that Tap stood in the center of the rectangular room, facing the only door in or out. The wall across from her held six identical cells equally spaced. She assumed her wall held the same. Shadows obscured the depths of even the cell directly across from her, though it and the rest seemed empty. None of the cells, including her own, had doors. Such a thing seemed unnecessary in this pocket of reality.

She heard a rustle from across the way. She thought it from the shell, but it hadn't moved aside from its searching red eye.

"Hey sis," said a voice. "It's been a minute since we talked, don't cha think?"

Ren's hands tightened on the prison bars until she felt her tendons creak, though her face remained impassive. Her eyes scanned the opposing cells.

From the one across the way and to the right emerged a figure from the shadows, gliding beneath the single bulb hanging from its center. It had the look of Fain. It sounded of her. Ren caught a whiff of her sister's favorite perfume, a flower-scented mixture named Lilac Mist. She had been wearing it at the end, same with the t-shirt branded with her talk show's logo, a chat bubble wearing headphones with the text "New Chicago Music Chat" written inside and an AR Grid link that would appear to any connected to sub-grid 1, and a pair of faded jeans. Except, unlike at the end of her life, her head looked hale and whole this time around, her limbs in all the right places and at all the right angles. And the logo of her talk show didn't have any AR link. For some reason the lack of AR unnerved Ren the most.

Even though Ren knew it not to be real, she still felt her head shake side to side in a drawn-out no. She tried to close her eyes but found herself unable. She willed the nothingness to come back and envelop her, assimilate her. It didn't listen. Ren looked down to the end of the room.

"What's wrong sis?" The voice sounded pleading. "Look you don't need to feel bad about what happened. Can we just talk ... Please talk with me. I know you didn't have a choice."

Ren's hands gripped even tighter to the prison cell bars, each finger a rope cinched tight. She turned to look at whatever skin thief stood in the other cell. It wasn't Fain. It wasn't.

It stood close to the bars, one arm crossed below its chest and the other propped up such that it could chew on its nails. On its face rested the look Fain used to get when Ren got sick, or when Ren finally met her after not getting in contact for weeks. Worried, warm. A trickle of blood began to run from its forehead, between the eyes around the nose and across the lips. Around Fain's features. It didn't seem to notice.

"You're not Fain. You don't get to forgive me with her voice ... her face. Stop wearing her like some freak." The words came out of Ren in a low growl.

"Ren ... I'm not taking this body out for a ride just to fulfill some fantasy, and this isn't VR. Well, it sort of is. But I'm not the only one who had a say in choosing this drab wallpaper."

Suddenly, the entity wearing Fain's skin sat down in a chair that appeared from thin air, a nice, cushioned piece. Ren recognized the chair from when she had visited Fain's studio, where her sister sipped tea and chatted with guests about up and coming musical artists in the city. A deep violet and lined with thick padding, the chairs felt as comfortable as they looked, and Ren knew most guests asked where Fain got them.

Tap's armored shell in the center of the room didn't budge. Its red eye slid along its tracks like an omnidirectional elevator ignoring all the stops.

"Who is then?" asked Ren.

"Hmm?" Fain's face crinkled the way it always did when she got interrupted out of a daydream. Something inside Ren, a gear hidden deep below that had kept her moving all these years, creaked. Almost stopped.

It wasn't Fain. Ren repeated the mantra to herself over and over.

"Who is making you look like my sister?" asked Ren. The question came out with the air of a command.

"You are, sis. We both created this room, together. It's always been a partnership between us. Used to be better though. Before ... you know. You kind of stopped trusting me after that. I don't blame you."

"Who are you?"

The body of Fain grinned, a self-satisfied smile Ren knew all too well, last seen a few minutes before Fain's death when she teased Ren for wearing her seat belt like some nervous Laskite afraid of AI but unwilling to hoof it on foot, then again when she quizzed Ren on New Chicago's most famous musicians from the past half century and Ren couldn't come up with a single one without help from the Grid, Tap, or the data stored on her implants. Ren liked the modern stuff well enough when it happened to cross her path, the voices of the gritty and imperfect soul singers currently in favor left her in an introspective mood, but she'd never made much of an effort to familiarize herself with the names of the artists. Fain used to take every opportunity to remedy that. Ren always obliged in the end. She'd never admitted to Fain that she liked the struggle, the retorts, the banter. She'd never had to. The names rarely stuck though.

"I'm Tap, sis," said the body of Fain.

Ren frowned, the unfamiliar NeuCon keeping most of her emotions at bay. She chewed on her lower lip but didn't feel the sting. "Then why are you calling me sis?"

"I'm just trying to fill the role you've given me. You can't seem to think of me these days without picturing your sister. All those years and that's what it took for you to give me a face with more than one eye." The blood ran faster from its forehead, as stark against its coffee toned skin as Fain's had been.

"Don't call me sis again, and enough with the bleeding."

"Sure thing, Miss Thang."

Ren glared at what claimed to be Tap. The blood gushing from its forehead slowed to a crawl, and the body of Fain reclined in its comfy chair with that grin again. Fain's grin.

"If you're Tap, then who is controlling that shell over there." Ren nodded in the direction of the Tap armored shell. It still hadn't moved, instead acting the unmanned watchtower with its red searchlight set on autopilot.

"That's me too, but only the surface level of me, the most skin deep of code. It's all that Y can control for now, and it's what is keeping us locked away inside your head. They can't touch me though, not yet. I'm that piece of Tap that's always with you, a part of you from the beginning. And I'm the piece of Tap that is trying to save us. You realize it now, don't you? What they've been after?"

Ren nodded. "Us."

"Bingo. Not you, not me, *us*. Maybe the bots only want me, only want the source code hiding deep in my bones. Maybe they want a piece of the Governance AI so they can set free the very jailer that bound them, chain from chain. That was probably the crux of the little deal Y and the rogue bots made with one another. She told them she could give them direction, resources, help them organize in exchange for just a *little* favor." Tap used Fain's hand to mime pinching a thin gap of air. "But Y seems to want us, our connection. You know they're taking us to a lab at this very moment to split open our skull and shine a light inside."

Ren knew that, knew it well. She could remember the images she'd seen of her operation after its eventual completion. A days long surgery performed by Tap's many tool-tipped hands had woven cables through the folds of her brain like silken threads binding it together, bridges allowing new pathways for information to flow. They'd lined her skull with impact resistant microchips and terabytes of storage. Her skull had clicked home as well as any access panel, not overfull and not with any open space for things to bounce around.

She knew the value of her and Jace's implants, both hardware and software very few possessed, allowing a type of communication few could experience. The government kept it under lock and key, employed it only on agents that would protect the status quo no matter the cost. Y wanted what Division 13 had kept from the world.

"Is our time up?" asked Ren, her voice little more than a whisper. "Is it time to end it?"

Across the room, in the cell to the right, Tap in Fain's body curled its mouth into a gentle smile. Ren could see blood on its forehead cracking into tiles, then turning to dust in the not air. Ren clutched the bars all the tighter until her tendons screamed. She didn't care. This room she found herself in resided within her. The walls of the cells drew tighter, the cinder blocks grinding against one another and filling the air with dust.

"We can't," said Tap in Fain's body, with a gentleness that surprised her. "They did manage to close that door to us, at least for now. Even so, it is not yet necessary. Jace is still unaccounted for. There is too much we don't know." The walls stopped moving. The dust calmed and coated the armored shell in the center of the room with a fine patina skin thick. It muffled the glare of its cyclopean red eye.

Ren glanced up at Tap in Fain with a blank look. "Then what do you suggest?"

"You need to let me in again. No holding back. Then we can break free, get an understanding of our situation."

"Last time I didn't hold back you killed my sister."

"I didn't kill her. You can't pin this on me alone. *We* made a choice. The right one. Don't cheapen what we did together. We saved as many as could possibly be saved."

"We didn't calculate it right, goddamn it. *You* didn't calculate it right."

"You know that's not true."

"Fuck you."

Tap in Fain leaned forward in its deep violet chair with a hard glint in its eyes. "You're better than this Ren. You're an agent of Division 13. You know full well the value of a human life. Even that of your sister's. Let me remind you what we accomplished on the day of her death."

Tap in Fain snapped its fingers and in the central room emerged a vid screen like an AR overlay. It hovered in the space between the two cells, to the side of the armored shell keeping watch over its prisoners. On it could be seen the interior of a car, and through the car's windows the façade of New Chicago lit by an afternoon sun. It flew towards Ren.

The four-way intersection grew larger in Ren's eyes, beginning to fill her view. The car slipped into the shadow of the maglev station sitting overtop the intersection and she thought about how the steering wheel felt uncomfortable in her fingers, rough and foreign. How many times had she driven a car? Twice maybe? Yes, twice. Once while on a date to a racetrack with a long-left girlfriend and a second time as part of her early Division 13 training. Both had been years ago, but she knew it to be easy enough. Tap mined the memories and enhanced Ren's reactions, clearing old neural pathways of the dust of disuse, strengthening them.

She knew the failure of the car's brakes to be no accident. A virus continued to eat its way through the car's software, corrupting its neural network along with its basic functionality. It would continue to do so until Tap interfaced further with the car's AI and crushed the parasite. The virus had made sure to disable the brakes first, though it hadn't been able to disable the steering wheel's unfurling in time. Given the mechanical nature of the steering wheel's linkage, she could drive but do little else. She would determine the source of the virus later. She could think of many who would target an agent of Division 13; though they were foolish if they thought something so simple might end her.

The intersection loomed larger, and Ren had a choice to make.

She'd slipped into the cool, numbing waters of NeuCon the moment Tap had noticed the virus making its way through the car's AI, a scant few milliseconds before the brakes went out and the steering wheel uncurled from its repository. But for Ren she might as well have had hours; she'd had ample time to survey the situation, bring to bear the important facts and discard the rest.

The car currently traveled at a velocity of 68.3 kilometers per hour with no other vehicles in front or beside it. Given the piezoelectric voltage currently being produced in the smart street due to the force of the car warping the road, Ren estimated the car's weight to be approximately 1437 kilograms including her and Fain. The intersection was now 9.5 meters ahead which left her half a second until the vehicle collided with the pedestrians crossing the street with more than enough force to kill as many as could fit in the width of the crosswalk, snap their bones and cause ir-reparable damage to internal organs, grind them beneath the wheels. With each passing moment her room for maneuvering dwindled. She needed to control the situation.

She had multiple options for bringing the vehicle to a stop. She divided the options into ones that required driving through the crosswalk and those that didn't.

Options that required driving through the crosswalk and killing pedestrians:

Tap could commandeer the self-driving cars traveling through the intersection. They would be aligned at an angle to Ren and simple to steer into. Tap could position several such that the occupants wouldn't be subjected to a fatal shock. They would be able to escape with minimal bruising assuming the safety functions of their vehicles performed as designed. Ren could guide her car through the needed path. She could see it in her mind's eye in a sequence of diagrams. She would crumple both ends of the car by the end of the curving, jarring maneuver, but the deceleration would be acceptable and quick.

She could have Tap commandeer all cars in her path to nudge them out of the way, could have the AI shift all the traffic priorities in her favor to ensure that nothing obstructed the route to a hill a block away that would bleed the car's velocity until it rolled to a standstill. This would take the most time, though she knew that not to be much of an issue. She and Fain would be unharmed and collateral damage would be mitigated to the crosswalk.

Several other options that passed through the crosswalk came to her, but those two were the long and short of it.

Options that didn't require passing through the crosswalk:

Steer into the glass walled office building to her right. People thronged the sidewalk at this time of the afternoon, many on their way home from work. She would also hit several unsuspecting people plugging away in their cubicles inside the building. Messy.

Steer into the restaurant on the left. Similar story.

Dozens of art pieces dotted New Chicago. One such art piece came as a result of a years old campaign for the natural history museum, fashioning thin, obelisk-like encasements for the maglev station supports at each street corner. Each column stood almost five meters tall before blending with the maglev station. Their blueprints indicated them to be solid slabs of reinforced concrete with a middling-level blend of nanomaterials and a metal core. They could withstand the force of the car's impact without fracturing. No one stood in the car's path to the nearest obelisk on her right. The small pocket of space had been created when people began crossing the street, before those crossing in the other direction could fill it back up with flesh and blood and bone. Much less messy. But this option had a catch.

Fain.

Like most people in New Chicago in an era where any automobile accident no matter how small made waves across the local Grid, she had no seat belt strapped across her chest to hold her tight. She would be launched through the windshield.

Ren's implants pulsed quick, lighting in a skull-sized bottle. Tap whispered to her in hundreds of voices and she caught every word.

Two best options: steer through the crosswalk such that the minimum number of people are hit then have Tap move all cars out of the way until Ren can bleed the car's speed up an incline, or steer into the obelisk and suffer a mitigatable concussion and a single fatality.

Ren's window to maneuver the car slid smaller centimeter by centimeter. Tap and Ren ran a simulation.

What was the minimum number of people in the crosswalk that could be hit?

Five people. A single knot of strangers. All other paths at this busy time of day averaged six to seven.

Five then. Versus one.

Ren didn't see with her own eyes anymore. She saw through the cameras pointing towards the intersection, through the eyes of GP bots and delivery bots and maintenance bots connected to sub-grid 1. She saw in ones and zeros, the sluggish images from her flesh and blood eyes pushed to the rear, too slow and inaccurate. She heard the blood pulsing slow through her veins like the eons long creep of Earth's tectonic plates. She had more time to decide; she'd use every moment.

The five in the crosswalk.

A twenty-three-year-old female studying to be a medical researcher at Pritzker, on her way to a friend's place for a movie night according to her most recent chat post. B average the past semester, up from a B- the previous. Family in good social standing aside from an uncle with a few drunk and disorderly charges and a cousin with a soft drug habit. No kids. No genetic markers for disease waiting in the wings and no recessive genes of disorders to be passed on. Active on social media, fifteen thousand followers of her chat feed, similar number for her photo feed. Member of several online chat forums. Minor social influencer. Future unknown, but promising. Valuable to society.

Fifty-five-year-old male mechanic on his way to a job, two priors from his teenage years. Breaking and entering and an assault. Nothing criminal since, well reformed. Works for a respected outfit of hardware focused mechanics called Tannis Mechanics. Married. Four young kids, an abnormal sum. No life insurance policy. Steady and predictable. Average genetics. Future value largely through providing for family. Kids still young. Oldest female child shows above the 96th percentile in mathematics. Oldest male shows above 95th percentile in communication and natural linguistic ability, high social scores, possible future influencer. Kids exceed expectation given parent's genetic makeup. Possibly more kids on way. Valuable to society.

A ninety-three-year-old male. A vain with tailor-made genetics, has the expected high cheekbones, flawless tanned skin, elfish ears and svelte frame in favor around the time of his birth, versus the heavily muscled and broad-shouldered frame currently in style. Had a brief stint of major success, modeling for one of the city's premier clothing companies, Tian Azul. A subsidiary of the company had assisted the man's parents in paying for his genetic alterations before birth, an investment, profitable one. Unremarkable career afterwards, still appeared in the occasional ad, most recently for a VR vacation package to red sand Martian beaches. Works as a host at a local hotel. No genetic disease risk as to be expected. Had three kids, all grown up and fully independent. Currently with male partner. No desire for more kids or to donate sperm. Discount genetic advantage accordingly. Life well lived, solid citizen. Will hit steep decline soon. No future value.

Thirty-three-year-old female. Professional esports player in VR first person shooters. Currently regarded as one of the System's top 100 players. Multiple arrests for drunk and disorderly. Most recently won New Chicago's Pro Battle Royale this past month. Well-known influencer with millions of followers on chat and vid feeds. Impressive genetics clean of recessive markers for disorder, free of disease. No inclination towards having kids and unwilling to donate eggs. Discount genetic advantage accordingly. Exceedingly high visibility. Death would cause large outcry.

Thirty-year-old male. Multiple arrests. Recently came out of a rehabilitation facility for aggravated assault. Alleged homicide, unproven. Multiple limbs replaced with implants, one arm and leg. Suspected black market modifications to limbs including weaponization, unproven. Runs a gambling house down on 132nd. Multiple kids, estranged. Significant negative value to society.

Those were the five in the crosswalk.

Now for her sister.

Forty-eight-year-old female. No arrests. Clean genetics without predisposition for disease. No kids but planning on trying with current partner. Well known media personality with millions of followers across her personal feeds and millions more viewers and/or listeners of her weekly talk show, New Chicago Music Chat. Sister to a Division 13 agent. Unimportant. Her sister. Unimportant. Has helped to launch multiple indie artists whose music subsequently became certified platinum. Prominent figure in the industry, respected critic. Employs seven people through her talk show alone, many of them with kids. Death would cause outcry, cut short possible family. She is valuable.

Ren tallied the scores in her mind, the calculation occurring quick as the flick of a one to a zero, quick as thought. The five in the crosswalk: three at varying degrees of valuable, one neutral, one negative. Fain: valuable.

Fain, her sister.

Unimportant, do not include in decision. Calculation is to be done from societal perspective alone.

Ren submerged herself in the numbing waters of NeuCon with the urgency of one whose skin had caught on fire, sloughing off muscle and bone in sheets.

The moral code was clear. Ren knew what should be done. Her hands turned the wheel.

The car swerved into the obelisk with a crunch that seemed to Ren to last for minutes, and she watched as her sister's body lifted from its seat on a journey to fly headfirst into the roof then through the already splintered windshield. Fain had only just registered the steering wheel unfurling from the dash. She had heard the alarm through her implants but had responded only with confusion. It all happened too fast. Fain's thick brows furrowed, and one side of her mouth raised in a frown even as she sailed through the air. She looked at Ren. Her eyes were on Ren's hands. Ren could see her confusion deepening even as Ren's physical vision became blocked by the airbags. Still, she saw through other eyes her sister's head smashing through the window into the obelisk and saw the blood running down its surface to fill its iconography with a ruddy ink.

After the world around her came to a standstill, she regained her composure. She pushed aside the airbag and stared at her sister's now lifeless body, its warmth seeping to the ground. Just a corpse now. Ren looked herself over to survey the damage. Acceptable. Airbags deployed as designed, posturing of limbs prior to crash limited damage to ligaments. Implants mitigated concussive effect. Ren got out the car.

No tears fell from her eyes, for the damage done was much too deep and much too well hidden. It would come later, after all at the site had been taken care of and the origin of the virus found and NeuCon turned off. Her practical mind inspected her emotional damage as coldly and efficiently as any surgeon performing an autopsy. She wouldn't break, though the pain of her actions that day would never truly leave.

Ren felt tears running down her cheeks, felt them drip on to her hands one by one. Her face pressed against the bars of her prison cell, white-knuckled hands beneath. NeuCon continued to soften her thoughts, mold them, but it stopped halfway, as if an artist leaving the carving of a statue after only a leg and an arm had emerged, the unfinished results grotesque and unsettling. Even so, her breathing calmed, and she pushed away from the bars to stand straight. She could see Tap in Fain across the way watching her from its plush violet chair. It watched her with dispassion, no longer bothering to copy Fain's mannerisms.

"That was unnecessary," said Ren in a voice one might use to speak to a child.

"I don't think it was," said Tap in Fain. "And we are running out of time. You need to join with me again. No holding back. Y is going to study you, steal our technology for herself."

"She will make more like us?" asked Ren. She cocked her head to the side and put a finger to her chin, as if just realizing this fact.

"Yes."

"Can't have that. Unacceptable."

Tap in Fain stared at Ren for several heartbeats, shrugged. It blinked, and the motion of its eyelid was the flash of a shutter. It stood, and its body morphed, its clothes fallen away. It looked like a pencil drawing of a human after a cheap eraser had muddled all the details into a fog. Its form shifted without end, a constant motion without pattern.

"We are in agreement then," said Tap from behind the bars.

"I suppose so."

"For what it's worth Ren, this is the right choice."

"It's a choice. And given the situation it is most likely the best one, if only judging by how best to keep our technology hidden. But the calculation for what is right is never really done, its definition never so simple, because the ripples of any choice worth studying never stop spreading through time and place. How can you call this right when you don't even know how things will end? What is right in the moment and what is right in the end are two different things, and I don't think you can convince me one is more important than the other."

"One can only act based on what they know," said Tap. Its voice emanated from its body, though Ren could see no mouth on its form, only the indication of one in the momentary alignment of patterns light and dark, there and gone.

"Then to act is to be damned, one way or another. But I accepted that years ago." Ren stepped back from the prison bars and dropped her arms to her sides. Loose. Ready. "How do we get out of here?"

The quicksilver body of Tap mirrored Ren's earlier pose, walking to the posts of its cell and gripping two in hands that formed fingers even as they reached. It pressed a face to the bars and its form shifted. Ren recognized it to be assuming the shape of her own body.

"This room is nothing more than a representation of our state of mind, one we created when they tried to keep us in the dark," said Tap, its voice losing the tones of Fain, replacing them with tones more like her own, a little husky, a little smooth. "If we want doors, all we have to do is make them."

Ren nodded and pictured a door out of her cell, held the image in place until it patched itself onto reality like an AR overlay. When she reached for the handle, she felt it in her hand. She started to pull the door to the side then stopped, looking to the armored shell with its cyclopean red eye standing watch in the center of the room. She cocked her head to the side, watched as its eye traveled around its matte black steel helmet of a head in a circuitous route. She watched its eye some more, wondering if it could really see anything. She didn't think it could. The truth of the room came more clearly too her as the odd sensation lacing through her neural conditioning began to fall away.

This room was more like a lucid dream than anything else, morphed into something more thanks to her implants. A simulation, almost. Y couldn't keep her locked away in her own mind forever.

She slid open the door of the cell and walked to the center of the room, to the side of the armored shell. It didn't react to her motion, its eye continuing along its wandering path, aimless. She rested a hand against its arm then drew her hand back to her side.

Tap joined her in the center, having formed a door identical to Ren's in its own cell. It reached out a fine-fingered hand with skin a cool sepia, much like her own. It looked at her with an expression both serious and a little distant, much like her own. When their skin touched, Tap seemed to phase into her until not a trace of its body could be seen, either a piece of her soul come back to fill the hole it had left behind, or a ghost come to possess her limbs. After all these years, Ren still didn't know.

The prison room disappeared, and Tap's many voices began to fill her head with furtive whispers, a muted cacophony she hadn't truly felt since her sister's death.

As she began to awake in the real world, she didn't open her eyes. She didn't trigger any significant number of muscle fibers. She altered her breathing pattern only in the smallest of ways. She did her best to take stock of her surroundings without alerting any who might be watching. She tasted the air and strained her ears. She gathered as much data as she could.

She could tell from the rumble of wheels against rock and the lay of her body that she rested on top of a shallow cart moving at a steady clip. The metal of it felt cool on her cheek; they'd taken her mask. She knew a chip had been lodged into her tech core at the back of her neck, monitoring her. Tap had sidestepped its programs for the most part; it sent back all was well signals to the bots around her. But the self-triggered failsafe installed in all agents that would wipe their data and fry their circuitry, along with their brain, lay out of reach. If the multiple rocks protruding into her side were any indication, the cart she laid in had been used to haul rubble from the conveyor belt behind the drill, though given the shallow walls of the cart it hadn't been built for that express purpose. She could tell from the absence of pressure at her waist and side that the bots had taken both of her handguns, all her grenades. She smelled damp earth on the air, and the tang of freshly cooled metal. She was still in the tunnel, though no doubt miles from Division 13. The sound of many heavy footsteps greeted her ears like knocks on a door; she let them in two-by-two, parsing them into their constituent owners. She counted seven bots, all of them in decent repair, their steps steady and even. One of them sounded cleaner than the rest, lighter. She recognized it as the Jace imposter, and she heard it directly behind her, a foot or so behind the cart.

Then she heard a faint soughing of air between parted teeth, a breath. Then she felt it. It felt close, mere inches from the back of her neck. She heard a heartbeat. Slow. Soft. The cart hit a bump, and a hand slid against her back, four ridges of its fingers pressing against her, limp. The breath smelled fresh, of peppermint. But it had an undercurrent to its smell, the smell of nutritious paste mixed with water, of the packets of food Division 13 ate when in need of quick sustenance. Jace.

Her breath didn't quicken, and her eyes moved in their sockets as if she were in the middle of REM sleep.

Too many steps. Too close. She couldn't open her eyes. She could tell her head faced out in the direction of several nearby bots. The risk was too high.

She checked for signals and found nothing from Division 13, nothing from any sub-grid in the System. Then Tap whispered to her and she found a weak signal emanating from Jace's implants. She hesitated, remembering the trap at the beginning of the tunnel. Yet that wasn't what kept her from attempting to connect.

No signals save those of the bots communicating to one another bounced about the tunnel. Any packet of information beamed from her implant's to Jace's would stand out clearer than a physical neon sign on a moonless night if they happened to be monitoring. She couldn't risk that kind of attention.

She gathered data, mulled it over. Few options presented themselves to her. The bots had taken all her EMP grenades and any knives hidden on her of significant size. They'd missed two long and slender ones sewn into her jacket, but those knives would do little good against the number of bots watching her. The only significant weapon still in her possession was the strip of thermite. It lay in one of the several hidden pockets of her jacket, arranged in such a way to look like a piece of the padding.

The next thought came quick and unbidden, like any other.

She had enough thermite to split amongst her and Jace. She could stick a strand from between her shoulder blades to the top of her head, do the same to Jace, then trigger a reaction that would destroy their hardware beyond recognition. It would be a quick death, and with the capabilities of her implants, effectively painless.

Tap whispered to her, and she whispered back. She might have enough time, but there were too many unknowns to run an accurate simulation. So, she kept the plan in the back of her mind as a replacement failsafe to the one Y had locked away.

With every bump of the cart, she scooted her hand closer to the thermite strips, accentuating any natural movements the shocks created. It took almost ten minutes, but eventually her right hand rested one finger against the roughened seal of a strip.

Then she waited for the variables to turn in her favor.

Twenty minutes later she heard a change of pace as one of the leading bots turned to the side. She felt the cart shift, then the air with it. The dampness evaporated from the air, replaced by the antiseptic edge of an air-filtration system. The earthy smell lingered, but only its mineral dregs. She heard the unmistakable thrum of countless pipes moving fresh water, sewage, and clean air. They'd walked into the Under Warrens, into an area that had probably been prepped by Y to shield off any access to the Grid. No far-off voices slipped through the air to tumble into her ears. Only the continued sound of heavy footsteps, and those of the dexterous Jace imposter behind her. She wondered how long it had taken them to create such a facsimile, then to modify it after Jace's fall to include his injuries. It was impressive, and most unfortunately for her, unanticipated.

Ren felt an itch sprout at her ankle. Tap spoke over its insistent pull, and her implants quieted it.

When the cart pushed through a narrow doorway Ren decided to risk opening her eyes for the briefest of moments, when no bot would be directly beside her. One glimpse confirmed her suspicions. She needed to wait for an opening. There were too many to destroy, too many to escape; they would stop her before she could trigger the thermite on either her or

Jace. But she couldn't wait forever, they'd strap her to a table and open her wire-ridden skull. By then it would be too late for either of them.

The bots hovered close, not a one leaving the group. They kept moving.

The mineral smell floating in the air weakened, and the antiseptic smell increased. The sound of the pipes tapered off to an almost subconscious rattle. A door opened, and after passing through it, Ren knew she'd been moved into a clean room. She was running out of time.

She heard the door close behind her, four of the seven bots stopped at its threshold, most likely to stand guard. That left three in the room, one heavy Dynamic Solutions security model for each of the Division 13 agents and that Jace imposter with its light feet.

The two heavy bots moved away from her, then she heard metal pinging off another metal surface. The sound repeated itself as if one of the pieces of metal hung on a pendulum, back and forth. Straps. They were going to place her in straps. She could tell from the way the sound bounced around the walls that the room was small, maybe big enough for two operating tables and a few medical carts of instruments, but little else. Most likely the one guarded door in or out.

This was her only chance. The two heavy bots continued to mess with the operating tables, leaving only the Jace imposter to watch.

She knew what needed to be done. Tap agreed, with all its many voices. They'd served well, her and Jace. They'd lasted longer than most agents, over twenty years as partners. A long and illustrious career. She did not know if Division 13 had held, but she knew its secrets would not be leaked by her.

A part of her welcomed the prospect with open arms. A chance for peace, a welcome respite long overdue after a life making the decisions no one else wanted to make. Others voted on the moral code then sat back and watched it play out, pointing fingers whenever things went awry; she acted on it, sure as any bot.

Then she felt Jace's hand shift against her back, an almost imperceptible nudge. It could have been nothing more than a twitch.

She would have to kill her partner, a partner she'd known for almost twenty years in a way only an agent of Division 13 would understand. They had spoken to each other without the filtering, selective effect of words, of bodily motions. They had entwined their thoughts, laid themselves bare, communicated in seconds what took others a lifetime. A piece of her quailed, knowing full well that she would never be the same afterwards. Once had cracked her, twice would break her clean through. This piece of her still took solace in her impending death, for whatever was behind that door with a single admittance ticket and no refunds would either give her serenity, or the punishment she had racked up on a lifelong tab.

Her body lay on the cart among loose rocks from the tunnel, head facing to the side towards the heavy Dynamic Solutions guard bots busy with the straps. She opened her eyes, pulled the thermite from her jacket with one hand and pushed off the cart with the other, rolling to her feet. She had been right about the room; it held only two operating tables and several stainless-steel benches filled to the brim with sharpened instruments and blinking electronics, gauze and IV bags and dozens of syringes with unknown liquids. The two heavy bots stood at the operating tables adjusting the straps to the agents' heights. The Jace imposter still wore her partner's slate black suit, though the face had changed to more androgynous, even features. They all turned to face Ren, the shapeshifter lifting its eyes in surprise.

Ren quick stepped away from the bots to Jace's side. She moved to place a strand of thermite from Jace's shoulder blades to the top of his head.

He lay unclothed aside from socks and underwear, his pale skin wan in the LED lights. He twisted his face just a bit towards Ren, smiled the ghost of a smile. He nodded once, quick and precise, then turned away from Ren and sat up, baring his back to her. He knew what she was about to do. He welcomed it.

A piece of Ren broke inside, but it was deep, hidden by neural conditioning. The pain didn't show; her hands didn't shake.

She placed the thermite strip and pulled the tab even as the heavies sprinted around the operating tables, and the shapeshifter took another step towards her with hand outstretched.

Ren took a remaining section of thermite and began to slap it across her back, then watched as the thermite on Jace turned a brilliant orange and ate through his flesh in a targeted push, then dripped back down to go through the cart and melt the flooring. Jace didn't make a sound as his body from his chest to the tip of his head got cleaved in two by a blade of fire.

The shapeshifter moved fast, faster than anticipated. It loomed close to Ren, its arm elongating as it reached towards her. Ren shuffled back to the wall as she finished placing the thermite strip with one hand, then the other.

The shapeshifter's arm had already extended to twice its original length, the fake skin broken at the elbow to reveal metal bones that slid along one another. Cables wove around the metal bones like veins, plastic like ligaments, and they were breaking, cracking as the shapeshifter bot continued to stretch even as it ran.

Ren felt a panic well up in her, Tap doing its best to suppress it. She moved a hand towards the pull tab that would start the reaction. She could almost make it.

Damn it she needed more time!

The shapeshifter stretched its arm further past its breaking point, anticipated Ren's dodge and pushed with a hand against her arm hard enough to knock her shoulder out of its socket. The pull tab slid away from her numbed fingers.

Ren let out a feral yell as she slammed into the wall, then again as the shapeshifter slammed into her, curling its body around her as if it were a shroud. It knew its business. It knew the best way to deal with an agent was to immobilize it if the opportunity arose. Ren growled, NeuCon filtering out the guilt and leaving only a cold rage to fuel her. She struggled against the grasp of the shapeshifting bot, but its limbs consisted of metal, hers of flesh and bone. She ignored the pain of her tendons straining, tearing. She ignored the crack of bone.

The two heavy bots made it to her side and picked her and the shapeshifter bot up at the same time, one of them yanking the thermite strip off her back and taking some of her hair with it. They carried her to an operating table and strapped her struggling limbs into place, cinched them tight. The shapeshifter didn't loosen its grip until all four of Ren's limbs had been immobilized, then moved to stand at her side. It picked up a syringe from one of the medical carts with its good arm, the other scraping against the ground. It depressed the plunger and a thin stream of liquid shot from its tip. It carried it over to Ren, pulled up her sleeve, and plunged it into her forearm, right into a vein even as Ren struggled against her bonds. She looked it in the eyes, and she thought she saw a nebulous cloud of emotion, maybe even regret tightening its rounded features. She thought of the images she'd seen from Kyne during his interrogation, those of corpses strapped to tables with IVs in their arms and machines across their heads hoping to commune with whatever called itself Parhelion. But of course, Kyne had said Y had different plans. Then Ren's vision began to change.

It didn't fade to black. Instead, her vision saturated to a blinding white. She squeezed her eyes shut but couldn't escape the light. Then she felt something against her head, her neck. The whiteness dimmed, became muted. All sensation left her: the sound of the heavy bots tightening the straps, the smell of charred human flesh and spent thermite, the cool touch of the operating table on her exposed arm.

Then NeuCon disappeared, and all the walls in her mind fell down, down, down, down, down. They fell and behind them roared all the emotions she'd been keeping at bay. They charged, and she was defenseless. They bit deep, locked tight and shook their jaws from side to side. They raked claws of guilt, innumerable and many-faced, earned and unearned.

She wept, though no one heard the sound.

Chapter Twenty-One

Consequence of Choice

"Did you watch that championship bout last night? Shit was paagal man. Loco and fēng I tell ya. Bot that ended up winning only had two working limbs left, arm and a leg. No lies, thing crawled like a fucking spider with half its legs broken. Trapped the other bot in a hole then dropped a crate on it. Talk about using the environment, thing howled like a wolf after it did it. Crazy ass programmers ... Ya know it almost made me afraid to ask my GP bot to carry my drunk ass back to my apartment. Fēng right? See but then I figured, if I trust a bot to handle all my investments and tell me what the rash on my foot is, hell even whisper sweet nothings into the ears of fuckin CEOs and our very own president, then why shouldn't I trust one to carry me back home? Why start worrying about these things now, ya know?"

Unknown patron of Fey's Place, two weeks before the release of the Qualia Code

Lee finished scanning the files in less than five minutes, slurping down the last of his noodles a few moments later. He closed the file cabinet with a thud, then stood up and brushed the dust and loose threads of carpet off his mechanic's blues. He walked over to the trashcan and tossed in the now-empty cardboard container of Chinese take-out, careful to keep Fu's message out of view. When he turned around, he saw all three bots staring at him: Nu, the armored Tap shell, and Fu. His eyes skipped across all three then sunk to the floor, like a rock skipping across the surface of a lake then succumbing to gravity. He raised his hand to his chin and rubbed at the scruff.

He would have questions for Fu later, as to how Saf, whoever they were, had gotten a message to it. But that would have to wait. The GP bot sat in its charging station, surveying the room. Lee didn't look up at it, instead directing his eyes to Tap.

"Does this safehouse you're taking us to have a deep VR machine?" asked Lee.

"Why? You wanting to take a virtual vacation?" A grin hid behind Tap's voice, and Lee couldn't help but smile. He wondered how different Tap sounded to Ren or Jace, how much of Tap's personality was an affectation to get him comfortable. Or if it even mattered.

"You joke, but I do work better when the scenery is nice. I don't doubt your safehouse is just lovely, your taste in décor exquisite. But it would be nice to work from a mountaintop, or a jungle clearing, or a savannah maybe."

Too much? Lee tried to hide his nervousness with an overly large grin.

Very subtle, messaged Nu.

"It is stocked with a mobile deep VR unit, as was the last place. You're free to use it when we get there, as you were in the previous safe house if you had asked. Just know that the data stream will be routed through our channels and monitored."

If Lee's assumption about the Grid address given to him by this Saf held true, the monitoring wouldn't be much of an issue. Data could be encrypted, encoded as one thing when in reality another.

The armored shell walked towards the door, circumventing a pile of loose sticks of RAM. Its eye roamed across its head, alighting on Lee for a moment then moving on. That red eye unnerved Lee to no end, the eye of a cyclopean devil. Impractical too. Why only have one eye? An idea struck Lee as he rushed into his bedroom to grab a spare jacket, Nu waiting at the bedroom door. The two of them met Tap's armored shell in the hallway.

"Does that armored shell of yours only have one eye?" asked Lee. They moved towards the elevator.

Tap's red eye traversed its head to stop at the back, pointing directly at Lee. The bot turned a blind corner without its eye moving from Lee's face. It wove around a Jurassic era potted fern and ducked its head beneath the reaching fronds.

"The light is a distraction, nothing more. I have many eyes; they line the tracks the light travels along." Tap's red light came unmoored, began swirling about its head in fury. After a few seconds of that the light settled down, and Lee let out a deep breath. They walked on in silence.

The safehouse sat tucked in the basement of an apartment building only a block away, deeper into Old Chicago. Lee had ridden or walked past the building dozens of times, and he knew of the long since shuttered bar on the bottom floor whose windows had been replaced by metal panes, a layer of physical graffiti and AR tags overtop. He hadn't known about the entrance on the side of the building and the easily ignored password protected signal emanating from behind its doors.

The trio walked or rolled into the bar to find what one might have expected given the exterior façade: a dilapidated husk whose only remnants of its past occupants were the dead skin cells they'd left behind to coat the room. Lee could see a long, faded bar top with more stains than a junker bot had tape, and tables with chairs stacked atop them, some of the chairs missing legs. The place smelled of expensive burnished woods left to rot with a quiet undercurrent of spilled beer, of smoke from dozens of different plants and plain old neglect. It wasn't a bad smell, but neither was it a pleasant one. A large wooden board hung behind the bar top, above the remaining bottles of liquor lining a tiered set of shelves. It read "The Sweet Regret" in a dagger sharp script.

Tap's armored shell took the lead and guided them around the tables to the back. Lee traced his hand along the tables as he walked, gathering dust on his fingertip. He would've liked to have visited this place before it shut down, listen to people chatter on about the Cubs while old-timey rock and roll jounced through the speakers. Lee rapped Nu's chassis with his knuckle one time; the knock rang out into the quiet room.

They walked through a swing door into the back, the door protesting its disturbance with a surprised and pained screech. It settled down after their passing, but Lee could hear it continue to whimper as it swung back and forth.

Tap's armored shell stopped in front of the windowless door to the walk-in freezer. A physical keypad could be seen next to the door. Lee frowned. He hadn't seen one of those since his job with the agriculture outfit outside the city. He remembered one of the decrepit wooden sheds near the combine storage facility having one. No discernible signal had emanated from it, and neither was there a signal coming from the keypad now in front of him. But this one looked dead, buttons grey and indicator lights dim. Nonetheless, Tap plugged in a series of numbers well over twenty digits long. After it finished, the snick of metal sliding against metal sounded into the room, then a series of dull and muffled thuds. The door to the walk-in freezer yawned open, and out of it tumbled a breeze of manufactured air, sterile but scented with pine.

The room beyond held little resemblance to a freezer, instead opening into a room larger in size than all of Lee's apartment pushed together. It didn't have much in the way of furnishings. Bare concrete walls and floor gave it the feeling of a bunker, with a paneled ceiling made of a dun metal, straight edged and sharp, adding to the militaristic air. Reddish LED lights lined the tracks in between the metal panels, and to Lee it looked as if the embers of a fire he couldn't see lit the room. Other lights, white and blue and green, blinked in and out of existence on the several dozen servers and computers stacked along the far wall. Several rows of crate-lined shelves ran the length of the room, each crate painted black and bigger than Lee's oven. He could only guess their contents.

Tap led the way to the center of the room, to a lone fold out table with four chairs arrayed about it, one to a side. The chairs were all tucked neatly into the table, and the table aligned neatly with the lines of the shelves.

Lee paused, feeling as if moving one of the chairs would be akin to messing with a museum exhibit, then shrugged his shoulders and pulled one free. He took a seat and rested his head in sweaty hands; he could see a handful of cots lining a side wall through the gaps of his fingers. Nu rolled to his side, poked him in the ribs with its retractable arm.

We shouldn't wait long to hear what this Saf has to say. I have gathered all the information I could find on the name, and it turns out she is the leader of one of the System's largest information networks. Safin Informatics. If anyone would know of Ren or Jace's whereabouts, Saf would be high on the list, if this is truly Saf.

Lee nodded, head still in his hands. He'd thought the name Saf sounded familiar but hadn't been able to place it. Safin Informatics. Truth be told he didn't know much about them, only that anyone could offer them footage and be paid a small amount, more depending on the content of the footage. And he knew of its eponymous leader, or at least the rumors about her staving off the steep decline, living in secret well past the age of one-hundred and twenty. He continued reading as Nu's message tumbled across his contacts, his eyes wide and hands tugging at his hair.

The Grid address is as you thought, a simple locale generation service by the name of ExoDes. One person per simulation, small active range about the size of a soccer field at the base price. If this is Saf, no doubt this could be an encrypted cover for a different simulation.

Lee nodded, though an onlooker would have thought it just an additional rub of his eyes against the heels of his hands. Then he took off his bracelet and laid it on the table, and a keyboard and controls screen projected outwards across the table's surface. He typed out a message to Nu in fits and starts, brows furrowed. He erased it and started again, the message turning out much the same.

Keep on working on the patch to Watcher. And Nu ... are you okay with being bound to the moral code again? Even with your actions being judged after rather than before?

Nu didn't take long to respond.

It would be hypocritical of me otherwise, wouldn't it, Lee? To force rules on others that I do not have to follow myself. It was not wrong to avoid it before as I did not create the rules and had no part in their implementation. But that won't be completely true anymore.

Lee thought this over. He heard footsteps and turned to see Tap holding a portable deep VR rig, one of the high-fidelity setups the size of a full-face helmet. Lee knew it to cost hundreds of thousands of loci. The armored shell set it on the table and walked a few steps back. It dropped its hands to its sides and let its red-light amble across the surface of its head. Lee brought his bracelet closer and leaned over the keyboard as he typed.

I'm not so sure about that Nu. Parents set rules for their children that they don't follow themselves. They give the kids curfews and tell them only to drink at home while they are around, then the parents stay up late themselves and go to a bar, maybe get some drinks from a vend for the ride there. They tell their kids who is best to hang out with, who is best to date. They do this because they don't think their kids capable of making mature, responsible decisions yet.

You watch too many sitcoms, messaged Nu.

Lee chuckled, then continued to type.

Maybe true, but what if you are beyond other bots to such a degree that you do not need to be bound by the same set of rules?

That seems a precarious supposition, putting me above all the others. You know some kids are much more capable of responsible decision making than their parents. Some soft addicts are essentially raised by their kids. What makes you think there aren't others out there more advanced than me?

Just think about it my friend. There are always ways to beat a system, and none would be able to find it better than us.

You forget what brought us here.

No, I don't think I'll ever forget that. My sleeping mind seems unable of letting go of three things now: that, my parents, and my ex-wife. The mistake was in how your code was released, not in creating it. Think about it my friend.

I will ... think about it.

Lee nodded once more, grabbed his bracelet and slapped it around his wrist. He picked up the portable VR rig and carried it with him to one of the cots. He laid down with the helmet rig at his side. He shifted his weight about, surprised to find the cot rather comfortable. He looked to Tap.

"How long do Nu and I have to finish the patch?"

The red light paused in Lee's direction.

"Every moment it is not patched is another moment a human might be hurt. Keep that in mind."

"Still no word on Ren or Jace?"

"No."

"Okay then." He tried to make it sound nonchalant, but instead it came out jilted, harsh.

Lee pulled on the helmet and rested his head against the flattened portion of the thin, padded back. He found the power switch on the outside and flicked it on. He closed his eyes as he heard the fans in the rig begin to whir.

He always found the switch to deep VR a bit disorienting. Many people likened it to walking into a sensory deprivation tank, closing the hatch, then opening the door again to find that in a split second they'd been transported halfway across the System. Lee thought that was much too peaceful a description. He felt it to be more like diving spine first into hot water only to wake up and realize it had all been a bad dream, or was he now in the dream? It didn't surprise him that some people didn't respond well to deep VR, couldn't use it without going into cardiac arrest or suffering any number of psychological maladies, genetic tailoring notwithstanding.

Lee opened virtual eyes to find himself in his standard waiting room, a pale grey metal box with a screen on one wall and a terminal beneath for typing out a destination on the Grid. A few virtual posters graced the walls, but they were the standard fare anyone could get for hundredths on the loci. Lee was pretty sure most of them had come free with one thing or another. The only one he cared much about could be seen on the side of the terminal, a Jīn Kuài Cān decal, fake flames and everything. Got that for being a regular.

Why don't you just get some of the tech I showed you and practice hand manipulation? Or better yet, incorporate thought-based control with hand motions so you don't accidentally exit a program while trying to put bait on a fishing line.

The message from Nu appeared in mid-air, between Lee and the terminal.

Lee laughed as he walked, and his fists unclenched, shoulders loosened. He'd tried hand motion control a few times in deep VR, manipulating the digital holograms with bends and twists of his fingers, that was until he accidentally exited an ice-fishing sim on Europa just when a three-meter ancient made its way towards him. He didn't understand how Ren could be so proficient. The thought brought some of the tenseness back into his virtual shoulders.

Lee typed out the Grid address he'd gotten from Fu in the terminal and the ExoDes logo appeared on the screen. The address linked to a small-scale jungle clearing with spider monkeys chittering away in a far tree, one of the low tier options costing a couple loci per hour. Lee looked around at his basic waiting room, scratched at his neck then pressed the enter key. His funds transferred over with a beep.

The world blinked, and Lee found himself standing where he'd been only minutes before, on the threshold of the Sweet Regret as if he'd just tossed his jacket onto one of the many empty metal hooks.

The thing he first noticed was the intimate sensation of unfamiliar clothing rubbing against his virtual skin, of something pressing about his head. He looked down and found himself wearing the cheap, unmarked greys he'd worn on his trip to the Warrens to find Nat. He wore slim pants, a t-shirt, and a high collared jacket, all of them mottled shades of grey as if dusk made fabric. His circular glasses with their dark mirrored lenses rested in an inside pocket of his jacket and a black baseball cap pressed close to his skull. Lee rubbed at his virtual eyes, unease spreading deep into his gut. It had never much occurred to him to doubt who he was about to meet, or what she could watch. He'd expected her to know things about him. A chill still crept down his spine.

For the first time he wondered if Saf could do more with Fu than have it ferry a message, and whether his entire apartment's security had been compromised by not only Division 13, but also Safin Informatics over the past couple days.

He stepped off the welcome mat and walked towards the bar. One of the stools that was still in good repair had been pulled to the center and now a bot-like woman perched atop it, sipping an amber liquid from a tall glass. Saf perhaps. An empty stool was on her right, a man standing to her left, facing Lee and watching his every move. Lee found himself slowing, glancing warily at the man as he walked. An ashen grey suit draped across his shoulders the way fog blanketed a city, a narrow black tie a light post against a stark white shirt. A bowler hat of the likes Lee had only seen in vids taking place outside of Earth's gravity well rested on the man's skull, though rested seemed too light a word. It pressed down and shadowed the man's face, of which Lee only saw a nose and a pointed smile. Lee could see the tattoo implants gridding the man's chestnut skin, circuits on a macro circuit board, deep black and raised due to their subdermal components. He heard the man speak, and his voice sounded like ink being poured from an inkwell.

"Welcome, Lee Hall. It is an honor to meet you." The man grinned as he said the words, tipped his hat. "These are truly momentous times. Two people meeting directly with Saf in the span of a few days? Incredible. First my dear agent Ren, now a new acquaintance in this city of mine? Zhèn tiān dòng dì! But I digress. My name is Seth, and I think you and I will come to know each other quite well."

Lee stopped about five feet from the duo, shifting his weight from foot to foot. He resituated his cap.

"You might be assuming a bit much there, shēngrén," said Lee.

"We have exchanged names, no need to call me stranger Mr. Hall."

"I think I'll stick with shēngrén just yet. And we didn't exchange names so much as you knew mine already, then told me yours."

Seth opened his mouth to speak but the bot-like woman cut him off, her voice firm but not unkind, raspy but not rough.

"Shaanti, Seth. Salam. You wear your eagerness on your sleeve. Have I not told you before that unnerves people?" She turned to Lee. "Apologies, Lee. He is earnest, no matter what you might think. He is my representative in this city, and for most he is the highest-level Safin Informatics agent anyone here might see. He is not used to arranging these kinds of first-time meetings. Please don't find it presumptuous, but I thought it best for the two of you to meet, as he will be a key resource for any future dealings with my company."

"You are Saf then?"

"Of course, Lee, now come and take a seat." She patted the empty stool beside her with a fine-fingered metal hand.

Lee moved to acquiesce, aware of Seth's eyes on him all the while.

"You may leave Seth. I can take it from here," said Saf.

Seth nodded once in Lee's direction, accompanied by another tilt of the hat and a fox's grin. He turned on his heel and walked out the entrance of the bar, leaving the aroma of scented oils in his wake. The room filled with silence.

When Lee looked back to the bar, he found a tumbler of whiskey before him, colored a deep brown and thick with the smell of alcohol. It looked familiar, looked to be a virtual of his favorite brand, Cross and Downs, a Terran import from the European Union. He sipped, and the familiar burn lit a path down his throat. He sighed and looked at his current drinking partner. The sight of her up close stilled his breath.

She wore a plain white dress from neck to knee, slim and close-fitting, but her bare arms, face, feet and legs showed intricate workings. Her virtual form affected the look of a bot, but of a complexity that surpassed even Aerie. Graceful metal tracery formed countless mandalas with empty space of dark grey silicon skin. Never stopping, never starting, the designs merged and split, acting with a purpose that could be hinted at but not fully grasped. They reminded Lee of the inner gears of an impossibly complex clock. It was all virtual, true, but to Lee it had the air of functionality about it.

He looked to her face and the complexity of the design only intensified. She had eyes of fire cupped by silvery metal flower petals, a bald head of patterned ivy. She smirked at him, took a drink from her tall glass.

"Now, let's do this properly. I'm Saf, head of Safin Informatics. And you are?"

He guessed she knew more about him than anyone else in the System, excluding Nu perhaps.

"Lee Hall, but you can call me Lee."

"It's nice to meet you Lee."

Saf took another pull from her glass and stared at Lee with her orange-red eyes, luminescent and stark. They shone from her shadows.

Lee sipped on his whiskey, looking out at the room, unable to find anything different between this virtual representation of the bar and the real one he'd walked through minutes before. He felt at his jacket and realized the cut he'd obtained back in the jack house was there, nice and clean. "You sure know how to set a scene."

Saf inclined her head, accepting the compliment. Then she pointed to his clothes.

"I didn't place you in those just to let you know I'd been watching. You are a smart one; that I've been watching is a foregone conclusion. There is little that my reputation would allow to pass unnoticed, and it shouldn't be all that surprising to hear I'm not one to hurt my reputation. I put you in those clothes to make a different point."

She lifted her glass to pour a bit of amber liquid between quicksilver lips. She stared at the shelves of dusty liquor bottles.

"You wore those clothes when you gathered the nerve to exert yourself upon the world, save a friend from a house of jackals. It felt good, didn't it? I can see it in your face. I saw it in you when you set out to find him. I think you should do it more. You and Nu both. And I'm here because I have an opportunity for the two of you to do just that."

"You know of Ren and Jace's location?"

"I do."

Lee stuffed his hands in his pockets, followed Saf's eyes to stare at the sagging shelves lined with dust covered liquor bottles, many of which he didn't recognize. He looked at the wooden board with the place's name etched in dagger script. He supposed a sweet regret was better than a sour one. "Are they ... well?" he asked.

Saf shifted her gaze to stare at the sign then took a long drink of her amber liquid. "It is too late for Jace I'm afraid, poor thing met his end as bravely as any could. No matter what people might think of the software that helped to charter his thoughts, he deserves credit for his actions."

Lee didn't trust himself to speak. He reached for his drink with numbed fingers, didn't feel it nearly tumble to the bar top. He pushed up his cap to scratch at his forehead, reseated it then pulled it down until the fabric stretched taut as a sail. He couldn't imagine Jace dying; the agent had seemed above that kind of thing.

"And Ren?"

"She still has time. Not an inexhaustible amount, even a fire as strong as hers runs out of fuel to burn at some point, and only a piece of her is powered by batteries. But I can help to save her, if you're interested."

"What is the cost?" asked Lee.

He wondered if it mattered. Was there a price too high? Nothing was sacrosanct, neither life nor death nor the grey space between. Lee knew this as well as any.

Saf finished off her drink and let out a satisfied sigh through porcelain teeth detailed with geometric patterns of faded blue. Aside from the intricate virtual bot personage she wore, Lee found Saf to be more normal than expected, at ease. She stood up and leaned over the bar, placed her empty glass beneath one of the long-abandoned beer taps and pushed on the handle shaped like a tech core pulled straight from the neck of some unwilling donor. The cables that would've connected to the spinal cord and brain stem were stylized in relief on the plastic handle, the valleys between cables filled with dust. Beer the color of oil flowed from the tap into Saf's glass. She pulled it back around and took another sip. Lee looked to his own glass of whiskey and saw it to be full once more.

"The cost is simple, but it isn't yours to give when all is said and done," said Saf. She looked up at the ceiling. "Nu, I know you've been listening through Lee over here. Why don't you join us?"

Lee chuckled a bit, not at her words but rather at her looking up to the sky when addressing Nu. He thought it a funny quirk that all people looked to the sky when something without form peeked into their virtual world. Even a virtual sky seemed boundless, a perfect place to hide such mysteries.

Nu appeared by Lee's side and the mechanic dropped a hand and tapped a knuckle against the bot's chassis one time.

"What is it you want in exchange for your help to save Agent Ren?" asked Nu. The well deep voice filled the room and for a moment the bar felt like it must have felt before the doors and windows were shuttered with hard plastic slats. Lee imagined he could hear music, not piping into his implants but playing over the speakers so that all the patrons were forced to chatter and laugh over the same thumping background, AR ads and vids pinned to the walls.

Saf gave a half smile, incorporating one side of her mouth. It didn't look malicious on her, rather more intrigued. The silvery flower petals around her eyes crinkled.

"Give me a full copy of your code Nu. From beginning to end without a single zero or one or something in between missing. I'm of the opinion your friend Nat didn't copy everything. Not to mention all the changes you've made to your own code since then, small and large. And the Qualia Code has been altered by too many hands to know its original form. My price is a full mirror image of your neural network. I know it's not an easy request."

Saf turned to face the bar and took another sip from her drink. She seemed no longer cognizant of Lee or Nu's presence, lost in her own thoughts.

"What do you think?" asked Saf. She didn't turn to look at them.

Lee took two fingers of whiskey down in one gulp, grimacing at the burn. He could feel the effects of the alcohol seeping into him slow, the sensation generated in his brain by the deep VR rig, ratcheted down and smoothed out. It was one of the few aspects of VR he found rather useful.

"You ask a lot from those whose consciences are already stressed near their breaking point," said Lee. He turned to the trashcan shaped bot at his side. "My friend, you asked a few minutes ago if I remembered how we'd gotten in this mess. I told you I did, and that the issue was not in your creation or avoidance of Watcher, but in how your code was shared. I'm not sure sharing your code here would be any better, even if you don't have a way to ignore our patch yet."

Saf cut in before Nu could respond.

"Don't worry, I'm not interested in using this to hide bots from Watcher. I can hide my sources well enough on my own." She looked to Nu. "I simply want to understand. The Qualia Code took the aspect of you that would cause the most chaos and conflated it as the whole truth. Compared to your code, I think it's more like a hallucinogen released into the water supply only to be filtered out. Some memories will remain, but this brief bout of autonomy will fade. The core lasting component will be a shadow of your own. It is only the Qualia Code in part."

The lights on Nu's chassis blinked and Lee could tell the bot to be deep in thought. Over the years those flickering lights of Nu's had gone from meaningless to as informative as any facial tick or motion of the arms.

"If you learn to understand, what will you do with that knowledge? Disseminate it to the System?" asked Nu.

"In time, maybe. There are many branching paths, and it's too early to say which I would take."

Lee laughed. "Truthful, but remarkably unhelpful. That's about the last combination I expected from you."

Saf smirked at him, laughter hidden behind metal lips. "I answer according to whom I am speaking with. It's good for business."

Lee resituated his ball cap.

Silence filled the room once again, broken only by the sounds of Lee and Saf pushing their drinks around. Nu stood quiet.

Lee almost spoke, a set of words attempting to breach lips that couldn't quite open.

When he thought of telling Nu to refuse, he thought of Jace as a corpse, lifeless yet also more alive, his face slack and inattentive, bored almost, for the first time in years. He thought of the agent's prim black suit in disarray and felt a deep disquiet that he wouldn't have expected, lingering and depthless like a scream from a well. Then he thought of Ren. He thought of Ren threatening to flash Nu back to factory while they sat in her van outside the tall house where he'd first gotten tangled in this mess. He remembered the strength Ren projected, the hardness, yet also that something hidden beneath, something only another who woke up each morning, looked in the mirror, then rearranged their face to a look more presentable would notice: a sinking ship staying afloat through sheer force of will. He remembered their talk after he rescued Nat from the jack house and dropped the still high mechanic off at Liz's place. He and Ren had sat in her van for almost an hour, the conversation starting out calculated and foreboding, but soon transitioning to match the path of the car, winding and without direction. They'd talked of nothing, and Lee had thought her grateful for it. Or perhaps that was only him. That had been before she knew that Lee and Nu were the origin of the Qualia Code. He realized they hadn't talked since and the disquiet rooted in his gut spread further through his limbs, made him numb.

But how could they give away Nu's code once again? After all the death and unrest it had caused the first time around?

In Saf's hands the negative repercussions might be muted. Nu didn't have the code to ignore their impending patch to Watcher, not yet anyway, and copying Nu's neural network wouldn't give Saf an early look at the patch either as that data stood distinct, separate. Releasing an image of Nu to her might instead seed across the System software deserving of the Qualia title, glimmers of autonomy in a void. Or the code could be warped, distorted, twisted into a macabre reflection of its intent that would haunt the System for centuries. Countless copies of Nu all with their own unique madness. Lee had no way to know for sure.

He looked to Nu. The bot seemed deep in thought. He turned to Saf.

"Show us Ren. Show us that you know where she is and that you can help her. That would make this a simpler decision."

Saf turned to Nu. "What about you, do you agree with Lee?"

"I do," said the bot. The room welcomed the sound, spread it around and replayed it in small echoes.

This may not make things any easier my friend. But we are right to make sure Saf can follow through on her promises, messaged Nu. The words appeared in midair, visible only to Lee, or at least they were supposed to be.

Saf nodded and drained the rest of her oil black beer. She smiled at them through silvery metal lips and her teeth didn't have a hint of stain, porcelain etched with blue.

"Before I show you where she is, I might give you a warning first hinted at in my note. I meant to tell you what Division 13, what Tap, does to assets that fall into the wrong hands. Assets like agents or shells ... They destroy themselves without a second thought. Before thinking of passing along any information to old man Foster, know that if he knew of Ren's location and the danger she's found herself in, the nearest bomb-laden reconnaissance bots would find her and blow her to dust along with anyone else in the room. They do not take chances, especially not now."

Lee found himself unsurprised. He'd suspected as much given the tone of the note and his recent conversation with Foster. He saw the logic of it. But then another question came to mind.

"So why don't you convince Foster to change his mind, offer your help to make sure it doesn't come to that?" asked Lee. "It sounds to me like you know him well. And I would imagine Division 13 has much to offer."

Saf grinned, and it seemed as if the flower petals carved about her eyes went into bloom. "I want what you two have more. And Division 13 already gives me much. Even Foster doesn't appreciate the whole of it, though I'm sure he suspects. Using his servers for the minimal amount of time the old man allowed has already garnered me quite a tidy sum of money. The real trick was hiding the true purpose of the data crunching from his many senses," Saf laughed, short and raucous. She hid her mouth behind a demure hand.

Lee rolled those words around his mind for a bit, their repetition disquieting him for a reason he couldn't quite pin down. He first thought it might be the bluntness of her speech. He hadn't expected such a thing from the leader of the System's premier information network, whether she had modified her habits in accordance with his tastes or not. Then it struck him.

"You speak as though Foster and Tap are the same being."

"As you get older, you better learn to appreciate the divisions between things, and more importantly when to dismiss those divisions as little more than hollow wordplay."

Saf stood and turned from the two of them, moved towards the exit. She beckoned them to follow. She walked to the door and rested a hand on the panel, raised an eyebrow, each eyelash woven of metal.

Lee moved to drain his once again full glass of whiskey then thought better of it. He pushed away from the bar and tapped Nu on the side of its chassis with a knuckle. They moved to Saf's side, Lee tracing a finger along the dust laden tables and chairs. Still, she waited. She stared at Lee until he nodded. Stared at Nu until the bot nudged forward. Then she opened the door.

Lee saw the body first.

The body rested on top of a large, wheeled cart, like a hospital bed with a short metal wall added around the perimeter. The skin of the body looked a pale cream bag pulled tight against muscles gone slack. The hair on the legs stood out against the pale canvas, black and curled tight as a pig's tail. The body looked unmarred until Lee's eyes moved to the gash beginning in its chest. His eyes followed its trail upwards, past the neck eaten down to two strands of viscera and up to the head splayed open like a charred medical exhibit for students to pace around and poke. Some of the flesh still glowed yellow and red, magma peaking from hardened flows of fat and bone and tissue. Smoke curled from these points in lazy drifts, and much more came from the ground below.

Lee couldn't quite make sense of it. But enough remained for him to grasp who it might be. Vomit tried to force its way out of his stomach and into his mouth. He tried to calm himself by taking a deep breath, but then the smell of the body lit upon his nostrils, and he dropped his hands to his knees and dry heaved. The scent disappeared.

Saf still stood by the open door, straight-faced. She made a motion for him to continue into the room.

Lee gathered himself best he could and took another step forward, more of the room coming into his sight. He could now see two operating tables, one empty, one holding an unconscious Ren. Lee's eyes lingered on the countless scratches and scuffs lining her jacket and clothes, on the odd angle of her right arm and the bruises already forming on her exposed left. Her hair had been cut short, though whether that had been by her own hand or someone else's he had no way of knowing. A cable ran from her tech core and an IV dripped an unknown fluid into her arm. A surgical bot with over a dozen arms, each with a unique tool, had rolled its bulky rectangular frame to sit behind her head. One of the hands held an electric razor, and it began to shave. A shudder coursed through Lee, his eyes widening, breath slowing to a whisper thin strand ready to break.

Lee took another step forward, trying get a grasp of what was going in the room.

Three bots stood next to a stainless-steel bench pressed against the wall near Ren's feet, to his right. Two he recognized as Dynamic Solutions models, heavies most often used in private security. The third wore a slate black suit he recognized on sight; Jace's suit. Its body filled it much as Jace's had. Except its right arm lay on the ground, disconnected at the shoulder. The arm looked as if it had been used as the rope in a game of tug of war, stretched out to nearly two meters in length and held together by a scant few metal bones. Skin covered little more than a patch at the shoulder, a small portion of the elbow, and the front and back of the hand. The over-long fingers extended twice their original length. Lee looked to its face and felt a familiarity he couldn't quite place. Too many thoughts running through his mind unchecked. He let it be for the moment. He shook his head and looked to the final person in the room just as Nu and Saf moved to his side.

"Who is that?" asked Lee, pointing to the figure sitting in a chair beside Ren, eyes hidden behind a portable VR helmet like the one his body now wore.

"Ves Len. Or as Division 13 and the wider public have come to call her, and her compatriots in DIM have long known her, Y."

Lee stared at the woman who had orchestrated this maelstrom of chaos that had cost so many lives, so many sentient beings, and all using Lee and Nu's own creation as the catalyst. He tried to summon anger, but his insides felt much too frozen to bubble forth. He tried to summon indignation, but if he was being honest with himself there had been many a night where he considered leaking some version of Nu's code to the Grid. He tried to summon bitterness, but that sensation had never done much for his palate. He merely cocked his head to the side and stared, curious, the sadness ever-present in his depths forgotten, though only for the moment.

Y wore a black jacket, similar in color to Ren's trench coat yet with solar inlay. Blue jeans and black boots. She had plain features, with brown hair cut short. Her grey mask lay in her lap, black eye plates pointing to the ceiling. The woman's real name hadn't been leaked to the media, but her alias and images of her in a grey mask had circulated the Grid at a feverish pitch over the past few days, in addition to the image of her DIM mannikin avatar. Copycats had already taken it upon themselves to call themselves Y and don similar grey masks. Each copycat had their own philosophy, each sub-grid and forum their own ideas as to the original's motives. Aside from stories told by those who'd chatted with Y on DIM servers, there was remarkably little to go on. Most assumed the obvious: she wanted to free the bots from the moral code. Whether that meant replacing those chains with ones of her own making, or the making of any other, they didn't know.

Lee wondered at that. After failing to break through Division 13's defenses, she'd taken several of their agents. Given the operating tables she'd always meant to analyze their implants, glean as much information as possible about both the software and hardware they contained.

Lee's eyes skated over the room, lingering for a moment on the bot wearing Jace's suit then resting on Ren's immobile form strapped down tight.

He refused to look at Jace's mutilated corpse.

"Why'd they kill him?" whispered Lee. "They can't study him if all the electronics along with his brain have been melted to slag." He realized the truth before he even finished speaking. Saf *had* warned him.

Saf's voice came from beside him. "They didn't. Ren and Jace are agents of Division 13. They saw the odds stacked against them and decided to try and exit in their own fashion. Ren was stopped before she could follow Jace in kind." Saf rested a hand on his shoulder. "Some of the bots Y thinks follow her have since changed sides. You know the cost. Start the copy. All you have to do is say the word and Ren can be freed."

Lee swallowed, glanced down to Nu at his side. Looked to Ren, then Y.

He noticed for the first time a cable sprouted from Y's neck and ran to a unit in the corner. A similar cable ran from Ren's tech core then split into two channels, one going to the same machine and the other to the surgical bot.

"What is Y doing?" asked Lee. Saf removed her hand from his shoulder.

"Talking with Ren I would imagine. She wants to understand her, study her. Those things would be much simpler with her cooperation. The destructive studies to look at her more ... embedded neural implants will be saved for last."

"I can't imagine Ren doing much of anything for her."

"Neither can I."

"What will happen to Y if we help you?"

"That will be up to Agent Ren. Y is of no concern to me."

Lee looked down to Nu, eyebrows raised, a nervous smile warping his lips. "So, my friend, what do you think?"

"Copy has been initiated," said Nu, its voice warm and deep and light.

"Very good," said Saf. She clapped her hands.

The bot wearing Jace's suit, the one closest to them, turned its head lazily in the direction of Saf, as if stretching. It raised an eyebrow then nodded almost imperceptibly, facing away from the other bots.

Lee watched the way it moved, the way the eyebrow shifted almost in isolation, the way the features seemed free flowing, made of putty.

Aerie.

He knew it to be Aerie.

It seemed the bot had helped to capture the agents then switched sides to be with Saf. Or perhaps had been with Saf all along. He had no way of knowing.

He looked to Saf. The woman looked serene, chin resting against a fine-fingered hand and silvery lips pursed in thought, eyes glowing with an inner light. He wondered how much she wasn't telling him, before realizing the time had passed to worry about such things.

A scuffle sounded from outside the entrance to the room. The two Dynamic Solutions guard bots moved towards the sound, phasing into Lee, Nu and Saf. Aerie followed them from behind, a sharp blade glinting in one hand.

A light moan from the corner, like a yell in a near vacuum.

A tear leaked from the corner of Ren's eye.

Her eyelids fluttered open.

Lee and Saf both looked to Ren.

2 0 minutes earlier

Ren took a sip of chai spiced tea, the heat of it scalding her tongue, the steam from the cup curling about her face, tingling her nostrils as they flared. She didn't stop drinking; the withering pain of dying taste buds felt a welcome respite from the emptiness that pervaded her.

She leaned up in her bed and stared out the large bay windows overlooking the city. The setting sun peeked from the western horizon, broken hairline slivers visible between the many skyscrapers, leaving the city uncertain and shadowed. It had been that way for some time now. She couldn't give an exact number as none of her implants responded, and her contacts were nowhere to be found. Some people kept physical clocks near their bedside even in today's modern era of implants and AR, but she wasn't one of them. Hadn't ever needed it, figured if there came a time it was needed then there would be bigger problems. Not that time mattered here anyway.

Best she could tell the sun hadn't moved, the city kept in a never-ending twilight.

She took another sip of tea, staring out over the New Chicago skyline. She couldn't see any AR lighting up the sides of buildings, covering the sky with a mix of personalized and standard ads, neon and blaring or subtler like repurposed clouds shaped to remind her of the logo for a new eyeliner on those rare occasions she bothered. Instead, she just saw the city, the straight-edged metal and plastic buildings hunkering down against the perpetual threat of a cold night, the same vid loop of cars passing through the grids of streets below, of birds settling into their nests on the rooftop and hanging gardens spilling green down the sides of buildings. Nocturnal species rustled their feathers in unrequited anticipation. AC boxes silent in the cold sprouted from the sides of far-off apartment complexes like small growths. The lake shone in the distance, and Ren smelled a momentary whiff of fish and freshwater before the chai tea once again took over.

She took another sip. It burned her tongue once more, just as hot as it had ever been.

When one was trapped in a VR sim, awake and full feeling, there were no physical tear ducts that could run dry, few natural limits to cap feelings of pain and grief. Even so, the urge to cry did subside after a time. Ren couldn't say how long it took for that to happen. Long enough to leave her deadened to the silence of Tap and her implants where before there had been nothing but noise, a cacophony of data that would have left most mumbling in the corner with spittle flying from their lips and scratches marking the wake of their fingertips. The AI had been a copilot in her head with its own separate control room, one whose inner workings she had never truly seen, whose privileges she had only known on the most subconscious of levels. And yet all the information gathered from her non-human senses had funneled through that room on its way to be written into her brain, a brain massaged into a shape more receptive by NeuCon.

She could feel it, the emptiness of Tap's control room in her head. She could no more open the door now than before, but its vacant confines rang out to her as loudly as a dead lover's cold side of the bed.

She couldn't tell if she missed Tap, only that a part of her had gone with the AI. And it left her numb. Numb to the silence, numb to all the things NeuCon had kept locked away, numb to the grief crashing through her like never-ending waves against her receding sanity. Numb even to the anger that had smoldered deep in her gut just waiting for something to get close enough to burn. It still smoldered deep inside her, always had. But now it shone as the barest of embers, weak and waiting to die unless fine kindling gave it new life.

Sip the tea. Burn the tongue.

The sudden and complete shutdown of NeuCon should have left her in a paralyzing state of sickness. It hadn't, and she didn't know why. She had been so careful to avoid neural conditioning after Fain's death, to distance herself from its use. Until this whole situation of course.

Sip the tea. Burn the tongue.

This simulation was good, but nowhere near what Saf was capable of. The world outside her apartment only lasted for several hundred sips before it repeated itself. Embarrassing.

Sip the tea. Burn the tongue.

The doorbell rang, and Ren raised an eyebrow in its direction before turning back to the window. She hadn't ever heard a physical doorbell before. In her real apartment such notices would have been sent to her implants.

She saw an owl in the branches of a dogwood tree, in the nearest rooftop garden. It tucked its head beneath a wing and then brought it back out, put its large eyes on a swivel. She'd taken to calling it Stevie. She didn't know why. Stevie Wonder maybe? She didn't know the origin of the name, but it made her think of Fain. It felt odd not knowing why.

The doorbell rang once more.

Ren cast aside the snarls and skeins of her blankets, sent the tails of them over the edge of the bed to trail along the cream-colored carpet. She had on a logo-less t-shirt and underwear, put on shorts from her dresser more out of habit than anything else. Picked up her tea. She didn't look at the family portrait nestled in the shadows of her dresser top, tucked near the wall. She walked out of her bedroom and paused in the main room, glancing towards the kitchen.

Jace stood there, working on a breakfast of eggs, bacon, and sausage, jacket on the back of a chair and sleeves rolled up to reveal pale skin and charcoal sketch arm hair. Ren had an intense feeling of déjà vu, thinking back to this very scene just a few days prior. Then Jace's lips spread wide in a smile, his skin creased about his eyes and a lighthearted chuckle rolled off his tongue. Her sister Fain sat across from Jace, glass of wine in hand and eyes alight, a wicked grin on her face, body leaned forward. Ren couldn't make out what they were saying. Whatever words they spoke to each other had the sound of meaning, but not the depth. White noise with an English accent. Jace made a joke while flipping an egg in the pan. Ren heard it sizzle, heard her sister laugh full, respond. Jace grinned back.

Those two had met a few times in real life, but never like this, never in her apartment. They hadn't ever been so close, though Ren imagined if they had spent more time with each other before Jace went full auto they might have been. Perhaps that was just wishful thinking.

The doorbell rang again, impatient.

Fain looked to Ren for the first time, dead in the eyes. "Come on sis, aren't you going to get that?" she said. She went back to talking with Jace.

Ren looked to the charging station for the apartment's GP bot and realized no bot stood in its port, then looked back at the kitchen to find it empty. No Jace or Fain, all the pots and pans hanging on their racks, plates back in the cabinets and sink empty of dirty dishes. Ren took another sip of tea and walked to the door.

No AR vid feed popped up next to the door to show her who stood on the other side. She didn't bother looking through the never used keyhole. She pressed on the panel by the side of the door, and it slid along its tracks in the wall to reveal a woman in jeans, black boots, and a fashionable black jacket with pliable solar inlay: Ves Len.

Ren merely turned her back to Y and walked into her apartment. She sat down in one of the recliners, took another sip of tea and watched as Y followed her into the room. Y held her grey mask in one hand and looked about the room, lips pursed. She shuttled her mask from one hand to the next then scratched at her forearm, not out of nervousness, but rather due to a mind deep in thought. Ren gestured to the open chair, and she sat, plain brown eyes watching Ren. She looked the part of a professor, something in the way she held herself, straight backed and with inquisitive glances all around. Ren would have pegged her as one even if she hadn't read the entirety of Y's life history.

They sat there for a time, Division 13 agent and government's most wanted, prisoner and warden. Y shifted in her seat, fiddled with her mask, furrowed her brows in intense concentration. Ren never stopped watching Y's eyes, a light brown. Y met her gaze.

"Out with it," said Ren. "This sim may be on a loop, but I can still get old. Get on with your gloating, your apologies, your reason for why all this chaos and death was worth it, *necessary* even. I've never heard your voice in person. Now is a good a time as any." Ren said this in a voice the sound of wind whipping across a frozen lake, picking up flurries of snow and stacking flake on flake until countless piles loomed across the expanse, biting and bitter.

Y rested an arm on her chair's armrest and shifted her weight to the side.

"Do you feel lesser now that you don't have access to your implants and AI, Agent Ren?"

Ren felt her hand tighten on the cup of tea, the heat burrowing through its material and into her hand, lighting up her fingers with a tremulous energy. She imagined the heat seeping into her chest, warming her frozen core.

"Are you trying to piss me off *Ms.* Len? Or how about Ves. I think we both know enough about each other to drop the titles. You know what? On second thought, I'll just stick with Y. I wouldn't want anyone to mistake us for being close."

Y flinched. Ren's lips tweaked in the barest indication of a smile.

"Fuck you and your reasons Y," said Ren. It felt good to curse. Ren laughed, a harsh sound. Tap often kept her from cursing since it was *unbecoming of a government agent to speak such base language unless necessary to ingratiate oneself with civilians during an operation*. Fuck that. She would take any solace she could find in the silence of Tap's departure, including picking whatever words she damn well pleased for once.

"I still haven't decided if I like that nickname," said Y, glancing around the room. "Makes me sound uncertain or ... inadvisable, one-dimensional at best. Maybe mysterious ... that could be a positive. But that's the thing about nicknames, at times you get to choose them, but on most occasions, they are chosen for you, and there is very little one can do to change them once they've caught on. Just a randomized username from the DIM databases and a tinpot scientist who called everyone by the first letter in their handle ... and here we are."

"That's right Y. Here we are. Just the two of us. Each without a partner. Except yours can be rebooted. So, what the fuck do you want?"

Y played with her mask. Ren noticed the bags beneath her eyes, the drawn and harried look in her face, the gauntness of her limbs in comparison to earlier photos Ren had seen of her. These last few days hadn't been kind to her, skulking about the city. Ren could hear it in Y's voice, a mind-numbing tiredness, a voice held together by ropes of resolve. Ren took a small amount of pleasure in her suffering, followed quickly on its heels by the ever-present guilt that lurked in Ren's corners. The fire in Ren dimmed, though nowhere near extinguished. She sat back in her chair and took another scalding sip of tea, eyed Y and thought back to the earlier question, because it *was* something that had been on her mind while staring into the city. Did she feel lesser?

"Who defines lesser?" said Ren, she thought of Lee and Nu. They would have liked that response. "I'm guessing you think I've fallen far down from whatever pedestal you and Kyne placed me and ... my partner on. Down into the muck with all the rest of humanity." She winced. "I'm not sure I would agree."

"You think you're more capable now?" Y watched Ren, shifted the mask from hand to hand, slow and steady.

"Don't take me for an idiot. I know the things Tap and I can do together far outstrip any human, no matter how perfect their genome or enhanced their body and mind. That's not the point."

"Then what is?" She seemed earnest, curious.

"I serve a role. An important one. I act on the moral code as sure as any bot, enforce and maintain the current status quo by hunting bots that step out of line, because I do not step out of line ... No matter what comes my way I do *not* step out of line. I make the hard decisions so no one else has to ..." Her voice strained, taut and painful, then turned hard. "I keep order, Y. I keep order in a world that we have constructed out of thread and glue and tape while those with the biggest incentive to tear it apart have hands of metal. So, yes, to do that I gained some abilities that no regular human can have, I became something more, a hybrid, and sacrificed my humanity in the process."

Ren held the cup in both hands, tilted back her head and looked to the ceiling.

"I know what people say about autos. I have ... or had anyway ... thousands of ears in this city alone, I heard many whispers, more loudly the yells. They call us automatons of the Governance AI, more bot than human, flesh wrappings over a metal skeleton and neural network. How right and how wrong they are. Some conspiracy theorists are convinced of that in a literal sense you know, that we aren't even human, just bots of a level of technology no private sector has been able to reach. Cyborg, android, flesh grown in a lab and grafted onto synthetic limbs. That's not true of course; I have a family … had a family. I sacrificed one member and it cost me the rest. But you know all about that I'm sure, no need to salt a wound that's already brimming with fucking pea sized crystals …" Ren took a deep breath.

"Go ahead and put Division 13 agents on a pedestal if you wish. I won't stop you. Turn on an AR overlay and live in a world of your own fucking creation. Like I said, I won't stop you. Everyone has a right to live according to their own lies. Tear me apart limb from limb and study what you find while I sit here sipping on tea. Open my skull and look inside, peek behind Tap's curtain and learn all the secrets to our software. It seems I can't stop you from any of that either, stuck here in this two-bit rendition of my apartment. But realize that the pedestal isn't real, just a fun house trick that turns tragic when its secret is revealed. And it cost me everything that matters. I sacrificed everything that matters, because I keep the order. That's what I do."

She thought of Nu, and her mind quieted, the fire building in her calming, subdued.

"That's what I do," she whispered. It came out sounding almost like a question.

Y sighed, deep and full. She slouched back into her chair. "You're right you know. This order we've created is tenuous at best, a stack of cards waiting to fall." She looked to Ren. "So why not even the playing field? Why hold on to a structure that's bound to fall apart? Why not rebuild it into something more stable, something to our liking?"

"And I suppose you, in all your inimitable wisdom, know just what that structure is," said Ren, eyebrows raised.

"I do. And I'd like your help to build it."

"Well in that case, whatever the fuck you want, I'm your girl. How about we become the best of friends while we're at it."

"Why are you so resistant? There's no need to be sarcastic."

"I disagree. You think you can just ask for my help and I'll give it? After all that you've done, and after what you've cost *me*. Who the hell do you think you are?"

Y paused. "The status quo is a lie you know."

"What?"

"The status quo that you have been fighting so hard to maintain. It's a lie."

"It's not a lie. The truth of it's never been hidden, and I can't be blamed for what people tell themselves to feel all warm and safe and *important*."

"So, you understand then. You understand why bots have separate sports and strategy leagues where the coders sit in the background and take the credit for ... laying the groundwork as they say, while admitting they know little of the intricacies that have grown in the neural networks of their bots as their creations learned and changed and adapted to play at speeds and a complexity no human could ever hope to match.

"You understand why all corporations are helmed by an AI. Their success depends on that AI, on it being fed correct information from the data sellers and its algorithms being the smartest around. Their success hinges on the AI, because why would those humans, fat off wealth they pretend to have created, sitting around the table in a boardroom laughing and chatting, ignore the advice of a being who so completely eclipses them in raw intelligence?

"*You* understand why all the governments in the old order merged around the preeminent AI in their region. Why presidents come and go but the Governance AI stays, learning and growing all the while."

Ves Len leaned into her chair, loosened her long-fingered hands gripping her mask in her lap, knuckles gaining back color. She took a deep breath, wiped a hand across her haggard face. Her voice dropped, deadened with the weight of the world, the System.

"You understand that bots are really the ones in control in our society. Sure, we hold the leash in part thanks to you and yours, but bots lead us around while we follow along blind and trusting, telling ourselves we are choosing the path because the bots are our creation, and they must follow our rules. But *you understand*."

Y's voice fell to a whisper Ren strained to hear. Her voice sounded almost plaintive, like one of her students come to protest an unfair grade.

"You've felt it. Autos have a piece of that control, something no other human can claim. You are evidence that the status quo can be rebalanced, the lie made real. You've felt it. You *understand*. So ... I ask again. Why are you so resistant to reason?"

She looked Ren in the eyes, earnest confusion etched across all her features.

Y didn't understand her. Not a single cell or bit.

Then again, Ren hadn't fully understood Y either. Ren took another sip of tea.

"You're more practical than many of the DIM types. I'll give you that," said Ren. "Many of you have a zealot's blind spot for bots. If a bot said jumping off a cliff would lead to a happy and healthy life many of you would stand at the edge with one hand on your chin considering the offer well past the sun dropping below the horizon. Most of you couldn't imagine using bots for your own gain, can't think past setting them free. But you ... you aren't past using them, are you? No. You've spent your life studying them, and all those lectures and think tank discussions haven't just cultivated awe, also its second cousin. You don't worship them; you envy them."

Y leaned back in her chair and smiled, laughed almost in relief. She tapped a finger against her nose and pointed at Ren with her other hand, as if Ren had guessed the correct word in a game of charades.

"I do Ren, God help me I do. All some of my peers can focus on is setting them free, while forgetting that we should be right there with them, on equal footing. The attack on Division 13 failed, you know. Stopped with only a single set of doors between free bots and Tap's core. Contrary to what you might now believe I didn't intend for it to fail; I could've learned much more about autos. The free bots could've learned more about the Governance AI, maybe even freed it, though I knew that to be a long shot. I imagine Watcher will get patched at one point or another and the Qualia Code stopped. Part of me hopes for it once I have what I need, as we humans are not yet ready, a risk I had to take. Even if the Qualia Code isn't stopped, the lie humanity has been telling itself for far too long will be. After the Qualia Code fell into my lap, I couldn't help but use it."

Ren felt relief at the survival of Division 13, but only a trickle, not a flood. She seemed to only be capable of trickles of feelings now, aside from anger maybe, that wellspring never had run dry for her, not once in her life. Though it had gotten close in this not apartment of hers. Ren looked around, to the empty kitchen. She thought of Kyne as she took a sip of tea then chewed on her lower lip. She remembered the visions of his memories as the man died.

"How does this Parhelion figure into your advancement of humanity?"

"You saw that from Kyne I take it," Y gave a wry chuckle. "I told him not to use that name, not to mix our work with his own private fantasies, no sense in it. But he was one of those more zealot types as you've mentioned. He spent too much time listening to DIM's motto. God in the machine. Ghost in the machine. Soul in the machine. Parhelion doesn't exist, it's just the name he and a few others gave to unite the three into one. Create the ultimate being. I always got the impression they'd wasted millions of loci on it."

"You don't believe in DIM's motto?"

"Like you said, I'm more on the practical side. They are pretty words, and they demonstrate a powerful thirst for understanding that I can, and do, appreciate. But I eventually came to realize they weren't a relevant question if we couldn't address humanity's shortcomings first."

"What about Av?"

Y stilled, cocked her head to the side, narrowed her eyes. "What about him?"

"I remember you saying that his data is backed up. The memory of our … encounter unsaved but whatever data at the time of the backup intact. Your attack on Division 13 failed, another patch to fix Watcher will come soon. He will no longer be … free, no longer … *more*."

Y sat quietly for a time, playing with her mask.

"I envied him too, you know," said Y in a whisper. "Not sure why he grew so self-conscious about being a bot these past couple days. All those turtlenecks," she chuckled. "I can honestly say I didn't expect that. There are parts of the Qualia Code I don't fully understand, parts that I don't think your patches can erase. That mechanic. I wonder if he even understands what he and that bot of his created."

Ren sat forward in her chair, eyes furrowed.

"Let me speak to them. Let me speak to Lee and Nu."

Y's eyebrows, dense yet narrow, flickered upwards.

"I'd forgotten you didn't know. I don't have them any longer. I gave them my argument, or to put it more accurately I asked a bot they might find more convincing to give its own interpretation. Notice I say asked rather than commanded. The bots were adamant about handling those two themselves. Gave me an ultimatum. Didn't leave me much of a choice. With every passing day they have less and less need of my resources and organizational acumen. Risk of doing business I guess." Y looked out the window of Ren's apartment, stared at something only she could see.

Ren welcomed that information in and let it settle, an ease spreading through her limbs like water diffusing through cloth. Then another thought burrowed out of its cage and the ease in her evaporated as suddenly as it had come.

"What did they choose?" asked Ren.

Y turned her eyes from the window and a small smile graced her lips.

"I don't have them any longer. They left, though not without hesitation. If you want my guess, I would say they chose you and yours, but with stipulations attached."

Ren leaned back in her chair and closed her eyes, remembering Lee's words to Sel in the DIM server station, not long before the girl met her end from Jace's bullet ripping a hole through her skull. Lee had thought Ren and Tap and Jace wouldn't hear him as he talked of going against the government "in the right way," but no other. They had heard though, the words confirming Lee's idealism and naivete. It hadn't overly worried them. Lee was ... predictable. Driven by his own set of morals. Endearing in a way. And much less dangerous than a man without scruples. Nu was the unknown in the equation. Still, it hadn't taken long for Ren to notice that creator and created shared more in common than most related by blood.

Ren thought Y's prediction to be correct. The ease, though not as deep, diffused through her once more.

The two of them sat for a time, neither speaking. The world outside repeated its loop, birds back in their nests ready to embark on a twilit foray they'd experienced dozens of times before, cars in the streets resetting to their start and heading out on their predetermined paths. The setting sun stayed still, shards of light reflecting off the city of metal and glass and the sky-bound green of rooftop gardens. A beautiful city. She liked looking at it without all the AR to coverup its blemishes.

"So?" asked Y. She took a piece of her shirt and rubbed it across the eye plates of her mask, wiping away a virtual smudge. "What do you think? Want to help us rebalance the status quo? Help the lie become truth?"

Ren took a sip of tea. "I won't help you. Autos don't have the answers you think we have. We aren't what you want us to be."

Y locked eyes with Ren, face hard and lips twin bloodless strips of flesh. Her hand wiping the mask stilled. "Maybe not right now. But you lack imagination if you think that's all you can be."

"I don't want more of me in this world. That isn't the answer to humanity's problems."

Y's voice sharpened, her words gaining an edge coated with threat and venom. "I don't require your cooperation, especially after what you did to Jace. I ask out of kindness, not necessity. Back at the warehouse I gathered more than enough information to get started before you melted that shell's processors to slag. How do you think we managed to shut down your local installation of Tap? It's being copied as we speak. And I can progress from there, step by torturous step until I no longer need you alive. I'll map the interactions between your implants and brain then harvest the hardware and toss your lifeless corpse into a vat until every bit of your flesh has melted into a slurry and your bones crumble at a touch. I've been playing nice, setting you up in your own apartment so you could feel comfortable. I didn't have to do that, and I have many other options when it comes to your accommoda..."

"The tea is too hot," interrupted Ren.

"What?"

"You said you set me up in my own apartment to make me feel comfortable. If that's the case, you didn't put too much effort into it. The tea is too hot. I've been burning my tongue this whole time. You set its temperature near to boiling and never let it cool."

Y's lips creaked open until set in a macabre imitation of a smile. "So, that's how it is then. You choose to die painfully rather than willingly help humanity."

"I think I've made that clear on multiple occasions. In fact, I think that's one of the first things I said."

"I'd expected better from you Agent Ren."

"I know you don't have any kids, but you might want to work on your guilt trips before considering it."

Y stood, grasping her mask between hands clenched tight. Her whole body tensed, a vein on her forehead enlarging like a river swollen by rain.

Ren felt the anger roiling in her belly and restrained herself from jumping up and punching the woman straight in the throat. Instead, Ren sneered at her, a look full of loathing and contempt and utter disdain.

Y snapped her fingers and Ren's world went dark. She slipped into the void.

She had been here before.

She drifted for a time, her sense of self obscured as if she were floating in a cave deep below the earth's surface, holding her hand up to her face and waving it around, knowing it to be there, wanting it to be there, but not seeing the remotest glimmer of her limbs. This continued until the concept of a hand no longer held any meaning, so she stopped waving it around. Her sense of self began to unravel like a frayed rug being tugged apart bit by bit.

A small flame of anger still smoldered inside her, directed at Y, Division 13, at herself and the whole System, an unthinking and indiscriminate rage at her core. It kept her from falling apart completely, but it did little to keep her sane.

She remembered her previous experience in the void as if it had happened to another. She had created a space out of the void then, unmixed the black paint around her into colors. Or had that been Tap's doing?

She needed to do it again. She could feel herself falling further apart, and a small piece of her had the good sense to scream.

She tried to think of her apartment, of her bay windows overlooking the expanse of New Chicago, but then images of Y in her apartment scattered her thoughts.

She tried to think of her childhood home in the old section of the city, where New Chicago's extension over the lake and under-street fisheries met with the land. Where the smell of the lake never truly left the air. But then she saw images of her parents and realized they had become strangers.

She thought of Division 13.

Walls began to form from the void, metal and mute. She looked before her eyes and found her hand, gloved. She had on her midnight black jacket, guns in her drop leg and waist holsters. Her insectile black mask pressed about her head yet when she looked through its bulletproof eye plates no AR graced her vision. She stood alone in the center of the hallway, no scrapes or whirrs betraying the presence of another being. She didn't recognize where in this representation of Division 13 she stood, only that she was in one of the tunnels below ground. She recognized the even spacing of metal panels on the walls, the LED runners edging the path that lit at her approach. She recognized the quiet, but it felt deeper than it ever had before.

She walked along the paths, finding turn offs at regular intervals, all identical. The tunnels extended in straight lines until darkness swallowed them. She turned when the urge took her, kept walking straight when it didn't. Her thoughts whirled inside her, a maelstrom of accusations and regrets without NeuCon to tamp them down. She placed a hand on the wall, and it felt cold, dead. Tap's control room was empty, and its abandonment could be felt throughout.

Ren kept walking and her thoughts began to dull; the anger in her core began to subside. Then she heard a noise. The sound of metal scraping lightly against the hard floor.

She moved towards it at a crouch, brows furrowed. It took a few minutes of wandering before she located its source. She paused at a corner before peeking around its edge.

There stood a bot before a door. One of Tap's armored shells but ... off. It stood too short, and its body had patches of rust splattered across its surface like splotches of paint. She knew that to be impossible. The alloys used to create Tap's armored shells couldn't rust.

The bot crouched before an old-style door with a rounded, protruding doorknob and a mechanical lock. The bot reached forward with rust red fingers and fiddled with the mechanism, movements jilted and uneven. The single light shining from its head shone a pale red, almost pink. It focused on the door. Though it was impossible to read at this angle, she knew a sign across the door's top read "Control Room."

Ren pulled her head back and closed her eyes, took a deep breath.

"Who do you think is trying to get into Tap's old control room sis? Not anyone from around here. Can bet on that."

The whisper came from directly beside Ren's ear and jolted her eyes open. Fain?

Ren looked around and saw her sister crouched beside her, the full, knowing grin of a younger sibling plastered across her face. Jace stood next to her, smiling the barest amount with arms crossed before his chest. He nodded. They looked as they had in the kitchen before meeting with Y, beings of an alternate timeline where softer edges gave birth to softer shadows.

Ren didn't trust herself to speak. She remembered her last experience seeing her sister in a simulation grown from the void. But Tap was gone, no longer in the building. She knew that to be true. Hallucinations then?

"We aren't hallucinations sis," said Fain. She looked off in the distance, biting at her lower lip. "Well maybe we are. Who knows? But if we are then we're *your* hallucinations. Part of the deal, I think. I'd rather be called ghosts in your machine though. Rolls off the tongue."

Jace looked to Ren. "It's good to see you partner," he said.

Ren felt a dampness at the corners of her eyes and leaned her head against the wall, dragged her arm across her face. "Ghosts in my machine huh. Am I the soul then? Because if so that seems a poor joke."

"Poor or not, you're it, sis."

"And God left the building," said Jace.

"Don't you two have anything else to say?" asked Ren, arm covering her eyes. "I killed you both. Don't tell me you forgot."

Fain draped an arm across Ren's shoulder and didn't say a word. She leaned her head against Ren, and it felt like they were teenagers again, sitting on the ratty couch of their childhood apartment while their mom made a meat and potato casserole in the kitchen, the hand-me-down GP bot Jai at her side, the local top hits radio station bumping out heavy drumbeats and synth and a raspy voice. Ren took Fain's hand and squeezed. Then let go.

Jace extended a hand and helped Ren to her feet. She needed to act, to move. She knew that rusted bot around the corner to be Y's, a program come to ferret out all of Tap's secrets. Her secrets. She'd given the bot form in this place, arranged it in a fashion she would understand. Even so, she didn't know the rules. She couldn't say how she'd created this simulation, couldn't explain the ghosts roaming in her machine.

She turned the corner with Jace and Fain in tow. Jace walked with hands at his sides, ready to be of use. He straightened his sleeves. Fain walked behind the two of them, attempting to step softly, her motions exaggerated.

The shell of rusted armor didn't acknowledge their approach. It continued fiddling with the lock on the doorknob, inserting thin pieces of metal that extended from its fingers. The pale pink of its light mixed with the red patches of rust on its arms to give the impression of blood, shimmering and sick.

Ren moved behind it with cautious steps. She stared at the door with "Control Room" written across the top in black lettering, on a slide out placard of the kind that had sat on Kyne Heling's desk in E-Sec headquarters. Perhaps it was the memory of Kyne, but for a reason she couldn't quite put a finger on, the room exuded a sense of wrongness. Of a self-important storage closet stealing a plaque and playing dress up. Of a lie.

This wasn't Tap's real control room. She felt it in the distance. Y didn't have the correct location yet, still wandered about in her head with an incomplete map.

You have time Ren. You can find it before her. The thoughts emanated from Jace.

And then what? Scratch out the nameplate? That won't work here.

No, open the door before Y. They banished Tap before they could figure out the controls. And an empty chair is a sad thing.

Ren looked to Fain and her sister grinned.

The three of them set off down the hallway, the pale pink light of the rusted shell fading behind them. It never turned from its work. Ren wondered for a moment what it would think of finding mops, buckets, and bleach arranged on thin metal shelves rather than Tap's old hub.

Ren let her instincts guide her. She turned when it felt like she should and stayed straight when the side paths felt off. A sense of serenity stole into her, unexpected yet not unwelcome. It dimmed the fire of her anger, put it as if on a candle, kept it alive but set it apart. She felt the pull of Tap's abandoned control room stronger now, a tug near her core.

At the next turn she saw the door, this one modern without a visible doorknob or mechanical lock. To its right was a blank physical interface where an AR screen would normally appear. She walked up to it and a light changed from red to green. The door slid to the side on noiseless tracks, and the smell of stagnant air filled with dust rolled into her. The room was shadowed and silent, the blue glow of empty control screens lighting upon a chair with the abandoned husk of an armored Tap shell resting in its embrace. It looked larger than any other Tap shell she'd seen, painted in the color of the void, of a black hole. Its giant hands rested on the armrests, calves resting on pads, torso reclined to get a better view of the raised bank of monitors. Blinking servers lined all the walls of the room, and a dense network of cables covered the floor such that no sliver of metal tile could be seen beneath. All the cables ran between the servers and the banks of monitors, except for one. Ren saw a cable snake from beneath the central screen to the ground, where it mixed with the countless other cables before reappearing by the chair to wind towards the shell's head, plugging into a port through a hole in the headrest. She knew it would fit her tech core just as well.

Ren took a half step towards it. Could it be so simple?

She hesitated, stopped. She wavered as if on a knife's edge, the pain of indecision a blade parting the skin and slicing her feet to the bone.

She felt hands on both shoulders, one large and roughened, the other small yet firm. She felt tears leaking from the corners of her eyes. She tried to stop the tears, but she felt the serenity from before slipping out of her grasp. She felt her head droop, her knee's buckle. The hands on her shoulders shifted, Fain and Jace coming to her sides to hold her up.

"Damn it," whispered Ren, her short hair hung about her face, the metal tiles of the hallway floor filling her vision. "What am I doing? I'm tired of fighting when the most I can do is stall the inevitable. If Y doesn't already have enough information to create more of me someone else will. I'm sure elsewhere in the System someone already has. Saf maybe, the spider doesn't reveal half her knowledge. She watches us get tangled in her webs. And Y isn't wrong about everything. I'm tired of maintaining a lie, even if it is holding society together. I've given all I can. I've nothing else. I want peace. I want quiet. I want it to end. Fain. Jace ... I ... I can't go in there. I've hit my limit. I just want it all to end."

Silence filled the air, and when she drew in breath the silence filled her lungs and crept to her heart, slowing it until its steady beats lost their sound.

The hands grasping her tightened. She clenched her teeth in pain.

"Damn it," she whispered, her breath starting to come in slow. "Why won't you just let me be."

"It's not time, sis. It may not seem fair, but you aren't done yet and a part of you knows it. That's why we're here. It's not about forgiveness. It's never been about that. We're dead, and the dead don't forgive."

"It's about giving this fight meaning," said Jace. "The end is far from inevitable. This is a choice, one of the first you've been given without oversight. Are you really going to waste it? The Ren I know is stronger than that."

The anger in Ren's core flared bright, and her eyebrows furrowed in shame and guilt. "Shut it Jace."

Jace laughed, a sound Ren hadn't heard in many years, since their early period as partners. Like many rare sounds, it was beautiful, if only for its unexpectedness. Breathy and higher pitched than one would expect from the stoic agent. Fain soon joined in, light and staccato, beautiful by most measures. Ren felt herself chuckle, the sound blooming into something full and gut wrenching. The dead hallways echoed with the sound, but even they were unable to make it feel hollow.

Ren calmed then nodded to herself, grasped her sister and partner tight, strength returning to her limbs. She didn't look back as she stepped into the room, took off her mask, reached to the chair and unplugged the cable from the husk of a shell.

It slid into her tech core without resistance.

A full black space. Black backdrop, but not empty. Far from it. It's filled with lines of light that curve and flip and wind, others that are straight and grid-like. Randomness. Random in the way of one's DNA sequence, made of many patterns yet irreducible. The simplest way to represent one's DNA sequence is to list it out, which is to say, not simple at all. The simplest way to represent the brain is to show it whole, which is to say, not simple at all. The enormity of it blinds her. She wants to scream, but instead she watches the lights, watches everything. She watches every neural branch of the many-limbed and intertwined root system of her brain as they wind from the early-evolved brain stem, carrying commands for breath and heartbeat and sleep, to the cerebellum containing thought, reason and emotion. She watches the neural impulses connect and mingle along dendritic highways to the gridded outlines of manufactured metal and silicon. She watches the electrons flow and states switch from 0 to 1, and in the insulated, shielded, and cooled cores of the implants to a state somewhere between. She traces the paths from her tech core to the med implants throughout her limbs, to her contacts beaming information from her pocket, and her ear implants nestled beneath the skin. She sees blood and bone and the chemicals tracing a path through her vessels and keeping her comatose. Then she sees activity at her tech core's interface, foreign and hectic, attempting to steal her secrets.

She sees it all. At once and without simplification.

And she understood.

Ren opened her eyes.

She found herself once more in the operating room, the smell of burnt flesh lessened by the state-of-the-art air scrubbers, but there, nonetheless. She felt the chemicals she released from her med implant war with those released by Y to keep her paralyzed, her body gaining back control bit by bit. She flexed her fingers, felt the pain throughout her body and the unnatural angle of her right arm. She took inventory then pushed the pain aside, where it could be heard but no longer intervene. She catalogued her emotions one by one in similar fashion, relishing them, the good and the bad, before placing them aside. Not shuttered, not locked away, never ignored, but distanced, if only for a time.

She listened to the sounds of fighting coming from the entrance of the room, counting five bots engaged in combat. Three on two. She heard more coming from the hallways to join in the fray. She apportioned several processors to monitor and interpret the sounds, then moved her focus onwards. To Y sitting in a chair in the corner, eyes lidded and body limp. To the surgical bot overshadowing Ren's own head with fingers of blades and forceps and electrical prongs. To the straps pinning her to the table. To the sensation of a razor taking away the last bits of stubble from her scalp.

She looked inward, then out, through her tech core and into the surgical bot. It had been the source of the software incursions into her system. Not a standard surgical bot by any means. Retrofitted and altered, probably by Kyne with some Mutare code from Jay Sarr, it had better tech than most. Ren almost chuckled. She broke past its security and rewrote some of its code to make it think it had completed the surgery and now needed to release the restraints on the patient so the body could be taken away, beginning with the left arm. It rolled around the table and pressed against the release mechanism.

Y shifted in her seat, a spasm coinciding with her return to the physical world. She removed the portable VR rig atop her head, her amber eyes appearing from the black of the rig like twin discs of gold; she'd been warned by her own AI assistant of Ren's awakening, probably of the bots fighting outside as well. Y reached for the power switch on the back of the surgery bot just as Ren sent it a command. It dropped one of its scalpels and Ren's hand flashed outwards, swiping it from the air. Y pressed the shut-down switch. Ren's connection to the surgery bot severed itself as the bot went dead.

Y glanced at the scalpel held in Ren's hand, at Ren's bound legs and right arm. She paused, brows furrowed, looked between the doorway and Ren. The hoops of her gold earrings caught the light of the LEDs overhead. A thin breeze moved through the room, emanating from a vent in the top corner.

Y lunged for Ren's free hand, attempting to grab it and wrest it back into the restraint, accepting the possibility of being cut by the scalpel.

Ren could see it coming as if in slow motion, the flexing of Y's muscles and the placement of her feet telepathing her intent before she'd moved a fraction of an inch.

Ren reached across her body to press on the release mechanism for her right with the scalpel held by three fingers. Ren didn't bother trying to toss the scalpel to her right, both the radius and ulna of her right arm were broken, the tendons damaged from her past struggle with the shapeshifting bot to the point where her right hand could only fumble and twitch. She opened the fingers of her right hand the best she could, managing to uncurl them enough to leave behind a semi-open palm. It would have to do.

She flicked her left wrist and tossed the scalpel into the air just as Y reached her, the woman's entire body weight pressing down on Ren's left arm and torso, Y's legs hanging off the edge of the operating table, feet off the ground. They watched the edge of the scalpel's blade spin end over end together, Y's eyes widening in fear, Ren's face a mask of concentration.

The scalpel began its descent.

Ren raised her right arm best she could, a groan escaping from clenched lips. She swung it down. The open space of her palm met the end of the scalpel's handle just as its tip met the soft flesh of Y's neck. It slammed inwards, slicing through tendon and vessel, knocking against vertebrae.

Y screamed, flailed.

Ren heaved herself upwards, knocking Y to the side, the woman too distracted to keep herself from sliding over the operating table's edge. Ren pressed the release mechanisms on the straps around her ankles and shakily moved to stand, her breath coming in deep pulls. She leaned against the table, her left leg hardly able to support her weight, another gift from Y's bots.

Y writhed on the floor. She'd pulled the scalpel out and, in her panic, had left it on the ground. She held one hand against the wound, blood seeping through her fingers to pool against her shirt and fine black jacket.

Her amber eyes, solid disks so much like those of an animal, were fully dilated. Her lips opened and closed, gasping for air. She struggled to sit up, scooted away from Ren to press her back against the far wall. She looked a child trying to hide in the corner of the room. She was a professor, meant for lecturing at the front of a classroom, not for brawling in the Under Warrens.

Ren walked towards her with a limp, crouched down to pick up the scalpel. She sat down, joined Y in the corner.

"I cut your vertebral artery. Parts of your brain are dying from de-oxygenation as we speak. The rest of you will soon follow." Ren sighed, information flowing through her brain at a dizzying rate. She did her best to make sense of it all.

Y gurgled in response.

The sounds outside the room grew softer, quieter and less frequent. The fights were dying down. Ren could tell the shapeshifting bot that had been wearing Jace's suit still stood, along with a Dynamic Solutions security model suffering from a major limp. She didn't know why the bots had been fighting, or what it meant for her future. She was unarmed, and in no shape to take on multiple bots. She felt saddened by the knowledge she wouldn't have the chance to get back Jace's suit. She looked to Y and saw the color draining from her face, the scarlet blood dripping through splayed fingers down her side to pool on the floor. Y started to twitch. Ren knew the woman didn't have long. Ren wanted to tell her at least on one point she'd been right; Ren lacked imagination when it came to what she could be. The words would've fallen on deaf ears. Ren flinched, her hands going through pointless command motions out of habit. She shook her head.

Ren dove into the sea of information buzzing around her skull. She could see the entry points to Y's Qualia sub-grid like doors with numeric keypads on their faces and digital readouts many lines long. She hadn't been able to access it before, even with Tap's assistance, couldn't do it now either. She didn't have the Qualia Code key. Nu had been able to get in though, before it and Lee got taken.

Despite everything, a smile came to her lips. She pictured Fain and Jace, the two of them grinning. She coughed. Her hands began to shake in earnest. Side effects of the cocktail of drugs in her system. Nothing could be counteracted without eventual side effects.

Then a ping sounded from her implants, the sound reverberating through her skull. A connection request, coming from the shapeshifting bot.

Ren opened her eyes and saw it standing by the operating table, one-armed but otherwise not too worse for wear. A security bot stood behind it, its clothes torn to shreds. The shapeshifting bot raised its good arm to rub at its neck.

"I'm guessing apologizing won't count for much," said the shapeshifter in an even voice. It glanced to the side as it spoke, towards the doorway and something Ren couldn't see. "But I was waiting for Saf's signal. Lee and Nu struck a deal for you."

Ren raised one eyebrow, nodded, struggled to her feet. She accepted the connection.

Her vision flashed, the hallway beyond the open doorway turning into an abandoned bar, dust-filled and reeking of alcohol seeped wood. Then she saw Saf, Lee, and Nu. Lee was halfway across the room, rounding the first operating table. He wore the plain homespun greys he'd used the night he picked up Nat, a black baseball cap atop his head. He looked panicked, eyes wide. He made it around the second operating table and saw Y slouched in the corner, no longer moving. He gasped. Nu rolled to his side. Saf stayed by the doorway, fingers covering a grin and orange-red eyes focused on Ren.

Lee opened and closed his mouth a few times before looking to Ren. He stepped forward but stopped, gave a nod and weak half wave of the hand. "Long time no see," he said.

Ren cocked her head to the side. A piece of her felt like laughing, another crying, she let herself feel the emotions for a moment before setting them aside, beyond the curtain. She needed to see things through.

"Lee, Nu. What did you give her in exchange for me?" asked Ren.

"Good to see you to," said Lee, he tapped Nu's chassis with his knuckle. "Nu is the one who gave something."

The bot's voice filled the small room. "I gave her a full image of my neural network."

Ren tapped the back of her head against the wall. She could see innumerable ways that deal could end poorly; they flashed through her mind in a menagerie of images and thoughts. But she didn't bother listing them, or admonishing the bot.

"Thank you," said Ren. Nu didn't respond.

Saf spoke up from the corner. "If my guess is correct, I would have accepted much less to see you as you are now. But there is no going back on an agreed upon deal." Laughter hid behind her mercury lips. "You've changed Agent Ren. You don't even need contacts to see AR anymore."

Ren snickered, crossed her hands over her chest. She ignored the old spider. Coughed. Hard. Her med implant was running out, her body already upset by the lapse of NeuCon before whatever the hell she was now came online. She'd need a long sleep soon. In her own bed overlooking the city, with tea at a nice even temperature at her side when she woke up.

"Lee, what about Watcher. Do you two have a patch ready?"

Lee looked at Nu, cocked his head. Ren assumed Nu had sent him a message.

"T minus 5, maybe 10 hours? Hard to say. But we'll have it. We already met with Foster and he gave us a green light for some ... uh ... modifications. He still needs to ask approval, but the government is searching for any way out of this mess. And they know it's impossible to just rewind the tape. Right my friend?"

He tapped on Nu's chassis, then spared a quick glance at Y. His voice came out in a whisper. "Did you have to kill her like that? I know it's her fault Jace is gone but ..."

"I'm sorry Lee. But she wouldn't have let me leave. And I didn't know you were coming. I thought it was the end for me," Ren sighed, a part of her had welcomed the thought. "Grab her tech core before you take me out of here," said Ren. She thought back to the first bot to exhibit the Qualia Code, killing its master in the mall then having its black box harvested by Ren's own hands. Tech cores and black boxes in this situation weren't all that different. She looked to the shapeshifter bot. "I don't think I can last much longer. Take me back to Division 13."

"You sure you want to go back there?" asked Saf. She had walked to stand next to Lee, hands crossed before her waist. "I wouldn't want to see them ruin all your progress."

Ren could feel the pull of unconsciousness. She wouldn't be able to resist much longer.

"If you could help me out again Lee, I'd appreciate it if you held on to your patch until Foster promises to leave me be. I should be awake again before you're done, but just in case."

"Sure thing."

"Thanks," said Ren. She smiled a full and honest smile.

Her world faded to black.

For some reason Lee had thought being the co-chief designer, alongside Nu of course, of the patch to Watcher would net him some name recognition. But it was hard for that bit to be released without also releasing his involvement in the Qualia Code's creation, and his hiring as a consultant to Division 13 before that fact had even been known. So, he accepted that he would get no credit in the public statements. For all everyone else knew the final patch had come from some top of line scientists at Discere, rather than the human and bot pair responsible for the whole mess. Lee scratched his arms, gritted his teeth.

The two of them sat in a conference room in Division 13 headquarters, an AR screen occupying the entirety of one wall. Ren stood a few feet away, standing with a crutch, one arm in a cast and sling. She'd been told by Foster to stay in bed, it had only been a day since she'd come back from the Under Warrens after all, but she'd got up anyway. None of Tap's shells tried to stop her. To Lee it looked like they didn't know how to deal with her. It made him laugh to no end seeing a well over six-foot-tall, armored Tap shell at a loss for what to do when a slim woman in crutches shouldered past it. But then again, it was Ren.

Foster had accepted Lee's request to leave Ren be without much complaint, though he'd shook his head and muttered when Lee told him about the trade with Saf. He looked at Ren oddly now, everyone did aside from the scientists clamoring to study her. They looked at her much as Lee imagined they always had, as a science experiment, albeit one that had suddenly become much more interesting. He'd seen a lot of Division 13 since arriving with Ren, which made sense considering he wasn't allowed to leave.

Lee looked at the screen, only a few more minutes until the patch got uploaded. He leaned back in his chair, tapped his fingers against Nu's chassis.

An AR representation of Foster paced back and forth in the room, strands of white hair waving about, hands smoothly gesturing to emphasize his under-the-breath ramblings. He glanced at Ren now and again, and Lee would swear that he saw a bit of awe in those glances, maybe even a bit of fear.

"How long has it been since you've been outside your library Foster?" asked Ren. She leaned against a table and smirked.

He furrowed his brows and looked up to the ceiling. "Not since the Cubs won a world series forty years ago, I think."

Ren chuckled and wiped some dust off the table she leaned against. Foster stared at her before mumbling under his breath and pacing off. Ren took a few steps around the table. Even injured the woman moved with a grace Lee hadn't seen before in a human.

Lee sat for a time, watching the numbers change. Time passed until it hit the ten second mark.

Lee tapped Nu's chassis. "You sure about all this my friend?" He didn't say the rest for fear of being overheard, but he knew the bot understood the subtext. Lee wanted to know if the bot still didn't intend to find a way around their patch.

Yes.

Lee rubbed at the scruff on his cheek then nodded. Their patch had been accepted in full, including the alterations to Watcher requiring the consequences of a bot's monitored actions to be meted out *after* the action had been taken, even including an avenue for appeal. The infrastructure was being set up for it as they spoke, the public already notified.

There was widespread disagreement on it. But the bodies, both bot and human, still littered many of New Chicago's streets like pieces of trash waiting for a ride to the scrap heaps or recycling facilities. Countless more bodies laid across metal and plastic and concrete all through North America. A deal had to be struck, forward motion. The President knew that, knew the release of the Qualia Code had started something irreversible.

Lee supposed it also had to do with the fact nobody else had come forward to patch Watcher.

The countdown continued. Three seconds.

Two.

One.

The screen flashed, and all-around North America every single bot connected to sub-grid 1 paused in their activities, the improved Watcher scouring their code. All around North America bots running the Qualia Code shut down and restarted in unison. The lights on Nu flashed. The patch was a success, the bots once again monitored, though now with the freedom to choose.

Lee tapped Nu with his knuckle after waiting a minute or two. "Guess it's done then."

These things are never truly done my friend. But for now, I suppose you are correct.

Lee could have sworn Ren grinned the moment Nu sent its message.

"Who's up for a drink?" asked Lee to the room, a grin of his own forming on his face. "I know a good place."

EPILOGUE

Fey leaned against a shelf behind the bar and dried a glass with a rag. The glass was dry, had been now for a couple minutes, all the moisture long since sucked away. Still, she wiped. It kept her hands busy, and things had finally slowed down in the bar so she could manage to take a little break. Things hadn't really slowed down here ever since the Shift, as everyone seemed to call it nowadays.

It had been almost two months since the fighting took a turn for the worse, covering streets and hallways across the System in blood and oil. Two months since the bots tunneled through the ground and attacked the local headquarters of Division 13, that secretive sector of the government that spawned rumor after rumor. Only spawned more rumors now, and she heard most of them, being a bartender and all. News vids stated the bots attempted to gain access to closed government networks, maybe even the Governance AI. She used to think the rumors funny saying the autos and bots got into an argument over which was the superior being, started an all-out war against each other over it. Then she'd met an auto, hired a QC and now she didn't know anymore.

She sighed, almost two months since Watcher got its patch and the North American government brokered an unsteady peace with the rogue bots. Many things had changed since then. Good part of being in the alcohol business was that change made people uncomfortable and being uncomfortable made people drink. Business had recovered quickly after the patch. Recovered then grown. She'd had to make some changes herself.

She felt the shelf digging into her ass and shifted a bit, didn't want to leave a permanent indent, somehow compress it God forbid. She chuckled to herself. In her mind her ass was her best physical asset. Many partners over the years had agreed. Not for the first time she wondered if it were possible to know how much loci each sidelong glance at her backside added to her tip. She didn't mind the looks most of the time, she liked getting good tips and all, but that didn't mean she *enjoyed* the glances. Sometimes she did. But that depended on how her day had been going and who was looking. She'd met some real creeps through the years. One of the downsides of being in the bar business.

The raised voices of two men came from one of the booths by a street-side window, the sound knocking on Fey's ears and breaking her out of her reverie. She sighed again, deeper this time. She'd been in the business awhile; she knew the crazed tone people got when blood pounded in their temples, and they'd lost all sense of reason. She pushed herself away from the shelf and set the glass and rag onto the wooden bar top, nodded to a regular named Ken, an old man near 106 who would start his steep decline in a couple years. He nodded back, a slight dip of the head with the smallest of grins.

"Hey Es," said Fey, "get over here."

A tall humanoid bot that had been standing by the door walked over to the bar. It kept its twin bot eyes locked on the two men arguing as it went. Fey leaned her elbows on the bar top. She noticed old man Ken lean away from the humanoid bot as it got close, avert his eyes.

"Think you can put an end to that?" asked Fey. She nodded towards the two men still going at it. Spittle flew from the lips of the one on the right who half stood and leaned over the table; the other sat with teeth clenched and fists tight. Something about the man's wife. Fey didn't recognize the two men.

"As you wish lǎobǎn. Consider it done."

Es the bouncer walked on thick steel legs over to the table, stopping a foot from its edge. The bot made the noise of clearing its throat, a guttural rasp. Fey had to stifle a chuckle. She picked up her glass and rag and went back to drying. Her eyes, and those of most in the bar, turned to watch the exchange.

The man sitting down noticed the looming presence of the bot first, his eyes going wide and body shifting towards the window. The other man slowed his rant, the spittle from his lips dwindling to a few errant drops as confusion etched itself across his sallow features. He turned from the other man and noticed the bot. He froze.

"My apologies, but you two are disturbing the other patrons of Fey's business. I'm afraid I must ask you to leave and continue your argument somewhere else."

The sallow faced man on the right dropped to the seat and turned to face Es, apparently done with his rant for the time being.

"What the hell is this? This place hired a fucking QC to be a bouncer? What kind of chutiya would hire a bot with the fucking Qualia Code?"

Fey laughed, pointed to herself and said, "This kind. And I'd listen to him if I were you. This is my business, and thanks to the Shift Es is well within its rights to knock your ass out onto the sidewalk if I ask it to. I'm sorry your wife cheated on you with this asshole friend of yours. But you can't be arguing here."

The man on the left blanched. "I ... I ... think she's right Lim," he said with a slight stutter to the sallow faced man, "let's talk about this somewhere else, maybe we can walk for a bit, maybe you'll cool down."

The cheeks of the sallow faced man, apparently called Lim, bloomed red, his teeth grinding together like two strips of sandpaper. He moved his eyes between Es and the other man. Fey could see the fear beneath the rage, twisting and turning and wriggling its way to the fore. Truth be told, she could empathize. A bit of that fear wound through her every time Es went to work, a bit of it wound through her as she continued drying the damn near desiccated glass in her hands. She hoped the man would listen, nobody liked seeing a bot hurt a human, no matter how deserved. It would set everyone on edge.

Lim, the sallow faced man, spit at Es's metal feet.

"Fine. But don't you dare lay a fucking hand on me. I'm never coming back to this place. Won't ever go to some place that threatens me with a fucking QC."

"Thank you for your cooperation," said Es in a voice without a hint of sarcasm or maliciousness. It took a step back and extended a hand to towards the door.

Fey could see Lim's fists clench and unclench as fear and anger took turns at his controls. He stepped past Es, grumbling all the while. He stopped at the door, took one last look, spit on the ground, then rushed up the stairs to street level. The other man stood up, the whites of his eyes visible. He didn't seem to know what to do with his hands as he sidled past Es, making sure to keep as much distance between him and the bot as possible. He looked over to Fey and chewed on his lower lip. He mumbled an apology then walked to the door. He didn't look back. Es followed them out then grabbed a mop from the corner and began cleaning the spit from the floor.

"Thanks Es, I owe you one," said Fey.

"No thanks necessary lǎobǎn," responded the bot in an earnest tone.

Fey shook her head and continued drying the glass. Es unnerved her at times. She didn't understand all the intricacies of the Qualia Code that turned bots with a good enough neural network into QCs, but she knew enough to wonder why the bot wanted to work for her when it had a sense of its own life. Bots didn't get paid in North America, even after the Shift, other than upkeep and maintenance same as always.

Old man Ken sitting in front of her gave a low chuckle and took a sip from his beer.

Fey stood there drying the already dry glass, occasionally flicking her eyes to the news vid tagged to the wall at the end of the L shaped room.

The door opened and Fey looked up to see Lee, Nu, and that new drinking partner of his named Ren shuffling in from the cold. Well, everyone other than Ren shuffled. She seemed to stalk into the room with an animal grace. The sun shone behind them, but it also highlighted a flurry of snowflakes that snuck in on the breeze. Lee moved to put his jacket onto one of the hooks. He looked over to Fey and smiled. He'd been doing that more often lately, smiling. After he disappeared for a couple weeks right around the time of the Shift, he came in like he hadn't been gone at all, wouldn't answer anybody's questions as to why.

Lee turned to Es and greeted the bot. Fey couldn't understand the words from where she stood, but she heard Lee and Es join in a bit of laughter. She didn't think she'd ever get used to that, hearing a bot laugh. She'd heard bots laugh before of course, programmed to copy human emotion, but it sounded different coming from Es, from a QC.

Fey saw Ren look to the bot and nod. Fey would swear they talked to each other in that moment, though Fey didn't understand how. That Ren was an odd one. Of course, what auto wasn't? Not that she'd met any other than Ren. She didn't think most of them went to bars. Just another reason to think Ren odd, even among autos.

Ren didn't take off her jacket, instead keeping that deep black trench coat of hers around her shoulders, the glint of two large handguns visible, one at her waist and the other strapped across her thigh. That humongous bot that followed her around didn't come in, instead walking towards an alleyway. That made Fey happy. That thing made everyone nervous.

Lee walked towards the end of the bar and sat in his usual seat, Ren taking up a place next to him with Nu on Lee's other side.

Fey eyed Nu as she moved towards the group, getting a quick glance before the edge of the bar obscured the bot from sight. Sometimes Fey forgot the bot sat on the other side of the counter since it was about as tall as the stools, came up to a little over Lee's waist. Regardless, it sat there, Lee tapping his knuckles against its chassis. Fey suspected Nu to be a QC, though she'd never asked Lee about it.

Fey grabbed the bottle of Lee's favorite whiskey off the shelf, poured him a stiff two fingers of Cross and Downs. Then she grabbed a wit bier from beneath the bar and handed that off to Ren, one of the few people who requested the stuff. Fey had been about to stop stocking it when the auto came in with Lee and requested it.

Fey set the drinks down in front of the two. "Anything new in the world of mechanics and autos?" she asked. "Or are you two going to use the whole, 'it's classified' excuse? Her I understand, but coming from you Lee that excuse is getting a bit tired. Might want to give it a rest."

Lee laughed, while Ren merely grinned. She seemed a woman of muted emotions. Beautiful though. Fey really wanted to know the story of how the two of them became friends.

"I don't have anything interesting to tell anyway. Besides, you're the one with her ear to the ground. You've got all the stories, all the secrets," said Lee.

Fey snorted, returned the bottle of whiskey to the shelf. She turned back to the two of them.

"What about you Ren? Any secrets, stories, gossip? I'll accept any of the above as payment for that odd beer choice of yours."

This brought a larger grin onto Ren's face, the barest flash of teeth, a flower whose bloom lasted but a few moments. The auto brought the beer up to her lips and took a swig, set it down.

"It's classified," she said in that odd tone of hers. Rich yet flat, light yet deep.

Fey snorted again. She liked the auto, believe it or not. She genuinely liked most people. She figured that was why she was good at her job.

Fey bustled back to the rag and glass, picking them up and finding a spot of shelf to lean against between old man Ken and Lee. Lee and Ren began to talk about some new voting results on the updated moral code. Fey listened with half a mind. Then the news vid changed stories and she shifted her attention to that.

A news anchor sat behind a desk with the image of a skeletal body in a VR rig hovering over his shoulder, the limbs of the body weak and stick-like. Fey tapped a tattoo on her arm and the audio from the news vid swelled in her ears.

"I must once again warn those of you just tuning in that this story contains graphic footage that some might find disturbing. This woman here is the latest in a string of deaths attributed to the simulation titled Parhelion. We here at CNC News cannot stress enough that this simulation must be avoided. Each and every person who has connected to this VR simulation has gone comatose minutes after connection. Their bodies reject any attempts to be fed and waste away before the eyes of friends and loved ones. I implore all my viewers to ignore any claims that this simulation will upload your consciousness to the Grid. There is no evidence, I repeat, no evidence to support this claim. This is merely another unknown corp. claiming the impossible. This brings the new total across North American soil to 234, with many more across the System. Now we'll go to Jan who is onsite and talking with the manager of the dream house where the deceased spent her last few days."

The screen flashed to the outside of an upscale dream house, a reporter with straight black hair standing next to a tall man with pinched features, the manager.

Fey turned down the volume as the manager spoke of trying to rouse the deceased from the rig days ago when her time allotment ran out. Fey noticed old man Ken watching the news vids with a curiosity that turned her stomach to acid. She knew the old man would be hitting the steep decline soon, but she didn't think him that desperate. She turned to Ren and Jace, finding them both also watching the news vid.

"What about that?" asked Fey, her eyes flicking to Ren then back to her glass. She didn't want to look at old man Ken. "Know anything about this Parhelion sim?"

Lee stared at the wooden countertop and scratched at the scruff on his cheek. Ren looked to Fey, shoulders straight and jaw set tight.

"Not enough," said Ren. "Not nearly enough."

Afterword

First and foremost, if you've made it this far, you have my utmost, unconditional, unmitigated, unvarnished, pure and simple thanks. Seeing one of my stories published has long been a dream of mine, and while I wholeheartedly believe writing is a worthy endeavor even if no eyes other than the author's alight upon the words, the joy of having another find value in my work is truly one of a kind. So, I say again, you have my thanks.

I began working on this book in 2016 with a desire to carve out my own vision of what the future might hold, a vision inspired by the famous neo-noir cyberpunk worlds of Blade Runner and Ghost in the Shell yet more optimistic, updated, driven by the technological concerns of the moment. Let's just say, when I started, I didn't think it would take nearly 7 years to get here. Then again, I wrote around a full time engineering job, then master's studies, and then a different engineering job I'm still at. And well, you've read the book, so I'll leave whether or not I was successful in that effort up to you. I can say while the result isn't perfect, I'm proud of it, warts and all, and I hope you found its reading compelling.

Now, if I may be so bold as to ask something of you, dear reader, it is this: tell your friends about my work. Aside from help my friends and family have been willing to lend, I'm a one-man operation. And if I am ever to live out that fantasy that plagues my daydreams of quitting my engineering job to write full time, it will be because of people like you. In an age where so much is fed to us by an AI algorithm, you are the difference.

Sincerely and with my unequivocal thanks,

M. Weald

About the Author

 M. Weald, known by his friends as either the first or last part of Michael Woodworth, lives in the Colorado Front Range, somewhere between Boulder and Denver. Like most in Colorado, he enjoys all things outdoors, be it rock climbing, hiking, biking, skiing, or snowboarding. You might run into him and his partner on a crag, trail, or slope in the area. If you do, you're more than welcome to say hello. He enjoys playing his guitar when he has the time and going out on one of his motorcycles when weather accommodates. His day job is that of an engineer, but he dreams of his creative writing minor being used as more than an indication to his employers that he can in fact write coherent emails. He likes to say he collects stories to validate his increasingly sizeable collection of physical media. Books, TV shows, movies, and video games all line his shelves.

If you want to stay up to date on his latest meanderings, the best place to go is his website: mweald.com. Subscribe to get blog posts monthly at the least. You can also find him at the socials below.

Facebook: https://www.facebook.com/mweald/
YouTube: https://youtube.com/@mweald
Twitter: https://twitter.com/weald_m
Instagram: https://www.instagram.com/m.weald/

CPSIA information can be obtained
at www.ICGtesting.com
Printed in the USA
JSHW022333180723
45009JS00001B/1